I0760787

A DEMON'S GUIDE TO THE AFTERLIFE

THE COMPLETE SERIES

KEL CARPENTER

AURELIA JANE

A Demon's Guide to the Afterlife

Kel Carpenter and Aurelia Jane

Published by Raging Hippo LLC

Copyright © 2023, Raging Hippo LLC

Proofread by Dominique Laura

Cover Art by Yocla Designs

All rights reserved under the International and Pan-American Copyright Conventions. No part of this book may be reproduced or transmitted in any form or by any means, electronic or mechanical, including photocopying, recording, or by any information storage and retrieval system, without permission in writing from the publisher. This is a work of fiction. Names, places, characters and incidents are either the product of the author's imagination or are used fictitiously, and any resemblance to any actual persons, living or dead, organizations, events or locales is entirely coincidental. Warning: the unauthorized reproduction or distribution of this copyrighted work is illegal. Criminal copyright infringement, including infringement without monetary gain, is investigated by the FBI and is punishable by up to 5 years in prison and a fine of $250,000.

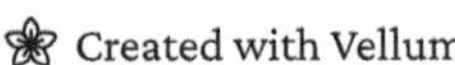

ABOUT THE AUTHORS

Kel Carpenter and Aurelia Jane are the hilarious team behind the international bestselling series, A Demon's Guide to the Afterlife.

They pride themselves in being absolute weirdos, spending hours on the phone coming up with detailed worlds, and laughing about crazy ideas for torturing characters. While they believe they each have the personality of a rabid badger, people still seem to like them okay.

They share a love of coffee, travel, and tacos, and they've made some adorable tiny people with their equally weird husbands. Best friends and work wives, Kel has the audacity to live in Maryland while Aurelia lives in Texas, but they try to see each other as much as possible.

Join Kel and Aurelia's Readers Group!

DARK HORSE

To Maegan,
You're to blame for the asshole crow. You're also pretty spectacular.
– Kel

To Patricia Browne,
It took eighteen years, but I kept my promise. You are missed.
– Aurelia

Hell is empty,
And all the devils are here.

— William Shakespeare, *The Tempest*

CHAPTER 1
FURY

"DINNER TIME, HUCK," I CALLED OUT, TAPPING MY FINGERS NEXT TO THE bowl.

A forty-year-old man came around the corner on all fours. His naked skin hung flaccid, and his knees stuck to the crappy linoleum floor. The tags on the dog collar around his neck tinkled.

Hate-filled, shit-brown eyes stared up at me. I grinned.

"You call that dinner—" he started.

I grabbed his face by the jaw and squeezed tight. "No talking back. Bad dog."

Indecision warred on his face. He wanted to hit me. Kill me, if he could. But he was thinking back to the last time he had made those attempts. It didn't end well.

For him, at least.

A moment passed, and he lowered his eyes. I dropped my hand away and patted his head mockingly. "Good mutt," I said without any of the positive inflection I'd use on a real dog.

I left Huck McKinley to his dinner of dog food covered in hot sauce, not feeling the least bit bad. Some would say I was more than a little fucked up. Cruel.

They were right, of course.

But I was a demon by trade. It was sort of in the job description.

A hundred years ago, I died. More accurately, I was murdered—by my ex-husband, to be exact. He was a piece of shit too, but that was a whole other can of worms I didn't often like to open.

The point was, I died and came to the Afterlife.

Because I wasn't in the bottom forty percent of humans that had to serve punishments for their transgressions on Earth, and I wasn't in the top one percent that automatically went through the proverbial pearly gates, I had to get a job. That's how I became a demon.

My time in the realm of the living had mostly held pain. It was what I knew. What I was good at. I took that pain and I turned it on assholes like Huck McKinley. He had also died, except he was a wife beater, and he ran dog-fighting rings that had killed hundreds of animals.

That was how he ended up here under my tender loving care.

Where is here? Hell.

Huck took a bite of food and gagged. He spat it out all over the floor, grasping at his throat. Murder shimmered in his eyes.

How cute.

"You bitch—"

"Ah-ah." I wagged my finger back and forth. "We talked about this. Dogs don't speak—"

He let out a growl that might have scared me a hundred years ago. Now?

I cracked my knuckles and grinned. He launched off the floor, saliva dripping from his lips, hot sauce mingled with bits of dog food staining his chest.

As he came up, so did my knee. I struck him square in the face. A crack echoed in the room. He flew through the air, crashing into the wall with a loud bang. He dropped to the floor, an indent of his disgusting body left in the drywall.

I tsk'd.

"Now you've done it, Huck." I walked over and picked him up by the back of his neck. My demonic strength was a godsend in moments like this. I tossed him in a wire metal crate and latched the door.

He groaned.

I hummed under my breath as I lifted my Apple watch to my face. "Play 'Baby' by Justin Bieber."

Huck let out a slew of profanities that were drowned out by the tween's obnoxious singing. I bobbed my head along to the music as I started for the front door.

"Wait—wait!" he yelled out for me. I paused at the exit. "You can't leave me like this. Please—" He cut off when I grinned maniacally.

"Should have thought about that before you were a bad dog."

With that, I stepped outside and closed the door.

All along the street sat ordinary cookie-cutter houses. They spanned miles. Every house was actually a prison containing a bad soul that had fallen into that lower forty percent of the human race that needed to be punished. How long each person served before being recycled and sent back to the realm of the living differed, but the houses didn't. The only thing separating each of them was the number on the door. Each one was special to the soul inside it. I was currently in charge of a dozen or so. People that ranged from pedophiles, to Huck McKinley, to emotionally manipulative twats that stole from their kids.

Each of their crimes were different in act and severity, but the outcome was not. They'd landed themselves in Hell, and it was my responsibility to punish and rehabilitate them before they were wiped clean of all memories and sent back to try again.

Two houses down, Malachi the Dreaded stepped out of a door. He let out a low sigh of exhaustion and straightened his blood-soaked tie.

"Long session?" I asked.

He took one look at me and wrinkled his nose in distaste. I knew what he saw. A twenty-something-year-old body with leather pants and a black corset. I wore knee-high black boots with a chunky heel. My red hair hung loose around my shoulders and not a weapon or speck of blood was in sight.

"Very," he said after a pregnant pause. "You?"

"Not terribly so. I'm enjoying this case. I've already got another fifty years planned out for this guy." I hooked my thumb toward the door behind me, and Malachi's eyebrows inched up in barely discreet incredulity.

"Hmm."

I had to give it to him. He didn't say what he was clearly thinking.

Must have learned from that asswipe, Karen. It wasn't exactly a secret that my methods of punishment were unusual. On the contrary, it made me an oddity for a demon.

It also made me the best at our job.

Anyone could hammer nails in a kneecap or shove bamboo under someone's nails. I was a true master of torture. A connoisseur, of sorts.

Not every demon saw it that way, though. Our profession generally attracted people that barely came in just above the forty percent. Shitheads that liked the idea of taking out their daddy issues on other people. People like Karen the Horrible.

A couple of decades back, I got assigned a case she wanted. Thinking she could get it back, she had openly challenged me to a duel. She and the others like her assumed I chose the punishments I did because I was weak. How wrong she was.

Malachi must have been there, or at least heard the stories. Then again, almost every demon had. The open snipes stopped after that day, even if the wandering eyes didn't. Oh, I heard the whispers through the grapevine, and over the years, several of the newbies had started to wonder. New demons always had something to prove. A bone to pick. It came with the territory. The demon guild was one of the most cutthroat in the Afterlife, and they had a tendency to judge or maim first and think later.

In that lay the problem. That behavior had broken way too many souls before their punishment was up. They weren't fully healed, and then those souls went back to the living realm to make the same shitty life choices that led them right back to Hell. Talk about a broken system.

Malachi idled warily, as if waiting for me to decide what I wanted. He likely didn't want to seem openly rude and run the risk of winding up on the other end of my legendary temper. Taking pity, or rather tired of my own mind games for the day, I waved at him and hit the home button on my watch.

My body de-materialized as I teleported into the demon dorms.

Several people took notice. I walked past the reception area where Diego the Dastardly was on duty. He gave me a wink and a sexy smirk, flirting shamelessly despite me having turned him down twice now.

Still, I smiled back and inclined my head toward the gawking new girl next to him.

"Fury," she said in a low whisper.

"In the spirit," I chimed as I went by. Diego chuckled, his deep voice following after me.

Some of the oomph left me as I climbed two flights of stairs, but I kept my shoulders back as people passed me in the hallway. Some idolized me, like the girl downstairs. Usually that worshipping phase wore off after they had a few years to settle in. Right about the time the punishing and their new reality finally got to them. She was as green as they came, but that wouldn't be the case for long, and when life after death became the new norm, it wasn't so easy for most.

There was a reason over seventy percent of our new recruits dropped out in the first six months and transferred to a new guild. Everyone was earning their way toward one of two things: retirement, or the chance to be recycled. Most wanted to be recycled.

In the Afterlife, everything was what you made of it.

On Earth, you get what you get by happenstance, but either way —you get it.

Money. Opportunities. Race. Ethnicity. When you were recycled, your circumstances and start to life were all completely random, and it was utter bullshit.

One thing I learned in dying was that most people preferred the bullshit. They'd rather play the lottery and hope they got an easy ticket in the next life, and maybe an easy ticket into Heaven.

I was never one for believing in chance. Whenever fate had a choice, it fucked me over. So, I opted to take the hard route.

Become a demon. Earn my spot.

My own little piece of heaven.

Literally.

I sighed at that thought as I opened the door. A full-size bed, half kitchen, and tiny bathroom. Everything I needed was in these four walls. By this point in my career, I could have left the dorms. Moved into my own little place in one of the lower circles of the Afterlife. Settled down with another demon and lived in . . . boring blah.

I refused. Instead, I was biding my time, saving every single second I earned for the big ticket. A place behind the golden gates.

On Earth, I'd been no one, but here—here I would be someone. Here, I already was.

Sort of.

It was an ongoing process.

I started for the bathroom, ready to strip out of my badass (and uncomfortable) outfit, run a nice hot bath, and drink a few beers.

Maybe whiskey instead.

It could really go either way after dealing with Huck all day.

I was just reaching for the zipper on my corset when my watch started to ring.

Incoming call from . . . Jake.

I threw my head back and groaned. Why? What could Jake from Afterlife Resources possibly want?

I weighed the merits of ignoring his call till tomorrow, but my curiosity got the better of me. I wanted to know what reason my resources officer would have for calling me this late in the evening.

My thumb hit accept before I could think it over more, but instead of a voice picking up on the other line, my body de-materialized once more.

I had only just registered that I was teleporting when I appeared in the hallway outside his office. His personal assistant, Francine, blinked in surprise.

"I'm sorry, but Jake is not available right now—"

"Well, I hate to break it to you, Francine, but I didn't come here by choice." I motioned to myself, happy I hadn't stripped first. I was so not feeling an orgy tonight.

Francine adjusted her glasses and picked up the phone on her desk. "Let me just call and see," she muttered, dialing his extension. Never mind that she could have just knocked on the door, or yelled, or better yet—Jake could have just given either of us a heads-up. I leaned against her desk and tapped my fingernails impatiently on the shiny veneer surface. "Your name is . . ." She left it open-ended, waiting for me to answer.

I gave her a hard look. You'd think I hadn't seen her once a month for the last thirty years.

"Fury."

She sighed. "Which Fury? Fury the Great? The Awful? Oh, I know—"

"*Just* Fury," I said, pinching the area between my brows and closing my eyes. A hundred years ago, I'd been an angry, murdered dead girl when I chose my name and profession.

How was I to know that Fury was essentially the 'Jessica' of the Afterlife?

"Oookay," she drawled passive-aggressively. We both waited for Jake to pick up. When he did, Francine said, "I have a 'Fury' here for you. She said you summoned her."

"Which Fury?" I heard him ask.

If my eyes could shoot fire, I would have melted the phone. I leaned forward over the edge of the desk and said into the receiver, "*The* Fury. The one you called after—"

The line went dead, and my lips parted.

Why that piece of—

His door opened. Jake stood there, wearing a wrinkled suit and chipper smile that always made me a little stabby.

"Hey Fury, why don't you come in and take a seat?"

I shook my head, heading into his office. The door closed behind me right as I sat in the metal-framed chair. Outside, the second sun was setting.

"Why did you summon me?" I asked, cutting to the chase. He hummed to himself the whole way to his chair and then took his sweet time sitting down. I waited expectantly.

Finally, Jake said the last thing I ever expected to hear.

"I want to send you back to Earth."

CHAPTER 2
FURY

I HEARD THE WORDS, BUT I COULDN'T FULLY REGISTER WHAT HE'D SAID. I stared at him, blinking, finally processing some sort of response.

"I'm sorry, what?" Okay, so it wasn't the most brilliant response, but it was all I had.

He pointed at me. "You." He pointed up. "Earth." He turned his hand to his desk then made his index and middle fingers walk across the surface imitating a tiny person. "I want you to go there."

I narrowed my eyes and my nostrils flared. "Right. I got that part —" I started.

"Then why did you ask?" he interjected, a slight sparkle in his eyes.

My head fell back, and my groan filled the room. If I were being honest, it was probably heard down the hall . . . and possibly the entire floor. I didn't have the patience for conversations like this.

It's not that it was a time issue. I had all the time in Hell. But that didn't mean I wanted to waste it going in circles with Jake—who liked to screw with me for the fun of it. It was different when I did it to him. That was funny. But right now I could've been in my bed, binge-watching something I borrowed from the Current Affairs department.

"Oh, you can piss off if you think I'm going back there."

Why would I go back? I mean, why in the *hell*—literally—would I go back to Earth? I'd been gone for so long I wouldn't recognize the place, even if I did keep up with the changes . . . the culture shifts . . . and the technology. Okay, I couldn't use that excuse.

But that didn't change the fact that Earth was where my ex-husband killed me, and I wasn't exactly excited to take a joyride back to the crime scene.

I knew it wouldn't be the same. Anyone and everyone I'd ever known was long gone. I'd heard about them when they crossed over. I'd looked for some of them. Found a few of them too.

I'd kept tabs on the only one I'd truly cared about, and that was really all that mattered. The rest of them were getting what they deserved, for the most part. I shook my head, clearing those thoughts and pushing them aside.

"So I'll take that as a maybe?" he asked, that stupid grin still on his face.

"Look, Jake, it's been a day, and as much as I love these shared moments between us, it's getting a little old after, what? A hundred and three years now?" I crossed my arms in front of my chest. "Spit it out. Why do you want me on Earth?"

He met my eyes but didn't answer.

I uncrossed my arms, moving them to the sides of the chair to push myself up as I said, "Okeydokey, I'm out—"

"Wait." There was something about the way he said it that had me pausing. "Just wait. Sit back down."

So I did. He had my attention. In the century I'd known him, he'd never once had a tone as serious as he did now.

Back when I first met him, he was falsely kind. Not in the human-backstabbing-drama kind of way. In the way you have to be when someone is newly deceased—his words, not mine—and you have to break it to them. Then you follow that gem up by telling them they have to get a job. With a pleasant attitude, he'd walked a murdered young girl through her options in the Afterlife. That had eventually morphed into the banter we shared as we laughed at each other's expense, more often than not.

But this? He wasn't pleading, but if I had to put a word to what it sounded like, that would be the closest thing I could come up with.

"What's going on, Jake?" I sat back down completely. "Answer for real this time. A bottle of whiskey and a bath were calling my name before you did."

He sighed. "Upper Management has a problem that needs to be . . . addressed." He twirled a pen around on top of a file I hadn't noticed before. "Ultimately, it ended up on my desk. So here we are."

"Upper Management?" I asked, raising my eyebrows a little. He nodded, lips pressed together. "Well, that's intriguing. You going to tell me more about it, or . . .?"

"There are some basics you need to understand first."

I cocked an eyebrow. Even after all these years, he was underestimating me. Still, I dipped my head, motioning for him to continue.

"Okay," he said with a sigh. "So as you know, there are hundreds of departments in the Afterlife. Lots of dead people, lots of roles to fill. It's simple enough once you accept it." I scoffed. Murdered, and I still hadn't been able to rest in peace. "One of those departments is Risk Management—"

"You mean the fortune-telling department. Future affairs. The risk witches—"

"They aren't witches," he cut in. I shrugged. "But yes, that department. I wasn't aware you knew of it. Most don't . . ." he trailed off, waiting for me to fill in the blanks with how and why I knew of the highly secretive group.

"I get around," I said suggestively, and he raised his brows.

I grinned, not bothering to correct his train of thought.

He pursed his lips and nodded. "Right. Anyway, so the fortune-telling department, as you called it, saw the possibility of something happening. It's big. Like, *end of the world* big."

"Okay," I said. "I'm not sure what that has to do with me. I mean, if the world ends, that means our workload doesn't even increase because no one gets recycled, right?"

"We're talking about the entirety of the living realm extinguishing. Imploding. You do know what 'end' means?"

"You mean how my life 'ended'? Ceased to exist and then I got dumped here?" I deadpanned. "Yeah, I'm familiar with endings, Jake. Get to the point."

He pinched the bridge of his nose and scrunched his eyes shut. "Listen. The living realm needs to exist, just like we need to exist. It's a symbiotic relationship. A cycle. Upper Management doesn't want this happening, Fury. It *can't* happen. They've sent countless angels to try to redirect this situation, but each of them has failed. Hell, none of them even made a dent."

"Wait," I drawled. "You want *me* to go back to Earth to fix something that the angels can't?" He nodded. "That doesn't even make sense. That's basically their entire job, isn't it? To go fix shit on Earth and deal with problems before they become bigger problems—"

"Fury—"

"I mean, that's what they do. They don't hate Earth. They like it. They like the people and the hope and the . . ." I grasped for a word that encompassed the bullshit way angels spoke about Earth, "the goodness of it all—"

"Fury—"

"And I don't. I don't like anything about it. This isn't my job. I'm a demon. That's the job I picked. Of course I could've taken some pencil-pushing job like you—no offense—but that just didn't suit my needs because I was *really* fucking angry at the time, and now I'm fine with it—well, mostly—but I'm earning my way to retirement because I just want to rest, for fuck's sake—"

"*Fury!*"

I stopped my rant, looking at him with wide eyes. I took a deep breath, cleared my throat, and clenched my teeth. "What?"

"This is different. The angels have failed. They don't fail. Not like this. The men they're trying to alter aren't the usual cases that end up on their desks."

I shook my head. There was something about this story I was missing. Something he wasn't telling me. Whether he knew and was keeping it from me, or he was in the dark too, I wasn't sure. But there was more to it. "I'm not sure how I can make a difference if they couldn't? I'm just a demon."

"That's actually *why* we need you on this," he said, slowing his speech as though he was searching for the right words. "The standard practice didn't work. This needs a special touch. A demon's touch."

I cocked an eyebrow and smirked.

He groaned. "Not *that* kind of touch, Fury." He leaned back in his chair, not taking his eyes off me. "You have the highest reform rate we've seen in eons. The other demons can say what they want about your methods, but they can't touch your success rate. Whatever it is you do, it works. And that hasn't gone unnoticed."

I sighed again and shook my head. "I hate Earth, Jake. I'm not going back. For a century, I've saved for retirement. I'm almost there. It'll be modest, but that's all I want. I just want to be left alone. For the rest of eternity. I don't think that's too much to ask."

And I meant it. He'd asked me before if I was content settling down by myself. The answer was always yes. I was fine on my own. I preferred it that way. Being with someone had landed me here. I barely had a chance in life. It was taken away from me. Taken by the person that was supposed to 'love me until the end of my days.' Hmpf.

When the time came and I moved out of the dorms, I'd go get myself a nice little unclaimed stray that crossed the rainbow bridge. Rest peacefully. Alone. It was true that animals had unconditional love to give.

"No," I said, breaking my train of thought. "I won't do it. Find someone else. Earth sucks." I got up, ready to walk out of his office so I could just materialize home. I touched the doorknob—

"You do this, and you retire when it's over."

I turned around and stared at him.

"Go on."

"You finish this job, successfully reform them where the angels have failed, and you get whatever you want. Full retirement, full benefits, anywhere you choose."

You choose.

Those words pinged back and forth in my brain.

This was too good to pass up. He had to follow through with his offer. That was how things worked in the Afterlife. I sighed, looking out his window. Not a bad view for Jake. I could have a view. Anywhere I wanted.

"All I have to do is reform these assholes, and I get whatever I want in retirement? That's it?" I asked, looking back at him.

He pressed his lips together and nodded. "That's it."

"Am I being recycled? Demons don't get to go to Earth. How would it work?"

He laughed. "No, you won't be recycled. Call it a special pass. From Upper Management, of course."

Of course. Upper Management could really do whatever they wanted.

"You'll go back as you. Your memories, your body, your charming demoness qualities. We need *The* Fury. No one else."

I gave him a deadpan look. "Laying it on kinda thick now, Jake." He shrugged. "Fine. I'll do it. For immediate and full retirement, I'll do it."

"Here," he said, handing me some files. "You leave tomorrow. You'll need to read up on current affairs and the intel we've gathered on your targets. It should help you locate them and get started on . . . whatever it is you do to fix people."

I grabbed the files and turned to walk out. "Pleasure as always," I said, shutting the door as he grumbled a response.

I glared at Francine as I prepared to send myself home, but a body materialized, and I stumbled back as someone plowed past me.

"What the—" I shouted. "Watch where you land, you wanker."

The girl was flustered, red in the face, and shouting at Francine. "I need to see Jake, *now*! When I said I'd take the job at the rainbow bridge, I *did not* agree to escorting spiders or snakes!" she squealed, her body shivering and squirming as she ended her sentence.

I busted out laughing.

Francine smiled at her. "People have pets of all sorts, Carly. Wait for the cockroaches. Entomologists love their pets too."

Newbies. I snorted as she screeched, reaching down to pick up my files and put them back in order.

A picture caught my attention, and my mouth dropped open a little. Three gorgeous men, each uniquely different from the other, stared back at me with piercing eyes. It was time to go home and study. Earth had just gotten a little more interesting if I could play with the likes of them.

CHAPTER 3
FURY

THE DEPARTMENT OF EARTH AFFAIRS WAS BUSTLING WHEN I TELEPORTED IN, but that didn't stop a few of them from staring. I wasn't sure if it was my blacked-out sunglasses and flask in hand that did it, or simply me. I was The Fury, after all. My trademark red hair and resting bitch face were unmistakable, even in the Afterlife.

So was my hatred of Earth.

"Fury," the front receptionist said, stumbling over herself to scan her appointments for my name. "I wasn't aware you were—"

Silently, I pulled a silver plate no bigger than a business card from my back pocket and dropped it on her desk.

The etchings that read *special pass* were unique. As was its holographic iridescence. Stardust, an extinguished soul, and metal harder than anything that existed on Earth went into creating them. It was the signature of Upper Management, and it was the greatest hall pass of all time.

"I see," the receptionist said, as understanding settled over her. "Come with me."

She stood and walked around the back of her long desk. Several people noticed as I took another swig of whiskey from my flask and followed her. We went through a set of double doors, down a long hallway, then cut in front of a line of people to approach another desk.

This one was smaller, less showy. Like the high school teachers' desks I'd seen in movies.

"Excuse me—" the girl first in line started.

Duke, the controller who handled all comings and goings between Earth and the Afterlife, lifted his hand to silence her. "Fury," he said with a soft smile. "How's it going, baby girl?"

I smiled back at him and lifted my flask. "About how you'd expect."

His smile turned a little sad. He knew.

Duke was one of my friends in the Afterlife. Hell, he was the first friend I'd made, and over the years, he'd turned into more of a father figure of sorts.

We'd bumped into each other that first day as I was leaving Jake's office. Turned out, we'd died a whopping half-second apart. Except where I'd succumbed to my ex-husband's fists, he'd been taken out by a brain aneurysm at the ripe old age of thirty-eight.

Duke and I had absolutely nothing in common. On Earth, I'd been a pretty housewife kept in a dollhouse cage. He'd been a steelworker with a wife and two little girls. If there hadn't been life after death, we never would've met, separated not just by the distance between our homes but by the color of our skins.

But here in the Afterlife, we were both dead and lost in our own ways. While I took a job as a demon and rose in the ranks through skill, he took a job with the Department of Earth Affairs, and his trustworthiness had led him to being the man in charge of the only way out of here and back to the realm of the living.

That job made him quite popular with all the wayward souls hoping to cheat the system. When he was alive, people had lifted their noses at him. Here, they fell over themselves to please him.

The receptionist flashed my hall pass. "*The* Fury has been assigned a job by—"

"I know," he said, waving her off as he stood up. "I was briefed when I came in this morning." Turning to the line, he said, "I'll be back in a few."

I saluted the crowd and followed him to a door marked with his name.

He motioned for me to take a seat, so I did. He had a comfortable couch, and I always enjoyed lounging when I came for a visit.

"How's the fam?" I asked.

He smiled. "Henrietta's good. The girls are still adjusting to the Afterlife. It's only been twenty years for them, and you remember how hard it is to get used to this place." He looked away, almost nostalgic. "But we're all together again. I'm happy about that."

Duke was maybe the only person I knew that meant something to me, and having his family together in the Afterlife was a big deal. People usually moved on in the living world. Humans weren't made to be alone, and the idea of soulmates seemed stupid. Call me jaded. But his wife had never remarried. Never looked for another partner. She loved him in a way that was rare and beautiful, and she'd waited to be with him again. Of course, she'd been expecting to be reunited in Heaven. But even though that wasn't exactly what had happened, she was still with him, and that was all she'd wanted.

"I'm happy for you, Duke. I really am. Not everyone gets the same ending you have. Not when we kicked it so early."

He laughed at me. "Always a way with words." I shrugged. "And yes, we're lucky. But it's not the ending."

"Isn't it, though?"

Duke shook his head. "You know it isn't. It's just the next step in our existence. Endings are permanent. Like the end of a book. You turn the last page, and the story has been told. We don't have that. We're still reading, waiting for the next chapter."

I couldn't help but scoff. "C'mon, Duke. The story *has* been told. At least mine has. My story is just sitting on the last page. There's no happily ever after for me. I'm just stagnant, waiting to retire from this life-after-death."

He frowned, looking sad. "Retirement is overrated. You're making a difference as a demon." It was my turn to frown. "Which brings us to why you're sitting in front of me today . . ." He trailed off, staring at me.

"What?" I asked. I knew where he was going; I just wanted to avoid it.

"Cut the shit, Fury," he said. "What are you doing? Going back to Earth," he huffed. "You said you'd never go back. Never be recycled.

And I don't blame you. Life screwed you over pretty badly. So what's the deal here? Why did I get a memo this morning about sending you to the living realm with a special pass? They don't exactly hand those out often."

I sighed. "I know, I know. I swore I'd never go back. But they offered me retirement, Duke. Full benefits. Anything and everything I want when I finish this job."

Duke raised his eyebrows slightly. He nodded his head, thinking on what I had just told him. Finally, he let out a deep sigh. "I can see why you took it, then."

"Right? I can't turn that down. Even if it does mean going back to that shithole." I fidgeted with my hands. That wasn't like me, but I needed to know what he had to say. I respected him. His was the one opinion that mattered.

He looked worried for me, as though he was thinking carefully about his words before speaking again. "Are you going to be okay up there?"

I smiled at him, appreciating his concern. "Yeah, I'll be okay. The file said I'm going to Houston. I never went there when I was alive, and it's been a century since I've been *anywhere*, so it can't be that bad."

I honestly wasn't sure who I was trying to convince. No, I wasn't going to run into anyone from my former life. I wasn't going to even recognize a lot, and if it weren't for the Department of Current Affairs, I wouldn't know about all the technology and advancements that had been made. I wasn't even going up north. No memories should be dredged up in the process. But it was still Earth. With humans. The same pieces of shit that found their way onto my roster. I got to deal with them day in and day out, but now I had to see them in the flesh. So to speak.

He looked at me like he knew I was full of it. "Mhm hmm," he muttered. "I read the file too. I won't talk you out of it, Fury. My role in this is to get you there. I'm your go-between. So that being said, do you have any questions?"

"Wait, you said you aren't going to try to talk me out of this?" I asked, surprised that he'd just moved the conversation forward.

"No one can talk you out of anything," he deadpanned.

I barked a laugh and smirked at him. "You know me better than anyone." It was true.

"I know," he said matter-of-factly. "So? Questions?"

"What's my timeline?"

"Dunno, actually. The risk witches have been having visions about this for a long time. Tried to take care of it, but nothing has worked long-term. With each attempt and failure, the visions increased. None of which are good signs. It was about twenty-five years ago that it altered so drastically that they haven't been able to adjust accordingly since."

"What does that mean exactly?" I asked.

He twisted his lips. "It means the frequency and the intensity of the visions increased exponentially, and the attempts they've made to correct it have only made it worse."

I sighed. "So you're basically saying the end of the world could happen tomorrow or a year from now. It's just a bomb waiting to go off, but there's no clock on the detonator."

He nodded slowly. "Pretty much."

"Great. No pressure," I muttered, shifting myself in the seat. "Okay, so the file isn't specific about information in regard to me. What about powers? Do I get to keep all of mine while I'm up there? If I'm going up against three supes, I need to know what I'm working with."

He nodded. "You do. Full capabilities. Just do me a favor and try to keep it under wraps as best you can. The living can't handle much in the way of what they call paranormal. They get weird and make TV shows out of it."

"Noted." I snickered, thinking of how they reacted to the poltergeists that worked in Current Affairs. "What can you tell me about this assignment? How I could go about getting this started, maybe? I can't just show up and go knock on their front doors."

He shook his head. "I can't help you with that. I've read the same file you have. As you move along up there, I'll know more, and then I can help you where I can."

It was my turn to deadpan. "Well, aren't you just immensely helpful."

He shrugged. "I do what I can." He reached into a drawer and pulled out a backpack-styled purse, handing it to me. "Here. You'll need this. It has the information you need to get around. ID, wallet, cash. We had an apartment set up for you and your access card is in there too."

I opened the bag, reaching in for the wallet and fished the ID card from its slats. "Wow, you really thought of—" I stared at the card, narrowing my eyes. It was my face, all right. Birthday that made me twenty-six human years old. But . . . "Really, Duke? You made my name *Jessica* Fury?"

He snorted. "You have to have a first name up there. You can't walk around telling people you are *The* Fury."

"Oh, come on. It's not my fault—"

"You picked the 'Jessica' of the Afterlife," he finished for me. "I know, I know. I've heard it for decades. You still needed a name, and I may be dead, but my sense of humor isn't."

"Fine," I grumbled to myself while he laughed. "How do I get in touch with you? You said you're my go-between."

"Ah yes . . ." He got up, crossed the room, and opened a door I'd always seen but never knew what was in it. It had markings scribbled on a plaque in a language I couldn't read. He disappeared inside while I waited. I didn't know what the hell I was actually waiting for because he hadn't said anything to tell me what was going on.

The silence was deafening. Awkward. I tapped my foot, looking out his window. He had a nice view. It made me question what Houston was going to look like. When I'd been alive, I'd heard it was filled with cowboys and horses. The file said it was a big city now. Like Los Angeles. I knew about L.A. I had a lot of charges from that pit. Everyone had sin. That place was teeming with it. But the most I'd read about Houston was that it had a lot of people, and most of those people didn't wear cowboy boots unless they were trying to complement the bedazzled asses of their designer jeans. I would not be dressing anything like that. That was a firm no. Sparkly wasn't my thing.

My thoughts were interrupted when I heard a loud squawk and Duke came back through the mystery door, a large black bird on his shoulder.

My mouth fell open. "What in the hell is that?" I yelled as it screeched at me again.

Duke reached up, stroking its feathers. "He's a crow. And he's yours."

I shook my head. "Um, thanks, but no. You know I'm more of a dog person . . . "

The crow snapped his beak at me, and Duke laughed. "It wasn't really an invitation for pet ownership. He's your go-between. This is how you will reach me."

Of course it was. A fucking bird. A big one, at that. I groaned and nodded, knowing that nothing I could say would matter, anyway. You couldn't really negotiate in the Afterlife.

The bird flew in my direction, and I scrunched my eyes shut as he landed on me. I turned and looked at him. "Shit on my shoulder, and I'm sticking you in a cage. Got it?"

He ruffled his feathers, lifting up a leg like he was thinking about testing me. I narrowed my eyes at him, and his body vibrated like he was *laughing* at me. This had to be a joke.

I looked back to Duke, scowling. "Right. So the plan is I send the bird back to you when I need something . . . because with our infinite wisdom and phenomenal powers, we can't find some better form of communication between realms. So we're just gonna jump back a few centuries and send the pigeon."

Duke opened his mouth to say something, but all I heard was an ear-splitting scream. My eyes crossed at the sound.

"I was going to suggest maybe not calling him that, but I think he already shared that with you," he said, chuckling.

"Yep. Got it. Thanks for that," I said, thankful living in the land of the dead didn't include getting tinnitus. "Anything else?" If I hadn't already resided in the Afterlife, I would've said the excursion I was about to embark upon was going to be hell.

He smiled at me, but it didn't reach his eyes. He wasn't saying something. I'd known him long enough to know his tells.

"What aren't you saying, Duke?"

"Nothing, kiddo," he said, smiling a little more. "I just worry about you, but I know you can handle going back. I'll miss our chats while you're gone." He jutted his chin out at the bird. "Send him if you need anything. I'm usually here, and he knows where to find me when I'm not."

Silence spanned between us.

He clapped his hands, grabbed my bag, and headed for another door in his office. "All right, let's get you out of here."

With the messenger crow sitting on my shoulder, I followed him silently, not having a clue where I was going. As a demon, my job was here in the Afterlife. I didn't leave. I hadn't been back to Earth since the day my life had been cut short with one final blow to the head. Down a white hallway, down another hallway, and finally to a single blue door at the end of a long corridor.

"This is it?" I asked, expecting something cooler. Like a portal. Not a freaking door.

"This will take you there," he said, handing me the leather backpack. "You've got what you need, and you'll manage to acquire the rest once you get there."

I took it, tossing it over my birdless shoulder. "Thanks, Duke," I said, throwing him a little salute. "Beam me up, fucker." I snickered. I'd wanted to say that since I'd watched a show years ago. Of course, I added my own little touch.

Duke laughed and shook his head. "Take care."

I walked through the door and saw a portal. Ha! Finally something that didn't feel so disappointing. Galaxy colors shimmered in a circular pattern, the edges moving like waves.

I held my chin up and stomped through, mustering the confidence I needed to go back. I was a motherfucking demon. I was The Fury. I had this. Do the thing. Save the world. Retire.

Then I stepped through.

I squinted as a blinding light assaulted my eyes. I felt disoriented, unsure of which direction I was facing. And it was loud. I was blasted in the face with steam. Jesus, was that *the weather*? Oh my god, where was that awful heat coming from? I felt like I was drinking the air. Where the hell had I ended up? The fucking sun?

I groaned, my senses adjusting and my eyes focusing. Being a demon with much more heightened senses than a normal person actually made the process take a second longer. I looked around, taking in my surroundings. Concrete. A lot of it. Incredibly tall buildings on all sides. And people walking and seemingly talking to no one in particular. I didn't see any steam, so the heat was the actual weather.

It was literally hotter than Hell. I'd know.

"You've got to be kidding me," I muttered under my breath. Why hadn't I been teleported to where I was supposed to be?

I pushed a button on my watch, looking at my notes. I needed to be somewhere cooler than this. I knew air conditioning was a thing. I'd read about it. And now I wanted it.

"Ah . . . okay, I need to be here," I said, tapping the watch and talking to the bird like he knew what I was saying and could help me.

I turned my head, twirling my body around to get an idea of my surroundings. I couldn't teleport unless I knew where I was. I needed both locations.

I saw some lights and signs, so I walked toward them and looked up to read. I was on Texas Avenue. How original.

A loud honking startled me, and I saw why. I quickly hit my watch to teleport myself, but nothing happened.

"That's not going to work," the crow said.

I turned my head quickly, looking at him. "Did you just talk?"

"You should move." He spoke again, flapping his wings and flying off my shoulder.

I jumped out of the way of the oncoming vehicle . . . and into another lane of traffic.

Tires squealed, and I looked over to see a massive bus . . . and I met it head-on.

Literally.

Fuck my afterlife.

CHAPTER 4
FURY

BAM.

My body landed on the tiled floor in a tumble, like I'd been a laundry pile dumped on the ground.

"Ugh," I groaned. I still felt pain, though it was generally a heavily muted form of it. More like a slight discomfort. This? It felt more like I'd been dropped off the side of the building.

"Fury, what are you doing back here?" an exasperated voice said.

I jerked my head toward Duke.

"You failed to mention that I can't teleport, and I got hit by a fucking bus," I grumbled as I stood and dusted myself off. "You said I would have my powers."

He pinched the bridge of his nose and then chuckled. "You do have your powers. Teleporting isn't one of them. That's a perk of being in the Afterlife, but it's not a power that demons have." He laughed again and shook his head. "But now you know. You die, you end up back here, in my office. I'll regenerate you and send you back up."

I stared at him wide-eyed as he tried to keep his laughter contained, but he was failing miserably. I threw my bag at him, nailing him in the face. That cut him right off.

"What the hell, Fury?"

"No, Duke," I said, pointing my finger up, "you mean what the Houston? Have you been there? It's ridiculously hot. The air is thick. How can air be *thick*?"

He busted out laughing again, throwing my backpack to me in return. "That's called humidity. I'm from Louisiana. I'm aware of what July feels like down south."

I caught it and then pointed at the crow sitting on Duke's desk. I gestured at him, raising my voice. "And you didn't say feathers over there can fucking talk, Duke. He *talks*."

"I know he does," he said.

"You didn't tell me that either," I shouted.

He shrugged, getting up and stroking the bird's feathers. "You didn't ask."

I groaned in frustration, long and loud. *It's fine. Everything's great. It's good.*

I straightened my shirt, picked up the bag, and tapped my shoulder. "You got a name, or do I just call you pigeon?" I asked the crow.

He flew over and landed on my shoulder, his claws pricking my skin a little harder than I thought was really necessary. But now I knew when he pissed me off, he would henceforth be known as pigeon.

"Hades."

"Cool, Hades," I said. "Try being more helpful about oncoming traffic next time, will ya?"

I looked at Duke, peacing out as I walked to the door behind his desk. "I know my way back to the portal. I'll be going now." I stopped, turned, and looked at him with a cocked eyebrow. "Is there anything I need to know about going back?"

A little twinkle appeared in his eye. I fucking knew it.

"Yeah, when you go back, you regenerate into a new body."

I nodded in understanding and sighed. "So I'm being sent back to the same place and there's a dead version of me lying in the road right now?"

"There is," he said, cracking a smile. "So don't go confusing people by sticking around too long."

Incognito it was then.

This time when I went through the portal, I was prepared for the god-awful heat and humidity. Last time, I'd been so assaulted by the weather and my surroundings, I hadn't noticed the instant frizz in my hair, or the way sweat slicked the undersides of my boobs.

I wrinkled my nose in distaste.

That was when the screaming registered. I flinched, side-eyeing the growing mob of people in the street. The man that I could only assume was the bus driver was sweating bullets as he spoke loudly about how I'd run into the road, others comforting him and saying they saw the whole thing. Sirens were going off left and right. That was my cue to get out of Dodge.

I pushed my sunglasses back on my nose and started down the sidewalk in the opposite direction. When I went to take another swig out of my flask, only bitter drops coated my tongue with disappointment.

Empty. Damn.

I sighed, stuffing it in my backpack.

This expedition to Earth was quickly proving why I wasn't a fan.

I needed to find my targets and nip their little apocalypse in the bud ASAP.

But where to start?

I looked around, peering up and down the street. My eyes lifted to a flashing neon crescent moon. Ugly pink letters that read *After Dark* triggered a memory. I'd read that name in the file last night.

A slow smile curled up the left side of my mouth.

"Take the afternoon off, birdie. I got a lead," I said under my breath to the crow still chilling on my shoulder. He let out an indignant squawk before flying off in a blur of black feathers.

I sauntered down the sidewalk and across the busy streets, careful to watch for cars this time. My boots clicked on the pavement as I approached the double doors. Two bouncers stood on either side, wearing full suits despite the awful heat. A carpet led off to the side of the building, like they were used to having a line.

There was no line now. Yet two bouncers were stationed here.

Hm.

I flashed them a pretty little smile as I approached the doors, tossing my shiny red hair over one shoulder. Both their stoic faces softened, becoming more approachable.

Bingo.

"Hey, big boys," I purred seductively. They puffed up their chests a little and internally I rolled my eyes but kept the smile plastered on my face. When I reached for the door, though, the one on the left stepped forward, crowding the entry.

"Club's closed," he said.

I might've believed it if I didn't know that was their standard line to non-supes. Little did they know, I had the password.

"Whiskers."

He blinked, stepping back. His hand dropped from the doorway he was trying to block. "You don't smell like a wolf," he said. He eyed me curiously.

"That's because I'm not," I retorted, smiling like I had a secret.

"Ears aren't pointed either," the other bouncer said with a jut of his chin toward me.

"You got a question there?" I said softly, leaning forward.

"What are you?"

"I'd tell you," I whispered to both of them, "but then I'd have to kill you."

His eyebrows drew together as if he was confused. The one on the left let out a barking laugh.

I flashed them a smile as I reached for the door again, and this time, they didn't press it. "Be safe now in there, little lady," the one on the left said. The bouncer on the right still seemed a bit unsettled as I opened the door.

I'd have to remember that for next time. Less smiling. Not so close. Demons carried an aura about them, similar to angels. While our holy counterparts typically handled business on Earth in all manner of ways, their goal was to make things better. Keep the world turning. As such, part of their charm was that people gravitated toward them. They couldn't help themselves. Human or supernatural, everything wanted to be close to divinity.

Demons weren't the opposite, but we sure as shit weren't the same.

Around us, emotions ran high. Chaos ensued. An unsettling sensation touched everything we breathed on. The bouncer's reaction was to be expected, and I would need to be more careful.

The glass door closed behind me, and the painfully bright sunlight winked out as a more muted atmosphere took its place. Blessed air-conditioning fanned my sweaty skin, and I extended both arms out and tilted my head back.

An unexpected and loud cracking sound broke the silence and made me tense. I loosened up quickly, taking a look at my surroundings.

A burly man was bent over a pool table, just shooting the shit with his buddies. They clinked their beers and walked with an air of confidence.

No, not confidence, I realized, after a closer inspection.

Arrogance.

There were a few others in the bar, men and women alike, but they gave these fellows a wide berth. I found that intriguing, given they looked like your run-of-the-mill chumps. In my time, these were the good ol' boys. They'd wear loafers and smoke cigars while making demeaning jokes about their wives and mistresses.

The more times changed, the more they stayed the same.

I sauntered toward the bar.

"What'll it be for ya?" a short woman with a killer afro asked. She wore a yellow bandana as a headband and a black T-shirt with a graphic that read *Nine Inch Nails.*

I liked her already.

"Gin Rickey," I said, leaning against the counter. "Make it a double."

To her credit, she didn't give me a dubious glance. She just got to work.

Thirty seconds later, she set a drink down next to my hand. I took a sip and sighed almost blissfully.

One of the patrons sauntered up beside me. "You're new," a nasally male voice said.

"Yup," I replied without looking at him. The four men at the pool table were being loud and obnoxious as they placed bets. I knew it wasn't really *them* that was bothering me. Just what they represented. Still, I couldn't help scrunching my nose.

"What's your name?" the nasally one continued, not taking the hint.

"Not interested."

Was it bitchy? Probably.

Did I care? Not one bit.

"Are you sure—"

A feminine laugh behind me drew my attention. "You heard her, Paul. Take a hike."

I glanced sideways at Paul. His thin lips twisted into a frown. "This doesn't involve you, Roxanne."

The bartender came up to the other side of the bar and leaned forward. "It does when it's in my bar. I won't have you harassing paying customers."

His face blustered as he huffed. "I was hardly harassing the girl—"

"Woman," I interrupted. "Don't call me a girl. It's rude."

Paul looked between Roxanne and me, as if weighing whether he still had a chance. She made a shooing motion. His fingers tightened into a fist, but he balled it up at his side and walked away.

Guess he knew a lost cause when he saw one.

Or Roxanne was a bigger badass than she looked.

Either was possible with supes.

"Let me know if he bothers you. I don't tolerate that shit in my bar," she said, wiping down the counter with a white rag.

"He's harmless," I said, turning back to the boys at the pool table. I jutted my chin toward them. "What's their deal?"

"You must be really new if you don't know them."

I cocked an eyebrow. "Am I that obvious?" I asked, taking a swig, and setting it back down on the bar top.

"Yes," she said flatly. "Try not to draw attention to that fact."

"I'll try to work on it." I leaned toward her. "Any tips you want to give me, then?"

She chuckled. "I'm the one who gets tips around here, in case you haven't noticed."

So that was how it was going to be. I pursed my lips and nodded at her, reaching into my backpack of magic tricks, and pulling out my wallet. I grabbed a twenty, and stretched over to a tip jar, ready to drop the money in. She quickly covered the top of it with her hand.

"Whoa, there," she said, shaking her head. "That wasn't me looking for a bribe. That was me being a smart-ass."

"Well, you made it sound like—"

"If I wanted you to pay me for information, I would tell you to pay me for information." She took her hand off the jar and leaned her elbows on the bar.

I smirked. "Straightforward. I like it. I can work with that." I looked around, glancing back at the guys. "So, if I were a new girl in town, what do you think I should know?"

She took a moment to appraise me before dipping her chin and nodding toward the pool table. "Those guys? They're the Dawsons. Shifters. I swear to everything holy that each one of them is an alpha because they all walk around like they have the biggest dicks in the locker room."

I snorted. "Anything to back that up?"

She huffed a laugh. Keeping her voice low, she said, "The one with the black hair is Taylor. He's technically the alpha. They run some territory south of Houston, but not Houston itself, and that pisses them off. Some of the packs are rivals, but most of them just bark. There are two packs that have a powerful bite."

"Let me guess. Another pack with big dicks in the locker room?" I repeated her phrasing. I was pretty sure I understood the context of it. I'd have to look it up later to make sure.

"Yes." A smile curved on her lips. "But they can back it up."

My eyebrows shot up. "I want that information next."

She busted out laughing, drawing attention from some other patrons. She cleared her throat and leaned toward me again. "At any rate, the Dawsons have hot tempers. They come here to intimidate supes and gamble. They're good at it too."

"Intimidating or gambling?" I asked.

"Both," she answered. "The local packs leave them be. If it's all for show, there's no reason to start a pissing contest over territory and shit. But don't play cards with them and don't drink with them. Just don't bother with them, honestly."

I was still scanning the room when I heard a sniff by my ear and turned my head to see Roxanne uncomfortably close to me. I could have sworn I heard her inhale my hair.

"Did you just . . . smell me?"

She shrugged. "Your hair smells nice. Good shampoo. Not something I've smelled before." She turned around to grab a bottle of gin and started mixing me another drink. "Where did you say you were from?"

"I didn't." And I wasn't planning on telling her either.

She raised her eyebrows and stopped pouring.

"But if you're asking, I'm from Indiana," I supplied, not actually lying.

She resumed pouring. "Never been up there."

"Not missing much," I mumbled, wanting to change the subject.

She topped off the drink with some club soda and handed it over. "So, woman-who-has-no-name, what brings you down this way?"

"Fury."

"I'm sorry, what?"

"My name is Fury."

"Is that your first name, or your last?" she asked, slight confusion coloring her voice.

"It's just Fury. I don't go by my first name," I said, trying not to grit my teeth at the idea of having to say what was on my ID.

"All right, Just Fury," she said, cracking a smile. I don't know what she thought was so damn funny. "So tell me. What brings you down here? I can't quite place you, and I'm pretty good at my job."

"I'm just here to have a good time. Make some friends, see the sights." I kept my features calm, and she studied me. I could tell she wasn't sure if she should believe me or not.

Finally, she nodded. "Okay. Well, I can't do much about the sights. But I like you, and you can have a good time in my bar. Darts that way, if you're so inclined." She cleaned out a glass, dipping her chin and nodding to a dark corner. "Cards are upstairs—buy-in depends on the supes you're playing with."

"And pool," I said with a mischievous grin.

"Mmm hmm. And pool," she repeated.

"So liquor and gambling. What else do you sell here?"

"I sell anything I want to. Humans don't regulate us, but I draw the line on what I will and won't have here. Why? What exactly are you looking for?" She eyed me with suspicion.

"Just something to eat. Whatever your favorite thing is."

"Oh. Sure, that's no problem. Anything else?"

An idea formed. "Yeah, do you have cigarettes?"

She wrinkled her nose and reached under the bar, slamming a pack of smokes and matchbook on top. "Knock yourself out. Away from me, though. My bar, my rules. It stinks."

"Fair enough." I grabbed them and my drink and stood. "I'll just go have one over there. Keep my tab open." I gestured vaguely and started to walk away.

"That shit will kill you," she called after me.

I looked over my shoulder and said, "So I've heard."

It had been over a hundred years since I'd had one. In the Afterlife, I'd taken to drinking my sorrows since cigarettes were banned. Go figure that I'd kick it during prohibition just to end up in another one after I died. I didn't know why I couldn't smoke in Hell. I didn't make the rules. I'd often wondered if there was contraband somewhere . . . I wondered if Duke could get me some. I'd never ask him, though. I didn't want to abuse his position or our friendship. He deserved better, and Roxanne was right. It stunk. Still, old habits died hard.

I walked over to the corner, swaying my hips just a fraction as I passed by the pool table.

"Hey, baby, you need a light?" Taylor said, stepping in front.

I grinned in a way he probably thought was flirty. "That would be great," I purred. Once upon a time, I would've been disgusted by his attention. The barely hidden predator beneath his leer would've set me off in a blind rage.

Luckily for him, I took anger management seriously and had gotten my shit together. Forever was a long time to suffer from PTSD, and I wasn't giving my piece-of-shit ex any more of myself after he killed me.

So instead of ripping his cock off and then choking him with it, I leaned forward as he pulled out a lighter and I cast him a demure look.

He lit the cigarette, and I took my first long drag.

Fucking perfect.

The only thing I needed to complete my day was an introduction to my first target.

"Heard you're new?" the man in front of me said.

"Mhmm," I hummed softly, blowing out a steady stream of smoke.

"What brings you to town?" he continued, ignoring his buddies who had stopped playing altogether to listen.

"Oh, you know. Same ol', same ol'. I needed a change of pace," I answered vaguely, gesturing with the hand holding the cigarette.

His black hair was oily from using too much gel to slick it back, like a shitty impersonation of *Grease*. The dark jeans and leather jacket didn't give him that badass vibe I suspected he was going for. Not when he talked shit about having a girl back home and already banging two random chicks while he was in Houston for the week. Someone should've told him to speak a little quieter in public places if he was hoping to pick up another hot piece of ass.

Fortunately, though, these types had a tendency to be ignorant of their own obvious faults, and they were far too arrogant to believe they weren't god's gift to the world.

"Change of pace, huh?" he asked, while looking at his pack. "You like pool?" He motioned to the table.

"I've played a few times," I said mildly, lying through my teeth. He didn't need to know that just yet.

"Wanna play a round with us?" he offered.

I turned to look at the other three pack members but kept an eye on him in my peripheral vision, not missing the way his gaze dipped to my cleavage before he licked his lips. Gross.

"I suppose I could . . ."

A pool stick was thrust into my hand. From across the room, a perplexed look crossed Roxanne's face. I would have apologized in advance if it wouldn't have fucked up my little plan. The unfortunate thing for her was that while she ran this bar, she didn't own it. Not really.

They went the rounds telling me their names, but I only partially listened while finishing off my cig. One of the Dawson boys racked up the balls. They lifted the triangle, and Taylor motioned for me to break. Internally, I snorted, suspecting he just wanted an excuse to look at my ass.

Giving him a show, I stubbed the cigarette out in the ashtray then leaned over the table, positioning the pool cue between the gap of my index finger and thumb. Taylor put the cue ball on the table, and I lined up the shot, but tipped it when I went to break. The ball rolled to the side, and I grimaced.

"Oops," I said.

One of the boys chuckled and said something under his breath about me being a woman. My back hand clenched the pool stick before releasing, as I stood up and shrugged.

"It's okay. Let me show you how," Taylor said gruffly. His pants were tenting like a twelve-year-old boy looking at his first porno. Talk about awkward.

This next part was my least favorite.

I acted like a shy little supe as I let him bend me over and cop a feel while pretending it was to help my stance.

Seriously. What a pig.

I was happy I'd picked these guys. They deserved what was coming.

He put his hand over mine, jerking it against the wooden pole like it was a hand job. "Not too tight now," he said in my ear. His breath smelled like sour whiskey and Cheetos. A disgusting combination. I actually had to work to keep the frown off my face as he took way too much time to hit the damn ball.

As soon as he did, a crack went through the club once more, followed by the pings of the others bouncing off the side. Two went in pockets by pure luck.

"See?" he said, reluctantly letting me up even if he was standing close enough to press his cock into the crack of my ass.

"I think so," I murmured. "Let me try again. Am I supposed to hit the striped ones or the solid ones? I never can remember."

A round of derisive chuckles followed my airheaded question. I let them mock me, pretending to be oblivious.

"You sank two stripes, so you're supposed to aim for those," Taylor said with another not-so-subtle lick of his lips.

"Oh, okay," I said softly, going to hit one that should've been an easy shot and then barely making the pocket. At least it looked believable.

"That was better," he said, grinning like a fiend as he went on to sink one solid then narrowly missed on the second. "How would you feel about a little wager?"

"Wager?" I repeated like he'd stuttered or something.

"Yeah, let's say if you win, I'll buy you a drink," he said.

Inside, I was smug as hell, but I simply said, "I'm listening."

"And if I win, you give me a kiss."

"Hmm," I murmured, like it was a tempting offer and I was playing coy. "What about your friends? Doesn't seem very nice to them if it's just me and you."

"You're right," he said, not at all surprised, though he acted like it. "How about—"

I stepped forward and ran a black-painted fingernail down his chest. "Let's speak plainly," I said in a deep, husky voice. "You're hard as a rock, and I'm here for a good time. You win, I'll suck your cock."

His eyes dilated. A smug grin turned up the corners of his thin lips.

"And if you win?"

I grinned right back. "I watch you suck one of theirs," I said with a thrust of my chin toward the other three.

"You're into that?" he asked, a little dubious.

I shrugged. "I'm into a lot of things. Mostly being straight forward. I don't like beating around the bush, and we both know where this is going. Now do you want me on my knees in the bathroom in ten minutes or not?"

He licked his lips once more and picked up the cue.

I was going to enjoy this.

CHAPTER 5
ROMAN

Two knocks on my office door made me pause. I lifted my head.

"Yes?"

The knob turned and in walked my beta, second-in-command, and closest thing I had to a friend. "Alpha," she said with a dip of her head.

"Caitlin," I replied. "Is there a problem?"

"I'm not sure . . ." she started. "One of the boys down at After Dark just called. Said a pretty little thing not from around here just showed up at the club." I lifted my eyebrows, silently asking her if she was really bothering me for this. Her cheeks darkened. "He said he couldn't identify her as a supe. She didn't smell like a wolf or have fae ears and her heart was still beating."

I tilted my head, waiting for more. It seemed that there was none.

"Please tell me you didn't just interrupt me when I asked for quiet to talk about a woman who showed up at one of my bars and could be any kind of supe. Witch. Succubus—"

"I know," she said. "It sounds like nothing, but Will doesn't call me for nothing. He said she has an air about her. Something not quite right. It reminded him of last time . . ."

I froze.

Last time.

She was talking about the creature that had killed my mate and unborn child.

I swallowed and then took a slow, steady breath. Thinking of them was painful, even three years later. I'd survived, and that was more than most wolves could say about losing a mate. I was here physically. But part of me hadn't made it. That part was buried in the same coffin. Six feet under and never returning.

"Pull up the video feed for After Dark," I said.

She gave me a tight-lipped, apologetic smile as she tapped a few buttons on her phone and then plugged it into a wire on my desk. A new screen opened, showing a live feed of After Dark.

I knew who they were talking about instantly.

Everything about her, from the flaming red hair to her full, luscious mouth, screamed trouble. And currently she was bent over one of my pool tables with that prick alpha from the Dawsons feeling her up.

My blood heated as something primal surfaced that I hadn't felt in a long time. My wolf looked out at the screen and found himself curious about the creature he saw there.

"How long has she been there?"

"Ten minutes," Caitlin said. "Maybe fifteen. You want me to send in—"

"No," I said, too sharply for what was warranted, but I didn't apologize. Alphas didn't apologize to anyone but their mate and parents. The former because they wanted to remain mated. The latter because it was owed. Caitlin was neither. "Let me make a call."

Caitlin hummed in acknowledgement. I pulled out my cell and hit speed dial two. Roxanne picked up on the third ring.

"What's up, loser?" she answered. The sounds of the club filtered through the speaker. From the muffled noise, I could tell she was holding the phone against her shoulder while wiping down the counter.

"Rox, what have I told you about—"

"No one can hear me. It's fine. What do you need, seriously?"

I sighed, my gaze still lingering on that unnatural red hair. I'd never seen a shade quite like it. While it was unmistakably red, the color was so dark it almost looked black when she moved around the table and into the shadows. She wore a devious little smile, and there was a wicked glint in her eyes.

"Tell me about the woman," I said.

Roxanne sighed. "She's new. Came down from the north, although her accent isn't quite right. She doesn't smell like a shifter, and I heard her heartbeat."

"So I've heard. You know what she is?" I asked, eyes narrowing on the loose hands that kept touching her slim waist. She touched a hand to Taylor's chest, and I had to work to keep my breathing normal.

That realization was alarming.

As was the recognition that my wolf wanted me to get up and go find her.

"No idea," Rox said. "She's got a weird aura . . ." My sister trailed off as if thinking. I breathed a little easier when the mystery woman and the Dawsons went back to playing pool.

Taylor went first, sinking a couple balls before missing. That bastard's greedy eyes roamed her body the moment she bent to line up a shot.

"Weird?" I repeated, mostly to keep myself focused on the conversation and not heading down to After Dark myself. It was only a fifteen-minute drive—

She aimed at nothing striped, and I frowned. When the cue ball bounced off one side and hit a striped ball, then pinged back and hit another, knocking them both into pockets, an uneasy feeling settled over me. Taylor's shocked expression confirmed it as she proceeded to clear the entire fucking table in one turn.

She never missed.

Holy shit.

"Roman?" Rox asked, coming back into clarity. Shit. I'd spaced.

"Yeah?"

"I said she feels like anticipation. Chaos. It's like there's a buzz of energy surrounding her."

"Uh huh," I murmured as the woman on screen turned to a slack-faced Taylor and then motioned to one of his men. He turned ruddy and started speaking in hard tones I couldn't make out.

She smiled scathingly and pointed out something in a quick

motion that had him clenching his fist. She turned to walk away, and he grabbed her roughly by the arm.

Whatever Roxanne was saying was instantly lost on me as red-tinted my vision. Blood pounded in my ears.

Taylor put his other hand on hers and then placed it on his cock.

Then my wolf lost his fucking mind.

CHAPTER 6
FURY

"YOU EITHER WALK TO THE BATHROOM AND GET ON YOUR KNEES, OR YOU DO IT right here," the sleazeball alpha growled.

I cupped my hand around his balls, fisting them tightly. I used my fingernails to dig into them.

He tensed, doubling over. "Bitch," he hissed.

"A deal's a deal," I said. "I was going to walk away, but then here you go, trying to force a girl. Is that how you got laid twice in the last week? You like throwing around those big, bad alpha vibes?" I asked him in a mocking tone.

Supes had a highly increased heal rate, but my demonic strength was definitely putting it to the test on his balls. "Logan. Owen," he wheezed.

A pack member appeared on either side of me.

I took a step back, releasing his family jewels, and my free hand went behind me.

They tried to grab my arms right as I closed my fingers around the pool cue.

Big mistake, boys.

"Hey, no fighting in here," Roxanne yelled.

One of them sent her a scathing look and walked over to the

counter in a way clearly meant to intimidate. The other two holding me just straight up ignored her.

"We got her," the one on my left said.

Taylor lifted his head, and anger mixed with lust shone in his eyes. "I was just going to get what was owed," he said, taking a step forward, "since you hustled me. But now . . ." He looked around, ignoring Roxanne, who was currently dealing with the fourth dude in their little gang. The rest of the club scattered like roaches. "I think I want a taste of it all."

"That's cute," I said. "I got a better idea."

"Oh?" he asked.

I smiled.

Then I headbutted him.

His nose crunched, and Taylor stumbled back, bleeding everywhere. Good god, he was a bleeder. I'd disemboweled people with less mess. The two holding me froze like idiots, which made it easy for me to tear myself away from them and turn around. I brought the pool cue up and smashed the thick end into one of their groins. The other rushed me, and I whipped it around to slam it into his temple. The sound echoed through the club like a gunshot, and he dropped right there.

"Lights out, motherfucker."

Two down. I turned back to Taylor, who launched himself at me. His anger made him sloppy. Dumbass. First rule of fight club was don't get mad.

Not unless you wanted to take a nap.

I cackled, and he stopped, completely confused. "I just came up with the funniest joke," I said, shrugging, then jabbed the pointy end into his kidney. "But you wouldn't get it. Inside joke, I guess," I added, laughing again.

I loved being a demon.

"Now," I mused, kicking his legs out from under him. "How about that bet, buddy boy?"

I was probably going a tiny bit overboard.

But, again, I was a demon. This was what I did.

I punished the guilty motherfuckers and made them repent for their sins.

Or something like that.

Taylor's knees hit the sticky floor. I tapped under his chin with the end of the pool stick, making him lift his head.

"I believe you promised to suck a dick if I won," I said, grabbing his jaw with one hand and prying it open. "I guess you can suck mine if you're so insistent on getting a little action."

I shoved the butt of the pool stick between his lips and let it slide back until I hit the tight barrier of his throat.

Taylor coughed, and his eyes watered.

"Uh huh," I singsonged, "I like it deep-throated."

I was still shoving the pool stick in and out of him when the door to the club opened.

A tingling awareness spread through me. Goosebumps lined my arms. I turned to look at the fourth member of the Dawsons, only to find him unconscious on the ground, bleeding from a head wound. Standing over him, a grim-faced Roxanne held a shattered Jack Daniels bottle and a phone to her ear.

Ah, that meant my first target was here.

Time to meet the big, bad Roman Mikaelson.

I dropped the pool cue and slammed my elbow into Taylor's temple. He slumped to the floor, lights out. I turned around, then placed my hands on my hips.

Ten feet away stood the man whose picture was in my file.

He was massive, built like a god—if there were any. Easily six and a half feet tall and all muscle with proud shoulders. His dreadlocks were pulled back, but a couple weren't playing nice and fell free around his face. They looked wild and fist-worthy. I could easily imagine his short beard brushing over the sensitive skin of my inner thigh. A tingle went through me that I shook off.

There was only one thing that really struck me as odd.

His eyes in the picture had been a warm brown.

Right now, they were ice blue and glowing.

The temperature in the room spiked a few degrees as he looked at me, and then in the deepest, most pained and husky voice, he said one single word that changed everything.

"Mate."

From the sidelines, Roxanne let out a low whistle. "Well, this just got interesting."

CHAPTER 7
FURY

Mate.

Um . . . no.

The word echoed in my head. The tingling electricity I'd felt moments ago buzzed along my skin in awareness. It traveled the length of me, leaving shivers in its wake.

Roxanne stood by her bar grinning like the cat that got the canary. Bitch was just missing feathers sticking out of her mouth. Another woman with ebony skin and curly brown hair streaked with silver halted at Roman's side. Her deep brown eyes were wide, and her mouth hung open slightly.

Then there was Roman.

I cleared my throat.

"You mispronounced Fury," I said, finding my voice. I had to get control of this situation again. All it had taken was a single word for me to lose the upper hand.

His hands were tightened into fists at his sides, and I heard a deep rumbling in his chest. The sound did things to my body that I wanted to ignore.

"Nice place you got here." I looked around, surveying the damage I'd done. "I'd be lying if I said I'm sorry about the douchebags I left on your floor. You really should be more careful about who you let in."

Roxanne barked a laugh and waved her broken bottle at me.

"Boss . . ." the other woman next to him whispered. She carefully placed a hand on his arm, and I found myself not liking that she'd touched him.

What the fuck was wrong with me?

Whatever sway she had, it must've been big. He turned his head ever-so-slightly, never taking his eyes off mine. The intensity of his stare weighed on me. I liked it, and every physical part of me wanted it. Except the rest of me didn't.

"Tell Will we're closed," he ordered.

The girl I could only assume to be his beta nodded, then turned to walk out the main door.

"You," he said. "Sit. We have to talk."

I narrowed my eyes and crossed my arms. "What's the magic word?"

Roxanne snickered, turning and walking back behind her bar. I watched her as she shook her head. "I'll get that food you asked for, Fury." She went to a door on the side, calling to Roman as an afterthought. "Regular for you, brother?"

Fuck me, did she just say brother?

This entire scene was catching me off guard. I was losing my touch. Flustered and heated by his mere presence. And frankly, that picture in his file didn't do him justice. Parts of my mind told me he looked like he'd be fun. That I'd like to lick him, maybe punish him a bit too—and not in the way I was supposed to. I scolded myself silently.

He grunted in response to her question, but I was still waiting for him to speak to me again. I raised my eyebrows at him expectantly.

His fists shook, and he said through clenched teeth, "Sit." He inhaled deeply. "Please."

"Now was that so hard?" I said, moving to a table that wasn't knocked over. I sat down, crossing my legs, and leaning back in the chair.

Roman covered the distance between us in a few large strides. His presence was imposing. Then he took a seat across from me and I almost felt like we had an even playing field again.

Almost.

"Who are you?" he asked. His deep voice was strained, and it called to me.

"Fury," I repeated. "I believe we already established that part."

"Not your name. *Who* are you? What are you doing here?"

I cocked an eyebrow, leaning forward and putting my elbows on the table. "That's not the same question . . ." I trailed off, waiting for him to give me his name. He just stared at me fiercely. "I'm sorry, I didn't catch your name. I'm assuming I shouldn't call you brother or boss."

"Roman," he answered. "But I wonder if you already knew that."

"Roman," I repeated, ignoring his slight. A rumbling sound vibrated in his throat as soon as I said his name. My core tightened at the sound, and I dug my nails into my arm. I schooled my features as best I could. "I'm from up north. Looking for a change. Something new to hold my interest." The tenor in my voice wavered as I aimed for snark but came closer to seduction.

"And have you found anything to hold your interest?"

"You could say that . . ." I responded.

"You're my mate," he said matter-of-factly.

A part of my body hissed *yesssss,* and it sent a bolt of electricity to the apex of my thighs. The rest of me said to get that bitch in check.

I shook my head. "I, uh, I don't do the mate thing. Polite pass."

His brows furrowed. "It wasn't a request."

I looked at him in surprise. "Mmm," I hummed. "I'm not exactly down for that kind of commitment." My stomach rumbled, and I looked away, wondering if Roxanne was coming back. It would seem my body was betraying me in multiple ways.

"You aren't really aware of how mates work. It's not a request, nor is it an order from me. It just *is,* Fury."

Holy shit, I liked the way he said my name. Sin and seduction and images of sweaty nights rolling in sheets flashed in my mind. I coughed, choking on the want that filled me.

"But I don't know what you are, and neither do the people who work for me," he continued. "So . . . what are you? You're not a shifter, and you aren't fae . . ."

"I couldn't tell you if I wanted to," I said cryptically. "I was born human. Then at the age of twenty-three, I changed."

"You . . . you were born human?" he asked, clearly shocked. He looked like he was conflicted, trying to make sense of what I'd said. His eyes raked my body.

I nodded.

"How old are—"

"My turn," I said, cutting him off. He growled. The motherfucker *growled* at me. I raised my eyebrows at him. "Tit for tat, Roman. You're calling me your mate—"

"Because you are." His hands were wrapped around the edge of the table on either side. He gripped it harder, struggling to keep his calm.

"So, it sounds like I'm entitled to ask some questions of my own."

I'd played out so many scenarios in my head. And this was never one of them. I was in completely new territory, and I wasn't quite sure which direction to take it.

Wing it. That was the best I had.

"Well, I've told you who I am. Where I'm from," I started. "What about you? Who are you, exactly? You just walked into the room, acting like I'd done something wrong when all I was doing was handling some unwanted attention."

"You beat four shifters in my bar—"

"Three," I interrupted.

His eyes flew open, seemingly shocked that I'd spoken over him again.

I pointed to the dude on the floor in a puddle of blood and whiskey. "I didn't do that. That was your sister." I shrugged one shoulder. "And let's get something cleared up here. You really have some fuck-me vibes going on, but you also have this dickhead attitude problem. Stop getting your panties in a wad when I speak. I've had enough of that in my lifetime." I leaned back again and crossed my arms.

"Noted," he said. No apology, no nothing.

Also noted. Prick.

"You beat *three* Dawsons in my bar"—his gaze finally left me, diverting to look at Taylor on the floor—"and throat-fucked one of them with my pool cue, apparently."

I wiggled my eyebrows. "Well, he lost a bet."

"What kind of bet did he make with you?"

"I don't think you really want to know the answer."

"Try me," he said, the muscle in his jaw tense.

"Fine," I said, tilting my head to the side. "Just a friendly wager on the game. If he won, I'd give him head—" Roman's sudden anger was palpable. Something vibrated off him in waves, penetrating my pores and crushing me. "And if I won, he'd give one of them head," I said, gesturing to the knocked-out shifters on the floor. "He was a pretty sore loser, though, so . . . I think you're up to speed."

"Were you going to give him head?" he demanded.

"Not that it's any of your fucking business, *wolf*, but I wasn't going to lose," I snapped.

The table rumbled, and a crack resounded through the quiet bar. A piece of wood came off in his hand.

"Hey!" Roxanne shouted as she reappeared carrying two plates. "What the shit, Roman? Stop breaking my tables."

He whipped his head to look at her. "They aren't your tables."

She set the plates in front of us. "They most certainly are. I run this place for you. All of it. Watch me walk and see what happens."

Now, I was no shifter, but I knew enough. Alphas didn't take that shit from anyone, sister or not. I couldn't figure out the dynamics, or why he didn't lose his temper right then and there.

But for whatever reason, he dipped his chin, ceding the argument as he gave her a non-verbal acknowledgement that she was right.

"Roxanne, do you mind getting me another gin?" I asked. "It'll be nice to have something to wash down these . . ." Boat-looking things. Folded sandwich? What the hell are these?

"Tacos," she said, giving me a weird look. "Jesus, you really are from up north. Don't even know what a taco is," she mumbled as she went back to the bar.

I shrugged and picked one up, taking a bite. It was good. There was a spice to it I'd never experienced before . . .

Fire.

I'd swallowed fire.

It consumed my mouth, my tongue, my throat.

I felt it in my nose.

I coughed, and my eyes watered as I pounded my own chest.

Roman stood up in a flash, bellowing to Roxanne. "What the hell did you give her?"

Roxanne came over, putting my drink on the table, and beside it, what looked like a glass of milk. "Oh, calm down. They're chicken tacos."

"Chicken and what?" he asked while I coughed.

"Drink the milk. It'll help," she said, nudging it to me. She looked at her brother. "And mango habanero salsa."

I gulped the milk down, feeling a cool and soothing sensation.

"What the fuck?" I croaked. "It's like swallowing a fire poker . . . that still has flavor, somehow. I can't even explain it. It's like sorcery."

"Taco sorceress," Roxanne snickered. "I am using that."

"That's enough," Roman said. She rolled her eyes at him, pulled up a chair, turned it backwards, and straddled it. She crossed her arms over the top.

"Look, Fury," she started, "my brother isn't exactly used to entertaining company, so I can see how he comes across as a dick who doesn't know how to actually talk to a woman, but he says you're his mate. That's not a thing we shifters take very lightly."

Roman bristled at her words but stayed quiet.

"Right," I said, finally feeling like I could drink some gin. I wasn't touching the devil food anymore, even if it did smell divine. I took a sip and held the glass up in a cheers to her mixing skills. "I appreciate the pep talk and the attempted murder by tacos, but I'm spent for the day. I'd love to chat more, so maybe I can drop by tom—"

"You're not leaving," Roman said.

I sighed. Really?

This was supposed to be more meet and greet style, not down and heavy. Ugh. I needed to prep for the deep shit. Being a hundred and twenty-six, I just didn't have the angst of these young people to do this all willy-nilly.

"I am, actually," I replied as I stood up.

Roman moved his body, blocking mine. Our proximity was too much to bear. I could smell him. Rugged and earthy and dripping in sex appeal.

My mind and body were at war. My mind shouted warnings and memories of my past. My body ached in places it shouldn't. Not over him. A deeper part of me whispered a reminder that he may be blocking my way, but he wasn't using force. He hadn't touched me yet.

"You aren't leaving my side," he growled. "Not until I know more."

"Move aside, Old Yeller. I'm not going home with you," I said, sidestepping him just to find him in my way again.

He grabbed my arm, and I inhaled sharply, tensing, and ready to rip his arm off his body.

I wasn't here to kill him. That was not the job. I also wasn't supposed to reveal my powers. But anger coursed through me at his audacity, and I didn't know that I could hold back.

"Buddy, I don't care how hot you are or who you think I am. Grab me without my permission one more time and you're going to get very well acquainted with my foot up your ass. So unless you wanna be tasting shit for the next week, I suggest you take your hand off me and step the fuck back."

His expression shuttered, and I sensed that wolf of his peeking out. It wanted to play. Too bad for both of them I wouldn't fuck targets.

There's a saying about mixing business with pleasure. Don't. It makes things messy. Complicated.

I wouldn't let that happen here. Not with retirement at stake.

Even if I was his mate, which was hard to believe given he had a mate already.

She'd died, and she sure as fuck wasn't me.

"Roman," Roxanne said in a curt voice. He didn't lower his hand, but he looked away for a fleeting second and narrowed his eyes. A predatory response. He obviously wasn't one hundred percent in charge of that wolf of his right now. I tilted my head to the side, studying him. "Can I have a word with you?" she asked.

Clearly debating, his gaze flicked between me and her.

The woman who'd come in with him stepped up. "I'll keep, uh . . ."

"Fury," I supplied.

She beamed at me like I was helpful for offering my name instead of being called 'uh.' "I'll keep Fury company."

Roman seemed to debate it for a moment. Meanwhile, his touch against my skin was doing wicked things to my mind. It was always fifty-fifty with me and men. Half the time, their touch disgusted me. The other half, I found myself enjoying it. In this case, it was a little more than that, and had he not been my target, I would've been all on board to explore how deep that savageness went.

Unfortunately for both of us, he was.

I lifted three fingers, and his eyebrows drew together.

"Three," I said, ignoring the rush of heat that had coursed through me at his first touch.

"Two," I continued, lowering one finger. A giddy sort of excitement fueled an adrenaline spike I hadn't felt in a few decades.

"One," I whispered, lowering one more finger. I half hoped he'd hold on, but that was crazy, right? Maybe it was some aftereffect of being alive again.

Roman made the right choice and dropped his hand. "Stay here. I'll be right back."

"Mhmm," I hummed. His piercing blue gaze swept over me once more, both drinking me in and assessing me—for what, I wasn't sure. He stepped to the side and followed Roxanne behind the bar and into the back, giving me a nice view of his ass as he went.

"He's a stubborn one, isn't he?" I mused to the woman who'd said she'd watch me.

"You'll need to forgive his aggressiveness," she said after a moment. I turned to her and arched an eyebrow, listening. "He lost his first mate."

"Lost?" I repeated, knowing full well what she meant.

"She died," the woman added. "Killed by another supernatural. We never found the murderer, and it's eaten at him ever since. For fate to give him a second one . . ." She trailed off. "You're either a blessing or a curse."

Her earnest eyes held depth as she stared at me, as if weighing my worth. I was immediately intrigued, because out of everyone I'd met since coming back, she was the first who seemed to see something past my fake smile and blasé attitude.

"Which do you think it is?" I asked, out of curiosity more than anything.

She smiled faintly. "If what I've seen is anything to go by, probably a bit of both."

I smiled back, slightly amused. She was wrong.
I was a dead girl walking.
A demon sent straight from Hell to be his worst nightmare.
Being his mate wasn't a blessing because I was his curse.
He just didn't know it yet.

CHAPTER 8
ROMAN

My blood soared.

My pulse thundered.

My wolf was raging with a need to be near his mate.

But instead, I was in the back room with my older sister and resident pain in the ass.

"You need to chill," Roxanne said, turning on her heel and crossing her arms. "I can sense your wolf. It's been a long time since he's been this close to the surface. I understand that he wants his mate—"

"No offense, Roxanne, but you don't understand shit right now." A flash of hurt crossed her face, but she pushed it back and replaced it with a hard glower. I scrubbed a hand down my face, then sighed. My body was angled toward the now-closed door that led to my mate. I was mostly one foot out the door, ready to leave, even as I looked at my sister. "Maya died. My wolf lost his damn mind and . . . killed so many people after that. Now I have a second chance. A new mate . . . I don't know if I even wanted one, but I sure as shit can't leave her alone now that she's here. He won't have any of it."

"And you, Roman? What does the man want?" she asked, playing the part of older sister and life coach to a grown-ass alpha. I didn't need it, per se. But it helped. We'd lost our parents young, and all I had was Rox. She might not be alpha of the Western Riders, but she was still owed more for all that she had done for me.

"I . . ." I opened, then closed my mouth, and my gaze gravitated toward the door once more. My wolf let out a growl. An itch had settled under my skin from the very first look. One I couldn't deny for long. "I don't know what I want, but I can't let her go. I have to keep her close, Rox. Keep her safe."

Safe.

Like Maya should've been.

Pain lanced through me at the reminder of Maya, and while my wolf felt it, the current bond was pulling at him too hard for him to lose himself in the loss and grief.

When he looked at Fury, he saw redemption and companionship. He saw his future. His whole fucking world.

But I was worried she would be our end.

And what about Maya? My first mate. The love of my life. She was supposed to be it for me. That was how it was supposed to go. But it didn't.

Could I really *replace* her?

The very idea made me recoil.

"Look, Roman, you're clearly fucked in the head right now," she said with a sigh. "I get it. I do. But that woman out there, baby bro, she isn't going to be Maya. She won't sit by and let you trample your way in. I've known her all of twenty fucking minutes and I can see that."

I clenched my jaw because she was right. Hell, I'd talked to her for five minutes and that was becoming painfully obvious.

"My wolf—"

"Will ruin this if you let him have control," she said. "After the San Jose massacre, you locked him out. I'd bet it's been a hot second since he tried for control. You've gotten used to his complacency, but right now he's riding you hard. I can see it on your face. Your eyes have been blue since you stepped into the bar."

Shit.

"I still don't know what she is," I said. "And it's driving me crazy."

"Yeah, well, it looks like it'll keep driving you crazy. You need to lock him down and find another solution to control your urges until you figure out what you wanna do with her," she said, making entirely too much sense and yet none at all.

My attention gravitated toward the door once more.

The scent of coming storms, fall leaves, and chaos calling to me like a siren.

Crack.

The echo sounded first, before the realization that Roxanne had slapped me.

I turned to her, glowering. "What the fuck, Rox?"

She shrugged. "Call it bar preservation. You looked like you were going to start pissing all over it. Your wolf in check now?"

Yes. Yes, he was. Albeit more than a little agitated.

I nodded once.

"Good. Now, what are we going to do about your mate out there? You know next to nothing about her, so you can't just take over her life. Maybe start slow. Ask her to dinner?" she suggested, trying to read me at the same time. The lilt in her voice told me she already knew I wouldn't be able to put the brakes on this that much.

And part of me didn't want to.

A dark, wicked side wanted to see that red hair wrapped around my fist and my cock pulsing between those cherry red lips. Physically, I couldn't deny that. I was rock hard now, tenting my pants like a fucking adolescent. In front of my sister, no less.

Thankfully, she took enough pity on me not to make a snide comment about it.

"Not good enough," I said. "I need her close. Beyond getting to know her, I need to know she's safe. At all times. The only way I can guarantee that is if she's with me."

"Roman." She sighed. Whatever else she was going to say didn't come out.

Footsteps started toward us, moving too fast. The door opened.

Caitlin burst in and came to a grinding halt. The guilty expression told me everything. "She's gone," my beta said. "She—"

"Where?" I asked, going hyper-alert as I started out the door with a single-minded purpose.

"The bathroom," she said. "She said she needed to take a piss. I let her go, not thinking . . ."

My feet were already moving, tracking my mate's scent.

Behind me, Roxanne groaned. "Damn it."

"I'm sorry, Roman," Caitlin stammered as I came to a full stop in the bathroom door.

I knew immediately what had happened. The tiny window, hardly bigger than an air vent at the top of the wall. The screen popped out. Written in lipstick on the mirror: *Sorry, not sorry. See ya later.*

I didn't realize I was growling under my breath until Caitlin stepped back.

"Roman," Roxanne said in warning. She sensed the shift. She knew what was coming.

My mate had run from me, and the last thing you should ever do with an alpha predator is run.

We give chase.

CHAPTER 9
FURY

I STARED AT THE KEYCARD IN MY HAND AND THEN SQUINTED UP AT THE matching sign on the building. It reminded me a bit of the demon dorms in its blocky gray atmosphere. Houston was hotter than Hell, though, and I couldn't figure out how to operate the damn sliding door. There was no place to insert the card. No sliding keypad. I'd observed two people entering about five minutes apart, and they'd just walked up, angled their hip toward a black box next to the sliding door, and it had simply opened.

After standing there bumping it with my hip—and no success—I was confused, exhausted, and about ready to put my fist through the glass just to get inside.

Then I felt eyes on me. The hairs on the back of my neck lifted. I whirled around and stopped straight in my tracks.

Blond hair. Blue eyes. Chiseled features. His lips were parted, taking me in. For a moment, I did the same, his similarities reminding me of another face from another time. A time where pale hands had beaten me black and blue. Where pouty lips had turned snide and cruel.

But there were differences too. His cheekbones were higher. Eyes a shade darker, more lapis lazuli than powder blue. His hair was lighter, closer to white-blond than honey.

I blinked, then remembered my senses.

"Do you need something?" I asked, pointing my thumb at the black box beside the door I was certain was my way in.

"No—I . . . well, this is going to sound crazy, but you look just like someone I used to know," he said.

"Oh?" I asked, twisting my lips. His easy smile made me settle. "Someone good, I hope."

He chuckled, a deep, earthy sound. "I wish. Old girlfriend," he said. "Things didn't end so well between us."

"Ah," I drawled. "I see. Your fault or hers?" I couldn't help myself. I was nosy by nature, and over a hundred years of digging into people's psyche just to tear them apart had made it worse. I half expected him to frown and walk away, but he surprised me when he laughed.

"Bit of both, I think. It takes two to tango," he said with a shrug. "I didn't love her enough. Took for granted what I had. Didn't realize that somewhere along the way she'd stopped loving me too."

"You don't sound too torn up about it," I said, blowing a sticky strand of red hair out of my face.

"It's been a while. Had a lot of time to think about it. I'd try to get her back if I knew how, but she won't give me the time of day . . ." He trailed off and then smiled again, offering another shrug.

"Hmm." It sounded like they probably weren't good together to begin with, not that most people liked hearing that, in my experience. "Well, good luck with that." I turned back toward the door and debated kicking the damn thing open just to get out of the blasted heat.

"Use the keycard," he said.

"What?"

"The keycard." He came around to my side and lifted the hand holding it to the black box. The light at the corner buzzed from red to green. The doors slid open, and a rush of cool air-conditioning hit me.

"Oh," I said, not-so-subtly pulling my hand away when he didn't let go.

I side-eyed him, wondering if we were going to have an issue, but he backed up and smiled.

"Have a good one," he said with a wink.

"Thanks, you too . . ." I turned from him to the door and back, but he was already gone.

Huh. Weird. I was still shaking my head when I walked into the reception area. A younger guy with dimples and light brown hair looked me up and down, appraising.

"Can I help you?" he asked in a way that made his intention clear.

What the hell was it with dudes today?

I looked down at my high-waisted pants and crop top. My guild brand marking me as a demon was displayed openly on my shoulder, looking like a strange tribal tattoo when really it was the language of the dead.

Sure, I was fit and had nice tits. My legs were shapely. I was a redhead, but man. This aura shit the angels talked about was no joke.

"You could have helped me when I was struggling with the door," I deadpanned, tilting my head.

He looked taken aback then cleared his throat. "We have a policy not to allow anyone in—"

"Whatever," I said, bringing the small backpack around and taking out another keycard with a note saying 621. "Where are the elevators?"

"Down the hall and to the right," he said slowly. "Do you have proof of identification? I haven't seen you before, and—"

I whipped out my ID and tossed it on his table. The plastic *tink*ed as it landed. The guy pursed his lips, clearly not liking the way I didn't have time to flirt. Or maybe he didn't like that I was irritable and coming off like an asshole. Who knew? I wasn't going to bother asking.

He turned to the tablet and started typing my name. It only took three letters for it to pop up, and there in the picture was my unsmiling mugshot from the last time Jake and Duke had made me get my guild registration updated. I looked about as done with it as I felt right now.

His gaze flipped from my picture to me as I placed both hands on the edge of his desk and leaned forward. "We good here?"

His pupils dilated with fear and arousal. "Y-yes."

I smirked to myself as I took my ID and backed away. He was adjusting himself when I turned the corner, and I rolled my eyes.

Earth was different than it had been in my time, and somehow still the same.

The roaring twenties, as they later became known, weren't half as thrilling or freeing as today. But some of that probably had to do with me already being dead. My time here was temporary. A mere stepping-stone to the next place.

Life was fleeting and exhilarating because of the unknown, but I preferred the devil I knew—and in this case, that was me.

It took me a moment to operate the elevator. Apparently, the fancy keycard was needed to open and close every door in the building. Soft, jazzy music meant to soothe surrounded me as I rode up. I side-eyed the speakers because it was a shitty knockoff of actual jazz, and it annoyed me more than anything. As the elevator came to a stop, the doors dinged before opening. I followed the signs down the hall to the door that read 621.

Given how unimpressive Houston seemed so far, I wasn't expecting much in terms of accommodations. I turned the knob, leaning into it with my shoulder as I pushed the panel open.

The sprawling apartment with high ceilings, marble counters, and a wall of glass overlooking the concrete jungle was a surprise to say the least. I stepped inside, a grin working its way up my face as I kicked the door shut behind me.

"Now, this. *This* is what I'm talking about," I breathed. A record player in the corner played King Oliver, a favorite from my time.

I listened to "Dippermouth Blues," bopping my head along as I gave myself a tour of the spacious one-bedroom apartment. I walked into a room with a king-sized bed overflowing with fluffy pillows. A door led to a bathroom with a big soaking tub, and a mini fridge full of gin. I knew without a doubt that was Duke's doing. He'd arranged a lot of the go-between from the Afterlife to the living realm, and that included more than just the portal. He would have been the one to set me up here if Jake didn't, but Jake wouldn't have been so thoughtful as to include booze. And he sure as shit wouldn't be playing my favorite music. We were cool with each other, but not on that level.

I was admiring a massive flatscreen and considering parking my ass in front of it for the evening when there were two taps against the window. I looked up, and my dream of being alone and catching up on *Grey's Anatomy* was shot.

I sighed when I realized who my 'visitor' was.

Walking over to the window, Hades tapped again.

Impatient bag of feathers.

I slid it open, and he flew right in in a flap of black feathers.

"Your next target is located in the south side of the city . . ." I let him ramble on while I grabbed a gin out of the mini fridge and started running a bath. I lifted some bath salts from the side of the tub and sniffed them.

Mmm. Lilac. I dumped half of it in the water and grinned when it turned a deep shade of purple. I put my hair up and started to strip.

"Are you listening to me?" he asked after a long pause.

"Mhmm."

"Then why are you getting undressed? You need to be working on introducing yourself to your next target—"

"Listen, birdbrain, I don't want to be here any longer than necessary either. However, I've got a real body now that has real needs. One of which is a bath, and it's calling my name. Come back to me during work hours. Wait—I don't get up at nine. Let's say eleven to seven, Monday through Friday, shall we?"

I dropped my pants, and he groaned. The bird actually groaned.

"It's five o'clock on Tuesday," he said.

I rolled my eyes. "Fine, work hours starting tomorrow. I need a short day today." Which I did. In all honesty, finding out I was Roman's mate was going to put a kink in things. I needed to process that and work through how I wanted to handle him, and the best place to do that was a hot bath.

"Fury, this isn't a vacation. You're on the clock the entire time you're here—"

"Don't you have french fries to steal from someone?" I said lightly.

He hovered, and I could've sworn he was plotting something behind those beady little eyes. Given he was just a bird, forgive me for not being all that worried when he said "fine" in a way that would've made Karen the Dreadful proud, then left me in a flap of wings.

Padding across the tile floors barefoot, I swayed to the music. My tub was steaming hot and half-full by the time I returned. I dipped one foot in and sighed blissfully, then stepped in with the other. It only took a second for me to lower myself into the water and then settle back against the cold tub. The first bite against my skin made me stiffen, and then the porcelain warmed. I found myself relaxing again.

I basked in the tub for a few minutes before my thoughts inevitably turned to Roman.

Much like the birdy, I was a workaholic. I just worked in different ways. Namely, alone. Like everything else I did that was unorthodox for a demon, I liked to mull over my cases. Each of them was a bottle of wine, and I had to figure out the best way to age it.

Normally, it wasn't too difficult. But when I thought of Roman, it wasn't the cool, professional detachment I usually felt. It was replaced by heat. Lust. His file said he was the alpha of the Western Riders. It was the largest pack in North America and ran the west from Houston to Alaska. There had been mentions of an older sister, though Roxanne wasn't named. His parents had died young. Another alpha had challenged his dad to power, and his father lost. The new alpha killed Roman's mom to set a precedent, and really just ended up setting off a twelve-year-old Roman.

He killed a man three times his senior and then took control of the Western Riders.

Despite his dark beginnings, nothing I read led me to think he was evil. He'd been a good, if somewhat inattentive, mate before his was killed. He ruled his pack fairly. All things considered, out of the three, he was the one I'd most wondered about because he didn't have the track record to make me think he'd want to end the world.

The more I considered it, the more I thought there was something I was missing. While I definitely saw he had a dangerous edge to him during the brief time we interacted, there were no alarms going off in my mind. No signs of cruelty or true apathy to humanity. None of the detachment or sociopathic tics it seemed the other two had.

He was all alpha, the most powerful known to have existed at that.

But he was still just a man.

So what would bring him to the decision to end it all? What was his trigger? His weakness?

His first mate had died, so that couldn't be it.

His parents had died, and that was so long ago it couldn't be the catalyst that would set him on that path.

And while he seemed close to his sister, something told me she wasn't it either.

Hm. I needed to get to the bottom of it and figure out what made Roman Mikaelson tick.

He did seem very sore about the mate concept, and that wolf of his wanted me something fierce. I saw his arousal the moment our eyes met. Maybe I could use that. Get beneath the skin. Who better to open him up than his mate?

I frowned. Clenching my hand into a fist.

That was cold, even for me.

But I was a demon. It was my job to dig deep and poke and prod until I found something. If I weren't his mate and he was simply attracted to me, that wouldn't be so bad. But supes took this mate shit to a new level. I knew that much, even if I only felt an inkling of what he currently was dealing with.

He had to be pissed after I left him a message in lipstick and crawled out the bathroom window. When he found me again . . . I grinned, my hand opening and skimming across my bare stomach. My fingers dipped lower into the plum-colored water as I slid them through my wet folds. I lightly pressed against my clit, thinking about that big, bad beast of a man and what he'd do when that time came.

There was going to be hell to pay.

CHAPTER 10
ROMAN

Her scent called to me as I combed the streets, tracking her and following her path. It was faint, sometimes erratic, like she'd been trying to evade me. Turning corner after corner then back again before going in another direction.

Roxanne was right. I needed to push the wolf down. Keep him under control. But neither of us wanted to be without her. She needed to be with me. Safe. It would be hard to keep him in check when we essentially wanted the same thing. I could feel him beneath the surface now, irritable that she wasn't close.

A gust of hot wind pushed between the buildings, dragging the smell of her further away. I growled in frustration, trying to find her trail again.

It was gone.

Anger rose and my chest heaved as I took deep, ragged breaths. I wanted to shred something.

The pounding of my blood throbbed in my head.

"She gets under your skin, doesn't she?" an unfamiliar voice said.

I furrowed my brows, looking around. A crow was nestled on a stair railing that led into a building. I turned my head, looking up and down the sidewalks, but no one else was nearby.

"You can keep looking around, but it's just us here," the crow said.

I could still feel my wolf bubbling beneath the surface, but I was taken aback with the situation unfolding before me. It was a momentary distraction.

"You're a crow," I said. "And you're talking . . ."

"And you shift into a wolf," he retorted. "This is a world of supernaturals. Don't act so surprised there, alpha. It makes you look stupid."

I sniffed the air and narrowed my eyes. "You aren't a shifter, crow." A predatory growl erupted from my chest. "Where is Fury?"

"Calm down, Roman. We're on the same side, you and me. Mostly."

"And what side is that?"

"Take a walk with me," he said, flying down to the ground. "We'll talk on our way there."

"I'm not following a bird walking around downtown." Confusion and distrust warred with the desire to find my mate.

"Good point. Thanks for offering the ride." He flew up and landed on my shoulder. I tensed, every muscle in my body going rigid, telling me to rip the bird into pieces. "Head north," he said. When I didn't move, he threw his wing out, nodding his little head. "That way, alpha. I thought wolves had a sense of direction."

"Look, crow, start talking before I rip your feathers off," I said through clenched teeth.

"Start walking, *dog,* and I'll explain."

I closed my eyes, tightening my fists at my sides. I sniffed the air again but didn't find her scent. I nodded and started walking.

"Oh, grab that little doohickey right there," he said, dipping his head toward the stoop he'd been perched on. It was a keycard of some sort. I reached down, picking it up.

"Now what?" I asked.

"Now put it in your pocket," he said. "Thought that one was obvious."

Smart-ass. This damn bird was a smart-ass.

"I'm Hades."

"What?" I snapped.

"My name," he said. "I assume you'd rather I call you Roman instead of dog, so . . ."

"Fine. *Hades*."

He held out a wing again. "That way."

I huffed, but headed north, waiting for him to say something. I felt his claws prick my skin. I wasn't exactly comfortable with a fucking talking bird—crow—Hades—balancing on my shoulder.

My wolf was momentarily quiet, assessing the situation with me.

"Take a left up here," he said finally, breaking the silence.

I huffed, my nostrils flaring. I didn't tolerate anyone giving me orders. "I thought you were going to explain something," I said, my irritation coming through loud and clear.

Hades ruffled his feathers, lifting a leg to scratch his neck. "I did say that, didn't I?" He put his leg back down, resetting his balance on my shoulder. "What do you want to know?"

"I want to know where Fury is," I growled.

"Calm yourself. That's where I'm taking you," he said.

I had to admit, there was a lot about this situation that was taking me by surprise. I hadn't been expecting help. I'd been expecting riddles. Tricks. Deceptions.

"Did she send you to find me?" I asked. I found myself hoping the answer was yes. I turned, taking the left he'd indicated.

He squawked in something vaguely like laughter. "No, decidedly not," he said. "Fury is . . . well, she's a pain in my ass. But you know how sometimes people need help even when they don't realize it?"

My heart skipped a beat, and I stopped. "Is she in trouble?"

"What? No. Take a breath, alpha. I mean, like, mentally. Emotionally. She's stupid—did I mention she's irritating?" He looked forward. "Three blocks, take another left."

I continued down the sidewalk. "And?"

"And I knew you were looking for her. I just happen to know where she lives."

"Are you her . . . pet?"

"Something like that," he said, then snapped his beak.

Suddenly, my wolf rippled beneath my skin and the hair on the back of my neck stood up. I smelled her; catching her scent on the wind just as I came to the corner. I picked up my pace, the crow pushing off my shoulder and taking flight. I ran, following him until he came to stop before a residential building. Her scent was strong. She'd been here, not long ago.

I tried to pry the sliding door at the seam, but it was locked. I shook the door, rattling it violently against its lock, but it didn't budge. I peered inside, seeing a male sitting at the counter. He made eye contact, then looked down. Daring to ignore me. No one would stand between me and protecting my mate. I would break the door, and then I would break his skinny neck for hiding her from me—

"Yo, Roman."

"What?" I yelled, spinning to look at Hades. He'd perched on a bench next to the entrance.

He nodded toward my pocket. "The thingy I told you to pick up? Use it. It's a lot easier than dealing with the cops for breaking and entering and—"

I reached into my trousers, pulling out the keycard, realizing what it was meant for. "Thanks," I muttered, swiping it, and entering the building.

"Six twenty-one," Hades called out. "Meet you there," he mumbled as the door shut.

I looked at the boy at the counter as he cowered. I sniffed the air. She'd been here. Right in this very spot. I leaned over the counter. I'd better not smell her *on him*.

"C-can I help you, s-sir?" the boy said.

"Elevators."

"I need to see some identification—"

I slammed my fist down. "Elevators, boy. Don't make me ask again."

His gaze shifted, and I looked in that direction, seeing the sign telling me where they were located. I turned and walked away.

"Sir, wait, I need to check you in—"

I ignored him, walked into an open lift, pushed six, and waited for the doors to close. She was here. In this building. I could feel her nearby. Everything inside me was on the verge of exploding but finding her would calm some of the rage. It would do nothing for the desire, but it would put the wolf to rest. For the moment.

I walked onto the sixth floor, finding apartment six twenty-one. I swiped the keycard and entered.

Her smell was overpowering. It was everywhere. I stiffened at the arousal permeating in the air. She was alone, but the scent was potent.

I stood in the entry with my eyes closed, breathing it in deeply, feeling it flood my veins. Then I heard a moan coming from down the hall. I snapped my head in the direction of the sound, rushing to the door.

I was not prepared.

Her body was draped in a bathtub filled with light purple water. Her legs spread wide, one hanging over the side of the tub. Her eyes were squeezed shut as she fingered herself, breathy moans escaping her lips.

I watched as she plunged her fingers in and out of herself. Her other hand gripped the edge of the tub, holding on as she writhed against her own ministrations.

My cock throbbed, heated and hard and ready. I wanted more than anything to rip her from that water and finish her off myself. Lick every last drop from her body. Fuck her until she came undone. I grabbed the doorframe in restraint, indecision warring within me. The wolf clawed to the surface, demanding we claim our mate. I pushed him down, the prospect of betraying Maya and what she meant to me was ever-present.

Her breathing became ragged, and her jaw clenched. I stared at her as her leg twitched, her mouth fell open, and the speed of her hand increased.

I watched her on the verge of release. I watched it climb. I watched her explode. Her eyes flew open and met mine. Staring at me, she let out a final moan and then screamed as she came. The sight of her getting off was too much for me to handle. My grip on the frame tightened, and it broke off in my hand.

"What the fuck are you doing here?" she growled when her tremors died down.

Reality slammed into me. Why I was here?

She looked down at my groin, at the straining bulge, and she lifted an eyebrow.

I cleared my throat. “You ran from me.”

“Well, this is unfortunately burned into my memory now,” Hades said, flying in and landing on the bathroom counter.

CHAPTER 11
FURY

"ARE YOU KIDDING ME?" I SNAPPED, STANDING UP IN THE BATHTUB, LOOKING between that goddamned crow and Roman. "Running from you isn't a reason for you to break into my apartment."

"I didn't break in," he said. I watched his chest rise and fall as he struggled to maintain some sort of control over himself. This was so not good.

Roman's eyes were ice blue and heated. The dichotomy was striking. It also told me he was having difficulty beyond what I felt like dealing with. I reached for a towel, stepping over the edge and onto a bathmat. I wrapped it around myself. I wasn't shy in the slightest, but wolfman was clearly having to restrain himself.

His body was tense, and he was packing something impressive beneath his trousers. There was no doubt my fantasy assumptions only moments before weren't far off.

I'd known he was there from the moment he entered the apartment. At the time, though, I was close to the edge. Knowing he was there, then seeing him as I pushed myself over . . . well, torturing him a little made my orgasm ten times better.

Now that the lust had cooled, and I was thinking straight again, I realized that tempting him like that after taunting him may not have been a great idea.

I looked at the gaping hole in my doorframe. "Oh yeah? Well, you're holding a piece of my door, so tell me again how you didn't break into my home?"

He didn't speak as he held up a hand. He kept his eyes on mine, but I looked to see what he was holding. My damned keycard.

I shot my eyes over to Hades. He nodded his little head side to side, clearly pleased with himself. "You're an asshole," I said to him, lowering my voice.

"And you're a pain in the ass. Get to work," he whispered in return, jumping off the counter and taking flight out of the bathroom.

I looked back up at Roman.

Shit.

He looked like he was going to explode any moment. I couldn't figure out if he wanted to fuck me or fight me. I'd be lying if I said a little bit of both wouldn't be fun.

But this wasn't the time.

This mate thing complicated a lot, and I hadn't had enough time to process it.

"What do you want, Roman?" I asked, trying to exit the bathroom, but he blocked me.

"You ran," he answered, unmoving.

"Yeah. And?"

"What do you mean *and*? You ran," he repeated. When I stared at him, he added, "You're not supposed to run from me."

I sighed. "Well, I'm not running anywhere naked, and now that you've come here, I have nowhere to run to. Thanks for that. So fucking move." I stepped forward, glaring at him. I would stand my ground.

"Lead the way," he grunted, barely moving enough for me to get by.

"Whatever," I mumbled, squeezing by him.

Our bodies brushed against each other as I slipped between him and the doorframe. The contact left a trail of goosebumps that had me clenching my teeth.

That was enough of that.

I pushed by quickly, padding down the hallway and into my bedroom. He was on my heels the entire way but stopped at the doorway and didn't follow me in. He stood at an angle, his back to my room as he averted his eyes and stared into the hallway.

I rummaged through a drawer, turning my head to glance at him over my shoulder. "Not worried that I might jump out the window and run from you again?" I asked, taking a tank top, shorts, and bra, and setting them on top of the dresser.

He exhaled roughly, still keeping his back turned.

"I mean, you already surveyed the goods, so I'm not sure why you're trying to be a gentleman now."

He said nothing, only clearing his throat in response.

But a quick look at his hands showed white-knuckled fists.

I'd known there would be hell to pay when I wrote the message in lipstick but seeing him in person so soon after was a little too much. His eyes were glowing blue, and the subtle growling hadn't stopped since he showed up. Whether or not he knew he was doing it, I still heard it. Roman Mikaelson's wolf wanted to mark me and never let me go. Completing my mission would be near impossible if I let him. Mates were complicated. Messy.

I dropped my towel and grabbed the clothes I'd laid out.

"What are you doing here, anyway?" I asked, slipping my underwear up and around my hips.

"You r—"

"Oh my god, yes, I ran from you. We've established that." I grabbed the spandex running shorts, putting them on. "But *why* are you following me here?"

A moment of silence spanned between us. It couldn't be that simple. He looked like he had so much more to him than a caveman mentality. So help me, if he said 'you ran' one more time, I'd club him over the head.

He risked a glance over his shoulder, his eyes raking my body before he turned away again. "I was going to say you *really* don't get it, do you? I'm here because you are my mate." He took a deep breath. "Yes, you ran, and I can't . . . I can't let you go unprotected."

It was hard to hold back my laughter. Walking dead girl, demon extraordinaire, did not worry about protection. I'd already been hit by a bus, and the day wasn't even over yet.

I sighed. "I don't need you to protect me. I'm fine on my own."

"It's not that simple. My wolf . . . our desire to protect you overrides what you think you need. I have to keep you near me. Keep you safe."

I pulled my sports bra over my head, adjusting my tits until they were comfortable. I slipped a loose tank top over it.

"That's a nice sentiment and all, but you can't stay here," I said. "You can turn around now," I added.

He turned slowly, taking in my form. He nodded. "I wasn't going to stay here."

Finally, we were in agreement—

"You're coming with me," he said.

I put my hand up, palm facing out. "Hold up. Rewind. Also? No. That's not going to happen."

I heard a rumbling in his chest as he furrowed his brows.

"Did you just growl *at* me?" I asked. "Let me explain something to you. I'm not leaving. This is my bed, I'm sleeping in it, and you can fuck right off thinking you can haul me to wherever you and your wolf want me to go."

"Am I interrupting something?" a female voice said.

I looked over, seeing Roxanne standing in my bedroom doorway. Roman practically snorted at her in response.

I threw my head back and groaned. "What are *you* doing here?" I asked. "Please don't tell me it's because 'I ran'," I said, using air quotes in what I hoped conveyed my extreme annoyance.

She cocked her head to the side and scrunched her nose, pulling her cheeks up in a face that said 'yeah, kinda.' "But I did bring drinks," she offered, holding up some bottles. "Thinking maybe the three of us can sit and chat. Again." She threw a glare over at Roman.

"I can't with you two," I said, walking to the door so I could go to the kitchen.

But Roman blocked me again, unmoving.

I pinched the bridge of my nose and squeezed my eyes shut. Taking a moment to think. "Kitchen, Roman. Glasses for drinks. Chairs for sitting," I grumbled.

He moved aside.

"Working on your people skills, I see," Roxanne muttered to him as they followed me to the other side of the apartment.

I grabbed some glasses and ice, bringing them to the living room and sitting as far away from them as possible.

Roxanne filled my glass with straight gin. I took a sip and let it roll on my tongue, pleased with how smooth it was. I looked at a ship on the bottle's label, unfamiliar with the brand. I had to admit, she had good taste.

I sighed. "The pigeon tell you how to get here too?" I asked Roxanne.

Her face scrunched up in confusion. "Huh?"

"Never mind. How did you find me?" I asked, taking another drink, and leaning back in my armchair.

She gave me an incredulous look and pointed to her nose.

Wolf. Right.

"I followed Roman's scent. You r—" My eyes went wide, and I glared daggers at her. She snickered, but instead she said, "wrote—you wrote on the bathroom mirror before leaving. He followed you, I handled a thing, then I followed him."

"And here we are," he said, finally joining in the conversation.

I looked over at him. His eyes were still blue, but he seemed to be breathing normally at least. "And here we are," I repeated.

Silence. Uncomfortable silence.

"Okeydokey," I said, breaking the tension. "So, I'm not good at entertaining, or whatever this is. I'm also not big on staying up super late. I may not look it, but I'm old and tired, and just grouchy in general. I also like my personal space, so . . ."

"I already told you, you aren't leaving my side," Roman said.

"And I already told you, I don't need protecting, and you aren't staying here," I said, anger starting to fill me again.

"Hey, hey, do you mind if I translate here?" Roxanne interjected.

"Translate what?" I asked.

She looked at Roman, and his jaw clenched. She widened her eyes at him, and he nodded.

"You know, just help the lines of communication between mates," she said.

I pressed my lips together and flared my nostrils as I exhaled. These two wolves . . .

She put her hands up in surrender. "I'm just trying to help. Sorta seems like maybe you're going in circles." She looked at her brother. "Am I on the right track?"

We both nodded.

"Okay," she said. "Now we're getting somewhere." She rubbed her hands together, scooting herself to sit on the edge of the couch. Roman sat in an armchair across from me on the other side of the coffee table.

I took a drink of my gin and set it down on a table next to me. I looked at her, motioning with my hand to continue.

"I think you've gathered by now that Roman isn't going to just give up. He says you're his mate. We don't take mates lightly. He can't just let it go, walk away, and leave you here," she said. "But I also understand that you don't exactly want to be caged, so to speak."

"You are correct," I said, crossing my arms over my chest. "So what do you suggest?"

"Well, I think I have a compromise. Neither of you will like it, exactly, but it's better than what you've achieved so far, which is a whole lot of nothing." She looked between us and waited for some sort of pushback. When neither of us said anything, she continued, "Roman, you don't want her left unprotected." He dipped his head in agreement. "But Fury doesn't want you up in her shit. She barely knows you." She looked at me, and I acquiesced with a single nod. "Then maybe you can stay with me."

"What the hell—" I started.

"Absolutely not—" Roman said at the same time.

She stood up and pointed at Roman. "When have I *ever* let you down, hmm? I get that she's your mate but get your shit in check. Under control. If you want to do this right, then fucking listen to me."

I waited for her to finish her rant before I cleared my throat and said, "I want to do this right as well, and that way is my way. That's where both of you leave, and I go to bed. Here. By myself."

Roman began to protest, but Roxanne spoke over him. "It's a fair offer, Fury."

"Horseshit, it's fair," I argued. "Why do I have to leave?"

She shrugged at me, crossed her arms, and asked, "Did you have a solution you wanted to present?"

"If I can't get rid of either of you, it seems like *fair* would be you staying here since you're both imposing on me one way or another. The least you could do is go out of your way instead of making me go out of mine."

Roxanne made a show of looking around, twisting her head in opposite directions, then turning her body in a circular motion. "Here?"

I nodded.

"Where?"

"I just said here."

"Right, but I thought maybe you were hiding a guest bedroom somewhere, so I wanted to check. Unless you were suggesting we share a bed, but I'm fairly certain you weren't heading in that direction."

I pursed my lips. She had a point. I nodded my head in the direction of the couch. "You can sleep there."

She barked a laugh. "Oh no, that's not gonna happen either. I'm inviting you to my home. With your own room, your own bed. And frankly, the city grates on my nerves."

I couldn't disagree with her there. "Well, it's hotter than Hell here, so I can see that."

"It's also the sound. It's non-stop." She pointed to her ears. "I need a break from it. I'm just south of the Beltway. Nothing fancy, but it's quieter."

"I don't know what that means, but I'll take your word for it." I huffed out a sigh. These fucking wolves. "Well, the city doesn't bother me, so it sounds more like a *you* problem. I think the couch is more than acceptable when I'm not the one who wants to leave here. So . . . are we done?"

Subtle rumbles came from Roman.

I rolled my eyes.

She pinched the bridge of her nose and took a deep breath. "Look, I am trying to help you. Him, of course, but also *you*. I'm not saying let's stay up and braid each other's hair. And if you want to smoke, go outside and keep it away from me. You have a cute setup here, really. Nice place. But the options are me, or him. You wanna stay in the city?

Cool. I'm for it. Let's shack up here. He lives in the city," she said, pointing at Roman, "so if we stay here, he's not far from you. Ever. We're wolves. You're his mate. Do the fucking math and quit being a pain in the ass, for the love of god. I'm tired, I'm hangry, so you can either go with my plan, or fuck him and get it over with. Take your pick."

She plopped back down on the couch and reached for the bottle of gin. She brought it to her lips, tilting her head back and taking an impressive drink. She slammed it down and looked at us, waiting for an answer.

Roman's knuckles were turning white as he gripped the arms of the chair. He closed his eyes, exhaling through his nose loudly. Then he nodded.

I raised my eyebrows in surprise. Their dynamics were something else.

Roxanne gave me a questioning look, waiting for me to answer.

I narrowed my eyes. "I—ugh. Fine. I just want to go to sleep. If this will shut both of you up for now, then so be it." I pushed myself up to stand, and Roman did the same. "Calm down, Lassie. I'm going to get my bag."

I stormed into my room then started tossing things into my backpack. I wanted to pluck Hades' feathers out and throw him in front of a bus. See how he liked dropping into a heaping pile in front of Duke's desk before he came back. At least I thought he'd come back . . . surely, he would. We were from the same world. That was how it worked. Either way, this was his fault. Showing Roman where I lived. Ugh. I'd grab his skinny little bird neck and strangle him.

I heard faint footsteps down the hall. They came to a stop at my door. I looked up to find Roxanne leaning against the frame. "Knock," she said.

"Wants eyes on me packing my bag, does he?" I asked. She winked at me, smiling. "This shit is going to get old."

She nodded. "I know. This is just so we can get to a better place and talk this through. Compromise and all." She took a couple of steps forward, picking up my boots and handing them to me.

I grabbed them, stuffing them into the bag.

"It won't be that bad," she said, trying to make amends. "I have booze, and I make killer tacos." She chuckled, clearly thinking about my reaction to her tacos earlier.

"Do you have any pets?" I asked, zipping up the bag.

She looked at me, confused. "No," she finally answered. "I work a lot. And I'm a shifter. Territorial by nature. Pets aren't my thing. I suppose I could have a goldfish if I really wanted something."

"Well, I hope you like birds," I said.

"Yeah, sure. They're okay, I guess," she responded as I slung my bag over my shoulder.

"Not this fucker," I muttered as I turned and walked past her, heading for the door.

When I got to the living room, Roman stood up, and a rush of heat flooded me. *Down, girl.*

He opened his mouth to say something, but his phone buzzed in his shirt pocket. He pulled it out reluctantly, and pressed the button, then held it to his ear. "Caitlin. What is it?"

I had a heightened sense of hearing too, despite what the wolves may have thought of me. His beta needed him.

"I'm in the middle of something. I can't leave right now—"

A look from Roxanne cut him off. "Go, Roman. I've got this. She's with me."

He didn't answer her. Instead, he just looked back and forth between us, his eyes flashing between brown and blue.

"Goooo," she said, the annoyance in her voice matching my general mood.

His shoulders tensed more, if that were even possible, but he finally exhaled and grunted into the phone, "Be there in ten."

I looked at his sister. "You said I get my own room, right?"

"Mhm." She turned to the door so we could head out.

"Does it have a window?" I snorted to myself when Roman's nostrils flared.

He took three long strides, coming to stand in front of me. His body invaded my personal space, and a very bad part of me wanted to keep pushing his buttons. "You will not run from me again. I will find you," he said, his chest rising and falling with his heavy breathing. His eyes flashed with hunger and anger.

"Calm down, Roman. I'm just yanking your chain." I looked down at his groin, then back to his face. I winked at him and turned to follow Roxanne.

I couldn't resist a bit of fun, and tempting the wolf certainly fit that description, but it was playing with fire.

Good thing I was familiar with the burn.

CHAPTER 12
FURY

Roxanne pulled her car up in front of her house. I flung the door open and slid out, landing on the ground. My head was spinning, and I was pretty sure my stomach was in my throat.

"Oh my god, I thought you said it wasn't far. Just a little bit south," I managed, swallowing bile.

She closed her door and came to stand by me. "Sorry. It takes about an hour to get from Houston to Houston."

I looked at her in confusion. "What?"

"Traffic. I mean, it's a big city. Like, fourth largest, I think? Something like that. Either way, driving takes a while," she said, leaning against the car and crossing her arms. "You didn't say you got car sick, otherwise I would've warned you."

Well, that was because I hadn't known either. One, cars weren't much of a thing when I was alive. Two, Duke failed to mention my human-ish body would come with those perks. I couldn't even die. But I could feel nauseated? What kind of sick joke was this?

"It's a new development," I mumbled. "Guess we know now, don't we?" Now that I was on solid ground, the waves of dizziness subsided, so I stood up slowly, dusting off my knees. "Well, lead the way. As pleasant as this day has been, I'm pretty much over it now."

I looked up at her home. It was cute. A little bigger than I'd thought, and it sat on a nice piece of open land. I hadn't expected that. Roxanne walked up the front path to the door, and I followed. She punched some numbers into a keypad on the handle and walked in. This new world was weird. It was one thing to watch some of these advancements on television shows acquired by the Department of Current Affairs. But now I was in it.

In the foyer, she pointed up the stairs. "Your room is up there. Go right, first door on the left. You have a bathroom attached too."

I nodded, taking in the tile floors and high ceilings. "Not a bad place you've got here. Is it just you, or should I expect you to have a friendly, furry visitor?"

She shot me a look. "It's just me."

Noted.

I started up the stairs. "Well, I'm—"

"I'm pouring myself another drink and ordering some takeout."

I spun myself around, stepping back down to the ground floor. "I'll be joining you for that drink."

"Are you hungry?"

Thinking about her fire tacos, I narrowed my eyes. "I'm not sure."

She laughed, knowing where my mind had gone. "C'mon. I'll get you something less spicy."

I walked into a large, open kitchen. It was so cozy. A little rustic. Open shelves lined the walls, but everything was organized and had its place. The wood block countertops and farmhouse sink were modernized, but they felt familiar. Like home. An odd feeling of nostalgia washed over me before a bitter memory ended it.

Roxanne grabbed a bottle from the counter and took two glasses from a shelf. She poured two fingers of whiskey in each, then pushed one over to me.

I saluted her with it. "Cheers." I took a sip, savoring the burn. "About that food . . ."

"Ah, right." She pulled out her phone and tapped on it for a minute. She looked up. "How about a chicken burger?"

I stared at her. "I thought burgers were made of cow."

She stared at me in return. "Chicken burgers it is." Then she went back to her phone. When she looked up, she pocketed it and then pointed to a living room with comfortable leather sofas. "Go. Sit. Food is on the way. You'll like it."

She was ballsy in an annoying, yet somehow endearing kind of way. Or maybe it was just because she was feeding me. But with that kind of bossy attitude, one might think she was the alpha instead of her brother.

With the bottle on the table, we sat across from each other, waiting for the other to speak.

"So. Didn't you say something about a pet bird? You didn't bring a cage or anything, and I didn't see him . . ."

I groaned. Hades. He had to have followed me.

"Um, yeah. So don't be shocked when he just happens to show up here. He's irritating like that."

"I thought . . . he just flies out on his own?" she asked.

I rolled my eyes and nodded.

"What the hell kind of bird is he?"

"Crow."

"You have a *crow*?"

As if the feather duster had been listening to us, there was a rapping on the glass.

Tap. Tap. Tap. Tap. Annoying-fucking-*tap*.

"Speak of the devil . . ." I said, getting up to let him in.

Roxanne watched me with confusion and intrigue as I opened the window. "How did it find you? I've never seen a pet crow, much less one that tracked its owner." She took a sip of whiskey.

"*He*, not it," Hades said, landing on top of a wingback chair. "And she doesn't own me."

That did it. Roxanne's whiskey got caught in her throat and she coughed, spewing liquid all over her marble coffee table.

I sighed, getting up and smacking her back while she tried to get air. "Roxanne, Hades. Hades, this is Roxanne. Don't be a douchebag, pigeon."

"I'm sorry, he fucking *talks*?" She coughed.

"Yeah, it gets old real fast," I said, glaring at him and sitting back down. I jerked my head, gesturing to tell him to go away. "Go somewhere and nap, will ya? Or do whatever it is that birds do."

"Tick tock," Hades said, pushing off the chair and taking flight.

I narrowed my eyes at him, watching him disappear. By this time, Roxanne had managed to catch her breath.

"He's an asshole. I'd apologize, but it's not my fault," I said, raising my glass.

"Care to explain that one?" she asked me.

"What? Why he's an asshole, or why it's not my fault? Because I honestly figured both were pretty obvious."

She shook her head. "Not that. Explain how you have a talking crow. He's yours, so I assume the asshole just comes with the territory," she quipped.

"Point to you," I said, acknowledging the quality of her jab. "Got him from a witch, actually. Lost a bet."

Her eyebrows knitted together in confusion. "You . . . *lost* a bet? I don't understand."

"What's not to understand? I lost and got stuck with him. Like a bloody curse."

She started laughing. "Well, that's just fucking mean."

Didn't I know it.

The doorbell rang, and Roxanne got up. I listened to her open the door, tell someone thanks, and come back in. She set some bags down on the counter and gestured for me to get up and come to the kitchen.

I walked over and grabbed the box she handed me.

We ate silently while we stood, leaning against the counter. I finished off my fries first, loving the taste of salt and grease. It tasted better in a human body, even with the whole being dead thing.

I took a bite of the chicken burger, feeling some heat as I swallowed. "This is spicy."

"This is Texas," she said in response.

"It's good," I commented. "I wasn't complaining."

She nodded, finishing her burger and wiping her hands on a napkin. "So, what's your story, Fury?"

I wiped my hands off too, then used the napkins to clean the corners of my mouth. "I already told you at the bar. There's not much to tell."

"Sure you did," she said, her tone indicating she didn't believe a word I'd said. "You're young, pretty, but you don't appear to be stupid."

"Why, thank you," I said, bowing my head. I walked over to the couch again, taking my seat next to the whiskey, and she followed me. "What about you? You're young enough. Pretty. There's no Mr. or Mrs. Roxanne?"

She smirked at me. "I like my privacy."

"That makes two of us, and yet here we are," I said. I thought about where to go with the conversation. If I was going to be stuck with a babysitter, at least I could take advantage of the situation and get the information I needed to move forward. "So I figure, as my captor, you owe me a little bit of background, am I right?"

She threw her head back and laughed at me, pointing to the door with the hand holding her glass. "Door's right there, doll. Feel free to leave, but I will have to call Roman. The choice was him or me, remember?"

Well, she had me there.

When I didn't move, she took a sip, and said, "What do you want to know?"

I smiled. "I'm so glad you asked." I leaned back into the cushions and crossed my legs. I draped one arm over the back of the couch, and I held my whiskey on my lap. "So he says I'm his mate—"

"Do you deny it?"

I pursed my lips. "So with that . . . declaration, I figure it's probably good for me to know what the hell this family is all about. I mean, he's the alpha of the pack. I'm no shifter, but I understand the importance of what that title means."

She nodded. "Fair enough, but I don't hear a question."

"Tell me about your family. About the pack."

She cocked an eyebrow at me. "Our father was the alpha of the Western Riders. He formed the pack in his youth, and it grew in numbers and strength. Our family bloodline was strong . . . some said it was too strong." She traced her finger over the rim of her glass as she spoke. I didn't interrupt, even though I knew all of this. "There was always this stupid rumor of ancient magic, but that's how jealous people talk. My father was a good leader. He had a firm, commanding presence, but he was also fair. He had a stubborn streak in him, one that Roman inherited." She smirked as she said it, clearly thinking fondly of something he'd done to gain that same label.

"I think that may have passed on to both of you, but what do I know?" I smiled a little.

She huffed a short laugh. "At any rate, every story has a villain, right? A wolf named Marlon challenged my father to gain status as alpha. None of us really know how my father lost, but he did. And for Marlon, it wasn't enough to kill my father. He wanted to set an example. His great show of power. Marlon killed our mother in front of hundreds of Western Riders. He put us up front to watch, no doubt planning to kill us too. Everything changed that day. Roman was just twelve at the time. Not yet a man. The wolves holding Roman back never saw it coming. The pure unbridled rage that exploded from him the moment our mother was killed was unlike anything we'd ever seen before. He killed Marlon first. Then he slaughtered his followers—every single one of them—in seconds." She stared at her glass, not making a sound.

I uncrossed my legs, leaning forward and putting my elbows on my knees. "He killed everyone when he was twelve?"

She nodded, her eyes unfocused, reliving the past in her mind. It was a look I was all too familiar with, having worn it many times myself. She shook her head, as though it would remove the thoughts, then looked at me. "He's been alpha ever since." She slammed the rest of her whiskey back.

I whistled low. "You're telling me a twelve-year-old took over as alpha and no one tried to challenge that?"

She snorted. "If you would have seen what he did that day, you wouldn't have challenged it either."

I tilted my head to the side. "No, I suppose I wouldn't."

That was probably a bit of a lie. That kind of strength was intriguing. Not that I wanted to challenge him, but I wouldn't be opposed to seeing that side of him. I got to deal with dead, boring shithead people who were as awful as they came. They didn't have any spunk to them. Not really. That was reserved for the living.

"So after that—"

"My turn," Roxanne said, taking the opportunity to change the subject. "Normally, I'd play the big sister role and ask what your intentions are with my brother. But this is different."

"Have this conversation often, do you?"

She shrugged. "He's rich, and he's powerful. A lot of women want him."

"And what about him? Does he want a lot of these women?"

She leaned forward, pouring more in her glass, and then laughed. "Roman used to be quite the ladies' man. I've had that talk more times than I care to admit, but not since . . ." The look on her face changed, and a dark shadow came over her features. I knew instantly what would have caused this shift, and why it would affect even her.

"Caitlin mentioned his mate died," I said softly.

Roxanne nodded, taking a deep breath. "She was killed. Murdered, actually, by an unknown supernatural. We never could figure out what kind of supe they were, or what the motive was. No faction came forward. No one challenged Roman or tried to gain power or the allegiance of the Western Riders. No one came for me. No one came for the rest of the pack. Just Maya and the baby . . ."

What?

The baby?

Those two words hit me, though I tried to hide it. Parts of my own past writhed from the memories, making me nauseated again. "The baby?" I whispered.

"She was eight months pregnant with their child. My niece . . ." She shook her head.

I could hear the insurmountable pain that was coursing through her. A feeling I wasn't familiar with crept through my veins, even as I tried to tamp it down.

"What did he do?" I asked, taking another swig to rid myself of the emotion I felt like I was absorbing from her. I couldn't help but wonder if this was what I was missing. That thing that just felt off . . .?

"Christ, what didn't he do? He lost it. He lost himself in his wolf. Killed more people in his blind rage than I care to think about. He was at war with himself, and he almost lost the pack because of it. He's pushed his wolf down ever since." She stopped to take a drink, holding the glass at her lips for a moment as though she were seeing something in her memories. "That is until you came along."

My gaze flew up to meet her stare. "I didn't actually *see* his wolf," I said. I wasn't sure why I thought I was being blamed for something, but it did sound that way.

"You saw those icy blue eyes, yeah?"

I nodded.

"Meet the wolf. You can see why he's hesitant to let you out of his sight."

Interesting. It certainly explained the difference between the real Roman and the picture I had in my file. It wasn't simply a trait, and it provided information that helped me understand a few things.

I wasn't sure how to feel about any of it. He claimed I was his mate, and there was some heated thing inside me that acknowledged a connection between us, but I couldn't let it happen. It fucked with entirely too much. Besides, I was dead. A demon. Pretty sure some wires had gotten crossed somewhere because demons and shifters weren't mates.

"You're right. I can see it." I stood up, ready for this weird day to end. I had my work cut out for me. "I'm going to go to bed. That's a lot of information to process, and I was tired hours ago when he busted into my bathroom, so—"

"Fury?" she said, interrupting my attempt to get out of the room.

"Yeah?"

"Please don't run again. Don't fuck with my brother. He's all I have left. Like it or not, he says you're his mate. A second chance at having a mate is rare. So rare it's more like legend. So do me a solid and don't piss off the wolf, okay?"

I gave her a non-committal hum because it was the best I could do.

"Good night, Roxanne," I said, walking out of the room. I paused, holding the doorframe. I turned and looked at her. It wasn't often someone did something nice for me. "Thank you for . . . well, for everything tonight. I appreciate it."

"Rox," she said. "My friends call me Rox. And you're welcome."

I pressed my lips together in a tight smile as I left the room.

First, I had a mate. Now, I had a friend.

This shit just kept getting harder and harder.

CHAPTER 13
EZRA

I PISTONED IN AND OUT OF HER ASS. THAT TIGHT HOLE CLENCHED AROUND ME. My cock throbbed as she moaned, "Yesss."

"Yes, what?" I purred, nearing the edge. She might be a quick fuck, but that didn't mean I wouldn't make it good.

Footsteps approached the couch where I had her bent over. My second-in-command, Kendrick, coughed twice under his breath. Whatever he had to say, he wanted her gone.

I groaned, picking up my pace. "Yes, what?" I repeated, a hint of irritation coloring my tone.

"Yes, Daddy!" she cried.

I went limp.

My eyebrows drew together, and my lips parted as I stared at the twenty-something vampire with complete and utter disgust. She had been hoping to gain my favor. Behind me, Kendrick chuckled, knowing exactly what had gone wrong here.

I pulled out, and she looked over her shoulder, dazed and heated with desire.

"We're done here," I said, dismissing her.

The colored lights of my club, Bite Me, danced over her skin as she frowned in confusion and hurt. I took a step back, not liking the emotion on her face.

"But—you said—"

"I have many kinks, girly, but that isn't one of them. Now go on, I'm busy." With that, I turned my back on her, tucked in my cock, and zipped my slacks.

Kendrick waited for her to walk away before speaking, but the mirth in his expression annoyed me.

"You needed something," I said, pouring myself a drink. All around me, blood and other body fluids were being exchanged. Bite Me was the most exclusive sex club in the city. Partially out of human curiosity since it catered to very specific tastes, namely the supernatural.

"One of our scouts discovered something very . . . intriguing this afternoon," Kendrick said. I took a sip of the rye whiskey and lifted an eyebrow, waiting for him to go on. "Roman Mikaelson has a second-chance mate."

I paused, then set the glass back down on the polished end table.

"That *is* intriguing," I purred, my sour mood waning at the possibilities that development presented. "How did the scout come to learn this?"

"He was at the elder Mikaelson's bar when a fight broke out. Supposedly, the girl was the reason. Roman showed up, and our guy watched the mate bond snap into place."

I stroked my jaw, running my thumb over my chin in contemplation. "A new mate," I mused. "Fascinating. Especially so close to the summit. Tell me about the girl. Who is she?"

"No one knows," Kendrick said. "She seems to have come out of nowhere, but news of her is spreading quickly. Apparently, she handed the Dawsons their asses shortly before Mikaelson showed up."

"All of them?" I murmured. There was an itch inside me. A thread that needed to be pulled. After all my years, things had started to fade. Pleasures merely brought contentment. Sex and blood and other frivolities helped keep me here in the moment instead of drifting.

But for the first time in decades, I found myself curious.

It was a dangerous thing.

"Taylor and his three goons. Get this, shortly after Roman made everyone leave, she came out of a window alone. No one's seen her with him since, but she was seen with the elder Mikaelson heading out of the city."

"You've done well, Kendrick," I murmured. That itch burrowed deeper. I needed to scratch it. A second-chance mate that ran? Now that . . . that was just too good to pass up. "Send the twins to pick her up. I want to meet this girl."

Kendrick nodded. "Consider it done."

As he turned away, another thing occurred to me. "Do you know her name, at least?"

"Fury," he said after a pregnant pause.

"First or last?"

"Both, it would seem."

Hm. Very curious, indeed.

CHAPTER 14
FURY

I ROLLED OVER ONCE MORE, CURSING INTERNALLY WHEN SUNLIGHT PEEKED through the windows.

My first day back on Earth had been an utter shitshow, and the second wasn't shaping up any better after a night of endless tossing and turning. A thin sheen of sweat covered my skin. My dark red hair lay in messy strands across my pillow and eyes. My muscles were sore, and my throat was dry.

I felt hungover. Or maybe it was withdrawal, given I'd barely had anything to drink since coming back. It was hard to tell.

I was debating the merits of a shot for breakfast when something tapped on the window. I rolled over again and groaned into my pillow. Maybe if I ignored him, he'd go away . . .

Tap. Tap. Tap.

Motherfucker.

I flung the sheets aside and dragged my ass out of bed. The cute little clock on the nightstand read six thirty. In the morning.

At this rate, I might as well call it a double.

"You better have a damn good reason for getting me up this early," I grumbled as I undid the latches on the window. Hades flew past me in a flurry of black feathers and settled himself on the twining metal bed frame.

"Your next target—"

"Oh, for fuck's sake," I snapped, dragging my fingers through my tangled hair in frustration. "Listen here, because I'm only going to say this once. Duke sent you here to help us communicate. Not hound me. Not help my targets—which in case you forgot are going to end the fucking world—and not to wake me up at six thirty in the fucking morning."

Hades blinked. "Well, *you're* clearly not a morning person."

I facepalmed and gritted my teeth. "I'm not an anything person, pigeon. I don't like people, and that includes talking crows. So unless you have a message from Duke, fuck off. Next time you piss me off, I'm going to go bird hunting and we'll see if you come back."

Hades stared at me, not saying anything. The silence dragged on, and he didn't move.

I cracked. "Are you going to say anything?"

"I was waiting to make sure you were finished," he replied.

I closed my eyes and tried to remember all those anger management classes I'd taken in the Afterlife. Remember what Vlad the Impaler, my sponsor, had said.

Count to ten.

Then stab.

In hindsight, I probably shouldn't have picked one of the most notorious demons as my mentor. In life, he'd been an angry man with more than a few screws loose. I really wasn't sure how he'd passed the forty percent mark given his track record, but Jake said times were shittier back then. Standards and the way they were measured were different. Either way, in death, he made a weird kind of sense and gave seemingly good advice.

He also didn't try to fix me or look at me with pity.

Hence why I'd picked him.

So, taking dear old Vlad's advice, I closed my eyes and counted to ten.

I made it to eight before Hades said, "What are you doing?"

"Counting."

"Why?"

"Because if I reach ten and you're still being a dick, I'm within my rights to stab."

Hades sighed. "Fury, that's not what I'm—"

Two knocks on the door made us both pause. The knob turned, and Roxanne peeked her head in.

"Everything good here?" she asked.

"Why are you up so early?"

"Heard noise," she replied, rubbing her eye with the back of her hand. "I'm a light sleeper. Since I'm up, you want breakfast?"

My stomach gurgled in response.

She laughed. "I'll go get us some coffee and donuts. There's a place a few miles down the road that's pretty good, and they don't judge when I show up in pajamas."

"You don't have anything here?" I asked.

She shook her head. "Apart from some protein bars and a jar of peanut butter—no. I spend most of my time at After Dark, and cooking is work."

A-fucking-men to that.

"I like cake donuts. If they don't have that, get me a maple bar," I said.

"Make that two," Hades chimed in.

I side-eyed the pigeon, and Roxanne lifted an eyebrow.

"Uh huh, we'll see what they have."

With that, she closed the door, and it was just me and Feathers again.

"Last I checked, donuts aren't part of a crow's diet."

"Coming from the girl who lives on alcohol," Hades scoffed.

I narrowed my eyes. "Doctors say a glass a day helps the heart."

Hades cocked his head mockingly. "A glass of wine, not a gallon of hard liquor."

Semantics.

"Are you ever going to get to the point? You woke me up and—" I paused when I heard a loud thump downstairs.

Hades groaned, a sound somewhere between a weird purr and a growl. "That's what I've been trying to—"

I held up a hand. "Roxanne," I called. Not a shout, but louder than I had been.

No answer. My skin prickled. I slowly turned to the door.

My footsteps were soft but not quite silent as I started toward it.

Over a hundred years of practice had given me a grace I hadn't had in my twenties, but I still wasn't a born supernatural. I was just a dead one.

My fingers brushed over the cool metal. I turned the knob slowly, wincing when it squeaked. "Rox?" I called again, feeling like the dumb girl in a horror movie who goes to check only to become a victim herself.

Least I wouldn't stay dead, I thought on a sarcastic, cheery note. That would really suck for Roxanne, though. Doubly so because supernaturals didn't get to go to the Afterlife. Their souls couldn't make the journey. Something about their magic extinguished them instantly, meaning if she died, she'd be dead-dead.

That sobered me instantly, and hangover or not, I pulled my shoulder back as I inched the door open.

"Hades, I need you to fly downstairs and tell me what you see," I said quietly.

"We're a little too late for that."

What?

I turned around only to find myself staring into a pair of orange eyes.

"Sorry about this," the man said. A needle jabbed into my arm.

I moved quickly, stomping on his foot then throwing my forehead into his nose. A wicked crack sounded that would've made me gleeful if not for the sluggishness quickly washing over me.

"What did you do to me?" I breathed as black spots formed in my vision.

A nap sounded really good right about now. Under different circumstances.

"Just a little drug to help you sleep," he said, catching my shoulders even as he bled all over me. His grip was strong, but not painful.

Well, at least my kidnapper was a gentleman.

That had to count for something.

CHAPTER 15
ROMAN

CRACK.

My fist connected with Taylor Dawson's cheekbone. His head snapped back, and he groaned, taking his punishment as silently as he could.

"Really? You said that? Just . . . 'you ran'?" Caitlin asked as she leaned against a table, arms crossed.

Crack.

Taylor's nose exploded and he grunted, and I could sense his wolf begging to surface. But Taylor was smarter. At least in this. I'd watched the security footage. Heard him. I knew what he'd intended to do to Fury. What they'd all intended to do. Yes, she was my mate, but that aside, I didn't condone rape. Especially not in my establishments.

I took a handkerchief from my pocket, wiping the sweat off my forehead and dabbing at the blood on my hand.

I nodded, acknowledging Caitlin's question. "Yes. Three or four or ten times. I don't even know."

I sighed, and she snickered. "Roman, come on. You've got to do better than that."

I gave her a deadpan look. "I'm well aware, but when she's

around, I'm at odds with my wolf the whole time. I end up focused on tamping him down and then I can't even string a sentence together."

Caitlin sighed. "True as that may be, she's not going to give you the benefit of the doubt. She's not a shifter."

Crack.

My fist connected with the side of Taylor's head, knuckles to temple. His neck strained as his head whipped around like a bobble before smashing into the back of the chair. A low groan of pain left his lips before he went silent. Still conscious but starting to waver. I needed to get on with the actual punishment for his crime, but I couldn't deny my wolf's need for blood. In truth, we both needed it. This male had meant harm to our mate. He was lucky I would let him leave here alive.

I needed him to send a message. Besides, death would be too easy.

"Shifters aren't the only ones who have mates," I pointed out to Caitlin. Turning my back on the alpha strapped to a metal chair, I walked over to the fireplace. Two fat logs glowed bright orange, flames leaping off them into the air. I picked up a silver branding iron.

Pain prickled in my palm, the silver agitating my skin just by touching it. I'd used this tool often enough in my first years as alpha that the skin on my right hand was completely calloused over and nearly as hard as the rocky fireplace.

I dipped the other end in the flames and waited for the metal to change color.

"We may not be the only ones, but something tells me she doesn't come from a kind that does. All of us that do have a natural inclination to form a pack and stick together. We don't do well alone." She glanced at Taylor. His head was bowed, and sweat-slicked hair hung forward in straggled pieces. "I get the feeling she's used to being alone."

"You're not wrong," I agreed reluctantly. "My mate . . ." I trailed off when the image of Fury was replaced by Maya in my mind. Her light blonde hair was already being eclipsed by Fury's red halo, and it wasn't just powder-blue eyes that haunted me in my sleep now, but the darkest shade of brown I'd ever seen. "Fury is unlike anyone I've ever met. Will was right that there's an air about her that's familiar to what was left behind . . . to what we felt at Maya's death, but it's not the same. While I gravitate toward it, Fury's feels more honest."

"It's not as deceptively inviting," Caitlin agreed. "I don't feel like she's going to pull all of my secrets out of me by making me trust her. It's more like you know you can't, but you want to be near her anyway. She's a flame you want to run your hand over just to see if you can without getting burned."

I lifted my eyebrows at my second-in-command, and she averted her gaze.

"Put a lot of thought into her aura, have you?"

Caitlin lifted her shoulder in a half shrug, the apologetic look leaving her eyes. "Normally you have better judgement than anyone, but in this, it will be impossible for you to be impartial. Someone has to look out for you and the pack when you can't." She smiled to cover up the awkwardness of it.

"As long as I don't have to concern myself with my second vying for her attention," I replied smoothly, the rest of it forgotten. "Then again, Rava may skin us both alive if that happened."

Caitlin chuckled under her breath. "That was one time, Roman. One, and you'd already moved on to another she-wolf. I was just doing my job and picking up the pieces." She gave me a sly smile.

"It was only one time because you mated her."

She shrugged again. "You're just lucky you'd already moved on. I would've taken her from you in a heartbeat, and neither of us could've stopped it." Her carefree jest fell flat when my own predicament became an uncomfortable comparison. With one big difference: Rava had been head over heels in love with Caitlin from the first moment they saw each other, and Fury most definitely was not.

Something I both appreciated and was frustrated by.

"I have to see her again today," I said after a moment, my mood souring. "Can you call Rox and ask her what time she's coming in? I'll meet them at After Dark and pick Fury up there."

Instead of giving me shit like before, she dipped her chin in understanding and moved away from the table. "You got it," she said, before stepping out. Her footsteps faded, and then it was just me and Taylor.

I glanced down at the branding iron and lifted it when the metal glowed the same orange hue as the logs. I turned back around, and Taylor lifted his head.

Before, there'd been anger and pride and even acceptance on his face.

Now it was just fear.

He knew what was coming. I could tell by the way he thrashed against the silver cuffs that held his arms behind his back and legs to the chair.

"You don't have to do this," he said. "I learned my lesson. I promise. I'll never touch the girl again. I'll—"

"You'll never touch her again because I say you won't," my wolf said, speaking through me in a gravelly tone. The word of an alpha was law, but my word? It was unbreakable. "Taylor Dawson, alpha of the Dawson Pack, son of Cherise and Milo Dawson—you have been found guilty of plotting to rape and coerce a female, a behavior unfitting of any pack member. You were an alpha. What you do bleeds into your pack. You're meant to care for them. Lead them. It's unbecoming to abuse your power." As I spoke, his wolf started to surface. Blue flickered over his irises. The chains on the chair rattled.

"You can't do this," he started, voice rising in tandem with his panic. "You can't—"

"You're hereby sentenced to live as a rogue for the next two hundred years. You will be exiled from all pack lands and unable to shift. This is the punishment I give to you."

With the words spoken by my wolf and sealed with his magic, I grabbed a fistful of Taylor's hair and wrenched his head back. Then I pressed the silver emblem to his forehead.

The next part was more unpleasant than the first.

If not for the scent of burning flesh, then because his shrill screams grated my ears. My wolf wanted to shove the rod straight through him and be done with it, but I had to grit my teeth and keep my hold steady because that wasn't the way we did things here.

I waited as long as my wolf would allow before pulling the branding iron back.

A circle insignia now darkened the flesh on his forehead between the eyes. Even blistered and bleeding, the 'R' on top of my family's crest made it painfully clear who and what he was.

A rogue.

An outsider.

Someone who was no longer welcome, and barely a shifter in his own right. If he survived his two-hundred-year exile without any further issues, I'd reconsider. Until then, it was done.

I didn't hear Caitlin enter amidst his screaming, but she was standing at the door when I turned to place it back on the metal rack. I paused, noticing the carefully blank expression on her face. I'd only seen it a handful of times in my life, and none of them had been good.

Fear gripped my heart, the worst coming to mind immediately.

"What happened?" I said, in the same growly tone of my wolf. Normally, I made a point not to use it on her, but the heightened stress my wolf was under had left him impatient.

He wanted answers now.

Neither of us were prepared for what came next.

"Vampires took Fury."

CHAPTER 16
FURY

My body went airborne, slamming into something hard above me shortly after I came off the ground. I groaned.

Where the hell am I?

My eyelids cracked, and past the fogginess still weighing me down, I registered the compartment I was being kept in as the trunk of a car.

"Son of a—" My curse cut off as the wheels slowed then jerked to a stop.

My shoulders were painfully stiff from having my arms tugged harshly behind my back and secured at the wrists. I tugged lightly. The biting feel of the plastic told me they were zip ties.

I wasn't scared, really. Considering I was already dead, there wasn't much left for me to fear. It was mostly the situation of being drugged and kidnapped that I found off-putting. The ties were a bit tight for my liking, but I was familiar enough with the feeling that I could ignore it for the most part.

There were no footsteps. No sound of warning. One moment I was on my side in a—thankfully clean—trunk, and the next the hatch lifted and two boys who couldn't have been older than eighteen or nineteen peered down at me. Their matching orange eyes and pale skin gave me a good idea of what I was up against.

"Oh, good," the one on the right said. "You're awake. Sorry about that. Had to make sure you wouldn't try anything funny while I was driving. Safety first and all that."

My eyebrows inched higher. "Right," I drawled. "Listen, I don't know who you two are, or why you want me, but—"

"Name's Tony, and that's Alphonzo. We call him Al for short," the other one said with a boyish grin. He was the one I headbutted. Blood smudged his pale skin around the neckline of his black shirt. He'd cleaned up hastily. "It's not us who wants you—nice on the eyes as you are. Our boss hired us to pick you up. He wants to meet you."

The first one leaned over and lifted me out of the trunk, taking care not to bang me against anything. With his thin frame and average height, the kid was definitely a vampire. There was no way he would've been able to lift me so easily otherwise.

"Why are you being so nice?" I asked skeptically. "I mean, I'm not complaining, but you did kidnap me, and I headbutted Tony over there."

"Boss didn't say he wanted you roughed up," Tony answered as Al put me down nicely, giving me a second to regain my footing as a wave of vertigo crashed over me. "We bring you in all scratched up and bruised, and it'll be our fault. No can do. The De Luca twins do the job right. Besides, you can be forgiven for trying to defend yourself. We *did* kidnap you, after all." He smirked. How had I ended up with the world's nicest kidnappers?

"You still haven't mentioned who your boss is," I pointed out as Al led me through a brightly lit parking garage. It was half empty, but the cars that were here were *nice*. Whoever he was, the guy was loaded.

"Isn't it obvious?" Tony said, as we approached an elevator that was manned on either side. Also vampires.

A creeping feeling was working its way over me as they pressed a button and the double metal doors slid open. We stepped inside with only a nod of acknowledgement from the guards. Al hit the button for the second floor, and my curiosity piqued.

"If it is who I'm starting to think it is, drugging me was kind of a dick move. I would've come voluntarily," I said, as we came to another stop.

Tony chuckled as the double doors slid open once more.

Music played softly in the background. Softer than I would've expected given the faint red glowing lights, scantily dressed people, and—oh yeah—fucking. Certainly one way to start the day.

Beside us, a group of five were getting it on. One female was sitting on a guy's face while sucking another's dick like it was an Olympic sport. Dude number one ate her out while a second chick sucked his cock on all fours as she got plowed from behind. Judging by the dark red smudges on their skin, there was a little more going on than my initial take.

This was *definitely* who I'd thought it was.

The De Luca twins escorted me through the sex club without pausing. Their professionalism was really something, because no matter what their flavor of kink was, this place had it. That was for damn sure. The Afterlife had similar places. I'd even been to a few, but too many demons frequented them, and I wasn't big on mixing business and pleasure. If I was going to fuck someone other than myself, I wanted to be sure I wouldn't have to see them semi-regularly. The same went for watching or being watched. The last thing I wanted was to be on the brink of getting off then catching sight of Karen the Horrible spreadeagled. Gag. No thank you.

We turned the corner and came to the end of our little tour. A wraparound set of lush black couches were pushed all the way back against the wall. Four men and one woman sat on them, but I barely noticed any of them.

Not when Ezra Xue peered up at me and sucked the breath from my lungs.

He was tall, but not large. The lean muscle apparent beneath his suit hinted at a different sort of predator than the wolf alpha. Where Roman was a wall of muscle with biceps the size of my thighs, Ezra was a lithe panther who would stalk me from the shadows. His shoulders were wide, his hips narrow. Dark hair that was so inky black stood apart from everything else. His skin was a shade more amber than the De Luca twins, but only by a touch. Despite all that, the thing I noticed most were his almond-shaped green eyes. They were the same color as polished emeralds, and they were currently narrowed on me.

I lifted an eyebrow in condemnation. "So this is the big, bad boss who sends a couple of kids to do his dirty work?"

Tony and Al's objections were white noise to me as a slow, sexy smirk spread across the alpha vampire's face.

"You must be Fury," he said, his lips caressing my name with an almost possessive lilt I hoped I'd imagined. "I must say, when I heard the wolf had another mate, I expected you to put up more of a fight—"

I pulled my wrists and the zip ties snapped. Tony's eyes widened a little in my peripheral vision, and Ezra chuckled. Unbeknownst to all of them, demons outclassed every supe in the living world and the Afterlife when it came to strength. It was our greatest asset. One I enjoyed thoroughly abusing when it suited me.

"Call me curious. I wanted to see who went through the trouble of kidnapping me." I paused, a flush creeping across my skin. My heart was beating hard despite the lack of danger or anxiety surrounding my situation. "Now that I know this is a petty jab at Roman, I'm bored."

"You don't care for the wolf?" Ezra asked, leaning forward. His elbows rested on his knees, and he laced his fingers together in front of him.

"Did I say that?"

"You ran from him," Ezra mused, drawing a long eye roll from me. What was it with everyone focusing on that? "I want to know why."

"Mighty bold of you to expect I'll answer. Is that an alpha thing?" I asked, dangerously close to the edge of flirting. Where my body *wanted* Roman, his brutish demands grated on me. With Ezra, I could see some of the same brazenness, but it was more a request.

"Probably." He shrugged. "I'm used to getting my way." Ezra unlocked his fingers and stood, slowly walking toward me. "How about this? Answer my questions, and—" His smooth velvet tone came to an abrupt halt when we were only a few feet apart. He paused, nostrils flaring. A hungry look entered his eye.

"And?" I prompted impatiently.

A tense moment passed where it was unclear if he was planning to eat me or fuck me. It faded when his head dipped, and a dark chuckle slid from his lips. He must've been more unstable than the file let on.

This guy had issues. Somehow, though, I still didn't see that kernel of dark that made me think he'd end the world. That bothered me. I considered myself a good judge of character with a sixth sense for sorting bad people from less bad. I'd met demons worse than these guys, which really affirmed I needed to find Hades and get him to send a message to Duke.

"Well, this is interesting. Unexpected." He nodded to himself. "But not unwelcome."

"What?" I squinted. His words only added to my theory that he was a few screws loose.

Ezra Xue stepped forward, eating the distance between us, and inclined his head. I blinked, waiting for the moment where he stopped and tried to use his closeness to intimidate me. It never came.

His lips crashed into mine. Cool, but firm. He licked the seam of my mouth, and when that didn't make me open up, *he bit me*.

Not hard enough to draw blood, but enough to make his intentions clear. He cradled my jaw with one hand, his thumb slightly too tight on my neck to be sweet. The other he threaded through my hair, pulling me closer.

I reached up to grab his hair, planning to wrench him away. Instead, my fingers wrapped around his silky black locks. He sucked on my bottom lip, making my mind falter. The attraction between us flared, heat coursing through my veins.

He was a target . . .

But it was just a kiss, *right*?

There was no harm in a little fun on the job, and when someone kissed like he did . . . My lips parted, and I felt his answering grin. His tongue met my own, making me wonder what else he could do with it. I groaned, settling into him, not minding the audience when I knew I'd never have to see them again after this job.

He slipped his hand from my hair to run it down the length of my back. He grabbed a handful of my ass and pulled me into him, making me feel his erection.

I bit him back. I needed to slow this down, but something inside me was screaming not to.

Then the music cut out. The club fell silent. An inhuman growl came from only ten feet behind me.

"Get your hands off my *mate*." Roman's voice sent a shiver through me, especially when Ezra did no such thing.

The vampire lifted his head, releasing my lips and giving me a saucy grin before turning his cheek to look at the werewolf.

"I think you mean *our mate*. Looks like you're not the only one who got a second chance."

CHAPTER 17
DORIAN

THE FAMILIAR RHYTHM OF MEASURED FOOTSTEPS ECHOED IN THE HALLWAY, interrupting my thoughts. I didn't need to look at the clock to know what time it was. James's routine was as rigid and by the book as my own. I kept my arms crossed, staring out the library window at the manicured green lawn of my estate.

The door opened, and James entered silently.

"Morning, James." I took a deep breath, turning away from the window and walking to my reading chair.

"Good morning, sir," he said, placing a tray on the side table as I sat down. The *Wall Street Journal* lay folded next to a cup of Earl Grey tea. "Do you have any exciting plans for today?"

"You know I don't."

"Can't blame me for hoping, sir," he said, clasping his hands behind his back. "Breakfast will be up shortly. Is there anything else I can get you beforehand?"

"You mean beside the copy of How to Navigate Tinder that you left in my bedroom? No. Just the eggs Benedict," I said, raising an eyebrow in reference to his suggestive reading material.

There was the slightest twinkle in James's eyes as he nodded. "Very well, sir." He turned and walked out of my library, leaving me with my tea and my thoughts.

How to Navigate Tinder. It was an absurd suggestion, and a remarkable reminder of how the world had evolved. I'd watched humanity change for centuries. The wars, the famine, the death . . . the progress. Despite what that hopeful fae thought, I didn't need a date. Or to get laid, since I knew very well what that app was for. Of all the things I could possibly want in this world or the next, that was not it. Across the decades, across the world, sex was by far the easiest thing to find.

I picked up the cup, sipping the hot tea. I wasn't sure if I even enjoyed it anymore. It wasn't bad. It was just routine. I wished I could have said I looked forward to it every morning. I'd hear humans discuss their love affair with coffee, claiming it was their addiction. At times, I pitied their ignorance. Other times, I envied it. Nothing so trivial could've made me happy.

Few things in the world had ever brought me true joy, and the one who truly had died over a thousand years ago, taking all echoes of happiness with her.

The same footsteps sounded in the hallway, interrupting my thoughts again, but this time they had an urgency to them. I looked up at the door as James entered.

"Sir, you have a call from Roxanne. I believe you'll want to take it," he said, extending a phone to me.

I nodded as he exited the room. Putting the phone to my ear, I greeted one of those few that had brought me a semblance of joy. "It's before nine a.m., Rox. Are you ill?"

"God, I wish. Maybe then this would all be a fever dream," she answered. Her voice wasn't its normal pitch. It was scratchy and dry, and not full of snark and life.

"I'm listening," I said.

"I'm sorry to bother you, Dorian, I really am. But I need your help. Favor for a friend," she said.

Roxanne never asked for help, unless it was picking out artwork, or an evening gown.

"What's wrong?" I asked.

"It would be much easier in person. Can you come down to Bite Me?" I could hear the hesitation in her voice.

"You can't be serious," I said. "You want me to come to Ezra's place? Ezra's. Why would I do that? And furthermore, what are you doing there?"

"I—" Shouting erupted in the background, cutting her off.

I pulled the phone from my ear in surprise, and a buzzing sensation crept across my skin.

"Will you all shut up for, like, three minutes, please? I'm on the phone trying to get some answers," she yelled.

"Oh, is there a hotline for troubleshooting supernatural love connections? I must've missed that in my Houston Tourist Guide."

"Could you *not* be you for just a hot second?" I heard Roxanne say in response to an unfamiliar female voice.

"Rox," I interjected. "I need more information. What exactly do you need from me?"

She groaned. "We have a situation, Dorian. You've been around a long time, seen a lot. Have you ever heard of two alphas ending up with the same second-chance mate?"

Did she just say . . .? Ezra *and* Roman?

Silence spanned between us as my mind raced for the first time in hundreds of years. Shouting filled the background of whatever room they were in at the club. My curiosity was piqued. I wanted to know more. I wanted to see it for myself. If anything, it would be entertaining.

"D?" Roxanne said, derailing my train of thought.

"I'll be there in five minutes."

For the first time in a millennium, I didn't know what to expect.

CHAPTER 18
FURY

WHO COULD TELL WHICH WAS WORSE: FINDING OUT SOME WIRES WERE crossed in the fabric of the universe and I had two mates on this assignment from . . . well, Hell, or being in the middle of a shouting match after a night of drinking and a morning of getting drugged? The only silver lining was that Roxanne somehow knew Dorian Radcliffe and had called him. I no longer had to orchestrate some happenstance meeting between us. Which was good. I'd been working out how to manipulate a secluded fae who was older than dirt and kept coming up short. The downside was, well, the rest of this situation.

I pinched the bridge of my nose while Roman and Ezra had a pissing contest over me. I needed a drink.

"It isn't possible," Roman repeated, sounding like a skipping record. He struggled to control himself, and his wolf. His muscles vibrated, taut and tense.

"What would you know about what's even possible for supernaturals, shifter? You're like, what, thirty-three? You haven't seen shit in your lifespan," Ezra said.

Roman rumbled as Roxanne interjected. "Oh, c'mon, Ezra. You mean to tell me you've seen this? You know damn well you haven't heard of this either."

He shrugged, walking over to a small private bar in his office. 'Office.' It was a mini lounge, private and clearly off-limits to anyone at the club. I leaned against the edge of a green couch, wishing I could teleport out and sleep off this nightmare. Was retirement really worth this job?

Ezra picked a bottle of good gin and poured the clear liquid into a chilled rocks glass. He twisted a lemon into it and walked back over to me. At least he had good taste in liquor. Score one for things in common, I suppose. He leaned against the couch as well, surprising me when he handed me the glass.

"Looks like you needed a drink," he said with a wicked smile and flirtatious wink.

"Well, cheers to you for being perceptive," I said, holding up the glass in thanks before drinking some.

Roman seethed at Ezra's proximity to me, and Roxanne clearly judged me for my choices. Walking toward me, she said, "You do realize it's only a few after nine in the morning, right?"

"Liquid breakfast never hurt me before," I said. Which was, in fact, true. Demon perk.

"Mmm hmm. Given I was drugged about three hours ago and never got donuts—I'm starving," she said, looking up at Ezra with annoyance.

I held my drink out to her, and she pressed her lips together pointedly. Okay, then. I turned to Ezra, and asked, "You did drug my friend and deprived us of our donuts. You owe her. Do you have food here? A not-vampire menu?"

"Of course. It's early for the kitchen, but they can bring something," he said, pulling his phone from his pocket. He tapped out a message.

"If you bring her dog food—" Roman growled, his eyes shimmering an icy blue.

"Calm down, I wouldn't dream of it. My mate has asked me to bring her friend food, and that I will do," Ezra purred.

I sighed. Loudly. "Thanks for that."

He chuckled as he put his phone back in his pocket, then crossed his arms.

"You drugged her?" a voice said from the corner behind us.

I jumped a little at the unexpected intrusion. It would seem our fae had arrived, and he was stealthy. I tucked that piece of information away for later.

Dorian walked out of the shadows and I drank him in.

Oh. My. Upper Management.

His picture didn't come close to doing him justice either. My files were worthless. Supernaturals may have been an accident. A break in the human design. But that body and bone structure were not.

His steps were measured. His shoulders were broad and muscular, accentuating the V shape of his back and torso. The way he kept one hand in his pocket as he strode forward exuded confidence. Even in a dark charcoal gray suit, he radiated power and strength. His white-blond hair was almost a pale blue in the right light, and his amber eyes surveyed the room while I admired the sharp angles of his squared jawline.

I took another drink of my gin, electricity buzzing across my skin.

"Top o' the morning to you too, Dorian," Ezra said.

"I asked you a question. Don't make me ask again," he said.

Ezra rolled his eyes. "No, I didn't drug her."

Roman scoffed, and Dorian raised his eyebrows, looking at Roxanne. "He didn't. His little henchmen did," she said.

Ezra grinned and shrugged, pushing himself off the couch as he walked past everyone. "I answered the question you asked, your mighty lordship. I'd like you to remember you're in my club. The rules apply here."

"I was invited, and I understand the rules. They were written before you were made," Dorian said, staring the vampire down. His tone was so cold it filled the room with a chill.

"Of course they were." Ezra smirked, turning to me. "Fury, this is Dorian Radcliffe. An old friend of Roxanne's, apparently, and probably the oldest fae out there."

I drained my drink in two swallows and placed the glass on the dark mahogany desk with a clink. "Well, then, now that we've established that." Dorian snapped his head up to look at me. Glad I had his attention. "Can we move this little get-together along? It's been a peachy start to the day, what with waking up early and being kidnapped, but I'd like to figure a few things out, and Rox says you're the man—err, fae—to do it. So . . ."

"Impossible . . ." he whispered, narrowing his eyes. "You're . . ."

I paused, narrowing my eyes in return.

Did he know what I was? If he outed me, this job was over. His file had said nothing about being a mind reader. Or knowing how to identify supernaturals and demons. What had tipped him off? Or did that special ability come with being the oldest living fae in the world?

He took a step toward me.

I stopped leaning on the couch and squared my shoulders, taking a defensive stance. "What's impossible?" I asked him, trying to ignore the way my skin began to itch.

He stopped in front of me, his towering height not intimidating me in the slightest as he looked me up and down.

I stared at him, waiting for a response. "Let's do this. Say what you need to say, Dorian." The second his name left my mouth, that buzzing itch on my skin rippled across my entire body, setting my skin on fire in a cold flame unlike anything I'd ever felt.

He closed his eyes, angling his head upward, taking a slow, deep breath and exhaling, as though preparing himself. He opened them again and stared at me as he said, "You're my mate."

This could not be happening. A loud ringing in my ears drowned everything out.

As my mind tried to process the words he'd just said, I heard Ezra laughing. "Well, I have to admit. I didn't see *that* coming."

Roman shuddered as Roxanne grabbed him, whispering harsh words about control. She looked over at Dorian incredulously. "What the hell is going on?"

He kept his eyes on me, never so much as glancing toward her. "I'm not entirely sure. You both claim to have a mate bond with her. It would seem I do as well."

Roman managed to speak through his visible anger and frustration. "This doesn't make sense, Dorian. We can't all have the same second-chance mate. It's unheard of."

Ezra laughed again, and we all looked over at him.

"Something funny?" I asked him, seconds away from knocking that smug smile off his face.

"Surely you see the humor in this. It's as fucked up as it gets." He crossed his arms and looked down at his feet, his shoulders lightly shaking from his laugh. "None of us likes the other, and fate decides to throw us the same mate? What are the odds of that happening?"

What were the odds, indeed? And where was Hades? I needed to talk to Duke, and soon. This wasn't supposed to happen. Once was a problem, but three times was—as Roman kept pointing out—impossible.

"Dorian, have you ever heard of something like this happening?" Roxanne asked, sitting back down, and rubbing her temples. "I mean, *before* it was complicated. Now? I dunno. You're the most knowledgeable supe, and you've been around the longest. What do you know about this? You can see for yourself that it's real."

Dorian walked over to Ezra's bar. "Do you mind?" Ezra shook his head, gesturing for him to go on. He poured himself a club soda and took a sip before he began. "Second-chance mates do exist in the scrolls, but they're so rare they've essentially become legend."

His honeyed voice mimicked the words Roxanne had said to me the night before. I wondered if he had said them to her before.

"Roxanne said you lost your mate too," I said, interrupting them. I had some questions of my own.

Dorian glared at me. How someone could look at me with a heated intensity that felt ice cold was beyond me. "I did. Over a thousand years ago."

I looked over at Roman, feeling somewhat bad for bringing it up after my heart-to-heart with his sister. "I know what happened to Roman's. What happened to yours?"

"She was killed."

I sighed. "Who killed her?"

"Does it matter?"

"I suppose not." I took a deep breath. "Ezra, what about you?"

"She rejected me," he said without emotion.

"Okay, so that means this isn't a second-chance situation, right? I mean, if she rejected you, then you were never—" Roxanne cleared her throat, and I looked to her. She shook her head slightly, her eyes widened in a silent warning. Oh . . .

"It means that whatever controls mate bonds didn't break when she rejected me." Ezra shifted his weight and looked at the other guys. "It doesn't matter anyway. She was killed a year later."

"Okay. So, how many second-chance mates have you seen or read about in your lifetime?" I asked, looking over at Dorian.

"Until today? It's happened sixteen times in the past fifteen hundred years that I know of, so no, I haven't seen or heard of two alphas sharing one, and certainly not three. The timelines didn't overlap so it wasn't a possibility." Dorian sipped his drink, walking around the bar and sitting in a chair at a small table. "I'm surprised, and somewhat disappointed, really, that no one is going to ask the real question here."

"How is that not the real question?" Roman said.

Dorian tapped his finger on the table, then looked up at me. "Fury?" The way he said my name sounded strained. "Care to ask the question?"

I cocked an eyebrow. This hot fae was calling me out. I just didn't know if he knew the full extent of it or not. He was cold and calculated, and I couldn't quite read him. Out of all three alphas, he seemed to be the only one who could blow. But the others? Not so much. Either way, I knew what he wanted from me in that moment. "What happens when a fae, a werewolf, and a vampire walk into a bar?" I answered, purposefully walking around it, and buying myself time to think.

He huffed an unamused laugh, raising an eyebrow in my direction. I looked around the room. "We can play it that way if you want. Tell me, what does happen when a fae, a werewolf, and a vampire walk into a bar?"

"They apparently end up mated to me," I mumbled, avoiding what he wanted me to say.

Ezra laughed again while everyone else looked in my direction.

"Why is that, I wonder? Three different supernaturals find themselves mated to the same woman . . ." he mused.

"My charming personality and tight body? You have to admit, I have a great ass," I said.

Dorian looked at me, point-blank, tired of my games. "What are you?"

A knock at the door saved me from answering.

"It's just someone bringing food," Ezra said, then yelled for them to come in.

A vampire wearing a white kitchen coat brought in a large tray filled with assorted breakfast items. "Sorry for the wait. We had to send out for the additional pastries and fruit you requested, sir." He nodded to Ezra and exited the room.

"You had them get donuts?" I walked over, excited enough to see food that I momentarily forgot the tension in the room. Hangry was not going to be a good look on me.

Roxanne got up, and scooped scrambled eggs and bacon onto a plate before shoveling the food in. I reached for a donut and shoved half of it in my mouth, moaning around the sugary dough. I took the next bite and swallowed, then picked up another donut and bit into it.

"Answer the question, Fury," Dorian said, bringing us back to the impending conversation.

"I can't," I said around a mouthful of food. I swallowed and took another bite, knowing full well how rude I was being. I didn't want to exactly make myself attractive in the moment. I wanted to find a way out of this situation, but I didn't see that happening without a miracle. "I already had this conversation with Roman. I was born human, and something changed when I turned twenty-three."

"What changed?" he asked.

"I became not-human," I answered. "I thought you were the smart one."

Roxanne got up and headed back to the food tray, looking more like herself. "We had this conversation with her, Dorian." She picked up some fruit and a donut and put it on her plate. "We got the same answers."

The room swayed a little, and I started to lose my balance. Ezra caught my elbow and righted me.

"Fury?" Tingling prickles traveled over my skin. Dorian needed to stop saying my name. It was doing something to me, and it was making me lose my concentration.

Sound went fuzzy and my lips felt numb as a cramping sensation ripped through my stomach. I watched as Roxanne took her donut and sniffed it, then began yelling as she threw it to the ground.

Dorian, Roman, and Ezra grabbed my body as I fell, the world spinning at an impossible rate. I was fairly certain she said 'poison' in her shouting . . .

I'd thought I needed a miracle to end the conversation. Turns out I just needed to be poisoned. Good. I hope it killed me. I had a bone to pick with Duke, and I needed answers.

CHAPTER 19
FURY

My body slammed into the ground in Duke's empty office. The lights were off, but a nice evening light filtered in from his window. I decided to stay on the ground for a moment and groan. Maybe nap.

"Are you just going to lie there, or did you plan on being completely useless in the Afterlife too?"

I lifted and turned my head, looking at a perch in the corner. "Hades, you undersized turkey, where the hell have you been?"

"Well, after I tried to warn you about the vampires with syringes—"

I propped myself up on my elbows and glared at him. "You *knew*? Why the—" I groaned. "Why didn't you tell me?"

He turned his head to the side, looking at me for a moment before answering. I could've sworn he narrowed his beady little eyes at me. "I can't imagine why. Maybe I was trying, but someone was busy interrupting me and serving up idle threats? I wonder . . ." he mused, then reached a claw up to scratch his neck.

"Oh shut up. You could've saved me the headache of being drugged and stuffed in a trunk. I needed you before I died. Now I'm here, and man, do I have some questions for Duke."

"He'll be here in a minute."

I looked around the dark office. "How do you know that?"

"It's the Afterlife. He knows when someone's in his office," he scoffed. "Honestly, Fury. They told me you were the best when they assigned me to you, but you really do keep those stupid human qualities even in death, don't you?"

I scrambled to stand up, intending on strangling the crow. He couldn't die, but I thought it might make me feel better. "I am the best, you pigeon. I just didn't plan on being blindsided by three mates —" I said, stomping across the room before the lights came on and I walked right into Duke's chest.

"Ow, Duke! What the hell?"

"Nice to see you too, Fury," Duke said, rubbing his chest where my face had planted. He looked behind him then back at me. "Ah, it would seem I came before you were going to . . . what? Strangle Hades?"

"Yes, actually. Now, if you don't mind giving us a little privacy—"

"Leave him alone, Fury," he said, moving to sit at his desk. He clapped his hands, and the lights came on.

I laughed. "You have The Clapper installed in your office?" I asked, somewhat surprised he would use one.

"Sure, why not? Unfortunate name, though. The Clap. The Clapper. Someone kept their mouth shut in that marketing meeting, am I right?" he said, lifting his legs to rest them on the desk. "So what brings you here this time, kid?"

I gave Hades a dirty look. "I guess pigeon forgot to fly his feathered ass here and tell you that this mission isn't all it's cracked up to be."

The crow rolled his eyes.

"I read the files, Fury. You knew this wasn't going to be an easy one. If it were, the angels would have—"

"I'm their mate, Duke."

I watched his expression carefully. Much as it pained me to admit, I had to ask myself, *did he know?* Because someone had to. Dorian said himself that second-chance mates were rare. Legendary.

Yet, I was one to three of the most powerful beings in the living world.

"Fury, I . . ." He let out a tight breath, his eyes wide. "That's . . . I had no idea," he said softly after a moment.

I believed him. Plopping down in the chair across from him, I sighed deeply.

"How is that even possible?" he asked. "You're dead, and beyond that, shouldn't they each have had a mate already? I thought they did. I could've sworn I read that in the files—"

"Three mates," I said, holding up three fingers. "Each one of them was killed. I'm their second-chance . . . and I was sent there to punish them."

Duke cursed under his breath. I could've really gone for a stiff drink right about then, but he didn't keep alcohol in his office. While I'd gone one way after dying, drowning my anger in liquor, Duke had gone the other and stayed away from it. He said it wouldn't do his problems any good, only make them worse.

I knew there was logic in the old man's words, but I couldn't seem to stop myself.

"That's . . . that's a tough one, kiddo. I have to hope that Upper Management didn't know about this, because if so—"

"It's fucked up," I said, speaking plainly. "I'm a demon, and even I think it's fucked up. I also have a really hard time believing that no one knew. The risk witches saw these guys ending the world, yeah? Then they sent angels? All three of their mates were killed." *And Maya had a baby . . .* I didn't say it because I couldn't let that get to me now, but it sickened me to my stomach to think about. "They're powerful, Duke. Dorian alone . . . it's not adding up. Mates don't just die. Mates to powerful people aren't just killed. It's not that easy. They have guards. They have power of their own—"

"You think angels killed them?" he questioned incredulously. "That's a bold claim, Fury. Those mates were innocents."

"C'mon. You have to see that something isn't right," I said.

"Even so, it doesn't mean the risk witches saw this coming," he countered.

"Bullshit," I said, slamming my hands down on the edge of his desk in frustration. The surface split, long jagged fissures running up the wood grain from each of my hands. It groaned before toppling over in a plume of dust and debris.

"I'm sorry," I said, getting to my feet and tugging a hand through my hair. "I'll fix it—"

"Sit down, baby girl. It's fine." He motioned to the chair across from him like I hadn't just collapsed his desk. It wasn't exactly the first time my temper had gotten the better of me, but I'd worked on it. I'd put in the time with Vlad at anger management. It had been over three decades since I'd snapped, and that thought cooled the fire burning in me. I couldn't let my anger have this power over me, and giving in was doing just that. "You're angry, and rightfully so in this case. Whether they knew or didn't, they've put you in a bad situation. So what are you going to do about it?"

I sat back in the chair, drawing my legs up to cross them. I rested my elbows on my knees and propped my chin on my right hand. "I don't know. This job just keeps getting more complicated. It's not just the mate thing. They know I'm different. They just don't know how—and now I died right in front of them, so if I go back there, I'll show up in a new body. That means more questions. I'm not sure how I'm going to play that and turn the tables, especially when I now feel shitty about what I'm doing."

Duke nodded and ran a hand over his short, buzzed hair, down the back of his head. "Well, I can understand that, but they're also supposed to end the world. As shitty as it seems, think about all the people who would die if that happened—in their world and ours. The Afterlife and the living realm will cease to exist. You, me, Henrietta, and my girls would be extinguished. Jake. Demons and trapped souls awaiting punishment or recycling, for better or for worse. They succeed, and everything we know is gone. We got to live our lives, but what about the people on Earth? What about all the kids, the babies, the families? It may seem like you're in a bad place right now, but the risk witches saw them ending it *all*. What about *them*?"

My chest tightened uncomfortably.

"I wish they could find someone else to do this job," I said.

"You can still back out. Keep at it here and you'll get to retirement by putting in the work."

I laughed caustically under my breath. "No," I breathed. "I won't. That's the thing. The files—Jake said they've tried everyone. No one could do it. And meeting them . . . I kind of understand why. They're different. They don't even seem like bad guys, for the most part. I don't think they would've ended up in the bottom forty percent if they were human. Which means whatever brings it on is complicated, but it's there. Buried so deep even I can't see it yet." I dragged in a breath of air, trying to make my lungs expand despite the pain in my chest. "If I walk away now, I don't think they'll find someone who can get to the source of the issue and fix it. There's a reason they brought me in, mate or no mate. I *am* the best. I can find it and stop it, but if I walk away now, I don't think I'll get my chance to hit retirement. Even if I do, eventually they'll blow—and then what was it all for?" I shook my head. "I can't let my feelings be the reason the world ends."

Duke pressed his lips together in a sad, knowing smile. "It sounds like you've made up your mind."

I had, but I also wondered if there was ever a choice, really. Not even a selfish person would walk away now. It would still mean their end eventually.

"I have to go back," I said quietly. Neither of us moved.

Duke reached across the space where his desk had been and grasped my leg, giving it a comforting squeeze. "I'll be here when the job is done. No matter what. You'll have the time to heal and know that you saved other young women like yourself from dying too young."

My throat clogged with emotion, and I swallowed it down. Where were my blackout aviators when I needed them?

I took his hand in mine and held it, drawing strength for what I had to do.

Pigeon was remarkably quiet through the exchange. Thank fuck. I was grateful I was allowed to have a moment every now and then.

I got to my feet, and Duke followed me. Hades flew over and perched on his shoulder as we started down the hall. When we got to the portal room, I paused before stepping through. "How long has passed since I died?"

"A few seconds, but you really need to be more careful. It's not just the alphas who'll take notice when your bodies start to pile up."

I nodded to myself, making a mental note to be more careful. Maybe there was something to be said for Roman's overprotectiveness.

"I take it there's no way to send me back to the same body?"

Duke shook his head. "That vessel is gone. You have a soul, and the portal gives it back its flesh form, but we can't put you in a dead one."

I nodded. Yeah, the corpse was going to make this a bitch to explain. I might need to just play the mysterious card for a bit. Maybe that would make them keep me closer and I could start digging . . . The thought made my chest ache, but it wasn't as bad.

I started for the portal, and then paused again.

"Are you sure you got this?" he asked one more time.

I took a deep breath and lifted my arm. Hades flew over and settled on it, a begrudging respect in his beady eyes.

"I am," I said, feeling more grounded than I had since the night Jake pulled me into his office.

Then I stepped into the portal.

When I opened my eyes, it was total chaos.

CHAPTER 20
EZRA

Sometimes being a mind reader had its perks.

Like when your mate dropped dead less than an hour after you'd found her.

Roman was losing his mind, the shift taking over. Roxanne was giving the corpse chest compressions, and when that didn't work, she switched to jamming her fingers down her throat—as if throwing up would save a body that was already dead.

Even Dorian, the oldest fae in living memory, and probably oldest supernatural altogether, was tense. His pale hands were gripping my office desk hard enough it might have crumpled already if it weren't reinforced with steel, per my request after I'd broken it one too many times.

Alas, being supernaturally strong had its drawbacks on occasion.

I rose to my feet and walked out of my office. Kendrick was nearby.

"We've already narrowed down the suspects, but they ran. I have people out searching for them now. Do you need anything—"

"A pair of blacked-out sunglasses and a tablecloth or blanket of some sort. Maybe a tarp?" I mused.

Kendrick did a double take, then took a moment to stare blankly. "Ezra, I know that your way of handling grief—"

"You, there." I stopped a vampire girl walking by.

"Sir?" she replied in a high-pitched squeak.

I reached out and cupped her chin, turning it. "These will do," I murmured, then plucked off the sunglasses she'd pushed up above her forehead. The hair it held back fell forward, and her lips parted in surprise, but she didn't argue. She knew who I was. All of my species did. I made an example of those who broke my rules.

The kind no one could forget.

I turned back to Kendrick. "Get me the tarp and compensate her."

My attention turned back to my office, where things had gone silent. I had a feeling my mate had made her grand reappearance.

I walked back and slipped inside, releasing the tight breath I'd been holding since her body dropped.

She sat in my chair, boots kicked up on the desk and her red hair pulled back. I looked forward to the day I got to pull that hair and take her cherry mouth . . . but there would be time for that later.

I set the sunglasses down and pushed them across the desk, silently.

Her eyebrows quirked up. Then she narrowed her gaze. I—and every other alpha in the room, no doubt—heard her heart rate pick up, but she took the glasses with a muttered "thanks."

I inclined my head and gave her a confident smirk before moving away, toward the window.

"So," she drawled, filling the heavy silence. "You guys going to do anything about that?" She jutted her chin out toward the dead body on the ground. Her dead body.

A knock at the door had the other alphas on edge. Roman stepped closer to her, Dorian toward the door. I sighed.

"Come in, Kendrick."

My second stepped inside, then froze in his tracks—the same thing everyone else had done. I suppose it would've been a jarring thing to experience. I may have had the same reaction had I not been reading her mind from the second she walked into my club.

Normally, I tuned out because I had no interest in hearing what others were thinking. Their thoughts bored me. Most things did. It was always the same. But not this delectable little . . . *demon*.

No, she was different in every way—down to her soul.

Because she wasn't a supe in the true sense, nor was she human.

She was dead, and she'd come back a demon.

One intent on punishing me—and her other mates.

I hadn't figured out why, not until she returned with a renewed sense of purpose. I couldn't really hold it against her, though. Not when she thought we were going to end the world.

On the contrary, it made me more intrigued. More curious. More . . . obsessive.

Fury wanted to play games with us. To tie us up in knots over her and figure out each and every little weakness.

Little did my mate know, I loved playing games just as much as she did.

And thankfully, I didn't have to play fair.

CHAPTER 21
FURY

The man Ezra had called Kendrick stood at the door, frozen, carrying what looked like a canvas tarp. No one moved. No one spoke. What was there to say? I'd died right in front of them. My body lay on the floor in the same room. And here I sat, legs kicked up and a smile on my face.

"C'mon, I wasn't gone that long. Say something." I wasn't entirely sure how to start it off either, if I were being honest. "Oh, and cover that," I added, gesturing to the expired version of myself. "No one wants to see it anymore."

That did it.

The room exploded in a frenzy of shouts and curses. All except Ezra. He didn't strike me as the silent type, yet here we were. Through all the shouting, aimed in my direction, he looked at his friend, and said, "Leave the tarp, and make sure no one comes in." Kendrick blinked a couple of times, then nodded, leaving it on a table and walking out the door.

I held up my hand to stop the onslaught of questions. "Can I get a drink?"

Roman looked at his sister, then back at me. "Are you serious right now?" he said through clenched teeth. His muscles were still trembling with the need to shift. Clearly his wolf had almost taken over at my death. He had more control than he'd realized if that hadn't fully set him off. It was something for me to consider.

"Yeah, I'm serious. I just died. I think I can have a drink." I looked at Ezra since he seemed to be fine giving me hard liquor at early o'clock. "Gin?"

"Hold up," Roman said. "I have some questions that need to be answered first. You—" Roxanne grabbed his arm as though she was trying to calm him. "No, I'm fine. Stop." He looked back at me, twirling his hand in a circular motion around the scene before us. "Explain this. Now."

I looked him up and down, trying to figure out how he was managing to be calmer than he ever had before. "You first. Why are you fine? I can see you shaking. Part of your suit is ripped. You almost shifted. Why should I talk right now and risk you going wolf-man on us?"

I gazed around the room. Ezra inclined his head in agreement while Dorian seemed content to glare at me like a particularly tricky experiment he wanted to dissect. Roxanne's eyes were wide with unshed tears that she was trying to cover as the shock and adrenaline started to come down.

"I'm . . . I can see you're safe. So can my wolf." He looked away for a second, and I could tell that wasn't all, but neither Dorian nor Ezra would push it. "Now answer *us*. What the hell just happened?"

I pulled my legs off the desk and sat forward. "It would seem the alphas have spoken," I joked.

"Stop it," Roxanne said, almost shouting. "What the hell, Fury? You just *died*. Your body is right there, so *stop*." She looked over at the dead version, then back at me. I felt a sudden pang of guilt. She'd been desperately trying to save my life. She didn't know. She thought she was going to lose a friend—her brother's mate—and she was the only one actively attempting to bring me back to life.

"Point taken." I nodded. "I'm sorry, Rox." I got up and crossed the room, picking up the thick tarp. Walking to my prone body on the floor, I shook and fanned the cloth sheet out, dropping it over dead-me. The slack-jawed face and wide-open eyes were really not helping anything here.

I sat on the couch, knowing this was only going to go one way. If I focused on that, I was still in the driver's seat. Or whatever the saying was.

Dorian came over and sat down across from me. I looked up, meeting his gaze.

"How did you do that?" he asked, probably thinking it was the best way to get me to answer.

"I didn't," I said. "I have no control over it."

"Bullshit."

"Okay," I responded. "Do you want me to lie? Make up some elaborate story about witchcraft and tarot cards, or that I made some deal with the devil to sell my soul and get three mates?"

Ezra snorted at my retort. Roman and Dorian stared me down before the former spoke.

"When I questioned you in Roxanne's bar, you said something happened to you when you were twenty-three that made you not-human. You said the same thing to Dorian. What was it?"

I pointed at the dead body. "That."

"What do you mean 'that'?" Dorian asked.

"I mean, my body died. And then it came back," I answered, motioning to myself. This was where it got tricky, but it was best if I tried to keep things as vague as possible. Feigning ignorance would help. They may not believe it, but right now it was the best I had.

Roxanne stood up, wiping her eyes with the back of her hand. "But how, Fury? How did this happen? What are you? What does this even—"

Dorian placed his hand on her arm and shook his head. There was something between them. Something deep. Solid. Similar to what I had with Duke, but not the same. Part of me was glad for it. Each of them would need someone when the job was done and I had disappeared for real. The thought caused a pang inside me, but I pushed it down, the conversation with Duke still fresh in my mind. I *had* to do this. It was the only way.

"I don't know what more I can tell you. You know what I know. Now you've all seen it for yourself."

"I don't accept that as your truth. There's something you aren't telling us," Dorian said.

I sighed, throwing my head back. "Okay, so it was witches and tarot cards, and I sold my soul to the devil for three mates. Happy?"

Roman stood with his arms crossed, looking down at the ground. As though he'd had a sudden and alarming thought, his head popped up. "Does anyone else know about you?"

"You mean does anyone know that this happens?" I motioned between me and the tarp. He nodded. "No. I'm not from around here, remember?"

"This has happened before, though. So someone could know about it," Roman surmised, looking at Dorian.

"I took care of it up north. No one there knows," I said. It was a lie, but also a truth. Not a single soul alive knew about me and my life up north. Nope. That miserable life was long gone, as were all the horrible people in it.

Ezra came over and handed me a gin with a twist of lemon again, right on cue. "Explains why you drink so much."

I snapped my head up. "What does?"

He looked over at the dead-me. "That. Because it won't kill you."

"Oh, yeah," I said, realizing what he meant. I raised my glass. "Cheers to that." It came out drier than I'd meant it to, but the eyes in the room were watching my every move.

Ezra sat next to Dorian, throwing his arm across the back of the couch, and crossing his legs, looking thoroughly bored. "We need to figure something out. She isn't going to answer questions to your liking right now, and we can't all just live here in my office."

Roxanne interjected, "Probably shouldn't forget the important detail that someone just tried to kill her."

"How do we for sure know they were trying to kill me?" I asked. I'd barely been there for a day. The thought was somewhat troubling. Dying clearly wasn't an issue, but someone was trying to cause problems, and that meant they were getting in the way of me doing my job. That just complicated things more.

All four of them glared at me with annoyed looks that said 'really?'.

Dorian leaned forward, propping his elbows on his knees, and clasping his hands. "Roxanne is right. She'll come home with me."

"Wait a minute," Roman said, his voice turning to gravel. His wolf was driving him hard. I wondered how much of the man also objected. "Why you?"

"Do you want me to list the reasons, shifter, because I figured they were blatantly obvious to everyone," Dorian said, looking at Roman's ripped suit from his almost-rage-shift.

"I'm fine with that," Ezra piped up. Everyone looked at him, and he shrugged. "Dorian has a point. Deny it all you want, Roman, but right now, she's probably safest with him."

I watched with curiosity as Roman's anger struggled to the surface, his eyes swirling between icy blue and a warm brown.

Dorian stood up, facing him. "We may not be friends, but I'm not your enemy. We are somehow mates with the same woman, and I can't explain why yet. She isn't human, but none of us knows or can feel what she is—and Fury isn't being forthcoming." He shot me a look I dismissed. Damn right I wasn't. The living weren't supposed to know about the dead. "This isn't a pissing contest. She was with Roxanne when she was kidnapped—"

"By him," Roxanne sniped, pointing at Ezra, who grinned his agreement, tilting his head to the side.

Dorian nodded. "But she was still kidnapped, and you were drugged in the process. She was poisoned here, in the vampire's club. Tell me why she's safer with any of you," he said, looking around. "I'm listening."

"Not that anyone seems to care, but I'm fine with this arrangement," I said, joining in the argument.

Four supernaturals stared at me, wearing a variation of shocked faces.

Dorian narrowed his gaze at me. "Why?"

"Does it matter?" I asked him. "It's what you wanted, anyway."

"Enlighten me," he said.

I rolled my eyes and sighed. "Do you really want me to go through a checklist, because I thought you just made the 'blatantly obvious' points to everyone?" I said, throwing his words back at him.

"My focus right now is finding out who poisoned her. Someone went after her, and they did it on my territory," Ezra said, his tone darkening. He cracked his knuckles, exuding confidence and complete assuredness when he looked at me. "My guys are already on it. We'll find them."

Roman grunted in frustration. "I want to be here when they're questioned."

"As do I," Dorian added.

Ezra dipped his head. "I'd expect nothing less. But until then, she can't be with me. Not when I can't trust my own people."

Roman looked at Roxanne, and she nodded in agreement. "I hate to say it, but Dorian and Ezra are right. Your wolf wants her safe. More than anything, I know that's your struggle. She will be." Dorian raised his eyebrows to her. "Oh, stop it. I've agreed with you before. We've been friends for a long time. I know when you're right, even when you piss me off. And right now, you're right. Keep her safe." She looked at me with a tight-lipped smile.

Probably not the time to mention that keeping me safe wasn't really a priority when I could come right back. Though, the dead bodies *were* becoming a problem.

Roman sighed. "Fine. I agree."

I clapped my hands, then rubbed them together. "Great. Now we have the custody agreement all set up—"

"Wait," Roman interjected. "You won't answer why you're in agreement. Is this a game to you? Part of some plan you have to run off and send us all on a chase? I can't deal with that right now, Fury. This is harder than you can imagine."

I held my hands up in mock surrender. "I'm not going to run off or plan some elaborate escape."

Dorian cocked an eyebrow at me. "Why should we believe you?"

"You can't, I suppose," I admitted. "Guess you'll just have to trust me."

Ezra snorted, and Roman let out a harsh breath.

Roxanne stood up, walking to me, and looking me straight in the eye. "I asked you once already, and I'll ask you again. Please don't run." Her eyes widened slightly, reminding me of the rest of our conversation. A vulnerable conversation she wouldn't share in front of three alphas.

Last night I wasn't as committed to my answer. I had loose plans, then. I was working on finding a way to bring Ezra and Dorian into my life. By some glitch in design, that had happened. Albeit in a monumentally screwed-up way. Now I had to stay, and I could at least give her that. "I'm not going anywhere, Rox." I nodded slightly and gave her a tight-lipped smile in return, keeping eye contact to let her know I understood exactly what she meant.

"How do we do this?" Roman asked, ending the moment between me and his sister. "Does she stay with you for a few days, then we trade? Keep her moving?"

Dorian ran a hand through his neatly styled hair. "Possibly. Ezra, do you think it will take long to catch who poisoned her?"

He laughed. "Probably no more than a few days."

"Good. We have the summit coming up, and that problem needs to be dealt with before then. If you need assistance, I'll send you some fae. We need to get this under control," Dorian said.

"I have shifters who can help too, if needed," Roman added reluctantly.

"So . . . I'll spend a few days with each of you until we make a new plan?" I asked, mentally calculating how long I would have to work around them. It would be easier if I had more than a day, so I wouldn't complain if that was what they gave me.

"I think it may be best," Dorian answered, looking at my other . . . mates. "Ezra, keep us updated with what you find. We stay in contact."

The guys shook hands in agreement, but Roxanne shocked me when she came up to me and wrapped her arms around my shoulders, pulling me close in a tight hug. For a moment, I stood there, unsure what to do. I hadn't been hugged in longer than I could remember. Not even Duke did that. And the fuck buddies I'd found in the Afterlife weren't really the hugging type either.

I hesitated, an unnamed emotion clawing at my insides, before I reached my arms around, hugging her in return.

"Thanks for trying to save me earlier," I told her. And I meant it.

Releasing her, I nodded to everyone. "All right, Dorian. What next?"

Dorian said nothing as he grabbed my hand and a whooshing

feeling shot through my body. My stomach jumped into my throat, and my head spun in circles.

Teleporting on Earth caused motion sickness. Awesome.

It wasn't even noon yet.

I really needed to catch a break.

CHAPTER 22
FURY

We reappeared in a garden that could have rivaled Versailles.

The marble fountain of baby cupids and sirens shot water fifteen feet in the air to land in the crystal-clear pool that was easily twenty feet in diameter. Rose bushes and other flowered plants lined the walkways. I took it in as I bent at the waist, hands on my knees, breathing hard.

"Are you all right?"

"Dizzy," I grumbled, turning to look off to the right. The garden just went on and on, as far as I could see. And while my sight wasn't as impressive as my strength, I'd had 20/20 vision when I was alive—before my shithead ex punched me too hard and damaged the cornea. Thankfully, in death they'd reverted to pre-asshole quality.

"Interesting," Dorian murmured. "You can't sift?"

I could tell he was digging. That was obvious. I'd expected it, and fortunately he was unlikely to ever find the answer, even with me telling him the truth.

"No," I grunted. "I also get motion sick easily, so I'd prefer to stick to my own two feet as much as we can." I stood up, looking in the other directions. It was much of the same–winding paths in a garden of flowers—apart from the mansion.

It stood extravagant and proud. Colonial style, despite the clear updating on the outside to make it look less like, well, a plantation.

"Not what I expected."

Dorian lifted an eyebrow. "Oh? And what did you expect?"

Sweat was forming on my brow, and I swiped at it with the back of my hand and pinched the front of my shirt to fan myself. "Less Anne of Green Gables meets The Secret Garden set in Hell, and more —" I broke off, twisting my lips as I considered. "Castle on a cliff. Somewhere it's always gloomy. And cold. Like you."

His lips twitched as he lifted his eyebrows. I could tell he was amused, even though he hid it. I'd guessed right, of course. Then again, I did read in the file he lived on an island off the coast of Scotland. In a castle on a cliff. Very doom and gloom.

"Well, you're right about one thing," he said, then started walking. I had to jog to keep up, making the sweating issue worse. "This place is Hell." He got to the door first, but instead of entering like I expected, he pulled it open and sidestepped, waiting for me somewhat impatiently.

"Then why do you live here?" I asked, knowing he didn't but needing to play the game. I walked inside and sighed in bliss as the air conditioner hit me. I almost didn't hear his answer because I was so wrapped up in the cool feeling on my skin.

"I don't."

"This isn't your house?" I asked without looking.

"It's an estate I have to stay in during the summit. That's it. Texas wasn't my first choice for neutral ground. I wanted Quebec, but neither Ezra nor the wolf alpha at the time went for that. I was overruled."

"Overruled," I mused. "Does that happen often?"

"No."

Simple. Straightforward. Resounding.

I sensed a hint of something. "But it did this time?"

"When you get to be as old as I am, you pick your battles," Dorian replied. "The location of an event that's held once a decade is not one of them."

"Hmm," I hummed, a little put out. He was self-assured, and while that wasn't a bad thing, it wasn't the most workable. They tended to be harder to break. Not impossible—no one was. Just harder.

I perused the room. Old paintings scattered the white walls. Dark hardwood floors were hidden beneath a large Persian rug. A wing-backed armchair that looked old but well-maintained sat next to a hardwood end table that had been carved in the image of a stag. Its horns came up and wound together to form the tabletop.

"You have expensive tastes," I mentioned casually.

Dorian stood at the door, staring at me with unnerving amber eyes. "It's only worth something because the creators are dead."

"What is?"

"All of it. Worth is relative. I furnished my estates with things I found in my travels, but as time went on, the people who made these things died. Their death made the items they left behind valuable because they could no longer create." He shrugged.

"Our lives must seem so fleeting to you," I said softly, taking a closer look at the pieces in the room. "You step through them and take your piece, then carry on."

"Some might say I'm bringing them meaning by carrying on these artists' legacies."

"By your argument, meaning is only found in death. If that were the case, living would be rather pointless."

When he didn't say anything, I slowly smiled.

I'd found a truth buried beneath his cold exterior.

"Perhaps it is," he said quietly.

The weight of the moment was lifted when a young man made his way toward us from down the hall behind Dorian. "Sir?" he said with barely contained excitement. "Might I ask who your lady friend is?"

"I'm—" I started.

"This is Fury. She'll be staying with us a few days," he replied.

I lifted my eyebrows. He hadn't called me his mate. Did I detect some hesitance there? My, my. This was shaping up better than I'd expected. It seemed I'd hit too close to the truth, and now he was running.

I smiled again, and it only served to agitate Dorian further.

His lips flatlined and those amber eyes turned hard. "Don't touch anything that looks expensive. Don't leave. Don't bother me. You think you can handle that?"

"Where are you going?"

"Work. The fae don't run themselves. I'll see you for dinner."

Then he was gone, and it was simply me and my babysitter.

The other fae smiled in apology, his bright purple eyes kind. "Dorian Radcliffe is . . . a hardworking man. Devoted to the responsibilities he's found himself committed to."

It was a poor justification for his even poorer manners, but it wasn't this guy's fault. "I can see that," I said. "How long have you known him?"

"Oh, a few hundred years or so," he answered happily. "My name is James. I'm his personal assistant and the keeper of his estates. I could give you a tour of the mansion if you'd like?"

I smiled like a wolf in sheepskin. This was exactly what I needed. "I'd like that very much."

CHAPTER 23
DORIAN

I PAUSED MID-SENTENCE, THE HUSKY SOUND OF HER LAUGHTER ECHOING DOWN my halls. My cock hardened. The point of the pen dug too deep into the report I was checking over and the middle snapped in half under my crushingly tight grip. Ink bled everywhere, and I cursed.

Eight hours.

This had been my life for *eight hours*.

I'd struggled to get into my work, thoughts of our conversation and everything I'd seen today nagging at me. Eventually I would find a way to concentrate, but it wasn't for long.

The sound of her voice called to me.

A siren I was fairly certain would drown me in her depths.

If it wasn't her voice, it was her scent, and when James came to deliver lunch, she'd followed him. She'd walked around my office in loose pants and a tank top. She'd stopped to touch something here or there. Commenting on it. Ever since that moment, I found my attention had gravitated to every object she took notice of. Asking myself what did she find interesting about it? Why? Could it somehow give me a clue to what she was, or why being in her vicinity was driving me *insane*?

I was an old supernatural. The oldest. If not untouched by time, then hardened by it. I did not grow fascinated easily. I did not obsess. My attention did not wander. And yet, it was.

I dropped the broken remains of the pen in the trash and glanced up at the clock. Dinner would be ready at any moment, and with it, a mental sparring match with my mate would be served.

That word silenced my other thoughts. Drawing mixed emotions. While I felt an innate pull toward her, a desire to protect her, an even greater one to fuck her, it didn't instantly create feelings.

It simply created possibility.

Last time, I was a young fae and fell head over heels in love. Morvain had been a kind woman. Soft. Easy to love and hard to lose. Her death tore me apart. My life had been boiled down to two distinct phases.

Before . . . and after.

The after was cold and lonely and desolate. There was no possibility.

But now . . .

I shook my head. My jaw clenched hard.

I needed to get to know the girl. To learn who she was. *What* she was. My instincts would drive me to protect her whether she needed it or not, and perhaps, I may even fuck her. Anything more was out of the question.

I left my office with a purpose. Agitation still gnawed at me. I hadn't felt that emotion—or much of any, really—in so long that it was harder to grapple with than I'd anticipated. But if fifteen hundred years had given me anything, it was the ability to play a part.

I trailed down the hall, following the sound of her voice. When I walked by the dining room and found it empty, uncertainty filled me. James was never late. Dinner was always at seven thirty, sharp. So where . . .

I didn't have the chance to finish the thought. I rounded the corner into a sitting room with a large television. I often forgot it existed since I never had the desire to use it.

"*Previously on* Grey's Anatomy."

Sitting on the oversized sectional, James was passed out. I frowned. Clear bottles littered the floor in a path from his side to Fury's. She sat at the opposite end with her knee propped up and a half-empty bottle of gin in hand. Her eyes were surprisingly clear, though dilated.

I let out a harsh breath. "What happened to James?"

She ignored me, but I could tell she heard by the slight twitch of her lips.

I stepped in front of the TV and repeated myself, something I almost never had to do. "What happened to James, Fury?"

"He's a lightweight. Who knew? Anyway, can you be a window instead of a wall and step two feet to the left?"

I gritted my teeth. She truly was nothing like Morvain. Where my mate had been sweet, Fury was prickly. Morvain was selfless, Fury inconsiderate. I stepped forward, blocking the screen entirely, and it was only then that I remembered their greatest difference.

Morvain had been innocent.

The devilish glint in Fury's dark eyes showed she was anything but, and she knew exactly what she was doing.

I snatched the remote off the couch and squinted at it.

"Big red button on the top right," she said.

I stilled, realizing that she knew why I'd paused. I'd only used a television a handful of times in the last few decades. I hadn't known which button, and she'd read that on my face as easily as if I'd said it out loud.

I cut the power, and the sound stopped, leaving us in the quiet with James's tiny snores and the crickets for company. "How'd you know?"

"Seen the look before," she muttered. "Ex-lover had the same expression on his face when going down on me."

I blinked, and she snorted then stood. "You must really know how to choose them."

Our bodies were only a few inches apart when she looked up. This close, I could tell that her eyes weren't actually dark brown like I'd thought. They were black. Truly black.

"I did say *ex*, didn't I?" She smirked before stepping around me.

I looked at James, debating the merits of waking him up.

"Leave him," she said from the doorway. I looked over my shoulder. "I'm pretty sure this is his first break from making you dinner in a century. Let the guy sleep. If you're hungry, we can order," she paused, as if looking for the word, "takeout. I think that's what Roxanne called it. The food that comes to your door? Anyway, unless you want a liquid dinner, I wouldn't recommend me cooking."

Without turning back, I followed her out into the hall, my curiosity driving me forward. "Where did you say you were from again?"

"Up north."

I sensed the truth, even if she was evading. This girl was skilled at twisting her words. I'd figured that out quickly but relearned the lesson several times over on each occasion we spoke. "They have takeout up north," I replied, calling her on it.

She smiled like she found something funny. "Not when I was there. It's a pretty remote area."

As strange as it was, again, she was telling the truth.

And for the first time, I thought I'd learned something valuable.

Fury wasn't as young as she looked. Nor was she apathetic enough to be truly old. She hadn't questioned how James had been with me for a century, and for a born-human-turned supernatural, she didn't seem at all surprised by our ages. The question was: exactly how old was she?

She continued down the hall before turning into the kitchen. I trailed after her. The scent of coming storms and fall leaves pulled at me, demanding I follow her.

"Tell me, Fury-from-up-north, what kind of food do you eat?"

"No tacos. I'm not feeling like a masochist tonight." She scrunched her nose and took another sip straight out of the gin bottle. By sip, I mean drained another quarter of it in one go.

"Have you ever died from alcohol poisoning?" I asked mildly. She really did drink a lot. In the nine or so hours I'd known her, the only thing she'd consumed was alcohol and poisoned donuts.

"Nope," she said. "But I'm not afraid to try."

I narrowed my eyes. While I wasn't truly worried about it—knowing she'd come back—I wasn't in the mood to test it. Walking over, I reached out to pluck the bottle from her hand. When it didn't move an inch, I stopped pulling.

"You're strong," I noted.

"How observant," she said dryly.

"Yet you die."

"Oh boy, here we go again. Why don't you order that food we were talking about before you try to jump down the rabbit hole?"

"You understand modern slang and like television, yet the word takeout is foreign to you," I continued, ignoring her. "So contradictory," I said, more to myself than her.

She lifted an unamused eyebrow. "Are we still on this?"

"You could tell me what you are and save us both the trouble."

She narrowed her eyes, then yanked the bottle away from me and drained the rest. When it was empty, she set it on the counter and said, "Are you going to be a gentleman and buy me dinner, or not?"

I chuckled under my breath.

"What?"

"I'll get you dinner, Fury," I said, leaning in close. "But you came to the wrong place if you wanted a gentleman."

My eyes dipped to her lips. She licked them, her tiny pink tongue darting out.

The urge to bite her surged, but I stepped away.

My desire to fuck her was strong.

But my need to break her open and learn every little secret—that was stronger.

CHAPTER 24
EZRA

"I'm heading out. What's the status on our poisoners?" I asked, still staring out the window. Kendrick had just stepped into my office; his reflection met my eyes in the glass.

"They've fled Houston. It seems they had help, though we don't know who from, or if they're headed to the source."

I nodded once. "How long until they're apprehended?"

Kendrick sighed. I wasn't going to like the answer. "Likely a day. Maybe two. They initially took a bus, but they think they're clever, hopping around from one mode of transportation to the next. We're currently tracking the latest. Getting them without causing collateral damage takes time."

I dipped my chin. "Keep me updated. I want to know when they're caught. Have you finished combing through the rest of our staff and security?"

"Yes," he said, sounding a bit surer, if not tired. It had been a long ten hours since Dorian took my mate and sifted out of my club. "Three of them had doctored stories with false records. They've been let go and told to leave the city before the summit. None of them had anything indicating involvement, however. It seems to be just the two who fled."

Hm. "I suppose we'll see once they're brought in for questioning."

Kendrick didn't say anything. This was usually when he nodded and stepped out. Back to work. Always work. After so long, even play had become work in a sense. I wondered if he felt it as much as I did. Perhaps even more, given he was twenty years my senior.

Kendrick was my second-in-command, but he was also my maker and my friend.

"We'll find them," he promised quietly. "I won't rest until they're captured and we know *why* they came after her to begin with."

"I know." He wasn't lying. He was good like that. When Kendrick said he would do something, he did it. That was why he was my second. "Speaking of my mate, I need to check in with her. See how Dorian has been. He's got a cruel streak in him. Runs deep."

"You think he'd use it on her?"

"No," I said, shaking my head. The city lights made my own green eyes more impossibly bright in my reflection. "I wouldn't have relinquished her so easily if I thought otherwise. She may not be able to die, but that doesn't mean she can't be hurt. I'm hoping some time with him wears her down before she comes to me."

"So, you plan to pursue the bond?" Kendrick mused, stepping further into my office.

"Yes, but not immediately. There's work to be done before I can bond with her fully."

My old friend lifted his eyebrows, his lips twisting together. "By work, I'm assuming you mean there are games to play?"

"It's all the same," I answered with a grin. "Fury is different. She's not like Lenora."

"Because she hasn't rejected you?" Kendrick replied. To some, it might've seemed a little callous, but there was no love lost between me and the woman who'd been my mate.

"Because she won't," I said. "Not when I'm done. I don't care if she accepts the other two. That's her business with them. But between us . . ." I said. "I'll be her confidant. Her friend. Her lover. She won't turn me away by the time I'm done."

"Mhmm," Kendrick replied uneasily. I could understand his hesitance, in a way. He cared for me. He didn't want to see me get hurt again.

Despite my and Lenora's lack of feelings, the severing of our bond when she rejected me—and then died—was the catalyst for a very long stretch in that dark place we all knew deep down. Normally, we could forget it was there. Let the music drown it out. Let sex and blood fill the void.

Not then. When she died, nothing could fill the hollowness that consumed me. I was truly empty for the first time in what would become my hundred-and-seventy-year-long existence.

The things I'd done as a result were truly . . . horrifying.

While the world didn't know how much some of those events troubled me still, Kendrick did. I'd lost control of myself so thoroughly that it had taken fifty years to find myself again. I wouldn't have been able to without him by my side. Of course he wouldn't want to see me in that place again.

I turned my back on the glass wall overlooking the concrete jungle below.

"This time will be different," I told him, putting my hand on his shoulder.

I was out the door when he quietly replied, "For both our sakes, I hope you're right."

The sounds of orgasms and soft, sultry music followed as I walked out of Bite Me. I took the elevator down and nodded to the club guards when they lowered their eyes and dipped their heads in respect. A quick, fleeting look at their minds told me they were both loyal. The one on the left had joined my clan with his mate for protection. The one on the right was ambitious and hoping to gain power by moving through the ranks. Both were standard reasons for joining and neither were worth a deeper look nor would be considered a cause for concern.

The parking garage was uncharacteristically half empty. Word had gotten around about what had happened to Fury in front of me and the other alphas. It made us look weak. Incompetent. Some people were staying away because they were scared to get caught in the crossfire. Others wanted to sit in the shadows and see how this played out. Either way, Bite Me had dropped in business considerably over the last ten hours, and the walk to my Audi R8 was uneventful. I unlocked my car and opened the door, the scent of leather and chrome enveloping me. I started it up and pulled out onto the road before turning my thoughts to Fury.

The image of her eating steak au poivre with that pompous asshole Dorian filled my mind. I narrowed my eyes and put my foot on the gas, listening to their conversation play out.

"*What do you do for work?*"

"*I work in a prison,*" she said in response. "*Out of state. I'm afraid I can't disclose any details.*"

I chuckled.

"*What do you do there?*"

"*Rehabilitate.*"

That earned a snort.

While technically, yes, she rehabilitated, her means were certainly unconventional. Humans would never approve of her methods. She would make a fine clan enforcer, however. I mulled that over as I got onto the highway, listening to their conversation in the back of my mind.

Dorian asked her where she came from, what she did, what she liked and what she didn't. For the most part, she gave him half-answers. Bullshit truths that weren't outright lies but they might as well have been.

By the time I got to my apartment on the west side of town, their little dinner had come to a close and he was escorting her to her room. After a few awkward moments and a dismissive goodbye on Fury's part, she was finally alone, and so was I.

I took the elevator up to my penthouse suite after parking. Without turning the lights on, I unbuttoned my shirt and stripped out of it—tossing it over the back of an armchair. My black tattoos reflected in the glass door that led out to the balcony as I padded across the living room and into the kitchen to pour myself a glass of O negative.

At the same time, my mate was stripping out of her clothes for a little *me time.*

Intrigued and already hard at the thought, I took a seat in the armchair and closed my eyes.

Pale, creamy skin filled my vision. She brought the water in the bathtub to a near boil before stepping in. Fury lowered herself into the water and moaned softly, making my cock twitch.

Unable to help myself, I purred, *Need some help?*

CHAPTER 25
FURY

I LOST MY GRIP ON THE SIDE OF THE TUB, GASPING TO SCREAM, AND GOING under the water all at once. I flailed around like a cat tossed in, trying to regain my composure and find my bearings.

Finally, I sat up, wiping the suds and water off my face, and all I could hear was laughter echoing in my head.

"What is going on?" I said out loud, looking around the bathroom.

There was just one problem. No one was there.

I just wanted to offer my assistance to finish what we started earlier.

Ezra. The voice in my head was the vampire.

"I wasn't aware you could read minds."

Not many are. That said, I would've thought something as powerful as Upper Management would do a better job at collecting information for you.

Oh fuck.

He knew about Upper Management . . . which meant . . .

I know everything, or most of it. I've been listening in since you entered my club earlier. Who would've thought that there really is an Afterlife—

"Shut up," I snapped. "I need you to stop talking for, like, ten seconds."

He laughed again, a deep chuckle that reverberated in my skull.

I wanted to scream and claw at my head, but instinct told me that was pointless.

I took deep breaths, sitting in the water of my once relaxing bath. Any attempts I might have made for an orgasm were long gone, scared off by a voice in my head. Literally.

It doesn't have to be that way, he purred in my mind. *You like to be watched. I like to watch. Touch yourself for me. I'll make you see stars.*

My core tightened at his insinuation, and while my body was curiously on board with that suggestion, the part of my brain that recognized I was in *deep* shit said now wasn't the time.

"It doesn't work that way," I said, trying to formulate something meaningful. The only thing that truly came to mind was the obvious . . .

My mission was a complete and utter failure.

Everything I'd learned about them. Every inch I'd gained with these boys . . . men . . . was for nothing. Ezra knew my secret. He knew who I was, and why I was here.

How could I fix them now?

It was hard to break someone who knew that was what you were doing.

You've never let that stop you before, the voice in my head taunted. *Every soul you've been assigned, you've told them the truth. That they'd died and gone to Hell. You still broke them.*

"I'm confused," I said into the quiet. "Whose side are you even on?"

Yours. His answer was immediate. Unshakable.

"Why?" I asked. "Is this because of the mate bond? You barely know me. Why not reject me and be done with it if you know why I'm really here?"

Because I don't want to. What you are and why you were sent here don't matter to me.

"I don't understand," I breathed harshly. "It should matter to you. If I break you, it's going to hurt. If I fix you, I'll still have to leave in the end. There's no happy ending for this—"

I don't care.

I rested my forehead against my knees. The water was cooling, but I didn't have it in me to move.

"Then you're a masochist who's signing yourself up for pain."

Maybe I am, his mental voice mused. *You could use that.*

I wanted to bash my head into the tub. His reaction to this wasn't sane.

I wouldn't recommend self-harm . . . unless you're in the mood to talk to Dorian.

"Does Dorian know about this?" I asked aloud into the empty bathroom.

No. Neither does Roman. I've gone to great lengths to keep this particular gift of mine a secret.

"Clearly it's worked since my file didn't say anything about it either. Fucking poltergeists. They have *one* job, and they can't even do that," I grumbled under my breath. I could blame them. That part was easy. And in truth—this wasn't my fault. I didn't fuck up. They did.

Unfortunately, there were no do-overs like when I died. I couldn't go back and restart my mission. In both worlds, time moved linear progression, and the only way I could go was forward.

"Are you going to tell the others?"

Roman and Dorian? No. I enjoy watching you fuck with them too much. Not much rattles that old fae bastard. It'll do him good to have something to focus on.

Well, I suppose as far as mind-reading vampires went, that was about the best I could hope for. I narrowed my eyes, another thought occurring to me.

"What do you want in return?"

Tell me about the Afterlife and Jake from AR. I want to know what it's like being a demon and part of a guild. You spent the last hundred years in an entirely different world. A world no one even knows exists. Tell me about it, and I won't breathe a word of this to anyone.

All things considered that wasn't a bad deal. How many times had I already wanted to talk to Duke about things? Sending the crow wasn't enough, and I couldn't just keep dying. I had to be careful, or too many people would take notice. Having someone who knew —*really knew*—who and what I was could come in handy.

"And if I don't tell you about those things?"

I felt his mental shrug, as if it ran through me. *You think a lot. It's only a matter of time before I'd hear it all, anyway.*

I glowered at the tile wall, feeling obstinate when I knew this was only an illusion of choice. "I could train myself to not think of it. I'll think about Dorian's abs instead."

A feather-soft touch ran down my thigh. I could've sworn it was actually there.

Will you? his taunting, teasing voice whispered through me—followed by the feeling of fingers trailing down my back then over my breast.

I sucked in a sharp breath. "You didn't say you could do this." I gasped as his mental hands ran down my abdomen and over my legs. He touched me everywhere . . . and yet not where I wanted him.

I prefer show versus tell.

I felt his smirk right before a psychic tongue flicked over my nipple. It pebbled instantly, and my legs stiffened.

"Stop," I hissed between my teeth as a moan built in my throat.

The torturous touching stopped, and part of me wished it hadn't.

"You've made your point, and I'll accept the terms of the deal if you're honest with me. I want to know what you can do—and what you know about Roman and Dorian. If you know everything, then you know why I'm here."

We end the world, he said in a far more serious tone. At least he understood the gravity of that.

"Yes, and I have to find a way to prevent that, or everyone dies."

I stood up in the tub, flipping the knob to drain the water. Wrapping a fluffy towel around me, I walked from the bathroom into my room and sat on the bed to dry off.

I'll help you, Fury. Contrary to what the angels in your Afterlife have said, I might be a monster, but I'm not evil. There are shades of gray in everything, but not in this. Whatever happens, I will help you and won't get in the way.

I sighed again, unwrapping myself then squeezing the water from my hair into the cotton towel. I ran a comb through my tangles slowly. "And there are no ulterior motives?"

I didn't say that.

I huffed a laugh and tossed the towel onto the floor. Reaching over, I clicked the light off and pulled my legs up and under the soft covers. "I suppose I should've expected that. You like to play games, and I didn't need the file to know that bit of information."

His deep laugh filled my mind, and sleep washed over me, begging to pull me under. My thoughts slowed as I started to drift.

Sleep tight, kitten. You and I are going to get to know each other. And lucky for me, you can't lie.

No. No, I couldn't.

CHAPTER 26
FURY

Banging jarred me awake, and for a brief second, I thought I was back in the demon dorms where Barb the Bitter and her ex were at it again, fucking in the early hours loud enough to wake the dead.

I blinked twice and rubbed the sleep from my eyes.

The silk sheets that pooled around my waist and the billowy white curtains reminded me this was most definitely *not* the dorm.

"Sir, the lady is sleeping—"

"She's been asleep for eighteen hours. Either she drank herself into a coma, she's dead again, or she fled. I'm going in."

I lifted my head at the sound of Dorian's voice. The door opened, slamming into the wall, and cracking the plaster. The big, broody fae stepped in, mouth open to yell at me when he caught sight of my naked body and pert breasts. The ladies were standing to attention this morning under his watchful gaze.

"I— you—"

"At a loss for words?" I mused, reaching up to stretch my arms. His amber gaze turned hard. "Color me surprised. When was the last time that happened? Hundred years ago? Two?"

"At least a hundred and fifty," came James' weak reply from the door. To his credit, he kept his eyeballs off my tits, instead focusing on the patterned ceiling fifteen feet above us.

"A hundred and fifty," I repeated. "Well, that's gotta be a new record."

"Fury," Dorian said through clenched teeth. "Why are you naked?"

"Because I bathed and then realized I didn't have any clothes." I shrugged. "Besides, I sleep naked most of the time. I've lived alone for —" My words fell short, and my jaw snapped shut. Nope. I was not starting off the morning accidentally giving away my age. He'd undoubtedly figure it out eventually, but I needed to keep him guessing. Especially when I had Ezra to deal with.

Dorian sighed. Instead of pressing for what I'd been about to say, he asked, "Why didn't you open the door when I knocked?"

"You call that knocking?" I replied with a lifted eyebrow.

James let out a choked sound, making Dorian press his lips together.

Hmm. Angry fae. Do I poke or do I let it lie?

"Answer the question."

"If you must know, I was asleep until about two seconds before you opened the door. In case you'd forgotten, I was kidnapped and drugged at the ass crack of dawn yesterday, and I didn't get to sleep until late."

"Why not?" A pucker formed between his brows in confusion as he stared at me unhappily. His chiseled jawline was doing bad things to my already wound-up body.

"I had to take care of some things."

"What things?"

James tried to come to the rescue, reading between the lines where his dense-as-fuck master could not. "I think the lady—"

"Can tell me herself," Dorian said in a hard tone. "What things?"

I looked between the two of them. James' cheeks were beet red. He glanced down from the ceiling momentarily to flash me a look of apology. Meanwhile, Dorian stared coldly, my tits forgotten.

I grabbed the end of the sheet and tossed it aside, slipping my bare legs down the bed. My feet touched the cool floor, and a chill spread over me—though that might've been Dorian's gaze.

"I was talking to the voices in my head, and then they offered to give me an orgasm," I replied before walking into the bathroom and closing the door firmly behind me.

I heard Dorian's muffled complaints through the crack but tuned it out for the most part.

I recall you turning me down, Ezra chimed in. Figured he'd been listening in.

"He doesn't know that," I said under my breath as I rummaged through the cabinets to find an unopened toothbrush and toothpaste.

"What was that?" Dorian called, and I knew damn well he could hear me crystal clear at this range.

"Just talking to the voices," I called back, before flipping the water on.

Ezra's dark chuckle in my mind drowned out the sound of the faucet.

Just think it. You don't have to speak. I'll know. Dorian's old, and I have no doubt he's seen mind readers before. He'll grow suspicious if you keep speaking aloud.

I swished a mouthful of water and then spat. *Don't you have a job to be doing? Poisoners to catch?* I thought in his general direction. Least I felt like it was. I wasn't the mind reader here.

I'm multitasking. It's one of my many admirable qualities.

I rolled my eyes but got no response. I guess he took the hint and stepped out. Or he just made me think he did. There was no telling until he made his presence known, and I didn't have it in me to keep worrying over it. I wiped my mouth with the back of my hand and walked over to the door.

I turned the knob and cracked it open. "While I'm not modest, I'm pretty sure James doesn't feel like seeing my naked ass all day. Care to find me some clothes?"

Dorian turned to glare at me, and clothes appeared on my body.

I blinked, staring down at myself.

Damn. Those files really didn't say shit, did they?

I opened the door slowly. "Thank you," I said, still a bit wary. He'd dressed me in pants, a long-sleeved shirt, and a white puffy vest. The only problem was that it was summer. In Houston.

"We going somewhere?"

"Yes, I have urgent business to attend to, and you're coming with me."

"Oh? I am?" I questioned. "Where?"

He grabbed my elbow in a tight but not painful grip. The fabric between us was a stiff barrier, but my skin still warmed beneath his touch. “My home. My *real* home.”

Then the ground disappeared, and my heart started to hammer. I felt hot and cold. My vision turned black. Solid ground couldn’t rise up soon enough, but when it did, I collapsed onto my knees. My hands fell with me as Dorian released me upon landing.

I registered the cold first. It was bone deep, a chill that wouldn’t lift. The stone beneath me was frigid to the touch, like ice, but harder. Colder.

The next thing I registered?

The cliff I was kneeling on that overlooked the ocean. A salty spray whipped my face as the waves crashed against the unyielding base.

“Welcome to the Isle of Glass. You might know it as Avalon.”

CHAPTER 27
FURY

Dorian burst through the double doors at the front of his castle, and I followed in his shadow, taking in the scenery. I held my hands behind my back, looking around at the opulent rugs and decor. Above us, grand iron chandeliers hung from the ceilings, their candles giving off a magically enhanced light.

Fae bustled about, left and right, obviously in a rush. I knew fae weren't all as grouchy as Dorian, so it was clear they were upset about something. Maybe it was that his sudden return had ruined their short vacation from him. I could see that.

"Tristan," he yelled into the foyer before moving swiftly down the hall.

Artwork and ancient tapestries lined the walls, and I wanted to get a better look at them when we weren't in a hurry to go . . . wherever we were going.

A beautiful fae man appeared next to us, walking in step with Dorian. A navy uniform hugged his lean frame. Olive skin accentuated the contours of his high cheekbones, and his purposeful blue eyes never once gazed in my direction.

"Sir, Elaine and the guards are in your study awaiting your instruction," he said.

"Which wards were tripped?" Dorian asked.

"The northwest corner of the island, sir," Tristan replied. He waited a moment before adding, "They found tracks as well, sir. Footsteps."

Dorian's pace slowed a fraction, clearly affected by that new piece of information.

I pursed and twisted my lips, not understanding much of what was happening.

We crossed into what was apparently Dorian's study when he stopped suddenly, turning around.

"What?" I asked, looking behind me to see what he was looking at.

"Tristan, take her upstairs to the green sitting room."

"Wait a minute, you're the one who said I was coming here with you," I argued, crossing my arms, and jutting out my hip. "Can you make up your mind?"

He stepped toward me, and said, "Not now." Looking to who I assumed was his second, or a really handsome butler, he added, "I'll call for you when I'm done. Keep her company." He stepped back into his office where I saw a tall, beautiful woman in armor and six male guards standing at attention.

Then he shut the door in my face.

I spun on my heel, taking in my surroundings and my new comrade. "Okay, hot stuff. Looks like you're my new babysitter. Show me around."

A look of shock crossed Tristan's face before a laugh escaped him. "You are most certainly *not* what I was expecting," he said, as he began walking down the hallway.

"Don't sift out of here. I can't follow," I told him, making sure he didn't just disappear and leave me lost in a castle.

"I know." He held his hands behind his back, turning a corner and going up a set of stairs.

Since my files were absolute garbage, I needed to know what I was dealing with, and I had to do it casually without being obvious.

"Reading my mind, or can you just read my powers?" I teased, playfully elbowing him.

He scrunched his eyebrows together. "Fae can't read minds."

Well, thank the stars for that. A bit of tension I was holding in my shoulders relaxed. If he'd said otherwise, I would've had to consider the option of jumping off the impressive cliff outside and just calling the whole thing off.

"Ah, so you're saying my lack of powers are really just that obvious," I said, taking a turn down the hallway and following his lead. The place was a maze.

He stopped. "Ms. Fury—"

"Just Fury."

He hummed. "Fury . . ." I nodded, and he continued. "Dorian has told me about you. I know you're an unknown supernatural, that you are his mate, and that you're quite smart, and dare I say, cunning. As his second, he has filled me in."

I cocked an eyebrow and tilted my head. "Point taken, Tristan."

He smiled slightly, dipping his head, and turned to continue walking.

"So, where are we going, or did you plan on walking me around until he's done with the knights of the round table in there?"

He huffed a laugh. "I was taking you to a sitting room where you would feel comfortable waiting."

I started to respond but stopped short when I saw some of the tapestries lining the walls. Tristan took notice and returned to me. Standing still, I stared up at the grand and detailed needlework. I looked left to see that I'd passed two others, then I moved down to look at them.

"They're quite beautiful, aren't they?" he asked me, breaking the silence as he stood next to me.

"They are," I said, drawn in for reasons I couldn't explain. Something about them called to me. "Who made them?"

"Many different fae. They tell the story of our people. War, peace, love, triumph, loss. The stories you know in the human world are nothing compared to the truth of Avalon, or the fae." Tristan looked at the tapestries with reverence and respect.

I was itching to touch it, and that made me want to know more about it.

"Somehow, I can't picture Dorian doing needlework in his downtime," I mumbled, as my fae babysitter coughed to cover the barest hint of a laugh at his sour leader's expense. I pointed at the one in front of us. "Will you tell me about this one?"

Tristan turned his attention to me and smiled. Pointing at the intricate border, he said, "Here. If you follow this pattern, the knot-work used tells us this story was from the seventh century." His finger trailed the symbols in the corners and my eyes followed. "Those symbols are—"

"Pictish."

He looked over at me with his eyebrows raised in surprise.

I shrugged. "I'm not much of a people person, so I read a lot."

"Well, you're right. They're Pictish. This one tells the story of a hunter's family. See the animals?" he asked, pointing to various figures.

I nodded, moving slowly to the next one. "And this?"

"Ah, I've always loved this one. This is the Wild Hunt," he said, his own eyes roaming over the tapestry in admiration.

Never before had any kind of art spoken to me or kept me enthralled to this degree. I couldn't explain it. I stopped in front of another as we crept down the hallway to the sitting room.

An embroidered fae with glowing amber eyes stood out in the middle. The golden thread used matched the color exactly, and I felt like I was looking at Dorian, just without the chill he managed to elicit all the time.

The scene on the tapestry pulled my gaze away from the center fae, and what I saw was . . . curious.

Pain and . . . destruction.

"Tristan?" I nodded to the one I was in front of. "What happened here?"

I hoped he'd give me some insight into the story being told. Did it tell me something about his powers? Was it something far more sinister? Was it representative of Dorian just being a moody prick?

Any of those things were possible, especially the latter. Without words, it was up for interpretation. That was what pissed me off about art sometimes. Sometimes a flower was just a flower. Why did it have to also be a vagina? The tapestry said something about Dorian. I needed to know what.

Tristan hesitated. "I'm not sure I'm the one who should explain this particular piece. I believe you'll need to ask Dorian that yourself."

"Oh, c'mon. It's just a story, right?" I flung my hand out toward the wall. "I'm not asking for the password to the secret vaults."

He shook his head.

"What's she asking for?" Dorian asked, appearing next to me.

"Nice of you to join us," I said. "Tristan was just telling me about some of these tapestries, but he got cold feet when I asked him about this one." I jutted my thumb at the wall next to me.

Dorian's eyes darkened when he saw the one in question. "Tristan, will you ask a steward to bring us the order I requested from the kitchen? Have it sent to the sitting room, please."

"Yes, sir." He inclined his head. Meeting my eyes, he dipped his head again. "Fury. It was a pleasure." And then he disappeared.

"You really know how to run 'em off, don't you?"

Dorian's cold stare gave away nothing.

I sighed. "Cool, if you don't feel like talking to me, maybe you could take me back to Houston and ignore me there? It's about the same."

"I'm not ignoring you. I'm thinking."

I raised my eyebrows. "This is thinking? Well, hot damn. What does it look like when you're dragging someone halfway across the world to not speak to them? Asking for a friend."

He put his hands in his pockets and cleared his throat. "Will you join me in the sitting room now?"

I walked past him, waving my hand. "It was supposed to be green, right?" I asked, seeing a set of open double doors that led to a large room I assumed had been prepared for me.

I whistled softly when I entered. The fireplace was huge. So big I could've walked into it. Its heat filled the room, warming the air and ripping away the cold that seemed to follow me. Green and cream oriental rugs covered the stone floors. Artwork with ornate gold framing adorned the walls, and oak bookcases held what had to be a thousand books.

A table near two wingback chairs had a silver tray sitting on top. On it were plates covered with silver domes, and what looked like a wine decanter and two glasses.

Dorian came up behind me and gestured for me to sit.

I twisted my lips, thinking about him telling me he wasn't a gentleman. If it quacks like a duck . . .

"Thanks." I reached for the decanter, then hesitated. I really didn't like wine all that much. I wanted something less fruity and more . . . hard liquor.

"It's fae wine," Dorian said, sensing my dilemma. When he saw the question in my eye, he added, "It's much better than the swill humans drink. And far more potent, so please don't guzzle it like you're trying to impress the rest of the frat house."

I glared at him and poured a large serving. I raised my glass in a toast and took a drink.

Damn. He wasn't kidding. Potent was an understatement.

He sat next to me, pouring his own glass, though it was a much smaller serving.

From our seats, on the opposite side of the wall, was a painting. It was placed as the focal point of the room, as though one would sit in these very chairs simply to look at it. She was a stunningly beautiful fae with white hair and soulful blue eyes.

"Who's that?" I asked, raising my eyebrows in the direction of the painting while I took another sip of wine.

Dorian sighed and raised the goblet to his lips, sipping his wine, taking his time to savor it before swallowing. He traced the tip of his glass with his finger, drawing out the silence between us. He inhaled deeply before he said, "My daughter."

CHAPTER 28
FURY

I CHOKED ON MY WINE. THAT HAPPENED. PROBABLY HADN'T EVER HAPPENED before, but if anything could cause me to choke on alcohol, it was hearing that Dorian had a daughter.

The poltergeists were fired. Not that I *could* fire them. But *if* I could . . .

"Where is she?" I asked, looking around.

Part of my mind imagined a little girl with a white dress and pink ribbons running around the corner and jumping into her father's arms. But the picture before me wasn't a little girl. She was a young adult. Who knew how old, really, but she didn't look as old as the other fae did when they stopped aging.

"She's here, but she won't be coming to join us," Dorian answered, staring into the fireplace. "She's in stasis."

What the hell was that?

"In stasis?" I asked. "Care to explain a little bit more there? I'm not exactly up to date on fae culture." Apparently.

He took a drink. "Stasis is an in-between for fae. An undisturbed, dreamless sleep where we skip generations of time—centuries—in peace. It's rejuvenating, and it gives us time to . . . take a break from the living world. We live a long time . . ." He trailed off, staring at nothing in particular.

I waited to see if he was going to continue, and I shifted my weight in the chair so I could face him. When he didn't speak again, I nudged his arm gently. "Dorian?"

"Hmm?" He looked up, meeting my gaze.

"You didn't finish. You said, 'we live a long time' and then you stopped." I could tell by the look on his face there was more to say.

"We do. We live a long time, and it can become monotonous. Exhausting. Joyless. At a certain point, it's just . . ." He took a moment, closing his eyes and inhaling a deep breath. "Existing. So we enter stasis to rest, and then we can return to the world refreshed."

The weight of his words were heavy, and our conversation at dinner the night before echoed in my mind. I hadn't understood why he seemed so cold until that moment. To live so long and just feel like you were taking up space in the world and nothing more . . .

I'd only been dead for a hundred and three years. It was a drop in the bucket for him. But I had to wonder, was that what my afterlife would look like? The ancients I knew didn't seem to act this way. Vlad was pretty content, which said a lot for a guy who'd lived during the Middle Ages. I wasn't sure about my own future, and I didn't like that I was suddenly thinking about it.

I chewed on the inside of my cheek while I thought, my eyes roaming, then coming to rest on the portrait again. "You said your daughter is in stasis?"

He nodded. "Yes." Something shimmered in his eyes. A memory. A longing. It was clear as day.

"You miss her, don't you?"

His voice was quiet when he answered, "Every day that goes by." He took a small sip of his wine, then rubbed his thumb up and down the side of his glass. "That's why we're here."

Was she coming out of stasis? I immediately questioned if this was about to become a weird situation where I met the daughter of a fae I'd planned to break. That wouldn't be awkward or anything.

Dorian read the look on my face and shook his head. "You misunderstand. Tristan came to inform me that wards on the island were triggered. Someone came here, and they were looking for something."

"Here? On . . . in Avalon? I didn't think humans knew it existed. Surely, you have it concealed. If whatever enchantments you have didn't work, I'm sure the weather would turn them right off. I thought Avalon was supposed to be green and pretty. Not so cold and bitter that nomads in Siberia would vacation here for the warmth. If someone ended up here, it was an accident, and they were looking for a phone to call for help."

He glared at me, and I shrugged.

"You might be right. It has happened over the years a time or two. However, this time is different. Elaine and her guards found footsteps. Whoever they belonged to, they had purpose, and they were entirely too close for comfort."

He gave me a disapproving look as I poured more wine. I returned it. I didn't need him judging me. "What were they too close to?"

"Where we keep those in stasis," he said, his tone turning somber.

"I don't understand. If they accidentally woke people up, couldn't they just go back to sleep?" Unless someone was there to kill the sleeping fae . . . but that sounded insane. Who even knew where to look for them? Or that they went into stasis?

"It doesn't work that way. It's more complicated than that." His expression looked simultaneously pained and angry. I couldn't get a read on him.

"Uncomplicate it for me," I suggested.

He chose instead to look at me, contemplating something. I'd counted to thirty-seven in my head before he finally spoke again. "I believe you'll think less of me if I do."

That statement shocked me more than I would've expected. Warring parts of my mind said I wouldn't—and another part said this was information I needed.

"Do you care if I do?" I asked, skirting around his statement. "You may claim I'm your mate, Dorian, but I'm not sure you care one way or another what I think."

The tiniest hint of a smile peeked on one side of his lips. "I do find you fascinating, Fury. Know that."

Skirting around my statement as well. Interesting.

"Why don't you try me?"

He sighed. "Lyra, my daughter, can't wake from stasis. She didn't go into it willingly."

I sat back in my chair, waiting for the ball to drop. What had he done?

As though he'd heard my question, he said, "I had to."

His icy exterior broke for a fraction of a second. The tiniest crack in his voice and slip in his tone. It was barely noticeable, and a human never would've caught it. But I did. He was . . . heartbroken. Somehow, I felt it. This ache in my chest I couldn't explain. I knew what emotional pain felt like, and I knew this pain wasn't my own.

"She was mentally unstable. I had to put her in stasis for her safety, and for the safety of others," he finished.

Was this what the risk witches had seen? Dorian, leader of the fae, would help end the world . . . because he'd forced his daughter into stasis? Would he do it to others? It was certainly unorthodox. Then again, so was I. Feeling torn between how to view that revelation, I sat quietly. To compel someone to stop living their life, forcing them into what was essentially a coma against their will . . . it was monstrous on a grand scale. And yet, I saw what it did to him. His mate had died, and he was alone, left with a mentally unstable child he had to protect. And what does a parent do? I wouldn't know. Some deeper part of me that I never spoke to anymore knew that I would have done anything to keep my child safe. Maybe that was what he had done . . . and that didn't seem so monstrous.

Dorian broke my train of thought when he spoke again. "Change how you see me?"

I huffed a humorless laugh. "I honestly don't know what to think. I can't imagine having to make that choice. I'm, um . . . I'm sorry you had to."

His head tilted to the side in surprise as though he was searching for a lie in my words and coming up short. It was probably the most honest I'd been with him. No false truths or twisted words. His lips were tight, and then he slightly dipped his head in thanks before he stood up and walked across the room, coming to a stop in front of the fireplace.

I took a deep drink and then another. I felt dizzy, then remembered how strong fae wine was. I probably should've eaten something. I'd been asleep for the entire night and most of the day before he'd decided to drag me to the Arctic Circle. I reached over and took the silver dome off a plate in front of us to find a spicy chicken burger with fries.

I looked up. "You made this for me?"

He turned. "Well, no, I didn't. I had the kitchen make it for you. You said you enjoyed it at Roxanne's."

His random thoughtfulness surprised me. I smiled at him and dug in. I downed the entire thing in six bites. After stuffing my face with fries, I dipped a couple in the wine. It wasn't the best taste. Better to drink the wine instead. The decanter was empty, so I looked around to see if there was any more.

Dorian caught my eye and realized what I was looking for. "I can have them bring some hot tea, if you'd like."

I frowned. "Not exactly what I was looking for."

The look of disapproval came again. "You drink too much."

Whatever moment we'd shared earlier was gone, and the icy wall that Dorian surrounded himself with was back up.

"It's not as bad as it sounds. You should try it sometime," I said, eating another fry.

He glanced at her portrait, then went back to looking at the fire. "I have." A few moments passed before he drank the rest of his wine then threw the glass into the fire, the delicate crystal splintering as it collided with the stone. The sound of it shattering echoed in my ears.

I opened my mouth when his phone rang, and he answered it.

At the same time, Ezra whispered in my mind, *See you soon.*

"They have them," Dorian said, putting his phone in his jacket pocket. "Time to go."

CHAPTER 29
FURY

Fae wine and sifting did not go together.

We landed on the bank of a river outside an unmarked warehouse where I doubled at the waist and emptied my stomach.

"I told you not to drink so much," Dorian said, completely unsympathetic.

I wiped my mouth with the back of my hand and glared up at him. "It's not my drinking that's the problem," I growled. It wasn't completely accurate, but blaming it on the wine would just highlight my crutch . . . one I'd found myself leaning on more and more since returning to Earth. Also, Dorian would be right, and I couldn't have that.

"Hm, could've fooled me," he answered dryly.

I hauled myself up and rubbed at my tender stomach while he strode away. "What about my clothes?" I called out, motioning to the long sleeves and puffy vest. I already had boob sweat, and I was pretty sure the tiny hairs around my face had started to curl.

Dorian glanced at me over his shoulder and the clothes disappeared, replaced by a loose tank top and linen shorts. I eyed the strappy new wedges, noting that he'd put me in heels.

I lifted an eyebrow at him in question.

A subtle, almost non-existent smirk was all I got in reply before he continued.

Fucker.

At least he had good taste in shoes. The clothes weren't exactly my style, but they were light and airy, letting my skin breathe in the humidity instead of dying from it.

I followed him, picking up the pace when he reached the door. Two guards stood outside once again. They were different vampires, but still seemed to be on the up-and-up and didn't question my presence, instead just nodding at me in respect.

We entered the darkened warehouse. The sounds of screaming and bones cracking were the first thing to greet my ears.

Dorian glowered in the low light, following the noise down two rows of unmarked crates.

Our two poisoners sat back-to-back in plastic chairs. In front of one of them, Roman stood with bleeding knuckles and a grim expression. Ezra was off to the side, leaning against a wall of crates. His sharp eyes caught sight of me first.

I opened my mouth to say something when a shadow moved. I turned my head to catch the flapping of wings. Hades landed on my right shoulder; his beady eyes narrowed on me.

I groaned.

"Don't act so surprised to see me," the crow muttered in annoyance.

"This isn't my surprised face," I replied. "I was hoping you'd be roadkill by now, pigeon."

"I'm a bird. I don't walk across the street. I would have to be supremely stupid to get hit by a car—" He broke off sharply at the look on my face. Yup. The insult had finally hit.

Hades let out an irritated squawk in my ear. "Keep it up. I'll shit in your liquor."

"Do it and we'll find out how many lives you have, birdie. I'm not afraid of going hunting. You'd look nice mounted on Dorian's wall."

With that, Hades took off, flapping his wings and knocking me in the head as he went to oversee us from the safety of the crates.

It was only then that I noticed all eyes on me. My mates and my killers.

How sweet.

"You have a talking crow?" Dorian asked.

"Lost a bet with a witch. Got stuck with the pigeon," I muttered, repeating the lie I'd told Roxanne and hoping Dorian wouldn't call me out for it. It may as well have been true. I would not have picked an asshole crow for a go-between. He was useless at his actual job. Like the poltergeists. God, when I was done here, I was going to put in a complaint with Jake about giving the Afterlife an overhaul because there were way too many slackers not doing their damn jobs.

Ezra chuckled, only a second too late to be laughing at my comment. Must've been listening in.

I'm always listening, kitten. Your thoughts . . . they're refreshing.

"Shouldn't we be interrogating these guys?" I asked, clapping my hands to bring us all back to the important thing: the people trying to kill me.

"It looks like the wolf got started without us," Dorian said, a chill entering his voice.

Ezra shrugged. "I gave Roman a heads-up before calling you. I knew you'd sift in and do whatever you wanted. Besides, the dog needed to get out his aggression."

Roman bristled at Ezra's jab.

I rolled my eyes, ignoring the shifter's comeback insult. While the one he'd been working on looked pretty roughed up, the other did not. His eyes were sharp. Keen. He watched me, his lips pulled back in a snide expression.

"Did you get anything out of him?" I asked Roman, jutting my chin toward Pulpface, as he would hereby be dubbed until his inevitable death. It was healing quickly because he was a vampire, but still resembled a misshapen lump of bloodied meat more than a face.

"No," Ezra replied before Roman could. "He won't talk."

Their minds are also being blocked somehow. Spells can do that, which implies they're working with a witch, he added in my mind.

Do they know you can read minds? I asked.

Unclear, but also highly unlikely.

Hm. Looked like this wasn't a cut-and-dried hit-and-run. No one would've bothered with that sort of protection if it were.

I moved toward them, walking around them both, hands behind

my back. They usually started to sweat when I didn't dive right into questioning.

"We'll see about that," Dorian said, tugging the sleeves of his shirt up his forearms. "Fury, you may want to step out—"

"Not a chance," I said before he could finish. "Besides, I have a feeling you'll need me."

"Doubtful," the fae replied with complete and utter arrogance.

I stepped back and motioned for him to come forward. Dorian knelt in front of the non-pummeled vampire. His amber eyes glowed brighter for a moment. "Why did you try to kill Fury?"

Our vampire glared back with a hatred in his eyes I recognized all too well. It was almost like being back in the Afterlife.

Vampire Number Two reared back to slam his head into Dorian's nose but the fae saw it coming and caught him by the throat.

I tilted my head, curious about his method.

"I said, *why did you try to kill Fury*?" His eyes burned brighter this time.

Still no response.

I shot Ezra a questioning look.

He can make those weaker than him do what he wants by commanding it. They should have no choice but to answer.

That was terrifying . . . and intriguing.

He could've tried to use that power to make me spill my secrets.

He hadn't.

I'm not the only one who likes games. Dorian's just forgotten the thrill. He's finding it again, with you.

Goosebumps formed on the exposed skin of my arms, and Roman saw them, his eyebrows drawing together in concern. "If you need to step out, no one will judge you—"

"Oh, for fuck's sake," I grumbled. "Roman, I'm fine. Dorian, get on with it or step aside." I motioned with my hand and then crossed my arms.

Dorian narrowed his eyes at me.

"You think you can make him talk?" he asked, not questioning my abilities, but instead inciting a challenge.

A part of me knew I shouldn't rise to the occasion. He was only doing this because he wanted to learn more about me, after all. But, well, the thing was—I was a demon. This was what I did. While I didn't *love* the Afterlife, I truly didn't mind my job. There was a sort of comfort in it.

After so long *rehabilitating* souls, my fingers itched to be back at it.

I couldn't handle the guys that way, but these schmucks? They were getting in the way of my actual job. They were no one. Just a means to an end, whether I got the answers I needed or not.

Nameless, faceless vampires meant to do the dirty work and take the fall.

They didn't seem particularly confident, which made me think they knew there was no getting out.

The real mastermind wasn't going to save them.

And yet, they didn't seem overly fearful either.

A curious combination.

Instead of answering him, I strode forward. He backed away, giving me space.

"Pain will not work on us," Pulpface said, his jaw finally healed enough to speak. "Neither will fear. We have nothing to lose. You can break us, bind us, but you will not win."

"I know." I nodded slowly. "You're not hired help. This is personal. You'll see this through to the end," I said quietly.

Vampire Number Two blinked, evidently a little surprised by my fast deductions.

"I admire that, in a way. The ability to carry out orders and do what you say you will. It's hard to find good lackeys these days." And, man, did I know it.

"Who said we were taking orders?" Vampire Two chimed in.

I smiled but kept my face devoid of any true emotion. He paled. "You're here. Whoever orchestrated this, it wasn't you two. Someone smart enough to cover their tracks doesn't get caught. Not easily, anyhow. If I had to guess, I'd say you're just the beginning of a problem for me. But to what end?" I mused aloud, watching their reactions closely.

"We have seen the truth," Pulpface said. "We know what you are. We know what you will do." He recited the rhetoric smoothly, like a true zealot. For a fleeting moment, I wondered if he knew.

"Oh?" I questioned. "What am I?"

"A devil," Vampire Two spat. "Straight from Hell."

If I hadn't already considered the possibility that he knew what I was, my heart might've skipped a beat. But instead of giving myself away, I smiled. "That's a new one. I like it. So I'm a devil from Hell, and that's why you want me dead? Seems a bit hypocritical for vampires."

"He told us you'd do this," Pulpface said.

He. Now that drew my interest.

"Do what?" I asked, instead of poking at the more obvious question. People tended to reveal more when you didn't do exactly as they expected. Unpredictability threw them off.

"Gaslight us," he grunted.

"Gaslight?" I repeated, unable to help the chuckle. "I haven't said you're crazy yet, but could you truly blame me after you tried to kill me?"

"We know the truth," Vampire Two said again. There was some sort of resolution on his face. As if he were ready for something.

"You keep saying that. Do you mind enlightening me?"

While I'd prepared myself for the slight possibility that they somehow knew I was a demon, I hadn't considered what would happen next. Nothing could've prepared me for the words that came out of his mouth.

"You're going to end the world," Pulpface whispered cruelly.

I froze. Shock filled me, though I quickly hid it.

"But we are not the ones to stop you. We're only the messengers."

"What's the message?" Dorian said, finally choosing to speak at the very moment it seemed I'd lost my voice.

I'd barely recovered when they both turned to look at me.

Whatever they had to say, it had to be good.

Or in this case, so very bad.

They spoke in unison. "Welcome back, Sunny."

My face blanked. My heart dropped. I stepped forward, wrenching Vamp Two from his seat—despite the fact that he'd been chained there. I grasped him by his front and pulled hard enough the metal bent and squealed.

"What did you say?" I whispered low, my control hinging on nonexistent for the first time in a very long time.

Instead of an answer, I got a bloody smile and a rasping laugh.

Then blood started pouring from every orifice of his body.

It stained his eyes and ran down his cheeks.

It leaked from his ears, dripping onto his black T-shirt.

It gushed from his nose as if something were forcibly emptying him of it.

He was dead in the time it took for me to drop him. So was his buddy, by the looks of it.

My hands fell to my sides, clenched into fists. I bit the inside of my cheek, tasting blood. Those words replayed in my mind even though the messengers were dead.

"What the—" Roman started.

"Spell." Ezra sighed. "They must've just been waiting to trigger it."

Mentally, I was fading. Receding. The desire to fight or flee was surfacing.

Bile climbed back up my throat . . .

"Who's Sunny?" Dorian asked.

I wanted to tell him now wasn't the time. Not to push this. In the same way his daughter was off-limits, so was this. But I couldn't even say that. "No one."

"Bullshit," he said, calling me out. Little did he know, it was the wrong time to make a stand. "Is your real name Sunny?"

My breathing grew thin. Not frantic but panicked all the same.

I strode up to him and tilted my head back.

"I'm only going to tell you this once, so listen closely." I closed what little gap was still between us until we were only inches apart. "My name is Fury. You can call me that or any number of things, honestly, I don't particularly care. But if you ever call me Sunny, it'll be the last word you say."

With that, I stepped around him and started down the aisle of crates. I only paused when I reached the end, looking up to see Hades staring down at me, unmoving. The crow had heard, and I could see he was unsettled by the revelation. He angled his head, and I nodded once in confirmation, jerking my head to the side toward the exit. Hades had a job to do. As he took flight, I turned, peering at the guys over my shoulder. "It's time to switch. I'm going with Ezra today."

If my words hurt him, he didn't let it show. Dorian's face turned as cold as I felt. "Very well."

I walked out of the warehouse without another word, and I didn't look back.

CHAPTER 30
EZRA

Fury's mind was racing a million miles an hour. Images clashed. Memories attempted to surface. She battled them, trying to stuff them all down.

I sighed heavily.

"I see her time with you hasn't done much to soften either of your demeanors," I quipped to Dorian.

The fae bastard looked torn between chasing after her and leaving it be. I needed to divert his attention. "She's hiding something," he replied, ignoring my comment entirely.

"And which of us isn't hiding things from her?" I said quietly. That did the trick.

He turned away from staring at the spot where she'd rounded the corner and disappeared from sight.

"That's—" Roman started. I already knew what he would say without needing to read his mind.

"It's not different. Neither of you like it. *That* is the only difference."

"People are trying to kill her for it," Dorian said.

"People try to kill us all the time. At least my people do." I shrugged, feigning disinterest in them. "There will always be a threat, but something tells me our little kitten has claws. Push her too much, and I suspect she might actually use them on you."

Something I wasn't opposed to watching, though I'd much rather she used them on me—preferably while I was balls deep inside her.

"Some people need pushing," Dorian replied in a dark voice.

"And how well did that work out for you? Last I checked, she's opting to stay with me—but what do I know?" I nodded once in their direction. "Now if you'll excuse me—"

"Do you think they were telling the truth?" the wolf said.

I froze mid-stride. "You think she's a devil sent from Hell?" I said mockingly. "Or that she's come to end the world?"

"I didn't say—" Roman blustered, though Dorian was notably silent. Knowing that asshole, he was waiting for me to slip. While Roman was young and still prone to displays of emotion, Dorian was a more cunning sort.

"No, you didn't *think*," I sneered. "Really, look at the two of you. Dorian's being a demanding prick when something happened here that clearly triggered her. Meanwhile, you're over there listening to the words of two very obviously brainwashed puppets." I shook my head, completely unremorseful for gaslighting them both. "It's no wonder she chose me, given the options."

I skimmed the surface thoughts in his mind. Unlike Dorian, who either had a natural resistance to my talents or had a block put on himself before I met him, Roman was an open book. Anger and guilt swirled inside him as he warred with the wolf.

"Whether she chose you or not, you'll still need to trade with Mikaelson before the summit," Dorian said. "I expect to be taking her back during that time. Try to make sure she doesn't die or run off before then."

The bastard sifted out before either Roman or I could reply.

"I'll be in touch when she's ready," I said over my shoulder, walking to the exit with my car keys in hand. "Oh, and you may want to work on shit with your wolf before then. If you keep trying to protect her, you'll be the one who gets hurt."

CHAPTER 31
FURY

Welcome back, Sunny.

Those words played on repeat in my mind. A never-ending loop of anxiety and confusion. For the first time in a very long time, I felt incredibly lost and more than a little angry.

Because someone—somewhere out there—knew about me.

Who I used to be.

The victim of domestic abuse.

The housewife from the roaring twenties who was depressed and browbeaten, living her shitty life in a shitty world where women's only roles were to cook and clean and please their husbands. Nothing more than a prize to be won. A trophy to show off. I got married, and he carted me off, locking me inside a little yellow house with a white picket fence. A façade. A cage. My prison . . . with nothing but liquor to ease the physical and mental pain and suffering. It may have been my husband who abused me, but it was society that allowed it. The outlook that women were property and meant to be loyal as dogs wasn't new or specific to him.

It was a mentality as old as time.

But then I'd died. I'd stepped outside time, pushing that past as far away from me as I could. Stuffing it down so deep that I would never have to see it again. I broke the glass ceiling and became the best damn demon in the Afterlife. I was so good even Upper Management wanted me. They'd sent me here to do a job . . . one I was now fairly certain I was failing.

I threaded my hands through my hair and pulled.

When had things gotten so complicated?

Was it truly during the interrogation? Or before that?

When Dorian told me I drank too much, I felt called out and seen for the first time.

When Ezra spoke to me until I fell asleep, I felt less alone.

When Roman spoke of protecting me, I felt guilt about what I was doing to him when all he cared about was my safety. When had anyone besides Duke ever cared about my safety?

Fuck me, this mission was doomed from the very beginning.

Kitten, Ezra's mental voice prodded me lightly, but not gently.

"Go away," I grumbled, lying down in the giant white bed. The ceiling fan hummed as it blasted cool air at my face, pushing loose hairs over my face and around my eyes.

No can do. I've given you time to brood, but you're spiraling.

Spiraling? I narrowed my eyes at the door that led to the rest of his penthouse.

Would you rather I say you're being overly dramatic? Don't get me wrong, I love a good moping session, but you're beating yourself up for shit that isn't your fault.

"Go away," I huffed, throwing a pillow at the door. It exploded in a shower of feathers.

Oops.

That wasn't nice.

"You're not nice. You're invading my privacy by being in my head, and I can't even get away from it. Now's really not the time to test me, Fangs."

Fangs? He mentally scoffed.

"I should be calling you stalker right now. Don't push your luck."

Look. Ezra sighed. *In most cases, I can simply tune it all out. Even if I try to ignore your thoughts, though, I find it incredibly difficult the closer we are. It's a side effect of you being my mate.*

I rolled my eyes. "Well, it's not like *I* can control it, nor do I have a witch on hand to help me like those fuckers who poisoned me did."

Silence wrapped around me for a suspended moment. I thought Ezra might've gotten the hint. Then he asked, *Do you want to talk about it?*

"Fuck no," I groaned. "I don't want to talk or think about anything. I just want to be left alone."

I heard the latch turn and then I was being picked up. Strong arms wrapped around me, cool to the touch. If I hadn't already known it was him, the scent of blood, leather, and whiskey would've given it away.

"Ezra, so help me god—"

"There isn't a god. You've said so in your thoughts. Makes that threat a bit weak, don't you think?"

I gritted my teeth. "Put me down."

"Or?"

"Or I'm not responsible for what happens if you don't," I answered tartly.

His full lips twisted into a smirk. "Well, when you put it that way . . ."

I didn't register that we were moving at first, and when I did, it was already over. Black dots appeared in my vision as vertigo made my head swim.

They cleared just in time for me to look up into the night sky. The dark abyss opened over me. The air was thick with tension and heavy clouds sat over Houston.

"Where are—" I started to ask.

Then he dropped me.

My fall was short and broken by the crash of water enveloping my body. Being mid-sentence, I sucked a mouthful of it in before I realized my mistake.

My eyes flew open. I was disoriented for only a moment, before the blue lights of the pool registered. My butt hit the bottom, and I righted myself, pushing off the glass floor with my bare feet.

Pressure built in my lungs, the air expelling outward when my head broke the water. Cool droplets fell down my face, curving around my neck, straight toward the plunging V of my now soaked and see-through white shirt. I ran a hand over my eyes, pushing the stray hairs away from my face.

Ezra stood on the side of the pool. His suit jacket was gone, as were his shoes and socks. He was pulling off his button-down shirt when I said, "What are you doing?"

"You know what I'm doing. Don't be dense."

My glare sharpened. I strode toward the edge of the pool, moving only a little slower since I had to wade through water to get there.

His shirt was off, and his pants unbuttoned by the time I reached the edge.

My fingers curled around the siding and I hauled myself up with ease, a torrent of water pouring off of me while I did so.

Ezra dropped his slacks, kicking them away.

"Why are you being such an ass?" I demanded, lifting my hands in the universal sign of 'what the hell?'

Ezra turned his chiseled jaw without fully circling around, giving me an angled display of his fully inked back. A dragon wrapped around his torso; with Chinese characters I couldn't read filling up almost all the space it didn't.

I took an unconscious step forward, tilting my chin to get a better look.

"Because it's what you need right now. You don't want to talk? Fine. I'm not going to make you. If you wanted someone to push you over that edge, you would've gone back with Dorian. I'm also not going to treat you like you're made of glass because we both know you're not. The silent treatment won't work on me like it does with Roman, and you already know that."

I frowned, taking a step back. He moved faster than I expected, turning, and grabbing me. His hard forearm looped around my waist, pressing my front to his. The ink that traveled up his sculpted chest to his neck had me swallowing. I really was a sucker for a nice body with tattoos.

"I don't do relationships with targets, Ezra. For someone who seems to know so much about me, you'd think you'd know that." The words were acidic. Biting. I wanted to get him away, to create space, give myself room to breathe—and remember why I'd come down here to begin with.

"This isn't a relationship. It's a solution," he said in a deep voice. He inclined his head forward, those emerald eyes piercing straight through me. "You said you don't want to think, remember? I can't help listening, and you can't help thinking. So I'm giving us both something else to do. Now are you going to get in the fucking pool, or do I have to throw you in again?"

My breathing went shallow.

I felt hot and cold, but it had very little to do with the winds whipping around us.

"Okay," I said, taking a step back.

He released me easily and motioned for me to get back in the water.

I padded over to the edge, careful not to slip and crack my head open on the side of the deck. I may be dead, but I didn't heal like the rest of them, and a dead body was honestly the last thing I needed right now.

I squatted next to the water and then slid back onto my butt. I kicked my legs over the side and made the snap decision to pull my shirt off. Given I could see the outline of the lacy white bra under it, the material wasn't doing much to hide things, anyway. I opted to keep the shorts on since Dorian had put me in a thong when he changed my clothes earlier.

Behind me, a breath hissed between Ezra's teeth. One that made me realize he was listening once again.

I slid over the side and into the crystal-clear water.

It had been a long time since I'd been in a pool. Over fifty years.

A serial killer who liked to lure away and drown little kids who didn't listen to their parents. He'd killed twelve before he was caught.

It had been difficult keeping myself in check on that job.

Too many times I'd come close to breaking him, and not in a productive way.

After that, Jake had stopped assigning me assholes who killed or hurt kids. I had a harder time remaining indifferent enough to keep the game going and rehabilitate while punishing. In that particular case, it hadn't helped that Vlad was encouraging me to impale him on a pike. He'd insisted it was good for the soul. I was pretty sure he meant his own, but still . . .

"Punishing souls truly doesn't bother you, does it?" Ezra asked quietly, standing right behind me.

"No," I said. "If anything, I find redemption in it." I shrugged softly. "I'm good at what I do."

"What makes you so good?" he asked.

"I turn people's vices on them and make them empathize with their victims. You never truly understand someone until you've lived through it, so I make them do that. Again and again. It's a ritual of sorts. The repetition . . . it works. I pick apart their lives then break them down to those pieces—so that when they're rebuilt to go back to Earth, they turn out all right." I lifted my chin to stare up at the clouds. A misting of warm rain started to fall. "I don't think I'm making any Gandhis, but over half the people I send back make it over the forty percent mark the next time around. Of the ones who don't, half of them I'd asked for their sentences to be extended. They weren't ready to return yet, but Upper Management overruled me."

"Why?" he asked, moving around me to stand a few feet away.

I watched him with my peripheral vision. "There's a system in place. Every action gets points given or taken away. If someone comes in below the forty percent, then those points are converted into time. Every bad thing makes it longer, but the good things shorten it. The problem with the system is it doesn't account for individuals." I'd had this argument with Jake many, many times. It came up annually for us at the very least, and every time Jake said he'd take my notes to the ones upstairs—but that's the thing with bureaucracy. It doesn't change. By the time it gets through the chain of people, assuming it even does, the last thing anyone wants to do is rock the boat. What we have works, right? Why fix what's not broken? I never understood that logic when playing with morality. It seemed . . . lazy. "It's made to make all things equal, even if one person needs more years than another to truly reform, they do the same time regardless of where they're actually at by the end."

"And the souls who fall below the forty percent, but aren't ones you requested more time for?"

"Irredeemable," I answered simply. "Some souls truly lack the ability to feel empathy or remorse. Without that, the odds of actually doing better are less than one percent. I usually recommend those souls be exterminated. Extinguished permanently. Sometimes they listen. Sometimes they don't."

Such as the case of my child serial killer.

Despite how hard it was for me, I did everything right. But he wouldn't break properly. The pieces he was made of didn't possess the ability to. The fabric that made up his soul was completely incapable of feeling remorse.

When they sent him back to Earth, despite my strong urging to exterminate, I tried to wash my hands of it. Then the reports came in of who he'd become in his next life.

Jeffrey Dahmer.

After that, Jake tended to back me up when I was certain there was no coming back for a soul.

"It's truly that easy for you to make the call? Knowing that's the true end to someone's existence?" he asked, not judging but curious.

"It is," I said, weaving my hands through the water. "When a soul twists, there's nothing to be done about it. In the same way it can happen and create a supernatural, it can also create a psychopath. I don't make the call lightly, but when I know, I know."

"Where do supernaturals go in the Afterlife?"

I didn't answer immediately, but as usual with him, he heard it in my mind.

"Ahh," he said. "I see."

"Your magic is different from that of the Afterlife. They don't run on the same wavelength. There's this giant system, but supernaturals are a glitch in the coding, essentially. You all get to live preternaturally long lives and have these bomb-ass powers on Earth—but this is it for you. No do-overs, I'm afraid." I offered him a half smile, but he didn't return it.

"You're wrong there."

I blinked. "About?"

"The no do-overs part. In that, we're a lot alike." I drifted closer to him. A shiver worked its way over my arms. While the heat was unbearable, the gusts of wind this high up could make it feel chilly.

"You die and come back?" I asked, lifting an eyebrow.

"I can't die. Period."

My lips parted.

Because that, well, it certainly wasn't in my fucking file. That was for damn sure.

Ezra let out a deep chuckle, clearly having heard my thoughts. "What is actually in your files?"

"Clearly not the important shit," I griped. "One would think knowing that one of my targets can't die . . ." I trailed off at the expression on his face.

Then it clicked.

"None of you can," I whispered. "That's why nothing they sent worked. I wondered why they were bothering with me instead of just having you all taken out . . ." The pained smile he gave me said it all. "They tried, didn't they?"

"If it was 'them', I didn't know it. But yes, I should've died hundreds of times over my lifetime. Dorian, probably thousands. Same for the wolf pup. He was ripped apart at twelve. Did you know that? They tore him to pieces, and that motherfucker healed and then *slaughtered* them. I wasn't there when it happened, but I was involved in the cleanup." Ezra wore a faraway expression, like he was seeing something that wasn't there. "After that, I've had no doubts he's the same as me and the old bastard. Clearly, I'm right since your Upper Management sent you down here to fix us."

I felt horrified and yet relieved at once, but I wasn't entirely sure what type of response I was supposed to have. It was a strange thing, knowing what had happened to them.

"I don't want to talk about that tonight," I reminded him.

His chin dipped in acknowledgement. I knew that wasn't the end of the conversation regarding my job and assignment, but he was letting it slide for now.

"What would you rather talk about, kitten?" he said, in a devilishly flippant voice that did things to me. Bad things. The way his sultry mouth curved up didn't help.

"Tell me about your tattoos. Why a dragon?" I jutted my chin toward his chest. The beast's head ended on the left pec, the characters I couldn't read on the right.

"Dragons symbolize power in my culture. Sovereignty. Strength. When I was turned, I became the most powerful vampire in the world, and I was still just a kid at the time. I didn't want to forget who I was, so I had Kendrick put the dragon on me." He brushed his hand down one scaled side that slanted toward the V of his hips.

"And the characters? What do those mean?" I asked, swimming closer to get a better look in the bright pool lights.

Ezra stood at ease, letting me drift close while I reached out to touch one. "They're dates. Each of them was a life-changing event for me—for better or worse."

"So you don't forget," I surmised.

He nodded once. "Do you know how old I am?"

"A hundred and seventy?" It came out more like a question than an answer.

"Close enough. Do you know how old Dorian is?"

I let out a low whistle. "Old. Roughly fifteen hundred years was what the file said, but it could be more given how not-accurate those are."

"If it's not exact, that's close. Dorian is a supernatural who can't die. He's seen some shit, probably done some shit too. But instead of using his past to ground him, he's drifting aimlessly. The guy can pass weeks sitting in his study staring out the window. He's hollow."

My hand paused on his chest, fingertips just barely grazing his skin. "You worry that's your future," I murmured.

"I take steps to make sure it's not," he said. But that wasn't the same as saying no. He'd evaded answering. I couldn't blame him, knowing that I would ultimately use everything I learned to break them.

We had an agreement. No thinking. His thought whispered through my mind, deep and husky. I felt those phantom hands tug my chin up.

I was unprepared for the intensity I saw in his eyes. *I can't help it,* I thought back. *I told you that.*

He leaned forward, bare chest nearly touching mine. He twisted a lock of hair back behind my ear. I let out a shaky breath, trying not to let him rattle me.

Feather-soft lips brushed against my lobe.

"Let me help you," he rasped, his voice husky.

CHAPTER 32
FURY

The word "no" teetered on my tongue.

He sucked my earlobe between his teeth, and warmth shot through me. My core tightened. I drew in a sharp breath as my thoughts scattered.

"See?" he murmured against my skin. "I told you I could."

He grasped my hips, pulling me closer. The hard bulge of his cock pressed into my lower stomach. *Jesus, he's huge.*

"No Jesus here, kitten."

His fingers pressed into the bare flesh of my sides. My body moved through water at breakneck speed. My ass hit the deck in a wet smack and my legs parted of their own accord.

Meanwhile, everything was spinning.

"This isn't a good idea, Fangs," I said, drawing on the new nickname I'd made for him. "You're a target, *and* my mate. This," I motioned between us, "it's bound to just complicate things further."

Ezra gave me a few inches of space, opting to put his hands on either side of me instead—even if he still stood between my legs. "What you and I are feeling right now is lust—and because I can read your thoughts, I'm well aware of how much you are thinking about it. This doesn't have to be complicated if you don't make it that way. It's just sex. Hard, mind-blowing sex. We don't have to complete the bond. And maybe we'll both be able to think straight for two seconds if we get it out of our systems," he said. He was just close enough that his scent was intoxicating, drawing me in, but he toed the line, not getting close enough to be pushy and set me off. It was . . . unpredictable.

"And if it doesn't work?" I found myself asking. Instantly, I wanted to kick myself for being so weak when a big dick with a hot body came along.

Ezra snorted a laugh. "I haven't heard that one. That's new. But to answer your question, if it doesn't, we fuck again. And again. And again. We're both more than old enough to know how this works, Fury. You're here for a job. There won't be any of the messy complications afterward because I know what this is from the start. So why not indulge?" His voice was like warm honey flowing over me.

"And you think you can manage this without biting me?" I mused. I knew the only way to truly complete the bond was to bite and mark your mate. That was true for all three species of mine: vampires, werewolves, and fae. But we had even bigger problems if he bit me.

Ezra tilted his head to the side. "I'm not looking to lock you down when I know how this whole thing ends. I won't bite you unless you ask, but something tells me you won't have much to say once I'm balls deep in you. The choice is yours, but I've already kissed you. Teased you in the tub. Drawing the line at sex seems like punishing yourself, and I didn't take you for a masochist."

Well, when he put it that way . . .

Against my better judgement, I lifted three fingers.

"You don't bite me, *even* if I ask. I know how this mate bond shit works. The endorphins from skin-to-skin contact are meant to make the female laxer and more accepting of it. No bite."

He quirked an eyebrow. "We can still bite without completing the bond, Fury. Sometimes a little nip is just in good fun." He grazed the tip of his tongue over a fang.

I shook my head. "It's non-negotiable, Ezra. You *can't* bite me. What I am . . . biting won't change me the way you think it will. It's dangerous. Just trust that." I dropped the first finger and waited.

He observed me for a moment, surprising me when he chose not to probe at my thoughts. Then he nodded his understanding. "No biting. You have my word."

"No hitting, slapping, spanking, or using an object to do any of those things. You *will not* like the results if you do." I was very, very serious about this limit. It was a boundary I could not cross, and it was the one thing I told every man and woman I took into my bed. Raise your hand to me, and it was over. I wasn't into it, and I never would be.

"Understood," Ezra said solemnly, not asking why, though I suspected after the afternoon we'd had, he already knew. I dropped the second finger. "Your last condition?"

"I can be a Dom. I can be a sub. The second you tell me to call you Daddy, I'm out."

Ezra tilted his head back and let out a deep, rumbling laugh. "Kitten, on that, we're in complete agreement."

I lifted a dark red eyebrow. "Then what are you waiting for?"

In that moment, the skies opened, and rain poured down.

But when his lips crashed into mine, all I could think about was how I wanted *more*.

I moved forward to press against him and he pressed against me in return, crowding my space with his much larger body. My legs came up to wrap around his waist, drawing a groan from him.

He pushed me back, putting the bulk of his weight on his hands that were still on the deck. My back hit the cool stone tiles, and I stared up into a dark and stormy sky while he worked his lips down my neck. Kissing. Sucking. Nibbling—but not biting.

His fangs stayed clear of piercing my skin, true to his word.

He moved down my chest, pausing at my bra.

Slowly, he dragged his teeth down the slope of my right breast, fangs catching on the lacy fabric. He tugged it down over my hard nipple and under the curve of my breast, pushing it up more.

Then he turned to the other and did the same.

"Much better," Ezra purred.

I opened my mouth to tell him he hadn't fucking done anything yet, but that sly bastard heard it coming and ducked his head, taking my hardened nipple between his lips. The first long pull made my legs stiffen. The second made my back bow. When he released it with a pop just to whorl his tongue around the stiff peak, I let out a moan.

My legs became a vise grip around him. I lifted my lower half and pressed into the thick bulge beneath his boxer briefs.

"Such a needy little thing," he groaned, rolling his hips to meet mine. The friction was exactly what I needed to drive me even more wild as I chased that release.

"You're damn right," I breathed.

He wasn't even inside me, and I was on the verge of losing it.

"Not so fast," he murmured, giving my other nipple a quick suck before lowering himself back into the pool, forcing me to release my hold on him. He grasped my knees and spread my thighs as wide as they would go.

Then he grabbed the waistband of my shorts and pulled.

The storm overhead drowned out the rip of the fabric. Water poured down me, following every curve and contour of my body. Ezra threw the soaking wet fabric onto the deck, letting out a purr of approval for my lacy white thong.

"Dorian has good taste," he mused. Instead of ripping the thong off, he pushed the thin scrap of lace to the side. His nose dipped over my wet cunt, inhaling deeply.

"You scream when you come, or next time I'm not so nice. Understood?" His green eyes flashed. While he didn't have a wolf inside him like Roman, he was very much a predator in his own way. Arguably more of one because there was no separation between man and monster. He was one and the same.

I nodded once, mouth dry.

"I want to hear it," he said.

"Yes."

"Yes, what?" he prompted.

Part of me was tempted not to say it. Just to see what he would do.

His lips curved, amusement showing in his expression. "Try me. My body can go a lot longer and a lot harder than yours. See what happens when you don't play nice."

I swiped my tongue over the bottom of my teeth. I toyed with it but decided maybe next time—if there was one.

"Yes, Sir," I said.

Good, kitten.

He parted my folds, licking and pushing his tongue into me. Heat rushed through me, and then he pressed the flat of his tongue to my clit. The rough friction of it made me jump the first time he dragged it over me. The second time, I squirmed.

The third, I pushed back.

Overhead, thunder boomed, and lightning streaked the sky.

He switched to sucking on my clit while twisting his mouth. The sensation pulled a gasp from me.

Two blunt fingers pressed against my wet entrance. He thrust them in easily, curling to tap my G-spot.

Scream for me, he ordered.

Then he sucked me again.

I broke apart, and the next clap of thunder echoed my release. My channel tightened around him while my legs stiffened, then unlocked.

Heat rushed through me, engulfing everything. I was in a haze of wind and rain and stars. Lightning flickered behind my eyelids, but all I heard was that initial boom that went off as I did.

Ezra took me through the aftershocks, waiting until my vision cleared, and the tremors faded. I sagged in a puddle against the wet ground, only then realizing how hard the rain was coming down.

"As much as I want to fuck you right here in the middle of a thunderstorm, your body is human, and the wolf will never let me hear the end of it if you get sick. Let's do this inside."

I sat up as he hoisted himself out of the pool and then picked me up. He carried me with one forearm under my knees and the other banded around my back. I squinted up at him when we stepped inside. The lights flickered on, detecting motion.

"I can walk, you know."

"You can also fuck yourself, but instead I'm taking care of that."

I bit my tongue instead of telling him he'd yet to actually fuck me. Then again, there wasn't much point to biting your tongue when the person you're wanting to tell off can hear your every thought.

Ezra pulled his arm back, letting my legs drop to the floor abruptly. I'd barely caught my balance when he twirled me around, splaying a hand on my back and pushing me until I was bent over the kitchen table, my cheek forced against the surface, my arms spread on either side of my head.

"What was it you were just saying?" he asked, keeping his palm firmly pressed on me as he reached down with his other hand, lightly scraping the back of my leg. His fingers trailed toward my inner thigh, teasing dangerously close.

"That you'd yet to fuck me," I said, struggling to concentrate and form words as he touched me.

He curled his fingers around my thong, barely grazing my sensitive skin as he hooked the fabric.

"I fucked you with my fingers," he said, twisting his hand so his knuckles pressed into me but didn't give me what I so badly wanted. "I fucked you with my tongue, did I not?"

I groaned, trying to get the contact I needed for friction. It was so deliciously close.

Not the same, I thought.

He nudged my legs apart with his knee, and I spread them willingly.

"So tell me, kitten. I fucked you with my fingers," he said, slipping a finger from his grip on my thong to run along the wet seam of my pussy.

I moaned.

"And I fucked you with my tongue," he continued, leaning over, and grazing his tongue over my skin, following the trail with his teeth.

I hummed in response, and he fisted the fabric, ripping it from my body in one swift move.

With one hand still pressing into my back, he used his other to rip his boxer briefs off.

"What do you want me to fuck you with now?" he asked, sliding his tip against my entrance, teasing me.

"I want you to fuck me," I growled impatiently, trying to push myself back into him, but he held me firm.

Say it, he whispered in my mind. *Say what you want. I want to hear you.*

"I want you to fuck me with your cock," I said, my voice hoarse and my frustration leaking through.

Ezra rumbled a growl of approval, pushing himself into me fully. A loud moan of pleasure and pain escaped me as his impressive girth stretched me out. I could've sworn my eyes crossed.

"Yessss," I hissed as I tightened around him in anticipation.

He slid himself in and out slowly, coating himself in my wetness as I adjusted to his size. I ground against him, encouraging him to give me more. God, I wanted more.

He moved faster, pacing himself as he picked up speed. With each thrust, I groaned, scratching my nails into the wood. He pounded into me from behind, reaching down and hooking his arm under my right leg, giving him deeper access, filling me more than I would've thought possible.

The pressure built in my core, and a thin sheen of sweat covered my body, my cheek sliding over the tabletop as he slammed into me. I clawed at the table as his fingertips pressed into my flesh, holding me in place.

"Do you want to come again?" he asked between ragged breaths.

"Don't stop," I said, my voice strained. "I'm so close."

Ezra took his hand off my back, scooping his arm under my torso and lifting me up. I threw my arms out, supporting my weight. He never broke his rhythm. With one foot on the floor, half bent over a table, and the other leg held up, he gripped my hip and fucked me, just like I wanted him to.

Heat pooled in me, and I felt the telltale tingling flutters of an oncoming orgasm. I closed my eyes, dipping my head back, the pressure building—

He let go of my hip, reaching around to rub my clit in harsh, fast circles. My eyes flew open and my mouth opened in a silent scream as he thrust into me harder.

No longer a slow and steady climax, the intensity of the combined movements pushed me over. I screamed, a deep, guttural moan echoing in the kitchen. I squeezed my eyes shut and my inner walls clenched around him, pulling him in deeper as I came. Ezra pressed against my clit, and the muscles in my legs tightened and my body trembled as white dots exploded behind my eyes.

A wave of aftershocks rode through my system as Ezra pounded into me, finding his release.

My arms gave out, and I slid forward on the table. I tried to calm my breathing, but it was heavy and uneven as my heart thundered in my chest.

My mind raced at the strength of my orgasm. I wasn't sure I'd ever felt one so acutely. It had left me a trembling mess . . . but I wanted more. If they were like that, I wanted so much more.

Ezra ran his fingers through my hair, pulling the strands away from my eyes. The side of my face was exposed, and I could see him in my peripheral vision as I rested on the cold, flat surface.

He looked at me with a devilish smile, and I wondered what he was thinking.

Leaning forward, he grazed my ear lobe with his fang, then purred, "I told you I'd make you see stars."

CHAPTER 33
ROMAN

I LISTENED OUTSIDE EZRA'S DOOR AS HE FLIRTED WITH HER. NO DOUBT HE could hear when I'd arrived, and he was tormenting me on purpose.

I heard her laugh, and my wolf stirred. He'd been agitated at our distance from her, but there was nothing we could do about it.

She'd been at Ezra's for five days. I hadn't expected her to stay that long. For five days I'd been itching to see her. Talk to her. Smell her. I wanted more than anything to touch her.

My wolf nodded in approval.

I breathed in deeply then reached out to knock on the door.

Moments later, Ezra opened it wearing nothing but jeans.

I glared at him, knowing his game. "It's five in the afternoon. Can't find it in you to wear a shirt, or were you hoping to put on a show just for me?"

Leaning against the doorframe with an arm overhead, he winked at me. "Hey, Roman. Didn't know you'd be here this early."

I sighed, looking past him to see Fury. Her jeans hugged her body, and she had a small backpack. She walked up to me, smirking . . . until she saw my motorcycle jacket and her face fell. I tossed her a helmet, and she caught it.

"Nice reflexes," I said, and pointed to it. "You'll want to wear that."

"Great," she mumbled, walking out the door.

Ezra cleared his throat. "She's feisty, but she's a fun one. Be careful."

Fury and I groaned at the same time, but she spoke first. "Try not to piss on each other, will you?"

Ezra chuckled. "Not my kink, but I'm not one to judge."

"Ugh, really?" she said to him, walking out the door and waving at him over her shoulder in dismissal. "See you later."

"You really are a dick," I told him.

"She likes it," he said knowingly.

"Mmm." Time to change the topic and get out of here. "Call if you learn anything new. My rangers are still looking for anything out of the ordinary. There are packs running the borders in all directions."

His eyes darkened, and he nodded. "I have six crews out. Nothing yet."

He was just as unhappy as I was about it. "I'll update if we find something." I turned to leave.

We silently rode the elevators to the parking garage. When the doors opened, we stepped off, and she tensed in hesitation as she took in my motorcycle.

"Roxanne said you get motion sickness, but I don't think you'll have a problem here."

She swallowed thickly. "What makes you so sure? To be honest, I'm a little worried about puking inside my helmet. I can't die, so how about I don't wear the helmet, and if I throw up, whichever car it hits, it's their problem."

I couldn't help the small laugh that escaped me. The mental image was too much. "Just wear it. I'll feel better about it. You'll also appreciate not getting pelted in the face with a loose piece of gravel. It'll get better once we're out of the city."

I straddled the bike, putting on my own helmet. No, I couldn't die either, but she didn't know that. Aside from the possibility of shredding my face to pieces and having to heal from it, I also didn't care for pebbles or gravel, and with the number of cars on the interstate it was bound to happen.

"Wait, we're leaving Houston? Where are we going?"

I grinned at her apprehension. It was a nice change to be the calmer one. Usually, I felt as though I were pulled too tight, like a cord about to snap. From the moment we'd first seen her beating the shit out of the Dawsons in Rox's bar, my wolf had been right beneath the surface, testing my limits of control, desperately trying to rip the binds I held him with. The power struggle had taken some time to even out. Longer than I would've liked, given she'd opted to stay with the fucking vampire a few extra days.

The desire to protect her and be close to her was ever-present. But the reality of it was she wasn't Maya. For one, she couldn't die. For another, I was more likely to lose her by treating her like they were the same.

"I don't live here," I answered. "I sleep in the office if I have to stay for some reason. On the rare occasion, I'll stay at Rox's, but she stays with me more often. I keep a house on a lake, away from the city."

She grumbled incoherently and put the helmet on, straddling the bike behind me.

"Tap me twice if you're going to throw up. Otherwise, hold on." I didn't give her a chance to respond. I turned the bike over, and a loud rumbling filled the garage. It was awful in such an enclosed space, but to a wolf, everything about being in the city was too overwhelming. Sensory overload to the extreme.

She wrapped her arms around my waist the best she could and turned her head, putting one side against my back.

Everything about riding was exhilarating. The wind was so loud, it somehow made things peaceful and quiet. It was a strange combination. Like how sound disappeared under water and things felt calm.

Usually, my mind ran with a million thoughts, twenty-four seven. It never slowed down. I had to find ways to calm the storm inside and keep my sanity. I didn't want to end up like Ezra, a loner detached from anyone and everyone.

She kept her arms wrapped tightly around me as I sped like a bat out of hell, seemingly content to watch the scenery change as we left the city. Multi-laned gray concrete morphed to double lanes surrounded by tall trees. The air changed, no longer feeling so dense, but rather thick with the scent of nature. Cleaner.

After an hour, I pulled up to the house and cut the engine, taking off my helmet. She threw her leg over and lost her balance, but I grabbed her quickly and let her use me for support.

"Thanks," she mumbled, taking her helmet off too. "I just need to get my bearings. My legs feel numb from vibrating for so long. It's bizarre."

"But you don't feel nauseous, do you?" I asked her, curious to see if riding a bike helped her motion sickness.

She smiled, and it reached her eyes. "Surprisingly, no, I don't. That's a nice change," she mused. She tilted her head up, but she was looking behind me. "So, uh, Ezra said you had a log cabin by the lake. That's not a log cabin." She pointed to the house.

"No, not in the traditional sense," I said, getting off the bike.

"Then in what sense would it be?" she asked.

"It's a luxury log cabin, if you want to give it a name." I pointed south. "Houston is that way. This is Lake Conroe." I held my hand out to the nature surrounding us.

"Fancy," she said, but I didn't miss the snark. How could she go to *Dorian's* and then snark at me that I was fancy?

I frowned, feeling like I'd missed something. "I'll show you to your room."

I walked up the steps and through the door, wondering what she was thinking. I wasn't trying to impress her with *fancy*. I just wanted to get her away from the city. Have a minute to think around her. Breathe a little deeper with her near me.

"Why are you grumbling?" she asked from behind me as we walked up the main stairs in the house, heading to the second floor.

"What? I'm not grumbling." I looked at her over my shoulder.

She gave me a flat look. "You weren't saying words, no, but you're grumbling about something."

I grunted, going down the hall to a door, and turning the handle to open it. "It's Roxanne's room when she stays here, but if you don't like it, you can have my room across the hall."

Her lips turned up, and she quirked an eyebrow. "Was that a sly way to offer to share a bed, Roman?"

The wolf inside me went still at the thought. My cock twitched, and a rush of adrenaline swept through me at the thought of claiming her. The rest of me shoved it away, flustered that she thought I was trying to bed her instantly. "That's not what I—"

"Relax. The room is fine. Lighten up, Roman," she said, a smile on her face. "I'm just giving you a hard time. I don't know if you can tell or not, but I kind of enjoy it."

I looked at my feet and cleared my throat. "Right . . ." I grabbed the back of my neck, rubbing. I had no plans. No idea what to do. Aside from being mated, what was there between us? Nothing. I had nothing to offer her. I knew nothing about her. "Well, the sun hasn't gone down yet. Would you like to take a walk around the lake?"

She scrunched her nose at me, and I hated how adorable it looked. "Have you seen what nature does to my hair? Or my sweat glands, for that matter?"

"So that's a no. Got it."

"I'm not very naturey," she said.

I nodded. Okay. No walks in nature. Noted.

"I like baths . . . but you already knew that," she said, winking at me.

Didn't I know it. The first day we'd met, when she stared at me while fingering herself in the tub . . . it had been in the back of my mind since. The thought of her dark red hair wrapped in my fist while I fucked her from behind had started to replace the image of Maya's blonde locks. When the nights were empty and I woke up hard, it was her lips I started to envision moaning around my cock. Her dark eyes watching me.

Her.

A loud, thunderous sound interrupted my thoughts. Fury looked at me in confusion and moved to the window. Over her shoulder, I could see that seven motorcycles were pulling into the long driveway. "Were you expecting company?"

"Frequently," I said, hovering nearby. I could smell her shampoo. And she smelled entirely too much of the vampire. "We're shifters. Wolves. We run in packs. I usually have company. There's comfort in it."

She spun on her heel, moving to the bed, and tossing her bag on it. "Yeah, I think I'll stick to the bath, then." She bent over to take off her boots. "I don't much like crowds."

Her words clicked. A piece of information about her she hadn't given to me before. Had she given it to Dorian or Ezra? I didn't know, and I wasn't going to ask. What I did know was that she kept secrets. Secrets she wasn't willing to share yet. Secrets about who she was, and more importantly, *what* she was. I wouldn't find the answer easily, but if she left me enough breadcrumbs, I would figure it out.

I walked toward her, slowly, my skin buzzing with awareness. My voice went dark, and low. "What is it that you aren't telling me?"

"Hmm?" she asked, looking up to find me closer to her.

"I find it an odd choice, coming to Houston, when you don't much like crowds. But then, by your own admission, you also don't like nature. So, I have to ask: what is it that you *do* like, Fury?"

CHAPTER 34
FURY

He towered over me, imposing in my space bubble. His voice had gone dark, and his eyes glittered. His proximity and the husky tone in his voice had made something inside me stir.

I did my best to school my features. He wouldn't trap me in this.

"Jumping to conclusions, Roman?" I asked, tilting my head. "I honestly can't even figure out which direction you're heading with that. But to answer your questions, a person can like cities without liking crowds. I like convenience, for one. And cities have that. I also like solitude, but solitude doesn't have to equate to nature. Furthermore, nature around here is a whole different ball game. You can't argue that with me. You roam up north. I know you know there's a difference."

I could tell by the way his posture didn't change that he didn't believe me one bit. That was okay, as long as he dropped it. He couldn't dispute what I'd said.

He shifted his weight and crossed his arms. "The pack is making dinner tonight. You'll join us. Take a bath before or after, I don't care which. You're here. Try to enjoy yourself." He turned and walked out the door. It closed with a loud thud.

I sighed. Well, that had gone okay for about five seconds. I scrubbed my hands down my face in frustration.

Dorian was cold and distant, but he had moments of clarity where I felt a connection with him, even if it was only in short bursts. Ezra was the easiest. It was nice to have someone to talk to. And someone who let me not think about things in too much depth.

But Roman? How did I find a way to connect with him? It was hot and cold, and I didn't know what to do with it. How could I when I was certain part of the shift in his hot and cold attitude had to do with his wolf? Sure, we had attraction, but I didn't understand him, nor did he understand me. Not yet.

I looked toward the bathroom, thinking about ignoring him completely. He'd busted in on me taking a bath once before, so he wouldn't hesitate to do it again. Last time, he'd been on edge, desperate to find me and keep me safe. This time, he'd just be pissed off. Really, if I wanted to get away, a bathtub wasn't my best choice. It would just end with a relaxing soak being ruined.

I looked out the window again, watching the shifters gather around and greet each other. They all looked happy. Like family. It wasn't something I could relate to.

And there it was. A piece of the puzzle. That thing about each other we didn't understand. Or one of them, at least. If I was going to get the job done, I had to learn more about him, and this was a step in the right direction.

I leaned down, retying my boots, committing myself to socializing with wolves for the night.

Leaving my room, I could hear voices downstairs. I took the steps slowly, gauging the response as some of the voices trailed off when they saw me.

At the bottom step, I surveyed my surroundings. A familiar face caught my attention.

"Caitlin," I said, somewhat surprised. "Good to see you again."

"Is it?" She laughed, standing in the doorway unmoving. "Last time I saw you, it was before you crawled out a window on my watch."

I lifted my shoulder in a shrug, putting my hands out in mock surrender. "Nothing personal. Just, well, it was a weird day. Besides, you look like you came out of it okay. It wasn't your apartment he burst into later."

"No, I'm the one who got my ass chewed out for losing my alpha's mate." She crossed her arms and looked me up and down. "You plan on sticking around this time? Or are you having another weird day?"

I gazed through the large windows, taking in the wooded area, listening to some birds chirping. "Oh, it's weird, all right. But I'll stick around. Besides, judging by the ride to get here, it's a long walk to Houston." I pointed down at my boots. "Plus, wrong shoes."

She huffed, moving aside, and throwing her arm out to let me by, several pairs of shifter eyes following me.

What was with the cold reception? I snuck out a window *one time.*

I made my way outside, where a bonfire was being lit and several shifters were moving seating around.

I realized Roman was behind me, and he'd been watching the entire exchange between Caitlin and me. "She's not that bad, you know," he said. "But she does hold grudges pretty well."

I sniffed. "I'll get over it." I held grudges too. Long ones. I was a pro. I'd been holding grudges longer than they'd been alive. I snickered at the thought.

He put his hands in the pockets of his dark jeans. The black T-shirt he wore was tight and showed the contours of his chest and abs. It was such a different look than his suits. It was nice. Down to earth. "I'm sorry if I was too aggressive earlier. I—"

I turned to face him, putting my fingers over his lips. "Don't. Let's not do this, okay? Let's just do this thing you wanted to do with your pack, and I'm here to just . . . hang out, so let's not get serious with this. I think the last thing you or I need is too much serious."

He smiled. "Fair enough."

I clapped my hands. "Good. Now what?"

He barked a laugh. "Good speech, but no follow-up, I see?"

"I'm new here. Aren't you the host?"

Seeing someone over my shoulder, he yelled for one of the shifters to come over. A young shifter with tanned skin and jet-black hair followed orders, stopping in front of me and Roman.

"Sir?"

"Fury, this is Andy. Andy is going to be cooking the steaks tonight. How would you like yours?"

"Oh, um, medium rare, but closer to rare if you can. There's this sweet spot that's perfectly in the middle of the two if you can find it," I said to the kid. He couldn't have been a day older than nineteen.

He smiled and nodded. "That's easy enough."

"Is it? I thought I was being difficult."

"It's the same as Roman's, ma'am, so—"

"Mmm, none of that. Just call me Fury."

His fearful eyes shifted to Roman, who nodded to give him the okay.

After the kid ran off, I walked over to the bonfire and sat, Roman following in my shadow. He sat next to me, and I had to comment on the exchange.

"I approve of your temperature choice in steak. But I have to ask, is that how it always works with you? It's my preference, but they need your permission to call me by my name?"

He shook his head. "No, I imagine you caught Andy off guard. No one needs my permission for a choice you're going to make about how you want to be addressed, or anything else like that. But to have a woman say she doesn't want to be recognized and respected by title, especially the alpha's mate, I think you scared the kid. He probably thought he was being tested."

I laughed at the thought. "Testing the members of your pack is definitely not on my agenda."

As I said it, several of them looked my way, and I suddenly realized why there'd been such a cold reception in the house earlier. They were testing *me*. Sizing me up. I was the intruder. I hadn't had that with the few fae that were at Dorian's, and no one had been at Ezra's house.

I see.

Caitlin chose that moment to come up to me and Roman. "Mind if I steal her away, sir?"

He shook his head, gesturing for us to go on.

I shot him a look, but I got up and took a walk with her.

"Look, if you're going to give me the 'best friend' talk, don't bother. I got the sister talk from Roxanne, or some version of it," I said, hearing the icy tone in my voice.

She shook her head. "Nope. I was going to apologize about earlier in the house, but now I'm reconsidering my decision."

"Wise choice. If you apologize to me, I'll remember it and hold it over you for eternity, never letting you forget the time you told me you were wrong," I said, walking slowly to who knew where in the woods.

She laughed and stopped in her tracks, causing me to do the same. When I faced her, she looked relieved, somehow. "You have an honest streak about you that I can appreciate. You might be pretty rough around the edges, but you don't beat around the bush."

"Why is that comforting to you?"

"Because you aren't going to bullshit him. He likes honesty. I mean, who doesn't? But some people value certain traits more than others. Roman values honesty. To him, honesty and loyalty go hand in hand. It's hard to find that once, but twice? He's lucky."

It seemed that Roman and I valued the same things. I hated being lied to. It made me want to stab things. But then the comparison hit me. Maya. She was honest. She was probably kinder about her honesty, but Caitlin still believed Maya and I shared that trait. That stung more than I wanted to admit.

I wasn't as honest as she thought, and there was some guilt lingering inside me as I heard her words. I didn't want to hurt him, I just wanted him to not hurt others.

We hadn't walked far; I could still see the bonfire in the distance. Roman wasn't hard to spot. The massive wall of muscle, his smooth, dark skin, and his long, clean dreads. He stuck out in a crowd. I could've found him anywhere.

A chill went down my spine, reminding me where I was. If Caitlin wanted to go deep, she needed to pick another night. So I did what I did best. Deflected. "Well, Second, to tell you the truth, I'm not sorry I climbed out a window. You don't have to be sorry for being mad at me for it. You had every right to. But we can move on. I'm not crawling out any windows tonight, and you aren't on babysitting duty, so we're square. I'll even let you find me a drink," I said, winking at her.

She laughed, and the tightness in her shoulders eased slightly. "C'mon. I'll get you a whiskey. That's what I drink, so that's what you'll have too."

I could see the smirk on her face as she said it.

Size me up all you want.

"Four fingers, no ice," I told her.

She raised her eyebrows in appraisal, then nodded once.

A flapping of wings caught my attention, and I slowed my pace. "Go on ahead. I'll be right there," I called out. She turned and looked at me in question, and I smiled. "I'm good. Just not used to big crowds. I'll walk a little slower."

She looked unsure, but I gathered she didn't sense anything out of the ordinary and she went on ahead, occasionally turning her head to keep me in sight.

As Caitlin went into the house to get our drinks, I took slow steps, waiting. I couldn't see him, but I knew he was there.

"I wondered if you'd find me out here," I whispered.

"Please," he scoffed. "Unlike you, I actually do my job."

I rolled my eyes. "Keep your voice down. Shifters have remarkable hearing." He clicked his beak in what I assumed was acknowledgment. "I haven't seen you for five days. Did you find anything?"

Hades flew down from a tree, and I stuck my arm out for him to land. He cocked his head to the side and squawked at me. "Five days, huh? I wonder why you haven't heard from me in five days. What is it about five days?" he mused.

"Oh my god, what is it you want to say, Hades?" I motioned for him to get on with it.

His feathers poofed up, and he shook his head. "Forgive me if I didn't want to interrupt your fuckfest with Ezra. Which reminds me, close the curtains. No one needs to see that side of you."

I couldn't help but laugh. "He lives in the penthouse. We didn't need to close the curtains."

"I assure you, you do," he said dryly.

I sighed. "Fine, get to the point. You know how to track Roman and give him my keycard, but you couldn't find a way to peck on a window or sneak through the door when we were in the pool. You can get anywhere you want to, Hades. I have no doubts about that. So why haven't I heard from you in five days?"

He stretched his wings out then pulled them back in, shifting his weight. "Nothing of consequence to report. I went to Duke, and he was clearly upset. He's looking into how anyone in this realm could possibly know your name."

"That's not—"

He let out a shrill squawk, cutting me off.

I shushed him.

"Don't be obstinate. It *was* your name. Duke doesn't want you here anymore, but he knows why you're staying. Supernaturals are flooding into Houston for the summit, but I haven't caught wind of any plans or conversations that explain what happened in the warehouse. No one even knows about it, as far as I can tell."

I frowned. That wasn't good. "Okay. Keep me posted. The guys haven't found anything either. I listen in when they talk about updates, whether they know it or not. I'll be here for a few days, I think."

"What about them?" he asked.

I sighed. "Nothing yet. I know what the vision said, but they just don't seem like they'll end the world."

He snapped his beak at me twice. "That isn't for you to decide."

"Fuck off, pigeon, I know that. I'm making a point. I haven't figured it out, but I'm working on it. If I don't know what's broken, I can't fix it."

"Tick tock."

"No 'tick tock', asshole. Aren't you listening? The visions have always shown the three of them combined ending things. I'll be more concerned for our timeline here when they finally start showing me something that indicates they're going to blow."

Hades puffed up his feathers again, reaching his leg up to scratch his neck. "Fine. I'll relay that message."

I rolled my eyes. "Tell Duke hi. And let me know if you see anything with those annoying and beady little eyes of yours. You know where to find me. Tap on a window."

He glared at me. "Which window?"

"Look for closed curtains." I grinned at him, letting him think whatever he wanted.

He grumbled, and I held my arm away from my body so he could flap his wings and get enough air to take flight.

I picked up my pace and made my way back toward the bonfire, crossing several small groups of shifters that were deep in conversation. I was heading toward Roman so I could sit next to him when I heard a familiar voice. I couldn't help but smile.

Roxanne had a beer in her hand and was telling a story when she caught sight of me. "Fury," she yelled. "There you are. Roman said you were off with Caitlin, but I saw her go inside alone." She ran up to me and embraced me.

The icy parts of me that wanted to keep a wall up were hard to maintain when Roxanne hugged me. She managed to knock my guard down when I least expected it, and I'd known her for less than two weeks.

I hugged her back. "Caitlin is off getting me a drink now. I was headed this way when I got a visit from the crow. He's hard to shake," I supplied, assuming I'd been seen with a bird on my arm. She snorted, but before she could question me about him, I asked, "When did you get here?"

"I've been here for a while. Just visiting a friend at another cabin that way," she said, jutting her thumb in a random direction.

"You're friends with Roman's neighbors? Are they shifters too?"

Roxanne scrunched her eyebrows at me, turning to her brother and then back to me. "He didn't tell you?"

I frowned and shook my head.

"He owns about sixty percent of the land surrounding the lake. Part of it is investment. The rest is a place for the pack to live. There are houses scattered all over the place. There's easily a dozen cabins nearby on this piece of property alone."

A lot of shifters had shown up to the bonfire. Now I knew why. It wasn't a party. It was their neighborhood. Family.

"I hadn't realized," I admitted, looking over to him. He was watching us, but his face remained neutral.

She waved her hand. "It's not a big deal. I just figured he explained the setup around here." She took a drink of her beer, tossed it in a green bin, and grabbed a bottle of water from one of the coolers. "Anyway, I wanted to tell you that we're going shopping tomorrow."

I cringed. "Shopping?"

She looked at me, confused. "Yeah, shopping. You have something against shopping?"

"Sometimes, yeah. What kind of shopping are we doing now?"

Her eyes widened, then she looked past me, and I could tell she was glaring at her brother. When I had her attention again, she said, "Dress shopping. For the summit."

"We wear dresses to the summit?" I asked.

The truth of it was, I'd read about the purpose of the summit. The frequency. The duration. The politics. But nothing more. And there was a good chance everything I'd read in my files was crap, anyway.

She looked at me incredulously. "You've spent time with all three guys, and not one of them has told you anything, have they?"

"Not really, no. Certainly not about what I should be wearing."

"Night one is a black-tie dinner, so we dress to impress," she said, winking at me. "Though you'll be on the arm of three, so I don't know how to coordinate that."

I stared at her blankly. "If they're wearing tuxedos, why does it matter? Aren't they all the same?"

The look of admonishment said I was wrong. I mouthed, 'Okay.'

"I made an appointment at a custom dress shop that serves supernaturals, so—"

"We need an appointment to buy clothes?" I asked in genuine shock and curiosity.

"Sometimes, yeah." She took a deep drink from her bottle. "So, shopping tomorrow. Dresses. You and me. It'll be fun."

"I don't know about fun, but okay. Dress shopping it is," I mumbled. I knew she heard me. The wolf ears all around probably heard me.

Pulling me from my internal grumbling, Roxanne grabbed my hand, and tugged me along with her, walking around trees. "Let's go throw some shit."

I allowed her to drag me along. "I'm sorry, what? What are we throwing?"

As we came to a small clearing that was marked off by reflective tape, she stopped short, picking up a weapon off the ground.

"Axes," she said, with a wicked grin on her face.

I smiled. "Okay, now we're talking."

I grabbed one and observed the setup in the forest. Two wide oak trees had massive boards in front of them. The boards looked heavily reinforced with multiple layers to take the impact of a shifter's throw. The tree was simply to hold up the board.

Each board was marked and painted for points, and each board had a measured distance from the throwing line to the target.

"You first," I said to Roxanne.

She walked up to the line, drink in hand, and called out, "Third line." She threw, the axe making a whooshing sound as it sailed through the air and hit the third ring from the middle. "Ha!"

"Not bad, not bad," I said, picking up one of my own. "Third line." I threw, my axe hitting my board on the same spot as hers.

Caitlin came with my whiskey, along with one of her own.

"Nicely done," she commented, handing me the glass. "Can I watch?"

"If you keep the drinks coming, you can do whatever you want," I said, taking a heavy drink and swallowing, savoring the burn. It was spicy on my tongue and warmth bloomed in my chest.

"Bullseye," Roxanne shouted before releasing the axe. It smacked into the board, slightly off center, marking both the bullseye and the first line. "Damn it."

I repeated her call for my board, sending my axe flying and hitting the bullseye clear in the middle. "Oooh," I called out. I slammed back the rest of my drink and told Roxanne she was up.

Before long, we'd developed a crowd, and I hadn't paid much attention to how large it had truly gotten. I wasn't sure how long we'd been going for.

"Kill shot," she yelled. Behind her, money was exchanging hands and bets were being made.

"Not a chance," I mocked her, egging her on. I secretly wanted her to get it. She was a badass, and every single guy here needed to know it if they didn't already.

Thwack.

Kill shot.

Roxanne tossed her hands up in the air in victory then pointed at me as she walked in my direction. "You're up, buttercup."

I bowed to her, chuckling. "Gladly. Step aside, milady. I have a kill shot to make."

She returned the laughter and bowed out of my way. There was more murmuring in the crowd, and more money changing hands.

I lined up my aim and threw.

Kill shot.

I whooped, and Roxanne high-fived me. I met Roman's eyes at that moment, and I felt a tightness in my belly I couldn't explain.

As she picked up another axe, someone whistled and caught the attention of all the shifters surrounding us. Which, now that I was looking, was a lot. Then a call for dinner came, and the crowd dispersed, heading back to the bonfire.

We dropped our weapons, grinning from ear to ear. "I'm starving," I said, as I picked up my glass and she picked up her water bottle.

"Me too." She wiped her forehead with her wrist. "And I am sweating like a farm animal."

I belted out a laugh. "I'm sweating in places I didn't know could sweat."

I looked around the ground, stopping when I realized I hadn't had another drink.

Roxanne must've realized what I was looking for. "You only had the one," she said, casually.

"Yeah," I said, trailing off. "I just wanted to make sure I cleaned up after myself. Thought I had . . . two." *Or more.*

We walked side by side as we headed back. "Caitlin brought you one, but you never drank it. So she did." Roxanne shrugged.

Oh. Was she sure? That didn't sound like me at all. I scanned the ground and replayed the sequence of events in my head.

"Hey . . ." she started.

"Hmm?" I answered, mildly distracted.

"Thanks for throwing with me. I had a lot of fun."

I saw her out the corner of my eye, and she looked happy. "I did too. I haven't had that much fun in . . ." I trailed off. "Well, it's been a long time."

"You're the only one who throws with me and doesn't keep track of points."

"There was a point system?" I said, looking shocked. When she looked at me in surprise, I added, "I'm joking. I know there was."

"I mean it, though, Fury. I don't think you understand how much that means to me. Shifters are competitive by nature. *Everything* is a competition. Sometimes a girl just wants to have fun without it being a pissing contest."

"I think there's a pop song about that first part." I snickered, and she side-eyed me and laughed. "Well, then I'm glad you finally had someone to throw with who wasn't trying to make it about who comes out on top."

"You and Roman," she said.

"Me and Roman what?"

"I meant that you and Roman are the only other people that throw for the enjoyment you get from it. No one else does." She sighed. "What can you do? C'mon. Let's get dinner. Then I'm crashing in my room with you. I'm beat."

She looped her arm through mine and we made our way to the gathering.

Roman watched me walking with his sister. I couldn't read his expression, and I couldn't help but wonder what he was thinking. There was so much about him I didn't know, and so much about him I couldn't figure out how to reach.

What I did realize was that I'd seen more of him through other people's eyes, and that wasn't something I'd expected.

CHAPTER 35
FURY

INHALE.

Exhale.

Inhale.

Exhale.

Deep breaths, Fury.

I could do this. It was just a car ride. While I sat in the backseat. And some really nice shifter named Owen drove. Roxanne had called a car company for black car service. Whatever that meant. What I knew was that I was in a fancy car, it was black, it wasn't hers, and death felt better than motion sickness. How did I not have a hangover, but driving in a car made it feel like I did?

She patted my thigh. "We're almost there."

I mumbled incoherently in response as she looked at her phone. The idea of looking at something like that made my stomach roil again.

I didn't even want to go dress shopping. I could dress as a waiter for the summit and be content. For the love of anything they considered sacred in the realm of the living, I just wanted the car to stop.

Owen pulled into a spot, and as he put it in park, I flung myself out of the vehicle and onto solid ground. I landed on my knees, and the concrete scraped my skin. I ignored the burn, focusing on taking steady gulps of air.

"Ma'am, you're going to get burns from the concrete. It's too hot here," Owen said.

"Ugh, don't call me ma'am," I groaned.

"Uh, I'm sorry, Miss . . . um—"

"You're fine, Owen. Just call her Fury," Roxanne whispered to him. "You didn't do anything wrong; she just doesn't like it."

I grunted as I put my hands on my thighs and pushed myself up, wiping my palms on my shorts. I smoothed my hair out of my face and looked at the two shifters waiting for me. Roxanne was leaning against the car, calm as ever. Owen looked worried that his driving had caused a problem for me, and that he might suffer the wrath of my mate.

"It's not your fault, dude," I said to him, holding my stomach. It felt tender and far too sensitive. "I don't do well in cars at all. Doesn't matter who's driving."

Roxanne looked up, meeting his worried eyes. "It's true, and it isn't a secret. Roman knows." She clapped him on the back. "You're good. Give us some time to shop. We'll be here for a couple of hours. There's a café right there," she said, pointing to a tiny restaurant a block down the street. "I made you a reservation so you'd be comfortable. I'll call you when we're wrapping up."

The kid beamed at her. "Thank you, Ms. Mikaelson," he said, nodding and looking at me. I waved him off with a forced smile.

When he was out of a normal range of hearing, though he probably heard me anyway, I hissed, "A couple of hours, Rox? Don't people just pick out a dress and buy the damn thing? How does that take two hours?"

"Oh, stop complaining. It won't be that bad," she said, turning on her heel to walk up to the storefront.

I looked up but there was no signage to attract customers from the street. Barely any indication of where we were. Lettering on the door read *Kelly Lee Boutique*, but other than that, it was a nice building that no one would have a reason to stop by and visit.

Roxanne opened the door, and I followed her, standing in the entry with my arms crossed and feeling incredibly uncomfortable from the moment I walked in.

I didn't belong here. At all. I hadn't felt so out of place in a hundred years. Not only was everything pristine, but it also looked like someone else should be wearing these clothes. They were frilled and feminine. Pretty. Flawless.

"Don't be intimidated, Fury," Roxanne whispered, reading me like an open book. "You could rock any number of these dresses."

Taking in a pale pink ball gown with its billowing skirt, I said, "I'm not so sure about that."

"Roxanne," a woman said as she walked up to us. "I heard you come in. I was so glad to see you on the books today. I was wondering when you'd be in. I almost thought you were having someone else dress you this year." A tall woman with creamy skin and long black hair leaned in to kiss Roxanne's cheek, and I took a step back in case she tried to do that to me.

"You know I wouldn't dream of it, Kelly." Roxanne kissed her cheek in greeting. "A lot's been happening lately." The knowing look they shared told me that Miss Dress here knew all about Roman Mikaelson finding his second-chance mate. "I'm sorry we're cutting it close, and I imagine you've been busy fitting people for the summit, but I knew you'd be able to take care of us."

Kelly's gaze shifted to me—my posture tight, arms crossed, knees skinned and bleeding—and she didn't turn her nose up at me. "Fury, it's a pleasure," she said, holding out her hand. I uncrossed my arms to shake her hand, surprised to find her genuinely kind and unassuming. "I'm happy to dress you both. But first, your knees. What happened? Did you fall outside?"

"I tripped getting out of the car. Lucky the ground was there to break my fall," I said.

"Well, let's get you cleaned up first." She ran to the back before I could say anything.

I looked at Roxanne, and she shook her head before I could argue my case about not needing a Band-Aid. "Don't get blood on her dresses. Just let her clean you up."

"Fine," I mumbled, sarcastically. "I suppose that makes sense."

"You can't die, Fury," she whispered, pointing to my knees, "but you can still get hurt. Even if it's a little blood, you haven't healed yet. So your healing powers are slower than mine, it would seem."

"Okay, stop being all logical," I said under my breath.

"Shopping really brings out the best in you, did you know that?"

I glared at her as Kelly came back out, waving at us.

"Come on back to the room. I have you all set up," she called from an archway.

I followed Roxanne through a rainbow sea of dresses and silky fabrics, still certain I would do better as a waiter at this shindig.

We entered a room with a plush couch and other seating. On a carved wooden table sat a tray of hors d'oeuvres and two flutes of what I assumed by the bubbles to be champagne.

"What kind of dress shopping is this?" I whispered to Roxanne.

She huffed a laugh. "The best kind."

I looked at the spread of food that had been laid out. Tiny sandwiches, a fruit salad, and a dish of pastries. Real dishes and linen napkins. I went over to the table to pick up a glass. "Is it free?"

She looked at me wide-eyed and shushed me.

I threw my hands up at her. "I'm new to this," I hissed at her. "And I feel really weird right now, okay? I like my jeans and Docs. They're comfortable. I like your brother's leather jacket. I wouldn't have thought it at first, but Dorian has pretty good taste in loose-fitting, comfy clothes too." I took the champagne and drank it down.

Roxanne sighed and smiled at me. "I know he does."

Before I could comment, Kelly returned to the room with someone. "Roxanne, Fury, this is my assistant, Jovie." A remarkably beautiful girl with high cheekbones and flawless skin waved at us. Vampire. Her pant suit was feminine, but sharp, and her eyes were focused. "She has keen taste when it comes to fashion and design. You should see what she's been working on. This fabulous spread she's called Evening through the Ages. It's simply stunning."

Jovie smiled and dipped her head. "I appreciate you saying so." She looked at Roxanne. "I have something special for you that Kelly thinks you'll like. I'll be back in a moment with a selection for you to try on." She left, and I sat on the chaise longue, propping my legs up and crossing my ankles.

Kelly came to sit next to me, and I tensed. She saw my hesitation and pointed at my knees. "May I?"

"Oh yeah, I forgot about that," I said, moving to make room for her.

She waved her hand over my knees and her eyes glowed silver for a brief second. She whispered a few words under her breath, and I looked down at my scrapes. They were gone. She moved away, pleased with herself.

"Thank you," I said, realizing the sting was gone and inspecting her handiwork. "Roxanne didn't mention that you're a witch."

"Oh?" she asked, looking to Roxanne for clarification.

She shrugged at me, unapologetic. Looking at Kelly, she said, "Fury lost a bet with a witch once, and she got stuck with a mouthy talking crow as a result. She sounded sour about it, so I didn't want her to toss you in the same pool."

Kelly laughed, nodding. "Was it my sister? Because that honestly sounds like something she would do. But seriously, it's okay. We aren't all that awful. We get a bad rap, but I suppose every supernatural does to an extent."

Speaking of the crow . . . I needed to figure out a better way to keep track of him. He was my link to Duke, but that only worked if he was with me. Now I had him on a mission looking for anyone who knew about the two fuckers in the warehouse. He knew I was at Roman's now, but where could I find him? It wouldn't surprise me if he were sitting in a tree waiting to shit on my head, to be honest.

"Fury?" Roxanne's voice pulled me from my thoughts.

"I'm sorry, what?" I asked, refocusing on my surroundings.

Both women looked at me with concern. "Kelly was just asking you about your style," she prompted, taking a piece of shortbread and eating it.

"Oh . . ." I trailed off. "My style?"

"Yes, your style. What fabrics do you like? Will you be dancing? Here, stand up and let me look at your shoulders and frame. We wouldn't want to put the wrong cut on you. It's important we accentuate and work with your bone structure and your features, not against them."

"Uh . . ." I looked to Roxanne for help.

"Yes, I imagine she will dance. Something that moves easily. Nothing too tight or stiff. Nothing with a corset," Roxanne offered. "Oh, and the guys will be wearing Ralph Lauren."

"Which one?" she asked.

"Black Gregory Handmade Shawl," she answered.

I looked at her with my brows furrowed. What was she even talking about?

"Good. Yes." Kelly held her fist under her chin, humming and nodding as she took in the information. "Is there anything you've seen before that you like? From a movie or an award show?"

A switch flipped. I met her eyes. "Yes. *The Great Gatsby*."

"Gatsby?" She tapped her lips, her eyes twinkling. "Give me a moment. I have some ideas." She shuffled out of the room.

Roxanne gave me a look of surprise. "I didn't picture you going that classic. *The Great Gatsby*. That's the 1920s, right?"

"I'm an old soul, what can I say?" I shrugged. "You can't deny that the look would fit me though. Loose fitting. Not tight or stiff. Just enough edge to be dark, and just enough class to be sexy." I smiled, no longer hating the idea of a dress.

She smiled at me and shook her head. "I won't disagree with you. I just didn't picture it." She took a sip of her champagne, then said, "Dorian probably did. He has an eye for things like that."

My interest was piqued. "What, fashion?"

"No, not fashion. Just . . . reading people, I suppose."

I looked at her knowingly. "What happened between you two? You had a thing with him, that much is clear."

She threw her hands up. "Oh, no you don't. I am not falling in that trap. This is weird enough already on so many levels. I'm not going to kiss and tell."

Just then, Jovie came around the corner, holding a selection of dresses for Roxanne. "Kelly told me you love long skirts and form-fitting bodices. I have some here for you, but I think you may find this one to your liking. I have some standard go-tos, and a phenomenal two-tone trench gown. But this one here," she said, pulling out a shiny black number, "this is the one I see on you. Square neck, duchesse satin, classic black. I say we add pink pumps for a splash of color."

Roxanne ran her hand over the gown Jovie had suggested. "Oh, this one . . . it's beautiful," she whispered.

I smiled at the way she lit up. I nodded to her. "Go try it on. I want to see you in it."

She grinned, taking the dress, and walking into a changing suite right as Kelly came back with a little surprise of her own.

She held up a gown of liquid silver dotted with tiny beads in an intricate pattern. She began to fill me in on the details I could already see. "Yes," I breathed, as she talked up the cap sleeves and floor-length material. It would hug the body then drape loosely starting at about mid-thigh.

"It's the closest I have to hitting that Gatsby, 1920s era you were looking for. Jovie was working on it, but with a few touches, I can have it in time for the summit without a problem. It's not ready to try on," she said, pointing to some pinned areas and unfinished bead-work, "but we can get your measurements, and have it done before you leave."

Witches worked quickly, but not as fast as fae, apparently. Dorian could've just made the dress appear finished with a single thought. But I wouldn't complain. Not one bit.

"Done," I said, as Roxanne opened the door from her suite and came out in her black dress. She poked her foot out, clad in pink high-heeled shoes that looked like they were meant to be the death of someone. I pointed to them. "Can you walk in those?"

She smirked and strutted across the room, her curves and figure showing they were made for the way that dress clung to her every move. She stopped in front of Kelly and me, then looked at the beaded beauty hanging over the shop owner's arms.

"Is this yours?" she asked in awe. I nodded. "This is so . . . it's you. You were right. I haven't even seen you in this and I can tell it's meant for you."

I winked at her. "I know. It's like I know what I like, or something weird like that."

She whacked my arm and looked at Kelly. "Can I look at clutches and accessories?"

Kelly's eyes sparkled. "You always know how to make me smile. C'mon, this is my favorite part." Jovie came to take the dress from

Kelly, but she held on to it. "I'll take this up front. We're going to take some measurements and get this one tidied up for Fury. Will you take care of that while I pick out a clutch with Roxanne?"

She dipped her head. "Of course."

Roxanne put her hand on her hip, jutting it out like a model. She spun on her heel, shaking her wild hair, and making sure to accentuate the swing of her hips. "Too much?"

"Go pick out a purse," I told her, rolling my eyes.

She laughed, walking out of the room, calling over her shoulder, "It's a clutch."

I huffed, and muttered under my breath, wondering if she heard me mocking her. The distinct lack of shouting said she either didn't or chose to ignore it.

"If you'd like to step over here, I can get your measurements," Jovie said, pointing to an area in front of a wall of mirrors.

"Yeah, sure," I said, making my way over to her. "What am I supposed to do?"

"Just stand here." She pointed to a circle on the floor.

I did as I was told, and she stretched a measuring tape from my shoulders to the floor, making a mental note, I assumed. She didn't write anything down.

"Arms out," she said, and I held them out, parallel to the ground.

She first measured across my back, and then from shoulder to fingertip. I scrunched my eyebrows together, catching our reflection in the mirrors.

"Why did you do that?" I asked, cautiously.

"Hmm?" she hummed, looking up into the mirror to meet my gaze.

"You measured the length of my arm." She stared at me blankly. "For a dress that has cap sleeves."

For a moment, she didn't respond. Then she laughed, looking down at the floor. She put her hands on her hips before looking up at me again. Jovie's eyes darkened and the pleasant smile fell away. A look of blind hatred stared back at me.

She opened her jacket, revealing a small bomb wrapped around her waist.

This wasn't happening again. Really? Was one day without death threats too much to ask? I took two steps back, putting distance between me and the kamikaze vampire. My back bumped up against the heavy changing suite door.

"Time's up, Sunny," she said, a feral grin on her face.

I heard that name, and her choice of words echoed the vampires in the warehouse, and my mind was torn as I processed them. I stared at her for what felt like entirely too long, though it couldn't have been more than a second. "What the fuck did you just call me?"

At that moment, I heard Roxanne's voice on the other side of the main door. "Fury? What do you think of this clutch and these earrings?" she called, getting closer to us.

I made a snap decision when I saw Jovie's lip curl slightly, revealing a touch of her fang. Time was indeed up.

I turned around and ripped the heavy door off its hinges, shouting to Roxanne to run and get out. I'd be back soon, and this vampire bitch would be dead, but Rox needed to be as far away from the blast as I could get her. I swung the heavy wood into Jovie, sending her crashing into the wall in the far corner.

The room exploded, and my body flew back, crashing through something hard.

I landed with a thud, a heavy object on top of me, my head slamming into the ground.

The wind was knocked out of my lungs and my entire body hurt from the impact.

Time crawled in slow motion.

From a distance, I heard muffled screaming. Voices that were far away and calling my name.

Whatever was on top of me was pulled off. My vision was blurred, as if a haze filled the room. Roxanne's panicked look didn't register as real, and I could barely hear her screaming my name. I groaned, reaching up to touch my ears and pulling away fingertips wet with blood.

I tried to move, but my muscles protested, and my bones cracked.

"Kill me now," I muttered to Roxanne, and I was dead serious.

"Shut up, Fury, I'm not going to kill you," she said, yelling something I couldn't understand to Kelly.

Was Kelly a traitor too? Was Rox still in danger? I couldn't even get up to help. Ugh, this human body sucked so bad.

Roxanne hovered over me, pressing something to my leg, and dialing on her phone with one hand. She put it to her ear, and the last thing heard before I faded out completely was the sound of her voice.

"Dorian? I need you now."

CHAPTER 36
EZRA

Roman sat on a couch in his living room with his elbows resting on his knees and his hands running over his dreads. He was struggling to keep his temper in check. Keep the wolf down.

Dorian stood next to a large window overlooking the lake, his arms crossed, lost in thought. Who knew how he was actually handling it? The fae was made of marble ninety-five percent of the time.

I sat in a high-backed chair, my head tilted back.

"I don't understand how the witch knew nothing of that vampire," Roman said to no one in particular.

"Kelly," Dorian said. "Her name is Kelly. Both Ezra and I interrogated her. She was completely unaware of the motives, and distraught that it had even happened. When I arrived, she had Rox and Fury shielded in an effort to protect them until she realized it was me." He sighed, still gazing out the window. "She's working on some of Fury's wounds right now."

Indeed she was. Which was why Fury was rambling and cursing up a storm, directing her angry thoughts at me through our connection.

"How did this happen?" Roman asked, looking in my direction.

"I have no idea. Jovie wasn't one of mine—"

"But she's under your jurisdiction. She is your faction, your responsibility—"

"Don't lecture me, wolf. I'm well aware of my roles and responsibilities. Before you rudely interrupted me, I was going to say she wasn't one of mine, but nothing about her lines up. We keep track of every vampire who comes in and out of here. None of my men knew of her, didn't recognize the picture Kelly had of her, nothing. It's as though she appeared out of thin air."

Roman added, "What I don't understand is why the vampires are suddenly willing to just bleed out or strap a bomb to themselves. For what purpose? What's the point of trying to kill Fury?"

"Fae," Dorian interjected. "We could potentially be looking at fae. I had thought witches, but it could be fae. Spells or compulsion could be what's pushing them. These suicidal vampires don't necessarily have to believe in the cause, they just have to be controlled."

I held my hand out, gesturing to Dorian. "See? He doesn't know the motives either, and he has nothing better to do in life than stare out windows and think shit up." I craned my neck, stretching the muscles. "This involves more than vampires. We just don't know who else quite yet."

"Are we looking at a small cult, an army, a group of extremists? Who fucking knows anymore?" Roman started to shake, his eyes burning an icy blue.

"Rein it in, Roman. She's upstairs. She can't die. She's fine," I reminded him.

I'd be fine if you let me die, Fangs.

I believe the general consensus was no. I voted to kill you if that makes you happy.

She whined in frustration. *This witch is knitting muscle back together. My skin is on fire. It's painful to breathe—*

Pull up your big girl pants, demon. I thought she gave you something for the pain. You have a low pain tolerance for someone who—

I haven't been in pain for over a century, you hemorrhoid. I forgot what it feels like, but if you would. Just. Kill. Me, I could be back in a flash. No problem.

I broke our connection, shutting her out as much as I could until it sounded like a loud, angry whisper that was just a touch too far away. I refocused on the conversation between the fae and the wolf.

"What suggestions do you have?" Dorian asked, looking between us.

"Suggestions for?" I said, not having heard the topic we'd moved on to.

"Pay attention, Ezra," Roman growled, his fingers gripping the edge of his seat cushion.

I narrowed my gaze. "I'm thinking about a multitude of things, and I don't have time to coddle your temperamental alter ego there, youngling. Watch it."

Roman stood up, but I didn't budge. I moved faster than he did. He could bring it.

"Sit down. Now," Dorian roared, his voice booming. "This isn't between us. This just includes us, or have you forgotten? All three of us are on equal footing, and all three of us are mated to her."

I smirked, turning my head to Dorian, taking my eyes off Roman to remind him I was in no way intimidated by his show of power. "I voted to kill her and let her come back, but you two and Roxanne outnumbered me." I shrugged. "I put in my two cents."

Dorian pinched the bridge of his nose. "We've moved past that. The answer was no. It's not worth the risk. We don't need another one of her bodies to dispose of. We can't draw any more attention to ourselves than we already have, especially not the week of the summit. The bomb was at a public place. Human first responders are involved. Kelly is healing her to the best of her ability. Drop it."

No such luck, kitten. Tough it out, I said to her mentally.

A string of curses and creative ways to insult us bombarded my thoughts, causing me to almost laugh at her.

I exhaled loudly. "What was the other question?"

"The summit," Roman answered, his voice terse. "How do we keep her safe?"

"I don't know," I said, shrugging slightly. "I haven't really put much thought into it."

Roman looked at me incredulously, then looked to Dorian for help. "I know you don't care about mates, but this is callous, even for you," he growled, turning in my direction. "If you don't want the bond, reject her and move along. Just get it over with and get back to your club and endless, meaningless fucks. No one here's going to throw you a farewell party, but not caring about whether she lives or dies—"

"She can't die," I shouted, leaning forward in my chair, gripping the arms. "For fuck's sake, this has nothing to do with rejecting or having been rejected, you sanctimonious dickhead. Fury can't die, so excuse the fuck out of me for not running myself into the ground over how to protect her from *dying*."

"Yet," Dorian interjected, turning his head slightly before looking back out the window.

"What?" Roman and I said in unison.

"You said she can't die. Yet. She can't die *yet*," Dorian answered.

I sat back, massaging a temple. "Wait, what are you saying, Dorian? You saw what happens when she dies. You were there."

Roman groaned and scraped his hands down his face as if realizing something. I looked between them, waiting for an answer.

Roman looked up. "How many times should *you* have died in your lifetime? What about Dorian? And me?"

"We're only alive because nothing has killed us *yet*, and there's been no shortage of accidents or what should have been fatal encounters over the ages. We've questioned it before on how many occasions?" Dorian argued, looking over his shoulder.

I sighed. I knew more about her than they did. They couldn't understand. "It's not the same, though. We just regenerate and heal. She died and then *came back in a new body*."

"And when does that stop?" Dorian asked.

I stared at him blankly. "What'd you say?"

"I said, when does it stop? She can't die now. At what point does she?" He turned his head to look at us again. "Every supernatural has something that can kill them. It would stand to reason she does too."

"We don't," I said stubbornly. She wasn't the same as us, and I had no way of explaining it to them.

"Not *yet*," Roman said quietly. "But over the years, there've been enough attempts on us to know our enemies have certainly tried to find out what does kill us, right? It's only a matter of time before someone gets us with something we can't heal from."

A realization washed over me, and for the first time I acknowledged there could be a deeper truth to what they were saying. I didn't need them to understand her like I did. It was good they didn't. Where I had arrogance leading me to a false sense of security, they were able to see more clearly.

I leaned forward, running my fingers through my hair. Killing her body was easy. Could someone stop the demon from coming back? I didn't know the answer. She would tell me no, but their logic . . .

"You're right." I exhaled deeply then nodded. "It's always only been a matter of time for us. Now she's in the same place. We don't know anything about her enemy, but we know they want her dead."

"They're not going to stop either," Roman said, his elbows resting on his thighs as he clasped his hands together. "It could be tomorrow or a hundred years from now, but whoever is after her won't stop until they succeed, and they don't care about collateral damage at all."

Somehow, figuring this out had put him in more control of his wolf. I didn't understand that in the slightest. Now that *I* saw the bigger picture, a part of me was fighting against an unnamed emotion deep in my chest.

"What do we do?" I asked.

Dorian moved from the window, coming to sit in another chair near me. He crossed his legs, rubbing his thumb over his fingers repeatedly while thinking. When he finally spoke, he said, "She has to stay here until the summit. Roxanne said she isn't leaving the house, and that she is going to stay here as well. I have too much to do in preparation for the summit itself, in addition to jumping between here and Avalon while I deal with something." He looked at me, anticipating an argument. "Ezra—"

"I don't disagree. She needs to stay here. We don't know if fae or witches are involved. And seeing that we've had three vampires try to kill her, I don't know how far the betrayal runs or who I can trust. Kendrick's the only one I can say with certainty." I shifted my focus to Roman. "It pains me greatly to say it, but right now, the shifters are the most trustworthy."

Even the shifter driver, Owen, had shown his loyalty. Not only had

I listened to his thoughts, but he too had been guarding Roxanne and Fury when Dorian had arrived. A witch and a shifter, protecting a demon. It would've been laughable only minutes ago. Now? Concern and hesitation washed over me, and I pushed the new feelings aside, trying to focus.

Dorian dipped his head in thanks for my agreement.

I watched Roman. He'd been teetering on the edge of sanity since she'd arrived. I'd seen flashes and hints of icy blue in his eyes, the dormant wolf demanding to come out. Though he seemed more in control once he had a better understanding of the situation, I knew it would be short-lived. I only wondered how long before his wolf showed himself? It had been a long time . . .

"That brings us to the summit itself," Dorian said. "I can come get Roxanne and Fury. I'll sift and bring them to the summit directly. No driving, no go-betweens."

"Who do we have that we trust implicitly?" I asked, holding out my hand and raising my index finger. "Kendrick, that's one. Roxanne, and Caitlin . . ." I held up my second and third fingers, and Roman nodded.

"James and Tristan, for certain," Dorian said. "That's five. We have to move around and socialize. We don't want anyone to suspect there's something going on in the background. Roxanne can keep an eye on Fury when we aren't with her."

Thinking about the layout of the grand ballroom where we would have our first night of the summit, I said, "It'll be tough to limit entrances. We don't have enough people. James can be in the kitchen, watching what happens in that area. He'll blend in well."

"Put Tristan at the front door. Less likely to draw attention to himself," Roman added, sitting back in his chair.

"Put Kendrick on a side entrance. He's good at lurking in the shadows. Would Roxanne work best at the back? We can make our rounds, bringing Fury to her after we arrive," I said.

Dorian nodded. "That works well. They can alternate posts if they need to. Fury and Roxanne will inevitably move around the room, but we can limit their movement. Caitlin, Tristan, and Kendrick can rotate their assigned locations as needed."

Roman cracked his neck and sighed. "It's not enough."

"It has to be," I said. "It's what we've got. We keep close, and we can work out how to manage each day moving forward."

Dorian gazed between Roman and me, looking for signs of agreement. "Let's get through the summit. Then we figure out what the hell is going on. In the meantime, we keep her safe."

CHAPTER 37
FURY

I stuffed the last of the French fries into my mouth as Roxanne ran the rules by me one more time.

"I got it," I said through a mouthful of food.

"Repeat it, then," she said, hands resting on her hips. She was already dressed, with her hair styled and makeup done. She was just waiting on me to finish eating so I could get dressed. Why was I eating now and not at this grand dinner that was going to be held at the summit? Why was I eating a chicken burger—not that it didn't taste good—instead of indulging in a six-course French fusion discovery?

I recited the rules. "Don't eat the food in case they try to poison me. Again. Don't let anyone else get me a drink. If I set my drink down, don't drink from it again. Always have a babysitter with me," I mocked in a bored tone. "I heard you, Rox. For three days, I've heard you. And Roman. And Dorian—"

She held her hands up in surrender and blew out a deep breath. "Okay, okay. I'm sorry. I'm just worried. Feeling a little anxious."

I wiped my mouth off and stood, patting the little bulge on my belly. "Good thing my dress isn't as form fitting as yours, am I right?"

She huffed a laugh, but I could still hear her anxiety riding her.

"It's going to be fine. Of all the places to try something, you really think anyone in their right mind would try tonight?"

She glared at me. "Thinking like that will get you into trouble."

I shrugged, moving to the walk-in closet where my dress hung. "Yeah, but I can get out of trouble, so I'm really not all that concerned about it."

"You'll be the death of me, I swear," she mumbled.

I laughed, getting undressed and stepping into my new gown.

That psycho vamp had only blown up the back of the store where the changing rooms were. It was just enough to take us both out. Or it should've been, had that door not held up as a shield. Kelly had recreated Roxanne's dress and finished mine the day before, checking with Roman to see if she could hand deliver it.

I shimmied into the silky fabric, letting it glide across my skin as it settled in place. I slipped on the low, t-strap heels and walked into the bedroom. Roxanne let out a low whistle.

"You're going to knock them dead tonight," she breathed. "That looks stunning on you."

Warmth bloomed in my chest. It felt right, wearing this dress, even though the closest I'd come to something so luxurious when I was alive was in catalogs.

"Can I ask you a question?"

Roxanne looked at me in confusion. "I'm surprised you had to ask that question. I think we've been through a lot, yeah? After almost being blown up together, and all. I figured you knew you could ask me anything."

I cocked an eyebrow at her. "I asked you about your fling with Dorian, and you flat out refused to answer," I said, pointing out the contradiction.

"Mmm hmm." She nodded. "You can ask me anything. I just may not answer."

"Right." It was my turn to glare at her. "Anyway . . . Roman's your brother and you clearly had some sort of *thing* with Dorian you won't talk about. Doesn't it, I don't know . . . bother you that the three of them are my mates, especially when two of them mean something important to you? Does it bother you that your brother has to share me, and you have to watch it?"

Roxanne gave me a small smile. "No. It doesn't. It's not like you're playing the field. Bonds are . . . well, you don't get to make the rules. If you choose to accept or reject it, that's still on you, but can anyone force a bond? No." She walked over to me, straightening my dress, and smoothing out any areas that needed it. "Dorian and I weren't made to last, but that doesn't mean we didn't have fun. We were together so long ago. It was at the last summit. I love him, but not in the way you think. We made much better friends than lovers, and neither of us look at each other that way anymore."

I exhaled, not realizing my breathing had been slightly tense. I nodded. "Okay."

"Relax. There isn't one bit of anger or jealousy here. You won't get that from me. Ever." She smiled, but then frowned like she was thinking otherwise. "Well, maybe a little jealous that you can pull off that dress so well." She winked at me.

She was moving away from the emotional direction of our conversation, and I went with it. Relieved. I appreciated the deflection. "Please. If we want to discuss that kind of jealousy, I wish my skin tone looked as good with every color. You could wear something bile-colored and you'd still manage to make it look radiant."

"Ew," she laughed, "really? You went there?"

I shrugged, walking over to the dresser and grabbing the long, pearl necklaces each guy had bought me to match my outfit. I don't know who bought the first strand, but no doubt, when that was learned, the other two wouldn't be outdone. They couldn't claim me yet, but they found subtle ways to put their mark on me.

"Tell me about this hotel again. I honestly shut down when the guys were talking about it because we were on round two or three of the rules by that point." I hid my grin. Roman had to repeat it. Couldn't help himself. His desire to keep me safe was overwhelming.

"Of course you did." She snorted. "It's at one of Dorian's historic hotels downtown. It's supernatural staff only, but since this all happened, there hasn't been enough time to check everyone's background, whereabouts, dealings, and credentials again. Either way. First night of the summit is always the opening soiree."

"The meet and greet," I supplied.

"No, smart-ass, it's not a meet and greet. You aren't joining a glee club tonight. This is a big deal. This is the kickoff. The summit is tense and political. It really matters to supernaturals. This is our one night where we're all on even ground. We eat and drink—"

"I don't get to eat and drink," I grumbled, wondering where I could hide a flask in my dress. "Not unless an assigned babysitter provides me with said drink."

"Oh, look, you were listening," she mocked. "Anyway, as I was saying, we eat, drink, dance, have conversations. Schmoozing. It's political, in a way. Like sizing up opponents, but it's clean. I'll walk you through each day. Just stand with me, and you'll do fine."

I fixed my earring, thinking quietly about the job I'd been sent to do. Get through tonight and then learn more at the summit. If they were going to take it one day at a time, so would I.

Roxanne came and fixed the pin in my hair, sweeping up one side. It fell around my shoulder in loose waves. She wore a headband scarf in duchesse satin to match her dress, and it held the tight curls of her afro away from her face. Her lips were painted with a berry-colored lipstick, complementing the shade of her new shoes.

I held my arms out. "I'm as ready as I'll ever be."

We walked downstairs to find Dorian waiting for us. He was watching the sunset over the lake, adjusting his crystal cuff links, when he heard us and looked over.

For a split second, my heart stuttered in my chest.

We drank each other in, and I took back what I'd said about tuxedos looking the same. The way it was cut to his body was like magic. It had to have been. He wore a vest underneath the jacket, in a dark silver that matched the fabric beneath my beaded masterpiece.

Dorian's eyes traveled the length of my body, his lips parted slightly as his mouth hung open for a brief moment.

He cleared his throat, his voice taking on a husky tenor as he said, "Fury, you look . . . "

"Stunning?" Roxanne offered. "That's what I said."

"Breathtaking," he finished.

Never having received compliments like this, I had no idea how to respond. The best I could do was give a small smile and thank them both.

As we stared at each other silently, Roxanne eventually piped up, "So . . ."

"Yes," Dorian said, walking toward us. "Fury, we're arriving outside in case you feel sick."

My stomach twisted, knowing the sift was coming. "Oh, I'll feel sick, all right." I just wanted to keep the food down this time.

As soon as we arrived, my heart was beating faster, and my stomach threatened to empty itself. I held on to Dorian's arm as he steadied me, and I took a breath.

"Maybe we need to look into some motion sickness medicine or something," Roxanne suggested.

That would have been better to bring up earlier, and I would make sure we'd have that discussion at a later time.

"Shall we?" Dorian said, holding out his arms for each of us to wrap ours through.

We walked up the steps to the historic hotel and entered the lobby. It almost felt like a flashback. It wasn't quite 1920s, but maybe the 30s. It was old-fashioned, and I loved it. When I spotted Tristan's familiar face, I dipped my head slightly in greeting. He kept his features neutral upon seeing me, but I saw the tiny spark of acknowledgment in his eye.

We entered a room to the right of the entrance, and my mouth fell open. It had been called the grand ballroom in their discussions, but I hadn't understood why until that moment. I let go of Dorian's arm and looked around in awe.

The space was expansive, more so than the outside of the building had suggested. The floor was a beautiful cherry-stained hardwood. The windows were floor to ceiling, and warded, from what I was told. Cream drapes in a heavy, luxurious fabric hung, framing the glass. What must've been a hundred tables filled the room. Fine china and crystal glasses, gold cutlery, and opulent floral centerpieces. It was a lot to take in.

In all my life, I've never seen anyone look as beautiful as you do right now, a voice lightly touched my mind.

Smooth line for a player. I smiled and scanned the room, looking for Ezra. *Where are you?*

A hand lightly touched my waist, slid around my stomach, and pressed me to the hard body behind me. "Right here," he breathed in my ear.

My legs quaked, and a shiver of desire crept up my spine.

I turned around, and he kissed me on the cheek softly, still holding my waist, but only grazing his fingertips over me. The beads on my dress clattered together.

He stepped back, never taking his eyes off me. His tuxedo looked like Dorian's, but he had no vest and wore black on black. He kept me under his gaze for a moment longer before he turned to Roxanne, taking her hand in his, bringing it to his lips and kissing her fingers. "Roxanne, you look radiant, as always."

She winked at him. "I know."

"Rox, would you like to join me for a drink? Ezra and Fury can meet up with you in a minute, I'm sure," Dorian said. His voice wasn't cold, nor was it genuine. They were moving Roxanne to the back, where she'd keep her post, and where I would eventually follow.

Ezra nodded to Dorian knowingly, then put his attention back on me as they walked away.

He took my hand and placed it flat on his chest. I wasn't sure what his intent was until I felt a flask in his tuxedo pocket. His eyes sparkled with mirth, and I grinned at him.

"Sometimes we need a little bit to warm us up," he said, taking it out of his coat and unscrewing the top. He handed it to me, and I took a swig, feeling the burn of bourbon as it hit me.

"I appreciate the gesture," I said, taking one more and screwing the cap back on. He took a swig of his own then tucked it back into the lining.

He winked at me, his lips curling up in a grin, the tiniest point of a fang extending. Taking my hand, he laced his fingers through mine, walking me to the dance floor.

String music played, nothing too fast. Simple melodies to get the night started as people were arriving.

Ezra put his hand on the small of my back, pulling me close, swaying and moving our bodies in time with the music.

"I could get used to this," I said quietly, remembering what it felt like to be pressed against him in bed.

“I’d prefer it, honestly. But you’ll be passed between us tonight,” he said, looking around the room as we danced.

I cocked an eyebrow at him. “I knew you were willing to share, I just didn’t realize you were so blasé about it.”

His fingertips pressed into my back, and his eyes glittered with hunger. “You’ve been with the wolf for five days. I hate it.”

I shrugged. “Do something about it,” I challenged.

He opened his mouth when a deep voice came from behind me. “May I?”

Ezra grunted, seeing Roman. I turned around and had to catch my breath.

Roman’s dreads were pulled back, showing off his cheekbones and amber eyes. Up close, I could see flecks of icy blue within. His ever-present wolf on the watch.

He wore the same tuxedo as Ezra and Dorian, choosing to go for the classic styling. It hugged his muscles, but the cut was tailored to him and flowed naturally with his movements.

“Roman,” I breathed. “You look handsome.”

He smiled and reached out, tucking a stray wave behind my ear. “You look . . . beyond comparison.” He looked over at Ezra, nodding knowingly, and Ezra returned the gesture.

To be continued, he said as he walked away, mingling with supernaturals I didn’t know.

I took Roman’s hand in mine, and his other rested around my waist as we danced toward Roxanne’s assigned corner.

“Thank you,” he said.

I looked at him, confused. “For what?”

“For giving us the illusion of control with you tonight. For letting us keep you safe,” he murmured.

When his normally deep voice whispered, it vibrated over my skin and through my bones. I breathed him in, taking in his scent as I closed my eyes and he led me across the floor.

“What do I smell like?” he asked me.

My eyes flew open. “What?”

“You smell like storms and chaos. I want to know what you think I smell like,” he answered.

My stomach tightened at his heated gaze. I cleared my throat.

"Like . . . wind. The trees. Earth," I said, closing my eyes as I spoke.

"Ahem," Ezra said, "hate to interrupt."

Roman glared at him. "And yet, here you are instead of my sister," he grumbled.

"She said you took too long and went to the bathroom," he said. "I told her I would wait here."

"I doubt she said that first part," I said. "But I'll go to the bathroom too." They shared a look, and I saw the hesitation. "Guys, she just went to the bathroom. I'll only be walking alone until I get in there then I'm with her. It's okay."

"Ezra, you stay until they're back?" Roman asked, and he nodded in agreement. A small smile gracing his lips, he squeezed my hand before letting go and disappearing into the crowd.

"I'll be right back," I said, heading down the hall to the women's restroom, feeling Ezra's eyes on me.

I pushed the door open and walked in. A sitting area where women could touch up their makeup was empty, the plush couches untouched.

"Rox?" I called, walking into a stall, and shutting the door as I heard a toilet flush. I started to carefully pull my skirt up. "Rox?"

No answer.

A chill crept up my spine. This was wrong.

The skirt material fell out of my hands, back down to the floor.

I slowly opened the stall door, listening for sounds in the bathroom and hearing nothing.

I stepped out, checking the periphery first and only then looking forward.

A piece of folded white paper was on the counter. A tube of lipstick sat on top.

I rushed over to it, picking up the tube, seeing it smeared with blood. My breath hitched. My heart started pounding in my ears.

Carefully unfolding the note, I read the words written in a familiar berry color.

East side exit. A car is waiting. Get in. Alone. Or Roxanne dies, and she doesn't come back.

CHAPTER 38
FURY

I READ IT THREE TIMES.

Shock pulsed through me before resolve set in. I calculated my odds if I simply defied them and told the alphas. After all, there was strength in numbers, right?

That very logic made me hesitate. I suspected whoever was behind this had to have numbers too. A lot of them, by the looks of it. If they saw me make my way out of the bathroom and go tell Dorian or Roman—that would be it. I had little doubt they'd kill her to make a point. Then they'd wait to steal someone else or find some other plan to lure me out.

At least I couldn't die. Not permanently.

I could tell Ezra. Keep him updated. Let him tell the guys once I was wherever that car would take me. If they didn't release Roxanne, though . . .

Best-case scenario, I could play my cards right and find a way to save her.

Worst-case scenario, Roxanne died.

That wasn't an acceptable outcome. Emotion flooded me. Losing her . . . it would haunt me. She deserved so much more. I would do anything to get her back.

I swiped the bloody lipstick off the counter, folded up the paper, and tossed them both in the trash.

Ezra brushed against my mind. *Everything all right?*

There's been a change of plans, I thought back, turning for the bathroom door. I peeked my head out then exited and turned down the hall—for the back door that would lead to my getaway car.

Change? His mental voice took on a different quality. Sharper. More perceptive. *Fury, what the actual fuck are you doing?*

They took Roxanne. I was told to take the east exit where she was posted and head out back. A car will be waiting for me there.

"Fury?" a light voice called. I paused mid-step, stomach sinking.

"Yes?" I turned, plastering a smile on my face for Caitlin.

She smiled too, but the slight narrowing of her eyes told me she wasn't buying it. "Where are you going?" she asked, starting toward me at a still somewhat casual pace. "We were very clear on everything before we came—"

I lifted my hands in mock surrender, letting the tension ease from my shoulders. "I know, I know. It's just, I really don't do great with parties. Or crowds. Or people, for that matter. I just need a couple minutes of fresh air without one of the guys or one of their people breathing down my neck, ya know?"

I'm getting Dorian and we are coming to you, Ezra said, and it was a real effort not to let the annoyance show on my face. Caitlin's suspicions had lowered, and I didn't want to give it away.

If you get Dorian, you can kiss my ass and our deal goodbye. I'm a hundred-and-twenty-six-year-old demon that can't fucking die, Ezra. Roxanne can, and unlike me, she doesn't get to come back. You know this. I'll keep in contact with you, but we do things my way. I felt his hesitation, a mental pause as he considered it, and Caitlin caught up with me.

"Mind if I go with you, then? I could use some air myself." Instead of waiting for an answer, she continued past me and out the double doors.

I sighed. Just great. Exactly what I needed. Another fucking complication when I was trying to save Roxanne.

Ezra? I thought as I started for the door. *Are you with me?*

His answer was immediate. *I think this is a rash plan. You . . . There are things we don't understand about what's after you. You—*

They will kill Roxanne, *Ezra. I won't let her take the fall. Are you with me, or am I alone in this?*

You're never alone. I'll play along for now. For Roxanne. But the second I lose contact with you, I'm telling them, and we give chase. Do you understand?

That was a decent compromise and probably the best I was going to get, given I was his mate and all. *Understood. Now keep them distracted because I have to take out Caitlin.*

I shoved at the door a little harder than necessary and stepped out into the sticky embrace of the night air. It was thick with humidity, trapped by the clouds that told of a coming storm. It made my dress cling to me even more, and not in a good way.

"So," Caitlin said as the door shut behind me. She had a cigarette in hand and a lighter in the other. She flicked the top, and a small flame came to life. She touched it to the end, and it turned a burnt orange and began to glow. "Is this really about the party and your role as their mate being overwhelming, or were the last few days with us just an act? I can't quite tell, but I know you're a good actor."

Aw shit. That made me feel even worse about what I was going to have to do. I casually stepped toward her, scanning the street.

A black Honda Civic was parked down at the end. The lights were on, but the car wasn't moving. If I had to bet, that was my driver.

"Color me surprised. You don't seem the type to smoke," I said, coming up beside her at an angle.

She took a long draw then blew it out. "Working for Roman isn't always easy. There are a lot of shifters to be managed, and someone has to take care of the things he can't. I picked up the habit after Maya died and haven't quite been able to stop." She tilted her head to look at me out of the corner of her eyes. "You didn't answer my question."

I sighed. "No, it isn't an act."

The edge of her mouth tugged up. "I'm happy to hear it. I worried when I saw you heading for the door."

Normally, I would've asked for a cigarette and mentally taken a seat. Maybe even enjoyed the conversation. I liked her better when she was more direct and less uptight. Which made this suck that much more.

I moved closer until I could sling my arm over her shoulders. She gave me a strange look but didn't shrug me off. "Unfortunately for us both, the truth is I care a little too much." Her eyebrows drew together in confusion. I curled my arm inward, cutting off her air supply in an instant. "I'm sorry about this, really."

She tried to take in a breath and gagged.

I'd already maneuvered my position to be somewhat behind her so that when she reared back, trying to stab me with the burning end of the cigarette, I caught her wrist and twisted it. She hissed in pain, letting out more of her precious air supply. I was careful not to break it though, just bruise. I wouldn't hurt her any more than necessary. I just needed to get away.

They're starting to wonder. Need to hurry up, Ezra chimed in as Caitlin tried to stomp on my foot.

"I'm going as fast as I can," I grunted.

She used her free hand to reach behind her and grab a fistful of my hair.

Motherfucker.

"The hair?" I winced as she threatened to rip it out of my scalp. "That's a low blow."

She grumbled in reply. I took that to mean she wouldn't have if I weren't strangling her. It was a good point. Unfortunately, it wouldn't save Roxanne.

She doesn't want to hurt you, but she's going to shift to protect herself. Hit her in the side of the head and be done with it, Ezra said.

I pressed harder against her throat and the thrashing increased. "I'm trying not to hurt her. Turns out that's a lot harder than trying to cause pain," I groaned.

She's a wolf. She'll heal. Do it now.

Her body began vibrating, and her chest rumbled. Her wolf was coming out. I tightened my arm over her throat in a lock that would've killed a human. The shifting halted. Her thrashing movements slowed, becoming weak. Languid. Only when they stopped altogether did I start to relieve the pressure.

She didn't gasp or jerk to life. Her legs gave out, and she started to crumple. I let her down gently, hoping that he was right about her healing. Her pant suit was ripped, and her hair was a sweaty mess.

A sliver of guilt ate at me even as I saw the slight rise and fall of her chest.

Take care of her, I told him.

I didn't have time to stick around and keep an eye on her.

There was a car waiting for me.

All I had to do was take it.

I started down the street, walking as fast as I could in my heels. When I got to the end of the sidewalk, the blacked-out window rolled down.

"Get in the back," a man's voice said. I didn't recognize it, or him.

I reached for the handle then paused. "How do I know she's alive?"

He lifted a gloved hand, holding a cellphone. A few taps on the screen and Roxanne's face lit up. He turned it around to show me.

Her dress was torn, and her left eye was swollen and blackened. She had a split lip and heavily bruised jaw. She must've put up a fight. I couldn't figure out why she hadn't shifted.

"Rox?" I asked in a terse voice, noticing the rise and fall of her chest. She blinked a couple times with her good eye. "I'm coming to get you. Just hang tight."

"No," she rasped. Her vocal cords sounded shot to hell. They must've really done a number on her. She moved her mouth, trying to form words. What she could say came out in a slur. "Roman needs you. You're his last chance—"

"All right, chat time is over. Are you going to get in the car, or we gonna do this the hard way?" my driver asked in a deep voice. Given how rough Roxanne already looked, I wasn't sure she could handle the hard way.

"Nope, that's proof enough." I opened the back door of the car and slipped in.

His eyes met mine in the rearview mirror, cold and unflinching. At first glance I'd thought they were brown, but they were a dark shade of purple. He wore a hat that covered his ears, but I suspected fae. No one else had eyes like that.

He lifted his hand, holding a vial between his forefinger and thumb. "Drink this."

"Do I have a choice?" I asked, knowing it was a drug of some kind and doubting I'd get lucky enough for it to be poison.

"Do you want to see the she-wolf live? Or have you reconsidered the hard way? I don't believe wolves can regrow fingers and toes very fast. Pretty painful."

I sighed.

This is a bad idea, Fury. I don't trust it.

No shit, I thought back to him. *The point isn't to trust them. It's to make sure Roxanne comes out alive. Just stick to the plan.*

"Times up, Devil. Drink it or I have my friend get his pliers out and we can watch her lose them one by one."

I reached out and took the bottle in my hand. It was cool to the touch, but not cold. The liquid inside glowed a faint green, which meant magic was at play here. Not science.

"Bottoms up," I murmured, popping the cap with my thumb.

I pressed the rim to my lips. There was only enough for two swallows, but one swallow was all it took.

My head started to spin. My vision blurred. I expected to lose consciousness, but when I didn't immediately pass out, alarm bells clanged in my head.

My driver turned around in his seat, another object in hand. Even cross-eyed and seeing double, there was no mistaking the syringe.

"I really hate being drugged," I groaned. "Can't we do this the easy way where I just sit here—"

He moved faster than I'd anticipated, though in all honesty, I probably wouldn't have stopped him, anyway. I'd already come this far and swallowed the weird green potion. There was no turning back now.

The needle disappeared into my thigh. The twinge of pain that followed was so slight I wouldn't have noticed if I hadn't watched him push the stopper down.

"Time to take a nap," he said.

My eyelids fluttered. My thoughts wavered as Ezra shouted in my head. I counted the seconds, only getting to eight before blackness closed in.

CHAPTER 39
FURY

CARNIVAL MUSIC PLAYED SOFTLY IN THE BACKGROUND.

I tried to open my eyelids, but they didn't seem to be working right. The darkness still surrounded me, but that damning music grounded me in reality. I tugged at my arms, but they didn't seem to be working either. Neither were my legs. I tried to wiggle a single toe, but I wasn't sure if I actually did or if it was just my mind playing tricks on me.

The music continued to play all around me.

Left. Right. It went round and round and—

A wave of vertigo hit me. Or maybe it already had, and I was only now registering what it was. Vomit fought its way up my throat. The acid burned as it climbed.

The music kept playing.

And I kept spinning.

My lips broke apart as my body's natural aversion to movement sent the contents of my dinner spewing everywhere.

My eyes flew open.

Suddenly, the darkness was gone. Instead, bright lights assaulted me. They were everywhere. Red and white. Gold and blue. My head lolled as the spinning continued. My neck rolled and my head followed like a bobble, unable to stop itself.

My wrists were tied together over a golden metal pole that was moving up and down in a rhythmic motion in time with the music. I tried to regain control of my body, but that was a lost cause. My legs were strapped to stirrups. I was riding an animatronic metal horse.

Carousel.

I was on a carousel.

Ezra? I called out mentally.

My hope was already fizzling, but the silence dashed it.

Looked like backup wouldn't be coming.

I had to save Rox all on my own and figure out who the fuck was behind this nonsense.

My stomach turned again. With my dinner already gone, I retched up bile, dripping down my chin and onto the beautifully beaded dress.

I had to get off this fucking ride.

"The devil lives," a mocking voice announced like a loudspeaker at a show.

I tried to peer past the bright lights, but the spinning prevented me from truly seeing anything beyond the painted horses from Hell.

"What? No snappy comeback this time?"

I tested my mouth, and found myself able to open and close it, though my control was still weak. "Kill . . . you . . ." I ground out. Not the most terrifying, but it was the best I had.

"You're going to kill me?" the voice asked.

My head rolled, and I used the momentum to nod.

He let out a condescending laugh. "You hear this? Even drugged, covered in her own vomit, and completely at our mercy, she's still making threats." Several grunts followed. I had an audience. Great.

"Weak fucker," I replied, sounding surer. Whatever the asshole driver had given me was wearing off, and these dumbasses were just letting it.

"Weak?" he asked quietly. All the mocking was gone, replaced by utter seriousness. "Turn it off. I think it's time we send this bitch back to Hell once and for all."

The carousel slowed. I thanked my lucky stars. If they'd hurry up and kill me, I could come back not drugged and ready to rumble.

A loud mechanical clunking echoed in the night, and my horse finally came to a stop. Now that I wasn't moving, I could finally make out the silhouette standing at the edge of the ride.

He lifted an eyebrow. "Surprised to see me?"

"Tyler?" I asked, knowing that wasn't his name but wanting to egg him on. "Teagen? Travis?"

"Taylor," he said in a dark voice, stepping up onto the shiny metallic floor. "Taylor Dawson. I was the alpha of the Dawson pack. Until you came onto me and pissed off your *mate.*" He pointed at the darkened skin of his forehead. A brand if I ever saw one. The elaborate R was placed on top of a crest I recognized but couldn't place. "He branded me a rogue because of you. I can't shift *because of you.*"

I tried again to move my arms, and while I could, I definitely couldn't break my bonds yet. I needed more time.

"I tried to walk away. You tried to take something that wasn't yours. You only have yourself to blame," I mumbled. At least I was able to speak a little better than before. The rest would come. It had to.

Taylor's face hardened. "Untie her. It's time."

Time? Time for what?

A fae and another vampire came up from behind him. The vampire undid the bindings, and the fae grabbed my shoulders then roughly yanked me off the horse. I still couldn't fully walk. My legs were jerky, my limbs not complying when my body told them to hold me up. I started to fall to the ground, and he grabbed a fistful of hair, dragging me off the carousel.

Pain erupted in my scalp, making me hiss. My back arched when my ass dropped two feet and hit pavement, tailbone first. A searing pain lit that bone on fire, spreading outward.

Shit. I was pretty sure he'd just broken it.

Motherfucker.

"She's moving too much. Give her another hit," Taylor commanded.

A needle jabbed me in the arm courtesy of another nameless asshole.

I blinked while I still could and found there were a lot of them hovering near me. Easily several dozen.

The drug soared through my veins, quickly taking effect, causing my stupid human body to betray me.

"Where's Rox?" I forced the words out while I could still talk.

Taylor snapped his fingers. "I knew I was forgetting something. Thank you." He grabbed the attention of another minion, raising his voice as he asked, "Where's the bitch? She should get a front-row seat to this."

My body went completely limp and my eyes stayed wide open, frozen in place. I was trapped inside myself, unable to do anything.

The fae guy dragging me stopped, and I fell back on the concrete. The lights of the Ferris wheel and other carnival rides lit up the edges of my vision. Thick storm clouds sat heavy over us, watching ominously and waiting to open the floodgates. Not a single sliver of the moon was in sight.

"Get your hands off me, you fucking traitors," Rox said in a slurred, husky growl.

They'd suppressed her wolf somehow, and she had to be pissed. I couldn't actually see her. Just the lights against the dark. I really wished he would get on with the killing.

Knees smacked against the pavement near me. I recognized the sound as they popped.

"Fury?" Her voice changed. "Fury, what happened—"

Crack.

"Gag her," Taylor said gruffly. "I don't want to hear her bullshit."

Sounds of a scuffle followed, but it was short lived. Then it was just Roxanne's grunts, the carnival music, and Taylor talking.

"Wolf boy, can we get on with it? Her mates are looking for her, and I don't want to be here when they find the body. I get that you got a bone to pick, but this is about stopping her—not your petty fucking grudge."

Well, at least my driver was an asshole to everyone.

"Have you forgotten what her supposed mates have done to us?" Taylor replied in a low voice.

"No," driver man replied. "I'm well aware. We all are. That doesn't change the fact that I don't want to be here when they find her. The angel came to *us*. He showed us what happens. Get it over with."

The angel.

My mind was spinning like it was still on the damned carousel.

How could an *angel* have done this? Why? It didn't make sense.

Someone had to have told them the name Sunny, though. They couldn't have pulled that out of thin air.

So maybe there was something to it. Maybe an angel had betrayed me . . .

But why? I didn't know the angels. We had different jobs, but we worked for the same purpose.

Was this about the job? That they had failed, and I wouldn't?

That seemed extreme given what would happen if no one succeeded.

None of it added up.

I waited, hoping they'd drop more breadcrumbs. Maybe a name. A face. Could my mysterious angel be here right now?

I wasn't sure, but I needed to find out.

There was just one little problem.

I was faceup and unable to move.

Taylor leaned over me, a twisted grin on his smug fucking face. Behind him, something broke the pattern of the clouds. I focused on it. Trying to will myself to see.

It happened again.

Then again.

And on the fourth time, I was able to make out what it was.

A crow. Hades was here.

He turned in the sky and stared down at me with beady black eyes that I really hoped were saying he was going to get the guys. Then he twisted and flapped away.

"Are you ready to die, Devil?" Taylor asked me, as if I could answer. He knelt down, his face looming closer. He had a twisted streak in him, and for that alone I was happy we had an audience. I had little doubt he would drag this out if left to his own devices, but they wanted him to get on with it.

I could handle whatever pain he would throw at me. It would be temporary, and then I would die. I would come back, and I was going to question every single motherfucker here tonight because I wanted to know who this 'angel' was. They were dead supes walking.

"Our angel told us your secret," he said after a moment. "He told us the only way to actually end you."

Given they'd already tried poison and blowing me up, I wasn't exactly terrified.

"Goodbye, Sunny Adams."

Then he did the only thing I hadn't expected.

He bit me.

CHAPTER 40
DORIAN

I WAS GOING TO FUCKING KILL THAT VAMPIRE.

Then when he was dead, I was going to kill every other fucking person that even knew someone who was involved. I was going to wipe this little cult from existence.

And once I finished doing that, I was going to lock Fury up on the Isle of Glass until I got some fucking answers from her about who and what she was, and why so many people wanted her dead.

But first I had to find her.

Vampires were scouring the east of the city. Shifters the north and west. The other fae and I had taken the south, but I also sent half my men to the other sections of Houston because I didn't trust anyone. I had to hope more of my people were less corrupt than theirs.

I sifted mile by mile, searching the streets of south Houston for my mate, but Fury was gone. Ezra had told us about the trap they'd laid, but the driver wasn't actually a driver at all. The car was still sitting there when we started the search. It appeared that whoever it was had sifted her out. Which meant she could technically be anywhere.

Most fae weren't powerful enough to take another person outside Houston, and our attackers always seemed more interested in killing her than anything. I wasn't certain if she was even here, but I kept looking because it was all I could do.

The feeling of being helpless for the first time in over a thousand years was unsettling. Deeply disturbing. Panic inducing.

I wasn't familiar with those emotions. I hadn't felt them since Morvain died and Lyra fell into her downward spiral. But here and now, I felt them again.

Anger rode on their heels.

I sifted again, going closer to the shore. I scanned the horizon, listening for anything that would lead me in the right direction. But there were no screams. No fires. No dying or dead people are far as I could tell. Everything was seemingly the same.

"Dorian," a voice said, sounding breathless. I turned, but no one was there. "Up here," it said again.

My head tilted back.

It was the crow from the warehouse.

"Where is she?" I demanded. "Where is your master?"

The beast cocked its head, flapping its wings. "First, she's not my master," the crow smarted off, wasting my time. He had seconds to live if he didn't tell me what he was clearly here to say. "Second, she was taken by an angry group of supernaturals. They've been brainwashed into thinking she'll end the world. They have her at King's Pier."

"Where's that?" Not the most familiar with the area given I never stayed longer than absolutely necessary.

The bird turned as an explosion rattled the street.

I sifted toward the noise and reappeared in front of a tacky arch that read *King's Pier*. It was an amusement park.

And the Ferris wheel was currently falling out of the sky.

I pulled out my phone and hit speed dial as I walked into the park.

Ezra picked up on the first ring.

"King's Pier. Tell the wolf."

I didn't wait for a response before disconnecting our call.

Supernaturals were sifting away and running in my direction, but they didn't seem to notice me. They were too busy fleeing something . . .

I picked up my pace.

"Fury!" I shouted.

The boom of the carousel exploding was my answer.

CHAPTER 41
FURY

My limbs felt like they were being torn from my body.

My skin was on fire.

My very being was breaking down because of one little detail I hadn't anticipated.

The dead can't be turned. We're already dead. The magic that we gained upon entering the Afterlife wasn't meant to mix with the magic in the living world.

Over the millennia, a few had made the attempt. Tried to return to life on Earth. Return to the living realm permanently. Each time, the angel, poltergeist, or whatever else that did so ended up dying a horrible, painful death—a true death—as the magic that was their soul literally tore apart.

That was my future.

My ending.

Taylor Dawson was right when he said he'd kill me. Now that I understood just how much they knew, I was certain there was a traitor in our midst. Someone in the Afterlife didn't want me to succeed. For an unknown reason, someone wanted the world to end.

And someone had picked the wrong fucking demon to come after.

I wasn't *The* Fury simply because I knew how to break and fix people the right way.

I was *The* fucking Fury because I was the last person you wanted to piss off if you wanted to live, dead or not.

And if I was going down, I was taking these sons of bitches with me.

I had just enough clarity. Barely enough focus. I teetered on the edge of losing myself in the pain when an electric current tingled through my arms. It couldn't burn off the drugs, but it could kill the pieces of shit who'd given them to me.

"Look at that. Doesn't look so tough now, does—" Taylor didn't get to finish before his entire body exploded.

The people gathered around went quiet, only just beginning to realize their mistake.

I didn't need my demonic strength to end them.

I didn't need my cunning or hard-earned combat skills.

I was one of the most powerful demons the Afterlife had seen because of one little fact.

No one knew how or why, but I made shit go boom.

And one by one, they did.

I knew the general direction they'd taken Roxanne. I hoped what little control I had was enough to save her from my wrath. But the rest of them? They could die. I was going to, so it only seemed fair they joined me.

The most excruciating pain I'd ever experienced consumed me, flesh and soul. I felt like my cells were being ripped apart. It was worse than burning, or drowning, or even being beaten to death.

As the werewolf bite from Taylor Dawson infected me with venom meant to change me into a wolf, my soul began to die.

And my magic rose in response.

The control was gone.

Explosions went off left and right.

Shaking the ground. Rattling the stars.

Water rained down on me as I started to lose consciousness.

And that awful music cut out as wherever it was coming from detonated in a shower of flame and ash. Each explosion was bigger. Deeper. It was my soul crying out in a way that my body couldn't because of the drugs they'd pumped into me.

Tears leaked out of the corner of my eyes, mixing with the rain.

This was the end.

Whatever it was that I'd found both here and in the Afterlife was over.

It wasn't the end of the world that saddened me the most in my final moments. I hadn't felt true fear in so long that it took me by surprise. The thing I was most sad about was that I couldn't say goodbye—to Duke, the father figure who'd watched over me for a century. To Roxanne, my first best friend. To Roman, who just wanted to protect me. To Dorian, who would never have the truth he deserved. And to Ezra, who was unexpectedly my greatest confidant.

I hoped they realized I wasn't trying to be the stupid, self-sacrificing hero.

I'd just gotten played.

It could've happened to any of us.

Even the best, the strongest, and the most infallible had a flaw.

Unfortunately for me, my greatest strength and weakness were one and the same.

No matter how hard I tried not to, I cared too much.

And this time, it had gotten me.

CHAPTER 42
ROMAN

I RAN LIKE MY LIFE DEPENDED ON IT.

In a way, it did.

King's Pier was forty-five minutes by car.

Thirty on my motorcycle.

But only ten if I let the wolf out.

I knew the consequences if he was in charge. I knew what was at risk. If we found her dead, if whoever was after her had succeeded, the last bits of sanity would splinter. We'd go feral. Rogue.

So I ran.

Rain poured down, filling my coat with water. It slowed me, but not by much, because I ran without caring who saw me.

My paws ate the distance, a fast and rhythmic sound as they pounded the pavement.

Lights were the first thing my wolf picked up on.

An illuminating blast lit up the sky like a firework show, except the boom that followed rumbled the earth. Explosions rocked the ground the closer I got. Tremors vibrated the streets, shaking anything in its path.

I extended my claws, tearing up gravel in an effort to keep myself grounded despite the quaking pavement and thunderstorm raging around me.

I closed in on the pier.

I burst through the entrance, muscles burning and mind so hyper-focused on getting to my mate that the ground breaking apart beneath me didn't deter me. Not one bit.

I leapt over the ten-foot hole in the pier where churning waters thrashed underneath. The closer I got, the worse the destruction was.

Until I reached her.

Everything in me clenched tight.

My sister, Dorian, and Ezra all knelt around an unmoving body.

I padded up to them, and Roxanne was the only one to lift her head.

My sister's icy blue eyes said it all. "Something's wrong."

I shifted in an instant and went to her side.

Rain poured down on us, dirt and gravel mixing as it sloshed against Fury's pale skin. Her eyes were wide open, but she didn't move.

I would've thought her dead if not for the slight rise and fall of her chest.

"What happened to her?" I demanded, my voice more animal than man.

"She was drugged," Roxanna started. "Then Taylor bit her—"

A thunderous growl built in my chest. I should've killed him when I'd had the chance. I should've—

"She killed him. She killed all of them. The explosions . . ."

"I think she's dying," Ezra said after a moment. "Actually dying. What she is, it's not meant to cross with our kind."

"What the fuck—"

"You know what she is?" Dorian said, lifting his head. He looked like he was already feral. His amber eyes wide. The cat-slitted pupil dilated.

Ezra nodded. "I can't tell you—"

"Tell me how to *fix* her," he growled. It resonated with the wolf.

Ezra lifted his hand to Fury's cheek. Beneath the pale skin, lights were dancing. Her normally black eyes were bright shades of yellow and orange, swirling like the colors under her skin.

"I don't know how," he yelled back. "All I know is she's not from here. Her magic is different. Her body is different. This body should die so she can go to another one, but it was bitten by a wolf and she's dying inside it."

"We could suck the venom out," I said.

"It's too integrated already," Dorian said. "We suck it out and we'll likely kill her in the process, but she may not come back from it."

"She's not coming back from this either," Ezra argued.

"What if all three of you changed her?" Roxanne said softly.

I didn't think it was possible for me to go more still.

"Rox, if this is how she's reacting to a wolf bite from a mid-tiered wolf, I can't imagine she could survive transitioning into a three-way hybrid at once," I said.

"Normally, I'd agree. But there's magic here we don't understand, and you're her *mates*. Some part of her resides in each of you. Use that," Roxanne said, running her hand over a purple-splotched wound on Fury's thigh. "Before it's too late."

"Would it work?" Dorian said, staring straight at Ezra with an intensity that made me fairly certain if it didn't, Ezra might wish he could die.

"I don't know," the vampire said honestly. "I can't reach her, even now. If I could, we wouldn't even be having this discussion."

Dorian clenched his hands into fists. Meanwhile, the lights within Fury were growing brighter, moving under her skin like lightning. The pier shook harder.

"Do you *think* it will?"

Ezra went quiet for a moment. We all stared at her face, hoping for some sort of answer. But she lay as unmoving as before.

"I truly don't know, but we don't have a better idea, and that glowing light beneath her skin looks an awful lot like the explosions that are happening. I think we should try."

"Then we try," Dorian said.

"Wait," I interrupted. "This could kill her instantly—"

"Do you have a better idea, wolf?" Dorian snapped.

"No—"

"And are you prepared to let her die *permanently* because you're too scared to try anything?" Dorian continued.

His accusation stopped me in my tracks.

This whole time I'd been terrified that I wouldn't be able to keep her safe. I hadn't, and now there was a chance that she could die.

I could do nothing. Wait and see. But in all reality, what was happening right now was beyond explanation. It was unlike anything any of us had ever seen. Something was horribly wrong with my mate, and it had been set in motion by Taylor's bite.

And maybe, just maybe, the three of us could save her if we tried.

Or kill her, a small voice in my mind whispered.

I knew enough now to realize that voice was fear, and I couldn't listen to it any longer.

"No," I said solemnly. "I'm not."

"Good," the fae replied. He reached beneath his tux for a chain he kept underneath. He lifted it over his head, revealing a slender vial at the end. "Because I intended to try either way."

He whispered ancient words under his breath that I couldn't make out. The vial glowed. He twisted the top off and then grabbed Fury's jaw to part her lips.

As he dumped the contents into her mouth, Dorian said, "If any of you ever breathe a word of how the fae are made, you'll wish for death by the time I am finished with you."

I lifted Fury's wrist to my lips.

Then I bit her.

Her body jerked once and the lights within her turned brighter. Blinding. It hurt to watch, but I couldn't look away. I wouldn't.

"I hope this works, kitten," Ezra murmured. The vampire sank his fangs into his wrist, pulling and ripping open a gaping wound. The blood flowed heavily. He pressed it to her lips, letting it drip into her mouth. Her heartbeat thundered like a racehorse's hooves. It beat heavily against its cage of blood and muscle and bone.

On a broken and crumbling pier, I sat at my mate's side and prayed this wasn't it. That we weren't making the greatest mistake of our lives.

Ezra cupped her cheeks, and both Dorian and I tensed. My wolf screamed inside, clawing at my mind. I swallowed thickly.

We knew what was coming, but we agreed to do this, we had to let it happen. We had to let her die.

Ezra snapped her neck.

A crack echoed as lightning struck.

Her heart stopped.

The storm continued to rage.

Time went on.

Seconds passed as all four of us held our collective breaths.

"It didn't work," Dorian growled. He stood up and kicked a hole through a building so quickly that I hadn't realized he'd moved until it was too late. "It didn't fucking work!"

My breathing grew ragged. That thin tether of control I held began to fray as my anger and fear and emotion took over.

I'd thought it was just the wolf that wanted her. I still loved Maya. I still missed her . . . but I could have loved Fury. I could have built something with her. I could have done a million things differently. Been less guilt-ridden and less focused on betraying Maya's memory. Less overprotective. Less wishy washy. I could've tried harder. I could have. I could have. I could have—

A single thump stopped me.

I looked at her face. She hadn't blinked, but there, beneath her skin—the light started to fade.

Dorian turned his head to look at her, and Ezra froze.

Her chest rose and fell once.

Then she gasped.

I stared in stunned silence, torn between grabbing her, kissing her, and wringing her neck for dying on me to begin with.

She blinked a couple of times and reached to her face to wipe her eyes. Then she stared at her hands like they belonged to someone else. Another second passed, and she slowly lifted a hand to brush her hair back and feel the now-pointed tip of her ear.

Her eyes, still yellow, went wide.

"You're fae now," Dorian said, standing closer than before.

"And a vampire," Ezra added.

"As well as a shifter," Roxanne said softly, speaking when I couldn't.

Fury dropped her hand. A quiet laugh bubbled up on her lips. She tilted her head back in the rain, and all I could think was that she was the most beautiful, enigmatic creature I'd ever seen.

And I was so fucking lucky that I had a second chance.

"I should've died," she said.

"Technically, you did," Ezra said grimly.

"You don't understand." She shook her head. "What I am . . . what I was . . . we can't become supes. We die whenever someone tries. This shouldn't be possible."

"Neither should having three mates, but here we are," Roxanne said. She hugged Fury tightly, and Fury hugged her back. "You had me worried," my sister continued. When they pulled apart, she punched her in the arm. "And don't you dare ever try to save me again."

Despite the atmosphere, I couldn't help but chuckle. So did Fury when Roxanne shook out her hand.

"Damn, what are you made of now?" She looked her up and down.

Fury did the same. "I don't know. This defies everything I know."

"Speaking of," Dorian interrupted. He crouched down, coming face-to-face with her. "You have some explaining to do."

She sighed. "I suppose me almost dying from being bitten gave it away . . ."

"Who are you? *What* are you?" Dorian asked, recovering rather quickly for a guy who'd been on the edge only moments ago.

"My name is Fury. Just Fury. I'm a demon sent from the Afterlife."

My lips parted, but credit where it was due, Dorian didn't react one bit.

"Why?" Dorian asked.

"Wait, the vampires trying to kill you were telling the truth?" I looked up and narrowed my eyes on Ezra.

He averted his gaze. He'd known about it, and still he'd tried gaslighting me into believing I was a horrible mate for questioning the things they'd told us about her.

I looked back at Fury. "Are you going to end the world?"

She blew out a tight breath.

"No." She shook her head. "You are. I was sent here to stop you."

CHAPTER 43
AN ANGEL

The Isle of Glass was dreary, as always. Cold. Brutal. Though not unpleasant.

Most of the guards had been called away to deal with the search for Sunny, and those who hadn't were now dead. The isle was near empty. But not completely.

There was still one who slept within these halls.

One who'd witnessed divinity and lived.

Deep within the castle on the cliff overlooking the ocean lay a maiden so old she was near ancient. A woman who'd been forced to sleep for over a thousand years. Trapped in a tomb. Imprisoned in her mind.

While many believed her father to be more powerful than all, they were mistaken.

I took the stone steps that circled down several levels. So deep that if the rock were to fail, we'd both be buried down here for eternity. There were no windows. No light.

It would've been utterly silent, if not for the softest sigh of breathing.

I reached the bottom step and entered the chamber.

The floor and ceiling were crafted from the finest marble. Precious gems lost to the world ages ago were inlaid in the walls, framed by gold designs. It was as if he'd tried to cleanse himself of the guilt, adorning her prison with treasures and bestowing on her more riches than one could spend in a lifetime.

In the center of the room was a single stone tomb with a glass lid.

I approached it, taking in the veil of white hair that splayed across the silk pillow. Blonde eyelashes fanned out over her closed eyes. Her skin was unnaturally pallid, not having seen the sun in over a millennium.

I remembered what she'd once looked like, though.

How her light pink lips curled into a smile. How beautifully red had stained her pale skin, and how the angels who looked down had wondered if it would ever lose its taint.

She was a sleeping beast.

A monster.

She was the daughter of the man I wished to punish for touching what was mine. For saving what was mine.

He had no right to take her from me.

Now I was going to take something in return.

My hands touched the cool glass, and I pushed it off the tomb in a single motion. It hit the floor, shattering like a thousand crystals as the sound broke through the silence and reverberated off the stone walls.

"Lyra," I said, speaking in her mother tongue. "It's time to wake up."

White Raven

To my husband
For reminding me I'm a motherfucking shark. Or a honey badger, depending on the day. –AJ

To Matt
For keeping me sane and healthy. –KC

I don't care about whose DNA has recombined with whose. When everything goes to hell, the people who stand by you without flinching—they are your family.

Jim Butcher, *Proven Guilty, The Dresden Files*

Hades

Didn't expect me, did you?

Well, I'm here for a recap. If you remember what happened, you can move right along. But for those of you that have a shit memory or have just slept since you last saw Fury, this summary is for you.

We start in the Afterlife. It's like it says. It's where you go after your life ends. Your concept of Heaven and Hell? Not a thing. Anyway, Fury is a demon. She reforms bad souls before they get recycled for life again, or just get flat out terminated because they suck too much. Well, she got sent to Earth because she's supposedly good at her job. (I'm not sure about this, but Duke—he runs the Department of Earth Affairs—says she's the best. Upper Management says she's the best. I have some reservations, but I'm just working here.) So, she's sent to stop the end of the world. It's been foreseen that the apocalypse will be brought on by three ultra-powerful supernaturals. Dorian—he's the broody fae, Roman—he's the overprotective and grieving wolf shifter, Ezra—he's the mouthy vampire with an appalling sexual appetite. (No, I didn't mean appealing. I'm not Fury.) These dudes can't die—at least they haven't yet.

In case you need this pointed out, the apocalypse is bad. It's the end of *all* things, the Afterlife included.

Bang, crash, burn, fire, explosion, implosion. Darkness. The end.

Bad. Clear? Okay, moving on.

Stopping them should be an easy task for someone who's "good" at her job, right? Of course not. Because somehow Fury is mated to all three of these guys. That's unheard of. And she's somehow a second-chance mate to all three as well.

It's irritating because I'm stuck as her go-between for the Afterlife and her job on Earth. She can't die—demon, remember?—but the only way for her to go back to the Afterlife is for her vessel to die, dumping her soul right back into Duke's office. It's pretty funny to watch. But the bodies she leaves behind can become a problem. That's where I come in. The go-between. *Not* a pigeon, despite what she tells you. Apparently I'm the go-between here too.

So, she meets all three of these dudes. Lucky for me, she only has a sexfest with one of them. But someone is trying to kill her. They succeed once, killing a vessel. The next time she just suffers injuries. The problem? The assassins have called her Sunny Adams.

Who is Sunny Adams?

That was Fury when she was alive. A twenty-three-year-old girl in the roaring twenties that died at the hands of her abusive husband when he beat her to death.

It's been one hundred and three years since her dickhead husband killed her. So, what the fuck, right? Yeah, we're still trying to figure it out too. Since then, she's been working as a demon. She also drinks to the point of absurdity, and it hasn't gone unnoticed by anyone except her.

Now, add in that Fury has befriended Roxanne. She is Roman's sister. Roxanne gets kidnapped. Wolfnapped? Whatever. It was the kickoff night at the summit—a once every ten years gathering of the fae, shifter, and vampire factions. First night was a fancy banquet. Dinner, dancing, etc. Could that be uneventful? Of course not. This is Fury we're talking about. So that night, Roxanne gets taken by some rogue shifters that Roman pissed off after, well, after branding them rogues. Literally. No, really. He branded it right there on the guy's forehead.

Right. So Fury goes to save Roxanne. Surprise! It's not just shifters. There are some fae and vampires in this group of rogue assassins. Why? Beats me. But they're there. They subdue Fury with some *really* good drugs, stick her on a creepy carousel with creepy clown music, and then cryptically say they know how to kill-kill her. Stop her from existing. Make her for real dead. How? The shifter bites her. See, demons can't be "changed" into supernaturals. The magic from the Afterlife and the supernatural world can't be mixed. The two forms of magic violently collide. In her dying state, she finally exploded in power, killing each and every one of those that hadn't sifted or run far enough away.

Yours truly leads Dorian, Ezra, and Roman to her location. You're fucking welcome. How did they save her? Well, the shifter bit her, the vampire shared his blood with her, and the fae did a thing that's a secret and we don't talk about. Three different supernatural species, each her mate, tying themselves to her indefinitely to save her life—or death. It's complicated when I word it that way. She didn't die-die. But she's changed now, and only because they were, in fact, her mates. Ta-da!

Now you're all caught up.

Oh, and there was some mention of an angel that told the rogue supernaturals how to actually kill Fury's soul and then that angel woke up Lyra in a crypt below Avalon where Dorian lives and Lyra is his daughter that he had to force into stasis because she went crazy and she is fucking dangerous.

And now we're here.

Carry on.

CHAPTER 1
FURY

My feet pounded against the ground, sending shots of pain reverberating through my legs. Heart pumping, I sucked in short breaths to keep pushing forward. Another cluster of leaves smacked me in the face as I ran through the trees, cutting my cheek, but I didn't stop. I couldn't.

Roxanne's screams guided me. I had to find her.

Fire raged in the forest surrounding Roman's lake house. *Where the hell was he?*

I turned my head in the direction of another scream as more panicked howls pierced the air.

"Rox! I'm coming!" I called, running once more, pushing myself harder.

I looked around frantically for Roman. Ezra. Dorian. Anyone. Ezra wasn't answering me when I reached out to him mentally. What was happening here?

A malicious cackling in the forest diverted my attention. It echoed, as though it were bouncing off the trees. Seeing the clearing ahead, I pushed myself faster. I had to find them. All of them. I had to save them from this.

Crossing the forest threshold to the lakeshore, I came to an abrupt halt. I couldn't believe my eyes. The lake was no more. The earth had split open, the water drained into the gaping crevice it created. A cliff rose from the once level earth. An eerie orange glow flickered against the rocky sides and suffocating heat rose from the caverns.

I turned my head, searching for Roxanne, but I couldn't get my voice to work when I tried to call her name, choking on the thick, smoky air, coughing and sputtering. That's when I saw them.

Bodies.

Hundreds of them. Thousands. Shifted. Partially shifted. Still in human form. Large. Small. I walked toward them slowly, catching a glimpse of a body with dreadlocks.

The bile rose in my throat, and I couldn't stop it. I fell to my knees, emptying the contents of my stomach as I held myself up on all fours.

"Fury, help me!"

I snapped my head up, searching for Roxanne. She cried out again, and I ran to the edge of the former lake. Holding onto a root, she hung over the side, the river of lava below her mocking her mortality.

I dropped to the ground, reaching out. Tears streamed down her cheeks, carving a path through the blood and ash caked on her face.

"Grab my hand," I told her. "I'll pull you up. I've got you."

She shook her head. "I can't let go."

"You can," I shouted. "You have to. I won't lose you, Rox. I *will* pull you out. You have to trust me. Please, Rox . . . "

She pressed her lips together and nodded. She swung an arm up and I caught it, starting to pull her up as an earth-shattering scream pierced the sky.

A dragon swooped down, raining fire on the already ravaged forest.

"Roxanne, climb *now*," I urged, grunting as I pulled her up. Her foot found purchase briefly before she slipped, but I didn't let go as her body slammed against the side.

She looked at me with wide eyes, the tears spilling out. "She's here," she whispered. "This is your fault . . ."

I faltered. "No, it's not, I swear."

"See what you've done," she said. "*Look*."

I choked on a sob as I shook my head.

That same awful laugh echoed, and I saw a petite figure in a white cloak standing on the cliff; long strands of white hair escaped and danced on the wind. Dorian was next to her, resting on his knees. A sword was pressed to his throat, a thin line of red already shining beneath the blade.

"You can't save us," Roxanne said, slipping from my grip.

"No," I grunted, refusing to let her go.

"Sift," Dorian shouted as the woman beside him cackled.

"I can't," I yelled back to him. "I don't know how!" I met his gaze and held it, watching his amber eyes glow with power.

"SIFT," he bellowed before the blade sliced across his throat.

I screamed, the anger and the fear burning inside me, bubbling up in furious rage as explosions detonated beneath my skin.

I looked down to Roxanne, begging her to not let go as her hand slid another fraction through mine. I mentally called for Ezra, pleading for his help.

As she slipped through my fingers, and I cried out to her, Hades flew toward me as though he would crash into my face if he didn't veer away.

"Tick tock."

~

I GASPED.

Then I fell.

My body hit something soft before bouncing. My stomach roiled violently, and I sat up, only intensifying the sudden dizziness. Blinking rapidly, I looked at my surroundings.

No fire. No smoke. The air was cool. The fabric touching my skin was soft. My eyes adjusted to the faint glow in the room.

"Nice of you to drop in," Ezra said sleepily. He lay on his bed next to me, the black sheets pulled up only to mid-torso, his bare chest and tattoos on full display.

I scrambled out of his bed, my body covered in sweat and my breathing ragged.

"What the fuck just happened?" I asked. "I was . . . I was at Roman's. I was . . . dreaming." I let it sink in, thinking about the series of events in my nightmare.

It wasn't real. That meant Roxanne was okay. And Dorian . . . Roman . . . they weren't dead.

A loud pecking on Ezra's window pulled me from my thoughts. I rushed over, pushed the heavy drapes aside, and opened it up to let Hades fly in. Early morning light filtered into the room as downtown Houston began to wake up.

"Now you've done it," he said, landing on a chair. "Every shifter in a fifty-mile radius of Roman's is looking for you."

I sighed. "Not now, asshole. I'm trying to figure some things out."

"Like how you ended up here?"

"Wait." I glared at him. "How did *you* know I was here?"

He fluffed his feathers in his version of a bird shrug. "I know a lot of things. If you were nicer to me, I'd probably tell you. Alas . . ."

Ezra chuckled, sitting up and swinging his legs over the bed. He picked up his cell phone. "Incoming," he said. A second later it rang, and he pressed to answer it. "She's fine. She's here," he said.

I could hear commotion and yelling in the background before Roman's voice filtered through. "How?"

"Pretty sure she sifted. Call the fae if you haven't already. This is his area of expertise. We'll head your way shortly." He ended the call and stood up, the sheets falling to the side. He looked at me as he said, "So much for rest before the interrogation."

My eyes raked his naked body, and he winked at me as he walked to his closet. A small laugh escaped me. Only Ezra would be so calm about me unexpectedly dropping out of thin air and into his bed.

"Keep it in your pants," Hades said.

"Ugh, go away." I frowned at him, and he narrowed his little eyes at me. "No one said anything about sex."

"I saw the look on your face," he said. "And he's over there swinging it around—"

"Enough," I said. "Don't you have something else you should be doing right now?"

"Not really, no."

"I find that hard to believe."

"I found you. That was what I needed to do."

"Lucky me," I said. I threw my arm out and pointed toward the window, away from the building. "Go talk to Duke. I need answers."

He narrowed his little bird eyes at me. “I don’t answer to you, you realize that, right?”

“You do, actually. You’re the go-between, right? So *go*. I can’t exactly go myself right now, and you know damn well we *both* need answers. If you’re going to be up in my face telling me to do my job, go do yours. Find me when you know something.” I couldn’t have suppressed the venom in my voice if I wanted to. Which I didn’t. I’d just had the nightmare of all nightmares, which ended with his stupid ‘tick tock’ bullshit in my face, and then somehow sifted while sleeping.

“You also broke windows and started a small fire before disappearing from Roman’s house,” Ezra said, clearly having listened in on my thoughts.

My mouth gaped open. “I what?”

Hades snickered in his birdy way. Flapping his wings, he took off without another word.

Ezra came out of the closet dressed in jeans and a black T-shirt. Handing me some clothes, he said, “While I think the underwear and tank top are adorably sexy, you’ll want to change.”

I took the shorts and shirt from him. “Wait, you said I—”

“You did. Get dressed. Dorian has a lot of questions for you, but this just got more complicated.”

CHAPTER 2
FURY

I FELT THE INTENSITY WHEN HUNDREDS OF PAIRS OF EYES FOCUSED ON ME AS I walked up the steps to the porch in some weird version of a walk of shame. Every shifter in the pack must have been jolted awake by Roman's frantic demands to find me, and here I was. Just fine.

Roman and Dorian stood at the open door, side by side.

"Fancy seeing you here," I said, trying to break the tension.

Ezra snickered behind me, but not a damn thing from Roman or Dorian.

"Tough crowd," I huffed as I walked in between them and into the open living room. I took a seat on the couch, pulling my feet up to tuck them under my legs.

As the guys followed in, they silently sat down and watched me.

I looked around at them, but no one spoke. Ezra seemed bored. Roman appeared conflicted. Dorian was standing by the window overlooking the lake, seeming pissed as always.

I sighed. "Okay, I guess we can keep playing the quiet game, or one of us can talk. I'll be the bigger person here and go first," I said. "I have no idea what happened this morning. I'm really sorry to have scared everyone, and I didn't mean for everyone out there to spend their time looking for me. Don't know what else to say."

"No one is pissed at you for that," Roman said, taking a seat in a high-back chair.

Roxanne's voice carried from the kitchen. "Speak for yourself, Roman. My favorite comforter was in flames."

"Okay, Roxanne might be pissed at you for burning the bed, but that's not what this is about," he said.

"But it does complicate things," Ezra interjected.

I snorted. "That's an understatement."

Dorian turned around, crossing his arms and resting his shoulder against the glass of the window. "As far as we can tell, you sifted this morning. Have you noticed any other. . . changes?" he asked, leveling me with his signature stare of cool detachment and utter arrogance.

"Other than the slightly pointed ears and permanently yellow eyes?" I deadpanned.

"Yes, other than that," he answered, unflappable despite the undercurrent of annoyance I sensed.

"It's only been, like, what, ten hours?" I shrugged, leaning back. "I can see farther. My canines are a little longer, but I'm not feeling a craving for blood if that's what you're getting at."

"Noted," Dorian said. "But your vampirism isn't the only change you've undergone. You're now a shifter as well. Have you sensed your wolf yet?"

"No."

"Hm." He narrowed his eyes.

"We're still two weeks from the full moon. Not sensing anything right away is normal. The closer we get, the more her wolf will try to surface. She should stay with the pack as much as possible," Roman said. "In case the shift is triggered early for some reason."

"Wait, does that happen sometimes? It just comes out of nowhere?" I asked.

"Fine," Dorian agreed, completely ignoring me.

"As long as sleepovers are allowed." Ezra flashed a cocky smirk. I rolled my eyes. "She is a vampire too, after all. When the time comes, I'll be the one to guide her through it."

Despite his easygoing demeanor, the possessive tone sent a bolt of heat through me. I wanted to shift my weight, feeling my body's aching response between my legs. I tried to ignore it, and I hoped for the love of all that was dead, they'd do the same.

Ezra winked, his psychic hands grazing the inside of my thighs with devious intent. I stiffened, flashing him a glare.

"If you're done with trying to impress her with your *boyish* antics, we can move on," Dorian interrupted. Was that a hint of . . . jealousy?

The corner of my mouth curled upward.

"Just because I'm not old as dirt doesn't mean I don't know my way around the female body, Dorian," Ezra replied without missing a beat. "Or Fury's, for that matter."

"As fun as this is, the summit is starting in two hours, and there are a lot of things we still need to discuss, so if you can both stop swinging your dicks around and save the insults for later, it would be appreciated," Roxanne said pointedly before taking a seat on the arm of Roman's chair.

"Right." I nodded to her, happy to be moving away from the subject of me breaking my own rules and fucking Ezra . . . again. "You said you had questions. Where do you want to start?"

"Why were you sent here?" Dorian asked, point-blank.

"I told you—"

"No," he interrupted. "Why were *you* sent here?"

I sighed, leaning back into the couch and resting my elbow on the arm, propping my chin in my hand.

"There's a group in the Afterlife that I call the risk witches," I started. "They're not really witches. More like the fates from Greek mythology." Namely, speaking in riddles and enjoying the power trip that comes with making everyone in the Afterlife do what they want. "They're basically fortune tellers that predict catastrophic events on Earth, and then they tell the powers that be to go fix it before it comes to pass. Beyond the usual doom and gloom, they predicted you guys would end the world. Like end it for good. And the angels couldn't stop it—"

"The angels?" Roxanne asked.

The question was there on each of their faces, all except Ezra.

"My divine counterpart that deals with things here," I said. "Contrary to legends, demons don't actually come earthside, or at least they didn't . . ." I trailed off. "Until now."

"What exactly do the angels do?" Dorian asked. He walked away from the window, coming to sit in a chair near the rest of us. He sat back, crossing his legs, his amber eyes narrowed in speculation.

"Same thing I do in Hell," I replied, taking a deep breath. "They fix things. Demons have a longer time frame to work with. Angels work quickly. Their brand of fixing is supposed to be more of the do-gooder variety, but not always." As the words came out, the latter part was spoken quieter than I intended. What I suspected, it was grim. The conversation was treading into dangerous waters, and I was acutely aware of the growing tension in the room.

"How did the angels try to *fix* this 'prediction'?" Roman growled. I swallowed hard, taking in his taut biceps straining against his T-shirt. His eyes were flickering between brown and blue.

"I *believe* they tried to kill you," I said quietly. "Indirectly or not. That's usually how they *fix* this sort of situation."

"My mate . . ." Roman interjected.

I wanted to look away from him, but I didn't as I said, "I'm so sorry."

I meant it, even though it wasn't my fault. Roman's eyes turned wholly blue, and he stormed out of the room. The door slammed behind him. Roxanne got to her feet, giving me a sad smile before following after. I sighed.

"You believe they killed his mate?" Dorian continued without missing a beat.

I pursed my lips and nodded slowly. "The more I've thought about it, I think they killed all your mates."

The silence was deafening. I almost missed that pigeon's incessant blabbing. Just something—anything—to lift the heaviness away from the conversation.

Other than the slight stiffening in his shoulders, Dorian didn't let on how the information affected him. "Let me make sure I have this straight. The 'angels' have been trying to kill us, and when that failed, they killed our mates, all to end some prophecy that suggested we'd end the world?"

I shifted my weight, sitting cross-legged on the couch. I clasped my hands together and cleared my throat. "Correct."

"What did our mates have to do with this?"

I shook my head and took a deep breath. "I don't know the answer to that. This is what I have pieced together as I've learned more about you three." I huffed, thinking about how little I still knew.

"So I'll say it again. Why were *you* sent here?" He repeated his earlier question with more ferocity.

"You all lived. They failed," I said simply.

I could recognize where his line of questioning was coming from. How did I, someone who happened to be their mate, end up involved in this? After all, I was a demon. By my own admission, we didn't come to Earth.

But here I was.

Not far-off in the distance, I heard things breaking. Wood being ripped apart. Pained growls and angry roars, coupled with soft words as Roxanne tried to coax him down.

It occurred to me that I'd never been able to hear this easily. Advanced senses were not a perk of being a demon—we didn't need it—but it was for fae, vampires, and shifters. The thought made me shift uncomfortably because the current predicament I found myself in made my reasons for being here infinitely more complicated.

Dorian's eyebrows furrowed. "I am rapidly losing my patience with you. You have not answered the question."

"I know what you are getting at." I narrowed my eyes at him. "Despite our bad rap on Earth, a demon's job is to fix people, Dorian. Bad people. Most of my guild has forgotten that over time and a good portion of them prefer to punish blindly. I don't." I shook my head, thinking of Karen the Horrible. "I've dedicated my afterlife to actually rehabilitating the fucked-up people I get assigned. Souls get recycled and sent back. It's up to my guild to send them back so they are better when they live on Earth. My cases have the lowest recidivism rate and I have the best track record they've seen in a very long time. Simply put, I am the best at my job. That's why they sent me—to see if I could succeed where the angels failed."

"Not because you're our mate?" Dorian prodded.

"I don't know," I said honestly, shrugging. "They didn't tell me that. They didn't tell me a lot of shit," I grumbled.

"Upper Management didn't brief her properly before she came

down here," Ezra said from his seat, finally choosing to back me up. "She was as surprised as we were to find out we are all mated."

The front door slammed once more, and a booming voice followed it. "You knew about this?" Roman roared.

Rounding the corner, he didn't seem anymore under control than when he'd left. Eyes flickering again between brown and blue, he glared at Ezra with deadly intent.

"Yes, I knew," Ezra replied, meeting his stare. "I was trying to help her."

"That's a bit of a stretch," I said under my breath.

"I didn't tell them why you were here, did I?" he retorted.

I rolled my eyes.

"Your kind killed my mate," Roman yelled, turning to me. Emotional turmoil was eating at him. "Killed my child." My heart hurt for him. It did. But there was a fundamental problem here that I couldn't let go unaddressed.

"No," I said softly. "Angels did." He narrowed his eyes. "I'm a demon. My kind have never been to Earth. You can be pissed at them. I'm angry about it on your behalf. For all of you." I motioned to the three men gathered around me. "If they actually did it . . ." I shook my head. "There are bad eggs in every department. I am truly sorry they killed them. I am. But don't blame me for this. I would never do that."

"Not even to save the world?" Dorian asked darkly; emotionless as he was persistent in his questioning.

"No. I can't—" My hands tightened as I kept them clasped. I straightened in my seat. "There are some lines I will not cross. Children are one of them." I hesitated to say the next part. To give them a piece of truth, of vulnerability, that could very well come back to bite me. I needed them, especially Roman, to understand that this wasn't me or even my kind. That I wasn't lying to them. There was more at play here, and them doubting me now, when the situation was already so far beyond fucked, it just wouldn't do. "I—I know what it's like to lose a child. I would *not* do that to someone."

Roman looked away, a sliver of guilt coloring his expression. Ezra's eyebrows raised slightly as he read my thoughts, learning that new bit of information.

"What is your assignment now?" Dorian asked, leaning forward in his chair.

I took a deep breath and exhaled, trying to ground myself. "The same as it's been since I got here." I shrugged. "Fix you three. Stop the end of the world." The job was supposed to be simple. Then again, maybe it might've been if the stupid poltergeists had done their part and gathered information that would have been useful.

"And how's that going for you?"

"Poorly," I deadpanned. Leaning forward, I put my elbows on my knees. The position brought me and the moody fae bastard eye to eye with only a coffee table in between us. "Seeing as you all know why I'm here, I couldn't imagine how it could get worse. Oh wait, except I'm now changed into some demon-fae-shifter-vamp hybrid thing"—I motioned to myself—"and no closer to figuring out what it is that sets you three off to make everything go *boom*."

His eyebrow twitched. "Interesting choice of words given your ability to make everything go 'boom'."

I shrugged.

"Is that a demon ability?" he continued.

"No," I said. "It's a Fury one."

He hummed in response, pursing his lips slightly. "Speaking of Fury—that's an interesting name. I can only assume it wasn't given to you as a human."

I stared at him, showing fire and steel in my gaze. "It's the name I chose."

"Sunny Adams—" he said, eliciting a growl from me.

"*Is dead,*" I snapped. "You'd do well not to talk about things you don't understand."

His features softened ever-so-slightly. "I'm trying to understand."

"You're trying to pry," I corrected, raising my voice. "There's a difference. I've told you about why I'm here. Why I was chosen. But who I was before all of this—that's my past and I want to keep it that way."

Dorian sighed in frustration. "What if it has something to do with—"

"It doesn't," I said firmly.

"It might," he replied through gritted teeth. "Whoever wanted you dead referred to you as Sunny Adams. That's not an accident."

"And I'm not discussing this," I replied, leaning back and crossing my arms. I needed space from him. From this. From the constant push and pull I felt when I was around him.

Dorian opened his mouth, probably to argue some more, when Ezra interjected. "I wouldn't push it right now if I were you. We have plenty of other issues to focus on for the moment. I think Fury can keep her privacy a little longer."

"Easy to say when you can read her mind," Roman replied, still bitter about that turn of events.

"Yes," Ezra said haughtily. "It means I know when our mate is at her end. Contrary to what you both like to believe, she has a limit, just like us. Who knows what the fae prick is hiding? And you get all pissed off anytime you talk about your mate—"

"Careful with your words," Roman growled. "This is still pack grounds."

"Easy boy. My point is, she is entitled to some secrets."

"When those secrets put her life at stake—"

I was done in. The cold laugh that bubbled in my throat wouldn't be denied. I tilted my head back to let it out. "I need a drink," I said through the chortles.

"What's so funny?" Roman frowned. Ezra sighed.

"This." I motioned to them. "You all. I'm one hundred percent in danger of actually dying because you lot changed me. Something I shouldn't have survived to begin with, mind you." I twisted a lock of my deep red hair, watching it move from near-black to the color of flame depending on where the light caught it. "That's why Taylor Dawson bit me. Whoever wants me dead knew the only surefire way to extinguish me was to try to change me—because the Afterlife and the supernatural don't mix. Our magic is fundamentally incompatible. It's the reason supernaturals that die don't cross over. You know what that means?" I stood and walked over to the liquor cabinet. I plucked a bottle with green liquid from the shelf and read the label. Not recognizing it, I shrugged and took a swig.

I made a face, setting the bottle back. The taste was fruity.

"Odds are if I die now, I'll probably stay dead. No Afterlife for me,"

I finished. Searching for a bottle of something I recognized, I muttered to myself, "Dead, dead, dead."

Retirement was now a fleeting memory. One I was still coming to grips with. That was easier to take than the rest of it, though. No Afterlife meant no Duke. No jesting with Jake. No strays from the rainbow bridge. Everything I'd known and worked so hard for over the last hundred years was gone . . . unless I somehow found a way back.

"Looks like you get to be all alpha protective over me, after all, Roman," I said, holding up a bottle in cheers and then drinking from it. I winced at the burn as the tequila went down.

Roxanne grimaced at me. "Don't be a dick, Fury. This isn't easy for any of us. I don't know what you are going through and that's fine. If you aren't ready to share that with us, you don't have to. But with the exception of Ezra," she shot him a glare, "this is news to us, and it's not exactly the kind of news you want to hear. It's a hard pill to swallow, okay?"

I softened. She managed to bring out the best in me. She was like Duke in that sense. Logical. Kind. Genuinely caring. I set the bottle down and sighed. "I know," I whispered. "Believe me, I know." I looked at her, meeting her glassy-eyed gaze.

She blinked a few times, pushing back the tears that threatened to fall. Clearing her throat, she said, "Okay, then. Let's move on. We know more now and got some questions answered, right?" She looked at Dorian and he took a moment, but finally dipped his head in agreement. "Good. First things first. You're a super hybrid . . . ish. I don't know what to call it. Do we know anything about that?"

Dorian shook his head. "Two specie hybrids aren't uncommon. We all know that. But not even the fae knew demons or the Afterlife existed until now."

"The scrolls?" Roman suggested.

"I can search, of course. Even if I find something, it certainly wouldn't include a three-way hybrid with a demon. But it's worth a look to see if any multi-hybrids have ever existed."

"Rava has extensive knowledge of two-way hybrids, and I can send shifters with you if you need help researching—"

"That won't be necessary," Dorian said quickly. "If I find anything,

I have no qualms about sharing it with you. I'll bring everything we have to Rava. It would benefit all of us to be informed." He shot a glare at Ezra, who raised a single shoulder in response.

Roxanne frowned. "Fury, if you're a hybrid, that has to give you some level of protection. Fae, shifter, and vampire are the three strongest factions in the supernatural world. On Earth, I mean. And if you have any demon left in you, maybe you aren't as easy to kill as we think."

I took another drink from the bottle, wiping off my lips after I swallowed. "We can try—"

"We are not going to try to kill you," Roman said. Ezra laughed.

I rolled my eyes. "Don't be so dramatic. I'm not suggesting you shoot me. I was going to suggest starting small. We cut my arm and see if it heals."

A buzz on Roxanne's phone interrupted us. She looked down and grunted. "Rava said they're arriving at the summit."

Hades' annoying 'tick tock' seemed appropriate right about now.

I walked back to the couch, setting the bottle down and taking a seat. I opened my mouth to say something but was cut off when Ezra moved faster than I expected, using a long nail to slice my arm.

"Motherfucker!" I yelled, grabbing the bleeding wound, and pulling away from him. Roman flew out of his chair, and Roxanne slammed her hands on his chest, showing more strength than I knew she had. "What the hell was that for? I wasn't ready, you prick."

"If someone comes for you, you won't be ready then either. Need to test this both ways. You expecting to be injured, and also not. We don't know what your powers are. Maybe you heal differently when you expect it. Maybe you have a way to shield yourself. Best to find out," he said, sitting back in his chair.

"Asshole," I muttered.

Dorian pulled a handkerchief from his pocket, leaned forward, and extended it to me.

"Thanks." I took it, pressing it to my arm.

Ezra picked at some lint on his pants, then looked up. "As Fury said, someone knew how to make her death happen. What do we know about Taylor?"

Roman shook his head. "He wasn't the mastermind. He was too

low-level. And stupid. Someone else found him and used him. He never would've known to call her Sun—" Roxanne elbowed him, "—by a different name."

"Exactly," Ezra said. "So whoever is trying to kill her knows they didn't succeed. Again. That's what, three attempts? They all failed. Best to assume they're going to try again, and that this time, she'll die."

"We can't postpone the summit," Roxanne said, frustrated. She looked at me with apologetic eyes. "It's bigger than us. Putting it aside could cause an all-out war between the factions—"

"I'm not offended, Rox. I wouldn't suggest postponing the summit," I said, peeking under the cloth to check the cut on my arm. The burning sensation was still there, but it was starting to heal. That was good news. I held it up for them to see. "Hey, look."

All eyes turned on me, inspecting the handiwork. "That's a good start," Roman said.

Ezra pulled out a small pocketknife. Nothing huge, maybe three inches long. As he approached me, he said, "Do you want to do it, or do you want me to?"

I scrunched my face in disgust. "I don't really like pain, so inflicting it on myself isn't going to go well."

"Suit yourself," he said. "Hold out your other arm."

I groaned, extending it as he requested. Turning my head so I didn't have to watch, I felt him grip under my armpit, then press the blade to the upper muscle. He sliced quickly, and I hissed in pain.

"Calm down, it's superficial," he said quietly, pressing a towel to the wound.

"Tool," I mumbled. I didn't even have much of a reason to be mad. This was my idea. It was a theory that needed to be tested, but knife wounds burned like there was no tomorrow.

I sat there grumbling to myself when Dorian stood up, walking to the window again, staring out at the lake. "There's some healing ability, and that's good to note. Until we know more, she'll need around-the-clock protection."

"This again? I don't need a babysitter, Dorian."

"Clearly you do," he snapped. "Last night, you snuck out of the hotel, damn near got yourself killed—"

"To save Roxanne, you condescending donkey." I stood up as I shouted, throwing my hands out. "Would you rather I had let them kill her? Are you seriously going to chastise me for *saving* her? What the hell is wrong with you? I had one person in my human life—*one*—that gave a shit about me. I am thankful every day that she lived a short, beautiful life before she died. She was that small percentage that moved on to a peaceful resting place. If Roxanne died, she doesn't get the Afterlife. None of you do. Do you get that? Supernaturals don't pass go. They don't collect two-hundred dollars. They just. Fucking. Cease. Existing."

Dorian tried to speak over me, likely answering my rhetorical question, but I didn't let him get a word in edgewise.

"There was absolutely no way I was going to let Roxanne die because of me, so before you go treating me like a child, I knew exactly what my choices were, and I had no problem making the one I did, and I would do it again. Don't stand over there judging me for it, acting as if I'm stupid and can't take care of myself. I'm not as selfish as you think I am, and despite whatever you think of me right now—"

"I'm sorry," Dorian said, cutting me off.

"Don't interrup—wait, what?"

Completely caught off guard in my tangent, I stopped yelling and didn't move. Dorian walked over and stood calmly in front of me. He tilted his head down, lowering his eyes, then looked back up to meet my gaze. "I said I'm sorry. Truly. You're right. Despite all, I know what it's like to have few that care for you, and to have few that you, yourself, care for." He looked over at Roxanne, who had tears running down her face, then back to me. "I am grateful you saved Roxanne. She is very special to me, and of course to Roman. Our lives wouldn't be the same without her. So, thank you."

"I, uh . . . you're welcome." It was all I could manage. I had no idea what else to say.

Dorian took a step back. "With that said, and with all due respect, it is still in your best interest—and ours—that you have one of us with you. For your protection, and for Roxanne's. They used her to get to you once. They won't hesitate to do it again."

I grumbled, wishing I had more time to relish in his apology. Every now and then he'd break through his cold demeanor and show some humanity. Or whatever the equivalent word would be for a fae. More than anything, I hated that he was right too.

Ezra chuckled.

"What's so funny?" Dorian asked him.

"She doesn't disagree with you, much to her chagrin," he answered.

I glared daggers at him. "Rude, much?"

He shrugged.

Anger roiled through me. I just wanted five minutes to think by myself. Was that so much to ask? I checked my upper arm, seeing the cut had healed. It still hurt, though. Of course it would. I couldn't get lucky enough to not feel the pain.

"It doesn't change the fact that I feel imprisoned when someone is watching me and I can't even go to the bathroom without an escort," I said, returning to the conversation. I wouldn't live like that. We had to come to some sort of an agreement. One where I had a choice in the matter.

"You're healing against these minor injuries, but that's not enough for us to go on, Fury. We need to know more, but at this moment, there isn't much time to test further," Dorian argued.

"She knows that," Ezra said. "She's also still feeling the residual pain even though she's healed."

I swear I could feel flames on the side of my face. My nostrils flared as I breathed deeply and looked at Ezra. "Stop. Doing. That."

"You aren't being honest right now," he said.

"It's not your place to speak for me," I seethed. "No one asked me what I was feeling. I didn't volunteer to give a play-by-play report. Being cut hurts. I'm healing. The end. If this is what it's going to be like, I'm putting my foot down and I'm not going to the summit. I'm not agreeing to any of this. I will walk out that very large door over there and there is nothing you can do to stop me."

A cacophony of loud voices filled the room. Frustration, anger, outrage—welcome to the club, boys. They yelled over each other, arguing with me that I wasn't being reasonable, and that I wasn't making this easy, and blah blah blah. I grabbed the bottle of tequila and walked away while they went on. I tipped it back, taking a big mouthful before swallowing.

This was too overwhelming.

"Stop," I said loudly, feeling a little twinge pound in my head.

Silence. They stared at me, waiting. I inhaled deeply, counting to ten. Don't stab. Stabbing won't help. Breathe out. Count to ten. They mean well. They're just acting stupid, I reminded myself. But some things would need to change.

"I want you out of my head, Ezra."

"I . . . can't do that," he admitted, and his eyes hardened.

Don't do this, he said mentally. *Don't ask this of me.*

I glared at him in our private conversation. *I'm not asking you. I am telling you. Unless I invite you in, get out. I need space. Privacy. You told them I needed it. It's true. But I also need it from you. It's hard enough to wrap my head around what's going on without feeling safe to think.*

He sighed, closing his eyes. To everyone else, we were having a standoff. Maybe it looked like he was giving up, but he opened them, pleading with me. *I can't turn it off. You're my mate. From a distance, it's more manageable, but since we met, the connection is increasingly stronger. When I'm near you, I can't stop. I always hear you in the back of my mind, even if it's only a whisper. I'm sorry. I don't want you to feel unsafe around me.*

I sighed. *It's not* that *kind of unsafe. It's just . . . I don't know.* I growled in frustration, wishing I could just feel a measure of peace.

I can give you that.

I huffed, knowing he heard my thoughts. He gave me an apologetic look. I gestured for him to go on, seeing Roxanne and Roman look around the room pointlessly in awkward silence. Dorian surprisingly gave us space, having walked back to that window he liked to look out of.

I can give you a measure of peace.

How?

I may not be able to stop hearing your thoughts, but I can stop reacting as I do. I won't speak for you. I won't let you know I'm listening. An ignorance-is-bliss sort of thing. If you don't feel that I'm listening, perhaps that will give you the measure of peace you're looking for. When you invite me in, so to speak, then I'll make my presence known. Within reason. Emergencies don't count.

Deal. I pursed my lips and nodded my head a few times. It was better than nothing. A phantom hand cupped my cheek, a finger grazing my skin affectionately. He smiled, but it didn't reach his eyes.

Ezra cleared his throat, speaking out loud. "I think it's best we figure out who she needs to be with first. We'll all be at the summit intermittently, so we can all escort her during panels."

Dorian's phone buzzed. He reached into the breast pocket and pulled out the device, looking at it with furrowed brows. "To Roman's point earlier, you should stay here to start. We can change things as we go, if needed, but the full moon is in two weeks' time. No matter what, you have to prepare for that, and there is no place safer for it."

Roxanne looked at the time. "We have to get ready, guys. We're pushing it as is."

"I'll meet you there. I have some things to take care of in Avalon," Dorian said. His cold eyes met mine, softening for a fraction of a second before any hint of emotion had escaped. He sifted, disappearing from the living room without any further discussion.

Roman looked pained as he struggled through everything that had just happened. He pinched the bridge of his nose. "Okay. We've got twenty minutes to get ready. Let's move."

Ezra took the bottle I had and silently raised it, putting the rim to his lips, and tilting it back.

My soul felt like it was being crushed. My heart felt like it was being tugged in three different directions. I'd hurt Roman and Roxanne with the truth of their loss. I'd pushed Ezra away, demanding his role as my confidant be silenced. I couldn't read Dorian's emotions, and that bothered me more than I cared to admit.

I wished I could talk to Duke about all of it. My breath caught in my throat, feeling the shattering ache all over again as I thought about my friend I may never see again.

CHAPTER 3
DORIAN

THE MOMENT I SIFTED TO AVALON, I FELT IT. A SHIFT IN THE FRIGID AIR. A buzzing undercurrent of something sinister. The scent of death carried on the wind.

I crashed through the double doors, ready to yell for someone to tell me what had happened. Tristan stood there, waiting. The silence in the foyer was deafening.

"Where is she?" I asked. My voice vibrated with an anger he didn't deserve.

"We don't know, sir." He shook his head, his saddened blue eyes meeting mine. "The island was breached, and the intruder knew where she was. Her coffin was destroyed."

"How many are dead?" I walked past him, taking note of every detail in the castle as I passed through, checking if anything was out of place. A clue. Insight to who had come to my home and done this.

Tristan followed behind me, his footsteps heavy. "Three dozen," he answered.

I stopped short, turning around to look at him. "All of them?" The words were barely audible.

"I'm afraid so. No one had a chance. Had you not called everyone to come to Houston in the search for Fury and kept us all there for her security detail during the summit—I fear they would be dead too. It likely saved their lives."

My brows pressed together, and I closed my eyes, recollecting who I had left there. When Fury had gone after Roxanne, I ordered the search. Roman, Ezra, and I each did the same. Except I chose to keep them there after she'd been located. We'd spent the hours overnight mapping out their security orders to watch Fury from the shadows over the course of the summit. I'd left thirty-six on Avalon. Their lives were my responsibility. They were my people. Dead. Slaughtered. And as I had come to find out, stricken from the universe. No longer existing on any plane. There would be no reunion of any kind with the ones they loved. Extinguished, she'd called it. I inhaled deeply and exhaled, shaking with barely contained rage.

"Everyone's names. What's left of their family line. I want it all." I turned, continuing to my destination.

"I've already started," Tristan said. "The general is waiting for you. You'll want to hear what she has to say."

I moved through the castle with purpose, my mind racing and trying to piece together the timeline of events. I exited the back of the castle, stepping out onto the moor.

Elaine stood in her armor, her blond ponytail high on her head. Hundreds of fae surrounded her as she spoke.

"Strengthen the wards. All of them, including those around the castle. Pull every resource you have into it. Double the number of guards at all points of entry. Sifting is now restricted to the southern entrance, and I want warning triggers on that ward amplified tenfold," she ordered, addressing a group. "You." She pointed at a soldier. "I want you to oversee the collection and preparation of the fallen. You have a dozen men you can take with you."

The man nodded.

"An extra-tropical cyclone is headed this way. Your time is limited," she said. "Go. I want it done." Her troops dispersed with precision.

Tristan signaled to me he was leaving, and he followed the soldier to gather information on the dead. Elaine turned around, the wind blowing her hair behind her, accentuating her high cheekbones.

"General." It was the best I could do for a greeting.

"Sir," Elaine responded. "I . . ."

"Don't. It wasn't your doing." I held my hand up, stopping her from walking down that path. That was not what we were here for.

Her blue eyes hardened, and she nodded. "Understood."

"Fill me in. What do we know?"

She put her hands on her hips and looked toward the castle. "I sent Markus back to collect some texts from the library. Information we could use during the summit. He came back to the Houston mansion almost immediately. It didn't take him long to find that everyone was dead."

My heart twisted as I prepared to say the next words. "Lyra . . ."

She met my gaze. "Gone. There is no trace of her."

"And the catacombs?"

"Destroyed," she answered. "And the footsteps leading there are the same as last time."

"Did they come from the same location?"

"No." Elaine pursed her lips and her brows furrowed. "They just . . . appeared near a cliff edge."

I narrowed my eyes. "What do you mean 'appeared'?"

"I mean just that. Nothing off the side of the cliff. Nothing before the footsteps started. No markings of any kind on the shores or the land. Then a set of footprints appeared like they came out of thin air."

"Like someone sifted," I said. Thunder clapped heavily in the distance, warning us of the incoming storm.

"Yes, but not at one of the entry points. They appeared midway through the northern and western entrances." Elaine pointed in the direction she was referring to, a look of frustration on her face.

I could see it. She was thinking the same thing as me. That shouldn't be possible. I had the island warded to prevent trespassing fae. No one could come and go by sifting unless they arrived at one of four entry points. The magic in the wards demanded it.

I ran my fingers through my hair, turning away from my general. My mind was reeling with the possibilities, but nothing was making any sense. I pinched the bridge of my nose and paced, trying to work it out. The cold wind whipped around us, mimicking the turbulent emotions cycling through me.

Elaine's posture slackened, and she stepped forward, dropping all pretenses. "Dorian, whoever did this knew about her." The urgency in her voice was grave. "They knew where to find her, and *worse*, I think they knew how to wake her up. I'm not sure if they knew how uninhabited the island was at the time, or if it was pure luck for us that they came when they did, but they are going to use her as a weapon. There's no other reason to wake her, and I don't think they've done it yet. If she's as bloodthirsty as she was last time, who knows how long we have until she starts leaving a trail of carnage behind her."

I stopped and looked at her. "Are you saying this isn't a trail of fucking carnage, Elaine?"

She looked at me with thinly veiled anger. "I was the second one that arrived here, right after Markus. You haven't seen the bodies yet. I know what this is. I'm saying she didn't do this. Whoever came here killed everyone on the island first, then they took her."

"How do you know she isn't awake? That she didn't do this?" I asked.

She was struggling to keep her composure. Struggling to focus as she looked at me. "I trained my sister to fight. And she's one of the thirty-six that died. I know what Lyra does when she loses her mind. She is like a cat with a mouse. She likes to toy with them. Play games. Give them hope. Then she slaughters her prey. This was not the same. I'm telling you, the intruder killed all of them first. My sister didn't have a chance to pull her sword. None of them did. That's not the Lyra we know."

The crushing loss in her voice jolted me. "My apologies, Elaine," I said, and sighed. "I'm sorry about your sister. Truly. Forgive me. I didn't know Aerinn was one of the fallen."

She straightened her shoulders and dipped her chin, acknowledging my poor excuse for an apology.

"I trust your judgement. I always have," I continued. "When they wake her, they're going to use her as a weapon. Why, or what for, remains to be seen."

"You know what this means, Dorian."

I did. And I hated it. "Only a fae is able to wake Lyra. No other faction has the magic capable of stasis, or its reemergence."

She pursed her lips in response, agreeing with me.

I sighed. "Get a track on her."

Elaine cocked her head and looked at me in question. "How on earth can we track her? She's disappeared without a trace."

"Find Rya," I answered. No one was going to like it, least of all—

A subtle groan behind me caught my attention. I turned around to find Tristan had returned.

"Do you have something to say, *second*?" I asked, raising an eyebrow.

He schooled his features quickly. "No, just . . . Rya. Surely, we can get—"

"Find Rya," I repeated, harsher, and leaving no room for discussion.

"Consider it done." Elaine and Tristan responded at the same time.

The clouds rolled in ominously, rumbling in warning. I heard the crashing of the waves against the cliffside far off in the distance. Storms were not unusual. It would rage and destroy whatever it could. It would pound against the earth, wreaking havoc as Mother Nature often did. But with nature's destruction, life was born anew.

The tempest was an omen, but it was a cruel reminder that Lyra wasn't of the same force. Nothing good could come of her storm, for she only brought death.

"I'll be in my study," I said, turning on my heel and walking into the castle as raindrops started to fall.

I walked with purpose. I needed to think. Quietly. Alone. The way I preferred it. I needed to work out how to manage the summit, the vampire, and the shifter . . . and Fury. It wasn't something I would bring up to them just yet. This was fae business.

I couldn't help but recall the last time I saw Lyra. The glow of her skin was no longer present. Her eyes didn't shine as they had before but were instead filled with hatred and anger. Her shoulders carried a weight I would never understand. I couldn't save her from whatever monster ate away at her psyche. I couldn't protect her from herself. I couldn't save her mother. I couldn't save those she hurt, just like I couldn't save my people today.

I forced her into a dreamless sleep. Put her in stasis unwillingly until I could find a way to heal her mind, even if it took forever. I needed rest, but I wouldn't take it until I could give her back her life.

Now I feared that opportunity was gone. I feared that I'd failed her again. Failed to protect others from her.

Failure . . . an old friend.

I looked up as James came running down the hall, skidding to a halt when he saw me. "Sir, you need to see this. Your study."

I picked up the pace, following after him. It was no use to ask what I needed to see. James was clear. I needed to see it for myself. It would happen soon enough.

The doors to my study were open. I turned the corner, entering, stopping to look around. Not a thing was out of place. Every book was on its shelf. Every paper sat neatly organized, just as I'd left it. The rugs weren't stained or tarnished. The chairs and furniture weren't overturned. It was immaculate.

Except the painted portrait that hung on the wall. It had only faded slightly over the years. Magic had protected it. I looked at it daily. Morvain and I stood beside each other proudly, her black dress a beautiful contrast to her creamy skin. Lyra sat in front of us, angled toward her mother's side, a modest smile on her lips, the blue of her dress matching the color of her eyes.

A jagged rip was torn down the middle of the canvas, now separating me from my family. There was no need to search for the weapon used. The dagger sat embedded in the portrait, centered over my heart.

"Well that answers that question," I said softly.

James scrunched his eyebrows together. "What question was that, sir?"

"She's awake."

CHAPTER 4
FURY

I SAT IN THE FRONT ROW WITH MY LEGS KICKED UP ON A CHAIR I'D TAKEN, sipping whiskey from a flask I'd refilled before we left. Roxanne kept shooting me not-so-subtle glances from my left. Caitlin sat on my right, and her annoyed glares were a hair more judgmental. Over the course of the past week, my boredom increased while their patience with me dwindled.

On stage, at a rectangular table, my mates sat in a row with microphones and were listening to horribly tedious debates over border disputes, resource allocations, and requests to grow territory. Four days now. If there were a god, I would thank them for this almost being over.

Roman seemed the best at listening to the lot of them and attempting a fair compromise in most cases. Ezra was struggling to give a shit, and I didn't need to read his mind to know that. The flirty, challenging looks he kept sending me followed by yawning when anyone called on him made it easy to see.

Still, the one that left me the most curious was Dorian.

He arrived late that first morning, storming through the doors and declaring the floor open for discussion. Since then, he'd barely said a word. Unlike Ezra that was pointedly disinterested, Dorian's mind seemed elsewhere. Actively preoccupied by something, and like the nosy demon I'd been for a hundred years—I wanted to know what.

"Does Dorian seem off to you this week?" I whispered to Roxanne, trying to keep it quiet enough so even supernatural ears wouldn't hear me.

Rox tilted her chin back and examined the fae with a touch more interest.

"Not particularly," she said after a moment. "Why?"

"He seems broodier than usual. Not to mention distracted."

"Dorian's never been particularly talkative during the summit," she replied. "I think he views it as a minor inconvenience he has to sit through, much like Ezra in that."

I hummed in response, not completely satisfied. There was more to it. The stiffness in his shoulders and the way his hands kept clenching said something was bothering him, and I'd watched it progress each day.

I took a deep breath and recrossed my ankles for the hundredth time that afternoon, reminded why I never, ever wanted to be in charge. You couldn't pay me enough to do this kind of work. Not here. Not in the Afterlife. Ruling might mean getting to break the rules because you made them, but the responsibility that came with it wasn't my schtick.

I was more of a break-the-rules-now-and-ask-forgiveness-later sort.

Stretching my arms above my head, I casted a glance of the room when a flash of black caught my eye. I frowned, tilting my head at the window when something dropped down into view again.

Hades.

He might be a crow, but he still managed to use his beady eyes to catch my attention across a room full of people. Could it have been another bird? Absolutely not. They didn't usually carry a look of pure exasperation. No, I knew he was my crow, and right now he was trying to get me to notice him.

I dropped my legs to the ground. Beside me, Caitlin huffed, "Finally."

Then I got to my feet.

Despite some whiny vampire lamenting about the big bad wolves that were stopping him from having an all-you-can-eat buffet in bumfuck-nowhere Iowa, almost every pair of eyes shifted my way.

Hades is here. I need to speak with him, I silently sent my message to Ezra. He nodded to me as Roxanne and Caitlin popped up dutifully at my sides.

Judging by the way Roman's eyes flashed in alert, Ezra relayed as much to him. The wolf alpha leaned to his left and whispered something in Dorian's ear. The fae got to his feet, excusing himself without a word to the attendees.

I guess I wasn't the only one wanting answers right now. That or they didn't want to leave me alone with just Rox and Caitlin. It had been uneventful so far, but it didn't surprise me that they wouldn't want to chance it.

So it was going to be a group outing.

Yay for me.

I strode down the aisle toward the stairs and ascended them quickly, my boots stamping against the steps as I exited the auditorium. Rox and Caitlin followed at my heels without question, and Dorian was waiting in the hallway when I stepped out.

"Does this building have a roof? I need to have a word with the pigeon."

"We'll take the stairs. Three doors down to the right," Caitlin said, having memorized the building and every window, door, or stairwell in it five times over.

"Thanks."

I started down the hall and sensed both Rox and Caitlin falling a little behind as Dorian loomed closer. His shadow dwarfed me like a moody cloud that dampened anything he got near. I snorted.

"You think the bird will have answers for you?" he asked, nodding to a fae that stood by the exit.

"He'd better," I answered, wrenching the door open to the stairwell after the guard stepped aside. "You seemed distracted in there," I continued, not subtle in my pushing. "And you were late again."

"Business on Avalon took longer than expected," he said, his voice turning almost brittle.

Something was definitely eating at him. Consider my curiosity officially piqued.

I slowed my pace as we ascended. "So you mentioned the other day. Care to talk about it?"

"No." He sifted to the doorway at the top of the stairs and flashed a keycard that turned the buzzer on it from red to green.

Well then. If he was just going to disappear when I asked a question, I wasn't going to get very far. But it did make me somewhat excited for when I learned to sift. To literally disappear when they were pushing me too hard? Oh I liked the thought of that.

"You know I'll find out eventually, right?" I pointed out as I stepped onto the roof. Wind whipped my hair back from my face, providing a brief relief from the stifling atmosphere of the summit, then the Houston humidity bore down on me like a heavy blanket. I frowned. A really *damp* blanket.

"For both our sakes, I hope not." The words were murmured so quietly I would have missed them if not for my heightened senses. I pivoted to dig a bit deeper when a loud squawk made me jump.

I ground my teeth together.

"Pigeon," I said, reeling back around, my hair getting in my eyes. I pushed it away and crossed my arms over my chest to properly express my annoyance. "Where have you been?"

"In the Afterlife. Where you told me to *go*, remember?"

Ah, perfect. He was actually being useful for once.

"And?" I asked, dropping all the snark. It was time to get serious. "What did Duke have to say?"

The bird sighed, dropping down onto the ledge of the building to perch. "They're just as confused as you are. No one knows why you didn't die, and no one knows how to get you back."

My lips parted, and I couldn't keep the disappointed expression off my face. Turning quickly, I tried to bury it by swiping the back of my hand over my forehead. This was bad.

"All right, that was not what I was hoping to hear. Anything else?"

"Duke is searching in the Library of Anomalies, but in the meantime, your mission is still on. The clock is still ticking." I turned to give him a sideways glare. Now was not the time for him to say his catchphrase. Strangely, it didn't appear he was going to. He cocked his head to the side, saying nothing more.

I closed my eyes and rubbed my temples with my fingertips.

This is just great. While I was happy Duke was actively looking for a solution, why was I not surprised that the parting line was that there was still work to do? Or that I still *hadn't* succeeded? Of course I hadn't. I still didn't understand what made them collectively lose their cool in the first place. If you can't find the trigger, you can't dismantle the bomb.

"What is the Library of Anomalies?" Dorian asked, interrupting my train of thought.

I ran a hand through my hair and turned to face them. "One of the nine Divine Libraries. It tracks abnormalities and inconsistencies that pop up across history—both in the Afterlife and on Earth. Specifically for cases like this on the off chance it happens again." A thin haze was starting to obscure my vision. I took a wobbly step. Something felt off.

"Who documents them?" Rox asked.

"Scholars department," I murmured, touching my lips. My mouth *ached.* I ran a finger over one of my elongated canines, liking the pressure I felt against them when I did. "They take the case notes from poltergeists and angels, then translate them into the books and then categorize them."

Was this a weird vampire thing? Did I need to eat?

The very idea of drinking blood made my stomach turn.

Nope, definitely not. I swallowed thickly, feeling another throbbing in my head. I'd heard enough about the thirst to know this wasn't it.

I could tell they were still talking. Voices drifted in and out, but whatever they were saying didn't reach me over the sound of my own heartbeat.

My face felt hot, not warm, but *burning.* Blood rushed to my head, and I took another step. Spots danced in my vision and the shapes around me distorted and warbled like a funhouse mirror.

The humidity was oppressing.

I ran my hand over my upper lip, wiping away the perspiration—

Then I froze.

Red coated my fingers.

Blood.

I realized what it was just as a wave of crimson gushed from my nose, covering my front. It soaked my shirt, dripping wet, sticky drops onto the pavement.

"Ah fuck," I slurred.

Light exploded in my vision.

The world spun in a violent circle.

I felt a tiny measure of relief as everything went dark.

CHAPTER 5
ROMAN

THIS SUMMIT PANEL WAS NOTHING MORE THAN A PISSING CONTEST. THE entire schedule was full of whiny leaders with minor territories, insisting they be given more. Not one of them had earned it. Not one of these groups had put in the work to rise in ranks. They just demanded to be handed more simply because it's what they *wanted*. Like a child. And I had to sit and listen to them complain like I cared.

I did better at it than the other two did. Dorian had been sitting through it with thinly veiled disdain. Ezra was so disengaged he would've been better suited in the audience. The one thing I could at least give him was he didn't discriminate in his apathy. It wasn't just shifters he was bored with in this discussion. He couldn't have cared less about the vampires arguing their points either. The way he saw it —the way we probably all did—was a lot more would get done if they just followed the rules and presented their cases for compromise rather than just trying to get their way.

I picked up my water glass and sipped it, taking in a breath, and exhaling deeply in a long sigh. I was at the end of my patience. I felt the light throb of a headache coming on.

I turned to glare at Ezra, expecting to see him with his arms crossed and snoring. Instead, his eyebrows were pressed together, and his body was tense. A sharp inhale of breath. A quick flair of his nostrils. His eyes met mine.

Fury.

I stood up abruptly, interrupting the speakers.

"I'm calling a short recess. I think it would be good for all parties to take some time and gather their thoughts. Come up with some practical solutions. We're all here to work together," I said quickly. "Let's break for an hour and then regroup." I looked over to Rava and nodded, knowing she would handle the rest.

Ezra was already out of his seat, walking off the stage and to the side door. Caitlin came rushing through it, her eyes wide and sweat dripping down from her forehead. "You guys need to come upstairs."

Then I saw it.

Blood on her hands.

Splattered on her shirt.

The scent of it was off when it reached my nose, but I knew it was my mate's. A deep growl rumbled low in my chest.

"Easy, Roman," Ezra said, putting his hand on my shoulder. "It's not what you think."

"Then what the hell is it?" I growled, pushing through the door, and heading to the stairwell.

"He's right," Caitlin said, following close behind. "I mean, we don't know what it is, but she's with us. She wasn't attacked. She just started gushing blood out of her nose and ears, then fainted. Dorian has her in the presidential suite."

I took the steps two at a time, Ezra right beside me, climbing to the top floor. When we reached the top of the stairs, a fae guard stood watch, preventing any uninvited guests from entering—and judging by her weapons, preventing anyone with ill intent from getting the chance to try.

"They're expecting you," she said and dipped her head, moving aside to open the door with the swipe of a key card.

I muttered my thanks as we passed through.

Fury's scent and that of her blood washed over me.

She lay on a couch, a red-stained towel being held to her face. Roxanne was next to her, holding Fury's hand. Dorian stood over both of them.

"What happened?" I asked, storming to the couches in the center of the living room.

"Ugh, I'm fine," Fury mumbled. "I just fainted, I think."

Dorian gave her an unamused, sideways glance. "We were on the roof, and she looked disoriented. Nose started to bleed, followed by her ears . . ." He trailed off, and it was no surprise. Bleeding out of the ears was never good, even for supernaturals. "Then she passed out."

"I said I'm fine," she repeated, moving to sit up. She grabbed the edge of the couch and closed her eyes. "Okay, maybe I'm not fine yet." She laid back down, scrunching her eyes shut.

I frowned. Aside from the situation seeming a bit unusual for her, something else was wrong. I came in closer, leaning over her and sniffing.

"You smell it too?" Roxanne asked as she looked up at me.

I nodded. "I do."

"Smell what?" Dorian and Fury asked at the same time.

I sighed. "I don't know. Something about her blood smells off. But I couldn't tell you why."

"Poison?" Dorian asked.

I shook my head. "I don't think so. It doesn't smell like any poison I've ever known. Poison has a sweet scent to it. Subtle and enticing. This is off-putting. Stale."

"Wow. Thanks," Fury grumbled, pinching the bridge of her nose.

Ezra moved around the couch to stand by Dorian. "She hasn't eaten much today. She's mostly been drinking. I can't imagine that's helping her right now."

She glared at him. "You promised you wouldn't—"

He pointed to her flask in her pocket. "You were drinking it in front of everyone. I was stating the obvious out loud, considering the circumstances."

She pursed her lips, and she looked away from him, mumbling to herself about his rudeness. I couldn't say I disagreed, considering his blatant disregard for protocol and showing his boredom during the entire summit.

I made eye contact with Caitlin. "Will you get Fury something to eat? Sugar and carbs. And water." She nodded and went to the kitchen.

I reached down and plucked the flask from her pants as Fury protested. "You've had enough of this today. For fuck's sake, Fury. You've been drinking since this morning. This is already half empty."

"People drink all the time at breakfast, Roman." She tried to sit up again, and this time Roxanne helped her. "You know, mimosas, bloody marys . . ." She trailed off mid-sentence, looking like she'd thought of something, or maybe just wished she had those drinks.

"This isn't brunch," I said, taking her silence as an opportunity to respond. I handed it over to Ezra. "Dump it, will you?" Turning my attention back to her, I squatted down and met her at eye level. "Drink some water and eat something. This isn't the cause, but Ezra's right. It's not helping anything."

"Oh, repeat that for me," Ezra drawled as he tucked the flask into his back pocket. "I want to hear those words come from your mouth again."

"No." That pompous fucking vampire. I growled at him in frustration, and he chuckled.

"Enough, you two," Dorian interjected. He looked at a pocket watch, checking the time. "Roman, have you ever smelled blood that was stale before?"

I raised my eyebrows and shook my head, bewildered. "I haven't."

Dorian looked to Roxanne and Ezra and they both confirmed the same as me.

Caitlin came back with some croissants, fruit, and a glass of water, setting it all down on the center coffee table. "I'll be outside if you need me," she said, walking to the double doors that lead into the hallway.

I silently watched Fury with interest as she picked at some food and took sips of her drink. Her hand shook slightly, and she'd squeeze her eyes shut and open them again.

My wolf desperately wanted to protect her. But neither of us knew how. I didn't know what she needed protection from. I just knew that there was more to this than I wanted to admit. We could brush off a nosebleed. But ears? And the smell . . . no, this was something worse.

"What did you feel like before you fainted?" I asked her, sitting on the couch across from her.

She chewed thoughtfully, turning her head side to side slowly.

"Just off, I guess. Kind of fuzzy. A little dizzy. Then I felt really hot. Oh, and my mouth started to hurt. Then the lights went out."

I looked at Ezra and Dorian. "Does any of this happen to vampires when they are made? Or . . ." Dorian cleared his throat, and his eyes flashed a warning. A reminder not to say anything about how he had made Fury in what we perceived were her final moments the first night of the summit. My eyebrows furrowed at being chastised by the fae. "*As I was saying*, have you seen any fae experience symptoms as they grow in their powers?"

Ezra pressed his lips together and shook his head. "No, this doesn't happen to vampires. We don't feel anything in our mouths, and our bodies don't exactly reject blood. We prefer to drink it. We don't expel blood or faint. That's . . ."

"A human trait, though not to this extent," Dorian finished. "And no. As fae mature, they don't experience anything like this."

My senses were on edge. There had to be something more to it. I just didn't know what questions to ask that would lead me to the right answers. "What was happening when it started?" I asked her.

She wiped her mouth with the back of her hand and sighed. "I was talking to that damn bird—wait, where is he?"

"He flew off after you fainted. Said he would be back. Maybe he went to tell your friend Duke about what happened?" Roxanne answered.

"Figures he'd leave. He was giving me news that wasn't that great, to be honest. The Afterlife doesn't know what I am, why I didn't die, and they don't know how to bring me back—"

"You want to go back?" I interrupted before I could think better of it. Yes, a part of me struggled to accept her as my mate. The truth bomb she'd dropped about how Maya had died—how all of our previous mates had died—didn't help that internal battle. But the other part of me knew I would do anything to keep her here. I could argue with myself all I wanted. At the end of the day, she was my mate. Hearing that she had the desire to leave Earth—had the desire to leave *me*—I felt an ache deep in my chest.

"I want answers," she said. When she met my gaze, something in her reacted. She looked conflicted.

"So do I." My muscles tensed.

"We need a witch," Dorian said. He looked at Roxanne and asked, "Do you mind calling Kelly? Tell me where she is. I'll get her and bring her back here."

She nodded, meeting my glare and shrugging as she stepped into another room to make the call.

"A witch again, Dorian? What the hell?" I asked. I didn't like trusting witches, especially not when Fury was involved. Witches were too unpredictable. They didn't like to make friends, and they often played both sides in a conflict.

"Kelly is different," he said, as if reading my mind. "She protected Fury once already, and then she stitched her back together after that bomb exploded at her shop. She can be trusted."

I looked at Ezra, hoping for some backup. He shook his head at me, but a stiff expression marred his face. He wasn't comfortable with it, but clearly I was on my own in pushing back. I opened my mouth to question more, but Roxanne came back out, putting her phone in her pocket. "She's at her house. She said she's ready to go when you are."

Dorian thanked her, then disappeared.

If we kept bringing others in, it was harder to control who could get to Fury, and if they had easy access, they could hurt her. We still didn't know enough about her healing. Fuck Dorian and Ezra. I know they wanted what was best for our mate, but so did I.

Rox? If she told me she trusted someone, I believed her. Without question. Aside from the fact she'd never led me wrong before, she had a sixth sense about people. Where I knew my anger and my biases could cloud my judgement—especially when my mate was involved—my sister could see clearly.

"Roxanne, you trust her with this?" I asked.

"I do, Roman. I always have. I know how you feel about witches, but she's one of the good ones. You weren't there. If she wanted Fury dead, believe me, she had the opportunity. Instead, she was ready to die protecting us." She gave me a small smile. I huffed in acknowledgement, leaning back on the couch and crossing my arms.

"Not that anyone asked me, but I thought she was all right too," Fury piped up, crisscrossing her legs and shifting her weight.

Ezra barked a laugh. "Glad you are willing to cooperate."

She shot him a look. "Piss off, Fangs. I want my flask back."

Before he could respond, Dorian and Kelly popped into the room.

She stood there in a flowing royal blue skirt and black blouse. Kelly gave a warm smile and a small wave. When she saw me, she said, "Don't worry, Roman. We will find out what's wrong with her."

I twisted my lips and looked at my sister. When I looked back at the witch, I motioned with my hands for her to get on with it.

"Hey, Kelly. Long time no see. Did you bring me any of those little pastries you had at your shop?" Fury took another drink of her water and smiled.

Kelly and Roxanne laughed. Dorian looked at me in question and I shrugged my shoulders.

"I'm afraid not. But next time I see you, I promise to bring you some. Let's get started, though. The tension in this room is unbearable. I don't know how you manage around all three mates," she said, making sure we all heard her. "That aside, I know they're concerned for you. *That* is evident. I'm going to try a couple of things first. See if I can pinpoint any magic coursing through you. Do you feel better lying down or sitting up?" she asked.

"I'm okay both ways. Sitting up is fine, I guess," she said, leaning to set her water glass on the table. When she sat back, she rested her back against the couch cushions and closed her eyes.

Kelly moved her hands over Fury's head, hovering closely but not quite touching her. I felt zaps of electricity in the air, and my wolf stirred, questioning if that should be happening.

The witch's eyes were closed tight, her eyebrows bunched together as she focused. Her hands traveled over Fury, never touching, but always knowing where she was. She moved over her body once. Twice. Three times.

Kelly stopped, putting her hands in her lap with a huff. Fury cracked an eye open. "Did you find anything?"

Kelly looked unhappy. "No," she muttered. "Not a damn thing."

"How can that be?" I asked, frustration filling my tone.

The look she gave was sympathetic, and it made me angrier than I already felt. "Because there isn't a trace of magic that I can detect. She has no spells on her. No curses, no charms, not even protections." She shook her head. "Roxanne said the blood that came out of her was unusually heavy. And it smelled off. But it's not poison, I can assure you of that." She reached over and grabbed the towel that had been used to clean up Fury's face and staunch the bleeding. She sniffed it, wrinkling her nose. "It *is* stale. Like it's. . . old." She looked at Fury incredulously.

Fury raised her eyebrows, looking around at everyone. "I don't know what you want from me. I have no answers right now, and the one feather-brained jerk I was relying on had nothing useful either."

Kelly looked at me. "Dorian mentioned a wolf called Taylor. What do I need to know about him? He just bit her, right? Was there anything more to this?"

I leaned forward, resting my elbows on my knees, and clasping my hands. "Low level. Branded a rogue. Couldn't even shift anymore. He was a nobody."

Kelly pursed her lips and hummed. "I need to go through some texts. Spell books. I can't detect anything here, but clearly there's something that isn't revealing itself to us."

She stood up, grabbing the towel with blood. "Dorian, do you mind taking me back? I'll call you or Roxanne after I've had some time to research." She turned to Roxanne and kissed her on the cheeks. "Fury, Roman, Ezra, I will see you soon."

She walked to Dorian, and they sifted out of the room just as a knock sounded. Caitlin opened the door and popped her head in. "Twenty minutes till showtime, boss. Rava said tensions are high after you called that unscheduled intermission."

I sighed. If it wasn't one thing . . .

Dorian reappeared. "Well that didn't answer any of our questions," he grumbled. "However, she's going to keep me posted on whatever she finds."

"Or doesn't," Fury added. She looked around at all of us. "Come on, guys. Do you really think a witch from this world is going to be able to find out what's wrong with me? Even Duke and Hades don't have a clue, and they're from the Afterlife." She looked down at her lap and shook her head. "No. Kelly isn't going to find out what we need to know."

"What are you suggesting?" I said, curious to see where she was taking the conversation. This was Fury. I was learning very quickly that she had several cards she had yet to reveal.

Ezra pointedly looked away to the balcony where Hades had just landed and perched himself on a chair near the window. He had an idea of what she was going to say, but he was clearly giving her the space he'd promised.

"Enlighten us. If Hades and Duke can't help you right now, and you're saying that a supernatural can't help you, then what other options do we have?" Dorian asked, taking a step toward the couch where she sat.

She looked between the three of us before she answered. "I need to talk to someone between our worlds."

Roxanne looked just as confused as the rest of us. "I'm sorry, *between* our worlds?"

Fury nodded. "Yep," she answered, popping the 'p'.

Outside, Hades squawked and flapped his wings in what appeared to be outrage.

"What exactly does that mean?" I asked, voicing the same question we were all thinking.

She took a deep breath and sighed. "Have you ever heard of Bloody Mary?"

CHAPTER 6
FURY

"THE DRINK?" ROX ASKED, CONFUSED.

"The queen?" Dorian suggested.

"The legend," Ezra said.

"Bingo," I said, pointing at him. "That one. Although technically the drink plays a role in this too. The legend of Bloody Mary is actually sort of true. 'Sort of' in that chanting her name thirteen times into a bathroom mirror doesn't do jack shit, *but* that there is an entity where that legend came from. She's real, and she exists in a mirror dimension. She's a poltergeist."

"A poltergeist is a ghost?" Roman said.

"Not really. The human idea of ghosts are dead people that linger around for unfinished business. A poltergeist is a job in the Afterlife. It's in the Department of Current Affairs, and they flit between realms to gather information for the Afterlife." It was also an offensive name to some of them, depending on who you said it to.

"What makes you think this poltergeist would have the answers you're looking for if your Divine Library doesn't?" Dorian asked, crossing his arms.

"One," I held up a finger, "we don't know if it does. It's a rather large library. It'll take time for Duke to search. Two," I held up another finger, "I think she might because she's no longer part of the Afterlife."

That got everyone's attention for sure. Furrowed brows and confused looks filled each one of their faces.

"How?"

"She left," I said simply. "Disappeared and never came back. Upper Management considers her a traitor. They sent people after her, but mirror dimension. That's not a poltergeist ability, just like exploding things isn't a demon ability. It was specific to her."

Dorian appeared to be deep in thought. I watched him carefully, looking to see what I could learn about his behavior. I just wanted to be able to read him better.

"If you don't go back, will they send people after you?" Roman asked quietly. The way he asked the question made it clear he was contemplating my future and what punishments Upper Management may send my way.

"I don't know," I said honestly. "If I can't, I suppose that's different. But they may not see it that way."

"If this Bloody Mary was branded a traitor, what makes you think she'll help you? Assuming she can," Dorian said.

"I don't know if she will or not. She's helped a fellow poltergeist here and there over the years, but it's impossible to catch her. All you can do is summon her and ask. She'll either show up, or she won't." I shrugged. It's not like this was supposed to be part of my job. I was supposed to be focusing on the guys. Trying to prevent the apocalypse. Not teaching Afterlife 101 and figuring out what was wrong with me.

I looked over at Hades. He was shaking his head. I knew he was judging me for it.

He wasn't wrong. Asking Bloody Mary for help was desperate. A stretch, really. I had no reason to believe she would listen to me, or help. But if I was supposed to save the entire universe—no pressure—I needed to figure some of my shit out too. I couldn't walk around, fainting and bleeding all the time. I needed to try whatever I could.

I rolled my eyes and waved for him to come inside. Ezra opened the balcony doors, and he flew in, landing on the coffee table in front of me.

"I hope you know what you are doing," Hades said, fluffing his feathers up. "You know what she can do."

I widened my eyes at him, pinning him with my stare. "Yes, thank you, bird. You have any better ideas right now? Tick tock, right?"

He snorted through his beak and scratched at the table with his claws. That was the best he would give me in answer, which suited me just fine.

Dorian glanced at the time again and frowned. "We don't have time to . . . do whatever it is you need to do to summon her. After the summit . . ."

The woozy feeling had dissipated, and I felt more stable. I leaned forward to stand up, and everyone moved to help me.

I waved them off. "I'm fine now. Let's get back so we can get this day over with."

"Not going to happen," Roman said. "You can't go down there. If that happens again, especially in that room—"

"I'll take her to the clan," Ezra said. I looked at him in mock surprise, and he winked. Of course he was fine leaving this boring summit. Roxanne wasn't kidding when she said the first night was meant to be fun and then it got down to business after that. I thought for sure she was downplaying it. Nope. That was a negative. Not that our first night was what I would call fun. Banquet-turned-kidnapping-turned-attempted murder-turned making me a hybrid demon. The turmoil of that night aside, it really was straight and narrow after that kickoff.

"Oh, don't go out of your way for me," I said dryly. "I'd hate to impose on the leadership responsibilities you have to your fellow vampires."

Ezra laughed. "You should be with me if something happens. I am the one that can communicate mentally. I can call for them, but they can't call for me if I'm not listening," he pointed out.

Dorian and Roman looked at each and nodded in agreement. "Go," Dorian said. "We'll handle the rest of the sessions today."

I pointed to my bloody shirt. "Mind giving me something clean to wear?" I asked Dorian. "Pretty sure it's the wrong attire to hang out with vampires. Or the right one, I suppose. Depending on who you ask."

In a second, my soiled clothes were gone, replaced by a simple sundress. Not exactly my type, but it was airy and light. I smiled my thanks at him.

Roman's heated gaze made my skin break out in gooseflesh. I could see it, then. Tiny icy blue flecks flickered in and out. He didn't want me out of his sight. He and that wolf of his wanted to protect me. Wanted to keep hold of me tight and never let go. There was something almost endearing about it. When I really thought about it, I hadn't ever had someone care to actually protect me before.

I felt Ezra's phantom touch skimming up my thigh, pulling me from my thoughts, and I swatted at it. Roxanne looked confused, but then she looked at the amusement on his face and she put it together. She rolled her eyes and huffed.

"All right, then," I said, moving around the table. "I guess that's me out, then." I went to give a little two-finger salute, but Roxanne stuck her foot out slightly and I tripped right over it, stumbling and crashing right into Roman's muscled chest.

His warmth enveloped me as he wrapped his strong arms around my body to stop my fall. The sudden contact and the intensity of his embrace sent electric shots through my veins. I looked up and met his gaze. I swear I could see fire in his eyes, and the flames wanted nothing more than to consume me. A part of me screamed to let him.

He leaned down, his lips grazing my ear as he softly breathed, "Be careful, little one."

"Yes. I would. Will. No, right." I cleared my throat, gathering words and straightening out my scrambled thoughts. "I mean, I will. Thanks for catching me," I mumbled. Glancing at Roxanne, I saw the little smirk on her face.

What. Was. That? The residual tingles of my moment with Roman buzzed over my skin. Stepping aside, I waved at Ezra to go. I needed to get some air. I wasn't so sure that would happen hanging out with a bunch of vampires, but I was about to find out.

~

STROLLING through Ezra's sex club proved to be more entertaining the second time around. It was strangely crowded for an afternoon. At least it seemed strange to me.

"Aren't vampires supposed to sleep during the day?" I mused as we passed cages of naked men and women on display. They touched themselves for the pleasure of the surrounding crowd that watched them with hungry eyes.

"Some do," Ezra said. "But don't the most delicious acts happen at night?" he questioned, a hint of something warm in his eyes.

I swallowed thickly. "Some do," I mimicked, voice coming out huskier than I'd intended. A fiendish smile stretched across his full lips.

"What is day if not the vampire night?"

I turned my cheek, looking anywhere but at him. It was easy to do in a place like this where there was so much to see. From orgies in one corner to a Dominatrix in another. The sub was spread wide by a St. Andrew's cross, his wrists held taut by suspended chains attached to the cuffs. I hid my flinch when she smacked him with a leather riding crop. The man on display moaned in ecstasy.

Ezra's fingers ghosted a touch over my forearm as he silently urged me on.

"Much as I would love to do some of these things with you," he murmured in my ear, guiding us deeper into his lair of depravity, "I'd want a safer location. Fewer prying eyes and fewer things that might distract you." Like that riding crop.

"Don't like being watched?" I said, easily imagining him in here with the rest of them.

"With you—I'm more particular about the audience," he answered, surprising me. We reached a door I recognized vaguely from my previous visit here. He opened it, motioning for me to go first.

"Particular?" I repeated back, entering the quiet office space.

"People I trust not to attempt to harm you, for one," he said, right behind me. My breath quickened as my heart sped up a fraction.

"And?" I forced the word from my lips in an attempt to think about something—anything—except the tingling of my skin and heated flush creeping up.

The hair on the back of my neck lifted. A cool breath brushed over the damp skin there, followed by the lightest touch of lips. I groaned, my head tilting back on its own accord as he went from my nape to just below my ear.

"Those that understand 'look, but don't touch'."

The sheer possessiveness of the statement rattled me. I turned around, facing him.

"I thought you didn't mind sharing," I said. Not phrased as a question, but the intent was there.

"The wolf and the fae are also your mates," he said. With surprising gentleness, despite the fierceness in his expression, he reached up to brush a strand of hair from my face. This wasn't the joking, playful Ezra—but the hundred- and seventy-year-old vampire alpha. "You have a connection with them as much as you do with me, and I won't come between you and a mate. That's your business."

"But?" I prompted, hearing it there in the statement, silent but lurking.

"The idea of someone else touching you makes me want to dismember them," he admitted. There was a vulnerability in that honesty that made me tread with caution.

"Ezra," I said his name softly, shaking my head. What happened to just sex? Where did the lack of commitment go?

"Before, you were going to go back," he said quietly. "Now you can't. As far as we know, you're here for good." He took a step forward, and I took one away from him.

"And I'm still trying to find a way to return," I pointed out.

"I know." He nodded. "And if you do, we'll cross that bridge when we come to it. But while you're here—I want to be with you. I'm not asking for forever. Just right now."

I pressed my lips together, feeling caught between a rock and a hard place. On one hand, I had no desire to run off and fuck other guys. It wasn't so much about the exclusivity that bothered me as opposed to *what it meant*. We were a thing. Not just whatever it was we'd already been.

It was scary to take that risk or even consider it when there was still a chance I could somehow find my way back, and then . . . I wasn't sure what came next. For so long I'd worked toward one thing:

retirement. But in my plans, it's not like I'd ever accounted for a relationship—or multiple relationships at that, and certainly not while on Earth.

Even if I did return to the Afterlife and somehow this couldn't last, did I really want to miss the opportunity when I had it right here in front of me? My twenty-three short years were all missed opportunities because of the life I'd been pushed into.

But I was not that girl anymore.

I hadn't been her in a long fucking time.

Ezra heard the change in my thoughts before the firm line of my mouth softened and my stance relaxed. He prowled forward, a gleam of victory in his eye.

"Don't make me regret this," I said quickly, taking another step back on instinct. My ass bumped into his desk. I curled my hands around the edge, holding my weight as I slid back onto it.

"Never," he said fervently. His lips came down on mine and I opened my mouth to him. His hands grasped the underside of my knees, using them to push me back further while spreading my legs wide. I groaned into the kiss, and he swallowed it down.

"Truth or dare, kitten," he murmured against my lips.

Uhhhh...

He grazed his fingers across my skin, then skated up the outside of my thighs, pushing back the thin material of my sundress.

"Dare?" It was an answer, but it came out like a question. He could read my mind. Truth wasn't really an option, anyway. I felt his smile against my lips, right as his fingers slipped under the edge of my thong. I started to lift my hips for him to pull it off when a loud rip made me jolt.

Ezra tore it off me and then pocketed it with a devilish grin.

The door to the office opened behind him. I jumped on instinct, but Ezra knelt between my legs with his hands clamped around my thighs, holding them there.

"What do you ne—" Kendrick, Ezra's second, broke off.

"Take a seat," Ezra said quietly. But his voice was a boom in my ears. My heart started to race, a thrill working its way up my spine as my eyes flashed between the two.

Ezra stared at me purposefully. Then I understood.

Truth or Dare.

"For your pleasure, I asked him to join us. Kendrick is going to watch me eat this pretty pussy." At my vampire's words, Kendrick slowly started toward the couch and took a seat, bracing his hands behind his head and legs sprawled out—at ease.

My breath caught in my chest as Ezra waited, silently, for any inkling of consent.

I bit my lip and spread my legs wider.

Ezra's gaze turned dark with hunger as he crooned, "Good girl."

He trailed light kisses and small nips up my inner thigh, making my back arch. Reaching the sensitive skin just a few inches from where I really wanted him, he sucked on a patch of flesh that made my legs jerk.

After the last few days I'd had, my body was wound *very, very* tight, and I needed this more than I cared to admit.

My hands tangled in his dark locks, I pulled tight as I tried to guide him where I wanted him to be. Ezra huffed a laugh against my center, a cool breath of air hitting my clit and making me stiffen.

I looked up to see Kendrick staring unabashedly. His dark brown eyes burned with lust, all the more inflamed when Ezra took my clit between his lips and my mouth dropped open in a silent moan.

I bucked up, urging him on. Ezra rewarded me by pushing two fingers inside and using the flat of his tongue to scrape along that sensitive nerve bundle. I fisted his hair even tighter, using my sheer demonic strength to pull myself to him. He punished my clit in the best way possible, driving those fingers home with only the strength a supernatural could have.

It. Was. Heaven.

Heaven may not have been real, but this was as close to it as it got.

My legs shook, and my grip slackened. My eyes closed as I raced toward that edge of release. The feel of his teeth pinching my clit followed, but a soothing suck sent me careening over the edge.

"Ezra," I moaned his name, throwing my head back as I lost all control. My body flashed hot, then cold as my orgasm soldiered through me, taking no prisoners. He lapped at me, sending shock waves on the heels of the best oral I'd experienced in my long life. I writhed against him until the last of my pleasure died off, leaving me sated, but greedy for more.

Ezra stood up, pressing two fingers to my lips. I opened up without preempt and tasted myself on his skin. His green eyes smoldered with barely restrained heat as he said, "So fucking sweet."

I reached for his belt to return the favor, but he placed his hand on mine. "Next time."

I frowned and decided to mentally prod. *Why?*

Because the first time I take this cherry-red mouth, I don't want an audience.

My cheeks flamed a little as I realized how utterly serious he was being about why he brought Kendrick here. It really was for my pleasure, and perhaps, his way of showing me that being his mate didn't mean he would run around banging his chest like a fucking idiot every time another man looked at me.

Ezra smiled, his way of telling me I was right on the mark.

"Now, you had another reason for coming to see me?" he said, tugging my sundress down to cover my glistening center. I arched an eyebrow at him, and he held up my torn underwear, then turned as he not so subtly adjusted his pants.

"Right," Kendrick said, coughing once to clear the hoarseness in his voice. "There's been some accusations brought against one of the clan enforcers."

"Accusations?" Ezra asked, walking over to the bar to pour himself a drink. I noticed that he pointedly didn't offer me one.

"A dozen or so vampires claimed he took advantage of his position and raped them during their sentencing. Male and female," Kendrick supplied.

A shiver ran through me, and I slid myself off the edge of the desk, letting my dress fold naturally around me. "Do any of them have proof?" I asked.

Kendrick looked from Ezra to me, and instead of questioning it, he didn't miss a beat. "No," he said, "unfortunately not. Their stories all have one thing in common, though, and none of the victims have any record of knowing each other—which gave me pause."

"Oh?" Ezra chimed in.

"He only anally raped them."

I cringed. "Do you have the vampire in question in custody?"

"Yes," he answered. "He's being held in the dungeon. Ezra's ability to read thoughts should tell us for certain, but I suspect that he's guilty."

I lifted my eyebrows. "You're keeping him in a sex dungeon?"

Kendrick tried to hide his smile at my confusion. "Not *that* dungeon."

"It's below the club," Ezra said. "It's mostly used as a holding cell until judgement is passed. I actually have a specific den set aside for clan enforcers to do their punishing. It's a nice place. You'd like it." I snorted, amused by his assumption.

"My methods might surprise you," I said.

"My dear, I'd be disappointed if they didn't. You are *The* Fury, after all." I preened a little under his compliment.

"You said this dude is in the dungeons right now, yeah?"

Kendrick nodded. "I picked him up this morning during the summit meetings when he was blowing off some steam in the club. Haven't told him what for just yet, but I imagine he has an idea if my gut is right."

"It usually is," Ezra said, downing the rest of his drink.

"Then I say we pay him a visit."

CHAPTER 7
FURY

THE DUNGEON WAS APTLY NAMED.

Gone was the sexy glow of the dim lights and the leisurely atmosphere of the club. In its place was a cracked concrete floor, cinder block walls, and metal bars. "What are the bars made of that it keeps them inside?" I asked as we walked along a row of cells, mostly empty, but not all. Kendrick followed silently, several paces behind us.

"Tungsten," Ezra said. "One of the hardest metals on Earth. Just in case they are able to bend it, though, they'd have to break through it first. They're also chained to the floor."

I looked through a gap in the bars to see chains the same color as the metal attached to the concrete floors. Hm.

As a demon, I could most likely break those, but I'd never tried to bend anything that was Tungsten before. It was a long-standing tradition of my guild to test our strength and flaunt it at parties. I was the strongest in my age bracket, but not the strongest amongst all demons. The more one aged, the more their Afterlife abilities grew.

For demons, that skill was our strength. For angels, their ability was to manipulate minds. The rainbow bridge attendants could communicate with animals. Poltergeists were interesting in that their abilities largely showed on Earth. The older they got, the more physical they could become. It was rumored that if left to time, and their own devices, one could eventually flip back and forth between human and phantom. It wasn't exactly a secret that Upper Management tended to pull them from Earth before they were actually able to achieve that, though. Something about the temptation of life again being too great.

Before, I might have wrinkled my nose at the prospect. But now . . . my eyes ventured to Ezra's back. His proud shoulders and lush dark hair. I had something with him. Even if I couldn't feel the mate bond as he did, I felt something, and when I thought about it, staying on Earth didn't seem so bad.

"Robert Waters," Ezra remarked as we approached a figure at the end of the long row. He stood against the wall, smoking a cigar. His honeyed hair was gelled back, and his pinstripe suit was reminiscent of a time closer to my own.

"Finally," the guy huffed, blowing out a stream of smoke. "Boss, I knew you'd come clear this mess up," he said, stepping forward. The chain attached to his ankle dragged across the floor, scraping as he walked.

"Actually," Ezra hummed, "we have some questions for you first."

The easy demeanor he wore froze, a mask settling over as Robert repeated, "Questions?"

Ezra nodded, not seeming in any particular hurry. I wasn't sure if it was intentional or not, but I knew from experience the lack of a rush tended to freak people out.

"How long have you been working for me, Robert?" Ezra started, hands in his pockets, the picture of utter calm.

Robert sucked the air between his teeth, eyes darting toward the ceiling.

"Since the seventies. I wanna say 72', right at the end of my first decade after being turned." He scratched the back of his head.

"Do you know why I make the newly-turned wait a decade before they can become an enforcer?"

Robert licked his lips, a hint of anxiety creeping into his expression. He started to shift his feet. "So we know the rules and have the bloodlust under control."

Ezra nodded. "Partially, but not completely." He paused, taking a look around his dungeon, as if admiring the view. "I make the newly-turned wait so they have plenty of opportunities to see what happens when someone breaks my rules. Enough time to understand that any delusions of power they might have are simply that. To understand their place in this world. *My* world." He looked back at the man behind the bars, eyes hard. "Do you understand your place, Robert?"

He swallowed. "Yes, sir."

"Hmm," Ezra replied, as if he were doubtful. "And what is that?"

"A-as your enforcer, sir." He was already pale by nature, but his face seemed to go white as a sheet under Ezra's scrutiny.

"And what is your job as my enforcer?" Ezra continued.

"To enforce your rules. Give out punishments." He licked his lips again, something I figured out was a nervous habit.

"Tell me, what happens to enforcers who break the rules?"

Robert went silent, his mouth opening, then closing. "I'm not sure—"

"You're not?" Ezra asked, his voice sharp as a blade. "Well, let me remind you, then. I am hardest on those that have chosen to abuse their power when I have allowed them to enforce my law."

Robert swallowed, but stayed quiet. As I watched him, I assumed he sensed the end of the conversation and what it would mean for him.

"Have you abused your power, Robert?"

A pause.

"N-no."

Ezra hissed. "I don't like liars, Robert."

The cigar dropped from his fingers, and while I'd suspected partway through the conversation, I knew in that moment he was guilty.

"I didn't—I swear!" He jumped forward, fingers coming within inches of the bars when the chains around his ankles stopped him short.

"How many?" Ezra asked quietly.

Despite his attempts to look confused by the question, I saw recognition behind his dark brown eyes.

"Don't make me ask again, Robert. How many vampires entrusted to your care have you raped?" Ezra said, the first signs of his anger actually showing.

"I—you—I don't—"

"Seventeen," Ezra said quietly. "Kendrick, pull the files for every vampire he's had to deliver punishment to for more than a month. That seems to be when he starts up. They need to be aware their abuser is in custody and that I'm willing to provide every service available to help them move on from their mistreatment."

Kendrick stepped out of the shadows and nodded. "Understood."

"Fury," Ezra said as his second started down the hall, leaving us with the piece of shit. "What punishment would you give him if he were assigned to you?"

I blinked, not expecting the question. Instantly, my mind started turning with possibilities. I stepped forward, toward the cage, and I stroked the cold metal bars with my fingers. "I'd need his history to say for certain, but usually rapists are a combination of punishment and rehabilitation. Punishment, because they actually did it. But you need rehabilitation because the urge came from somewhere. It's long-term reconditioning, essentially."

"Such as?" Ezra prompted, less angry and more curious.

"I start with the punishment. Rapists have distorted views on sex. Power trips. They enjoy taking something from their victim; hurting them and watching them suffer. So I take that and turn it on them. I simulate the beginnings of a rape over and over again, where their victim becomes the abuser. This teaches him that trying to force someone won't go the way he expects, and he should fear raping someone. The entire time they are powerless. They hate it in the beginning, of course." I smiled. "Once they're broken down enough, I start giving them choices again, little by little. Recondition the way they view everything. So rehabilitation comes with finding power, control, and sexual gratification in consensual ways. Finding a new outlook that isn't distorted anymore takes time. Overall, I condition them to reject every notion of what they once were. Provided I had enough time and did my job well enough, when they're reborn, they break the mold."

"Interesting," Ezra said, as if considering. "How long does this process take?"

"It depends on the person. Between twenty-five to sixty years is about average. I imagine it would be at the higher end for this one because of his already longer life. Not to mention there's no being reborn, so I'd need to be confident in the level of conditioning that he could possibly re-enter society without relapse or being unable to function. It's a fine line and if I broke him too much . . ." I shook my head. "Unless my job is to torture and kill, that's not the way to go and it doesn't fix anything anyway."

"Do you think you could change him?" Ezra asked. The tone of his voice made me turn.

"Are you asking me to?" I replied. His green eyes stayed fixed on me, us both ignoring the man quietly freaking out in his cell trying to process what was happening.

"You're bored here, and you enjoyed having a purpose as a demon. You still can." He thrust his chin toward Robert Waters.

"I may not be here long enough to finish the job," I started.

"Then write down how. Create a guide for someone to finish the job, if for some reason you can't," Ezra said, taking a step closer. His scent was intoxicating to me.

"You won't like all my methods," I said quietly.

"You don't fuck your assigned cases. You told me that." My eyebrows lifted at the crassness in his tone.

"I have to put myself in compromising positions to do this job, and I'm not just talking sex." I crossed my arms, leaning my shoulder against one of the bars.

"Would you let him hurt you?" he asked.

"No."

"Then I trust you," Ezra said simply.

"I'll need his history," I started slowly, my mind considering the very real possibility and what it would take. "And a secure location, but not like this. It needs to be normal. Like a house or an apartment."

"The enforcer den has suites for the prisoners. I can have one assigned to you, just for him, without any others present," Ezra said with a dip of his head. "Is that all?"

"I have to be able to do this multiple times a week," I said after a moment. "While it's not a set schedule, a certain amount of frequency is needed to condition properly. I don't know how Roman or Dorian will take it, though, so I may need a ride if I'm not staying with you."

He nodded once. “Consider it done, and if either of them give you grief—let me know.”

I cocked an eyebrow in question. He flashed a mischievous smile at me before extending his hand. “Come,” Ezra said, taking my own. “Roman will be here to pick you up soon and I’m not done with you just yet.”

CHAPTER 8
EZRA

I RUBBED MY TEMPLES IN SLOW CIRCLES. I DIDN'T EVEN BOTHER TO LISTEN TO Roman as he spoke, closing out after the last speaker. One much-needed recess, then one more grueling, but thankfully short, gathering to send farewells, and the summit would be over.

Finally.

I was focused on more important things. Like Fury. I kept my promise and gave her as much privacy as I could offer, but I still heard her all the time. I heard the questions and the worry. The conflict . . . and the desires. She was trying to solve so many problems, and she was still trying to do it by herself.

I saw in her mind what Upper Management told her we would do. End the world. I scoffed. A bunch of soothsayers in the Afterlife. What a fucking joke.

I had once told her that I would help her complete her mission. That I would not get in the way. That was still true, but things were different after the night we changed her. I had changed.

Her internal struggles with the mission and the lack of understanding it had been steadily increasing with each passing day. So was my attachment to her.

"Ezra," Roman said impatiently, breaking through my train of thoughts.

"Hm?" I looked up to see him standing next to me, the crowd clearing out. "What?"

"I've said your name three times. It's time to go. Fury and Roxanne are upstairs waiting."

"Right." I slid the chair back and stood, reaching my arms up to stretch.

"I need to check something in Avalon. I'll be back in time for the final closing," Dorian said, looking at his phone. "Call if you need me."

He sifted without another word.

I cocked an eyebrow and stared at the spot where he had just stood.

Roman grunted. "It's bad enough that you're so disengaged. Now he is too."

I shook my head. "No, we're nothing alike. My lack of caring is pure apathy. He's preoccupied. Maybe distracted. You know Dorian. He stares out the window and just thinks or drifts off. I don't know. He's old as shit. Nothing he ever does surprises me."

Roman smirked. "I can honestly say the same about you," he said, crossing his arms. "Which brings up an excellent question. Would you care to tell me why Fury spent most of last night drawing up what she called 'a torture outline' and mapping a dungeon for punishment?"

I barked a laugh. A torture outline. How organized.

"I've enlisted her help as an enforcer, of sorts. We had a vampire abusing his power. Raping. I asked Fury what she would do and how she would handle it. She told me, and I liked what she had to say. I said it was her case to take." I shrugged, wondering what kind of pushback I would get from the shifter.

Roman looked unconvinced. "Do you think that's wise?"

"Why wouldn't it be?" I asked, leaning on the edge of the long table that sat on the stage, curling my hands over its side. The room was entirely empty. "It doesn't put her in danger. This was her job when she was in the Afterlife, and the place where she'll be doing the work is safe."

"I question that considering everything that has already happened to her," he said. Roman reached into his pocket for a rubber band. He pulled his dreads back, away from his face, and tied them off. "What's the purpose? There's something you aren't saying, so spit it out. We're in this together now, much as we don't want to be."

I crossed my arms. He was right about us being in it together. More than I wanted him to be, especially considering what he was to Fury. But that was part of it. I wouldn't come between her and a mate. Ever. I didn't want them to come between us either.

"I want to get her involved in something she finds useful. She's been gone from this world for a long time. She was important there. Respected. Good at what she did. She valued that more than you know. This may come as a shock to you, but I want her to stay here."

His brows shot up. "The vampire has feelings. Color me surprised."

I glared at him, and I could feel a rush of angry adrenaline push through my veins. "I didn't reject my mate if you recall. She rejected me. I can't claim to know your loss. Don't claim to understand mine."

While I silently cursed that I had allowed that to slip—showing more of myself than I cared to admit—my words had an effect on him. He nodded, a look of sympathy and regret shone in his eyes. He cleared his throat. "I'm listening."

"Let me ask you something, shifter," I started, my temper rising as I tried to maintain a measure of control. "What will make her *want* to stay, hmm? What about you is worth sticking around for? Yeah, she might like fucking me, but that won't keep her here long term." He narrowed his eyes, a bit of his jealousy peeking through. I had his full attention. "What are you—we—doing to make her feel like this is her home too? Now she may or may not get stuck here, unable to return, but what if Fury and that bird find a way for her to go back? We can't make her stay. She leaves. We all lose. Forget the end-of-the-world bullshit. She's *gone*."

A threatening rumble came from Roman's throat. The icy blue in his eyes flashed as he and his wolf heard the words I'd said. They knew I was right.

Some of my anger dissipated. I couldn't believe I was trying to side with a shifter, but I went on. "She has to belong here. This needs to be her home, and that's what I'm trying to give her. Where she comes from, mates aren't a thing. This isn't her world. It's ours. And her human life before . . ." I trailed off, knowing it was territory I shouldn't cross. "Well, it's not my place to say. It's her story to tell when she's ready."

Roman's jaw was clenched as he understood a small fraction of what I wouldn't say. He nodded slowly. "It's why she drinks, isn't it?"

I pressed my lips together in acknowledgement. I didn't need to say anything. He already knew the answer.

He sighed. "I figured."

"She still hasn't dealt with that yet, so she drinks to cope."

"That's a piss-poor way to cope. Doesn't fix anything. To make it worse, she's not a demon anymore," Roman said. "Whatever she is, the liquor has an effect on her. She's getting hangovers, even if she won't admit to that yet."

"I know."

"I don't want that for her. And I . . . agree with you. Given the possibility she could leave, we need to give her reasons to stay. Beyond the mate bond. She needs to make the choice," he said quietly. "I want her to stay too."

"Then we would do better working with her, not against her," I said. I considered my next words carefully. "And we would do better working together, the three of us. This goes beyond protecting her. If you don't want her to go back to the Afterlife if she finds a way, then you and I at least have the same goal in mind here. I'll have to ask the fae what he wants."

He huffed a humorless laugh. "I'm not sure Dorian even knows what he wants anymore." He sighed, sticking his hands in his pockets, and staring at the floor in thought. "If we give her more of a reason to stay, help her feel valued and part of this world—our world—then that's what we do. We give her what she needs. And I can support her doing whatever it is she has planned on that torture outline of hers."

I twisted my lips in a smile and reached out to shake his hand. Here we were. Alpha vampire and alpha shifter, teaming up to keep our demon hybrid mate on Earth. What was the world coming to . . .

CHAPTER 9
FURY

"What is taking them so long?" I asked, laying on the couch with my head hanging over the edge. "They recessed like fifteen minutes ago, yeah?"

Roxanne picked up a strawberry from a fruit tray on the coffee table and popped it into her mouth. "Yeah. We can go downstairs and get them," she said while she chewed.

"Finally. I'm starving up here. I want real food." Standing up, I readjusted my shirt, pulling a small gray feather off me. I groaned. "Ugh, is Hades molting and leaving shit on my shirt now?"

Roxanne glanced up and laughed as I tried to flick the feather off my fingers. "Hades has gray feathers under the black? Or is there some other bird you're hanging out with now and you don't have the heart to tell him?"

"Don't even joke about that. It's hard enough dealing with the one. He's driving me crazy," I said. "He's off searching for some answers with Duke, supposedly. But when he's here, I think he's sleeping in my clothes."

"Perhaps," Roxanne said, tucking her phone in her back pocket and grabbing another piece of fruit. "Maybe it would help if you made him a bed and didn't leave your clothes on the floor," she added with a know-it-all shrug.

I considered my response, then thought better of it. I was hangry, and when the hanger wanted to talk, it wasn't nice. I needed to be fed more often. Instead, I grumbled incoherently.

"You need a purse." Roxanne walked to the door and opened it. "That will help some of this."

I scrunched my eyebrows in confusion. "What? What does a purse have to do with anything?"

"A place for you to put snacks. You're a grouch when you're hungry. I can see it in your eyes. I don't need to be Ezra to know that," she said, waving her hand for me to exit first.

The guard at the door turned to us. "Shall I escort you and Fury down?"

"No, we'll just meet the guys downstairs, Frances. Thank you," she answered.

I followed her out and gave the fae a forced smile. She was right. I was grouchy. I was over this summit. It was days on end of doing what felt like nothing. I still hadn't figured out what would trigger the guys. I was no closer to getting answers on what the hell I was. I'd sifted into Ezra's bed, and bled like a stuck pig from my nose and ears, and we still had no clue what that was. Nothing else had happened yet, but it had only been a day since the last episode. Small victories, and all. I hadn't been alone long enough to summon Bloody Mary, and if I had, I wasn't sure what to ask her just yet, anyway. I didn't know if she would show up, and if she only gave me one question, I wanted to make it good. I didn't want to play that card just yet. It was pretty much the only one I had. If Duke and Hades didn't find what we needed, then I would take the risk.

I missed talking to Duke. I missed conversation and bantering with him. He was the closest thing I had to family, and more than anything, I missed that connection. I wanted his advice. I wanted to ask him questions I wasn't ready to even voice out loud to myself just yet, but it would be different with him. All I could do was hope he found some answers soon. In all my years in the Afterlife, I had inadvertently come to hate the unknown even more. I liked being in control.

I liked having a plan—even if that plan was winging it, it was still my choice to have that chaos as my strategy. I didn't feel like I was given a choice in what was happening now. At this point, any plan I might've had was shot to shit. I was truly flying by the seat of my pants, and I had zero control over it.

As soon as we entered the stairwell, I heard a cacophony of crashes and screaming. That was when I realized our other fae guard was not at the top stairwell post. Roxanne looked at me wide-eyed and I pushed past her to run down the stairs.

"Damn it, Fury, stop!" she shouted behind me as she followed. "Get back to the room—" She grabbed my arm, and I whirled around to face her.

"Fuck the room, what if they need us?" I said between clenched teeth.

"They want you safe. I can't let you run down there into whatever that is," she answered. She kept her grip on my arm tight.

I could have pulled away. Tossed her aside. It wouldn't take much effort. She was strong, and I knew that, but she wasn't as strong as I was. Every day I felt an increase in power, even if it was only a tingle. A tiny measure. I could hear just a little bit more in the distance. I could see just a little further or with a touch more clarity. My strength was there before the change. I could tear away from her, and she couldn't hold me back.

But this was Roxanne. I wouldn't do that to her if I could talk to her first.

"Why haven't the guys come to us? Why hasn't Ezra reached out to me? Where are they, Rox? Now let me go. Something is very wrong, and you know it. I wouldn't let Ezra stop me from getting to you the night of the banquet. I won't let you stop me from getting to them. I won't lose any of you."

Her grip loosened as she contemplated what I'd said, a slight flicker of her wolf flashing in her eyes so similar to her brother that it sent a chill down my spine.

She nodded. "Go."

I turned back and raced down the steps with Roxanne at my heels. The closer we got, the louder each shout and scream became. Reaching the bottom, I stilled, putting my hand on the doorknob and turning to Rox. She pulled off the purse she wore across her body and tossed it behind the stairs. She nodded silently, and I did the same.

I cracked open the door and saw supes running past us. They were all headed in one direction. Cool. That meant I needed to go the opposite way.

I flung it open and took off down the hallway toward the room where we'd held the panels.

I came to a screeching halt and Roxanne almost crashed into me.

It looked like the biggest bar fight I'd ever seen.

Countless supernaturals fought each other. Fists pounded into faces. Blood sprayed and bones crunched. Bodies were picked up and tossed into overturned furniture. Not a single table was upright. Chairs had been thrown across the room, some were still in the hands of those using the seats as weapons. Glass was shattered and broken everywhere, the light filtering in from the windows catching the shards and making them sparkle like jewels. Surveying the room, I saw there were entirely too many that lay unmoving, bleeding from gaping wounds or missing limbs.

"What in the hell?" Roxanne breathed behind me.

My mouth hung open before I could find the words.

"I don't know, but this was not what I expected to find."

"Where are the guys?" she asked, taking a step forward and standing next to me. "What happened here?"

I shook my head as I looked around. No one even seemed to notice us.

I saw a shifter stand up from behind a table she'd used for cover. Her green fatigue pants were covered in blood spatters, and her tight black shirt was torn in places. Whatever brief feelings of confusion I'd had dissipated quickly when I met her gaze. She walked slowly amongst the chaos, not paying attention to anyone or anything around her.

Something was wrong with her. I looked her in the eyes and what I saw was not a shifter. I didn't know what she was. Her eyes looked blank and hollow, but she was alive. There was no question.

Roxanne gasped when she saw her, coming to the same conclusion, throwing her arm in front of me like a mother would her child.

"Fury, go," she whispered harshly.

I looked over at her incredulously. "And leave you here? Fuck that."

Roxanne and I stood shoulder to shoulder, and she refused to take her eyes off the approaching imposter.

I turned my head a fraction, looking to see if we were going to be ambushed from behind, trying to formulate a way out. But where?

Ezra, now's the time to be prying in my head. Where the hell are you?

Slightly busy. A fight broke out. Roman and I are handling it.

Where is Dorian?

Avalon.

I placed my hand on Rox's arm. She shook her head slightly, never breaking eye contact. Don't speak. The shifter would hear us.

Ezra, this isn't just a random fight . . . main room . . .

Before I could finish, the shifter strode forward, cocking an eyebrow as her lip curled on one side in a cruel smile. I watched her fingers twitching at her side like she was eager to get her hands on something. I realized why. She moved lightning fast, reaching for a knife she'd kept at her side, and she threw it.

Everything happened so quickly, yet it felt like I watched it in slow motion.

The dagger sailed through the air, aimed directly at Roxanne's chest. Shoving my shoulder toward her and putting all my weight behind it, I pushed into her body, moving her out of the knife's path.

And into mine.

The blade sliced through my deltoid, and I felt the intense fiery burning that only comes with an open wound. The knife landed behind me, clattering to the floor. I screamed in anger and pain, grabbing my arm in reflex. Blood squeezed through my fingers and gushed down my arm.

That fucking bitch just cut me.

Oh hell no.

I heard Ezra's panic in my head as the events unfolded.

The shifter laughed, and she ran toward us, transforming into a wolf as she approached. I reached down to pick up the knife as Roxanne roared in response. Her brown eyes went so icy blue they turned white. Her canines grew, and she exploded into a monstrous wolf with black oak fur. She bolted forward with a deep growl, her jaws open as she lunged and met the attacker head on.

Were it not for the life-and-death situation playing out before me,

I would have marveled at Roxanne's beauty. The shine of her coat and the powerful yet graceful way she moved. But it wasn't the time.

The wolves clashed together in a frenzy, snapping and biting. I ran toward them, watching as the unknown shifter pushed up on her back legs, pushing Rox with her front paws. I dropped to my knees, sliding across the wood floors. I leaned back as far as I could, slashing the legs of the wolf as I glided right behind her. She collapsed, a distinct canine whine piercing the air. Roxanne jumped on top of her, jaws clamping down on her throat.

Ezra shouted my name through our connection as he saw what was happening, no doubt sharing it with Roman. It was then I heard Roman's bellowing reverberating through the walls.

My mates burst through a side door, knocking the fighting supernaturals aside with brute strength as they ran toward us. The fighting factions scattered, taking cover, or running off in fear as their enraged alphas tore them apart in an effort to get to us.

Ezra's strong, lean arms wrapped around me, pulling me away from Roxanne. "Let me go."

He held tight. "Just wait. He needs to calm her. Roxanne as a wolf is dangerous." I stopped fighting his hold and watched as Roman placed a hand on her shoulder, stroking the fur gently while he shushed softly. She growled in response, baring her teeth even more as they held the imposter. Then she looked at her brother from the corner of her eye.

Roman nodded in some sort of understanding as he looked at his sister. I realized he could communicate with her when she was a wolf. Would he be able to do that with me once I shifted? He pulled back his muscled arm, fist closed, then punched the subdued wolf in the head with a loud crack. The light left her eyes, and her breathing ceased. He'd killed her, taking the weight of that responsibility off his sister's shoulders. Roxanne let go, shaking out her body and rapidly shifting back into her human form.

"What in the world is going on here?" Roxanne asked her brother.

"I don't have a fucking clue." He ran both hands over the top of his head. "What did you mean Carly was like a zombie?"

"That one?" Ezra asked, pointing to the body as I pulled away from him. He took the knife from me, inspecting it.

Roxanne nodded. “Her name was Carly. She was a mid-level ranger in our pack.”

I scoffed. “Well, *Carly* looked blank. Possessed. Like she didn’t know what she was doing, but she was laughing after she threw the knife.”

Roman looked down at my bleeding arm and he grabbed it, looking at the wound. “It’s not closed yet.” He took off his shirt and ripped it, tying a piece of the cloth around the cut to staunch the bleeding. He cupped my face, stroking my cheekbone as he leaned down and touched my forehead with his own.

The serene moment was interrupted by a melodious laugh, echoing in the giant conference room like the peal of wind chimes.

We all jerked our heads in surprise, looking to see who it was. I turned my head around, not seeing anyone. Until I looked up at a chandelier. A woman in a red dress and white cloak sat on the curve of an arc. She rocked her legs forward and back, swinging like a child on a playground. She kept her head ducked down, the fabric obscuring her face from view.

“Come play with me,” she purred, curling her finger and beckoning me. “You’re mine, pretty girl.”

I crossed my arms. “I am not.”

She stopped her childlike movements, a low hiss escaping her lips.

I felt a tingling sensation on the tip of my nose, and I rubbed it. Then I sneezed.

“No,” she breathed. It was barely a whisper, but my enhanced hearing picked up on it.

Ezra—

I can’t read her. She’s blocked.

Of course she is.

I sneezed again.

“Stop making me sneeze, asshole,” I said to her, annoyance filling my tone. She growled at me in response.

Roman looked at me confused before recognition flashed across his face. “She’s trying to control you. A spell.”

“Fucking witches,” Ezra said through clenched teeth.

The woman jumped down from the candelabra, almost floating gracefully to the ground. She landed on one knee, her head down, looking at the floor. She picked up a shard of glass in one hand and squeezed it. Blood oozed from her hand, seeping between her fingers.

"Mortem. Exitum," she whispered as she started to look up. "Venit."

Crazy person speaking Latin about death and destruction was a bad sign. My mouth fell open as Ezra's voice drowned out my own thoughts.

She's after you. Go with Roxanne. We'll take her out.

Ezra flipped the knife in his hand, catching it blade side in preparation to throw it at our mystery witch. Roman's skin vibrated, his wolf itching to come out and fight.

The cloak fell from her head, settling on her shoulders, as Ezra's arm came down to throw, but I grabbed his wrist, stopping him from releasing the blade when her face came into view.

"Stop," I shouted. "Don't kill her!" My words came out quickly as I panicked, and I stared into her haunted blue eyes. A single tear ran down her bloodstained skin, leaving a clean path of white amongst the crimson splatters.

Ezra and Roman looked at me incredulously.

"That's Dorian's daughter."

CHAPTER 10
FURY

"WHAT?" ROMAN AND EZRA SAID IN UNISON.

"Impossible," Roxanne breathed, shifting her weight. She shook her head in disbelief, but her wide eyes said she knew I was right.

A million questions ran through my head. I tried to recall what Dorian had told me about her. We were in Avalon. I saw her portrait in the green room. Lyra. That was her name. He said she had been forced into a sleep to stop her from hurting herself. And others. What that meant, he never told me, and I didn't ask. As I looked at her bleeding hand, her tear-streaked face, and the crazy look in her eye, I now regretted suppressing those questions.

Dorian said she was in something called stasis. She couldn't just wake up on her own. Yet, here she was, standing before us, surrounded by destruction.

"You knew about this?" Roman asked his sister, turning his head a fraction in her direction. Anger rippled through his voice.

"Not the time," she answered through gritted teeth, her fists clenched at her sides.

I decided to take a chance. See if I could talk to her, or at the very least, get some answers.

"Your name is Lyra," I said cautiously as she approached us.

Her steps were slow, and her blue eyes flashed with an emotion I couldn't place. She masked whatever it was she felt, then drew her brows together in anger. That one I could read well.

I held my hands up in a peaceful gesture, and I hoped she would accept it. "I don't want to hurt you. I won't. I just want to know why you're here."

Her lips curled upward in a vicious smile. "Why, I'm here for you," she answered. "I was sent for *you*."

A thunderous growl emitted from Roman, shaking the ground beneath us. I didn't know he was capable of shaking the very earth in his rage, but it was something I needed to note for later.

"Ignore him," I said, waving off the alpha wolf, trying to keep her attention on me. I couldn't risk taking my eyes off Lyra. "Okay, you were sent to kill me. Got it. Who sent you?"

She shook her head, the white-blond hair moving around gently. Her pointed ears peeked through the strands. A humorless laugh escaped her lips. "I'm not here to kill you. I just want to play." She dragged out the last word, running her tongue over the tip of her slightly pointed canine.

A chill worked its way down my spine, but I didn't want to give away how her words affected me. The way Roman, Roxanne, and Ezra were frozen, I only imagined they were experiencing something similar. This fae wanted to do damage. She didn't want me dead. Whatever it was she wanted to do with me was worse than the simplicity of death. I didn't need to ask more questions to know that. But why?

Can you read anything about her yet? I asked Ezra. He stood in a defensive position, ready for the attack.

Nothing.

We need to get away from her. I don't know her powers, but I know she's dangerous. Tell Roman and Roxanne I want them out of here. They can call Dorian. Just be careful, and please don't kill her.

You're fucking kidding me, right?

Ezra, please. I hoped pleading with him would be enough. There was no way for me to explain it. I didn't even have all the information, but I knew she was Dorian's child. I knew she was ill. I knew he loved her more than anything. I heard the longing in his voice when he told me about her. I saw the sadness in his eyes. We couldn't do that to him. We couldn't kill his daughter. Roman was struggling to survive after the loss of his mate and child. I didn't want Dorian to go through it too. *I know you can hear me. She lives, do you understand? Promise me.*

Nothing but silence in return. Not once had she changed her speed as she approached, but she was too close, and I was out of time to argue with him.

"Here to play? I'm not much for games, Lyra. I'm more of a straight shooter."

She shrugged. "Suit yourself. Everyone breaks eventually," she said and lunged forward.

That Earth phrase about all hell breaking loose—it was an appropriate description.

I dove out of Lyra's reach as she took a swipe at me. I hit the ground, rolling with intent until I bumped into an overturned table. I groaned, quickly getting to my feet.

I had no idea how to subdue her. We couldn't kill her. We'd have to play her game until Dorian came, or until she was sated. I just hoped she wasn't planning on satisfaction via murdering us the time around. Maybe I could knock her out? That seemed unlikely, but I didn't have much to go on.

Ezra heard my thoughts and shook his head vehemently as he moved his position, circling her location with the knife still in his hand.

The floor rumbled and a furious roar filled the room. Roman and Roxanne shifted, exploding into their wolf forms in a matter of seconds. They stood side by side, hackles raised and baring their teeth as they growled in warning.

Lyra grinned in response. Looking above her, she reached a hand up, closing her fists, then pulling down hard. Her eyes darkened, flaring indigo in color, and I saw her intent. The chandelier she'd sat on earlier came crashing down. Both wolves jumped out of the way in opposite directions as it crashed on the floor, sending glass flying in all directions.

A piece of shrapnel flew outwards and embedded in Roman's shoulder. He shook his body hard, trying to dislodge it as blood coated the fur around it. All I could see in his blue eyes was rage.

A childlike laugh bubbled up and Lyra reveled in it. She spun around, looking for her next target.

Roxanne was by my side, but we had no way to reciprocate communication. I grabbed her giant muzzle, turning her to look at me, speaking harshly while I told her what I needed. "Go. Call him. We need him here. The longer we drag this out, the worse it could get. We don't know what we're dealing with."

She growled softly as we stared at each other. Several tense moments passed before she dipped her head and closed her eyes in an extended blink. She nudged me with her nose, pushing me toward an area of furniture. She wanted me to hide.

"Go," I whispered, pushing her away. "I'll be fine."

She grunted, turning away from me to run toward an exit, keeping close to the wall, her great paws thudding as they hit the wooden floors.

I scanned the room, catching Ezra's form as he circled behind Lyra while Roman prowled in front of her and snapped his jaws, his shoulder wound already healed.

"I know what you're doing, vampire," she said in a singsong voice, picking up her skirt and twirling it like she was dancing around a Maypole. She'd completely turned her back on Roman.

She was incredibly confident or overly stupid, and I was betting on the former. The little that I knew about her didn't suggest she was easy to take down.

Roman hunched close to the ground, but I held my hand up to him, shaking my head. He growled deeply, not liking my command.

Lyra held her hand out, turning it over front and back, admiring it. She grinned, then her claws extended slowly, long, pointy, and from the looks of it, sharp. "I have knives too," she said to Ezra quietly. "I bet mine are sharper. Would you like to see?"

Keep your distance, Ezra. Bide our time. I worked my way toward him slowly, circling the way he had.

Ezra flicked his gaze to me, then back to her. I saw the slightest twitch in his arm. I faltered, realizing what he was going to do. I burst into a sprint, hoping this weird supernatural hybrid magic would allow me to be faster than all of them.

I wasn't.

Ezra darted at an impressive speed, only to have her sift away from him. She landed four feet in front of me, and I tried to stop before slamming into her. A cruel smirk lit up her face when she turned and looked at Ezra over her shoulder. She tutted, then swiped her hand out, slashing across my stomach and digging into the corded muscle before she disappeared and moved to another location in the middle of the room.

Pain and burning ripped through me and I fell to the ground, crying out. I pressed my hands to wounds, pretty much hoping my insides were not on my outsides because the intensity of the fire I felt around it said maybe they were. Red oozed around my fingers, and I looked down, not seeing anything I shouldn't. Well, except the torn skin and pouring blood.

Roman roared, running toward Lyra as Ezra screamed a curse and ran to me in a flash. I rolled over to my knees, and pushed myself up, feeling every bit of the strain in my abdomen, and it freakin' hurt. He held on to me, trying to help me, but I pushed his chest away, yelling, "I fucking told you not to kill her. Don't engage."

He ignored me, reaching for my stomach, and pulling up the shirt to see the wounds knitting themselves back together. "It's healing," he said and breathed out in a sigh of relief.

Back in her human form, Roxanne burst through the side entry, shouting for Roman to stop, but he was too focused as he advanced on Lyra. He aimed low, looking to take out her legs, but she jumped in the air effortlessly, landing with an undeserved grace, her dress billowing in the air around her. Roman skidded, then turned to face her again, pissed he hadn't made contact with her.

There was a mischievous gleam in her eye as she smiled—then all her movements stopped. Her sapphire eyes flashed a deep indigo, then back to blue. The almost joyous look she had on her face disappeared and a single tear fell from her eye again. Her harsh gaze held mine as she opened and closed her fists.

"We'll see each other again soon. The angel calls to me."

My blood ran cold.

I knocked Ezra away from me and rushed toward her, shouting, "What angel? Lyra!"

In a split second, she sifted, leaving me running toward nothing.

The angels. This was about me. All of it. Again. I dropped to my knees and screamed in frustration as I pounded my fists into the ground over and over. A crack splintered across the room as I took out my emotions on the floor.

Roman shifted back, and I felt his and Roxanne's warmth next to my body. She knelt down beside me, wrapping her arm around my shoulders. Roman's strong hands stroked my hair. They were attempting to comfort me in the only way they knew how. Ezra was smart enough to stay away from me at the moment.

"You said to come back now. What the hell happened here?" Dorian's voice boomed in the expansive room.

I snapped my head up, and so did everyone else. He walked with authority and confidence, taking in the destruction surrounding us.

"Lyra happened," Ezra said, crossing his arms and cracking his neck from side to side. "Care to explain that one, *Dorian*?"

The fae alpha halted. His steps were no longer steady. His normally unshakeable poise wavered. Something troubled passed over his glowing amber eyes.

"No . . ."

Roxanne stood up beside me and stormed over to Dorian with purpose. Tears filled her eyes, threatening to spill over the moment she'd blink. She stopped in front of him, saying nothing. He said nothing in return. Then she slapped him across the face, the smack echoing in the silence. His head whipped in the direction she'd hit him, and still he said nothing.

"You said Lyra was dead," she said, her voice an angry whisper. "Don't you ever fucking lie to me again. *Ever.*"

I pushed myself up, wiping off my knees. Blood dripped down my knuckles from hitting the floor. "When Dorian? When did she wake up?"

He brushed his hand over his face where Roxanne had hit him, then ran his hand through his hair. "The same night the summit started. The night of the banquet."

His words played on repeat in my ears.

The same night Roxanne was kidnapped.

The same night I was bitten.

Lyra woke up that night. Every part of my senses were on edge, vibrating with barely contained rage. Even though Ezra wasn't pushing into my thoughts, I felt his presence. I shot him a look. It said 'back the fuck off.'

"When were you going to tell me?" I asked him. I gritted my teeth. The muscle in my jaw hurt. I knew what he was going to tell me. I needed to hear him say it. He was pushing me to be honest with them. Asking me question after question. Demanding answers. He chastised me for keeping my secrets, and my secrets weren't even all my own to tell. He judged me for the truth of who and what I was. And for a brief moment, I had felt badly for it. Now he was going to tell me what he was. And that was a goddamned fucking liar.

Dorian's features were cold and guarded. He narrowed his eyes a fraction but didn't answer me.

I closed my eyes and counted. Counted and breathed. When I opened them again, I met his stare. "When?"

Silence.

The anger inside me couldn't hold much longer. I clenched my fists and felt the prick of my claws extend into my hand. It pierced the skin, and I could smell the copper tang settle around me. My vision clouded in a foggy haze. "WHEN?" I screamed, drawing it out. My body shook as I allowed the violence I so badly wanted to unleash come out in my voice instead. It was better than the alternative.

Still. The windows shattered, and another chandelier shook precariously. The upturned tables and toppled chairs rattled against the once gleaming antique wood floors.

When the last of my echoing demands had abated, I stared at him.

"I wasn't going to tell you."

CHAPTER 11
DORIAN

The tension in the room was palpable. Roxanne's hurt was undeniable. I had lied to her. Probably my dearest friend in my long life, and I hadn't shared the truth of my loss. I had no doubt she was questioning my reasons for not trusting her.

Roman and Ezra were furious. I didn't care. They could go fuck themselves. I owed them nothing. I surely didn't know their most closely guarded secrets, and why should I? It wasn't my business.

But Fury. She looked at me with stormy eyes, seething. Her red hair clung to her neck and face with sweat. Her nostrils flared as she breathed in and out. I refused to look away.

"Why?" she asked, breaking the silent standoff.

I thought for a moment. It didn't matter how I worded what would come next. The anger she felt toward me would not be easily forgiven.

"Because I didn't want to," I said finally.

She huffed, "No, that isn't a good enough answer."

"I'm sorry you feel that way."

"Fuck you," she spat. "You aren't sorry for anything. Why didn't you want to tell me? To tell any of us?"

I straightened my posture, lifting my head up to look at the ceiling. The exhaustion of the week's events was taking its toll. My shoulders always felt heavy with the weight of time and knowledge. Mentally I was drained. I wanted to rest. I had wanted to rest for a thousand years, but I couldn't. It was my responsibility to take care of Lyra. To take care of those she had hurt all those years ago. To protect the living fae and honor the memory of the dead. I had no successor. It was my burden. My punishment for not being enough when I was needed the most. With that thought, I simply said, "It isn't anyone's business."

"Like hell it isn't," Roman roared. "You have some nerve saying it wasn't anyone's business. Look around you, Dorian." Roman threw his arms out as if I couldn't see the dead bodies and the room in complete disarray. "Tell me how she can destroy all of this, kill people, and come after Fury—come after *our mate*—and then claim it's somehow not our business."

Bringing my gaze to the shifter, I looked into the icy blue eyes of his unstable wolf. "She wasn't here for Fury. She came looking for me."

"That's not what she said." Fury's voice was quiet. Level. I considered, at that moment, that she may be a bit like me. The quiet in me was dangerous. It was when I was thinking. Strategizing. But it was also when the wrath was fed. When the tempest of anger in me grew. The quiet before the storm. Perhaps we were alike in that. Time would tell.

I glanced at Fury, taking my eyes off her face for the first time. Her arm was covered in blood. It coated her hands and clung to her clothes. Three slashes in her shirt exposed the bloody skin of her stomach. A deeper part of my instinct responded. The need to be near her. Heal whatever wounds she had. Protect her. It felt feral. Almost uncontrollable. Almost. I took a step forward, my hand reaching out. I pointed to her midsection. "You're hurt."

She followed my gaze and wiped her hand over it. "It's healing. I'm fine. No thanks to you."

"Did Lyra do that?" I asked. The muscles in my back tensed further. I knew the answer. My daughter had harmed my mate.

"Some of it," she said, wiping at the ripped shirt over her abdomen. "There was a huge brawl. Everyone was fighting. Like something out of a bad western movie. Nothing made any sense.

When Lyra made her appearance, she said she was here for me. Not to kill me. To play with me."

A harrowing cold descended on me. I felt it run the length of my body. Snapshots of haunted memories flashed in my mind. They never went away. Even when I slept, I saw the past. The bloodstained fields she'd left in her wake. I could see the trail of bodies. I could hear the screams of those dying, and agonizing wails of those clinging to their loved ones when we found her victims. The images would never leave me. Nor should they. It was my fault. "What else did she say?"

"She said she was *sent* for me. And right before you came, she said the angel calls to her." Fury watched me closely, no doubt looking for my reaction. "What does that mean?"

"I don't know." A truth I hated to admit. A second mention of an angel was only complicated by Fury's disclosure about our mates' deaths. I searched my mind for what it could mean, or why Lyra would say it, but it was a world I didn't know. That was her territory. Angels were unknown to us. Their lore was nothing more to us than a fairytale until Fury told us otherwise.

"Bullshit," Ezra said. "That crazy bitch showed up talking nonsense and speaking in riddles. We find out she's your daughter—something Fury managed to keep from me,"—he shot an incensed glance her way—"and you kept it a secret when she 'woke up', whatever that is supposed to mean. Why the actual fuck would we believe you now?"

"I had no idea she would come after Fury. She doesn't even know her—"

"But she did," Roxanne interrupted. "What is she capable of? And you better not lie to me. You owe me the truth."

"I think you owe us more than that," Roman said. "You told Roxanne she was dead. Fury recognized her, but seemed shocked at her presence. What's the real story here? Why did you keep this a secret?"

The vampire had looked over that detail in his tantrum. At the moment, he was too emotional. He had yet to look at my reasoning, only focusing on my action. Somehow, the shifter had. He surprised me at times, especially for one so young. His wolf was riding him, demanding answers. He barely had him under control, but his wolf and his strength were not the only reason he was an alpha, and whether or not he knew it, it was showing.

I had to decide how much to tell them. I found it curious that Ezra hadn't gleaned that little bit of information from her with all the mind games he played. I wasn't sure how she'd done it, but I wanted to know.

Fury kept quiet as she watched the exchange, and her silence did not go unnoticed. She raised a single eyebrow, challenging me to tell them before she did.

"Lyra is my daughter. My mate was her mother. Lyra saw what happened to her mother when she died, though I didn't. I found them afterward. After that day, she was broken. It sent her into a dangerous spiral of self-destruction. We tried to help her. Over time, the pain morphed into something worse. She became . . . not herself. I put her in stasis to keep her safe. To stop her from harming others."

I heard the questions forming in their minds. I suspected they were piecing it together. I knew what was coming.

"What does that mean?" Roxanne asked. The tears on her face had dried, leaving marks crusted on her warm brown skin. She'd never even bothered to wipe them away.

I tilted my chin up. "It means I forced her into a dreamless sleep until I could find a way to heal her."

"How long?" Roman asked. I met his judgmental gaze.

I inhaled deeply through my nose before speaking. "A thousand years, next winter."

Their curses and sounds of shock weren't hard to discern in the quiet of the expansive room. The high ceilings pushed the noise in circles, making sure I heard just how much they judged my actions.

"How is she out of stasis now?" Fury asked, crossing her arms.

I pressed my lips together and leveled her with a stare. "I . . . don't know. The magic and strength it took to put her in stasis was more than you could imagine. To wake her is . . . there are few in the world that could come close to having that kind of power."

"But someone did," she pressed. "And it wasn't you."

She hadn't asked a question, so I chose not to respond.

A realization sparked in her eyes. "The footsteps."

I inclined my head. "Yes, the footsteps. Whoever that was came back. Whoever that was woke her."

"Which brings me back to my question, Dorian," Roxanne interjected. "What is she capable of?"

I studied each of their faces, gauging how they would react to what I was about to say. They had no idea the havoc she could wreak. She fed on violence and bathed in blood. No matter how much I tried, I never understood why. I had spent a millennium seeking answers, but I came up short every time. I had tried to find a way to heal her mind without knowing what was wrong to begin with.

Roman, Roxanne, Ezra, and fae all over the world thought they knew the reasons for my intelligence and power. They were only partially correct. Yes, it was my job as protector and alpha to look after those placed in my care.

Without knowledge, there was no power. I'd spent centuries upon centuries pouring through scrolls, seeking wielders of old magic and new, learning legend and lore, accessing the secrets hidden within artifacts in mythology and religion—anything to give me a clue where to look next.

I still came up with nothing.

"Annihilation," I answered, my voice quiet. "And if for one moment you aren't fearful of what that means, you should be."

"You should have told me," Fury said.

"I had no way to know she would come after you," I admitted. "Nothing indicated a connection."

She rolled her eyes at me. "You're not as smart as you think you are if you actually believed this isn't connected. After everything I've told you—"

"Your arrogance almost got her killed," Roman said, his wolf sending a warning growl in his words. His eyes were a crystalline blue. The way his shoulders twitched told me he was on the brink of shifting. I met his gaze.

"I won't fight you, Roman, nor will I fight your wolf. Certainly not over this." I clasped my hands behind my back. "Take her with you, back to the compound. Keep her safe. Lyra is on the hunt now, and if she wants to find Fury, we need to be prepared to find her first."

"I thought that was what you were already doing," Ezra snapped. "Trying to find her and keep your dirty secrets safe?"

I quirked an eyebrow at his outburst. Mouthy vampire. Still . . .

"I could use your help. Roman and Rox can stay with Fury. You can come with me in the meantime. If I'm not mistaken, all Fury needs to do is reach out to you in the event they need us."

He squinted at my offer then gave a single nod. He briefly looked at Roman and they shared a moment, some unspoken understanding passing from one to the other. Curious that the vampire and the shifter were in on something together. It was not something I would have expected from them. I would take the opportunity with Ezra to learn more about what that meant.

I walked over to Fury and stood before her. Reaching up, I brushed my knuckles down her cheek. "I'm sorry Lyra hurt you. I *will* find a way to stop her."

She closed her eyes and leaned into my touch, if only for a second. "You should be apologizing for lying to me. To all of us." She pulled away, pushing past me, and heading for the exit. Roman huffed angrily, following at her heels. Roxanne passed me silently, looking at me from the corner of her eye before leaving.

I sighed. "It's you and me, Ezra."

"A thrill, I'm sure," he mumbled.

I hummed, pulling out my phone and hitting the speed dial. Tristan answered on the other line.

"What's your location?" I asked, motioning for Ezra to come stand next to me. "I have one stop to make, then we are coming to you. Lyra has been sighted, and it would appear she is back to playing her old games."

CHAPTER 12
FURY

I FIDGETED WITH THE STRAY LOCKS OF RED HAIR THAT ESCAPED MY MESSY BUN. Tonight was the ceremony for the shifters that died at the summit. Everyone from Roman's pack would be there, but it wasn't them that occupied my thoughts, but how they died.

Lyra was awake, and she was hunting. For me. Not to kill, but to play. The thought sent a trail of goosebumps up my bare arms. The Bruce Springsteen T-shirt had cutoff sleeves and a ripped midsection, putting both my demon brand and stomach on display. The three cuts I'd suffered earlier would have been fatal to a non-supernatural. Now all that remained were three very faint pink lines that would be gone by morning.

I tentatively reached down and brushed my fingers over the slightly uneven skin. This was what Lyra's version of play looked like. And to think, an angel sent her after me.

I knew one was behind the supernaturals before they kidnapped Roxanne and tried to kill me. But to wake Lyra . . . my hand dropped away. I couldn't understand this endgame. Before they wanted me dead, now they wanted to fuck with me? It didn't make any sense. If this were about the prophecy and the end of the world, I suppose killing me would have made sense if they wanted me to fail. But this . . . this felt personal.

Which was all the more confusing because I didn't know any angels. Not as anything more than an acquaintance, and no one in my human life would have been made one. That wasn't an option on the job roster. Angels were old. They'd been there since, well, forever.

So why come after me? And furthermore, I didn't know why the Afterlife hadn't stepped in to intervene yet. It's not like this was sanctioned. They'd sent me here for a purpose. Whoever was doing this had clearly gone rogue. But they hadn't been stopped yet, which made it all the more bewildering.

"Fury?" Roxanne called out before knocking softly on the door. "You ready?"

"Yeah," I said. "Coming." I took one last troubled look at the long mirror before heading downstairs. The house was eerily quiet compared to the usual chatter of people milling about. Rox must have seen the confusion on my face.

"Most everyone is already there. A lot of them had families that wanted to say goodbye before the burning." I followed behind her as we stepped out onto the front porch. The smoke from the fire hit me instantly, even though the plume rising in the sky was almost half a mile away.

"Did you know any of them?" I asked her as we started walking. The humidity still sucked, but without the sunlight, it wasn't quite as bad at ten o'clock at night.

"All of them," Roxanne answered quietly. "Carly and I went to school together. I dated her older brother for a while. He was supposed to be at the summit, but he got called away for work last minute." She walked at a gentle pace with her thumbs casually hooked in her pockets. She appeared at ease, despite the grief in her voice. "Most of the others I knew in passing. A few of them I was friends with. We're a pack. One way or another, I know everyone."

"Saying I'm sorry feels inadequate, but offering condolences just feels fake," I replied, kicking a rock out of the way with my boot. "I'm sorry I can't make it better."

"You're here," she said simply. "That's enough. I probably seem cold to some of the others because I'm not sobbing on the outside, but after watching my parents die and then what they did to Roman; Maya . . ." She shook her head. "I don't have it in me to cry right now.

I'm so sick of watching people I care about die, I can't even react to it anymore."

"There's a point where pain and suffering become too much. That you become so used to it, you grow numb," I said quietly. "I can understand if that's what you've had to do to handle it." I knew it from my own experience. Not grief in the same way she was dealing with, but a grief all the same. I mourned the loss of myself before I even died. I turned numb because it was the only way to survive, until one hit too many took me.

Dying was the best thing that ever happened to me. But it wouldn't be that way for her friends and family. There were no promises or silver linings that I could offer her, knowing what I knew. And I'd shared that information with her, so there was no doubt in my mind that she wasn't thinking about it too.

"I need you to promise me something," she said as the funeral pyre loomed nearby. I could hear others easily at this range, which meant if they were listening, they could hear us too.

"Hm?"

A cool hand grabbed my own as she pulled me up short. "Don't go to them. Don't let that bastard win."

"Who—"

"The angel," she whispered. A flicker of blue ran through her desperate eyes, telling me all I needed to know. "Today happened because of them. Maya happened because of one of them. I need you to promise me that you won't run into danger again, not even for me. Roman, Ezra, even Dorian—much as I'm pissed at him right now—I don't think they could survive losing another mate, and I don't think the world will survive them."

My mouth opened then closed. Her words clicked together the missing piece.

All this time, I'd questioned why.

What makes them lose it?

What could do that to all three of them that hadn't before?

The answer was so fucking simple, but I needed Roxanne to see it.

I was the piece that connected them. *I* was the only person that did.

Which meant I was the reason.

My death.

"Motherfucker," I muttered under my breath. Roxanne narrowed her eyes at me. "Sorry, I just had an epiphany." She lifted her eyebrows, urging me to continue. I shook my head. Now wasn't the time, not when she literally just begged me not to die. Didn't seem like a great time to tell her my end was inevitable. Probably.

"What is it?" she said, dropping my hand to cross her arms over her chest.

"Noth—" I started to lie, then stopped. Judging by her expression, she wouldn't have bought it anyway. "I figured out part of my case, but it's not important right now. What is—is that I won't promise you that." Her eyes flickered blue again, not liking that answer. "Not just because I care about you, but because it's not in my nature. Everything that's happening right now surrounds me, and I can't run away from that. I need to figure out what's going on and why an angel turned against the Afterlife. That doesn't mean I'll go to them or give up, though. We're playing with someone from my turf, and I need to be more careful than I have been because of that."

Roxanne let out a tight breath. Her shoulders sagged a little before she uncrossed her arms. "I suppose that's the best I'm going to get from you."

"It is." I smiled wryly. "Besides, the one sure fire way to kill me before won't work anymore. Given we don't know what will work, I can't imagine they do either."

She pursed her lips. "That's supposed to make me feel better?"

I shrugged. "I'm just being honest with you. Given I'm more likely to die-die this time, I won't hold back from using all the weapons I have at my disposal. People tend to back the fuck off when I can blow them up with my mind."

"I forget that, even though I shouldn't. It was scary as shit when you did it that night."

"It's a last resort. I prefer not to because of casualties. Demon strength also tends to be way more fun when it comes to handing people their ass." I smirked, and she rolled her eyes.

"You enjoy fucking with people too much," she huffed. I chuckled.

"I believe you meant to say I picked my job well, and yes, I did. That aside though, I think they're waiting for us." I thrust my chin toward the fire where a huge group of shifters were gathered. It was relatively quiet considering the number of people, and more than a few were staring at us.

Roxanne sighed; the ease we'd found began slipping away as grief took hold again. "Come on." My smile dropped away as soon as she turned around. It wasn't just burning the dead or what it meant to these people, but the realization that this really, truly might be me soon.

Despite dying once, and almost dying again, I never really thought it would happen. The Afterlife takes away all anxieties surrounding it and I'd been living in some existence for so long now that having to comprehend the finality I might have to face . . . it was deep. Thought-provoking.

The ceremony went by quickly for me. They burned the bodies of their dead while Roman talked about each of them. He shared stories about their lives, what they meant to him, and others. I could tell the shifters were moved by it. I had to keep myself from cringing every time someone said a prayer, believing they'd see their lost loved ones again in the end.

At some point when the mood was high, the atmosphere changed. Roman stepped down and people took their turns going up to the fire, then retreating back to their spots. Most people brought blankets and towels to lay out. A few trucks pulled up and dropped their tailgates open to reveal coolers of beer and soda, mini-grills for hotdogs and hamburgers, and a projector that they aimed at the side of the barn closest to us.

"What's going on?" I whispered to Roxanne.

"A celebration of life. When a shifter dies, we burn their body and then throw a party until dawn. We spend that time honoring them," she said. "I'm going to go grab a blanket for us. You want something to drink?"

"A beer sounds good," I said. "Wouldn't say no to a hotdog either if you were feeling nice. Ketchup and mustard if they have it."

"You got it," Rox said. She sauntered over to the group forming around the trucks. I stood there watching her for a moment. It was easy to see myself making a life here. Where Ezra offered me an escape from the ordinary, Roman offered a home. Safety.

I liked how down to earth they were. Their customs. The way they treated each other. It was so foreign to me. At the turn of the century, the portrait of the American dream hadn't even been painted yet. I was born into an authoritarian family that didn't share love, feeling, or emotion; that was our home. My father, the banker, my mother, the housewife. Support the household, raise the children. Those were their roles. My role was simple. Listen and learn. I was schooled on how to behave like a lady. To know my place in the world. It was the way of our social class in the early 1900s.

I scoffed internally at the absurdity of it all.

Everything about that life was hollow inside. Big empty houses filled with sad, empty people.

Here they lived and laughed and loved. There was no silence. No empty houses hiding secrets. They celebrated together, and they mourned together. They shared their grief and their happiness. They respected and protected one another. I loved that, though I'd never known it.

"I've never seen hair that shade of red before. Is it a demon trait?" The new voice that greeted me was high, feminine, flirtatious even—and completely unknown. I turned my cheek to a shifter with lilac hair and eyes to match who couldn't have been more than five feet tall. I might've questioned if she dyed it, if not for the faint purple sheen of hairs on her arms.

"Purple hair and eyes aren't a shifter trait, either," I said, tilting my chin to study her better. A wry smile flitted across her lips. She wore a red and black long-sleeved T-shirt and jean shorts that were fraying at the ends.

"I'm special," she said and smirked.

"Me too," I replied. "How do you know I'm a demon?" While my mates and those close to them did, it wasn't exactly common knowledge yet. Not in the least because the living weren't supposed to know.

"I'm Caitlin's mate," she answered. "Name's Rava." She stuck her hand out. I noted her nails painted with black nail polish, and the black lines of a tattoo peeking out of her cuff. I shook her hand, surprised by the strength. Nothing trumped a demon, but she was stronger than the average supe. That much was obvious.

"Fury," I supplied, taking my hand back.

"I know."

"I gotta say, I prefer being on the other side of this conversation." Her eyebrows drew together before lifting in silent question. "The side where I know everything, and the other person is stumped. This side isn't as much fun." Rava chuckled, pushing a strand of violet hair back from her damp forehead to behind her ear.

"I wouldn't say everything. Just more than most of the pack. I get perks from being her mate, but she told me I might be able to help you some too."

"Oh yeah?" I questioned.

"Because I'm also an oddity. Half-shifter, half-fae." My eyes flicked to her ears, now noticing their subtle points. Less than a full fae, but more than any other supernatural.

"I didn't know there were any hybrids in the pack," I murmured.

"Hybrids are everywhere, nothing quite like you—obviously—but those of us that were either born to mixed lineage or turned a vampire at some point have some experience with the in-between. Because of my heritage, I'm not the same as most wolves or fae. I exist in the middle, like you."

I nodded slowly, taking her in again. "They say I should shift in the next week, by the full moon, but I'm still not feeling my wolf."

Rava nodded. "I didn't feel mine at all until *after* my first shift—which was much later than most of the shifters. For a while they thought I might not be able to."

"Does it hurt?" I asked, not psyched on the prospect of pain but curious what her experience was, given I might be more like her than anyone else I knew.

"For me it didn't, but my shift wasn't conventional. Many need the full moon to shift the first time. It helps them cross that last little barrier. In my case"—she hesitated for a moment, debating how much to say. I narrowed my eyes a fraction before she continued. "I lost control. My anger and adrenaline powered it, which carried me through the pain."

"Ah," I said, because I wasn't sure what else to say. On one hand, I was curious what caused her to have that much anger and adrenaline. On the other, it was usually considered rude to ask if someone didn't volunteer the information. Might be good to ask Roxanne about it later. I could be nosy without being a jerk.

"Yours may not. You likely have greater healing properties being part vampire. They recover from wounds better than any other species." She offered the information half-heartedly as if it might make it better.

"I'm also part demon as you pointed out, and they don't heal for shit when in a human body."

That wry smile she wore when she first spoke to me was back.

"Half the fun of being so different is learning all the ways you truly are," she mused.

"For someone considered different, that's an odd opinion to have," I said. "Most people don't like their differences. I can't imagine growing up in a pack was easy when you didn't shift with others your age."

She lifted a brow, either amused by my observation or questioning my audacity. I wasn't sure which. "It wasn't, but as I got older, my perspective changed. My mother is a shifter, and my father was fae. While I was born from a one-night stand during a previous summit, they both took responsibility and co-raised me. I got to have a pack, but also see places like Avalon. And because of my fae tutor, I can now sift anywhere in the world. Differences aren't bad when you learn to appreciate them."

I hummed, tucking the information away as Caitlin and Roxanne walked up to us.

"I see you've met Rava," Rox said, handing over my hotdog and beer.

"I hope she hasn't interrogated you too much," Caitlin said jokingly, even if there was a serious note in her eyes when she looked at her mate.

Rava raised both hands as if in surrender. "We were just talking."

"Mhmm." Caitlin smirked. "You'll have to forgive my skepticism. Rava is a counselor that helps hybrids cope with the accompanying challenges. She's been very eager to meet you ever since I told her what you were."

Things clicked into place when she said that, and the bubbly yet straightforward personality made a bit more sense. "You fix people."

"Correction; I help people fix themselves—although fix isn't the right word. Learn to appreciate and be okay with themselves is more accurate."

Roxanne grinned like she'd seen this conversation before. "That's fair, I suppose. Fix usually implies that it was broken, and I don't think being a hybrid counts as that. You'll have to forgive my terminology some. I'm a bit of a fixer myself."

"Oh really?" she asked, her eyes lighting up. "In what way?"

"Just the usual shitbags of the world. Rapists. Murderers. Abusive people that need some modifying." I shrugged, not noticing how Rava's face paled. She sent a semi-alarming look at Caitlin, who grimaced. "I take it they didn't tell you what I did in the Afterlife?"

Rava shook her head slowly. "I knew you were a demon, but I assumed that human preconceptions were likely far from reality."

AKA she didn't want to believe I was a soulless monster.

"Yes and no, I'm afraid. In the Afterlife, the bottom forty percent of people are reconditioned and punished in an attempt to fix their souls at the fundamental level before they're sent back. Demons have the job of doing that."

"Well, that's just *fascinating*," Rava said, utterly serious. "You'll have to tell me more when there are fewer sensitive ears around." She flicked her unnatural eyes to the shifters around us. While no one seemed to be paying attention, she had a good point about subtlety.

"Anytime," I offered with a smile. I took a swig of my beer and sighed happily into the frothy, foamy goodness. It'd been a solid twelve hours since my last drink and I was dying. A small voice in the back of my head said keeping track like that wasn't a positive thing, but it was easy enough to shut it out with the sounds of a crackling bonfire and easy chatting around me.

"Have you guys seen Roman?" Roxanne asked as she spread the blanket out. "I haven't seen him since the burning ritual." Both Rava and Caitlin shook their heads. A worried expression crossed her face before she scanned the woods. "Maybe I should go look for him."

"I'll do it," I volunteered. "I need another beer, anyway." Roxanne looked from me to the half-full red solo cup that I promptly emptied to make a point. Her expression turned annoyed, but she didn't call me out on it. I had a feeling Caitlin and Rava were the reasons. More

Rava than Caitlin since Roman had no problem bitching at me about my liquor intake when she was around.

Rox tipped her chin. "Let him know I saved him a spot if he wants to watch the slideshow with us."

"Will do," I called, starting for the trucks. After a pit stop to fill up my cup, I took a walk around the whole of the fire, not spotting him anywhere. That seemed a bit odd since he was the leader of this pack, but perhaps he ventured off somewhere. Maybe back to the house to use the bathroom?

I walked around for a few more minutes, seeing if I just missed him the first time, but when he couldn't be found anywhere—and wasn't on the half-mile-long dirt road that led to here—I started to question myself. Logically I knew nothing could happen to Roman. He was unkillable. But that didn't mean he wasn't in a different sort of trouble.

Standing at the edge of the forest, I squinted my eyes to peer into the murky shadows. While I didn't see anyone, a glint of silver caught my eye before disappearing. I took one last look over my shoulder, still not seeing him, before starting toward it.

The mating call of cicadas quickly drowned out the party behind me while tiny flashes of yellow light from fireflies illuminated the forest floor. I was thankful to be wearing Doc Martens while stepping over fallen and rotting logs, not knowing what might be in the underbrush beneath. The last thing I needed was a frickin' snake to bite me. Watch my ass not be immune to poison, even if I could survive getting stabbed.

My gravestone would read:

Here lies *The* Fury
Demon
taken out by motherfucking snake

Talk about lame. If I were going to go out, I'd hoped my exit would be far more dramatic this time around. Considering it might be the key to bringing on the end of the world, I had high hopes.

At least Lyra offered that, though my heart hurt for Dorian if I died by his daughter's hands. Talk about a complicated relationship. He loved her unconditionally, as he should, even if he was an unrepentant asshole to me. I can't imagine killing one's mate would make it any better, though. Or that Roman and Ezra wouldn't hold back from trying to end her afterwards.

A shiver worked its way up my spine.

Definitely need to avoid that one.

A sharp thud drew my attention. While there was no glint of metal this time, it came from the same direction. Slowly, I crept forward, my heart racing at the prospect of what I might find.

Please don't be a dead body. More dead shifters were the last thing I needed tonight.

When a second thud followed up, my heart skipped. I quickened my pace.

"You might be a good interrogator, but you'd make a terrible spy," Roman's rumbling voice greeted me.

I stepped out from behind a bush and through the tall ferns, into a small clearing with tree stumps littered throughout. I looked from the forest floor to the hulk of a man standing shirtless with his back to me. His muscles rippled as he lifted an axe over his head and split the log in front of him cleanly in two.

"I wasn't spying," I murmured, walking around the edge of the circle.

"Could have fooled me."

"How'd you know it was me behind you?" I asked, crossing my arms over my chest. Roman reached down with two hands and grabbed either side of the split long, ripping it down the middle another time. His muscles bulged, making me want to run my nails down them.

"Your pace," he grunted, leaning down to rip the other in half as well. "You're heavy with your lead foot and walk with a sort of rhythm because you sway your hips."

I lifted my eyebrows dubiously. "That's very specific."

Roman shrugged, picking up another log and setting it on the stump. Without saying anything more, he went back to splitting them and ignoring me to his best ability.

"Do you pay attention to how everyone else walks?"

"No."

My cheeks warmed a little. "Anything else you notice about me you'd like to share?"

Roman swung the axe. It split with a loud thud, cutting clean through, and planting itself in the stump below. He looked up at me and lifted an eyebrow.

"What are you doing out here, Fury?"

My lips twisted at the tired note in his voice. "I could ask you the same thing." He looked down at the wood and back to me. I suppose it was fairly obvious.

Roman sighed. "If Rox sent you—"

"I volunteered," I interrupted. "What gives? Why are you out here splitting wood instead of with your pack, mourning and celebrating?"

His expression turned frigid, a hint of blue peeking through his gaze. "Can't say I feel much like celebrating," he answered quietly before going back to his pile. I grit my teeth in frustration.

"If you're upset about the shifters that died, I understand that, but are you sure that isolating yourself out here is the best course of action?"

Roman gave me a hard look. I wasn't used to this part of him. This cold. Roman was all hot blooded and wore his emotions on his sleeves. This . . . it wasn't right. "I think I'll take advice from you about how to cope with grief when you admit you're an alcoholic and you do something about it."

My lips parted. I would have been equally shocked if he slapped me.

Overtly conscious of the half a beer still in my hand, I said, "Now we're onto leveling me so you feel better about you?"

He closed his eyes and looked away, muscles tense. "I'm sorry. I shouldn't have thrown that in your face like that, even if it's true. You should go. I'm not . . . my wolf is close to the surface, and it's better if I'm away from everyone right now."

"No," I said, standing my ground.

Roman's jaw hardened. "I wasn't asking."

"I don't care."

The muscles around his mouth tightened. "You don't want to do this with me right now."

"Maybe I do," I replied. Dumping my drink out, I wrinkled the cup and let it fall to the ground, freeing my hands. "I can handle your wolf. Stop avoiding the question. Why is it better that you're away? Why do you think you should isolate yourself when your entire life is built on a pack mentality? This seems backwards to me, and your piss-poor mood has me inclined to think I'm right."

"Because I don't want to be around them." His fists clenched, and he took a step away from me. I followed, not letting up.

"Why?"

"I don't need a fucking reason—"

"Why?" I repeated harder, pushing him.

The dam burst as he towered over me, snarling under his breath. "Because every time I see them I'm reminded why I'm a failure as an alpha and a mate. Because I couldn't protect them any more than I could protect Maya. Because a fucking angel is hell bent on ruining me and I'm fucking terrified he'll find a way to take you away."

My lips parted. I'd anticipated some of that, but not all.

"Roman," I whispered.

"I keep hoping that if I put enough distance between you and me that it won't hurt so bad. It's tearing my wolf apart, making us crazy. I dream about fucking you like a savage and then I have nightmares about you being taken. I'm so hyper aware of your every move it borders obsession. I'm not . . ." He turned away, putting his back to me. "I'm not in my right mind, Fury—and you're not ready to take things where we need them to go."

I stepped forward without thinking. My hand grazed his back and Roman stopped, freezing against my touch.

"You don't know that," I said quietly.

He tilted his chin, permitting me a side view of his sharp cut jaw and ice-blue eyes.

"Don't give me hope unless you mean it. I can't play the games you and Ezra do."

I lifted my chin. "I'm not playing with you."

"Then you're ignorant."

He started to walk away again, and my own frustration bubbled over. I stomped after him and grabbed his forearm. Before Roman could respond, I forcibly turned him and then shoved his chest. He stumbled back into a massive oak tree. It shook on impact, branches swapping heavily above us.

Without wasting time, I gripped either side of his face and wrenched it down toward me as I jumped up, locking my legs around his hips. Roman caught me, hands grasping my ass.

"Does this look ignorant to you?" I snapped. Our teeth clanked as we came together in a kiss so vicious there was no stopping it. My tongue thrust into his mouth, and his was ready. In a battle of wills, Roman squeezed my ass with one hand and lifted the other to knot through my hair. He pulled on it, directing my head to the way he liked to give him the advantage as our tongues twined together. He tasted like whiskey, smoke, and regret. Not regret that we were finally doing this. Regret that we'd waited.

My hips rocked into him, feeling the hardness of his cock. Roman groaned, breaking off our kiss. He yanked on my hair, pulling my head back enough to look at him clearly.

"There will be no friends with benefits. This isn't just fucking. If I take you, you're mine, and you accept that claim for as long as you're here."

My throat felt thick. Commitment. That's what he needed. Not long ago I would have walked away. But after my chat with Ezra, and then figuring out my death may or may not be imminent, I wasn't wasting any of the time I potentially had left.

I had feelings for Roman. Maybe not love. I wasn't sure if I was truly capable of that anymore. Not after so long. But something more than lust or the pull of the bond. In him I saw a safe place. Shelter. Maybe even a home. I didn't have to be Fury the demon with him. I could just be me, as I was, whatever and whoever that meant.

I nodded slowly, swallowing hard.

"Say it," he growled, not a hint of give in his voice.

"I accept your claim."

CHAPTER 13
ROMAN

My head fell forward, touching her for a brief moment, eyes closing in sweet victory.

She accepted my claim. She accepted her place. By my side. As my mate.

I flipped around, pinning her back to the tree with her thighs spread wide for me. The tiny jean shorts she'd worn at the ceremony were bringing havoc down on me and my wolf through the burning. I had to catch myself several times from letting my mind drift to her and the way I wanted to bend her ass over the back of my truck. Better yet, have her ride my cock on top of my bike. One fantasy after the next played over, and I'd had many of them since the first time I saw her—but only now would I act.

Her breasts rose and fell, tight against my chest, I could feel her heat through the thin fabric of her T-shirt. My hips rocked inward, grinding into her delectable warmth, eliciting a shiver from my mate. Her head started to loll to the side, and I angled it with my hand in her hair. My lips skimmed up her cheek and down her throat in little nibbling sucks. My fangs sharpened at the taste of her. So fresh and sweet, like ripe fruit for the taking.

"You'll have to forgive me if I'm not gentle enough the first time," I rumbled against her skin. "It'll be impossible for me to rein it in."

"I can handle rough," she breathed. "Just no hitting or slapping. And no daddy kink."

"Noted," I hummed. That wouldn't be difficult for me, seeing as neither inflicting pain nor 'daddy' was a kink of mine. I let my hand slip free from her hair to grab a handful of her thigh. I loved that she was soft yet toned there. Her skin was supple and flushed.

"Shirt off," I grunted, not wanting to put her down. Fury arched up, grabbing the hem of the ripped T-shirt, and pulled it over her head. "No bra," I commented as she dropped it on the ground.

"Are you complaining?" she murmured, toying with me. I leaned down to skim the top of her breast with my lips. I lapped at her nipple and then sucked it softly, letting my front teeth scrape over the sensitive flesh. Fury's head hit the tree trunk as she let out a moan.

"You shouldn't sass me," I said, moving to her other nipple and repeating my actions again. I alternated back and forth every few moments, grinding my erection into her as I did. Fury's hands dropped from my face to my shoulders, nails digging into my skin.

"Fuck me," she demanded.

"No," I breathed, blowing a cold breath against her taut nipple. "I fuck you when I choose. Not the other way around, cherub."

A grin flitted across her perfectly fuckable lips. "Cherub?" she commented.

"Mm?" I hummed, debating how difficult it would be to get her home unnoticed if I ripped those tiny fucking shorts off her.

"Last I checked, I'm a demon, not an angel."

"Cherubs are cute and innocent looking. The opposite of an angel. You look like hell on wheels, but dig a little deeper and there's a heart of gold beneath that demonic aura," I said.

She lifted an eyebrow at me, but now wasn't the time to debate my name for her. The only name I wanted to hear was mine while I fucked her into the next morning. "Keep questioning me and you'll be doing the walk of shame in my T-shirt tomorrow."

"It's only shameful if you think it is. I couldn't care less what your shifters think of me." Her answer was music to my ears. My hand skated up her thigh to the waistband of her jean shorts. I pulled sharply, and the material ripped straight down the side.

Fury gasped, clearly not taking me seriously enough. I rearranged her weight, using that hand to hold her up so my other could do the same. With both the sides split wide on her shorts, all I had to do was reach between to pull the bunched-up material away.

Naked and bare to me, Fury trembled. She reached for my jeans with steady hands and quickly unbuttoned my fly, yanking the zipper down. She reached inside my boxers and ran her palm up and down my hard shaft.

"What happened to no games?" I hissed between my teeth.

She flashed me a coy look as she took my cock out of my boxers, but continued stroking me. Her thumb pressed against my head, wiping at the drop of pre-cum and using it to circle around again and again. "I'm just giving a little payback for how you treated the girls," she said, lifting her hand. She licked the pad of her thumb, then pushed it between her lips to suck.

I lifted her hips above me, positioning her over my cock. I let the tip rub between her slick folds, back and forth, eliciting small sounds of pleasure from her. Fury rolled her hips, trying to pull me in, and I let her, roughly pulling her down on top of me.

A groan escaped me as she took me to the hilt, then wrapped her legs around me.

"Be careful what you ask for." Not giving her a chance to reply, I pulled all the way out and thrust back in. Her warm heat enveloped me, her pussy clenching me tighter than a fist. Unable to help myself, I started pistoning in and out between her legs, fucking her so hard against the oak tree that its branches shook.

She arched back on her own accord, creating better friction between us for her clit. I didn't slow as I kissed her roughly before breaking away to lick the skin between her shoulder and neck. Fury's moans encouraged me, driving both me and my wolf wild with lust and need. I had to claim her in all ways. With my cock and my teeth.

I sucked at the patch of skin I picked to bear my mark. It occurred to me when I marked Maya, I chose her inner thigh. Somewhere away from prying eyes. It felt close. Personal. Much of my love for my past mate I treated that way. Something to be expressed when we were alone, and that was all.

But with Fury, my feelings were different. Complicated and messy and utterly unique. Wolves were possessive by nature, and with Maya

I wanted to hide her away. I kept that possessiveness to a minimum. With Fury, I wanted to bend her over and fuck her in front of my pack for all to see. I wanted them and everyone else to know she was mine, and that I'd rip apart any man or angel that tried to take her from me.

That's why I chose her neck, for all to see, and if she'd let me—it wouldn't be the only place I marked her. Even thinking about it had my cock stiffening further as I took her bare. I could feel her legs shaking hard as she approached the edge of her own climax.

My hand skimmed up the curve of her ass. I ran my index finger down the crack, feeling her reaction as the balls of her feet pushed into my lower back, guiding me onward. I pressed my index finger to her opening there, applying just a touch of pressure as I pushed it in knuckle deep. Fury moaned her approval.

"Roman," she whimpered, eyes closed and sweat coating her body. "I need to come."

Just what I wanted to hear.

I let my fangs fully extend before pricking her skin, then sinking them to the root.

Her body tightened like a vice. Her inner walls clenched, providing delicious pressure as I thrust into her furiously. The animal in me roared with dominance. Fury screamed bloody murder, a sound that I might have confused with pain if not for the way she clawed at my back, trying to pull me closer. Blood scented the air, mine and hers, as she broke skin.

It was a savage coupling, just as I dreamed it would be. But it was everything.

The aftershocks of her orgasm fluttered around me as I came. I stilled, and it was only when we were both sated that I retracted my fangs from her flesh.

The look on her face right then was something I'd never forget.

Sheer bliss. Sexy as all hell. It amazed me how this redheaded demoness came into my life, uprooted everything I knew, and somehow managed to realign my world surrounding her. When I fell asleep at night, it was her I was aching for. When I succumbed to thoughts of lust, it was her name on my lips. When I searched the crowd, it was her red hair that I was seeking.

Somehow, someway, she was eclipsing Maya. While she wasn't

forgotten, nor loved any less, Fury was filling the space she'd once occupied. In losing my first mate, I learned how precious having a partner was—and how much I would do to hold on to it and never lose that again.

Maya might have been my past, but Fury was my future.

The guilt of that still ate at me, and I turned my cheek to press it against her shoulder as I sighed.

Her body tightened, but this time she squirmed to get away.

"What did you say?"

"Hm?" I murmured.

"You—I—ugh!" She shoved against my shoulders, and I let her go on reflex. She dropped to the ground in a crouch, lethal in her elegance, yellow eyes narrowed at me.

"What's wrong?" I said, looking around the clearing, but there was no one here, save the cicadas that likely kept most of our fucking from my packs' ears. Probably not that climax, though.

"*You*. What the fuck, Roman? I can't believe you right now." She stood up with her jean shorts, eyes flicking to them for a short inspection before discarding them again. She cast a glance around the clearing, zeroing in on my button-down shirt I'd left hanging on a tree branch. Without asking permission, she marched over and took it, pushing her arms through the sleeves and haphazardly buttoning it up, albeit unevenly.

"What are you talking ab—"

"You said her name," Fury tossed out in an angry huff. "You called me Maya."

Fuck.

It wasn't what she thought. I opened my mouth to tell her as much, but she wasn't hearing any of it.

"I understand you still miss her and love her. I wouldn't expect any different, but I'm not a stand-in for her, Roman. I can't do this with you if I'm playing second fiddle to a dead woman—"

"Fury," I growled. "I wasn't calling you by her name—"

"But you did," she said. "And it's not fair to any of us. Me. Her. You. I fucked you and let you mark me because I thought you wanted something between *us*. But for that to happen, you need to accept that I'm not her and be okay with that. I don't need you to love me more or some bullshit like that, but if I'm always less than, I'm always in her shadow—and I won't be with someone that doesn't want to be with *me.*"

"I do," I argued, frustrated that she wouldn't listen for even two seconds.

"Then find a way to show it because right now I feel used."

With that, she walked away, and the chilled tone of her voice told me I'd be an idiot to follow.

CHAPTER 14
FURY

I PACED BY THE WINDOW IN MY ROOM, TIRED BUT RESTLESS. THE MOON HAD risen high in the sky, shining a pretty beam of light through the glass. The groups by the bonfires in the distance had quieted down. Nature's soft voice surrounded me; only the sounds of insect calls and nocturnal animals scurrying about filled the air.

It was almost maddening.

My mind raced. I was wound up, both emotionally frustrated with what had happened and simultaneously longing to be back with the one who sent me to this place to begin with. I traced the spot on my neck where he'd bit me, eliciting a shiver that made my skin tingle.

Stupid, traitorous body.

Like I would give in and sleep in Roman's room tonight.

He said her name. He held me, fucked me, marked me . . . but it wasn't me he had been thinking about.

I wasn't jealous of Maya. There was absolutely no reason to be. The poor girl had died. Killed by someone in the Afterlife. No, I would never be jealous of Roman's love for his first mate. I just wouldn't pretend to be her ghost for him either.

I was hurt that even if it were only for a second, he wanted me to be her instead. That he couldn't be with just me. I hated to admit it. I hated to feel it. I hated all of it.

Something festered inside me, and it felt an awful lot like human emotions.

Ew. No. There would be none of that.

I walked over to the bed and stuck my hand under the pillow. Pulling out the flask, I unscrewed the top and tipped my head back, swallowing a mouthful of whiskey.

My head and my heart had collided over many things in my past, and it finally felt like they were on the same page for once. I knew what I wanted. Maybe once, long ago, it was simply love that I had sought, but in all my long years, I'd finally realized I wanted something more.

Up until recently, I had only craved stability. Freedom. Independence. But never love. Never *more*. That was what my head said.

Now my head and my heart said belonging somewhere could also be good. My heart reminded me that what I saw tonight, and what I felt—watching the pack and the families come together in love and support—that was something I truly did want. My heart said I deserved it. Was worthy of it. Would it be so bad to be a part of something special? What would life be like to be loved that way?

I wouldn't know. Never truly experienced it. I had a baby sister once. She was beautiful and perfect in every way. I adored her, and every time she looked at me, I saw nothing but pure and unconditional love. A piece of me died when Spanish Flu took her from me.

It was the last time I had felt what it was like to be loved.

I only realized later that her death spared her a future like mine. Given away by our shitty parents to a man I hardly knew when I was barely seventeen, all for the sake of our family's good name. I took a backhand to the face the day my father told me my purpose, and I'd told him I'd rather die. Joke was on him, the bastard. I died anyway.

It was a hard pill to swallow when you realize you have no autonomy. That you are a tool used for closing business deals. That your ambitions are meaningless. You have a uterus, so your purpose is less than a man's. What was that old saying? Something about being pregnant and barefoot in the kitchen? That was supposed to be my future.

My family handed me over to John. He was handsome. Incredible lapis blue eyes and stark white-blond hair. His smile could light up a room, and he was extraordinarily charming. His work in real estate was demanding, often sending him travelling for weeks on end. It started off okay, but time changed him. I never knew who would walk through the door. Jekyll or Hyde.

Jekyll, who seemed as though he was trying to love me, but he was still a little distant all the same. He didn't know me any better than I knew him. He was kind, though. Thoughtful. He'd bring me flowers, shower me with generic affection, and thank me for keeping our home nice. I may have been miserable being forced into a life I didn't want, but those days were easier when it was that husband. Then he'd leave again, buying land and building his brand.

But sometimes Hyde came home instead.

He was the same charming husband. Kind and thoughtful, until he wasn't. Something sinister would flash in his eyes, and everything would change. His cruelty knew no bounds. I could still hear the way he'd laugh as he stood over my bruised and broken body while I gasped for air and coughed up blood. Reminding me that I was his, and no one else's. Telling me it was my fault he'd had to beat it into me. Blaming me for his anger. Swearing he wouldn't do it again, if only I understood how much I meant to him. How much he loved me . . .

I scoffed. *Love*. I wanted no part of that love.

I'd felt an inkling of bliss in my short, married life. Once. A flicker of life growing inside me. That was love. It was instant. It was eternal. And he'd made damn sure to beat that out of me too. He would not share me, he'd said.

I skimmed my fingers over my flat lower abdomen, resting my hand there absentmindedly.

I lifted the flask to my lips, taking another drink.

And another.

And another.

I sighed when it was empty, and I wiped my mouth with the back of my hand.

How had I gone from being with Roman to wallowing in my misery and thinking about my past? My stomach churned slightly. I shook my head and laughed a little. Roman had essentially done the same thing. He was tangled up with me, and for some reason he thought about Maya. No, I didn't think about my baggage while we were together, but I went there all the same.

The only difference was that he was crushed and lost when Maya had died. I, on the other hand, did a happy dance when that monster was exterminated.

I didn't want my ex back.

Roman did.

We were both damaged goods in the end.

A blurry figure swooped from the tree line and headed for me. Hades flew toward the window and I opened it, letting him in. He landed on a chair, pulled in his wings, and then hopped onto the windowsill.

"Had enough to drink yet? Or are you still trying to disinfect your internal organs?"

"You know what? Come here. I'm in no mood for your bullshit." I grabbed for him, and he jumped away as I kept swiping my hands at him. "Go sleep outside with the fucking mutant mosquitos—"

"I saw you," he interrupted. His eyes lowered, looking at my midsection, before he returned his gaze to me. "I know why you're drinking. I just don't know why you're thinking about it right now."

My mouth fell slightly open, shocked at what he'd said. "How'd you," I paused, stumbling for words. "How do you know about that?"

"I told you it was my job to know things." He settled, content that I wouldn't snatch his little body and chunk him out. He turned his head and looked out the window, bouncing on his little feet to move closer to me. Almost as if he were trying to comfort a friend. "We all have our secrets, Fury. I'm not telling anyone about yours. But you aren't going to find any answers or comfort in the bottom of your flask."

I bristled. "That's not what I'm doing."

He looked back at me and gave me a deadpan look. "Well, whatever it is you *are* doing, it's not good for you."

"Friendly advice, or is this a message from work?" I asked in an irritated tone.

Hades made an undignified sound. "We are not friends, so it can't be friendly advice, can it? It's just an observation."

I hummed in response, not believing him. "Sounded an awful lot like you cared about me there for a second," I trailed off, waiting to see if he would respond. When he didn't, I let it go. "All right, pigeon, have it your way." I turned away, watching the breeze as it rustled the treetops. "Any news?"

"None yet." He shook his head.

I grumbled in frustration.

"There's eons of history in those libraries, and not the watered-down version men write down."

"I know. I'm just . . . tired." I sighed. So bloody tired.

"What about the alphas?"

I glanced at him and twisted my lips to the side. "I had a small revelation tonight. Nothing so far has fit together to say they are going to lose their shit and destroy the world. There are fractions and pieces of their lives that are intense, but they've all been through some hellish experiences that should have triggered whatever it is inside them by now." I ran my fingers through my hair, tugging on some tangles while I combed it. "They don't even like each other in the end. They have nothing in common except the summit . . . and me."

"And you," Hades echoed, coming to the same conclusion as me.

I tapped my temple. "Exactly. I'm the key piece here. They've all lost their mates once already. If something happens to me, could they handle it? What would they destroy in their grief?"

He stretched, then tilted his head, thinking. "It's quite plausible. You do have a tendency to bring out the worst in people." He snickered, making a sound through his nostrils that sounded remarkably like a kazoo.

I barked a laugh. For a brief moment, I felt the flicker of a kinship. It felt good to laugh and forget for one second the weight of everything in my life. Afterlife-life. Whatever I was in now.

My smile faded, though. "What really confuses me is that the risk witches didn't say I was in the picture. They've been seeing versions of this for a long time. I've never been in the prophecy. Not once."

"I know." Hades nodded in agreement. "But it does make sense that you'd be the key to all this. Maybe they've been wrong all along and you're the one that ends it all. Maybe you are the one that explodes. Alcohol is flammable, right?"

This time I snorted. "You are literally the worst," I said through my laugh. "Here I am talking about the end of the world, and you're making jokes."

He did his little bird shrug. "What can I say? I have a sense of humor. It was hilarious for me when you got hit by a bus."

I glared at him, trying to be as serious as I could. A tiny smile crept up on one side. "Maybe it was a little funny. I might have laughed if it happened to someone else. Like you, perhaps."

I walked to the bed and stripped off Roman's shirt, replacing it with my own. The back of my head throbbed a little as I sat on the edge of the mattress, pulled my legs up, and stuck them under the covers.

"I made a bed for you," I said, pointing to the top of the dresser. I'd piled together some soft T-shirts and moved them around in a circle, making the best impression of a nest that I could.

Hades looked surprised. He flapped his wings a few times, gathering air to lift himself up there. He stepped inside my makeshift nest, scratched around, then settled down, wiggling his body to situate himself. "Thank you," he said. "That was . . . nice of you."

"What can I say? I can be nice sometimes," I said softly, laying on my side and curling up on the pillow.

My head wasn't entirely settled, but Hades coming and pulling me from the downward spiral of my thoughts helped quiet things just a bit. I closed my eyes and tried to fall asleep. I was tired. Sleep would have to come soon.

A CHILLING LAUGH ECHOED in my mind. I squinted my eyes and looked around, but there was nothing except fog settling over an open field. Dew formed on the blades of grass, and all of nature had fallen quiet. The moon was descending for its daily slumber, and the sun had not yet awoken on the horizon.

I turned, searching in all directions, trying to find where the laugh was coming from. It increased in intensity, the shrillness making my skin crawl.

I slapped my hands over my ears and screamed, trying to block it out.

"What do you want?" I shouted into the nothingness.

"Hybrid," the voice hissed.

The hairs on my neck stood on end. Goosebumps burst along my skin. Cold sweat dripped down my face and onto my chest.

I took off in a sprint, running toward the tree line in the distance. I needed to find cover. I pumped my legs and pushed off the ground as hard as I could.

Was this déjà vu? Had I been here before?

I checked my progress, gauging how much further I had before I reached my destination, but it looked no different.

A sense of dread washed over me as I felt an unfamiliar presence nearby. I turned my head over my shoulder to find what brought it.

A lone figure stood, tall and foreboding. A white cloak lined in shimmering gold obscured its face. An aura of light surrounded it, pulsing in time with my racing heartbeat.

"Fuck!" I yelled, trying to move faster, but it was useless.

The angel laughed and gave chase, catching up to me.

Spindly gray fingers with pointed talons gripped my shoulder, crushing down on the bone and drawing blood when it pricked my skin.

I screamed again, and the angel laughed. "Oh, Sunny, you are making this too easy."

My screams echoed in the room as I shot up to a sitting position.

I heaved deep breaths in and out, my hands curled into a death grip on the bed. Early morning light filtered in from the window. White and gray feathers were strewn about, some floating in the air. Feathers? I looked down to my claws, taking in the shredded bed and pillow.

Roxanne and Roman came bursting through the door, disheveled and clearly pulled from sleep. Roman's eyes were blue and alert, ready to let his wolf out at the first sign of danger. Roxanne held a fire extinguisher in one hand, and used her other to wave around, knocking the floating fluffies out of her face.

I frowned at the red canister, and she shrugged. I gave her an apologetic look in return. I felt bad that she expected another fire.

"What happened?" Roman said, his jaw clenched.

His voice washed over me, equal parts comforting me and annoying me.

"Bad dream," I answered. "I'm fine. Go back to bed." I turned away from him. I wasn't ready to confront anything. I felt like I'd been asleep for all of five minutes.

I glanced at the clock, unsure of what I wanted to see there. I felt exhausted. I wanted more time to rest, but if my sleep was going to be filled with nightmares, I'd rather push right past it and start the day.

"Fury," Roman said, his tone getting softer. "If you want—"

"I said I'm fine." I waved my hand around. "No danger. Just feathers. I'm *safe*."

A crease formed between his brows, the line deepening as he struggled with what to say. He straightened his shoulders, and with a grunt, he gave a dip of his chin. Turning on his heel, he stormed out of the room.

Roxanne whistled low. "Well, if that's not tension, I don't know what is."

I threw my legs over the bed, knocking feathers around. "Leave it alone, Rox. I'm not . . . I can't right now."

The voice in the nightmare rang in my ears. It called me a hybrid. The angel called me Sunny. Were they the same entities?

She sat down beside me and put her hand on my back. "You okay?"

Not even a little bit.

"I'm okay," I answered. Looking at Hades on the dresser, I met his calculating gaze. "What did you see? What happened?"

"Not a damn clue. I woke up because you screamed. I opened my eyes, and all I saw was an explosion of feathers filling the room. Wasn't sure what to think." He stood up in his T-shirt nest. "Worried something had happened to me, to be honest," he mumbled, lifting his wings and peeking underneath.

I grinned. "Hope you didn't shit yourself."

He turned around and looked down. I couldn't help but smirk at his expression.

Roxanne pressed her lips together in a firm line, trying hard to not laugh. She shook her head and stood up. “Can I get you anything? Like a new bed?”

There was no way I’d be able to get back to sleep. I had questions about Lyra and where she was. Who she was with. I wanted to know what I had been turned into. Were there others from the Afterlife like me? What it meant for my future. Would I ever make it back to the Afterlife? So many questions. I needed to talk to someone about all the things running through my mind, but no one would be able to give me answers. And that was what I needed more than anything.

Dorian’s lying by omission made my blood boil, even if I partially understood it. Ezra’s disregard for my pleading to spare Lyra made me want to hit him if I even looked at his face. Roman, well, I had already soaked in that emotional hell all night. It didn’t matter, anyway. None of them had the answers, but each one of them wanted to be a part of finding them.

But their actions said they didn't trust me, and they certainly didn’t trust each other.

Fuck them. I would do it on my own. I always did.

“I need a favor,” I started. Roxanne looked at me dubiously, her eyes flicking to the door and then back to me. “I need you to make me a drink.”

She groaned. “Fury, it’s—”

“It’s not for me, I promise.” She looked at me in confusion, waiting for me to give her more information. “I need you to make a bloody mary.”

CHAPTER 15
FURY

WITH THE SIGNATURE DRINK IN HAND AND HADES PERCHED ON MY SHOULDER, I walked into the bathroom and shut the door.

"You're sure about this?" my crow asked as I offered him my hand. He stepped onto it, and I moved him to the counter.

I looked at the lock on the door before I reached to twist it, and then nodded. "I am. What's the worst that could happen, right?"

"Um . . ."

I sighed. A lot. A lot was the worst that could happen. That was the answer. We'd all heard the stories, but I'd never met her. She had bolted from the Afterlife long before my time. Even there she was a legend. A legend I had only read about.

Bloody Mary's narrative on Earth was sparse, and her supposed history was muddled and had changed over time. No one really knew enough about her, so her origin story was made up. I at least knew the truth in that. Still, so often children and drunk teenagers tried to summon her. What they were hoping to gain, I wasn't sure. Since the legends said she would come and possess you, try to kill you, or just scare the living daylights out of you, I didn't understand the appeal.

I just needed her to show up and talk to me.

"Aren't you supposed to light a candle?" Hades asked.

"I just need to be able to see, that's all," I said. I clicked on my phone flashlight and turned it upside down, facing the beam upward before flicking off the lights. I looked at Hades. "Ready?"

He fluffed his feathers in response.

Standing at the sink, I moved the drink and held it in front of me. Taking a breath, I blew out, skimming across the top of it, pushing the scent of herbs, tomatoes, and vodka into the direction of the mirror. To anyone else, I would look like I'd absolutely lost my marbles. Maybe I had.

"A bloody mary for Bloody Mary," I said to my reflection. "I have a request."

The mirror warbled, and I heard a faint sound just as Hades mumbled, "She is going to be so pissed when she sees me."

"Wait, what?" I whisper-shouted.

"Too late," he said, tiptoeing to the side out of view.

An image finally appeared. A teenage girl with chestnut brown hair, rosy cheeks, and a heart-shaped face greeted me. She looked so young, but her soulful hazel eyes gave away her age. She'd been around for a long time. Much longer than most people thought.

"If it isn't *The* infamous Fury," she drawled, reaching out of her mirror dimension to swipe the drink in my hand. My skin tingled at the brief paranormal contact. She sniffed it deeply and smiled, taking a sip, and letting out a long sigh. "Oh, this is a good one."

I was quite curious to know how she'd heard about me considering she had left the Afterlife before I'd arrived. A question I would most definitely ask if I were given the chance in the future. For now, I needed to know something just a tad more pressing. "I'm glad it exceeds your expectations," I said.

She stirred it with the celery, and without looking up, she said, "I see you, Hades. You can't hide for shit."

"Hey, Dottie, how goes it?" Hades asked, cautiously moving back toward me.

I shot him a dirty look. He did not just say that. I would pluck out his feathers one by one if he'd just screwed me. Calling her by her living nickname was a surefire way to send her back into her world, never to return.

Her expression deadpanned. "I changed my name after I died, just like you did."

I couldn't say I blamed her. I didn't want the memories that came with my name either. Dottie, or Dorothy, was the youngest to be accused and jailed during the Salem Witch Trials. Her baby sister was born while her mom was imprisoned and later hung, found guilty for being a witch. It was a load of crap back then. None of the puritans were witches, but that didn't stop a bunch of lying shitbags from accusing innocent women and a few men of consorting with 'the devil'. I'd read up on those people and what happened to them when they came to the Afterlife. A few of those accusers were extinguished due to so many failed attempts at changing them. The remaining were rehabilitated and recycled. Their souls had come back a few times over, but I hadn't ever had one assigned to me. By the time I became a demon, those souls weren't in the worst-of-the-worst case files.

"I, uh, I didn't know you two had a history. Had I known," I narrowed my eyes at him, then met her gaze again, "I would have stuck him somewhere else."

"A cage, perhaps?" She waved it off, taking another drink. "It's fine. A story for another time."

I twisted my lips. "While he's annoyingly rude, he unfortunately brings up a good question. What would you like to be called? I know you don't like to be called Mary anymore—"

"You wouldn't either if you spent decades with people repeating your name over and over and over. It's like having someone open your windows and randomly shout into your house. It's very disturbing."

"So . . ."

"Juliet. Like from the Shakespearean play," she said, her voice a little dreamy.

"Wow. That's—"

"Romantic?"

"No, I was going to say tragic, honestly."

Hades shot me a look that said, 'now who's screwing this up?'

She furrowed her eyebrows. "I didn't insult your name."

"You could if you wanted. I was a little angry when I showed up. Duke says it's like the Jessica of the Afterlife," I grumbled.

She barked a laugh. "I suppose it is. But Juliet *isn't*."

In for a penny, in a for a pound, right?

I smirked. "It's not. But you picked the name of a thirteen-year-old girl that knew a guy for five seconds, claimed she loved him, and their so-called romance caused the death of six people, and brought down two prominent houses. That's a tragedy—the way he wrote it—not a romance," I pointed out. "I mean, if you wanted romance, Rosalind or Beatrice would have worked. You're headstrong and witty, or so I've heard."

I hoped my attempted recovery worked, and I waited silently while she considered my rebuttal.

"You make a good case." She looked at me and frowned. "You didn't strike me as a Shakespeare fan."

I shrugged. "I'm full of surprises. You should see me blow up." I waggled my eyebrows.

The corner of her lips curled up on one side. "I did, actually. It was quite impressive."

Hades stepped forward. "You were there?" he asked, dubious.

She waved a finger at him. "Enough about me. I concede your argument. Call me Jules."

I tilted my head to the side and crossed my arms over my chest. "That was an awfully quick change."

She grinned. "Someone I know convinced me to change it a while back. Same reasons you presented, actually. So you have my attention now if you'd like to make your request." She brought the glass to her mouth and took another drink, leaving a small line of red above her lip that looked remarkably like blood. She wiped it off with her fingertips. "I assume you have a question and that's why you summoned me."

I hadn't missed that tiny breadcrumb there. She said someone she knew. Who that someone was, I didn't know. No one could enter the mirror dimension, and she'd disappeared from the Afterlife over two hundred years ago. She had other people she visited, and I wanted to know who.

"I do." I nodded my head, contemplating which question was the most important. If all she gave me was one, I had to make it good. "You've seen a lot happen in the world. Been around for a while, right? Something happened to me, and I need help figuring it out." I lifted my top lip and ran my tongue over my elongated canine.

"You have my attention." The look on her face was filled with curiosity.

I hummed. "I'm sure I do."

I went through the basic parts of the story, omitting some of the heavier details. This was a need-to-know basis. She didn't need to know about the end of the world. She just needed to know I was on a special mission on Earth. Unorthodox for a demon, sure. But I was here, nonetheless. She'd already made it clear she saw me go boom, and I planned on bringing that one up in the future, so I picked it up from there.

"To save me, they changed me. I don't know what this means. No one in the Afterlife does either. But some strange things are happening to me, and none of it is related to what shifters, vampires, or fae experience in their youth, during the change, or while maturing."

She stirred the drink again with her celery and took a bite out of it, speaking with some still in her mouth while she chewed. "What is it you're asking of me?"

"I want to know if you have seen anything like this. If you know of anyone who is a multi-species hybrid. Or a demon hybrid. You have access to mirrors all over the world. If anyone knows, it's you." I gave her a twisted smile. "I was told demons don't come to Earth, but at this point, there's a lot that just doesn't make sense. The other poltergeists have done an absolute shit job at recon for this case, so I honestly don't trust anything they say or report to the Afterlife either."

She narrowed her eyes. "Wankers, all of them. They were a disgrace then, and they are a disgrace now."

Hades snorted, which still sounded more like a wheezing burp through a beak.

I side-eyed him. "I won't argue."

She sighed. "I don't have any answers for you. I haven't seen this before."

And there it was. I was shit out of luck. The one big card I had to play and—

"But I haven't been actively looking for it either. That doesn't mean I can't start now."

"Really?" Hades and I asked at the same time.

She shot a glare at my crow and narrowed her eyes before she looked back at me. "I'll help you. Bring me more of these tasty delights," she shook her almost empty glass, "and I will look around and see what I can find. It's a big world. Might take some time."

She looked happy as she drained the rest of her drink, clinking the ice in the bottom. She was far more pleasant than I expected, and I needed her more than she knew. It was a gamble, but one I was willing to chance. "There is another question I have for you."

She raised an eyebrow in surprise, the arch creating a striking angle. "Toeing the line, I see."

I raised my hands in a peaceful gesture. "I'm happy to keep bringing you whatever you need. Just say the word."

"Go on," she said. She listened as I told her about Lyra's awakening and the mysterious angel that she'd referenced in our encounter. Her features darkened as she muttered something in a language I couldn't understand.

"Does that mean anything to you?" I asked.

She shook her head. "Not specifically, no, but if angels are involved, it's seriously classified. We won't be able to find answers. They don't stay earthside. This one might, but there won't be others. Angels are more strategic than people think. That stupid image of halos and pretty wings is so far from the truth, it's laughable."

"It sounds like maybe you've had some rough encounters with our divine counterparts," I said, probing more than I probably should have.

She shrugged. "I have a tendency to break and bend the rules. They don't like that."

I didn't disagree. Clearly they had it out for me. Jules defecting from the Afterlife earned her a mark that would never go away. If they could find a way to rip her from her mirror dimension, they would do it in a heartbeat. "I don't know what they want with me, but something about the situation feels personal. I just don't know why. I'm hoping you can find Lyra. She may have answers."

She considered me for a moment. Eventually, she said, "I will think about it. First things first. Let's find out what you are. I'm intensely curious to know."

"The full moon is a week away. I don't want to put pressure on you, but I am on a bit of a time crunch. I haven't sensed my wolf just yet, but it's likely to happen any day now. The sooner I know more, the better off everyone will be. We'll have an idea of what to expect."

"Sure thing," she said.

"Wait, do you want me to um, summon you again?" I asked, not entirely sure what to call it. I couldn't exactly send her a text.

"Don't worry. I'll find you," she answered with a wink. The mirror warbled again, looking almost liquid in nature. Her voice sounded far away as she left, and the glass stopped shifting, looking as if it were solid once more.

"Oh, *now* you're paying attention to the clock," Hades mumbled.

"Tick tock, pigeon."

CHAPTER 16
DORIAN

"Monte Carlo?" Ezra asked me, confusion filling his tone while he walked beside me in dress slacks and a white shirt he kept unbuttoned at the top. We'd sifted to a copse of trees across the street from a famous hotel overlooking the Mediterranean Sea. We'd arrived to meet my second and find out his progress.

"Indeed." I straightened my tie and adjusted my collar, smoothing the vest of my three-piece suit. "It's the next location on his quest to find someone I need. A witch."

Ezra halted. "Why?"

I exhaled deeply through my nose, turning my head to look at the vampire I'd asked to come along. I was beginning to regret it.

"Because we need her to help us find Lyra," I answered. "Whatever it is with you and witches, let it go. It's not exactly like vampires have a good reputation, yet here you are."

He grunted, running a hand through his black hair. "Witches are different."

"They are. Especially the witches I know." Our footsteps echoed on the floor as we entered the lobby and headed to the elevator. I dipped my chin at the staff that made note of our presence and dress. Money always talked. "When we find this one, be careful. She's quite flirtatious, and she's incredibly powerful."

I pressed the button and the sliding doors opened. We stood in silence, side by side, waiting for our floor. I could tell he was concerned, just as Roman had been. I didn't know his history with witches, but he was hesitant to trust them. Even with his gift, he didn't trust them. When Fury was in the explosion at the dress shop, he'd read Kelly's mind and knew she was pure. Still, he was wary. Rya would be a treat for him. She teetered on the edge of madness, and he would have a difficult time trusting her. We needed her powers. She was the only one that could help me. Even Kelly's magic couldn't find Lyra. I'd already tried.

Arriving at the suite, we walked down the hallway and knocked on Tristan's door.

He opened it, greeting us, and moving aside so we could enter. The suite was large and had expansive windows, giving a panoramic view of the bright blue water. It almost looked teal the way it glittered in the sun. The living room was spacious, with two couches facing each other and two chairs facing the glass to overlook the sea. It was a stark contrast to the scenery in Avalon. Or Houston.

"Tristan, what news?" I said, moving to a chair and taking a seat as though it were the head of the table.

"I've been to London, Singapore, Bali, Hong Kong, Paris, Bermuda, and Rome. Nothing yet. She isn't responding to my . . . ads." He glanced at Ezra, unsure of how much he wanted to share.

Tristan was quite powerful in his own right, and I'd shared with him that the vampire's ability was reading people's minds. I couldn't leave my second without protection. He'd increased the barrier on his mind, guarding himself from the mental probing.

Ezra raised his eyebrows, realizing he couldn't get the information he wanted. He would be forced to use his words to get answers like the rest of us. "What do you mean ads?" he asked, clearly displeased by the discovery.

"Rya and Tristan have a long tumultuous history," I started. I knew Tristan wouldn't want to go into detail, and I would spare the aspects that weren't necessary. "When we have needed to reach her over the ages, Tristan uses creative ways to call her out of hiding."

"Such as?" he asked.

"Right now? Craigslist and Tinder," Tristan said.

"You're putting ads out for a fucking booty call, is that it?" He huffed a laugh and shook his head. Looking at me, he said, "Your daughter is trying to kill our mate, and some invisible clock is ticking for the end of the world, and your grand plan is finding a witch using hookup apps? Jesus Christ."

"Doesn't exist," I said. "He'll be of no help here."

He gave a deadpan look. "It's an expression and you know it. Don't be a condescending prick, Dorian. Basically, don't be you."

"Then don't question the methods we're using when you know nothing of which you speak," I countered. "Now, if you are done *whining*, we can move on."

He narrowed his eyes, considering me for a moment. I often wondered what went through his head. It had to drive him crazy that he didn't hold the upper hand when he was around me. "Fine. Tell me why those locations. What can I do to help?"

Moving to sit in a chair, I checked my watch. "Rya likes the finer things in life. Extravagance. She also likes to flirt and play hard to get. The ways to contact her have generally involved going to luxurious locations. Tristan then puts himself out in the open, both physically and via some type of announcement, so she knows it's him."

"Right." Ezra moved to the couch, taking a seat. "Because you two are ex-lovers," he said, looking at Tristan.

"Something like that," he mumbled. "It's complicated."

That was an understatement. Rya was complex. At her core, I believed she was a decent witch, but it was never safe to let your guard down. For Tristan, it became more personal. She had a flare for being dramatic. Relished in it. When it came down to it, she liked mind games, and Tristan grew tired of it. He'd never fully shared the details of their on-again off-again courtship, and I didn't push it. Their struggle was their own.

For me, it was business. Over the years we had need of each other's abilities. I would hear rumors of her dealings as centuries passed by. I knew what she was capable of. If I didn't know her as well as I did, it would be difficult to tell which side she was on. Rya would do what was best for Rya. The trick was figuring out what that was so we could entice her and benefit from her power. Lyra was a different case. Lyra was *always* different.

"And what exactly do we need her for?" Ezra asked.

Tristan's gaze shifted to meet mine.

I sighed. "Rya is the only witch capable of helping me put Lyra in stasis. We did it together once. We'll have to do it again."

He cursed under his breath. "This goes far beyond just tracking her down. You're telling me you can't stop her on your own?"

I pressed my lips into a firm line, drawing in a deep breath. "No."

A truth I absolutely loathed to admit.

We had little time. We had to work fast. We had one option. I always had a backup plan. Lived by the notion that one should always plan for the risks involved. When it came to Lyra, there were no backup plans.

"Lyra's power is unmatched. Not only does she carry magic similar to my own, but she also has hers as well. Lyra and I essentially cancel each other out. I battled her for years, trying to tame the monster inside her. Trying to cure whatever disease was eating away at her mind. I never succeeded. That was when I knew she needed to be put into stasis," I said. I interlocked my fingers and placed my hands in my lap. "When I tried, the outcome was worse than I had expected."

"I can't imagine why. You were trying to chain her, right?"

I sniffed and adjusted my posture. "The process binds her powers first, yes. Then she would enter stasis. It has always been a state we choose for rest or re-energizing. We live such long lives . . ." I trailed off, lost in thought. Tristan cleared his throat, bringing me back to my senses. "No one has ever been forced into stasis before. Not until Lyra."

"And she lost her shit, I assume."

Tristan snorted, crossing his arms, and looking away, clearly perturbed by Ezra's tactlessness.

"Yes, Ezra, she lost her shit. She slaughtered thousands in cold blood." I closed my eyes, wishing the mental image that had been burned into my memory would fade. A millennium and it still felt as clear as day. As though it had just happened. Every detail, every blood splatter . . . every single body. And equally worse, the picture of my once kind child standing in the middle of it, her hands dripping in red. I inhaled deeply and opened my eyes. "She didn't discriminate in who she played with before killing them. A family of prominent and powerful witches were amongst her final victims. Rya and her sister were able to escape, finding me when they were refugees seeking safety. It was upon meeting Rya that I realized she had the powers I needed to help me stop my daughter."

"So Lyra is unstoppable, and we can't do anything about it except sit here and wait for this all-powerful witch to answer Tristan's personal ads?" He glared at me wide-eyed, waiting for a response. I met his stare, unyielding. He scoffed. "Great. Just fucking great."

I rolled my eyes, wishing Ezra would just listen for a moment. This was the problem with him and Roman. They were so young and emotionally charged, whether the former was willing to admit it or not. His bias with witches was clouding his judgement and his ability to think logically about the situation.

A loud pop in the room stopped me from responding further. A giant plume of lavender smoke exploded, sparkling specs spewing in the air. I wafted a hand in front of my face trying to clear the debris. In the middle of the purple haze stood a tall figure, lean in stature, draped in a green cloak.

Ezra jumped off the couch, pulling a knife while he wheezed.

"Don't," I said, coughing and waving my hand at him to settle down.

Tristan didn't move a muscle. Except he rolled his eyes so far back in his head he likely saw the back of his skull.

"Why yes, vampire, I am fucking great," the witch said, twisting her arms and taking a bow.

I stood up, adjusting my coat, and running a palm over my clothes to wipe off the dust. I went toward her, reached out, and grasped the hood, tilting it back. Clever brown eyes twinkled with mischief when they met mine. Her plum-painted lips curled into a smirk, and she turned her head slightly.

I leaned down, lightly kissing her cheek. "Rya. It's nice to see you again."

She untied her cloak, letting it fall to the floor.

"Of course it is," she said, dusting off her white sundress.

"See, Ezra? Penchant for theatrics, like we said," Tristan muttered.

Ezra's brows furrowed, and he watched Rya cautiously. She

noticed the way he looked at her. "Oh, calm down, bloodsucker. You and I have no quarrel."

She clapped her hands together and looked at my second. "Well, Tristan, my love, you've been just screaming to get ahold of me. And you brought Dorian and a friend." She winked at Ezra, then walked toward Tristan, reaching up to graze her fingernail down his jawline softly. "What could be *so* important that you had to speak to me, especially after everything you said to me last time we saw each other?"

Tristan's internal struggle was put aside. He didn't vibrate in anger, and he didn't crumble under her gaze. "Lyra is awake."

Rya's flirtatious games halted, and she froze. "What?" she whispered, and he nodded in response.

She dropped her hands to her side, and turned around to face me, a questioning look on her face. "It's true, Rya. We have a lot to fill you in on, but not much time," I told her.

She threw her hands up in the air in exasperation. "Why didn't you just bloody say that, Tristan?"

He scoffed. "I can't exactly put that out in the open, now can I? Some Craigslist ad or making a Tinder profile saying Lyra woke up? Be serious. Supernaturals read those too, and some of them know who she is."

She gave him a deadpan look. "Next time it involves someone else, just say looking for a threesome with an old friend, eh?"

Tristan looked stumped. It wasn't a bad idea. Maybe not naming her directly, but still adding that third party for urgency. I shook my head, clearing my thoughts. "Let's hope we don't run into this situation again. Should there be a next time, we'll remember to do just that."

"Good. Now what do you need? Tell me where we're at," she said.

I filled her in on Fury, discovering we were mates, and the attempted assassination of Fury when she saved Roxanne. All about the footsteps on Avalon, the awakening and disappearance of Lyra, and then her appearance at the summit.

Rya blew out a harsh breath. "An angel? What in the hell is an angel doing involved in this?"

I shrugged, noting her demeanor upon supposedly learning about the Afterlife. She seemed shaken, but not as much as I would have expected. "None of us know that just yet."

"Well, let's see if we can start by finding her." She held her hand out to me in expectation. I reached into the breast pocket of my jacket and pulled out a small piece of white satin cloth.

"From Lyra's pillow," I said, answering the unspoken question. She nodded.

She grasped it, running her fingers over the fabric, and muttering some words softly as she closed her eyes. A crease formed between her brows and her lips pursed. An unnatural wind swirled in the room, tossing her jet black hair all around her face. What felt like minutes passed. Her sun-kissed olive skin glistened when she started to break out into a sweat, a small bead dripping from her forehead.

She let out a loud gasp, and the wind stopped. Opening her eyes, I saw the worry and the fear. "She's being blocked, Dorian. That's impossible," she whispered.

Tristan cursed, and I rubbed my temples, trying to think. Ezra looked at each of us, confused. "Has this never happened before?"

I raised my eyebrows. "No. We've always been able to track her with Rya."

"There's no one I can't find. I am the best at what I do. Even a thousand years ago, we were able to always track her. We always knew where she was. Stopping her was a different story, but I never couldn't find her," she said softly. Looking at me, she changed course. "This is magic beyond Earth if she is being blocked. I need to know *everything*. What more do you know of angels?"

"Nothing." I sniffed and looked out the window, taking in the beauty of the sun beginning to descend over the sea. "But I know someone that does. Brace yourself. It's morning in Houston, and Fury isn't exactly pleasant when she wakes up."

CHAPTER 17
FURY

I STOOD IN THE BATHROOM WITH MY HANDS PRESSED AGAINST THE COUNTER'S edge. My phone flashlight still illuminated the space, and the mirror only showed my reflection. I took some deep breaths. I didn't know what to do next, but I needed to sort that out.

My stomach rumbled loudly, reminding me that I hadn't eaten since the bonfire the night before. I grimaced and looked at Hades. "I'm going to get something to eat from downstairs. We need to troubleshoot some of this while we wait for Jules to get back with us. I'll bring you something. I read that crows will eat trash and cat food. Do you have a preference?"

He scoffed and flapped his wings at me in anger. "I will not eat either, you twat."

I laughed. "Fine, if you aren't willing to entertain me that way, then I guess I'll just bring you something normal to eat."

He huffed in response, but I didn't get the chance to speak. The air changed, and I stayed quiet. A tiny charge of electricity felt like it sizzled lightly over my skin. My mate was here. Dorian had come back.

I was equally intrigued and irritated at his presence here. I wasn't ready to talk to him, but time wasn't exactly on our side right now.

"The fae is back," I said to Hades as I reached for the knob to open the door and go into my room. "Stay here a minute, will you?"

The moment I stepped out of the bathroom, I heard a knock.

I knew it was him. I didn't want to see him. I reminded myself why. Lying sack of shit. Manipulative asshole fairy. Cold, guarded, moody jerk.

Stomping over to the door, I repeated the mantra in my head.

When I opened it, a burst of cool air rushed over my skin. Dorian's amber eyes took me in, perusing the length of my body. Having moved so quickly from my dream to summoning Jules, I didn't even bother putting on pants.

When his gaze met mine, his pupils dilated, and his nostrils flared.

"May I come in?" Without waiting for me to answer, he began to step forward, walking into my room.

"Apparently you may," I grumbled as he passed me, and I closed the door. "What do you want, Dorian? I really don't want to see you right now."

He stopped, taking in the feathered mess. Turning in a circle, he looked around. "What happened in here?" he asked, reaching down to pick up a feather and inspect it.

"I had a dream. Clawed the bed and pillows in my sleep, apparently. Now answer the question," I said, crossing my arms and jutting out my hip.

"At least you didn't sift and set something on fire. Small blessings, I suppose," he said, dropping the feather from his hand.

I rolled my eyes. "Everyone's got jokes. Final time. What do you want?"

"I came to talk to you."

I scoffed. "Oh, now you feel like talking to me? Sure didn't feel like that when you were keeping me in the dark about Lyra." I cocked an eyebrow at him, daring him to lie about his reasoning.

Dorian inspected his fingernails, not taking my bait. "You smell like the shifter."

"Maybe that's because we fucked last night." His eyes flashed when he looked at me, and his jaw tightened slightly. "Does that bother you, Dorian? It's hard to tell if you have feelings or not, so you'll actually have to use words to tell me." I heard the sarcasm and venom come out in my voice, but a tiny whisper in my head told me to ease up.

Still, he ignored me, not rising to the occasion. How did he do that? He grabbed the vanity chair and took a seat, crossing his leg over the other. He clasped his hands and stared me down for what felt like several agonizing minutes.

I wouldn't give in and speak first.

Tick.

Tick.

Tick.

I huffed in annoyance, sat on the edge of my mutilated mattress, and crisscrossed my legs while I waited in silence.

Tick.

Tick.

Tick.

"For fuck's sake, will one of you just talk already? It's boring in here," Hades griped from the bathroom.

"No, I will not, thank you very much," I responded to the crow while looking directly at Dorian. "He came here to talk to me, so I think this one is on him."

He raised his eyebrows in surprise. "Why is Hades in the bathroom?"

"Because we were calling Bloody Mary. Hung up just before you arrived," he answered.

I whipped my head around. "Shut up!" I hissed at him.

He flew out of the bathroom and landed in his nest. "Well, crow is out of the bag now, so I'm just gonna hang out here and watch the show, if you don't mind." I squinted my eyes and glared at him.

"Why did you call Bloody Mary? You were supposed to wait for us," Dorian said quietly. I could hear the irritation in his voice.

Returning my attention to Dorian, I said, "Are you serious right now? You aren't entitled to answers, fae. You have a lot to explain to me, and truthfully, I don't owe you anything. I guess you thought the same of me, otherwise I can't imagine why you didn't share what was going on with Lyra."

I looked out the window for a while, thinking about the way his lies made me feel. I hated it. It was lying by omission, but it was still concealing the truth. I didn't blame him for the death of those at the summit. That was not his fault. Lyra was going to show up whether we liked it or not. She was going to cause chaos and try to toy with me regardless. It wasn't Lyra's actions that were the issue. It was that none of us knew she was a potential problem. I don't know what that knowledge would have accomplished since she appeared to have an angel on her side, but at least we wouldn't have been in the dark.

That little voice in my head whispered again, reminding me of everything I thought about the night before. About all that I'd felt, and the realizations that had come to me.

I was here, and for however long that was going to be, I wanted to belong with them. I wanted to try. I couldn't very well make that happen while I sat here and gave him the cold shoulder. Nothing was ever solved this way.

I sighed. "It's hurtful, Dorian. You didn't trust us. You didn't trust me. You should've told me," I said, a soft anger in my tone. "I'm not asking for much, but I do ask that you don't lie to me. I already lived a life filled with secrets. I'm not willing to do it again."

He looked down at his lap and closed his eyes, taking a deep breath and exhaling. When he looked back up, I saw conflict. "My intention wasn't to hurt you, Fury. I would never do that on purpose. I kept it to myself for reasons I'm not ready to explain just yet. However, on the subject of trust, you were the only one that knew about her. Consider that."

"True." I tilted my head. "Why not Rox? You didn't tell her, and I thought you two were close."

"We are, but she isn't my mate," he said, his amber eyes flashing with a brilliant light.

I felt that tingle over my skin again, and a strange warmth spread through my body. Trying to ignore it, I pressed on. "But she is your friend. Friends trust each other."

He dipped his chin in agreement. "I suppose they do. It's something I'll address with Rox, though. Just as I wouldn't have this conversation with anyone else about you and me."

Fair enough. He respected boundaries with relationships, and that

I could appreciate. It spoke a lot to his character. I admired it, even if I was still pissed at him.

"Trust goes both ways. You came here to ask me questions, but you still won't answer mine." I picked at a feather that was on my leg, trying to flick it off my finger when it stuck. "I'd also like to point out that you demanded I answer everything when you interrogated me after you found out what I was."

Uncrossing his legs, he leaned back in the chair and looked at the ceiling. "I did. For the same reasons I expect answers now."

"You're unreal," I scoffed loudly. "How does that make any sense?"

Rolling his neck for a stretch, he took his time while I started to stew in anger again. When he finished, he sighed. "It's different." I opened my mouth to argue, but he held a hand up to silence me. I pressed my lips together and narrowed my eyes. "The questions I had then pertained to our safety, your safety, and to the safety of our people. Yes, you shared information you never had any intention of telling us, for reasons that were originally beyond your control. You had a job to do. I understood it, whether I liked it or not. The questions I have now also pertain to your safety, and the safety of others. If what you've said continues to be true, and it is prophesied that we'll end the world, then it would stand to reason that the protection of everyone overrides the desire to keep secrets. That being said, my reason for keeping Lyra a secret was purely emotional. There was no malicious intent. I acknowledge that I should've shared with you that she had been awakened. I'm sorry for that. I like to handle things on my own. I've been around a long time and that's how I've always been. I know that isn't an excuse; it is my reasoning, which I believe you deserve to hear. I don't think anyone knowing about her would have stopped her that day, but I know I'd be pissed beyond reason were I in your place. And perhaps theirs." He titled his forehead toward the direction of the living room downstairs, telling me all I needed to know. Everyone was here. I wondered for a moment if they could hear us or if they were minding their own business.

My mouth hung open for a bit. That may have been the most he'd ever spoken to me in one sitting.

"Okay," I said lamely. I waved my hand at him, motioning for him to carry on. "What do you want to know?"

A small smile graced his lips in response to my acceptance of his pseudo-apology. It faded quickly, and a more serious look washed over his features.

"I need to know more about angels," he said.

"Could you be more specific, or are you asking for a history lesson?" I asked him, quirking an eyebrow. "That's a lot of ground to cover. It'd be easier if you just asked me what you want to know."

Leaning forward and resting his elbows on his knees, he began to fill me in on Rya, and I listened to what I assumed was the CliffsNotes version of their time together, both past and present.

I learned she'd helped him bind Lyra and force her into stasis. That she was the best tracker in the world. And that she was Kelly's sister. That was definitely a conversation I wanted to have at a later time. But most importantly, I learned that Rya couldn't reach her. Never in all her years—which were apparently as long as Dorian's, yet another question for later—had she been unable to track someone, especially Lyra. She'd had a brush with death by her hands, her parents instead sacrificing themselves to save their daughters. Whatever spell her parents used sent Rya and Kelly to safety, but in doing so, it created an invisible marker between their girls and their killer. With the strength of Rya's tracking magic added to that obscure tie, she'd always been able to find her anywhere in the world, at any time. Rya had said she was being blocked. More importantly, she'd said it shouldn't be possible.

I cursed under my breath and stood up. I started pacing the room, feeling the feathers as they stuck to my bare feet.

I looked at Hades, asking a silent question. He knew. He knew as well as I did that this almost certainly confirmed the angel was with Lyra. He nodded his head.

"What does that mean to you, Fury?" Dorian asked. A tiny crease appeared between his brows as he looked at me with concern.

I exhaled loudly. "It means the angel is *with* her. He's cloaked her."

"What kind of magic is that? Do you know?" he asked. "If we know what kind of spell or charm or protection has been placed on her, Rya and Kelly can—"

I shook my head, cutting him off. "It's not as simple as a magic spell. It's an object. It's a talisman that angels use on Earth."

He considered my answer before asking why.

"It protects them from supernatural magic in this realm. Over the ages, religions have believed in all sorts of entities. Gods, angels, spirits, saints, devils, demons . . . furies." I smirked. "Anyway, man has tried time and time again to call on what they believe will help them. Call on their patron saints or ask for their god to give them a sign. Those sorts of things. Not like Ouija boards and stuff like that. Poltergeists always had fun with those, but they aren't meant to do anything real. But humans are foolish, and they always keep trying to reach the other side one way or another. It happened once. A drunken accident when a supernatural actually summoned an angel, ripping him into existence from wherever he was earthside to right in front of this moron. Wrong place, wrong time kind of thing, but it happened all the same. After that, angels carried a talisman to protect them from supernatural magic when they left the Afterlife. If Lyra is being blocked, that's why. She's most certainly wearing one. I just don't know how."

Dorian stood up and ran his hands through his hair. "How do we break through it?"

I pursed my lips and shrugged. "We can't. Not that I am aware of. But that doesn't mean we can't try to find out." I looked at Hades as he got out of his little T-shirt nest. "Will you go to Duke? Keep this as quiet as you can. Trust no one. If she has an amulet, you know there's some shady shit going on. I just don't know why. None of this adds up yet."

He snapped his beak in response as he stretched out his wings, preparing for flight. "Mind opening the window for me?"

Dorian was closest, and he slid the glass up for him.

"Be careful," I said.

He cocked his head. "Friendly advice?" he asked, mirroring my comment the night before.

I huffed a laugh. "Can't be. We aren't friends," I said with a wink.

"Talk to Jules. She'll be happier to see you without me around," he said, a small fleck of sadness briefly flickered in his eyes before it was gone. "I'll be back soon." With a loud caw, he took off, flying through the opening and heading back to the Afterlife.

Dorian closed it, and asked, "Who is Jules?"

I smiled. "Bloody Mary isn't her real name."

His mood darkened again. I was going to get whiplash.

This damn fae.

"About that. You were supposed to wait." He walked toward me slowly, but I stood my ground, unmoving. When he stopped in front of me, I craned my neck to look up at him while he towered over me.

"About that," I mocked, "you aren't the only one that likes to handle things by yourself. I needed answers, so I asked her for them. I didn't need you, Ezra, or Roman there to do it," I said.

"What did you ask her?"

I jutted my chin out. "I asked her what I am and if there are any others in the world like me. She doesn't know, but that's only because she's never looked before." I paused, waiting for that to set in when I caught the slight disappointment in his eyes. "And then I asked if she could track Lyra for me. Find out where she is."

He raised his brows in surprise, completely caught off guard that I would've been a step ahead of him. "And?" he asked.

"She's going to let me know when she finds her. Seeing as Rya can't find her either, I guess we're fucked, and we have to wait."

He hummed in response but didn't move.

"Any other questions, or did you get what you came for?" I still felt irritated with him. He'd apologized for part of his actions—part—but I wasn't sure it was what I wanted. I couldn't always read him, and it made my relationship with him more complicated than the other two. Sort of. Being called Maya certainly complicated *that* relationship.

"I didn't come here to use you."

I snorted. "That makes one of you."

The amber in his eyes turned a molten gold. "What does that mean?" he rumbled.

I shook my head and sighed. "Nothing. It means nothing."

He moved forward, causing me to take a step back on instinct. Not out of fear of his presence, but to keep from falling. I stumbled slightly, and he kept walking until my back was against a hard surface and I had nowhere to go.

He put his hands on the wall behind me, boxing me in and leaning down. His heated gaze sent goosebumps across my skin.

"I will not use you, Fury. For anything. Not for answers, and not for anything else. When I come to you, it's because I want to be near you. I make my choices. I know who you are, and I don't expect you to be someone else."

He had no idea the effect those words would have on me. He didn't know what had happened last night, or how Roman had fucked my body but had Maya in his head.

I swallowed thickly. "I'm still mad at you." I cringed inside when my voice came out huskier than I intended.

His eyes flicked to my lips. "You have every right to be."

With one hand still on the wall, he used his other to graze a finger down my cheek, tracing the collarbone, then down my arm. His eyes followed his hand, and I watched him, more turned on than I wanted to admit.

"Then why are you still here?" I asked with a shaky breath.

His large hand curled around my hip, his thumb stroking the skin as he held me firmly. "If you don't want me to be here, then I'll leave." His hand stayed curved, pressed against me as he dragged it up, feeling the contours of my body. Over my hip, across my ribs, and underneath my breast.

I wanted him. Oh, I wanted him. Even if I was angry with him, I wanted him.

But I also knew that it wasn't right. Roman had hurt me, and if I let Dorian have his way with me, there could be a part of me doing it for the wrong reasons. I didn't think that was happening, but if it did, I wouldn't forgive myself for it.

I slowly grabbed his hand, taking it off my body. He didn't try to stop me, instead respecting every action of mine. Placing it back on the wall, he closed his eyes and nodded slightly. "Okay," he said softly, opening his eyes and starting to step back.

Grabbing the back of his neck before he pulled away, I said, "It's not what you think." I struggled with the right words for the moment. I wouldn't share what happened between Roman and I, but Dorian needed to know this wasn't me rejecting him. "Trust me." It was all I had.

A look of confusion appeared in his eyes before he dipped his chin once in acceptance.

My heart thundered in my chest, and I was pretty sure we both heard it in the silence that spanned between us. I hadn't told him to leave, so we stood together, my hand on the back of his neck, his hands pressed on the wall beside me, our eyes locked in a heated battle.

A knock on the door made me jump.

"Fury?" Roxanne's voice came from the other side of the door.

"Come in," I managed hoarsely.

She opened the door and came in, coming to an abrupt halt when she saw us.

She looked away. "Ezra said it's time to go unless there's something angel business-wise that needs to keep you both here." She looked at her nails. "And he knows there isn't."

I cleared my throat, wondering how much Ezra had listened in on. "Tell them I need to change my clothes and I'll be down in less than five. And could you grab me breakfast to go, please? I'm starving." She mumbled a response, and turned on her heel, still angry with Dorian and not wanting to be around him.

"Where are you going that's so important?" Dorian asked when I moved to the drawers to find clean clothes.

"Turn around if you don't want a show." With my back to him, I took off my shirt and pulled another over my head. I bent over, changing my underwear, and shimmied my legs into some shorts. I heard a strangled groan escape his lips. He clearly hadn't turned around.

When I faced him, walking to the bathroom, I said, "I have an appointment to keep. In the meantime, I'll fill in Ezra, assuming the bastard doesn't already know. You stay here and fill in Roman and Rox. And fix things with her, Dorian. I mean it. You owe her that."

He furrowed his brows. "What kind of appointment do you have with the vampire?"

"Nothing much. Just a rapist to condition." I grinned and grabbed my boots, walking out the door.

CHAPTER 18
FURY

I PICKED DRIED BLOOD OUT OF MY FINGERNAILS AS I WAITED FOR THE WATER to heat up. When steam billowed from the shower, I opened the glass door and stepped in.

A loud moan escaped my lips when the hot water hit my skin. I just stood there, soaking it in, letting it drench me and roll off my body. I found it a little funny that something so simple was so very much needed. It was a form of self-care for me. Sometimes it was a shower, sometimes a bath. Depended on the tub, honestly. Either way, it was my quiet space. I liked the way my muscles loosened as they started to relax. I liked the way the water sounded as they hit the tile in fat droplets. I liked the smell of shampoo and soap. If calm had a smell, it would be the scent of *clean*. Silence enveloped me and I was left with my thoughts.

Lathering my hair, my thoughts drifted to the work I'd been doing with my little vampire friend. Day three with Robert, and he wasn't that complicated of a case. It was a textbook rapist study. He wasn't a case of past abuse continuing the cycle. He was just horribly damaged. He liked power, but he liked having power over people in truly dangerous ways. He got off on it.

I smiled to myself. He sure didn't today. Today he had the roles reversed on him. When he fought back, I hit him the same way he did his victims. When he tried to get away, I'd pin him the same way he did his victims. When he'd cry, I'd laugh at him—the same way he did to his victims. It would happen like this for a long time. He did everything I'd expected, and he'd likely continue to. Oh sure, every now and then they threw me a new bone to play with. They'd eventually find more creative ways to curse me. That was always fun. I liked it when they called me more than a bitch when they were angry. It was like a milestone of sorts. We'd see how he would progress over the next few years. I'd break him like all the others. I always did. I was The Fury. In the end, I'd win.

I rinsed my hair out and then squeezed liquid soap onto a loofah, rubbing it over my body and cleaning off the blood, dirt, and grime.

My thoughts strayed to the guys and the potential of my extended stay. What if Hades and Duke didn't find a way for me to get back to the Afterlife? Ever? Earth would be my home. *Again.* It wasn't that bad this time around, though. The food was better than it was back then, and the company had significantly improved. I felt a little torn. I missed Duke. I missed aspects of my Afterlife. I missed being someone there. I had damn well earned that. But even if it scared me a little, the idea of having to say goodbye permanently to Roxanne, Dorian, Ezra, and Roman hurt more than I wanted to admit. Even though tension with Roman was at its peak, they'd grown on me, and that would be hard to let go of.

Houston was as close to Hell as anything else. For now, I was here. I wanted to make the best of it. Rehabilitation work wasn't quite the same as it was in the Afterlife, but it was definitely nice to be back at it. For weeks I'd felt like I was floundering in my existence. I was the best of the best, and I was sent to Earth to do a job, but it felt like I was just fudging it up six ways from Sunday.

Meet guys? Check. Find out they're your mates. Erm. Not exactly part of the plan. Okay, moving on. Find out someone is after me. Seems weird. Ezra reads minds? Great. That doesn't get awkward when you're sent to rehabilitate them. Get called Sunny when someone tries to kill me—not even sure how that was possible. Get bit by some dickhead shifter then have all your mates change you in an effort to save your afterlife. Find out angels are sabotaging you somehow. Ugh.

In what world was that part of any plan? I grumbled audibly. I had one job. And I couldn't do it. I huffed out loud in frustration. The poltergeists had one job and look how much they screwed the pooch on that. Useless, they were. I wasn't useless, and I fucking knew it. I was being set up. It took a conversation with Rox to shove me in the right direction. Until that moment, I hadn't been able to figure out what finally set off the so-called bomb. Now I suspected it had to be me.

One of the many things that didn't make sense were the factors leading up to it. How in the world was I part of the prophecy? And if I were indeed the spark that would light the proverbial flame, did that mean I could in fact die? It wasn't exactly something I could test out.

And Lyra. Talk about not expecting that piece. I understood why Dorian kept it a secret. It didn't change the fact that I was pissed with him for it. It was information we needed to know.

Angels. Lyra. Imminent death and world destruction. Also, maybe, my imminent death and destruction . . .

All of these questions and no answers.

I finished rinsing off and turned off the shower. I stepped out, grabbing a towel to dry off. After I wrapped it around my body and tucked it under my arm, I went to the mirror to wipe off the steam.

As the glass was cleared, a face that wasn't mine popped in front of me.

"What's up, my demon?"

I screamed at her unexpected appearance as I jumped back, clutching my chest and dropping my towel. "Jeeeesus, Jules! You scared the shit out of me!"

She chortled, her shoulders shaking as she did so. "I'd say I'm sorry, but I'm really not."

I tried to slow my racing heart while I glared at her. "No, I don't imagine you would be sorry." I breathed in and out, convincing my blood pressure to calm down and not test the 'do I die or not' question that had been swirling around in my head.

Jules was the only poltergeist in the mirror realm. It was all her own. For that very reason, I'd never had anyone pop into existence in a mirror I was looking at. So yes, apparently *The* Fury could get scared and jump out of her skin like a kid at a horror film.

She shrugged. "When you're as old as I am, you have to get your kicks somehow."

"I'm sure you're out of practice, but that's not exactly how you make friends," I said, bending down to grab my towel off the floor.

"Is that what we are?" she asked. The tone of her voice shifted slightly. Almost hopeful.

I stood up, arching my eyebrow at her, and then started to wring out the water in my hair. "We could be, yes. Why not? You seem unsure about the prospect."

Jules shifted her posture, crossing her arms. "I don't really have friends. People want things from me. That's why you called, wasn't it? Because you wanted something from me. Not because you wanted girl chat."

"That's fair. I did call you because I needed something, yeah. I wasn't sure you would answer me. Or be willing to help in my cause. That doesn't mean I'm opposed to building a friendship. How do you think friends meet each other?" I asked, setting the towel down and picking up a wet brush for my hair.

She looked stumped. "I . . . I don't know. I didn't have friends when I was alive. And the Afterlife proved to be a joke," she huffed.

I laughed with her. "Well, you won't hear an argument from me. But to answer that question, people meet over work stuff, or they bump into each other at a place of interest. Sometimes they meet someone by asking them for help, or a favor. Sometimes you strike up a fun conversation and they try to kill you later with spicy tacos." She tilted her head in confusion. "Never mind, the point is that anyone you meet can become your friend if that's something you both want." I left it open-ended, waiting to see what she said.

A small smile crept up on her lips and she gave a single dip of her chin. "Okay . . . friend."

I smiled in return. "Something to know about friendships, though. It's not one-sided. Don't let anyone use you. If you try to be there for them and they are never there for you, that isn't your friend. There's give and take in every relationship, including friendships. Don't always be the giver, okay?"

I meant every word of it. I wouldn't use Jules for my gain and harm her in the process. People too often tried to be good for the wrong reasons, like there was some sheet being marked with all the good deeds they'd done in life. You either wanted to treat people kindly, or you didn't. Forget about who you think was watching you; it was always what was in your heart. And there were entirely too many hearts filled with hatred and ugliness. I knew all too well. I didn't want her to get hurt.

"All right," I said after she nodded in acknowledgement. "So what do I owe the pleasure of this unexpected visit where you almost sent me to another early grave?" I tugged at the tangles, then switched to the other side. "Or did you just want to see me naked?"

She threw her head back and laughed. "Well, I have seen my fair share of boobs since I escaped into the mirrors, and I must say, yours are quite nice. But that isn't the reason for my call."

I held a hand up. "I know we had an agreement, and I want to hear what you have to say, but I don't have a bloody mary with me. I told you I would keep them coming."

She waved me off. "Oh I know you'll pay up. We're friends, right?" She winked. "And if we weren't, believe me when I say I know how to get paid. You think that little appearance scared you? I can make your life a living hell if you fuck me over."

I silently stared at her for a second, realizing she was dead serious, but still in a joking way. But not really. "I have no doubts that's true."

She scrunched her nose in a quick and cute smile before continuing. "I found Lyra."

I dropped the brush and slapped my hands on the counter. "You what?" I said in shock. "Already?"

"Please." She flicked her hair over her shoulder. "Look, I know it was your second question. Your first is going to take time. That one is harder than you think. So I decided to make your second request my first priority. At the end of the day, it really is the more pressing issue, is it not?"

I frowned. I still wanted to know if there was anyone like me. Knowing Rava was a hybrid, and that there were many others like that, was helpful, but I just wanted to know more. Almost reluctantly, I agreed. "It is."

She twisted her lips. "I thought so."

"So where is she?"

"The Vatican."

I blinked several times, not saying a word. Finally, all that came out was, "I'm sorry, what?"

She creased her brows and tilted her head. "The Vatican," she said slowly, looking at me like I was stupid. "You know, the Pope's house?"

"I know what the Vatican is," I deadpanned. "I just . . . the irony is something I can't get past at the moment."

"I know, right?" she said. "Angels are so egotistical; it didn't take me long to find them. If you were a giant narcissist with a power trip, where would you go if you wanted to see how you've been portrayed and revered for a couple of millennia? It's their favorite place to talk about. Running joke and all that the guys there are in for a big surprise when they all kick the bucket."

I snorted. She wasn't wrong. But to think our mystery angel was hiding there with Lyra? Wow. I blew out a breath. "Okay. Okay. . ." I started thinking, my mind racing at an impossible speed.

"Stop thinking so hard. I can see smoke coming out of your ears. Don't worry. I have eyes on her."

That caught my attention. "What does that mean?"

I saw a mischievous twinkle in her eye, but she kept her lips sealed.

"Hmmm," I said in response. "We're not there yet. Fair enough." I grabbed my clothes off the counter and started dressing. "I need to update everyone. Will you find me and let me know if anything changes?"

"Of course. If you're near a mirror, I can always find you."

I smiled at her. "Thanks. I owe you that bloody mary."

"Damn right you do. I won't say no to cookies either."

I laughed, and when I looked back at the mirror, she was already gone. Shaking my fingers through my hair, I left the bathroom to go find Ezra.

And there he stood, the eavesdropping motherfucker.

"I already know," he said.

I narrowed my eyes, glaring daggers at him.

He held his hands up before I could rip him a new one for it. "In my defense, you screamed in the bathroom. What was I supposed to do? I listened in. You were okay. But I heard what your new friend, Jules, had to say."

I took in a deep breath, fully annoyed—even if I understood. Count to ten. Breathe out.

"Fine. But we need to get to Dorian and Roman and tell them now."

That's when I saw it. There was a look of shame in his eyes. It was a tiny speck of a moment, but it was there, and that's when I knew.

"You already told them, didn't you?"

"I've briefed them, yes."

I pushed past him, smacking his arm with my shoulder as I did. "Take me back to Roman's," I said.

"Fury, I—"

"*Now.*" I wanted to scream at him. "If you're as smart as you think you are, you'll know not to piss me off right now. And so help me, if I find out you're reading my mind, I will end you."

He opened his mouth to say something, but I held my hand up. "And don't talk to me either or I'll cut out your tongue."

Empty threats?

Yes.

The full force of my anger made abundantly clear?

Also yes.

I SLOUCHED in an armchair in Roman's living room, staring at the ceiling and twirling a lock of my hair. The guys argued back and forth, back and forth—around and around in circles. It was enough to make my eyes cross.

Rya pinched the bridge of her nose and released a deep sigh. She appeared just as annoyed as I was. I'd met her the day she'd arrived with Dorian. She seemed nice enough. I figured if he trusted her, that spoke volumes of her character and worthiness. Dorian didn't trust many people, as evidenced by his omission of Lyra.

Each of the guys thought they needed to go after Lyra. Dorian felt confident now that he had Rya again. Roman was just heated and thinking emotionally. Ezra wasn't that different from Roman if I were being honest. They both figured Dorian knew what he was doing when it came to his daughter, and I was surprised they were all on the same page for once. Did one of them ask me what my thoughts were? Or Rya's for that matter? Of course not. If they had, they would know I thought they were all dumbasses.

I raised my hand like a child and waved it in the air, waiting for someone to notice me. When they didn't even bother to look, I reached over to the glass of water on the end table next to me. I drank what was left, then took it and threw it down on the ground.

It shattered, and all the conversation around me came to a screeching halt.

"You about done?" I asked.

Three pairs of eyes stared at me when Ezra spoke. "Tantrum much?"

I shrugged. "Not one of you have asked what Rya or I think about this. Not one of you have spoken to us, and not one of you paid any mind only moments ago when I tried to get your attention." Glancing at each of them, it was clear they were finally listening. "So if you'd let the ladies in the room have a turn, we'd tell you that you're all a bunch of morons and you need to sit back and wait this out."

Rya's lips curved upwards, and the smile almost reached her eyes. Picking up her teacup, she took a sip and hummed into it. She was letting me have the floor.

Dorian was hard to read. His features were like stone, and when he spoke, his voice was flat. "Would you care to tell us why you think that?"

"I would, thank you." I straightened my posture, sitting in an upright position in the chair, and crisscrossing my legs. "I don't think you're thinking this through. Yes, we know where she is. That's great. You don't have a plan."

"That's what we've been—"

I held my hand up to Roman and shot him a look.

"Don't interrupt and mansplain to me the conversation I've just been listening to for the last half hour." Roman furrowed his brows and pressed his lips together. When I was satisfied he'd keep his mouth shut, I went on. "This isn't the same as last time. Lyra likes games, right? She's playing a new one now, but you're stuck in the past thinking it's just round two. It's not. There's an angel involved, and that changes the entire board. What do we know about it? Jack all, that's what. We don't know who the angel is or why they woke her up, or why they are after me. What we do know is that he's given her an amulet to protect her from supernatural magic. So tell me, what is your plan to get past that? Your magic won't work against her. Rya's magic won't work against her. She's untouchable right now. And you want to waltz up to the front door of the Vatican, bang on it, and piss her off? Leave it alone right now. We hold the cards, and you don't realize it. They don't know that we know where she is. They don't know we have someone on our side that can watch her for us."

Dorian raised his hand the same way I had. Did he see me do that earlier? Had he just *ignored* me? Now wasn't the time to address that. I needed them to hear me. I nodded my head toward him and asked, "Yes?"

"How do we know we can trust your friend, Jules? We've not met her. We know nothing about her. What if she's playing both sides?"

"She's not."

Dorian had been standing by the fireplace, but he came and sat in the armchair next to mine. "Ezra said she told you she could make your life a living hell if she didn't get what she wanted."

"Really?" I shot Ezra a dirty look before returning my attention to Dorian. "That was taken out of context." I sighed. "Look, Jules escaped the Afterlife. The only reason they haven't exterminated her in retaliation is they can't. We talked about this. They can't reach her in the mirror realm. It's her domain. It's her brand of magic. My magic isn't demon magic. It's unique to me. That's hers. She isn't going back; she isn't working both sides. She has no reason to. This may be hard for you, but you're going to have to trust me on this. Jules is on our side."

"So we're supposed to sit here and wait for her to attack you again?" Roman asked.

I shook my head. "No. We know where she is. We need to find out what we can in the meantime. We don't have a way to defeat her yet. Jules hasn't seen the angel she's with, so we don't know the motive or anything more than that just yet. Duke and Hades are working on finding out what they can too. We must play our pieces carefully. Moving too quickly on this will only end up hurting people."

"She's right, you know," Rya interjected. We all looked at her, surprised that she was finally weighing in. "I do think you're a bunch of morons. You aren't thinking ahead. Everything she said is correct, Dorian. This is a new game. One you and I don't know how to play just yet. We need more information before we can put her back in stasis. What if you and I aren't enough this time? What if we need more?" She turned her head to look out the wall of windows. The lake was calm and serene. You'd never know it felt like a sauna of death outside. "No. We play this safe. We may only have one shot at this. I agree with Fury, and you'd all do well to listen to her."

I grinned and held out my hand for a fist-bump. She looked at my extended offer and considered it. She tilted her head as though she was giving in for my sake. She fist-bumped me back. I turned to the guys and raised my eyebrows expectantly. "Well?"

Dorian took a deep breath. "Okay. We'll do this your way."

Roman and Ezra nodded silently in agreement.

"All right, then. Recon is already in place. Now I need to find out what's happening on the other side of the veil." I looked out the window, searching the trees. "Where's that pigeon when I need him?"

CHAPTER 19
FURY

THE SUN WAS SETTING WHILE I WAITED ON THE DECK OVERLOOKING THE water. Roman's lake house was quiet. Each of the guys had a home that was appealing. I couldn't say much for Avalon as a location, but Dorian's castle was fascinating and his mansion in Houston wasn't half bad either. That bathtub in my room was something else. Ezra's penthouse was stunning. The pool, the view; it was next to everything you could need, but so high up you still somehow felt alone. Roman's house though . . . the quiet was comforting most of the time. I closed my eyes and listened carefully. I could hear the shuffling of feet at other cabins. The pack. Not all of them lived here, but many of them chose to.

Even Roxanne had moved into a small cabin nearby. She slept in the main house just down the hall from me, but she had her own place when she wanted space from everyone. Her house south of the city was left for now, cared for by someone she paid to keep it up. As she'd said it, her place was here with me and her brother.

A breeze lifted my hair, flinging strands into my face and along my neck. That's when I heard it. A flapping of wings.

I opened my eyes and squinted them, putting a hand over my brows to shield the sunlight from blinding me as I searched the skies.

A familiar black dot came into view, quickly flying toward me.

I stepped back from the railing and let him land. He shook his body, then tucked his wings to his side.

"Trouble is stirring up," he said.

I frowned. "Nice to see you too." I crossed my arms. "What kind of trouble?"

"Oh, you know. Risk witches throwing out more prophecies, foreseeing doom and gloom. Upper Management is pissed you haven't done your job yet."

I threw my hands up. "For fuck's sake. Number one, my job takes time. Even if all this—I don't know, we'll call it weirdness—hadn't happened, I still wouldn't have finished. But the rest of it? Come on. It's not my fault. I can't control what's going on here. I was damn well set up. Mates. An angel sending assassins. Did the risk witches say anything about that?"

"You know they didn't."

"Did they see me in the prophecy this time at least?"

He pinned me with his stare and shook his head slowly. I cursed.

"Duke thinks we're on our own one hundred percent. He doesn't trust anyone right now. We're not sure if they're lying about the prophecies, or if something is missing and you aren't what sets them off."

I turned, gripping the edge of the railing. "What do you think?"

He tilted his head in confusion. "Are you asking my opinion?" I nodded. "I think it's still too early to tell, but I personally think you're the missing puzzle piece. You talk to them more than me, but I see them with you, and I watch from afar. Mates are a tricky thing. The Afterlife often overlooks what being mated and bonded truly means. It's not our way, so it's not taken seriously. Only fools write off what they don't understand."

Scratching at the deck with my fingernail, I considered his words. "Some humans experience it. They just don't realize it," I said quietly.

"How so?"

"Having a child. That bond is beyond the concept of love. Not all of them experience it. You and I have watched plenty of people harm their children, sell their children, or cast them out for being different. We've watched them disown them when they find out they're gay. We've seen them curse them and damn them in the name of their religion. For a hundred years I've seen it. I don't even know how old you are or how much you've seen, but I do know there are parents out there that have the epitome of unconditional love. We've seen that too. They'd walk through fire to save them, and if something happened to their child, they'd destroy everything in their grief and their rage if they were capable of it. Thankfully, they aren't."

He looked at me thoughtfully. "I believe you're right in that. I've seen all the things you speak of, and worse, and I've seen the bond too." He walked on the railing to be closer to me as he looked out at the lake. "Interesting that you're the first one to make that connection."

I shrugged. "I chose to be a demon because I was angry at my lot in life. I suppose I'm different because I'm not necessarily angry at my core. There's beauty in the world, and it makes me happy when I see it. Gives me a smidge of hope for humanity." I nudged him with my hand. "Don't go telling anyone, though. You'll ruin my reputation."

"Right. Dark and scary. Skulls and bubble baths. That's you," he said mockingly.

"Don't forget it. I'm not above plucking out your feathers when you piss me off," I added, and he chuckled. I smacked my hand down on the wood. "All right, all right. Moving on. We need to step up our game. I had a chat with Jules today."

I filled him in on my conversation with our favorite poltergeist and asked what he and Duke found out on their end.

"Duke started researching angels under the guise of looking into your hybrid status just in case he is being watched. That talisman makes this tricky." He sighed. "It's good that Jules can tell us where she is, but the fact that an angel is protecting her and the angel itself is protected, it just presents so many problems."

I pursed and twisted my lips, tapping my fingers against the wood as I thought. Hades was right. The shield that the amulet provided wasn't just for her. It was for the angel too. And for some reason, it was all connected. Angels, talismans, and prophecies, oh my . . . How could we fight that? What in the world could even—

I had it.

"I think I know what you need to look for." He perked up in attention, waiting for me to go on. "The amulet that angels use originally came from Earth."

He cocked his head and bounced around on his feet a little bit. "How do you know this?"

"Because I'm an anti-social introvert who has spent the last one hundred years being angry, punishing people, and reading both current events *and* history." I grinned, proud of myself. "Those talismans came from a supernatural source in order to protect them from supernatural magic. Like magnets. Magnets of the same pole reject each other. That's how these objects protect the user. By repelling supernatural magic."

"And you're saying we have to find . . ."

"The opposite pole."

"And we do that by . . ."

"Well, that's a bit trickier."

He narrowed his eyes at me. "Elaborate."

"We're going to need a source of magic from the Afterlife. That should cancel out the talisman's power, or at least weaken it. Earth magic doesn't hold a candle to our magic."

"I'm not sure I follow. I get the idea, but what is it you're suggesting? Where do we find this magic source in the Afterlife?"

I blew out my cheeks and answered quickly. "Jake's office."

He jumped back and flapped his wings. "What? Are you out of your mind?"

I held my hands up. "Hear me out."

"I'm still here, aren't I?" he said, the annoyance in his voice was clear.

"Jake is Afterlife Resources, but more than that, when you die, you end up dumped into the Afterlife with your resource officer's assistant in the waiting room, sort of unsure what exactly is happening. Jake was the one I met. He told me how I died. He told me how the Afterlife worked. He offered me the jobs that seemed to suit my personality, but he gave me options." I took a deep breath and kept talking, silently thankful that Hades was listening. "Up until the point you pick something, you're just dead. Not like a zombie, but you know, useless. When you decide what your job will be, Jake gives you your powers essentially. When I arrived, I was just a dead girl sitting in a chair. When I left, I was a demon, and I had powers. If that's not a source of Afterlife magic, I don't know what is. What we need is the object he uses to change you." I grinned awkwardly and fanned myself, trying to get a reprieve from the oppressive heat.

He blinked at me, staring wordlessly for what felt like an extremely long time before speaking. "You want me to break into Jake's office, steal from him, and smuggle *a thing* out of the Afterlife and bring it to you? Is that what you just said?"

I crossed my arms tightly. "Yeah, pretty much."

He shook his head and looked at the ground. Finally, he asked, "What is it I'm looking for?"

"Silver. About this big." I made a circle with my fingers, indicating its size. "It looks like a pocket watch, but it can be confused with a compass."

"Which one is it?" he asked.

I smiled. "Both. Time and direction are needed when you change into your Afterlife."

We sat in silence as he contemplated my request. "Fury, I—"

"Trust me, Hades. I wouldn't ask you to do this if I thought I was wrong. I know it's risky." I pleaded with him, knowing I probably sounded whiny, but my head was starting to throb a little, and the ache made me feel woozy. I tried to push the discomfort aside, needing him to agree with me before I went inside and cooled off.

He looked at me skeptically, then the tension in his body released. "You'd better be right," he said, and he started to take off.

"Be careful," I shouted as he flew away. He cawed in response, and it sounded louder than usual. Annoyed, probably.

I watched him fade into the distance as a lightheadedness swept over me. Texas heat was no joke. Maybe it wouldn't be some snakebite to take me out. It'd be heatstroke.

My vision warbled, and I knew it was past time for me to go inside. I turned, but the colors of the world started to swim around me in circles. I held the railing tight, waiting for the wave of dizziness to pass.

It didn't.

This wasn't the heat.

My mouth started to ache and my ears popped as the world spun harder. A cold, clammy feeling washed over my skin as a warm gush came out my nose.

Not again.

I reached up to my face, my hand coming away with blood.

Spots filled my spinning vision, and I tried to go down to my knees and call for help, but I felt myself falling and I heard a loud smack as pain radiated through my face as the world faded to black.

My eyelids fluttered open, and my head pounded in time with my heartbeat. My vision wasn't swimming, but it was far from clear. There was a slight ringing in my ears that I hoped would stop soon. Reaching up, I checked to see if there was still blood on my face, but it had been cleaned off.

I'd been moved inside the house, and everyone was around me, just as concerned as they were the last time this happened.

The fact that it had happened twice now was troubling, though I didn't want to admit that out loud, especially to the alphas. Maybe it was also somewhat alarming considering if it happened at the wrong time, I'd be fair game to anyone trying to kill me.

"Welcome back," Rox said, using a cold washcloth to wipe my forehead. I winced. There was a knot or something there that needed to heal a bit more. "You landed on your face again."

I swallowed, smacking my lips, and moving my tongue around trying to spread the moisture. It felt like I ate sand. "Go big or go home," I mumbled.

I tried to sit up, but she put her hand on my shoulder, putting just enough pressure to keep me down. "Give it a second. You bled a lot. It was your nose and your ears again." She frowned, then added, "And it came out your mouth too."

I groaned, realizing there was a metallic taste in there.

I tried to focus past the tinnitus to listen to the voices in the room that were talking about yours truly. Filtering out the distinct tones, I realized there was a person there I didn't expect. Rava argued passionately with the guys, moving her hands, and gesturing while she spoke.

"Are you certain? It seems odd that this would be the indication," Dorian said, scratching at the side of his temple.

I watched Rava give him a deadpan look. "What about her *doesn't* seem odd to you?"

I cleared my throat. "An indication of what?" I asked weakly. Rox handed me a glass of water with a straw. I gave her a smile in thanks and took a sip.

"That you need to bite someone," she answered.

My stomach roiled at the thought of blood in my mouth, and I shook my head. "Nope, mmm hmm, no—gross. That sounds terrible."

"I don't think it needs to happen after you've bled out. Your blood smells stale when this particular event occurs. That means it's past time to do something about it. I think when you feel this coming on, the bite needs to happen," Rava explained.

"This comes on and I have thirty seconds tops before I faceplant where I'm standing. There's no time," I said.

She frowned and looked at the guys. "When was the first time this happened?"

"Five days ago," Ezra said, running his tongue over his fang and looking at his watch. "Five and a half if we consider the time of day. Either way, vampires don't do . . . whatever this is. There's a thirst."

Rava rolled her eyes. "I know. I counsel hybrids, remember? Hybrids often present their powers and magic a little differently. Some don't. It's not exactly a science we can study."

Roman crossed his arms. "So what do you suggest?"

She paced the room, deep in thought. I closed my eyes and laid in silence while everyone else watched her. When the footsteps suddenly stopped, I opened them. "If it took five and a half days between these two episodes, let's assume we have that much time before another one. I'd say bite someone the day before, or maybe first thing in the morning. Both times this has occurred it's been in the afternoon. Let's cut it off at the pass and get ahead of it. She doesn't need to feed right now, especially not if the idea of blood is making her green in the face. Give her body time to recover, and it'll tell us when she's ready."

The alphas exchanged looks of doubt between them.

"She's right, you know," Rya said, walking down the stairs. Her skirt flowed behind her, draping over the stairs, and falling on the steps behind her as she descended.

"About?" Ezra asked.

"All of it," she said simply. When no one spoke, she sighed. "Rava and I have been talking. She knows hybrids. This is her job. You've created a hybrid the world has never seen before, at least not that any of us know of. Dorian and I are quite old, and this is an unknown to us. A demon-shifter-vampire-fae. She was *dead.* A creature from another realm. Be realistic. How do you expect any of this to go according to your expectations of your supernatural species?"

Ezra opened his mouth to answer, but she held up a hand. "No, no, dear. Please don't interrupt when I'm asking rhetorical questions."

I snorted my laugh while Dorian cracked a small smile. Ezra didn't seem pleased.

"As I was saying, Rava's specialty is helping those dual species learn to harness and cope with both forms. We all fit solidly into our powers, as we should. Rava's clients don't, and they never will. Rava knows this experience intimately. You're all incredibly lucky she had teachings on both sides and that she's dedicated her life to helping those like her. She's going to be the best bet you have in understanding Fury at this time, and you'd do well to listen to her. You're all smarter than this. I'm not entirely sure why you are pushing back to begin with."

"Because it involves our mate." Dorian let out a frustrated breath. Turning to Rava, he said, "Out of all of us here, you're the subject matter expert. You're saying the bleeding is due to her vampire nature, then that's the best we have."

Rava cocked her head. "It's the only thing you have," she said smugly. "You guys didn't have a clue what this could mean."

Ezra was put out. "How can you be so sure?"

"I'm not. I'm about eighty-five percent, but it's certainly not going to hurt anything. Doing nothing will. You can't just sit around and wait for her to start bleeding and pass out again."

"So by your estimate, she has less than six days before she needs to bite someone." Dorian's gaze shifted from Ezra to me, and his amber eyes darkened slightly. A shared moment between us from earlier in the week flashed in my mind. Me pressed against the wall, him towering in front of me. I shifted my position. "I'll take her with me, and we'll work on her fae magic until then. She needs to control her sifting. We know she can sift, so let's use the time to work on it." His lips curled slightly as he looked at me.

I finally felt a little better, and I sat up. The bump on my head didn't continue to throb, so at least that had healed enough for it to not be painful anymore.

"The full moon is coming up," Roman said. He tried to meet my gaze, but an instant irritation shot through me. I was still so hurt and furious with him all at the same time. How could you long for someone's touch while simultaneously wanting to throttle them and scream at them? I still didn't want to address any of those emotions, and I purposefully looked away.

"Fury said she hasn't felt her wolf yet," Dorian pointed out.

Rava shrugged. "That doesn't really mean anything. Fury and I have spoken about this. I didn't feel my wolf until I actually shifted. There was no indication I even had one, and then I just did. It'll happen when it happens. In the meantime, I think you need to work on your other powers."

"I concur," Rya added. "Not that anyone asked me, but if we have Lyra on watch, then Fury should be focusing on her fae magic before she needs to feed and before she needs to shift. Now is as good a time as any."

Dorian, Roman, and Ezra watched me. I raised my eyebrows and looked around, wondering why everyone had gone silent. Rox nudged me and gave a look that said, 'your turn'. Then I realized they were waiting on me to say what I thought of their plan. I shrugged. "Yeah, sure. Why not."

"It's settled then." Dorian strode across the room and wrapped his arm around my waist, scooping me up from the couch. I didn't have a chance to gain my footing as he leaned down and whispered in my ear, "You're mine for five days." Then the room disappeared.

CHAPTER 20
FURY

My brow scrunched in concentration. The faint scent of smoke from the fireplace and the crisp chill coming through the stone walls nipped at my senses. I squeezed my fists, feeling the slight bite of my nails push against the fleshy part of my palm.

Despite all the concentration in the world, I couldn't sift.

"If you hadn't done it already, I'd think you weren't capable," Dorian said. I opened my eyes to glare at him, the tension draining from my body.

"Maybe you're just not that good of a teacher," I huffed. "We've been at it for hours, and I haven't moved two inches."

"We've been at it for thirty minutes," he corrected. Huh. Well, it *felt* like hours. "But perhaps there is something to be said about you needing more motivation."

His amber eyes took on a dangerous glint.

"My motivation is just fine, thank you—" I didn't get to finish the sentence before he appeared before me. He clasped his hand around my waist, pulling me against him. In the next second, I felt the world turn upside down as he took me with him. My stomach hollowed as our feet touched solid ground once more, but the world kept spinning. My knees buckled, but instead of holding me upright—Dorian stepped away.

My shins slammed into hard stone. A frigid wind whipped through my hair, filling me with a truly bitter cold. I took a quick breath, calming my motion sickness, before looking around.

"Why are we outside?" The cocky look on his face and the arched eyebrow told me I didn't want to know.

"Motivation," Dorian said simply. "If you want to go back to the castle, all you need to do is sift yourself inside."

With that, he disappeared, leaving me to Avalon's gray skies and harsh winds.

I was going to kill him. He may not be able to die, but it wouldn't stop me from trying. Nope.

With great effort, I pushed myself off the steps and focused hard on moving myself from the extreme elements outside to the comfortable interior of the castle. Dorian said it was all about manifesting my own reality. As long as I'd been there before, all I had to do was envision myself there, and I should be able to do it.

So far this supposedly simple magic was proving extremely hard to grasp. And by hard, I meant impossible.

A tremble shook me as the glacial temperatures cut through my clothes, making it hard to concentrate. Dressed in high-waisted white pants and a tight long-sleeved shirt Dorian put me in when we came here, I was equipped for the cold inside the castle. Out here was another story.

I rubbed my hands together, trying to build some friction between them to stop the stiffness settling in my joints. I just wanted to warm up next to the fireplace. Motivation. My eyes narrowed on the set of double doors before me.

Inside, I told myself, imagining my body appearing on the other side.

My teeth clenched when nothing happened.

Inside, I repeated the exercise.

A sharp wind slammed into me from the front, knocking me back on my ass as if laughing at me. I slapped my hands against the ground, growling under my breath.

Inside. Inside. Inside—

The fire I'd been thinking about appeared before me. Burning logs and embers that only stayed that way for a moment were snuffed out from the winds barreling through.

Faint orange glowed from the coals at the bottom of the pile, while ashes and soot sprayed across my front. I frowned.

Not for a second did I believe Dorian sent the fire to me. Which meant I brought it to myself. Reframing my mind on that piece of information, I thought about Dorian's fae wine he sipped while attempting to 'teach me'.

Copying the same mentality, I imagined myself going to it.

Glass shattered before me, spraying my white pants with liquid.

My eyes snapped open, focusing on the plum-colored splatters now staining my outfit. It seeped into the cracks of the stone and pooled around me, dispersing faster while the wind whipped it across the ground.

A moment later, Dorian appeared. He didn't look amused.

Arms crossed, his eyes flicked toward the broken decanter, then back to me.

"How?" he demanded.

"I don't know what you're talking about," I replied, wrapping my arms around myself while I shivered.

"First the fire, then my wine," he answered. Taking a step forward, his boots crunched on the glass as he towered over me. He reached out, grabbing my chin between his index finger and thumb. "Now answer me, how did you manage to sift objects?"

"Take me inside and I'll tell you."

Dorian studied me for a moment. "Fine."

Turning on his heel, he strode to the double doors and pushed them open with a firm shove. My lips parted in shock. "They were open this whole time?"

His slight smirk was my answer.

I took the stairs two at a time, all too eager to get out of the cold. Once inside, he shut the doors firmly behind us.

"Where is everyone?" I asked, noticing the lack of fae soldiers and servants running around for once. The great hall was utterly empty.

Dorian narrowed his eyes, pointedly not answering. I sighed, running my hands over my arms, trying to warm them faster. "I was focused on sifting to somewhere warm. Preferably in front of the fire.

Then it appeared in front of me. Knowing you're not a kind soul that would send it, I tried again, this time thinking about sifting to your wine. Once again, it appeared in front of me."

Dorian's expression remained cool as he ran his thumb over his bottom lip in contemplation. "Fae can't sift objects. Only themselves and anything touching them."

"Except I'm not fae. Not fully, anyhow."

"Indeed," he murmured, falling deeper into thought.

"You going to tell me where everyone is now?" I asked, dropping my hands to my side now that the worst of the chills had passed.

"Sent them away," he answered, still seeming to pay attention only partially.

I frowned. "Why would you do that?"

"Lyra," he answered quietly, the fog clearing as he focused on me once more. "She and the angel know this place. How to get in and out. We reinforced the wards, but my general wanted to double our troops and protect all entry points. We did at first, but I thought my people would be safer if they dispersed for the time being. Besides, it's not like there's anything left here to guard."

"That's probably for the best," I said. "Angels aren't all-knowing. While they're good at finding out what they want, unless they're specifically looking for your people, they're probably safer away from this whole mess. Until we have a way to capture Lyra and deal with the angel, that is."

Dorian nodded, letting out a heavy sigh. "Enough about the angel for now. Until Hades gets back or Jules reports something new, we should focus on you, and help you learn your magic."

I twisted my lips, scrunching my nose. "We've established I can sift, but not when I'm trying, and I have better luck bringing objects to me rather than the other way around."

"So it seems," he agreed. "I'll want to test this more. Most fae struggle with sifting to some extent. Not as much as this, but I suspect you'll be able to sift on command, given time. We need to see if you have any other abilities."

"Such as?"

"Glamour, changing clothes, persuasion . . ."

I lifted both eyebrows on the last word, not recognizing it as a standard power the fae possessed.

"Both Lyra and I have the ability to take away free will. We can make someone do anything and everything we want—except you, it seems."

I took a step closer, hearing an undercurrent of something in his voice, though I couldn't tell what.

"Do you wish I wasn't the exception?"

"No," he said instantly. "While it would be nice to keep you from breaking rules left and right, I'd never want you at Lyra's mercy. It's a relief to me she can't persuade you."

I tilted my chin, noticing how he pointedly referred to being under her control, but spoke nothing of his.

"And you?" I asked quietly. "Would you want me at your mercy?"

His eyes darkened with lust. The tension between us came to the forefront at the sharp inhale of his breath. When he didn't immediately answer, I lifted a hand to run my fingers over his chest. His heart beat heavily, though his features remained stoic. "Well?" I prompted. "Would you?"

"You wouldn't survive my mercy," he said eventually.

I cocked my head, wanting a better answer from him. "Why do you say that?"

Dorian reached out, clasping a hand around my throat, not to choke me, but in a show of possession. His thumb skimmed my jaw softly, but the strength of his grip was anything but gentle.

"I'm not a soft lover. I want to find your limits and push you to the edge of them because I can." Heat pooled between my legs as I imagined what those words meant. "Because you'll trust me to. It won't be casual. When I take a lover, I'm committed, and when I take a mate—when I take you, I'll never let you go. I can't."

"Never let me go," I repeated, leaving it open-ended in question.

"Back," he answered. "To the Afterlife. Ezra and Roman will accept the present while hoping for more—but not me. I'm incapable of giving into this without taking everything in return."

My mouth parted, and he ran his thumb under my bottom lip, drawing conflicted emotions in me. "You don't want me to leave," I said softly.

"We should get back to training," he replied, taking a step back. His hand loosened, and I stepped into him.

"Stop it," I said. "We're talking about this."

"There's nothing to talk about, Fury. I know what I need from you, and if I didn't know better, I'd look the other way and take it. Take you. But you're not staying, and you won't—"

"You don't know that," I interrupted.

"Would you stay?" he asked, point-blank. "Would you agree to never return? To stay even if you found a way back? To remain on Earth even when your mission is finished, and the angel is gone, and Lyra is back in stasis?"

I licked my lips. "It's not that simple—"

"There it is," he said, smiling without joy. "I thought so."

"If there is a way, they may not *let* me stay. Hell, even if there's not —" I stopped abruptly, not wanting to finish the sentence or acknowledge the truth. The dangerous flash in his eyes told me I was too late for that.

"If there's not?" he prompted. I knew he knew, but he was going to make me say it.

"No one gets a free pass. The dead are meant to stay that way," I said quietly.

"They'd kill you if they couldn't drag you back." It wasn't a question, but I still felt like I had to answer.

"Probably," I said. "And because I've now got supe magic, it would be the end for me. The real end."

"This is what you want to return to?" he asked. "Why do you even want to?"

"I never said that—"

"But you do," he replied before I could continue. Dorian twisted so my back was to a tapestry and pushed me back against it. His arms rested against the wall on either side of my head. "You've made it very clear that if you can find a way back, you'll take it. Why? So you can live behind the pearly gates? Retire up in the clouds, leaving the rest of us here? Rox. Ezra. Roman. Me." I swallowed hard, not so sure now if I truly wanted this conversation. Perhaps he was right. I bit off more than I could chew with him, but damn me if a growing part of myself didn't want it. "You're willing to spend eternity away from your mates and condemn us to the same, for what? Retirement? Not needing to work?" He shook his head, letting out a callous laugh. "You wouldn't need to work another day in your life here. I'd take care of you. You could live anywhere in the world you wanted, have anything you wanted, and all you'd have to do is stay."

"And if I chose to stay, but they still came for me?" I asked, knowing it would show a card I hadn't revealed to the others yet.

"I'm not the same man I was when Morvain died. If they tried to take you—" He stopped suddenly, his eyes dilating sharply.

We stared at each other in silence.

He got it. He understood.

"You're the reason," he whispered.

I nodded, letting the truth sink in.

His head fell forward into the crook of my neck. "Fuck," he growled.

Fuck indeed.

"Do the others know?" he asked, lifting his head.

"I don't think so."

"How does Ezra not know yet?"

"I'm not sure," I admitted. "I try to shove some things away and not think about it when he's near me. I just thought it best not to say anything for the moment. We've got enough to worry about right now."

"Lying by omission?" Instead of looking judgmental, he seemed amused.

"Knowing doesn't change it," I said. "All it would do is cause more anxiety. I can't stop it if it's going to happen."

"It won't," he said, utterly serious.

"You can't know that."

"I won't let it," he replied. "If that means spending every waking hour you have making sure you can use your fae magic, then I will. If someone comes for you, whether it's the angel, the Afterlife, Lyra—you'll be able to sift."

I snorted. "That's a bold claim considering the last hour."

"Motivation," he said. "All I have to do is find yours."

I lifted an eyebrow. "What did you have in mind?"

CHAPTER 21
FURY

Bribing didn't work. Not even for alcohol.

Dropping me in extreme temperatures didn't do shit either.

After a day of trying and not getting anywhere—except for stealing objects out of thin air—I collapsed in Dorian's wingback chair, dead tired and wanting to sleep.

"Get up," Dorian said.

"No."

"Fury," he rumbled, his voice dark with intent. I didn't care.

"Fuck off. I'm exhausted." I kicked my legs up on the edge of the coffee table and tilted my head back, closing my eyes.

Cold water hit my face.

I gasped, sitting up in a flash.

"What the hell—" I growled, coming face-to-face with the fae bastard as he leaned over me, holding the sides of the chair, and boxing me in.

"We're not done here," he said sternly. "You can do this the easy way, or the hard. It makes no difference to me—but you *will* be able to sift by the time we have to go back to Houston."

I narrowed my eyes at him. "I'm not going to sift if I die of sleep deprivation."

Dorian scoffed. "You're hardly sleep deprived. I think you can put in the extra ten percent."

"Bite me," I snapped, crossing my arms and tilting my head back.

The scent of frost, mint, and fae wine registered vaguely—then a sharp pain in my bottom lip.

I opened my mouth to protest as his tongue grazed over it—soothing the pain and replacing it with something else entirely.

I leaned forward, slanting my mouth against his. Dorian didn't waste any time invading my senses. His tongue toyed with mine; devouring me, licking the inside of my mouth, and sucking my lip. The kiss lasted forever and yet only a blink when he started to pull back.

I reached for him on instinct. My hands knotted in his hair, pulling it tight.

A rough growl escaped his throat. He knocked my legs off the table, manipulating them to either side of him before grabbing my waist and hauling me up. I gasped at the feel of our bodies against each other. His chest to mine. Hands slipping to my ass and squeezing. His thick erection pressed into my belly.

My eyes slanted open as he started moving.

"Where are we going?" I asked.

"My chambers." His lips were back on me, even as he walked. The slight movement of his body caused me to sway back and forth, rubbing against him.

Somewhere in the back of my mind, I registered that something was off—but after weeks of wanting him and denying myself—it would seem we were both feeling a bit weak-willed. Perhaps the day of training wore me down, but I wasn't in the mood to fight it anymore.

Right when I was running out of air and needing to breathe, my back hit something hard. Dorian used the opportunity to rock into me, creating delicious friction between my thighs. I tilted my head back and moaned.

His lips trailed over my jaw and down to my ear, where he whispered, "If you have limits, tell me now."

My brain scrambled, but I managed to get the words out in a

semi-intelligible manner. “No hitting. No spanking. I’m not big on pain. I’ll snap.”

He kissed my neck, still working his hips into mine. If I could have spread my legs any wider, I would have. “That all?”

“No daddy kink,” I added.

He chuckled against my throat. Without replying, one of his hands left me for a brief second. The hard barrier behind me moved. Door, I realized. Must have been a sturdy one to not rattle with how hard he was moving against me.

Dorian’s fangs scraped the column of my throat, making my blood heat and my breath stutter.

“If I wanted to mark you, would you let me?” he asked.

I hummed my agreement, slipping one hand from his hair to his shoulder, letting my nails dig in.

“And if I want your mouth?” he continued.

“Make me come and it’s yours.”

The breath hissed between his teeth. Fangs pressing harder against my skin as he sucked on a patch of skin.

“What about your ass?”

“It’s been a few decades. You’ll need to go slow, but I’m down.”

“Being tied up?” he asked tentatively.

“As long as there’s no hitting, I’m open for it.”

“Fuck,” he murmured against me. “You’re going to make it hard to control myself.”

“Then don’t,” I moaned as my back hit something soft, certain it was a bed. “I just gave you permission to fuck me whatever way you want.”

Dorian sighed. He reached behind him to grab my hands, pinning them above my head. I let him.

Cold shackles clicked shut around both wrists at the same time. My eyes opened, distrust running through me for the first time.

“What are you doing?”

“Shh,” Dorian said, moving backwards on the bed. “We’re going to play a game.” He reached down to the left side of the bed and grabbed another cuff, putting it around my ankle. My heart hammered. He cuffed the second foot, leaving my legs spread and my arms pulled taut over my head.

"What kind of game?" I asked, suspicion bleeding into my voice.

His gaze was burning with lust and dark desire as he kneeled between my legs. My clothes vanished in an instant, but he didn't lower his eyes from my face.

Not even when he ran his fingertips over my stomach, down the curve of my hip, or the inner edge of my thigh. My chest rose and fell rapidly, waiting with anticipation for his next move.

His fingers skimmed over my pussy, and he lowered one blunt tip in between my folds, running from my wet center up to my throbbing clit.

I bucked against the chains.

Dorian didn't stop, nor did he speed up. Using only the tip of his finger, he ran it around my sensitive nerve bundle, agonizingly slow.

"Please," I muttered. I tried to break the chains, and they groaned under the pressure, but not even my own demonic strength would do.

"It won't work," he said, continuing his deliberate torture. "Once I learned you were stronger than me, I had them made from Tungsten. So is the bed frame. There's only two ways out of those chains."

I lifted my head to look at him. It was erotic to watch him—fully clothed, between my legs—playing with me, his amber eyes filled with such need and dark desire. "Either I let you out , or you sift."

Motherfucker.

"Please, Dorian," I moaned, trying to rock my body into him. Just a little more pressure and I'd get there.

"Please what, little demon?" he asked, voice husky.

"Let me out. Make me come."

"Which one?"

"Both," I said. He tutted.

"I told you, Fury, I'm not a soft lover. I take everything." As he spoke, my thighs began to tremble. The continued stimulation was getting to me. I was so close—

And then he stopped.

"I've offered you everything," I countered.

"Not true," he said softly. "But that's not the point right now. You need to learn to sift, and I think I finally found your motivation."

I growled, throwing my head up and down on the bed.

Motherfucker was becoming a mantra in my head.

"If you won't fuck me because I can't promise to stay, whatever, but this is just cruel," I snapped.

"I am cruel," he countered. Dorian crawled up my body. His legs straddled over my chest, he reached for my breast, lightly pinching a nipple. "But for this to work, you need proper motivation. The mating call will help. Your body doesn't want to deny me. That said, you need a reward. Escape the chains and I'll make you come, Fury. If you don't want to come, just say 'I give up' and I'll let you out."

"You're a bastard," I growled.

"I am," he agreed. "But in this case, it'll be just as hard for me as it is for you."

"I sincerely doubt that," I quipped. He twisted my nipple sharply, making me gasp. With a quick tug on his pants, he undid the front and released his cock. Hard and heavy for me, it jutted out of his boxers, the very tip touching between my breasts.

He lifted his hips, moving back and forth to run the tip over my sternum, between the valley of my breasts. Dorian grunted, a single drop of pre-cum welling at the tip.

"As you were saying," he said, releasing my breasts to shuffle off me and out of bed entirely. Seeing him only inches from my face and aching turned me on harder. Dorian walked around the bed and flashed me a cold smile. At the very end, he leaned over, beginning his ministrations to my clit once more.

This was going to be a very long night.

CHAPTER 22
DORIAN

She cussed at me. Called me a sadist. Threatened that she'd find a way to end me.

For all her cursing, begging, and writhing, she never told me to let her go—she never said 'I give up'—and I didn't yield.

She had to learn to sift, and we both knew this was the way.

I enjoyed torturing her like this. God, I did. The struggle for me was seeing her splayed open, crying in near ecstasy, begging for my cock. It made me want to take her like nothing else. I couldn't. Wouldn't. If the inevitable came—if she left us—I'd at least have this time with her. I wouldn't waste it.

After three hours of still not sifting, she started to drift, stuck between truly needing rest now and the mindless haze of being edged for three hours.

I backed off, giving her just enough reprieve to sleep before starting again. I waited, admiring her while she slept. The curves of her body. The slight rise and fall of her chest as she gently breathed. I wanted to burn the image in my mind. Her pussy was still glistening when moonlight filtered in the window, casting its glow on her form. It was time.

I woke her up with two fingers rubbing her clit, and Fury stirred on the brink of orgasm, moaning.

I stopped once more.

"You'll be lucky if I don't cut your dick off for this," she ground out in a husky voice.

"You won't," I said, completely assured as I switched to kneading her breasts, flicking my thumb over her sensitive nipple.

"I've done it before," she replied. "And because you can't die, you'd just be cockless and forced to watch while I fuck my other two mates."

Under different circumstances, I would've fucked her mouth. Considering the threat, I'd pass.

"It'd grow back—and I'd chain your ass up here and fuck you for good measure if you ever tried it."

"I'm chained now, and you won't even fuck me," she complained as I took her nipple in my mouth.

She liked this game. Loved it. While my little mate wasn't about pain, per se, she didn't seem to mind bites as long as I sucked them afterward.

I'd done it so much, her nipples would have been bruised if not for her advanced healing. That pleased me. Much as I wanted to mark her, bruises weren't the kind of marks I liked.

"I'd eat your pussy and lick you clean if you'd sift," I replied with her breast in my mouth, releasing it with a pop.

She groaned. Her eyebrows scrunched in concentration. She'd done it a hundred times now, attempting to sift. Occasionally she brought objects to the bed. Knives mostly. I didn't question where her thoughts were when that happened. I'd move them to the nightstand and then continue, though I did find it amusing.

This time, covered in sweat, breathing hard, her legs shaking, and her center dripping wet for me—she scrunched her face in real concentration.

I moved away from the bed, over to the decanter of fae wine that sat on a credenza.

"Sift for me, little demon. I want to watch you come. I want it as much as you do." I poured myself a glass of wine, turning my back on the bed for only a moment.

A damp hand grabbed my shoulder, turning me.

My surprise registered as Fury stood before me, raging mad. Her yellow eyes glowed near golden as she stared shrewdly.

She took the glass from my hand and drained the wine in one go before throwing it across the room.

"Get on your knees," she commanded, voice hoarse from all the screaming and cursing.

Yes. A rush of euphoric hunger shot through me. I smiled, satisfied, and eager to finish her off.

I grabbed her waist, spinning her body and switching our positions, pushing her backside against the furniture to prop her up. She was going to need it. I dropped onto the antique rug without question. She lifted one leg, slipping it over my shoulder—then grabbed a rough handful of my hair. While I normally wasn't the one in this position, for her—for this—I would gladly.

"Suck," she demanded as I grabbed her ass, pulling her closer to my face.

I parted the lips of her pussy with my tongue and wasted no time taking her clit between my lips. I pushed two fingers in her, filling that void. Fury's hand tightened in my hair and she held onto the side of the credenza with her other, leaning her head back, moaning low and long.

"Don't stop," she said with a shaky breath.

I whorled my tongue around her clit, then sucked sharply. She gasped, her channel clenching around my fingers.

"I need more," she begged, her breathing picking up. Giving her what she asked for, I added a third finger, sliding it in with ease as she coated my hand. Fury rocked against my face, both her legs shaking from the sheer exertion of what was coming.

I twisted my hand inside her, pressing my fingers together, adding my pinky as I fucked her hard with my hand. I kept my tongue pressed against her clit as I groaned against her.

Her hips jerked and her legs quaked. The hand in my hair pulled tight, sending pain scattering across my scalp. Her other hand dug into my shoulder, clawing at me as she came violently, pouring into my hand and down my arm.

Mouth open, she screamed. Her muscles contracted and spasmed while her orgasm tore through her, drawing out the pleasure and leaving ripples of aftershocks in their wake.

Her hand in my hair loosened, turning more affectionate as she ran her fingers through the strands.

The leg over my shoulder slipped off to the side, and she quickly lost all balance. I grasped her hips to steady her, using the furniture behind her to give stability.

"I don't think I've ever come that hard," she said in a raspy voice.

I glanced at the clock on the wall. "I edged you for over four hours."

Her lips pressed together. "I'm still pissed about that."

I arched an eyebrow, pointing at her wobbly legs and the wetness covering her thighs. "Mmm, I see that." I chuckled, ignoring the heaviness of my cock while I watched her secure her footing and test the strength of her legs. She stretched her arms and arched her back in a big yawn.

I took a towel from a nearby table, wiping her down and drying off what moisture still coated her. She remained silent and unmoving, letting me care for her. Lifting her up, I carried her to a lounge chair and set her down.

"I'll get you a bath ready. Does that sound like something you'd like?" I asked.

She hummed in agreement, still in her post-orgasm euphoria haze, and a small smile of relief appeared on her face.

"Anything else?" I offered. She appraised me, considering her options.

"Anything I want?" Fury traced the fabric on the chaise, but I wasn't sure what she'd ask for.

"Within reason, I'll give you whatever you want."

"Cheese fries?" she asked tentatively.

"I can do that," I replied with a small laugh. It wasn't what I expected. "We'll get you cleaned up and fed, then you need rest."

"And I want you to stay with me. Keep me company," she said, rolling to her side. "Where's the tub?"

"In there." I pointed to a door she hadn't noticed before. I bent down, sliding one arm under her legs and cradling her back with my other.

I walked to the bathroom, intent on making sure she recovered from a very long, very intense session. She needed to feel clean. She needed to be cared for. Worshipped. And she would be.

She also needed as much rest as I could give her. She didn't know what I had in store for the rest of our time together.

We'd only just begun.

CHAPTER 23
FURY

Crystal clear water tumbled from the cracks between the rocks and into the eight-foot stone basin that was the tub. I let out a low whistle, taking in the natural cut of the gray stone that revealed veins of silver and gold. A giant stained-glass window was centered over the space, melding the view of the island below in the blue, red, and purple panes of the design.

"This must have cost a fortune," I said, slowly stepping toward the tub.

Dorian shrugged as if it were nothing. "There's a cave on the island filled with several geothermal pools. Hot springs. My favorite looks similar to what you see here. It's actually a favorite amongst many of the fae on Avalon. I wanted one for my own private use, so I had it recreated."

"Not big on sharing?" I commented as I approached it. My own distorted reflection looked back.

"No."

I bent at the waist to grip the edge and slowly climb into the steaming waters. The first heated touch made me tense. The pool was fairly deep, coming up to mid-thigh. I stepped forward, wading through the clear water, and then lowered myself in, relaxing. A blissful sigh escaped me.

"That's a shame," I said, picking up our conversation again. While I wasn't looking at him, I sensed his eyes on me. "Sharing is caring."

"I can't say either of those are on the list of my better qualities."

"Are you good at sharing anything?" I asked, searching his face for a reaction.

He pinned me with an intense stare. "I'm possessive, so not particularly, no."

I snorted, reclining back in the bath. The hot water made my breathing slow and even, but heavy, making it difficult to float properly.

"How would you even handle it, then? If I stayed?" I posed the question nonchalantly while I stared at the rock ceiling.

"I would get over it this one and only time. You need your mates. After losing my own . . . I wouldn't try to separate you from them. But that doesn't mean I'm living with either of them. We all have separate lives. For you, we come together—but that's where the commonalities end."

"Hmm," I murmured as I thought about what that meant. "And what would my life look like? Bonded with three mates who don't care for one another?"

The whole idea was more theoretical than anything. The way humans would talk about what they'd do if they won the lottery. A dream so far off I could imagine it, but I couldn't actually imagine *living* it. After all, with a rogue angel, a crazy fae princess, and the Afterlife's own code—my chances of any future here were slim to none. That didn't stop me from thinking about it, pointless as it may have been.

"I imagine we'd find something similar but more permanent than what we have now. You'd spend time with each of us and our people, and at times we'd come together for you." He kept his hands in his pockets, turning to look at the images on the stained glass. "Why do you ask?"

I shrugged lightly. "I'm not sure. I think it's because I like to picture it. Play it through my head, like a movie. The dreams and ideas I have for my life. It's what . . ." I trailed off, realizing that I was coming uncomfortably close to rehashing the past.

"It's what you've done since your first life," he finished for me. "It's comforting."

I met his gaze, and in his eyes, I didn't see pity. I saw a hint of empathy. Understanding. I blinked, and it was gone, but I nodded slowly in response. "Yes."

"I think many of us do it. As much as you may feel like you are, you aren't alone."

I raised an eyebrow, surprised that he somewhat admitted to a vulnerability. I had the option to press on it, but I figured it would push him away if I did. For now, we were talking, and that was more than he usually gave.

"I've been alone my entire existence. I'm used to it. This," I gestured to him and then waved my hand about, "is new to me. I'm not entirely sure what to do with it all, but it's nice to think about, even if it sounds like you want to split custody with them when it comes to spending time with me." I splashed water at him, and he took a step back when it wet his pants.

"It's more complicated than that," he said, shaking his head. "Beyond basic personalities, we're different, Roman, Ezra, and I. Our species, our age, our histories, what we can give our mate. Could you see us all living in one house? No matter the size, it wouldn't work."

"Okay, fair point. No, I can't picture it." I huffed a laugh just at the mere idea of living under one roof. "What do you mean, though, about what you can give your mate?"

He considered me, tilting his head as he thought. "Roman and Roxanne could give you a family within their pack. It's what they are, and it's what they value. Ezra has made no attempts to hide that he's trying to mold you into a clan enforcer. You'd work without a set of rules or regulations the other vampires are forced to abide by."

"And you?" I prompted. "What would you give?"

"Whatever life you want," he said, walking toward the tub. His footsteps were soft, but sure. "We could live anywhere in the world at the drop of a hat. Go anywhere. See everything. The fae aren't affectionate in the same way shifters are, nor do I think you'd easily find a job you'd enjoy among my people—but we would have everything else."

I swallowed hard, my head bobbing below the water. I sat up, bumping into smooth rock beneath me.

"Material things," I murmured.

"Experiences and companionship. They're quite different. I'm not going to profess love or write you poetry. It's not who I am. But I will find what pleases you and give it to you, because in the end, it would please me too." I looked up at him. Dark, moody, his arms crossed over his chest as he leaned against the rock wall, watching me. He was shirtless, and across the ridges of his muscles, his pale skin reflected some of the light coming from the window and pool. Eyes burning, he stared with an intensity that rivaled the sun, despite his stoic face. "At least I would, if you stayed."

If I stayed . . .

Here we were again.

My heart pounded, and I could feel it in my head. I knew he heard it, but the conversation had taken a turn into something more serious than I'd anticipated.

"Well, let's focus on keeping me alive first," I said, backpedaling into more familiar territory. Dorian's eyes shuttered, putting me at a distance. I didn't blame him.

"Everything you'll need should be on that shelf," he said, pointing to the opposite side of the tub where a larger niche housed several bottles with white labels on the bottom. I nodded once.

"You're not staying?"

"I believe you were promised cheese fries," he said. A good excuse, even if it was just that. I went along with it.

"I wouldn't say no to a beer either. Or more of that fae wine," I suggested.

His lips thinned, not amused. "You need hydration after that session."

"I'm a supe now, right? I doubt dehydration could kill me."

"That's not an excuse to test it," he said.

"Or is it?" I drifted over to the shelf, plucking one labeled *shampoo*. "You said so yourself; you wanted to find my limits." Popping the cap open, I took a whiff. Oh, that was nice. Pouring a decent amount in my palm, I lathered it between my hands before moving to my hair.

"I'm not going to justify that with a reply," he said.

"You just did."

Dorian vanished, sifting out before I could push him any further.

I sighed to myself, taking my time to wash and rinse my hair, soaking for a bit longer until my fingers started to wrinkle. When I was just getting out of the tub, he reappeared with a Styrofoam container and a chilled bottle of water.

I pursed my lips, fishing the towel off a hook on the wall and wiping down my body.

Once I finished drying myself, I wrapped my hair in the towel and walked out into the bedroom once more. Dorian said nothing, setting my food on one of the small tables.

"You were gone a long time for cheese fries," I remarked, taking a seat. The cool air felt nice after such a warm bath.

"Fae or not, I still have to wait in line."

I cracked the lid, my stomach letting out a low rumble as the smell hit me.

It was perfection. The right amount of cheese spread over crispy fries and topped with bacon and chives.

The first bite had me moaning in a way that clearly did things to him. He reached down and readjusted himself, taking a seat across from me.

I lifted an eyebrow. "I'm surprised you haven't taken care of that."

"I did," he said. "Twice. While you were sleeping."

I swallowed thickly, and it had nothing to do with the ooey gooey goodness that coated my tongue.

"How is it?" he asked, changing the subject. Probably for the best. Orgasms versus greasy cheese fries was a tough call, and right now, my hunger for actual food was winning.

"Delicious. Incredible, really. Where'd you get them from?"

"A food truck in Austin. They're good, but wait another month for the Fort Bend County Fair," he said. "James dragged me to it a few years back. He insisted they had the best french fries."

"If they're better than this, I'll be shocked. This is to die for," I said around a mouthful. Dorian inclined his head. "Gotta say, I'm confused as to how James managed to drag you to anything. You're not exactly the dragging type."

He cracked the smallest hint of a smile. “Every now and then I can be obliging. He caught me on a good day.”

“You have good days?” I feigned mock surprise. “Will you make sure I get to see you on one of these alleged good days, or is it like an annual allowance and you only have so many to spare?”

“It’s a centennial allowance, not annual, and I’m afraid I’ve used up my allotted time for the current century,” he quipped.

“Ugh.” I snapped my fingers in disappointment. “So close.”

A small laugh escaped him before he cleared his throat and schooled his features.

I chewed silently, thinking about seeing Dorian at a county fair filled with children, cotton candy, and shitty games. What did this guy look like? I couldn’t picture it. To be honest, there was a lot I couldn’t picture about him.

“So going to county fairs isn’t exactly on the list of things you like to do in your free time. What is?”

He furrowed his brows in confusion, clearly wondering why I was asking.

“I mean, don’t answer if you don’t want to,” I said, sticking more fries in my mouth. “You can ask me questions too. I won’t promise I’ll answer them, which I imagine goes both ways.”

“Fair enough.” Dorian crossed his legs, leaning back in his chair. “I like art and I like to read.”

“Solitary things,” I said, nodding along. “I understand that. Any particular art or era?”

“I’m fifteen hundred years old. I’ve lived through the eras. What I enjoy is the evolution of art and what makes an artist. Even if I don’t like the work, I can appreciate it. The brushstrokes. The methods. The technique. Art is created from emotion, and it’s meant to evoke an emotion from its audience,” he explained, gesturing to different pieces he had on the wall of his room. “Art speaks differently to everyone. I find pleasure in that.”

I finished chewing my bite, licking the cheese off my fingers. When I started to ask another question, he held a finger up and wagged it at me. I snapped my mouth shut and held my hand out to tell him it was his turn.

"What is available to you in the Afterlife in terms of entertainment?" he asked.

"A lot of what is here, in a way," I said, wiping my hands on a napkin. I opened the bottle of water and took a drink. "Definitely more limited, though. We still socialize in the Afterlife. There are sex clubs and movie theaters; libraries and places to gather and eat. We have neighborhoods and pools; we can have pets if we want them." I shrugged. "We don't travel, though. It's the Afterlife. You are where you are."

"And what did you do with your free time?"

"I went to work, then I went home. I borrowed movies and shows. Television and film were such a great invention. The storytelling possibilities feel endless. I like reading too. Humans found a system for writing nearly fifty-five hundred years ago. It gives me a lot to read up on. Languages to learn. But on your point of emotion, I like music. The way you view art? That's music to me. That's what I collected."

"Collected?" he asked.

"Well, yeah. We had places where we lived. Possessions. I kept it small and uncomplicated, but I did allow myself to splurge on music. I didn't socialize much. I did sometimes, of course. The sex clubs were weird when I ran into co-workers, so that was an ick factor I couldn't burn out of my mind, but I got laid elsewhere. Never anything—" I stopped talking when I saw a possessive shadow cast over Dorian's face.

"Is there someone in the Afterlife?" he asked carefully.

I took a shaky breath, intrigued by the look in his eye. "Never anything serious was what I was going to say. And no. There is no 'someone' waiting for me."

"Good." He reached into his pocket and pulled out his phone. After he tapped on it for a minute, I heard the slight sound of speakers crackle as they came on, waiting for a song to play. A cello's dark timbre filled the room.

I smiled. "Bach." Dorian dipped his head in acknowledgement, then looked at a grandfather clock in the corner of the room.

"It's been a long day. You should rest," he said, turning the volume down.

I wouldn't argue. A yawn crept its way up and I covered my mouth with the back of my hand. "Will you leave the music on?" I asked. I drank the rest of the water and stood up, taking the towel off my head, and shaking out my hair. I ran my fingers through it and tried to separate some tangles while I walked across the room.

Flopping down on the giant bed, I stretched my arms over my head and then wrapped them around myself. After a warm bath, good food, and far too much exertion—my mind drifted quickly, sleep closing in fast.

I felt the bed dip beside me. A strong arm wrapped around my waist, pulling me in close. His lips pressed against my temple and the last of my consciousness fled.

For the first time in a long while, I slept without dreaming. No nightmares plagued me. No death or prophesized apocalypse. No fires and fear. Just quiet and calm bliss.

I was completely and utterly content.

I STIRRED when a cold shackle touched my wrist. I frowned in my sleep, mumbling that I needed five more minutes.

The clank of another one closing, this time around my ankle, brought me to. I blinked, trying to sit up. But I couldn't. My hands were trapped above my head and Dorian stood at my feet, securing my other ankle.

My heart started to pound, already knowing exactly where it was going.

"I'd say I'm sorry, but I'm not."

I tilted my chin as far forward as I could, my chest already heaving from the anticipation. "When I get out of these, I'm going to sit on your face."

Dorian smiled, equal parts playful and cruel. "I look forward to it."

His thumbs parted the lips of my pussy as he leaned forward and took a long, hard lick.

"You have three hours. After that I'm going to come on you and leave it there until you get out to clean yourself."

It was dirty. Disgusting. And hot enough to make me groan as liquid flooded between my thighs.

"Challenge accepted."

CHAPTER 24
FURY

Dorian sat on the edge of the cast iron clawfoot tub while I soaked in my bubble bath. Instead of his lavish hot spring replica, I'd opted for the en suite attached to what he said was my room.

My room.

He'd given it to me, telling me it was my space. I could do whatever I wanted with it. A place for escape and rest if I chose not to be with him. He understood what leading a solitary life meant. I couldn't always find comfort with other people. Sometimes I needed to be by myself. I was grateful for it. I hadn't even asked him for a place of my own, but somehow, he knew to give me that.

I sighed in contentment. The soapy water came up to my neck, my entire body submerged in its glorious warmth. I had my hair pinned up in a messy bun and my head rested against the soft pillow while he watched me quietly.

I found it almost fascinating how much he could say without using words. I liked to watch the details of his face as he thought, or reacted, or even as he spoke. Each little line that creased on his flawless skin. Each little twitch near his eye or around his mouth. His breathing and sounds would change as he considered something.

He didn't have to say much. He clearly held himself up well in conversation, but he was just as content with silence. I could see how after fifteen hundred years. I would probably like silence a lot too. I sort of already did, but that came more from my history and inability to trust people. I imagine a similar situation played a part for him, but also the amount of time he'd been on Earth. What did one really have to talk about after all that time?

I lifted my leg, poking my toes out of the water and nudging him. "Penny for your thoughts," I said.

He hummed lightly. "Nothing in particular. Enjoying the silence with you before we head back."

I adjusted myself in the tub, and the water sloshed around, echoing in the bathroom. "I would say that five days went by quickly, but that would be a lie. You knew how to drag it out," I said, raising an eyebrow at him.

He raised the corner of his lips ever-so-slightly. "I know." He clasped his hands in his lap, keeping his thumbs out as he tapped them together. "Though I don't recall you actually complaining. Threatening me and telling me you hated me, perhaps, but no true grievances. You seemed more than content to learn magic."

I laughed. "Yes. Learning magic. That's what we'll call it. The long, drawn-out orgasms played no part in my willingness." Placing my hands on the side of the tub, I pulled myself to a seated position, the water level just below my breasts. I watched him carefully, and his eyes didn't stray, keeping his focus on me.

"You learned to sift, didn't you?" he asked with a wry smile.

"That I did." I nodded. I may not have tried long distances yet, but I could finally control it. I could do it at will and to any location in the house. Even sifting one room to the next was a huge step. All things considered, learning how to do that in five days was quite the accomplishment for me. This wasn't my world, nor was it my magic. It was now, but everything was still raw and new.

I watched him for a moment, looking for the little movements on his face to see if I could figure out what he was thinking, but nothing came. I blew out a breath. It would take time to learn it all. If he got his way, we would have nothing but time. I had no way of knowing what would happen, but I didn't have high hopes. I hated having that conversation with him. The passion and the intensity in his voice when he talked about it was evident. He was a man that liked to have answers and be in control. Sometimes I wondered how much he teetered on the edge between control and chaos.

"Well," I said, "I have reached optimal pruning. We need to get ready to go." I moved to stand up, the water falling in cascades off my skin and splashing back into the tub. Dorian handed me a towel as his eyes roamed the length of my body. Stepping over the sides, I took it from him and smacked his hand away playfully as I walked to the mirror and took down my hair. "You've had enough. I need to be able to walk later, thank you."

Hunger flashed in his eyes, and he looked at me with a salacious smile. "Pity." Then he winked.

I stood there momentarily shocked. Did Dorian just . . . flirt with me? Did Dorian ever flirt? Did he know how to flirt?

His face was stoic again and it would have appeared the moment was gone, but I could see the twinkle of something there.

I opened my mouth to ask him about it, but the words were lost. In the blink of an eye, my towel was gone, and I was wearing linen pants and a light sweater over a camisole. "Really?" I deadpanned. "You have absolutely no patience."

He shrugged. "It's wasting valuable time."

Grumbling, I walked out of the bathroom while I ran a brush through my hair. I shook it out, trying to give it some volume.

When I entered the bedroom, I saw some packages left on the bed that hadn't been there before. I looked at him and he gestured for me to go on.

I tore off the pristine cream wrapping paper, opening a box that contained what looked like a smaller version of my phone. I heard his footsteps behind me as he came to a stop. Facing him, I asked, "What's this?"

"Turn it on and see," he answered, reaching for it, and pressing the button until the screen lit up. "It's for your music." He opened a tiny box with earbuds and handed them to me. "Keep those for when you travel, but when you're here with me in Avalon, it's connected to speakers in your room, as well as mine." He touched play and Saint-Saens' "The Swan" played softly in the background.

I scrolled through the library on the iPod and my mouth hung open. It was impressive. He had music from each decade, all categorized, each one filled with musicians, artists, and bands I liked. Everything from classical to 1920s jazz to 1960s funk to 1990s industrial metal.

"You have a rather extensive range in the types of music you appreciate, and there's plenty of storage space for you to add more. If it gets full, we'll get another, and another. You said you collected music in the Afterlife, so I wanted to give you that here too." He turned around and held his arm out, gesturing to a record player and a gramophone on the credenza. "The quality isn't the same, but I imagine it's more nostalgic to listen to certain artists the way you had originally in your first life."

I was speechless. As the days had passed—when I wasn't tied up and being edged, orgasming until I nearly passed out—we continued to talk. He showed me art he liked, and I played music I liked. Every emotion on the spectrum could be conveyed with both, I'd come to see. We were more alike than we often realized.

When I was alone by choice or by circumstance, I always had music. It was my one constant. Art was his.

I looked around at everything in the room, thankful for Dorian's gesture, but feelings of worry and disappointment were taking hold.

I silently made my way to the chairs by a large window, and I sat down.

"I've done something wrong," he said, not at all trying to hide the confusion in his tone.

I shook my head. "No, this is . . . this is really special." I swallowed.

"But?"

I put my hands in my lap and sighed. I would've much rather stared at my pants and picked at some imaginary thread there. Instead, I met his gaze. "My room. The clawfoot tub. This." I held up the device in my hand. "These are material possessions, Dorian. There's a lot that's out of my control right now, but when we talked about it, you said experiences and companionship. I can't help but wonder if . . ." I trailed off, not really wanting to say the rest of what I was thinking.

"Go on," he said flatly.

"Are you trying to buy my affection so I want to stay here?"

His mood darkened instantly. Shit. Nope. I'd misread this.

"That isn't what I'm doing." He went to the window and looked out over the moor. "They might be things, yes, but they are things you find comfort in. It's different."

"Oh," I whispered. I couldn't think of anything to say to him. I'd just accused him of trying to buy me, and I was way off.

"It isn't about making you want to choose me, or us," he started, coming to sit in the chair across from mine. "Whether or not you stay remains to be seen." The tone of his voice deepened as he considered what that meant. "Regardless, you're here now. You had built something in your afterlife, and for one hundred and three years, you've been set in your ways. The music you collected, the places you went, the solitude after a long day—it's all gone. While it was never our intent, all of it was ripped away from you. It's my desire to give some of that back to you. It's more than giving you gifts or buying material things for you. It's giving you a piece of what you left behind. You can have those things here too."

I sat in silence and considered his words. He was right. Remarkably so. None of these things held the same value to Rox, or Rava, or Caitlin. They were all things that were valuable to me. Yes, they cost money. Yes, it was tangible. But it *meant* something.

Thinking back to what he'd said they could all give me; I could see it more clearly. They were each trying in their own way. Dorian may have thought Ezra was just trying to make me a clan enforcer, but I could see his reasoning behind it now. I had a job in the Afterlife. A purpose. He was giving that to me because it would make me happy. If I stayed, he wanted me to do what I felt I was good at. It's what he had to offer me.

Roman could give me stability. A family. Something I had never known. Rox was already like a sister to me. If only Roman could just let go of his past, I could feel more like I was part of his pack.

And Dorian . . . I saw it now. It went beyond comfort. He was giving me the gift of security. In his own weird way, he was trying to give me a space to be myself. To be alone and to feel safe. To show me that if I stayed, I could still be who I was. I don't know that many would understand the gesture—could see beyond the monetary value —but it was powerful.

"Thank you," I breathed. "That means more to me than you know."

"I'm glad," he said quietly. After a few moments, he cleared his throat. "We have an hour before I have to drop you off at Roman's."

"Say no more," I said, getting up and scrolling through my new iPod library of treasures. Finding what I was looking for, I pressed play and Gershwin filtered through the speakers. I turned around and put my hands on my hips. "I'm going to get a drink, and you are going to dance with me."

He raised his brows in surprise. "Dance?"

I strolled to the credenza and opened a small door, pulling out a decanter and two glasses. Setting them on top, I looked into the mirror as I poured myself a drink. I held it up and offered him one. In the reflection, I watched as he declined. I shrugged, bringing the crystal to my lips, and tilting my head back for a big swallow.

"FURY!" Jules' voice screamed and her image appeared in front of me.

I inhaled in surprise, breathing in, and choking on whiskey. The heat of the liquor made my throat tighten as I coughed and spluttered, spewing it all over the mirror and the furniture.

"Fuck, Jules," I managed to say through a strained and hoarse voice, wiping my chin with the back of my hand and looking at the spilled drink down the front of my clothes. "Stop doing that."

"It's Lyra," she said in panic.

I snapped my head up, freezing at the urgency in her voice.

Dorian was beside me in an instant. "Where?" he asked darkly.

There was no time for introductions. I stared at Jules' wide eyes and my heart almost stopped when she spoke. "Roman's."

CHAPTER 25
FURY

I SWAYED ON MY FEET, RECOVERING FASTER FROM SIFTING WITH DORIAN THAN I probably ever had before. Adrenaline can do that to you.

On the shifter compound, everything was utter chaos, and yet nothing like the attack on the summit. People weren't outright brawling, but instead *running*. I followed the direction they were coming from, and my heart stilled at the sight of lavender hair.

Rava.

"I need to find Lyra," Dorian said, scanning the area.

"Don't try to face the angel alone if he's with her," I said quietly.

After a short pause, Dorian nodded. I wasn't sure if he would truly honor that, but I didn't have time to get caught up in our trust issues right then.

I took off in the direction shifters were coming from. It seemed to center around the cabin I knew to be Caitlin's. The she-wolf and Roxanne stood at the front, attempting to hold their ground and discourage people from interfering while a tense-looking Rava hulked out.

I didn't have a better way to describe it when she grabbed the railing of her own house, ripped it clean off, and used it as a spear to throw at Rox—who narrowly missed being impaled.

Fuck.

"What happened?" I called out, approaching the scene.

"Don't know," Rox said. "She came home early from work and started destroying the compound and attacking anyone she saw."

As if irritated by their presence, Rava narrowed her glowing purple eyes, and turned to heave a rocking chair over her head. Roxanne tried to push in front of me and shield me from the throw, but I stood my ground—letting her aim straight for me before catching the chair in my right hand. It was an awkward angle and uncomfortable at best. I dropped it to the ground immediately and kicked it to the side with my foot.

While we weren't sure how much I could survive, I think she and the others often forgot that first and foremost, I was a demon. My strength trumps all.

"You," Rava said in a visceral growl. Claws grew from her nails, long and lethal as she partially shifted. "This is your fault."

I was on my guard and didn't let the surprise show on my face. It was obvious she was out of her right mind. While not as blank as some of the others Lyra had influenced, the flat rage that seemed to consume her was all too familiar.

"Mine?" I asked, pointing at myself. "Pray tell, what did I do this time?"

She let out an outraged shriek as she launched herself at me.

"Rava!" Caitlin screamed, torn between interfering and not wanting to hurt her mate. It didn't escape my notice she already had blood on her and was limping.

"Get her out of here, Rox," I ground out, sidestepping the fae shifter.

"And leave you here with her—"

"Yes," I said in a hard voice. "You forget. I'm stronger than anything that walks this Earth, and I've been facing off demons for over a century. I can handle her." With that, I grasped the railing Rava had used as a spear and pulled it from where it was embedded in the ground.

It came free easily. Wielding it in one hand, I stared down my hybrid friend with grim determination.

"Don't kill her," Caitlin pleaded as Rox grabbed her around the waist and started hauling her away.

"I won't," I swore. That didn't mean I wouldn't hurt her. I didn't want to, but if she gave me no choice, I'd have to incapacitate her somehow.

"You are the cause," Rava hissed as she got to her feet once more. "The effect. The reason."

Her voice took on an eerie quality, making my skin prickle.

"For?" I prompted.

"*Everything*."

A shudder snuck its way up my spine as she lunged again. Faster than me, but not enough to disarm. She closed the space between us and swung her leg in a powerful roundhouse kick. Rather than taking the hit, I flipped the railing vertical to intercept. Her shin smacked into the wood, and it instantly splintered.

I grimaced as the chunks of it littered the yard.

"You're really going to regret this when you come to," I muttered, swinging the section of wood I still had like a baseball bat. When she wheeled back around for another kick, I stepped into it, swinging the railing straight into her thigh.

It hit like a boom of thunder, cracking through the compound.

Rava let out a strangled sound, falling forward.

I dropped the wood, catching her shoulders.

She stiffened, pulling back her lips in a snarl as she peered up at me.

"Angelus venit," she uttered like a curse.

Her incisors lengthened. She surged forward, snapping her teeth at my neck.

If not for my hands on her shoulders, she would've taken a nice chunk out of me, but I pushed her away.

She stumbled back several feet. Cold resolve hardened in her expression.

"The angel is coming," I repeated back to her. While rusty, my Latin was passable and downright flawless compared to people from the modern age. I spent a lot of time learning other languages in the Afterlife. The language of the dead being one of them. It was fitting. "Where's Lyra?"

I didn't expect an answer out of her. Not really. But the flat voice she used to reply left me chilled to the core.

"Hunting."

She lurched forward, swiping a clawed hand through the air, aiming for my jugular. I ducked—taking a knee to my chest. The air left me as I slammed into the ground, wood chunks digging painfully into my back. Her booted foot came down on my chest, holding me there.

She leaned over to pick up the railing off the ground where I'd dropped it.

My heart stuttered in my chest.

Just past her, on the roof of another building, I caught sight of a woman with flowing white hair. Lyra stood on the edge of the gable, deftly evading both Dorian and Roman.

Terror shot through me, because if Roman had the chance—he'd try to end her.

Rava lifting the rail over her head drew my attention back to my current predicament.

Sweat dotted her forehead as she looked down at me, the wood suspended above her, ready to pierce my chest any moment.

I grabbed her ankle, prepared to throw her off me the moment that railing moved. But the concentration in her brow made me hesitate.

"Rava," I said slowly. "It's not your fault. You can fight it."

"I—can't—ahh!" She gasped, the blank rage falling over her once more as she tried to slam it through my chest. I squeezed her ankle, crushing the bone beneath my fingers.

It cracked then popped, and I rolled sideways, throwing her leg outward.

The railing buried itself in the ground where my chest had been only a second before. Rava screamed in pain as she sprawled out beside me.

I crawled on top of her body, taking advantage of her disoriented state.

She looked up at me confused and yet conflicted, as if wavering in between the persuasion driving her and her own free will.

I gave her a sad smile. "I'm really sorry about this."

Then I slammed the side of my fist into the junction below her ear that connected her neck, skull, and jaw.

Pop.

The hit rattled through me as Rava lost consciousness.

I really hoped she woke free of Lyra's influence, but the only way to guarantee that was to get her away from here. I glanced up at the roof where they were still battling—if you could call it that. Dorian was trying to reason with her while Roman was aiming killing blows.

She evaded them both, dancing on a willowy frame that was utterly ethereal.

Gritting my teeth, I stared at the spot I wanted to be.

My stomach flipped as I sifted on the spot—directly in front of Roman's outstretched claws.

On instinct I jumped back, dodging a blow that wasn't meant for me.

"Fury, no!" Dorian shouted. The last thing I saw were his golden eyes blown wide with fear.

Then a soft hand grabbed my shoulder. My stomach flipped. I knew it was Lyra.

I didn't have time to respond as she sifted us out.

The world went black.

CHAPTER 26
ROMAN

She sifted in front of me. I'd damn near hit her, and then she was gone.

Disappeared.

Taken.

By Lyra.

And I couldn't stop it.

My world started to spiral out of control. Not again. I couldn't lose another mate.

"Where the hell is she, Dorian?" I roared, demanding an answer I knew deep down he didn't have.

Dorian grabbed his head, gripping his hair through his hands as he bent at the waist and let out a scream filled with fear and rage so intense it rivaled my own emotion. "Fuuuuuuuuuck!" The sound carried over the lake, disturbing the birds and causing them to fly off and leave their trees.

When he stood up, I could see that his eyes were glowing. His chest heaved as he took in short breaths in panic.

I clenched my fists, opening them and then tightening them again, trying to get the monster inside me under control.

"Dorian. Where. Is. She?" I asked through gritted teeth.

"I don't know," he said in a loud whisper. "We aren't going to find her up here."

He sifted, appearing on the ground below us and walking toward Caitlin and Rava's cabin. I jumped down, landing with a fist and a knee on the soft earth.

Roxanne came running out of the house, her eyes wide with fear. She'd heard Dorian. Every soul on this lake heard him. Still, she asked the question. "Where's Fury?"

I shook my head, unable to say the words. Every fiber in my being wanted to break down. I wanted to destroy everything. Everyone. But my sister grabbed my face, staring deeply into my eyes, speaking to me softly. "Roman, tell me where she is."

"Lyra took her," Dorian said from behind her.

Roxanne spun around, her mouth falling open slightly. Rya came running out of the main house and anger coursed through my veins. *The witch.*

"Where were you?" I growled, storming toward her. "Where the fuck were you when Lyra was here? Where were you while we fought her? Where were you when she sifted and took Fury with her?" Each question, my voice grew louder, echoing in the surrounding trees.

The witch straightened her shoulders and crossed her arms, unmoving. With narrowed eyes, she said coolly, "I don't answer to you, shifter."

Roxanne jumped in front of me, slamming her hands into my chest. "Stop it, Roman. Your fight isn't with her."

My sister's strength matched my own. She was my equal in that, and not many knew it. They all assumed I had the power, but the truth of it was she did too, with the exception of immortality. She was a better leader. More level-headed, more compassionate, less temperamental. She should have been my second, but it wasn't something she ever wanted.

She shoved me back, my foot sliding in the dirt as she pushed me. The rage I felt vibrated in my chest as I stared Roxanne down. "*No,* brother," she said, a stern and forceful tone taking over.

"Rya came with me," a voice called out. "I brought her here." My gaze shifted to Tristan. He came out of the house, pulling a sword, daring to challenge me on my own land. He didn't stand a chance. My wolf was breaking through. Fur erupted, covering my skin, my body shook, my bones popping and changing—

Crack.

Roxanne's fist made contact with my jaw, breaking it. My head swung around, pain radiating through my face, healing what was broken and damaged as quickly as it had happened.

"Get him under control, Roman," she yelled. "Do it for me."

Dorian held his hand up, calling to his second. "Stand down, Tristan."

"Caitlin is asleep. I cast a spell to calm her. Her mate was under Lyra's influence, and she was losing control. I can see that's common around here," Rya said, looking at her nails.

"Enough," a weak voice said, breaking through the chaos.

We all turned to see Rava, sitting up in a crouched position, her elbows resting on her knees as she held her head.

Rya strode past all of us, coming to her side, but at that moment, Roxanne grabbed my shoulders. "Look at me," she whispered. "I want my brother back. Get yourself together. Fight it. Whatever is taking over right now will not help Fury. It won't. *You* are the alpha, not the wolf."

My partial shift rescinded, the fur disappearing. I reached up and held her wrists that pressed against my upper body, closing my eyes. I exhaled through my nose harshly and nodded. When I opened them, she searched my features, seeking my wolf. When she didn't see him, she let go, walking past me to get to Rava.

I met Tristan's gaze, dipping my chin, and he sheathed his sword.

I cursed myself for what I'd almost done. Rya. Tristan. I was going to kill them, and anyone that got in my way. This wasn't their fault.

We surrounded Rava while the witch tended to her, placing her glowing hands over her head and her ankle. When the light faded, she stopped.

"I'm not the healer my sister is, but that should do it," Rya told her. "You've healed quite a bit on your own already."

"What happened?" Roxanne said, kneeling beside her.

Dropping her knees, she crisscrossed her legs, then looked up to Dorian. "Lyra happened." She suddenly realized one of us was missing as she searched behind us. "Did she . . ." Rava started, trailing off.

Roxanne nodded softly. "Yeah. She took Fury."

"I need you to tell me what you know," Dorian said to her, but my sister looked up to him.

"How are you in control right now?" Rox asked him, narrowing her eyes and searching his body language for signs. "Roman is about to lose control to a part of him that no one wants to see. I heard your scream. We all did."

He crossed his arms. "Lyra won't kill her. That's the only thing I know for sure right now."

"How do you know that?" I asked him.

He sighed. "Because Lyra likes to play games. If she wanted Fury dead, she would've tried to kill her. She had the opportunity when Fury sifted between you and Lyra, but she didn't take it. She used Rava as bait to bring us all here. She wants her alive."

"I want to find comfort in that, but forgive me if I don't share your assessment," I muttered.

"I think he's right," Rava said, putting herself back in the conversation. I raised my eyebrows to her in question, urging her to go on. "Lyra came to me at the clinic."

"She what?" Dorian's voice was soft. Confused.

Rava shifted on the ground, throwing her arm out for someone to help her up. I caught it, pulling her to her feet. She leaned over, dusting herself off before standing upright. "I had a new patient appointment today. Claimed she was a shifter-fae hybrid. Took me all of two seconds to figure out who she was, though I can't say she was hiding it much. She just needed to get close to me, and that was the easiest way to do it."

"Why not just sift and take you just like she did Fury?" Roxanne asked.

"That's not how the game is played," Rya answered. "Just taking Rava away isn't enough of a mind fuck."

"Bingo," Rava said, pointing at the witch.

"What did she say? I need to know everything," Dorian said.

She blew out a harsh breath. "I called her out on not being a hybrid. I figured I knew who she was. Rya and I have been working on figuring out Fury's situation, and she's also filled in the blanks about Lyra, so it was pretty obvious when the patient lifted her cloak and I saw her hair and eyes. The murderous grin was a big hint too." She ran her hands down her face. "I called her by name. I asked her what she wanted. She teetered between laughter and tears. There's a weird internal struggle there. It was hard to read." She looked at Dorian with sad eyes, but he remained unresponsive and unfeeling.

Roxanne put her hand on his arm and motioned for Rava to continue.

"She told me she wanted to play a game, and I said I would. I thought I could get some answers from her. I got some, but none of it made sense. She said some things in Latin I don't know. I think it was Latin. I can't remember what words they were. She said 'his voice. It plagues me.'"

His voice. I made a mental note, knowing Dorian was doing the same. My wolf stirred violently, furious and on edge with each passing moment.

"Lyra said the light was blinding, then she started laughing. It was madness. High-pitched and, well, crazy, for lack of a better word. It sent chills over my entire body. Then she disappeared."

"That's it?" I asked. Rava had lost her mind and attacked people, destroying everything in her path. There had to be more.

She shook her head. "No," she whispered. "I felt a gentle touch on my temple, and then I heard her in my head. She took control. Told me what to do." Her eyes welled up, tears sitting on the edge waiting to spill over. "I tried to fight her off."

Roxanne wrapped her arms around Rava, comforting her and soothing her worry. "This isn't your fault."

I looked away. Rox was right, but it didn't stop me from putting blame on Rava. She should've known better. She shouldn't have taken on Lyra by herself. She shouldn't have tried to talk to her. She should have called . . . should have . . .

I sighed, releasing some of the tension in my shoulders. Should have *what*? I asked myself. What could Rava have possibly done? Run away? Pretended she didn't know who Lyra was? Tried to stop her? None of it mattered. Lyra had a plan, and whether or not Rava called her out on it, she was going to manipulate and control her. She was going to use her. That was her purpose in going to the clinic. There wasn't a damn thing Rava could have done. I knew that, even if my baser instinct wanted to blame her, it wasn't her fault. My sister was right, even if my wolf didn't agree.

I met Rava's gaze, and her eyes were filled with guilt. She questioned if her alpha placed that weight on her shoulders too. "Roman?" she asked, her voice trembling.

"This isn't on you, Rava. Lyra is . . ." I trailed off, thinking of what I could say that would relieve her of the burden she was feeling. "Lyra is more powerful than any of us. I don't blame you for any of this."

She closed her eyes, letting the tears fall while Roxanne stroked her head.

"What did she say in your head?" Dorian asked.

Rava let go, removing herself from the embrace as she wiped her eyes and cleared her throat. "She blamed Fury for everything. She said she was the reason this was all happening. Her words came out of my mouth when I faced off with Fury, but they didn't make sense. Lyra was so angry. I've never felt a rage that strong, and it took over. I had no control of my actions, but I fought it as best I could. I almost came through, but her strength . . . the hold she had over me was too much. She was hunting, but I didn't know what for. She said the angel was coming, and then Fury knocked me out."

Dorian paced, scrubbing his hands down his face. When he stopped, he looked to Rya. "I know she has the talisman but try again. Just to see if you can find her. Try both of them. Rox, take her to Fury's room. She's going to need something Fury has touched. Clothes, a hairbrush, anything." They both nodded, turning on a heel and rushing into the house.

My arms stayed crossed, and I stared at the ground, my chin pressing into my chest. A thought occurred to me, and my head snapped up. "Does anyone know how to reach Bloody Mary?"

Dorian pointed at me in agreement. "Not the way Fury calls her, but there's the legend-way, right?" he asked.

"Yeah, saying the name thirteen times in front of a mirror or something like that."

"Tristan," he said, facing his second. "Look it up. Find out the way people normally do it. Her real name is Jules. Try to contact her. You're a friend of Fury's. She should help."

Tristan gave a single dip of his head and sifted.

"Where's Ezra?" I asked. I needed some good news. Anything to placate the storm flaring inside me. To calm the wolf's desire for blood and revenge, even if only a little.

"Right here," he said from behind me.

I turned, seeing him and James, Dorian's butler.

"Tell me you have something," I said, the desperation in my voice leaking through.

Ezra's eyes were haunted as he confirmed my fear. "I can't reach her. I can't make a connection to figure out where she is. She's blocked, or asleep, or . . ." he trailed off.

"Don't finish that sentence," I growled, red clouding my vision.

I couldn't take it. I couldn't bear the thought of it. I stormed off, ignoring them as they called for me. I heard Dorian tell him to let me go. It was in their best interests to leave me.

My feet pounded the forest floor, pine needles crunching and twigs snapping while I headed to nowhere.

The fear ate at my insides, tearing apart the little of me that was left. The nightmares were real. Foreshadowing what was to come. Fury being taken away. Of my failure. Of losing my mate. All of it rippled through me. I wasn't worthy of all that I'd been given. Earned. What I was born into. None of it. If I couldn't protect my mate.

I stopped, looking at my axe embedded in the thick trunk when I chopped wood.

Memories came flooding back to me.

I turned, seeing the tree where we'd been not that long ago. Where I'd claimed her as mine, marking her neck, thrusting into her with her back pressed into the rough bark.

Where I realized Maya was gone, not forgotten, and Fury had taken her place.

Where I somehow said Maya's name out loud while I was accepting the past and embracing the future.

Where I made Fury think she wasn't what I wanted . . . that she was second place and always would be . . . that I didn't love her . . .

That was the last thing she felt from me.

My body vibrated in a partial shift as I tried to contain it. Push it down. Not let him take over.

I clenched my teeth, stomping toward the tree, pulled my fist back, and smashed it into the trunk. I screamed, letting all my emotion come out in a feral roar as I hit it again and again.

The wood split, creaking as it tipped. I threw a punch into it once more, sending it over. The tree slammed to the soft earth, sending dirt and debris flying up in a cloud. A ferocious resounding crack went through the forest, mirroring the emotional turmoil that raged inside me.

CHAPTER 27
FURY

COLD WAS THE FIRST THING THAT REGISTERED.

Being shoved to the ground, the second.

I took a quick glance at my surroundings, surprised to find myself standing on the cliffs of Avalon again. The castle where I'd spent the last five days learning to sift was right behind me, but instead of Dorian for company, I was stuck with Lyra.

"Why are we here?" I asked, rolling to the side, and coming back up in a crouch.

I expected her to be positioning herself to strike. Perhaps preparing to toy with me. She'd been on the hunt after all, according to Rava.

Instead she hissed, looking away. "Capture Fury," she said in a lilting voice. "Play with Fury. Hunt Fury—but never kill."

Her neck twisted in a strange motion that wasn't natural.

"Why not kill?" I asked, seeing if I could penetrate the madness clearly eating at her.

Lyra lifted her head, eyes focused on me with more clarity than I thought she possessed. "Because then the angel would get mad, and bad things happen when I make him mad." She dropped her chin and started pacing. The billowy white dress flowed around her, sleeveless and light. It certainly wasn't enough to fight the chill, not that she seemed to notice.

"Why are we here, Lyra?" I asked again, hoping she might give me more.

"This is my home," she whispered. Lifting her chin, she looked out over the cliffs, her eyes beautifully and horribly sad. "But the angel's my home," she added, slipping back into her insanity. "The light. Look into the light . . ."

My chest constricted.

Look into the light.

Dorian's brief explanation of his daughter's descent into madness whispered in my mind. I had a horrible, awful feeling about what happened to her that might've caused her to change. To become what she was.

"Did the angel kill your mom, Lyra?" I asked, slowly standing up. I didn't wander closer, careful to avoid setting off her fight-or-flight response.

Her eyebrows furrowed together. She trembled.

"Mother," she whispered in Gaelic, a language I'd briefly studied and only knew enough for small talk. "Look into the light," she repeated in a shaky voice. Her features smoothed as if the phrase settled something within her.

I recognized the response for what it was.

Conditioning.

"What did he do to you?" I said, unable to help myself.

Her chin turned, and she regarded me with furious eyes.

"He saved me," she said, in a hauntingly eerie voice that was childlike and yet not. "Took away the pain. No"—she frowned at herself, hands curling and uncurling like a cat pawing at its tail—"he was the pain. He . . ." she trailed off as she struggled with words.

"Did he punish you for seeing him?" I asked her. "Did he tell you to look into the light?"

I wanted to go to her. To help. To piece together the shattered remnants of her mind and find out what truly happened to her—by who, and why.

But whoever this angel was, he clearly did a number.

"It's your fault," Lyra said without looking at me. "I slept. I was asleep, peacefully and blissfully asleep, and he woke me—*for you*. To play with *you*." Her head turned without her body moving an inch. "I'm his doll. A marionette. A puppet for him to play with . . . but you're mine."

Lyra sifted and the hairs on my arms stood on end.

"He won't let me go because of you," she said from behind me. I whipped around, but she was already gone.

"You're wrong," I called out. "It's not because of me."

She reappeared a few feet away and then sifted right in front of me, inches from my face. "Why?" she asked, her white eyebrows drawn together in concentration. "Why?" she repeated. "Why? Why? *Why?*" she said, raising her voice with each punctuation.

"Because he's a sick fuck that's hiding behind you—just like he hid behind the supes who died when they kidnapped me the night he woke you."

She blinked, like she was struggling to process what I'd just told her.

"Died," she murmured.

"Yeah. That's what happens to people he uses."

A cold wind whipped over the cliffs. That wasn't strange for Avalon by any means, but the chilling laugh that followed froze me more than the Isle of Glass ever could.

"*Lyra*," a charismatic voice said.

I stared up into the sky where a pair of ink black wings blotted out what little of the sun there was. He wore a cloak that flapped in the wind around him while keeping his face obscured in shadows.

"Finally," I huffed. "Why are you here? What have I ever done to you for you to fuck with my life like this? Not to mention the mission—"

A hand locked around my throat, squeezing.

Lyra had moved when I looked away. That was my mistake; forgetting she was still a very real threat even if she wasn't the one pulling the strings.

"We don't talk to him like that," she said as if she were scolding a child. "Ask for forgiveness."

"Over my dead body," I uttered hoarsely.

Her head tilted to the side. "You're a difficult one." Almost unbothered, she added, "No matter. There are other ways to make you behave."

Her hand tightened, threatening to crush my windpipe.

I struck out, slamming the side of my closed fist into her elbow. She hissed in pain, loosening her grip enough that I could sift away.

I reappeared on the castle roof. Swallowing hard, I thought of the knife I knew to be sitting on Dorian's nightstand and I sifted it to me. It appeared in front of my face, and I caught it.

The wind blew harder, making it more difficult to keep my balance at an elevated position on the battlement. I'd chosen the spot closer to danger—closer to the angel—hoping I could have the element of surprise. Or at least get in a good throw before he retaliated.

If I could get the angel out of the air, I knew I could take him. Getting him out of the air, that was another matter.

"Hey fuckface," I called over the wind. Both Lyra and the angel turned to me at once.

I threw the knife, aiming for a wing instead of his body.

He swerved midair trying to dodge my throw, and the knife nicked the edge of his hood.

Fabric tore right as another body barreled into mine. Lyra crashed into me and sifted us back down to the cliff. I pushed her off me just long enough to get to my feet, but she kept coming.

A rabid savageness seeming to consume her.

"We—" She slashed.

"Don't—" I ducked.

"Hurt—" She brought her knee up.

"The—" I used my forearm to stop it, punching her stomach.

"Angel," she growled in pain.

"He's controlling you," I said over the roar of waves crashing into the rocks below us. "Using you. He has you brainwashed—"

"It's no use," the angel called out, making the hairs on my neck stand on end because I'd heard that charismatic voice before. "Lyra's mine. My puppet. My pet. Her only desire is to please me."

I don't know how I didn't notice it the first time he spoke, but with every word he uttered now, it was a battle ram to the iron bars I'd kept around the bad dreams threatening to suffocate me. A key opening a lock on a safe I long since sealed shut, trying so desperately to never open it again.

I stopped without a single regard for the woman before me and stared at the figure in the sky.

The face that looked back at me was my worst nightmare. My greatest tormentor.

It was my ex-husband.

"That's impossible," I said. "I killed you. I—"

"You're as ill-mannered as you were in life, but far less breakable now." His lapis-colored eyes travelled my sweater-clad body, hungrily devouring it with a mere look.

My stomach twisted. Bile rose in my throat. I'd rather drown in the ocean than watch this.

It appeared I might get my wish.

"Punish her, Lyra. Be my good girl."

I didn't see it coming, but I could honestly say I wouldn't have stopped it if I had.

I was utterly and completely frozen in my spot as her bare foot came up and slammed into my chest.

The air left my lungs.

I went sailing through the air . . . but I never landed.

The angel's cruel, smiling face disappeared over the edge of the cliff, and only then did I realize I was falling.

CHAPTER 28
FURY

Down.

Down.

Down.

My heart thumped rapidly against my ribs as my inevitable end loomed near.

Who would've thought I'd be Sparta-kicked off a cliff?

Not me. At least it was far more dramatic than being bit by a rogue shifter. Not that I wanted to die. Just the opposite in fact. I'd only just learned how to live. Learned that I *could*.

And now, somehow, a monster from my past was back to haunt me.

Or end me, it would seem.

Black feathers appeared in my periphery. I flinched away, assuming it to be the angel—but the squawk of protest and talons that gripped my arm were anything but.

"Sift, Fury! SIFT," Hades yelled. "You lazy, good-for-nothing demon!"

His talons split the skin on my forearm as he tried and failed to pull me up.

The idea was endearing, really, and it didn't even hurt with all the adrenaline coursing through me. Then again, the pain wouldn't catch up. Not where I was headed.

The sound of the roaring waves grew louder in the space between one heartbeat and the next. I knew with some kind of certainty this would be it.

Death.

The apocalypse.

The end of everything.

Because my fucking ex.

Anger coursed through me. A fury, one might say if they were so inclined. It was the sort of anger that drove a woman to murder—or to changing her name to Fury.

It was a shade of red so vibrant and deep, your transgressions could never be wiped clean.

I was so pissed that I didn't realize I should have died already.

The fall wasn't that long.

I twisted midair and Hades' claws grabbed me again, only this time it worked.

My descent had slowed, and instead of crashing into the wicked-looking rocks below, I was being pulled away from them.

I turned my head, trying to grasp what was going on. Why there were white feathers everywhere—

"You need to lay off the beer and cheese fries," pigeon grumbled as he hefted me up and over the edge of a rock and dropped me unceremoniously. "Better yet, don't let yourself get kicked off a cliff."

I opened my mouth to snap back with something snarky and completely rude given he'd just saved my ass—but when I lifted my arm to get up, a white *wing* appeared.

What the actual fuck.

"Hades . . ." I said his name, but it didn't come out like I expected. A sort of growled croak sounded around me instead, echoing back. "What am I?"

"Not a wolf, that's for sure."

Blood rushed to my head. A sudden exhaustion hit that weighed me down. I just managed to angle away from the ocean spray that was misting around me when the darkness closed in.

And in the black abyss of my mind, the nightmares came.

CHAPTER 29
EZRA

I HEARD A TREE CRASH IN THE DISTANCE. ROMAN WAS LOSING IT. I LISTENED IN on his thoughts every now and then, checking to see when he'd explode. None of them knew just how close he was to the edge of insanity.

I'd learned quite a bit about him and Fury and what they'd shared. I'd learned his part of it. She had no idea what the truth was. If I'd made her feel that way . . . if that was our last encounter before this, I can't say I'd be much different from him.

He'd be back soon, though not even he knew why he was returning.

Dorian paced by the windows, quiet and stewing in frustration. This was out of his control, and for a fae alpha like Dorian, that wouldn't do. He managed to keep relatively calm, and I didn't know how or why. If only I could have read him.

Rya and Roxanne came up empty-handed in their task. It was a stretch, and we all knew it, but we still hoped she'd find a tendril of Fury to latch on to. They sat on the couch. Rya rested, exhausted from multiple attempts to locate her. She wouldn't give up. Roxanne stared at the floor, chewing her thumbnail, deep in thought.

Tristan had called the poltergeist, successfully summoning her. She had nothing, but she was searching. Every few moments I glanced at a mirror hanging on the wall by the stairs, waiting to see if she had returned with news. It was futile. She'd speak if she arrived, but it didn't stop me. I needed something to do.

I kept feeling for that connection. Reaching desperately for that tendril that linked my mind with Fury's. Anything to tell me where she was. Something. But I couldn't feel her. I couldn't hear her. I could read the mind of almost anyone, but something felt different with her. My mate. And that feeling was gone. It absolutely terrified me.

We were on the verge of cracking. The clock ticked and tocked, each moment that passed sent a spike of anxiety through me.

The door slammed open, Roman quietly seething and stomping through the house until he made it to the kitchen. He took a bottle of water, then returned, sitting in his chair and draining the water. His eyes looked like the blue of an iceberg, and just as dangerous as one.

Another tick.

Another tock.

Another glance at the empty mirror.

Another reach for that lost tether, finding nothing but silence.

A loud caw echoed over the lake, and each of us snapped our heads up.

"Hades," Roxanne shouted, jumping off the couch. "Open the door, the window, open it." Her scrambled words came out at a furious speed while Dorian wrenched the sliding door to let the crow fly into the room.

All of us were on our feet, looking at the bird as he landed on the back of a chair.

"Where's Fury?"

"Is she okay?"

"Is she hurt?"

"Where's Lyra?"

Everyone started shouting questions to him at the same time, myself included. Rava stuck her fingers in her mouth, letting out an ear-piercing whistle no shifter had the right to make. We all grabbed our ears as the sound ripped through us.

"Thank you," Hades said when the sound died down, dipping his head to her. "Fury's alive. She's shifted. Needs your help. Let's go."

"Where is she?" Dorian and I asked in unison.

"Avalon," he answered.

Adrenaline pumped through me. Alive. Shifted. But alive.

"You left her on Avalon with Lyra?" Roman growled, taking a step forward. "You left her to die?"

Hades flapped his wings, preparing to take flight if Roman attacked him. "Ease up, shifter. First of all, Lyra left. The angel showed up and 'poof' they disappeared. Second, what was it that you wanted me to do if Lyra was still there? I'm a *bird*. Want me to claw her eyes out? Pretty sure if you, the vampire, and Fury couldn't take her down, I'm shit out of luck in a one-on-one with señorita psycho. I came to get you three. That's what I should be doing, and I did it, and you're bloody welcome for it."

"So let's go," I said, looking at Dorian and Roman.

"I'm going too," Rava and Roxanne said.

Roman turned to them. "No. Stay here. That's an order." His eyes flashed. An alpha command. I'd not seen him speak to his sister that way. A crease formed between her brows, incensed he was holding that position over her. I had a feeling she could defy him if she wanted to, and I couldn't sense a lick of fear, but she didn't fight it. I listened in for a brief moment. She was doing it for Fury. No one else. She wanted her safe, and the sooner that happened, the better.

I wanted them to hurry the fuck up so we could get to my mate.

Rava surprised me, stepping forward, addressing Roman with both confidence and caution. "With all due respect, I can help. She's shifted. She's scared. This is what I do, alpha. I can help her through this. We all can."

Rava's thoughts were screaming for me to listen. She still felt somewhat responsible. A measure of guilt. But she knew Roman may be too emotional to help Fury shift. I couldn't, and neither could Dorian. If Roman didn't succeed, Rava would be there.

I took a risk, stepping in when I truly had no right to. I'd be pissed if someone stepped in and tried to make a decision for my clan. But this involved Fury. It was different. And I just wanted to go. "Bring her, Roman. She's earned it."

He turned his head slightly, glaring at me over his shoulder from the corner of his eye. He grunted, giving her permission.

"To Avalon," he said.

Dorian put his hand on Roman's shoulder, and Rava held her arm out for Hades to land on her. She reached her open palm to me, and I took it.

I felt like the ground was pulled out from under me, but then dropped from above, landing on the cold, hard earth.

A brutal wind cut through my thin T-shirt, freezing my skin. My teeth clattered together, and I crossed my arms, rubbing them for friction and warmth. "Well, this is a fucking nightmare," I said. "No wonder Dorian lives here."

He ignored my comment, staring at the castle. "She's not in the castle. I can sense her, but I don't know where," he growled, looking at me for answers.

"I haven't felt a connection yet. I can't find her," I said through chattering teeth.

Hades cawed, hovering over the edge of the cliff.

My heart dropped into the pit of my stomach. I think it did for all of us. We darted toward the edge, dropping to our hands and knees to peer over the edge, fearing what we'd see.

But we saw nothing. The face of the steep cliff led down to a rocky base where explosive waves collided with the stone. And we saw nothing.

No wolf.

No body.

No Fury.

"Where is she?" Roman called over the wind.

I pointed to Hades as he flew down the cliffside, taking a sharp turn and entering what had to be a cave.

"You've got to be kidding me," Rava groaned.

I turned to her. "What's the problem? Just sift us there."

"It's not that simple," Dorian answered. "We don't know where we're sifting. We haven't seen the location. We don't know what to visualize. We could sift into the rock," he explained, speaking loudly so we could hear him over the water crashing below us.

"*Into* the rock?" I repeated. "As in, we'd get stuck inside the rock for however long until we could break out or just live encased in it for fucking eternity?"

"Yes, that, except Rava would die since she's not like us," Dorian answered.

Roman's body trembled, and I doubted it was the cold.

Rava cursed, pinching the bridge of her nose, walking away from the cliff, further inland.

Dorian ran to her and grabbed Rava's shoulders. "I have an idea. You won't like it."

"Well, we're already on a winning streak with things I don't like, so no need to stop now."

"I need you to think of sifting to Fury. Not her location," he said, squinting his eyes, wondering if she understood what he was asking of her.

"That won't work." She shook her head when he tried to argue with her. "No, it won't. Listen to me. She's shifted. It's not her body. It's her wolf, and we don't know what her wolf looks like. We can't imagine shifting to her because if I think of her hand, it's not her hand. It's her paw. We don't even know the color of her fur."

I saw what he was getting at, which said a lot considering I knew nothing of sifting, but her point was valid. None of us knew what she looked like. Only Hades.

Hades.

"Sift to Hades," I blurted out.

"Holy shit," Roman said, his eyes getting wide, turning to Rava. "What he said. Do that."

"How do you know it'll work?" she asked Dorian, worry and doubt filling her voice.

"It's something Fury can do," he said. "It's how she started to sift. Thinking about objects and about what she wanted to be *next to*, rather than where she wanted to be. You're both hybrids. I believe you can do it too."

She frowned. "Maybe . . ."

I heard her fear. What if she screwed up? What if she failed? Fury needed us. What if she wasn't enough?

This shifter needed to get in line with those thoughts. We had the same things running through our heads. We were in good company.

Dorian put his hands on her shoulders and turned her around, facing away from us. He gestured for me to keep walking in the opposite direction, so I did. Leaning to her ear, he said, "Close your eyes. Picture Ezra. You don't know him as well as Roman, so choose him. Picture his black hair. Think about the tattoos on his arms. Visualize his green eyes. Picture him. He is your location." He paused, waiting several moments until she took a shaky breath and nodded quickly. "Now, sift."

She disappeared, and I slowed my steps, then she reappeared right in front of me. She peeked one eye open and saw me, realizing I had moved from the spot she'd last seen me. She shouted a brief whoop of excitement and relief. I didn't quite share the same enthusiasm, but I wanted to get to my mate.

"Do it again," he said. "Focus on Hades."

She blew her cheeks out. "Okay. Okay," she said, psyching herself up. She grabbed my hand, and Roman rested his on Dorian's shoulders.

God, I hope I don't fuck this up and end up in a rock, Rava thought so loudly I didn't need to listen in to hear her.

"What?" I said, and my eyes shot open right as the ground was pulled out from under me.

CHAPTER 30
FURY

I OPENED MY EYES, BLINKING SEVERAL TIMES AND WINCING AT THE POUNDING in my head.

Ugh. What happened?

I didn't know where I was. I needed to get my bearings, but my body protested, feeling lighter and weak all over.

My vision started to clear, and I could see things with an unusual clarity. Images were sharper. Focused. I was in a cave, I thought. I laid there, staring at the minute detail of the stone walls. The veining in the rock. The condensation dripping down the sides.

I lifted my hand to my face . . . and saw feathers. Bold, white feathers.

This isn't real. This can't be real.

Flashes of falling and seeing a white wing entered my mind.

I tried to sit, but tiling my head forward only allowed me to see small, black stick-like legs. Legs with three pointed toes. And claws.

There's really only one appropriate thing you can do when you see that instead of your own feet.

So that's what I did.

I screamed.

Except it came out in a loud honking squawk.

"That's the worst raven call I've ever heard," Hades said, laughing and snorting through his beak. The wheezing kazoo sound filled the cave. I turned and saw him standing nearby.

"I'm a *what*?" I said in panic. No, no, no, no, no, no. This wasn't happening.

"You're a raven," he chortled. "Oh my god . . . this is pure gold. It's everything I could have ever wanted. You're a *bird*." He dragged out the last word, losing the final enunciation to a fit of laughter. He tipped over, falling on his side. His wings flapped around while he got his entertainment at my expense.

"How am I a raven? What happened? How did it happen?" I blurted.

"Well, it happened when Lyra kicked you in the chest, right off the side of a cliff," he explained, getting himself up and finding a boulder to stand on. He kicked out a leg, making a 'hiyah' sound. "Then this was you, except with arms." He flailed his wings and yelled, looking like a right idiot. "You were screaming, 'save me, save me!' Then I came, you're welcome by the way, and I told you to sift." He puffed his body out quickly, looking like he swallowed a balloon, sending small feathers flying out. "And imagine my surprise when you shifted instead, and into a white raven no less."

Fractured memories came back to me. The Sparta-kick. Falling. Hades showing up. I was supposed to be a wolf. Right? I was a part shifter. Part wolf. But . . . I wasn't. I was a damned bird.

"A white raven," he said quietly, chuckling. "Talk about getting the fuzzy end of a lollipop. Your camouflage sucks."

A spike of anger ran through me.

"I'm going to wring your neck," I shouted, thrashing around, and flipping my body over upright. I wobbled at first, unsure about my center of balance.

"Gonna need hands for that, pigeon," he mocked, moving to a standing position, and flying up to sit on a rock. "You'll need to shift back for that."

I took a few steps, feeling far braver than I had any right to. "Ravens are bigger than crows," I reminded him. "When I catch you—"

"Fly up, then," he said. "C'mon. I'm right here."

"I . . . I . . ." My voice trailed off. I *what*? I had nothing. I didn't know what to do. I wasn't even mad at Hades, though him laughing at me didn't help things. In a way, I probably deserved it. I was woman enough to admit it. I was now a bird. Out of my element. In a cave, and I didn't really recall all of what had happened. I sighed, letting all the bravado melt away. "I need help," I finished.

"I know," he said. "I went to get your mates." He looked at the cave entrance. "Not sure what is taking them so long. They're up on the cliff right now."

"Thank you," I whispered. "For helping me not die. And for getting the guys."

"I'm sorry, what was that? I couldn't hear you," Hades said, lifting a wing to the side of his head where his ears would be if I could see them. "Waves are loud out there, crashing on the rocks."

I glared at him. "I said, thank you," I grumbled. "You don't have to rub it in right now."

"You're welcome, and I most certainly do have to rub it in. Don't tell me you wouldn't do the same. You're many things, but a liar isn't one of them."

"Fine," I admitted. "I'd one hundred percent be giving you shit."

At that moment, Ezra and Rava landed on the cave floor in a heaping pile. Dorian and Roman appeared, landing on a boulder, and tumbling off, grunting as they hit the ground.

Rava rolled off Ezra and looked around. A huge smile graced her face, and she whooped, slapping her palms on the ground. "I did it!"

Did what, I wasn't sure, but I'd never been so happy to see all of them.

Roman and Dorian pushed themselves up, wiping off their clothes; Ezra and Rava did the same.

"Where is she?" Dorian said to Hades. "You said she was here."

"I'm right here," I said. But no one paid any attention to me.

Hades turned his gaze from the group and looked directly at me. "She's right there. Look down," he said, gesturing with his wing. Then he laughed again, snorting.

I narrowed my eyes at him, then turned my attention back to the guys. "I don't know how to shift back," I told them.

But they stared at me. They didn't answer me. They just said nothing.

Ezra blinked repeatedly. "I can't hear her thoughts."

Roman's mouth gaped open slightly, and Rava hid a small smile behind her hand. "She's beautiful," she breathed. "I've never seen a white raven before."

"How . . ." Dorian started, but he didn't finish his thought.

"Can we talk about this later?" I asked. "I'm a bird. I'd like to be a person again."

"They can't hear you," Hades told me.

"She's talking?" Roman asked, surprise lighting up his face. "Nothing is coming through. Why can't I hear her?" There was a panic in his tone that wasn't at all comforting.

"Because she's not a wolf," Rava answered. "That's the best guess I have. But Hades seems to understand her just fine. Can you understand us, Fury?"

Disappointment was an understatement.

This is so humiliating, Hades.

I really had no way to respond. So what did I do? I bobbed my head.

And I squawked, wincing at the terrible sound I made.

"Or incredibly entertaining, depending on your perspective. Don't worry. We'll work on your caws and croak. That sound you make is horrific," Hades said to me before looking at the others. "And yes, she can understand you. She doesn't know how to shift back. She'll need your help, Rava. Roman looks unwell. I don't shift, so I can't talk her through this."

I huffed in annoyance.

What had happened? I couldn't sift right. I'd just turned into a bloody raven. What next? I needed to drink harpy blood to survive? Or maybe some terribly endangered, hard-to-find rainforest critter the size of a shrew. That'd be my luck.

What a clusterfuck.

Rava kneeled in front of me, inspecting my bird form. "Hey, Fury," she said, smiling warmly at me. I lifted a wing in an awkward bird-wave. "I need to walk you through this, but I've never been a bird, so I assume this is all going to be the same basic mechanics of shifting."

I tapped my feet a little bit, trying to let her know I was listening and ready to go.

"Okay," she breathed. "How did you shift when you turned into a raven?" She looked at Hades, waiting for him to relay my answer.

"She says she doesn't know. She was falling off a cliff, and she was angry she was about to die," Hades said.

Rava frowned, twisting her lips in thought while I patiently—not really—waited for her to tell me what to do.

She exhaled loudly, then looked at me again. "I need you to visualize being your human form again. Demon-hybrid form. However you view and define yourself, I need you to focus on that. Remind yourself that you're safe right now."

Visualize . . . myself. How did I define myself?

That was a great question, really, and that would've been better to understand and work on *before* I had shifted into a bird. Now didn't feel like the best time for a therapy session on self-discovery. I didn't know what the hell I was.

But apparently I needed to call it something right now.

Demon. I'd been one longer than anything else. Now I was a hybrid too, but I didn't know how to relate to my hybrid self at all. I was just starting to figure it out. I sighed.

"Stop overthinking this," Hades interrupted. "You're Fury. *The* Fury. Start acting like it."

How the hell did he know what I was thinking, anyway? I snapped my beak at him. "Shut up," I said.

But he was right. Once a human, then a demon, now a hybrid. I was still Fury. I pictured myself. That was it.

I nodded my head to Rava.

"You need to tell your body and mind to become that form again," she said.

Okay.

Shift.

I am Fury.

Shift into Fury.

Shift.

Nothing happened.

"She looks constipated," Hades said, laughing loudly again.

"Could you stop being an asshole for one minute? I am trying to concentrate!" I shouted at him. He shook his head, chuckling and making a high-pitched wheezing through his beak.

I closed my eyes, taking a deep breath.

Fury. I am Fury. I have red hair. Great tits. I'm *THE* Fury. I am the best demon the Afterlife has ever seen.

One, two, three, SHIFT.

Nothing.

Nooooow. . . SHIFT.

Crickets.

SHIFT, DAMN IT.

. . .

I flapped my wings in frustration.

Roman growled in frustration. "What's wrong?" he asked Rava, then looked at Ezra. "Why isn't she shifting?"

Ezra shrugged his shoulders. "I have no idea."

"I'm not sure," Rava whispered. "It's hard not being able to properly coax her through it while she struggles on the emotional side of it."

"Oh my god, I'm going to be a bird forever," I moaned, throwing my head back and letting out an incredibly pitiful sound.

"Stop bitching," Hades chastised.

I turned my head sharply in his direction. "Easy for you to say," I said, feeling my frustration rise. "You have no idea what I am going through. You're always a bird."

"I am. And if you don't get your shit together, you will be too," he retorted.

"NOT helping," I yelled at him.

Rava and my mates stopped making suggestions and stared at us while we had a conversation, and they only got one side of it.

"Ease up," Dorian said to him. "She's clearly struggling—"

"No," Hades snapped at him. "She's being a pussy. And she's whining."

Roman growled, baring his teeth, but Ezra put a hand over his chest.

"I'm trying, you stupid—" I said to Hades before he interrupted me.

"You're not trying hard enough. If you want to be a bird forever, then give up. Fine. But don't whine about it."

"I don't want to be a bird," I shouted.

"Then SHIFT and be your peachy demon self again or shut up and accept that you have only me to talk to for the rest of your fucking life." He threw his wings out, challenging me.

That. Son. Of. A. Bitch.

He was being a giant asshole and everyone in the room was just letting him.

My chest heaved with anger.

Rava leaned toward me, speaking in low tones. "C'mon, Fury. He's calling you out."

"She can't shift. She'll fail her mission. Just as useless as the poltergeists. The world will end, and it will all be because she's too—"

I was going to kill him.

Adrenaline shot through me, and my joints popped. I felt a gush of wind over my body as I screamed.

Then I heard it.

My scream, a real one, echoed in the cave, reverberating off the walls while little pebbles vibrated on the floor.

"Fury!" Rava cried out, throwing her arms around me while my mates let out a collective sigh of relief.

My contentment was short-lived when I saw Hades standing on the boulder.

I reached out and took a step, stumbling. I felt weak and tired, cold and completely uncoordinated. "You little fucker! I'm going to—"

Rava held me. "Don't, Fury. He helped you shift," she said quickly.

"I—what?" I furrowed my brows.

"You're welcome. Again," Hades said, taking a bow.

"I caught on to what he was doing. Ezra heard me and shared it with Roman and Dorian," she explained, releasing me only slightly. "You'd said you were angry when you shifted during your fall. He made you angry so you could fuel the shift back to yourself. It was worth a shot, and it turned out to be the right thing. We'll work on it more later, but for now, we have you back."

I looked at Hades with an apologetic smile. He tilted his head to the side, and I was pretty sure he knew that was my way of acknowledging what he'd done. Had he not been there, I would've died—if I could die. We still didn't know.

She let me go and I tried to steady myself. A burst of cold registered in my mind. I looked down. I shifted. I was myself. And I was also butt-naked. My nipples were hardened, and goosebumps pebbled my skin. I rubbed my hands over my arms and looked at Dorian.

"Right, of course," he said. "Sorry."

In an instant I had clothes. I breathed a sigh of relief. The guys moved toward me, but I held my hand up to them. "I'm fine, honestly. But give me a second to get acclimated."

"What happened?" Dorian and Roman said in unison.

"Did Lyra bring you here right after she took you?" Dorian asked.

I nodded. "Yeah. Not the cave, obviously, but Avalon. Outside the castle, near the cliffs."

"What happened? What did she say?" he pressed.

Fractured pieces of our cliffside standoff put themselves back together, playing like a film in my mind.

Her madness.

Her blame.

That voice . . .

My dead husband's face flashed in my memories.

A tremor shook my body.

The angel.

It was impossible.

"Tell them," Ezra said quietly, looking at the ground with his arms crossed.

I shot a glare at him, a spike of anger coursing through me before I let it go.

"Tell us what?" Dorian asked.

I looked at Dorian and I felt so much sadness. I didn't know where to start, but the beginning was probably the best place. "She's being used, Dorian. The angel controls her. Manipulates her. Maybe even the same way she does with her victims."

"Did she say that?" Roman asked, taking a step closer to me, his anxiety spiking.

"Not in so many words, but basically, yeah." I looked away. "It gets worse," I whispered. "I think . . . she kept talking about a light. Looking into a light. I think after the angel killed her mother, he punished her for it. It wasn't seeing her mother killed that sent her over the edge. It was him. And he's conditioned her to think he's taking away her agony, but he tormented her then and he's doing it now."

A darkness flashed through Dorian's amber eyes and a low rumble sounded in his chest.

Being clothed again warmed my body quickly, but I put my hands in my pockets anyway, rocking on my feet a little. It was an awkward feeling to pass on the news about his daughter being tortured. "She had moments of lucidity, though. It was extremely brief. Like she's still in there, but she's in an incredible amount of emotional pain and that outweighs everything."

Rava shuddered, clearly remembering something similar, though I didn't know what. "I tried to fight her control when she was inside my head. Maybe she's fighting the angel too?"

"You did," I told her, recalling the moment she'd broken through in our fight. "And I think you're right. If he's been at this for a long time, if it was him who started it, who knows how shattered her mind is."

Roman crossed his arms. "Why, though? Her downfall into . . . what happened a thousand years ago has nothing to do with right now. It has nothing to do with Fury."

I sighed. "The first event has nothing to do with me, but him bringing her back? That's one hundred percent for me." I relayed her message to me, trying to remember each and every word she said.

Dorian ran his fingers through his hair, pacing and grumbling. "This doesn't make any sense. Why? What does this angel want?"

I met Ezra's gaze and straightened my shoulders. I wanted nothing more than to pretend that never happened, but he already knew it.

"The angel showed up," I said.

All eyes pinned me with concern, anger, anxiety, possessiveness—you name it.

"And?" Roman said through gritted teeth.

"And he's making himself appear like my husband. Ex-husband. We didn't really divorce since he killed me, but I like to think of him as my ex," I answered.

Dorian and Roman froze. Even Hades didn't move. Roman's eyes didn't bother flickering. They just went straight to icy blue as he tried to suppress his response. The veins in his neck bulged, and the muscles beneath his shirt were taut as his body shook.

A cloud of something terrifying washed over Dorian. For the first time, his eyes took on a different amber hue. Gone were the warm shades of gold. An amber red circled his iris, eliciting a shiver to crawl across my skin. I'd watched his face. I saw the jaw tense. The eyelid twitch slightly.

Dorian moved a step closer to me but still kept his distance. Whether it was to give me space or control his emotions, I didn't know. "You said he's making himself appear to be. How do you know it's not him?"

I shook my head, reaching out to take his hand in mine. I held it firmly, meeting his swirling, violent eyes. "It can't be. John Adams was extinguished."

"He's playing a hell of a card in this game, then," Ezra said. "You froze when you heard his voice. Saw his face. He'll do it again to catch you off guard."

"Yes, thank you for that," I said with a clenched jaw. Annoyed as I was with him for reading my mind, he was right. No matter how much I knew the piece of shit was dead, the trauma . . . the history . . . it was always there. That moment I saw his face, it scared the hell out of me, and as much as I hated to admit it, hearing his voice sent fear through me that I'd thought was long gone. Turns out I was wrong.

Rava cleared her throat. "If this angel is the one that did this all to Lyra, is there a way we can reverse it?"

I smiled at her, ever the caring counselor. She didn't want to harm her. She wanted to fix her. We were on the same side in that. This wasn't Lyra's fault. It was the angel's. I didn't want Dorian to suffer the loss of his daughter. Roman and Ezra would respect that because that was what I wanted, and if they didn't, they'd hate the consequences. Hurting her would hurt Dorian, and that would hurt me. I flashed my vampire a look, making sure he heard every thought, and my threat. He blinked once slowly, audibly exhaling through his nose. I watched Roman's body language tense, and the muscle in his jaw tightened further. Ezra passed it on. Good.

"I don't know, but I plan on figuring it out," I admitted, answering Rava's question. "If I'm right and angel magic fucked with her head, maybe demon magic can fix it."

Dorian squeezed my hand back, silently thanking me.

"How do we do that?" Roman spoke carefully, testing the water to see how much input he had. I appreciated that he was at least trying to see my side. "I don't want to start off with the defeatist attitude here, but we can't capture her. We don't know where she is right now, and we don't have a way to subdue her."

"Jules can help us find her again. That's no problem. I'll have Roxanne whip me up a bloody mary, and we'll summon her." I shrugged and waved a hand. That part was easy.

"And the rest?" he asked.

I grinned, quickly glancing at the crow who had waited patiently. "Hades?"

"Oh, I found what you wanted. Stole it too," he answered.

I explained my theory on the amulets in Jake's office and the one protecting Lyra. No one argued with me, and why should they? It was better than anything else we had so far. I had confidence. I was rarely wrong with stuff like this.

"There's more to this thing than you knew," Hades added. I raised my eyebrows in surprise and gestured for him to go on. "If I'm correct—and when have I not been—this not only bears magic from the Afterlife, but it might be able to trap magic *from* the Afterlife."

For the first time in a while, I felt a huge wave of excitement. I wanted to know more. I had so many questions. How did he find that out? Was Jake in on this? Did he know? Did Duke tell him about it? How could we test it?

Before I could give voice to any of the thoughts running through my mind, exhaustion slammed into me. Any energy I had escaped me instantly, and even though I hadn't moved, I lost my balance. Dorian held me up. I raised my hand to the side of my head, trying to stop the room from moving.

"We need to get her out of here now," Rava said, holding her arm up for Hades to land on her. "She's going to pass out."

"No, I'm not," I mumbled incoherently. "M'mm just . . ."

Ezra and Dorian stood beside me, and Roman touched Rava's back.

"My place," Ezra said.

A rush of wind blew over me as I teetered on the edge of consciousness and my vision blurred.

Hold on, kitten. We're taking you home.

Home . . .

CHAPTER 31
FURY

Dorian sifted us to Ezra's place. The impact jarred my already weak body, and I canted forward. Ezra caught me around the front and Dorian grabbed my shoulders.

"I got it," my vampire said.

"She needs water and rest," Dorian said without releasing me. "Don't give her alcohol." I groaned. They both ignored me.

"You do realize I am almost two-hundred, right? I think I can handle our mate for a few hours." His green eyes flashed with annoyance. While age was a sore subject between them all, Ezra and Dorian seemed to go at each other on this subject quite a lot.

"Never mind that your mate is a hundred and twenty-six and doesn't need 'handling'," I griped. Sure, my weak knees disagreed, but once I laid down for a bit I'd be right as rain.

"No sex either," Dorian added, still ignoring me. "She doesn't need to be getting so worked up right after her first shift."

I might have called him a cockblock if not for the sudden wave of dizziness. My head lolled forward, and Ezra snatched me up, pulling my front firmly against him, before bending to pick me up.

"No shit, Dorian," Ezra snapped. "Now if you'll excuse us—I need to lay her down."

I saw Dorian nod out of the corner of my eye, then sift out. Ezra walked through the penthouse, carrying me to his bedroom.

The bed dipped under me as he placed me gently under the covers and then crawled in behind me. Despite laying still, the dizziness intensified. My head spun as my face grew warm.

"Ezra," I murmured. "I don't think this is from shifting."

Before I could even finish, I felt my canines sharpen, my mouth turning sore.

"Shit," he cursed. "The bleeding. You need to bite me."

I rolled over and opened my mouth to object when spots appeared in my vision. Ezra looped an arm around my waist and pulled me in, placing the crook of his neck where my mouth was.

"Bite," he commanded "Now."

Giving in, I braced myself for the bleeding to come. My lips peeled back as I pressed my fangs into him. His skin gave way with a pop, and Ezra tensed.

Then the strangest thing happened.

The pressure in my head *subsided.*

I wasn't drinking his blood by any means. It was more like everything building up in me released *into* him.

Ezra rolled, pulling me on top of him. I straddled his waist, locking my arms around his neck. He groaned then sat up, shuffling us both until his back was against the wall.

His cock hardened beneath me.

While biting him was helping me feel better, the taste of our combined blood on my tongue was not sexy. I lifted my hips so I wasn't pressing into him, and Ezra skated his fingers up my spine, soothing me and kneading the muscle.

"That's right, kitten," he murmured. His voice reverberated through him where my lips pressed to the column of his throat. "Get it all out."

He must've been able to tell from the lack of suction that I wasn't drinking either.

It made no sense. A vampire that didn't *drink* blood, but instead *gave* it.

Would violently expel it, apparently, if not given.

I would have shaken my head at my own conundrum if it

wouldn't have resulted in ripping a chunk of his flesh out. Ezra chuckled. "Much appreciated."

I let his obvious mind reading slip, at least this time. It had been a *long* afternoon, full of revelations and anxiety. Topped off with me needing to bite him so I didn't pass out and start bleeding out all my orifices.

Man, I really was a freak.

"Focus on the positives, Fury. We now have a solution to your predicament, and your animal has surfaced. You completed your first shift—"

I released his neck when the pressure completely faded, and my fangs started retracting. "Almost dying in the process," I added.

Ezra knotted his fingers in my hair and brought my mouth to his. He sucked on my bottom lip before licking my fangs clean of any traces of blood. While the blood giving wasn't a turn on for me, him licking me clean most definitely was.

I lowered my body down on him, rocking my hips against his. The bulge between my thighs twitched. My hand slipped from his neck, down his chest to the edge of his slacks. He grabbed my hand from between us, linking our fingers and pulling it away.

I frowned, leaning away from the kiss.

Ezra sighed. "Dorian is right. Your body has been through a lot. As much as I would love to fuck you and see how long it takes to break this bed—you need rest."

I narrowed my eyes at him. "I feel much better. Besides," I scooted back, a devious smile cracking through the frown, "I owe you for eating me out in front of Kendrick."

I dropped my other hand to the front of his pants, rubbing my palm over his thick length. Ezra groaned, tilting his head back against the headboard.

"You're wicked," he said. "Utterly evil."

I slipped my fingers just over the hem of his pants and pulled. They ripped down the center. "Well, I am a demon." I smirked, wrapping my fist around his cock. My fingers couldn't completely wrap around, but the strong pump I gave had him stiffening.

"Fucking hell. I'll never live it down if they find out—"

His protest turned to a groan as I bent at the waist, taking him in my mouth.

Ezra released my hand and knotted it in my hair. I half expected him to pull me back, but instead he pulled me forward, thrusting upward. I gagged on his cock as the head penetrated the tight barrier of my throat.

He rocked in and out in shallow thrusts until I couldn't breathe.

Bringing me back to the shallow end, he yanked upward, and I followed.

"You sure you're up for this, kitten?"

I licked my lips, feeling the first inklings of my crow outside my shift. While not truly invasive, it was like having a set of emotions that weren't my own and yet it also drove me.

And right now? She was feeling possessive over Ezra. He'd pleased her when he had me bite him. Now she wanted to own him.

In that, we were in agreement.

"I won't tell if you won't."

IN HINDSIGHT, I might have listened if I knew how much he liked being deep-throated. I was tuckered out. After a nap, then a bath, I sat at the kitchen bar while Ezra made me a bag of popcorn. Made was a bit of a stretch given he used the microwave, but I was still feeling boneless and not at all ready for the upcoming meeting. Hopefully, Jules could find Lyra again—and they could come up with a plan to capture her.

Not to mention the angel.

I really didn't want to rehash that again.

A bowl of popcorn appeared in front of me. I took a handful of buttery-goodness, munching on it idly while I worked through my thoughts.

"There's something we need to talk about," Ezra said. He crossed his arms over his chest, leaning back against the counter facing me.

I lifted an eyebrow, waiting for him to speak.

"Roman."

I tensed instantly. "What about him?"

Ezra sighed. "We need to talk about what happened the night of the burning ceremony."

My lips pursed. "You said you wouldn't come between me and my other mates."

"I'm not, actually. The opposite, in fact."

"Fine. What about it?" I asked stiffly.

"It's not what you thought it was," he said. "He wasn't calling you Maya. He was thinking about how what he feels for you is eclipsing her."

My mouth parted, not sure how to process the information.

"What do you mean by eclipsing her?"

Ezra ran a hand through his ink black hair, the dragon tattoo that wrapped around his chest moving as his muscles flexed. "It's not my place to say more, but you need to talk to him. You haven't given him the chance to explain. I know it hurt you, what you thought he was saying, but you don't want that conversation to be the last thing between you guys as we go into this." He motioned about, and I knew what he meant. This. The angel. Lyra. The inevitable fight that was coming, not including the Afterlife and their impatience with me for not having finished the mission.

"No, I don't," I agreed. A smidge of guilt ran through me for being unwilling to listen to him that night, and for avoiding him just about any other time we were near each other, but how else was I supposed to take it when he said another woman's name after claiming me? Especially the name of his deceased mate?

"Don't beat yourself up too much," Ezra said quietly.

"I won't." He gave me a look. "I mean it. I've got a lot on my plate right now, and I'm happy that's not what he meant—really—but I'm not going to lose sleep over it when we've got things to deal with that are way more important than my love life."

"I'd say that's debatable."

"Not really—"

"The angel," Ezra said. "He looked like your ex. Sounded like him."

I tilted my chin back, looking at the ceiling. "It's not possible," I said eventually.

"If it looks like a duck and quacks like a duck—"

"Not this time," I said. "There's got to be something I'm missing here, but it's truly *not possible* that it was my ex-husband."

Ezra narrowed his eyes, striding forward. "How do you know for certain?"

"Because—"

The clock ticked as it hit seven o'clock. Dorian sifted in instantly, followed by Tristan with Rya. Next came Rava with Roman, who dropped him off and then went back for Caitlin and Roxanne.

Ezra clapped his hands together, rubbing them in anticipation.

"It's a full house tonight," he said. "Feel free to help yourselves to food and drinks, but heads up, there's no alcohol in the apartment. Roxanne is only bringing what's necessary for Jules."

"Good," Dorian commented. "She doesn't need it." He looked pointedly at me. I stuck my tongue out in reply. I know, very mature.

"Why do you think I don't have any?" Ezra responded, surprising the hell out of me.

I turned my affronted face on him, and he winked, not giving a solitary fuck.

I was definitely regretting that blow job right now.

I should've bitten his dick instead.

Ezra choked on a laugh, clearly hearing my train of thought. I flipped him off as I slid over the edge of the stool. Roman stood off to the side, surveying the situation with stormy blue eyes and hunched shoulders.

He appraised me as I walked up to him and angled my head toward the hallway. Getting the gist, he followed me out of the room. I escorted him down the hall, away from prying eyes and ears even though it would be impossible to escape them all.

My room is soundproof, Ezra said telepathically.

Thanks for that.

I took Roman to the bedroom, hoping he couldn't smell what happened earlier. If he could, his face gave nothing away. He stood at the far end of the bed, watching me as I closed the door.

"We should talk about what happened . . . that night," I started. "I recently realized that I might have been hasty in refusing to listen to you."

"Ezra told you," he said, clearly not thrilled about the idea.

I bit the inside of my cheek and nodded. "Only a little bit. He told me it wasn't what I thought, and that I needed to come to you about it."

Roman sighed, his shoulders sagging, but whether it was from relief or feeling defeated, I wasn't sure. "Normally I'd want to rip his fangs out for interfering in our relationship." He scratched the back of his head, rolling his neck. "In this case, I should probably thank the bastard."

I gave him a wry smile. "What happened that night, Roman? Why did you call me Maya—or at the very least—why did you say her name when you were still *inside me*?"

His expression changed, dropping in shame, but he didn't look away or back down.

"I never meant to say her name. I wasn't thinking of her in that way, or imagining you were Maya. I just—we mated. Fully. I marked you. I fucked you—and it was everything that I never thought I'd have or feel again. It was *more*. What I feel for you is different from what I felt for Maya, but not any less. If anything, I felt guilty because these feelings I have for you are possessive and territorial and bestial in a way I wasn't with her." He exhaled a heavy breath. "I loved Maya, but it was the kind of love you have from being raised with someone and falling in love with them for the first time. I don't want to call it puppy love, because that disrespects her memory and the life we shared—but I can't help but feel like I didn't love her the way she truly deserved—the way I love you."

My mouth fully dropped open.

Speechless.

That was my name.

"You don't have to say it back. I'd rather you didn't until you feel it too. I just want you to understand what happened that night wasn't regret or me using you to replace her. I was caught up in all the emotions of being mated again and the realizations I was only just starting to piece together for myself."

Still struggling with how to respond but not wanting him to feel rejected, I walked up and pressed my lips to his. Roman melted beneath my touch. His rough hands grasped me around the waist, lifting me clear off the ground so he could kiss the hell out of me.

I wrapped my legs around his body and a chuckle slid from his beautiful lips.

"As sexy as you are, and as much as I've missed you—I can smell what you and Ezra were up to. I'm not interested in a quickie or fucking you on the same bed."

"Maybe one day you'll both fuck me in the same bed," I murmured playfully against his lips. His breath hitched, and I smirked. "But you're right. The others are probably here by now."

He slid me down his body until my feet touched the floor. While the wounds were still healing—for both of us it would seem—he'd managed to renew my fragile trust in him and make it even stronger than it was before.

Voices from the living room washed over me as soon as we opened the door, and the scent of the bloody mary Roxanne made for Jules reached my nose. Most everyone was seated on or around the giant sectional. A mirror leaned over the flat screen, balancing on the mantelpiece, and bracing against the wall.

I walked around to the front and kneeled to grab the drink off the coffee table. Roman took a seat between Roxanne and Caitlin, Rava making room for him by sitting on her partner's lap.

"Okay, I'm going to call Jules and we can see if she's found Lyra. If she has, we come up with a plan to separate her from the—"

The air shifted around me, and I stopped.

Everyone bristled with hostility, jumping up in reaction to whatever was behind me. I followed their gazes to just over my shoulder and slowly turned around.

The drink slipped from my fingers. Glass shattered and the bloody mary pooled around our feet like blood.

Duke stood before me, his friendly smile lighting up the room. "How's it going, kiddo?"

I threw my arms around him, blinking rapidly to stop the water that was building up in my tear ducts from falling down my face. Elated as I might be, I had a reputation to protect.

Clearly. I sniffed.

Duke hugged me back, letting out a boisterous laugh. When I released him, the tension in the room eased, but it wasn't exactly what I'd call friendly.

"Ummm, Fury, who's this?" Roxanne asked.

"This," I turned back to them, "is Duke. He's my oldest and dearest friend."

Duke snorted, slinging his arm around my shoulder. "We died a half second apart. Fury here kept me company until my beautiful wife and daughters passed on many years later." Roman and Dorian visibly relaxed upon seeing that we were very much in the only-friends category, despite being close.

"I'm happy to meet you. Fury's unintentionally told me quite a bit," Ezra said, sticking his hand out.

Duke took it, giving him a firm shake. "You must be Ezra. Your telepathy definitely threw the Afterlife for a loop. I've been saying for years the poltergeists have gotten lax."

"You're telling me," I huffed. Fucking useless was more like it.

"We've heard all about the poltergeists and issues with Fury's mission. I have to say, it almost seems like someone in the Afterlife wanted her to fail with all the things we've encountered," Dorian said slowly.

Duke nodded, his jovial expression turning muted. "You're not the only one who thought so. That's actually why I'm here. I started looking into things. The prophecy. Why Fury was chosen. Her history. Whatever I could get my hands on to try to see if she'd ever unintentionally had encounters with an angel."

My chest thundered. "And?"

He shook his head. "It's not good, kid. Upper Management has kept *a lot* of shit under wraps—"

"The angel," I said, gripping his forearm. "Tell me about him. Who is he? Why is he after me?"

Duke gave me a sad fucking smile that made my stomach bottom out.

"You might want to sit down for this one—"

"Tell me," I insisted.

"Azrael," Duke said softly. "The archangel of death. The wearer of a thousand faces."

I frowned. "I've never met Azrael. Not once—"

"But you have," Duke said softly. "You were married to him."

I reeled back, feeling the color leach from my face. "No-no—that can't—I extinguished him," I said in an angry whisper. Anxiety and adrenaline raced through me. "I watched the records. He died of a heart attack at fifty-two. They were going to let him in. He wasn't even going to be punished. I—I killed his soul, Duke. There's no coming back from that. For anyone."

Duke shook his head slowly. "Baby girl, you killed the wrong man. You married John Adams, but Azrael took John's place over most of the time you two were married."

Sound warbled in and out. I'd killed the wrong . . . *no*. It couldn't be . . .

"I don't understand," I muttered. "I . . . why?"

He placed his hand over mine as I held onto his arm firmly. "Azrael was sent to kill you. He deviated from his mission, but Upper Management had been turning a blind eye to his exploits for centuries. Until you got pregnant with his child . . . children from the Afterlife are forbidden, Fury. Exterminated when they're found without question or compassion."

I stumbled, reaching blindly for something to hold me up. Ezra was there. He caught me by the waist as my legs shook, threatening to give out. "I-I don't understand. Why was he sent for me? I was just a girl . . . no one. Why was he sent to kill me?"

Nothing on this world or the next could have prepared me for his next words.

"You weren't a no one. You were . . . forbidden. An abomination. A descendant of angels."

To be continued. . .

BLACK SWAN

To Uncle Chris
This world was too cruel for you.
If there's an afterlife, I hope you've found happiness in it.
-Kel

To my kids
You're my everything.
-AJ

The capacity for friendship is God's way of apologizing for our families.

Jay McInerney, *The Last of the Savages*

HADES

GOOD GOD, ARE YOU HERE AGAIN? YOU CAN'T REMEMBER WHAT HAPPENED, can you? I suppose you were expecting me this time around. Your memory is as bad as Fury's.

Okay, fine. I'll fill you in.

Where did we leave off?

Fury managed to get bit by her lover boys, and she was turned into some sort of majestic hybrid. Majestic might be a bit of a stretch. She still trips over her own feet. I guess you can majestically face-plant into the ground.

She started off in book two as a demon-shifter-vampire-fae. What does that mean? Well, her mates want to know too. The fun part about that is that no one knows. She finally spills the beans about who she was and what she was doing there on Earth. You know, the part where she's a demon that's come to rehabilitate them since they're prophesied to end the world? Yeah, that part. Ezra knew because he's the mind reader. Don't forget that tidbit. The other two were upset she'd kept that secret. Communication and honesty are important in relationships. But what would I know? I'm just a crow.

While our friend, Duke, searches for answers about what Fury is and why this mission has gone to absolute shit, Fury reaches out to someone that lives between worlds.

In the mirror realm.

You may know her as Bloody Mary.

She prefers to be called Jules.

Jules has access to all mirrors in the world. She's agreed to look for answers when Fury summons her.

In the meantime, Fury starts developing certain powers, and none of it makes any sense. Is our Fury graceful? Of course not. She starts haphazardly sifting in her sleep. She's bleeding from her nose and ears, fainting at random. And mysterious feathers are appearing. No, they weren't mine.

Why is this all important?

She's a hybrid. Weren't you listening?

Dorian teaches her how to sift, though she's absolutely shite at it. She was sifting objects to herself rather than sifting herself to locations. Although she was really good at slamming into things, much to my amusement.

They had their way of working that out and I am *not* sharing the details of that scene here. Go back and read it if you're thirsty.

What about all the bleeding? Fury has to be a special snowflake. She doesn't need blood like a vampire does. Nope. She needs to *give* blood. Ezra is good at being the recipient of that. You know, it works for them, but that bond isn't fully complete yet.

Fury fulfilled the mate bond with Roman and she accepted a mark from him. They have their thing going now.

As far as the mate bond goes, Dorian isn't willing to until she makes the choice to stay.

Now, in regard to shifting, that part is truly a work of art. See, Lyra —wait. I forgot to tell you about Lyra.

So Dorian's daughter is awake now, and let me tell you, that girl is a mess. She's under the influence of this angel, who at the time, we didn't know much about. Really. Who is this guy? What's his motive? Why's he such a dick?

Lyra's causing problems left and right, and she kills a good number of people. Shifters, mostly. Lyra grabs hold of Fury in a fight and sifts her to Avalon, where she Sparta kicks her off a cliff.

But not before the angel appears, wearing Fury's ex-husband's face. You know, the guy that killed her in her mortal life, beating her to death? Charmer.

Yours truly comes to the rescue, but she couldn't sift, and I couldn't really lift her.

So what happens?

She *shifts*.

Into a white raven.

And it was glorious.

Seriously, go back and read that chapter. It was fantastic, if I do say so myself.

Right, so back to story progress.

Lyra is being protected by an amulet given to her by the rogue angel, and no one can track her except Jules. Our girl in the mirror becomes a key player in this race to save the world.

Fury has an idea of how to cancel this amulet out. And she sends me back to the Afterlife to steal it. From Jake's office. (Jake is her Afterlife Resources caseworker, remember?) FFS.

Now we have a couple of things to figure out.

Number one, we need to neutralize Lyra. That's a big damn deal. But how do we do that?

Number two, why does this angel have this grand desire to kill Fury?

We all meet up at the end to figure out problem number one so that we can eventually solve problem number two.

And this whole time, the clock is ticking to the end of the world. No pressure.

Surprise! Duke shows up. *From the Afterlife*. And he brings some weird news.

The angel is none other than Azrael, the Archangel of Death.

Who also happened to be masquerading as Fury's husband while she was alive. Her real husband, John Adams, he never did those things to her. Poor dude was innocent.

Why, though?

What would cause Azrael to torment Fury in life, and then search for her in death?

She's an abomination.

A descendent of angels.

Dun dun dun.

What does that mean, you ask?

I'm not going to tell you, lazy ass. This is the part where you take over. I've done my part.

The setting where we left off?

Ezra's apartment.

Cast?

Duke: Dead dude from the Afterlife. Friend o' Fury's. Guardian of the portal to Earth.

Jules: Bloody Mary. Poltergeist. She lives in a mirror.

Tristan: Dorian's second. A fae. Pretty sure he and Rya banged for a while.

Rya: Witch that's almost as old as Dorian. Super powerful. Maybe a little dramatic. She and Dorian put Lyra into stasis a thousand years ago.

Dorian: An old fae asshole.

Ezra: A kink-crazed bloodsucking vampire asshole.

Roman: A wolf-shifter-thing with a growling-problem asshole.

Rox: The wolf-shifter-thing's much more tolerable sister. Great hair.

Hades: The most glorious specimen of wit, wisdom, intelligence, and humility that the Afterlife has ever had to contend with.

All right. Read on, people.

Tick tock.

CHAPTER 1
FURY

THERE WERE SOME THINGS IN LIFE—AND DEATH, APPARENTLY—THAT WERE best delivered with a strong drink.

One of those being that my ex-husband—the same man that beat me for kicks, tortured me in my mortal life, and ultimately killed me—was an archangel.

Not just any archangel. The Angel of Death.

That gem was followed up with learning he was sent to kill me because somehow, in my human life, I was the descendent of an angel.

I wanted to call bullshit. Would have called it. But I couldn't. I knew for a fact that angels were anything but angelic. The images humankind had conjured were far from the truth, and that could be said of everything that happened when one died. I wasn't immune to being surprised either, as luck would have it. I'd spent a hundred years thinking I knew how things worked. Assuming I understood the inner workings of what people called Hell. But in the last month alone, I'd had everything about my life and my afterlife turned upside down.

I died, then became a demon. Demon magic wasn't supposed to work with supe magic, yet now I was the only walking, talking, demon-shifter-fae-vampire—and evidently now angel-hybrid in existence. As far as we knew.

I was pretty sure none of that would fit on a business card.

One thing I'd come to realize was the more you think you know, the more you need to learn—and I don't know a damn thing about my life, or past life.

And my mates wouldn't even let it all sink in with a gin and tonic to numb the shock.

Fuckers.

I was seriously regretting that blow job I gave Fangs before this get-together.

A dark chuckle behind me broke the silence. Everyone in the room looked at Ezra like he was crazy, but I knew he wasn't responding to what Duke said.

"Only you would be thinking about how pissed you are at me for depriving you of liquor right now."

I pressed my lips together as Roxanne let out a sigh, clearly not amused.

I turned around to face Ezra, and he released me from his hold. "Just this once, I'm giving you a pass for intruding in on my thoughts and being so blatant about it, and only because I appreciate the distraction." I gave his dick a pointed look and lifted an eyebrow, making my meaning clear. *Next time you can take care of that with your hand.*

His lips twisted in feigned amusement.

In truth, my thoughts being listened to were the least of my concerns, but it gave me a moment to breathe. To process. Even if only for a moment, I appreciated it. Truly.

"You said Fury is a descendent of angels," Dorian said, apparently not needing the same amount of time as I did to recover. "What exactly does that mean?"

"The best place to start for that answer is at the beginning." Duke sighed. He gazed at me with a sad smile and squeezed my forearm. "Believe me now about taking a seat?"

I dipped my head in acknowledgement as Dorian sat, taking the only space on the couch available. He reached for my waist, pulling me down on his lap. I went easily, my back falling against his chest as he caged me in with one arm, letting the other fall to my thigh.

He wasn't the PDA sort. Out of all my mates, I'd have expected this from him the least. Under normal circumstances, I'd have questioned it. But right now, I had a feeling him touching me was as much for my comfort as it was for his security.

More so than Ezra or Roman, Dorian seemed to struggle with the idea of me leaving—by choice or otherwise. Hearing about a murderous sadist that wanted to kill me twice over? Probably a bit triggering, not that he'd show it through the cold mask he presented to the world.

"So about this beginning," Roman said, crossing his arms and looking at Duke.

"There's really no way to break into this easily. A thousand years ago, Azrael was caught breeding with humans," Duke started.

"When you say breeding . . ." I let my words trail off, not entirely ready to finish that sentence aloud.

"I don't know if it was consensual or not. Just as I don't know if he was doing it because he enjoyed it, or if he was breeding for a purpose. He'd created scores of half-angel children, generations upon generations. The Archangel Michael found out, and it was his duty to bring that knowledge to the other seven archangels. They unanimously ordered the immediate extinction of Azrael's entire lineage." Duke paused, taking a breath before continuing. "His punishment for putting Afterlife magic into the living world was that he had to carry out the execution of each and every one of his creations, all while Michael and the remaining seven watched."

My lips parted in shock, and I heard Rava and Caitlin gasp.

Oh my god.

I couldn't imagine . . . well I could, but only because he'd killed my baby before it was even born. Still, that was a thousand years—give or take—between the Azrael I met in my life and the Azrael that willingly created children. What was he like then? Did he laugh and enjoy it as he murdered them one by one?

Something told me he didn't.

"Is Fury," Dorian paused, and his hand tensed on my leg. What he was about to ask hit me, and with it came another wave of nausea. "Is she one of his descendants?"

Duke grimaced and shook his head. "Not that I know of. After the mass killing of his line, Azrael didn't father more children—at least as far as the person who wrote this was aware. If anything, the texts seem to suggest something in him changed. While children from the Afterlife were rare, they still happened on occasion. All the angels broke the rules. But there was a violent reversal in his viewpoint, and it was almost as if he declared himself the executioner. He tracked down every angel's hidden descendants and took them out. It was like he hated them and found joy in killing them."

"So having to murder his own line turned him into a sadist?" I asked, my voice terse and unforgiving. I might be able to see the gray in most things, but this was still the man that abused me. If he was sent to kill me, that's bad enough. But to spend years beating me? Deceiving me? To kill *our* baby while he stood over me and laughed? No. I wouldn't—I couldn't empathize with that.

"I'm not sure. I don't know who he was before, but he clearly was a sadist after."

"How did you find this out?" Ezra asked, eyes sharpening in a way that told me he already knew, and this rabbit hole was only getting deeper.

"I read through the journals of past archangels. Uriel, Gabriel, and Selaphiel. They all died within the last thousand years, and so did Michael—though he didn't have a journal in the Divine Libraries."

"That's . . . archangels don't just die. They've been around longer than living memory. They're eternal." I grit my teeth. "How does no one think this is odd?"

"Azrael's infractions weren't public knowledge; neither were the deaths of the archangels. It still isn't."

"But you read their journals in the Divine Libraries," I said in confusion. "How can that—" I met Duke's gaze and saw a slight twitch in his cheek. A shift in his eyes as his lips pressed together weakly. "Which library?" I asked quietly. "Which library did you read them in?"

He let out a long sigh before answering. "Bibliotheca Infernum."

"Only Upper Management has access to that library."

"Fury . . ." The slight pleading tone said it all.

I closed my eyes and turned my cheek. "You're Upper Management," I said. Part of me was hurt he hadn't said anything. The rest of me knew the facts: who was and wasn't part of the elite was a closely guarded secret. "I suppose it makes sense. They wouldn't leave just anyone in charge of the only portal to Earth. No. They'd need someone they could trust. That wouldn't be persuaded. It makes so much sense, but—" I broke off, because even as I pieced it together aloud, there was still one problem. "Upper Management gave me this mission. They assigned me because they thought I could fix things. They—you—did you know they were my mates when you sent me?"

"No," Duke said immediately. "I had no idea. If someone knew, that was kept from me, but to my knowledge, they had no idea. You wouldn't have been chosen. Them being your mates has complicated things. We never would have sent you if we'd realized." The arm around my waist tightened. I could sense Dorian's unhappiness over that declaration, and across the room, Roman let out a growl in response, equally as displeased.

They were irked someone would keep me from them knowingly . . . yeah, to say they weren't a fan was an understatement.

"And their previous mates? Did you know about the angels killing them when I brought that to you, and you told me that was a big accusation?"

"I didn't know. Not until after," he said, somewhat quieter. "I looked into it when you came to me. What you said, it made sense, but it also made me start to think something wasn't right. Too much was going wrong and was unaccounted for, and I realized someone in Upper Management was sweeping things under the rug. While angels are given cases that sometimes require euthanasia, it's rare. That it would happen to all three of you," he said, looking to each of my mates, "was no coincidence. So I dug deeper, and that's when I found out Azrael had been left in charge of this case for the last twelve hundred years. It was only recently that other individuals were brought in because the prophecy was getting closer."

I felt slightly better knowing he hadn't meant to betray me, and that he didn't lie to my face when I asked the important questions. I pushed aside my hurt. I didn't have time to think about it. Not right now.

"So Azrael killed their mates and also fucked with Lyra in the process." The hand on my thigh pressed into my skin, holding tight enough at the sound of his daughter's name that the mark was sure to bruise. I put my hand atop his, squeezing it just as tight. "He killed me after spending years torturing me because he apparently hates descendants born of the Afterlife now." That was a lot to unwrap, and I still wasn't sure how to piece the information together. I took a deep breath, trying to figure out what else there was to consider. "What about the archangels? Four have died in a thousand years. How did it happen?"

"Michael and Azrael got into it some three hundred years ago and dueled. Azrael extinguished him. Not surprising that Azrael held a grudge. The other three are more complicated. They all chose to be extinguished."

My mouth dropped open.

"Wait. Three archangels chose to end their existence, and no one thought that was strange?"

Duke's brows scrunched together in disappointment. "Archangels are the top of Upper Management. Everything else comes down from them. When one dies, the only people that could look into that are other archangels."

"And magically, almost half of the nine died in the past thousand years. That's probably a good motivator to keep the others quiet. If Azrael were capable of somehow causing that, who's to say what he could do to them too."

Duke nodded. "Which is why I'm here. Something's got to be done about Azrael, but it's clear the others aren't going to step in. Upper Management is pretending that nothing is off. Meanwhile, the end of the world looms closer, and that prediction hasn't changed. You're going to need all the help you can get if we want to prevent this prophecy and stop Azrael from doing whatever he's planning."

I nodded absentmindedly. Was this it? The fate of the world was in the hands of my mates, my dead friend, and me—an abomination with a giant target on her back. This was my army to fight against a prophecy and the Archangel of Death. It was a tagline to a bad movie.

It'd almost be funny if it weren't true. We had no choice but to succeed on both counts. If we managed to stop the world from imploding, but we didn't stop Azrael—he'd come for each and every one of us. No one was safe from him. A terrible thought slammed into me. "What about Henrietta? The girls?" I asked, jerking my head up to look at him.

Duke smiled, clearly having already thought of that. "They're hidden. No one on Earth or the Afterlife will find them," he assured me.

I lifted an eyebrow. No one in either place? That was a hefty claim. I wanted to know more, but I didn't expect him to reveal it in front of everyone. He'd tell me when he was ready.

"Good," I said. I hated to think they'd suffer in any way because of this.

"So now you know what I know. Hades has filled me in on where you are at with Lyra, but now is the time to fill me in on anything else."

"Exactly how much did Hades tell you?" I asked, looking over at the crow.

Duke gazed back and forth between us. "Judging by the looks you two are sharing, I have a feeling he didn't tell me everything."

I cleared my throat. "Well, I had an idea for how to—"

"I stole the starlight orb out of Jake's office," Hades interjected.

"Way to ease him into that knowledge, feathers," I snapped.

He shrugged his wings. "Time isn't exactly on our side here. Get to the point."

"Still. There was time to explain it."

"Tick tock," he said in response. I rolled my eyes.

Turning to Duke, I met his stare of shock. "You stole the starlight orb from the head of Afterlife Resources?"

I stood up, removing myself from Dorian's lap. "Yeah. That. I needed it. I have a theory on how it can cancel out the Afterlife magic that has a hold on Lyra. She's Dorian's daughter. I won't let Azrael hurt her anymore. So we're here to figure out a way to separate Lyra from him."

"All right," he said. "What's your plan?"

A small smile graced my lips. Duke was a true friend. He didn't question me. Shocked a little at the boldness of it, maybe, but he trusted me. If we were going to pull this off, I needed that trust more than anything.

"Jules?" I called toward the mirror. I didn't have a bloody Mary since it was all over the floor, but I'd make it up to her. I figured she would understand why I dropped it once she was up to speed on the details.

The mirror on the mantel warbled and shimmered. Jules' chestnut brown hair looked misty and far away before the image of her face came into view.

"You rang?"

CHAPTER 2
FURY

A few hushed whispers circled the room, which wasn't that much of a surprise. How many people had really seen a girl come to life in a mirror? I waved at her and started to speak, but Jules cut me off before I got a word in.

"It took you all long enough to finish talking. I've been waiting here forever. Had it not been for the really juicy information, I'd have taken a nap."

I stared into the hazel eyes of the young poltergeist. Well, young in appearance. She was anything but. "You heard everything?"

She flicked her long hair over her shoulder. "You mean the bit about Azrael being your ex, or the part where we only have five archangels left and we have no idea why?"

My expression flattened. "That about covers it."

"Then yeah, I heard. You invited me. You were late. I just kind of hung around until you were ready for me."

I huffed a laugh. "Okay, well, I'm ready for you. Let me introduce you to everyone."

I pointed around the room as I introduced her, purposefully skipping over Hades. I still didn't know what transpired between those two at one time, but I really wanted to find out. I would eventually.

First, I had to worry about a rogue angel and a dangerous fae. "You've met Tristan and Dorian, and this is—"

"Hey Duke," she said. "Long time no see."

"Jules," he said and dipped his head.

"You two know each other?" I asked.

"Does that really surprise you?" she asked me.

"Uh, yeah. It really does. Why wouldn't it?" I said, looking between them.

Duke grinned and his eyes twinkled. "Upper Management always viewed Jules as an enemy and a threat. I never did. I have my own way of doing things. When I learned about her history with the Afterlife, I sought her out to hear her side of the story. We're friends."

"Mm hmm." My hummed response was filled with skepticism. There were an awful lot of secrets going on. But if they trusted me, I needed to trust them too. "Fine. But I want details later," I said.

Jules waved me off, but I saw the hint of a smile playing on her lips. "So what's the grand plan you wanted to share with everyone tonight?" She frowned when she looked down at the floor to see the shards of glass and her drink pooled on the tile.

I ran my fingers through my hair. "Well, it's not so much a grand plan as it is an idea. I figured we could hash out the finer details together," I started. "So, the orb we have, its magic source is from the Afterlife, and it's significantly stronger than what is protecting Lyra right now. That amulet she wears is made of supernatural magic. Ours should be able to break through the hold Azrael's amulet has on her. Once we do that, we have a small window of time to protect her and stop him from manipulating her."

I'd felt infinitely more confident before Duke's truth bomb was dropped. Beforehand, it was getting Lyra to safety, then deal with the angel, then work on the reason I was sent to Earth to begin with, though I figured parts two and three were intertwined a bit. Those were the bullet points of my plan. Finding out who the angel was complicated things.

But did it really? The more I focused on that question, the more I realized the answer was no. Not really. What it did do was complicate my emotions. Which was further complicated by my past and my trauma. But the mission was still the same. The base facts of the case were still the same. Someone was fucking with me and trying to make me fail. That wasn't new. The *who*. That was new. I knew deep down the *why* was only the beginning. All of those revelations should help guide me to finding a way to stop it all, right?

"I'm keeping an eye on her. If she moves, I'll know," Jules said, breaking my concentration.

Ezra waved his hand, bringing the attention his way. "How do we use this orb you have?"

I looked at Hades knowingly. "All we need is to be close to her. Really close. I need its power source to negate the one around her neck. Considering she really wants to hurt me, I think that'll be the easy part."

"She's the bait," Hades added, angling his head in my direction.

"Like hell you are—"

"I'm not asking your permission, Ezra." I looked at my mates, making sure each of them made eye contact with me. I wanted everyone in the room to understand. "I'm not asking for anyone's permission. Lyra desperately wants to hurt me. She blames me for what is happening to her again. She threw me off a cliff. It's going to catch her off guard the moment she sees me, and that is the moment we strike. It's an opportunity we can't pass up."

Silence filled the room, but the tension was palpable. Roxanne fidgeted, pulling at a string on her shirt. Dorian pinched the bridge of his nose, and Ezra paced the room. Duke looked uncomfortable, but he was listening and learning. It was Roman that surprised me the most.

"She's right."

I jerked my head in his direction, raising an eyebrow in question.

He shrugged. "I don't like it. Not even a little bit. But it's a good plan. She won't expect to see you, and if that stuns her long enough for us to make our move, then so be it." His words weren't forced, but his voice sounded thick. He hated putting me in harm's way.

Ezra glared at him. "You can't be serious."

"I am. We all want the same things, right? So let's do what needs to be done to get there. She's our best shot at this."

A part of me warmed inside knowing that Roman was going against his wolf instinct. I needed him on my side.

My two other mates looked at each other and begrudgingly nodded.

"Good. It'll have to be timed and ready. We need to either lure her away—which I don't know how to do without dickhead tagging along—or we need to show up to her when Azrael isn't around. The former seems more likely," I said. "We run the risk of him showing up no matter which way we go."

"Then what?" Roman asked. He looked at Dorian and nodded respectfully before continuing, though I know he was hesitant to continue. "Her source of power isn't that necklace. You said it's only protecting her. She's incredibly strong and gifted in her own right, and she's—no offense—completely unhinged."

"Rya and I will be there to put her back into stasis," Dorian said, a hint of sadness leaking into his tone.

"Kelly has offered to help. It may take all three of us to put her back down," Rya added. "We don't know how much her powers have grown—"

"No," I said, stepping forward. "She's not going back into stasis."

A cacophony filled the room as everyone voiced their disagreement and questioned my reasoning—and sanity—all at once. I crossed my arms and breathed in deeply, waiting for it to die down.

Hades let out an obnoxiously loud squawk that left the shifters covering their sensitive ears. When the room quieted, he looked at me and whispered, "This had better be good."

I walked toward Dorian and looked up at him, craning my neck back in defiance. "You will not do it again."

"Fury, you don't know—"

"I don't know what? Don't know what she's capable of?" I asked, lifting my shirt to remind him of the wound she left on my abdomen. I pointed to Rava. "I don't know how she can manipulate people into hurting the ones they love? Or do you mean I don't know what her being in stasis has done to you for a thousand years?" I shook my head when he tried to speak again. "No, what we don't know is what stasis is doing to *her*. You don't know if you'll ever find a way to fix her broken mind. What I do know is that she'll never get better if she's put into a dream sleep. She's not at peace, Dorian. Convince me otherwise and I'll agree to letting you, Rya, and Kelly put her back into stasis, but it better be a compelling argument."

Dorian's shoulders tensed and he turned his neck, stretching as he considered his next move. "This isn't going to work."

I reached out, resting my hand on his arm gently. "It has to. Tell me how forced stasis is better than giving her death."

Dorian flinched at my words and shook his head. "I *will* find a way to—"

"When?" I asked. "*When* will you find a way to help her? It's been a millennium. You can't heal someone's emotional trauma while they're in a coma. Her mind has been shattered. He's played with her psyche. He broke her. Twisted and manipulated and hurt her. You can't fix that unless she's awake."

Trust me, I know. A hundred years later and it still haunts me, I said to myself.

"I need a moment with you," he said, signaling to Ezra as he was heading into his room. He grabbed my hand, sifting us there. One moment we were in the living room with an audience, the next we were in the bedroom, filled with privacy and soundproof walls.

"What the hell, Dorian?" I said, taking a step back.

"She has to go back into stasis, Fury," he said abruptly. "She can't die."

I stumbled backwards. "What? How . . . how do you know that?" I whispered, fear taking over my voice. "Did you try . . . to—" I couldn't finish. The mere thought that he'd possibly tried to kill her made me feel sick.

Dorian's brows creased deeply, and he shook his head. "Never. I would never." He sighed, his features softening into sadness yet again. "She tried to take her own life. Many times. Her pain was so great, the torture she was under was tremendous. She must've thought it was her only way. That's when she truly became what she is now. She couldn't break free in her mind, and whatever she was enduring caused her to crack."

"Dorian, I . . . I'm sorry." I sighed, now understanding another layer of Dorian's grief. I looked at the ground, thinking about Lyra on the roof. Worried that Roman would kill her. Seeing her in the ballroom, worried that Ezra would end up murdering Dorian's only child. "Why didn't you tell me earlier?"

"I'm telling you now," he said simply.

I wanted to argue. Remind him that keeping secrets did nothing for us. I wanted him to stop holding those things back. I wanted him to trust me. When all those thoughts came rushing through my head, a little voice reminded me this was him trusting me. This was him opening up and sharing a painful truth. As he said, he was telling me now, and that was what mattered.

I reached out, squeezing his arm, then wrapping myself around him in a hug. I didn't know what else to do or say. When I let him go, I looked up and met his gaze. "I'm sorry you both had to go through that." I turned my head, looking at the bedroom door. "I don't want to drag this out for you, but we have to tell them. They're in this fight too."

He nodded. "I know. I wanted to tell you first."

I pressed my lips together in a tight smile, whispering, "thank you," as he sifted us back into the living room.

I met the curious stares filling the room when we reappeared. Ezra's expression stayed flat, but I could see the twitch in his cheek as he read my thoughts, seeing the conversation that had taken place. He closed his eyes and breathed out for a moment. As respectfully as I could, I shared that Lyra couldn't be killed. The details of how it was known didn't matter. If Dorian wanted to share that later, he could. Rya's eyes told me she knew the missing information. After all, she was there a thousand years ago.

I turned in a circle, looking at everyone in the room. "I know you'll think I'm crazy here, but I refuse to accept stasis as the only way. We need another option. Anyone have anything? Something? A tiny spark of an idea?"

I was greeted with nothing but silence. Roxanne wouldn't meet my gaze. Tristan looked at the floor. Rava and Caitlin looked at each other. Everyone chose to focus on anything but me.

I groaned, running my fingers through my hair while I paced with heavy feet.

I stopped in front of the fireplace, turning my back on Jules to address everyone.

"We can't do this to her. It's no better than what Azrael is doing to her in the end. That's what he does. He takes away life, and if we capture her just to put her back in stasis, we are doing the exact same thing. She has the right to make choices and the right to live."

I thought of all the things John—Azrael, whatever his name was—had taken from me in life. I'd never known why. I still didn't. Not really. I couldn't save anyone he'd hurt before, but I had the chance to save Lyra. I felt the crushing weight of defeat starting to set in when no one made a suggestion.

"C'mon. We are a group of the most powerful supernaturals in existence, right?" I swung my hand around the room. "We have *four* beings from the Afterlife here, and we can't come up with one idea to subdue a single immortal fae?" I flung my arms up in the air. "Well that's just fucking great, you guys. Just great. If a group with this much power between them can't save one girl, then the world is just fucked," I said, my voice rising as my frustration climbed. "We're all—"

A loud sigh came from behind me before I felt a strong tug on the back of my shirt. My feet lifted off the ground. I was weightless, flying backwards, unsure what was happening.

A feeling like water rushed over my skin and I slammed onto the ground. My equilibrium was off balance, and I felt disoriented. My legs wobbled as I found purchase, trying to steady myself. The hold on my shirt lessened, and I looked to my side, watching as Jules released me.

"Will that work?" she asked.

My mouth fell open. "What in the actual . . ."

"Welcome to the mirror realm."

CHAPTER 3
FURY

I DID A DOUBLE TAKE OF MY SURROUNDINGS.

We were still in Ezra's living room. The mirror was still intact, but instead of being surrounded by my mates, friends, and everyone else that was working with us on the Lyra problem—it was empty.

I reached out, running my fingers over the couch to be sure it was real. "The mirror realm," I repeated. I thought only she could come here. I never expected to be standing on the other side of it with her. "So, what exactly is this place?"

I turned back to Jules, who now stood completely corporeal before me.

"My realm. Or, well, the realm I'm in charge of. No one can enter here without my help."

My lips parted and a sharp rap on the mirror to our left drew my attention. On the other side, Duke leaned forward, his knuckles tapping lightly on the glass. Mischief and amusement danced in his eyes. Behind him, Dorian, Roman, and Ezra had all jumped to their feet. While the former appeared concerned, the latter appeared puzzled, his lips drawn into a thin line and eyes flashing as he tried, and presumably failed, to find me. Roman's fists were clenched, nails sharpening to claws as he breathed heavily, demanding to know where I was.

"Might want to come back before these three lose it," Duke said into the mirror.

I shot a look at Jules. "He isn't weirded out like the rest of them. He knows I'm safe in here."

"Of course he does." She tilted her head to the side. "Where do you think his family is?" She winked at me.

Understanding of exactly what this place was only started to unravel as Jules extended her hand. "Just walk through," she said, touching my lower back and guiding me. "You'll be able to pass."

I took a tentative step and then reached for the glass. As my fingers loomed near, everyone on the other side froze, zeroing in on the movement. I tilted my head.

"They can see us?"

"Only when you're close to it. They couldn't when I pulled you through. Now they can. Like when you call me."

I lifted my eyebrows, taking a second look at Jules. I'd known she had the ability to pass through mirrors, but not how. The idea that she could bring others into her realm . . . it wasn't even a consideration.

My fingers passed through the other side and Ezra was there instantly, grabbing my hand and pulling me through. I phased from one side of the mirror to the other in a blink, landing against his hard chest. I took a couple quick breaths, pulling myself back to look at them. Each of my mates wore an eerily similar expression of fierce disapproval over what just happened.

"What the fuck was that?" Dorian was the first to speak.

Jules was the one to answer.

"That," she said in a singsong voice, "is the solution to your problem."

His eyebrows lifted slightly, dubious. "They couldn't hear us on the other side, could they?" I asked her.

"Nope," she said, popping the p. "They only see or hear us when we're within a foot of the glass, and that's only if I want them to see. Further than that and it's just their own reflection staring back."

"Care to tell me how you did that?" Ezra said, voice stiff. He gripped my upper arms like a lifeline, not easing up in the slightest. "I couldn't *hear* you. At all. There's nowhere on this planet that I can't—"

"That's because my realm isn't on this planet," Jules said. "It exists parallel to your world. It looks the same. Operates the same, mostly."

"Parallel?" Roman repeated. "Like a parallel universe?"

"I guess that's the best way to describe it. I was in Ezra's living room, only it was just me and Jules there. I could see you too," I told him. "On the other side of the mirror it's just like here, down to every detail." I turned, looking at her. "Is your world uninhabited?" I asked her.

"Not quite," Jules said as her lips twisted. "But close enough. Your girl will be safe there. Azrael won't be able to reach her, and she won't be able to reach anyone else."

"It won't work." Dorian sighed. I glanced over at him as he ran a hand over his jaw, his shoulders tense. "All Lyra has to do is sift. It would only confine her until she figured that out."

Shit. He was right.

Just when a seed of hope was starting to sprout, like we'd *finally* found one fucking solution to a problem, reality came to squash it.

Still, Jules was smiling, unbothered by his statement.

"She won't be able to sift," Jules said, shaking her head slightly. "Nor glamor. Or use any kind of fae magic at all. Supernatural magic doesn't work in my world. Only Afterlife magic."

I frowned, thinking of how easy it was for me to leave once I was there. "Okay, she can't sift, but couldn't she just walk out as soon as she comes across a mirror?"

Jules smiled, smug as ever. "The only reason you could leave is because I made it so. It's my realm." She wiggled her fingers at me. "Trust me. If I wanted you to stay, you wouldn't have been able to leave."

And just like that, my hope was restored. "She'd basically be a human in your world."

"Mhmm," Jules said. "Not even her fae strength will be of use, but she won't age here because it exists outside of time."

I frowned. "How is that possible? Even the Afterlife exists around time."

Duke cleared his throat, looking to Jules. “Mind if I cut in?”

She waved him on, unbothered. Hades fluffed his feathers, turning his head to look out of the window rather than engage in our conversation.

“The mirror realm is closer to a pocket dimension more than anything else. While nothing ages there, the surroundings shift to keep up with the current time on Earth . In that sense, it’s like a smaller version of the Afterlife—except the only person that’s ever been able to gain access to it is Jules. Humans enter the Afterlife upon death and no longer age, but the world still moves forward in time. It’s the same in the mirror realm.”

I sucked the air between my teeth, adrenaline coursing through me at the possibilities this presented.

Another Afterlife. Of sorts.

“Can people die in this realm of yours?” Dorian asked quietly. “If it suppresses her supernatural magic, and that’s attached to her being immortal . . .”

His expression gave away little to nothing, apart from the solemn way he spoke. What if she became mortal there? She’d attempted to take her life before. Would she do it again? The giddy feeling that was surging through me cooled, knowing what was fueling his question.

“No,” Jules said. “Not by your definition. People cease to exist on Earth, their physical body dying and their soul going to the Afterlife. In the Afterlife, souls carry on in a form of that previous body, but the soul can be extinguished. Neither can happen in my realm, but there is a form of dying, and there are consequences. They’d become incorporeal, like a poltergeist. Unable to regain form. If that happens, they can’t leave my realm. Ever.”

“Why?”

“They end up bonded to the realm, able to flip back and forth, but unable to leave. If Lyra were to somehow die here, she’d be stuck, and there’s nothing I could do about it.”

“But she’d live?” he questioned. “She’d be alive and conscious?”

“Yes,” Jules said slowly, watching him with a sort of sadness I couldn’t understand. “She would live. Forever. As long as Earth exists, so does the mirror realm.”

He fell quiet for a moment. I patted Ezra’s arm, silently urging him to let me go. Reluctantly the vampire loosened his grip but not before pressing a quick kiss to my temple. I turned from him, walking over to Dorian.

"This is our best shot," I said. "With me as bait, Lyra just has to get close enough so I can cancel out the necklace. We get her near a mirror and Jules can pull her through. She won't be able to live normally there, but she won't hurt anyone, and she won't be unconscious. I can work with her. I can't promise that she'll ever be the same as she was. The trauma she's endured . . . it's going to take time. And a lot of it. But I will do everything in my power to help her."

Dorian stared at me. There was something in his eyes, something intense and visceral and desperate. It was vulnerable, and yet strong. I didn't recognize it because I'd never seen that expression on his face. But something told me it was pivotal.

"One condition," he said. "We'll do this your way, but I want one thing at the end."

My chest squeezed. "What?"

"You stay. When this is over and done with, when Lyra is trapped and that fucker is extinguished, you do everything in your power to stay—even if the Afterlife wants you back, even if they try to take you away, *you choose to stay.*"

My mouth felt dry. My throat scratchy. Emotion clogged my windpipe, making it hard to breathe.

For weeks now I'd been avoiding this very question. Making no promises. No commitments. I'd danced the edge of what I'd do, constantly telling myself I'd cross the bridge when I came to it.

But that wasn't enough for him. Dorian wanted me to make a choice, whether or not I'd ever have to act on it. Whether the Afterlife came for me or not. Whether there was even a way back. He wanted me to choose them—choose him.

It was a monumental decision, not one I would have liked to make in front of so many people. Certainly not one without more thinking, then again, this wasn't the first time we'd talked about it. Maybe that was his way. He'd brought it up before to make me think, and now when the chips were down, he was asking me to lay out my cards. He was asking me for my answer.

I wanted his trust, their trust. I wanted their truths and their thoughts and their love, but I constantly held myself back. Giving the pieces that were safe, but not everything.

Dorian told me that things with him wouldn't be in half-measure. I wouldn't be able to dance on the line forever.

Here it was. The moment.

Either I committed to him and the life we had here, to staying, to fixing Lyra, to building something if we made it all through this . . . or I didn't.

For what? Retirement? To be a pawn forever? To be left alone for eternity, even though I had a feeling that wouldn't quite be the case given how much I was learning about Upper Management.

No. I may have wanted that once, but that's only because I couldn't even picture what I had now. I never imagined this future. As far as I knew, it wasn't within my grasp. It wasn't a possibility. That had changed.

I could fail. This could all be for nothing. But I was done being a piece on the board that others moved. I was done with accepting a half-future, and therefore letting Azrael win because I was too scared to care about someone.

I was done fighting fate.

"Okay," I said, my voice cracking. "I'll stay."

Dorian's expression didn't change, but there was an undercurrent of release. A tension that he'd been holding dissipated, and he wasn't the only one. Ezra's presence caressed my mind, and I felt his relief. Roman exhaled, and I knew without a doubt, the wolf inside him was sated. Their mate wasn't leaving them.

Without looking away, Dorian said, "Find Lyra and Azrael. Keep tabs on them. If Fury is going to be bait for this, we need to set the stage."

"Did you have something in mind?" Roman asked.

"I do." Dorian cracked a half-smile, holding my gaze. "I think Fury's decision is cause for a celebration."

I scrunched my eyebrows together and tilted my head, working through his words to decipher the meaning. As realization hit me, I opened my mouth to speak, but Dorian beat me to it.

"Roxanne, are you up for planning an obnoxiously large party?"

She smirked, crossing her arms, and cocking her hip. "What'd you have in mind?"

CHAPTER 4
DORIAN

"A ball?" Fury asked. "That's what you've been working on all night?"

Roxanne shook her head. "A gala. It's different."

Fury sat next to me on the couch in my lounge, leaning forward over the coffee table and flipping through the pages of Roxanne's notes with a frown. "How so? It looks exactly the same."

"It just is, okay? This isn't a ball. You're not Cinderella. The focus is on you and to celebrate you. Not just to dance and show off a dress," she answered with a huff.

Fury looked up, a flat expression resting on her face. "Thanks for clearing that up."

Turning to me, she mouthed, "It's the same thing."

I shrugged. "Perhaps it is." I met Roxanne's annoyed glance and gave a small shake of my head. "However, that's not the point."

"Enlighten me."

I stood up and walked to a table that sat near the window. I picked up a folder and brought it back to Fury, handing it over. "Take a look inside."

I watched her carefully as she opened it, thumbing through the photographs. Pictures of a location. A historic building that had been transformed into a ballet studio years ago. Decorative wooden columns supported the balcony overlooking the center space. Ornate carvings on the banisters and railing showcased the character details that so many older structures boasted. The dark stained wood floors were a stark contrast to the bright light that reflected from the mirrors lining each wall. Her eyebrows raised slightly, and her lips parted as understanding inched across her face.

"It's wall-to-wall mirrors," she whispered, tracing her fingers over the pictures. "It's perfect."

I looked at Roxanne and gave her an approving look. She was quite pleased with herself, putting her hands on her hips and accepting her praise. She'd always been good at these things.

"Rox is working on the invitations already, and Roman and Ezra are pulling every resource into getting this ready," I said, fixing my cufflink while I spoke.

Fury looked up and twisted her lips. "Why all the pomp and circumstance? Can't it just be a party? Send an evite."

I suppressed the urge to laugh as Roxanne cocked an eyebrow at my mate. "I would be offended at the suggestion if we weren't setting a trap. An *evite*," she muttered. "In all seriousness, though, it has to be believable. We don't know who he has control over. You've had how many supes come after you that know your old name? That was all Azrael."

"Okay, fair point," Fury said.

Duke had been sitting in an armchair, silently listening to our exchange until he cleared his throat. "If Azrael hasn't yet figured out that Fury isn't dead, it won't be long before he does."

I pointed at him in agreement. "Duke is right. And I know my daughter. There's no guarantee she'll show up if we don't make it a spectacle. Something this large? She won't be able to ignore the opportunity to show off and destroy everything around you."

"Azrael couldn't resist sending his minions the opening night of the summit ," Fury admitted, nodding along as she talked herself through it out loud. "And Lyra downright enjoyed destroying that ballroom and turning it into a bar fight. She used the chandelier as a damn swing." Fury's face fell and she ran her hands through her hair, the sunlight filtering through the window and catching the deep red and making it almost shimmer. "She also managed to manipulate a surprising number of supernaturals, and some of them ended up dead. We're taking a lot of risks here. I wish there was a way it could be just us," she said.

I sighed. It was a topic that Roman, Ezra, and I had debated all night. We were putting the lives of hundreds on the line for this plan. None of us liked it. I had little in common with the vampire and the shifter, and Fury aside, one thing did remain. We were alphas, and we had a responsibility to our people. We had to protect them. Unfortunately, we were dealing with matters that were far beyond our control. As Fury had said, first we subdue my daughter, then we deal with Azrael and the prophecy. She'd come here with a mission, and that meant we had to put the lives of our people at risk in order to save them. If we failed, everyone died.

Roman and Ezra didn't carry the same weight I did in making any of the decisions we'd agreed upon. I also had a responsibility to Lyra. She was my child. I was there when she came into the world, and I was there every time she tried to take herself out of it. I'd seen the devastation she'd left and the lives and families she'd torn apart, and still I loved her. I'd watched the evolution of a monster, and it shattered me into pieces that would never again be whole. But I never stopped loving her, hoping that I could find a way to save her. The love for a child was truly unconditional.

The fact remained, to protect our mate and to protect our people, we'd have to put them at risk again. All of them.

I shook my head. "We know the risks, and so do those attending." I held my hand up as Fury began to ask another question. "There won't be children. A great number of guests are soldiers and enforcers, and the rest are going to be volunteers, so to speak."

"I'm working on vetting a list that Roxanne gave me," Ezra said, sifting into the room with James. He patted my assistant on the arm, thanking him before walking to the couch and sitting next to Fury. He reached for her hand, grazing his lips over her knuckles, and kissing the top. Then he winked at me.

I stared at the spot on her hand and regretted inviting him. I never was much for sharing.

"It's a solid plan, then," Fury said. "Keep the furniture and everything away from the walls. We'll need to get her close so Jules can grab her. That would be just my luck to get her close enough to it but then get blocked by some giant floral arrangement on a table."

"Of course," Roxanne said. "But if you find yourself in that situation, you can always slap her in the face with a bouquet of flowers. Pretty certain she wouldn't expect that. Might buy you some time," she added with a shrug.

Fury crumbled up a piece of paper and threw it at Rox's head. She dodged to the side and smiled.

The circumstances were grim, but I was pleased they were able to smile in the face of it. It was more than I was able to do.

"Fury will carry the orb. Lyra will go for her, but on the off chance she wants to toy with others first, Fury is the only one that can sift it to someone else," I said.

My mate blew out a breath, no doubt wanting to practice that skill before putting it to a test. I had faith in her abilities. She was far more advanced than she gave herself credit for.

"We have a week until the date," Ezra said, leaning back on the couch. "We've got the guest list, Roman and the pack are handling the setup . They have the numbers to work fast."

"I've arranged a place for Duke to stay as needed," I added. "He'll be on the move but can reach us at any time."

"Hades and I have some digging to do." Duke smiled at her warmly, reassuring her that he was on board with everything. I could see that it mattered to her deeply, though I wasn't entirely sure why. They looked at each other, silently sharing some connection.

"Okay," Fury said after a moment. She rubbed her hands together and looked in my direction. "Where does that leave us?"

My lips curved up to one side. "You're staying with me."

~

Fury and I walked through the hallway after entering the castle on Avalon. Our footsteps echoed off the high ceilings, barely muted by the tapestries lining the walls.

She didn't argue when we told her she'd essentially be in hiding. It wouldn't have mattered if she had. I would always listen to my mate, but I had a feeling she wouldn't have liked our answers if she had chosen to disagree. We'd made the decision without her, and we were firm in it.

Ezra wanted Fury to himself just as much as I did, and Roman wanted more time with Fury to work out whatever issues they were having, but that wasn't my concern. The fact remained that Fury and I could sift, and they couldn't. She could communicate with Ezra from anywhere, but if Lyra showed up, I could sift Fury out of harm's way instantly. It was only temporary. She'd find us again, but it would give us a chance.

Ezra had certainly tried to remind me that Fury could sift herself to safety, but his point was moot. Fury could indeed sift, but she couldn't do it far, and she couldn't do it with a degree of certainty. We'd spent hours practicing her abilities. An entire night of edging her until she finally sifted out of her bindings. It was an unusual method. One that I didn't mind repeating if she were up for it.

Rounding a corner, we came to Fury's bedroom door. I turned the handle and opened it, gesturing for her to go in before me.

She stopped abruptly, pointing to a pale pink dress I had laid out for her. The bodice was a soft, pliable cotton with two thin straps over her shoulders. The skirt was a thick, billowing tulle that would sit at her mid-waist and drop to the floor. "What the hell is that?"

"Rox and I had Kelly make you a mockup dress for the gala," I answered, closing the door behind me. I put my hands in my pockets, dipping my head toward the garment. "She has your measurements on file. This is just a test run. You can change the color."

Her forehead wrinkled as she tipped her head to the side, considering it. "Why do I need a practice dress?"

I huffed a small laugh. "If Roxanne were here, you'd get an earful about it. You know that, don't you?"

"Oh, I learned that lesson already," she muttered with a smile. "But seriously. This isn't a real ball or gala or . . ." She waved her hand haphazardly when she couldn't think of another name.

"Try it on," I suggested. "Roxanne and Kelly ran through some details last night. They want you to be 'battle-ready'—that was the term used, I believe." I shrugged. "They designed it together, but if there needs to be tweaks made, we have more than enough time."

Instead she stared at the dress, looking back and forth between it and me. "I'm going to look like a ballerina." She grimaced and shook her head. "Is this Roxanne's theme, or whatever it is she calls it when she plans for a party?"

I tilted my head back and laughed. Fury did not seem amused. "It was her inspiration, yes, but stop complaining. It has a purpose."

"Ba-ller-in-a," she said slowly, enunciating each syllable. "What about me says delicate and graceful?"

"Literally nothing," I deadpanned, then snapped my fingers.

In an instant, Fury's jeans and T-shirt had been removed, replaced by the dress in question. She glared at me, putting her hands on her hips, preparing to yell at me. Her mouth opened, but nothing came out. I smirked as she looked down, realizing exactly what she was wearing.

She patted herself down, her hands grazing the curve of her body, under her breasts, over her hips, and down to her thighs. I wouldn't complain. I had every desire to do the same, but I kept my hands in my pockets and let her figure out what purpose that particular dress served.

She lifted the tulle skirt that pooled around her, sticking her foot out to see her Docs still on her feet. Her legs were covered in a skintight spandex, the same pale pink shade as the dress.

"It's a bodysuit," she mused, toying with the seam where the skirt met the waist. I smiled as she understood. "The skirt rips away, doesn't it?"

I nodded. "It does."

Fury turned, looking for her mirror. Standing in front of it, she twirled to look at the back. "Can I make some requests?" she asked, looking at me.

I took my hands from my pockets and strode forward. "Of course."

"Not spaghetti straps. They're going to break. Something thicker." I nodded, and she smiled. "Not so much tulle. Just a little less."

"Noted," I said. "Do you mind if I make a suggestion?" She raised her eyebrows in question and waited. "I would keep the same pink color on top, but I would suggest a black tulle. It'll be easier to hide your boots, unless of course you want me to change the color of them to match the pink."

"My boots?" she said, confusion filling her tone.

I hummed in response. "Roxanne said you'd feel more comfortable in your Docs, especially while fighting. The skirt is meant to hide every part of that."

"I'm good with black. It's dark and moody," she said, smoothing out the fabric. "Fits my personality quite well, don't you think?"

Standing behind her, I traced her bare shoulders while she watched in the mirror, waiting for an answer. I pressed my lips to her heated skin, looking up to see her eyes fluttering closed. "You are anything but delicate and graceful," I murmured between kisses. Her eyes shot open, her nose wrinkling, and I chuckled. I ran my fingers down the length of her arm, wrapping my hand around her waist and pressing her into me. "You are elegant and fierce."

"Nice recovery," she said, a hint of playfulness in her eyes.

"There's one more thing," I said, reaching into my pocket. "This is for you to wear."

I lifted my hands over her head and draped a necklace around her. A simple Celtic knot on a silver chain. It rested neatly on her chest, perfectly settled between the base of her throat and the top of her breasts.

"Knotwork has a long history with fae, dating further back than when humans think they discovered it," I said, scooping her hair aside and clasping it together. "Some knots are symbols for families or roles in society, some tell a story, and some have meaning beyond even that."

Her fingers reached up to touch it, tracing the lines of the metal. "It's beautiful," she said softly. "What does this one mean?"

I met her gaze in the mirror as something heated and feral coursed through my veins. She'd made the choice to stay, no matter what. To be with me. She wasn't going to leave.

"A knot has no beginning and no end. It's an interwoven continuous line, never breaking," I said, my voice thick. Grazing my fingers from the back of her neck, I wrapped my hand possessively around her throat, pressing my body to hers as my cock twitched. Her breath hitched and I waited in silence, feeling her heartbeat speed up beneath my palm. "This one means you belong to me."

CHAPTER 5
FURY

THE INTENSITY OF DORIAN'S WORDS SENT CHILLS OVER MY BODY. THE HUM OF his voice reverberated over my skin, and I shivered. The burning hunger in his eyes sent a shot of desire into my core and a throbbing ache to the place between my thighs.

"Say it," he whispered roughly.

I met his gaze, considering a challenge. Silence spanned between us, and I could hear the clock ticking softly. My heartbeat pounded in my ears. He waited.

In the past, I didn't want to belong to anyone. I was independent. A loner, graced with the free will to make that choice. Would I ever agree to belong to someone? No. Never again. But this? This was different, and I knew what it meant. It wasn't ownership. It wasn't patriarchal. It wasn't subservience.

It was mutual. Equal. It was unbreakable. It was my choice. *Our* choice.

If I belonged to him, he belonged to me.

I didn't break eye contact as I slid my hand over his arm, trailing my fingers up to his hand over my throat, placing it on top. I swallowed thickly, opening my lips as they peeled apart slowly after being pressed together for so long.

"I'm yours," I said hoarsely, my voice cracking.

A low growl in his chest rumbled against my back as the floor was pulled from beneath me, wind rushing around us and blowing my hair into my face.

I landed on my back, the soft bedding enveloping me as I crashed into it. I took in my surroundings, realizing I had no idea where we were. It wasn't the castle. We weren't in Avalon.

The room was brighter. Warmer. Modern.

I sat up, looking around the room. It was painted a soft gray. Wooden furniture with clean lines filled the space, and framed art decorated the wall. A chaise lounge sat near a dresser in the corner. Expansive floor-to-ceiling windows lined one side of the room, reminiscent of Ezra's high-rise without the balcony. Long, sheer white drapes hung on each side. The faint noise of a city made its way through the glass.

"London," Dorian said from the end of the bed, answering my unspoken question.

I started to ask more when he grabbed my ankles, pulling me to the very edge of the mattress.

"I bought it for us," he said, rubbing his hands slowly up the side of my legs, and pushing the tulle skirt up.

"No one knows about it." He bent down, kissing my calf, grazing his hand further. I exhaled a shaky breath, relishing the gentle touches for the time being, knowing that time with Dorian would always be a combination of rough play and soothing strokes. And I was all for it.

"No interruptions," he murmured against me, dragging his teeth over my skin.

I tensed, anticipating a nip or a bite that never came. Not knowing what was coming next increased my need for him to touch me, and I reached for him, trying to guide his hands to the apex of my thighs.

Dorian smirked and shook his head. "Same limits as last time?" he asked.

I raised an eyebrow, unsure of what he was aiming to do. He'd already edged me for hours on end. I had no idea what he had in mind. "Yes," I said finally.

He tilted his head and narrowed his eyes, catching the tremor in my voice. "Are you sure?"

I smirked at him in return. "Don't mistake my anticipation as fear. I said yes. I won't ever agree to something if I'm not ready."

"I'll remember that." Dorian grinned, an incredibly sexy and almost cruel smile. He grabbed my wrists, pulling me off the bed as I slammed against his chest. One hand cupped my face, and the other traced to the base of my neck, taking a fistful of hair. His lips crashed into mine, and I opened my mouth to his, moaning against the heat of his tongue as he devoured me.

Dorian reached between us, and he tugged at the tulle skirt, the sounds of the rip-away fabric echoed in the room. He tossed it aside, pressing his hands up against the curves of my body, following over my hips, across my ribs, and up to my breasts. He ran his thumbs over the fabric, flicking my hardened nipples and sending a rush of electricity through me. My breath caught, and I smiled against his mouth.

Releasing me, he hooked his fingers under the small straps of the bodice. I reached for his shirt to unbutton it, but he grabbed my hands. Shaking his head, he said, "Not yet. This is about you."

I wanted to argue. I wanted his fucking clothes off. I wanted to say if it was about me, then I wanted him to be as naked as I was about to be, but something about the husky tenor in his voice and his choice of words left a lump in my throat. For all the fire in me, all I managed was a measly "okay." Some demon I was.

He hummed in approval, taking the straps in his grasp once again, gently pulling them down my arms. The fabric slowly folded over the curve of my breasts, slowly curling over my waist. I pulled my arms away, moving to grab his hair and guide him down.

"Don't move," he ordered, placing kisses along my exposed skin as he dragged the bodice down. "If you move, I'm going to stop."

"You're a bastard," I muttered under my breath. His tongue ran a line down my skin, followed by a kiss, followed by tongue. I groaned, the throbbing ache between my thighs growing deeper.

Hooking his thumbs into the fabric of the leggings, he pulled it down my legs, just as slowly. Kissing and licking my skin as he went. Teasing. Never kissing or licking where I needed it the most.

I'd never once been undressed so slowly before. It was agonizing. I wanted nothing more than for him to touch me, or to at least touch myself. My fingers twitched at the thought, and I clenched my hands into fists at my sides.

The aching intensified. A flood of wetness coated my underwear.

Dorian was on his knees in front of me, the rest of my outfit around my ankles. He tapped my leg, and I lifted it out of the material, doing the same for the other side.

He took a step back, just staring at me as I stood there in nothing but dark green lace panties.

His eyes raked over my body, and I remained still, holding my fists together. The bulge in his trousers throbbed, his need for more just as obvious as my own.

"Fucking beautiful," he said.

Striding forward, he grabbed my jaw and kissed me, reaching between us, grabbing the lace, and ripping hard. The delicate fabric tore instantly, leaving a mark on my skin. My breath caught, not expecting him to drop back down to his knees and grab my hips. He pressed his mouth to my center, licking and pulling my clit into his mouth to suck.

"Oh fuck," I gasped, and my legs buckled. I wasn't ready for it. I was, and I wasn't. I wanted it so bad, and he'd dragged out everything so damn slow that I wasn't prepared for it when it finally happened.

I almost toppled forward, grabbing his shoulders and his head—anything I could use to balance myself. He chuckled against my core, the vibrations sending delicious sensations through me, and I moaned.

Grabbing one leg, he hoisted it over his shoulder. My balance was well and truly gone. I was damn near curled over his head, threading my fingers through his hair for support. He gripped my hips hard, his hands pressing deeply into my skin. In a swift move, he stood up, my other leg swinging over his shoulder quickly before he slammed me into a wall, the artwork rattling next to me.

My back hit the flat surface, giving me a place to balance as he held my thighs apart, his face pressed between my legs as he devoured me.

Each suck of my clit sent shocks through my system, pushing me to the edge of an orgasm. My legs tightened and started to shake; he pressed the flat of his tongue against me, and I bucked, angling my hips and grinding against his face, chasing the release I so desperately needed.

He moaned his approval against me, and I shattered, screaming as I flooded into his mouth. My legs quaked around his head, and I held his hair tight as I rode the waves, my body shaking.

He nipped at the inside of my thigh, then looked up at me. He pulled back, sliding my legs over his shoulder, and catching my waist as he set me down on unsteady legs.

I let go of his hair and grabbed his shirt quickly, ripping it open. The buttons popped off, clinking on the ground when they landed.

Challenge flashed in his eyes, and he pulled away from me, walking to a chest of drawers. My mouth fell open in surprise that he'd just leave me standing there.

"Where are you going?" I asked, my voice just as unsteady as my balance. I pressed my flattened palms against the wall, holding myself upright. My breathing came in almost panting breaths. I wanted more, and I wanted it now.

"I told you not yet, didn't I?" he answered. Opening a drawer, I watched him shuffle some items before pulling out metal locking wrist cuffs. He turned his head slightly, side-eyeing me to gauge my response.

My heartbeat fluttered and my pussy clenched. That's where this was going. A small smile crept up my lips and I nodded. "You did."

Striding toward me, I couldn't help but watch the way his trousers hung low on his hips. With his shirt gone, I could see every ripple of his muscular chest. Every bulge in his arms. The sexy lines that curved down the side of his lower abs, leading toward what I wanted the most right now. He towered over me, hovering. I looked up, jutting my chin out. I held my wrists out, palms up, waiting for him to make his move. I trusted him. The anticipation and thrill made me wetter, and the unknown sent my thoughts spinning.

He leaned down, kissing my wrist before putting the cuff on, clicking to lock it in place. I closed my eyes, and tilted my head back when I exhaled, loving the sensation as he repeated it on the other side.

My body jerked forward slightly, and my eyes shot open. He'd grabbed the middle that connected the cuffs and pulled it, testing its strength. Holding it, he lifted my hands over my head and slammed it against the wall as I gasped. Pushing his body against mine, he ran his nose over my shoulder, kissing the crook of my neck, his mouth hovered over my ear, taking my earlobe between his teeth and pulling slightly.

"Are you okay?" he asked softly, his hot breath sending a shiver down my spine.

"Yes," I said softly, trying to maneuver and spread my legs so he'd touch me.

Keeping my arms above me, he reached between us and unfastened his pants, pushing them to the floor. I tried to look down. Tried to see what he was doing, but he kept my head up, using his own body to block my view. I could feel his cock twitch against my belly, hard and ready.

"Spread your legs," he ordered, giving me space to move and follow through.

He palmed his length, running the tip over my folds, stopping on my swollen clit, then moving to press against my entrance. I tried to angle my hips forward, tried to slide him inside me.

"Not yet," he said huskily, teasing me, sliding it over me back and forth. "Tell me what you like, Fury. What turns you on?"

"You mean other than this?" I panted. He hummed in response against my neck. "Getting off. That turns me on."

"Wrong answer," he said, pulling his cock away from me.

I let out a loud groan, the lack of another release frustrating me.

"Tell me," he said slowly, enunciating each word. "What. Do. You. Like?" He shoved two fingers inside me hard, curling them and pressing into the pillowy G-spot.

I cried out, and instant electricity shot through me as my knees went weak. He pulled them out, depriving me of the oncoming orgasm.

"I like it when you lick me," I managed, wetting my lips with my tongue.

"Mmhmm," he responded, pushing his fingers inside my mouth so I could taste myself. "What else?"

It was hard to focus, and I cleared my throat, trying to buy time. "I like being shared. I like groups. I want to be the center of attention."

He rubbed beneath my thighs in slow, lazy circles. "What about that do you like?"

"I like . . ." I trailed off, my mind going blank in the heat of the moment. He bent down, taking a nipple in his mouth, whirling his tongue around the taut peak. Taking it between his teeth, he carefully pulled, not causing any pain, but definitely hitting some of that pleasure.

"You like?" he continued, my nipple still in his mouth. He pressed his fingers against my clit, rubbing until my legs shook. Then he took it away again. "Finish your sentence, Fury."

"I like being watched," I breathed out, my voice hoarse. "I like being on display."

"Interesting," he murmured against my chest. He stood up, turning his head slightly, a slow and intense smile curling his lips.

In a quick move, he put his shoulder into my belly, lifting me up and carrying me. I hung upside down, my hair creating a curtain around my face, not knowing where we were going. There was no one here. No one to watch us. He said no one knew about this place.

He palmed my ass while he walked, taking a handful, sliding his fingers down but never giving me the satisfaction.

"Close your eyes," he said, as he set me down.

The unknown elicited a flood of desire through me. I didn't know what was about to happen, but I knew Dorian wouldn't disappoint.

I kept my eyes closed while he held the middle bar connecting the cuffs, lifting it over my head again.

"Turn around, eyes shut," he said. As I did slowly, he held my shoulders, guiding me until he told me to stop. "One small step forward, then spread your legs again."

I stuttered a ragged breath as I stepped forward, then moved each foot to the side, doing as he had said. My heartbeat was pounding in my ears. Every part of me was shivering in anticipation of what he was going to do. There was a new chill in the air I couldn't place.

He licked my neck, and I tilted my head to the side, sighing. His hand grazed my belly, sliding over my skin, coming to rest as he cupped me between my thighs.

"Open," he said.

I did.

The pounding in my chest increased tenfold.

I inhaled sharply.

My pussy clenched and my clit pulsed and ached.

The floor-to-ceiling window was in front of me. The expansive glass overlooking a sprawling city. Buildings all around our own. Thousands of windows. Countless people. Bodies walking below, and those living or working in apartments across from us. Forty floors or more of nothing but people possibly looking at me right now, naked and entirely revealed, my cuffed arms held above my head . . .

"Like this?" he asked me.

"Yeah," I said thickly. "This is new . . ." I managed.

He chuckled darkly. "Good."

He nudged me forward carefully, and I faltered, the feeling of vertigo taking over.

"You're safe with me," he said softly, and I knew I was. His body pushed against my back, and I moved with him until my chest was pressed against the window. Dorian only put his weight onto me more, forcing me to turn my head and press my cheek into it.

I gasped as my skin flattened over the cold glass, my arms suspended and bound above me, unable to move. He gripped my hips, digging his fingers into my flesh, pulling my hips back so that my back was arched. Dorian angled himself behind me and took his length, rubbing the tip of his cock over me, coating himself in wetness. He slid in only an inch or two, then pulled out, repeating the shallowing actions several times over, but never once entering me completely. The teasing was so good it was almost unbearable.

"Fuck me now," I ground out. "Please fuck me now."

A dark chuckle escaped him, then he hooked his arm under my leg and lifted it, pressing it against the window too, leaving me to balance myself on one foot, my pussy perfectly exposed to anyone watching.

"Is this what you want?" he asked, positioning himself at my entrance.

"Yes," I mumbled, my face pressed against the glass.

"You like being watched? Then let them watch you," he said roughly.

He drove inside me, stretching me out, filling me more than I realized he would. I gasped and inhaled, my mouth forming an 'o'.

"Yes," I drawled out in a husky voice. This was what I wanted. What I needed.

Dorian moved slowly at first, dragging out the pleasure and the build-up as he found a steady pace. I tried to arch my back more, giving him better access as I felt the tingles of an orgasm start to spread with each thrust. I pushed myself against him, fucking him as he fucked me, meeting his movements as best I could in my limited position. He shoved in fully and stilled. My channel fluttered around him, begging for me.

"I love feeling you tighten around me," he said in a gravelly tone. Almost as if my body could speak, another spasm wrapped around his cock, and he hummed deeply in approval. He hovered by my ear, his breath heating my skin. "Keep your hands up."

I nodded, not trusting coherent words to come out while I practically panted with need.

He bit my shoulder, whispering against my skin. "Good."

I groaned when he let the cuff go but I kept my hands up, pressed against the glass. With one arm still hooked up my leg, he grabbed my hip to anchor us. I felt him twitch inside me and the anticipation made me clench around him again. He pulled out, then drove into me with a feral intensity I knew he'd been holding back. I exhaled in a loud cry, not expecting it, feeling the pain and pleasure all at once, but I didn't have time to recover before he did it again.

"Do you see them down there?" he grunted, sliding in and out of me. "Do you see them watching you?"

"Yes," I breathed out, my toes curling as I chased my release.

"When they look at you, when they see me fucking this pretty pussy, they know you're *mine*." His fingers and claws pricked my skin, digging in as he put emphasis on his last word.

"I'm yours," I moaned, another spasm wrapping around his cock.

"That's right," he rumbled and pounded into me at a fast rhythm, the sound of skin slapping skin echoing the room. Each time his body slammed into mine, the momentum pressed me into the cold window overlooking the city. Anyone looking would see me, my breasts against the glass, my legs spread apart and open as Dorian fucked me savagely from behind. They'd see each and every thrust, watching his cock slide in and out of me. They'd see my body move against the window, my face pushed against it, my cheek flattened and my mouth open as I panted in time with his movements.

With each pump inside me, with each thought of someone looking up to see us, with each time he slammed into me—his fingers marking my skin as he held on—the intensity of it all made the oncoming orgasm climb at an unprecedented rate. Tingling sensations ran down my legs and they started to shake. I could feel myself getting wetter, and my channel began to tighten uncontrollably.

Dorian felt it too as he started to fuck me deeper, dragging his cock over that spot inside me that made me damn near lose myself. I squeezed my eyes shut, a scream building in my throat as my body tensed.

"Come, Fury," he said, sliding his arm forward and reaching his hand over to pinch my clit. "Let them watch you come for me."

"Oh my god," I cried out, and an explosion hit me. White dots blocked my vision, my consciousness threatening to black out. I clenched tightly around him, pulling his cock in while a flood sprayed the window and dripped down my legs. My limbs shook, and the muscles contracted all at the same time. My fingertips went numb as I clawed at the glass, unable to do anything else with my hands.

Dorian grunted with a final savage thrust into me, leaning his weight into my back.

"I . . . I'm going to fall," I managed to say. I couldn't stand up anymore and I had only moments before my knees gave out.

He sifted us back onto the bed and I lazily mumbled my thanks, the post-orgasm exhaustion taking over.

"Not so fast," Dorian said, reaching up to unlock the cuffs.

I raised an eyebrow at him. He tossed them aside, then swiftly spread my legs apart, moving to settle between them. He ran his tongue over me, one long stroke from bottom to top, before he flicked at my swollen and overly sensitive clit, causing my hips to buck.

He grinned up at me. "I haven't licked you clean yet."

I opened my mouth to . . . what? Protest? I didn't know. But it didn't matter. He took my clit into his mouth and sucked. All that came out of me was a loud, completely undignified moan, and I shattered all over again.

CHAPTER 6
FURY

A DIM MORNING LIGHT STARTED TO FILTER IN THE WINDOW, RUDELY awakening me. I grumbled into my pillow and rolled over, crunching myself in a ball and hiding my face.

"I'm afraid it's time to get up," Dorian said. He sounded like he was on the other side of the room.

I peeked out of the covers, cracking one eye open and looking at him. He sat in a comfortable-looking armchair, having what I assumed was a cup of Earl Grey tea. "Why are you up?"

After a night of what felt like endless sex, I didn't understand how he could even be awake so early.

"It's eleven in the morning," he answered, not looking up from whatever it was he was reading.

"Really?" I moved to sit up, somewhat shocked. It felt much earlier than that. I looked out the window and frowned. The sun was fighting with the gray skies, finding little moments to break through before being cast out again. "It's still dark out. Well, darkish."

"It's London," he said, as though that explained it. "It's this or rain."

"Lovely," I mumbled, scooting myself down to curl under the covers again.

"Up, Fury." Dorian's tone took on a sharper quality, and I shot back up, the sheets falling to pool around my waist.

"Why?" I asked, pointing outside. "It's perfect weather for sleeping in."

He leveled me with an unamused glare and raised an eyebrow. "For one, you don't need perfect weather for that. You'll sleep eighteen hours if I let you."

I sighed. "And two?"

He set down his tea, and stood up, walking across the room to stand next to me. He reached out, caressing my hair. I'd been giving him my most annoyed look possible, but one of confusion took its place when he pulled out a white feather, then he held it up. "And two," he repeated, "you have a molting problem that needs to be looked at."

I grabbed the feather from him, turning to search the bed. There were more than I cared to admit. "I don't know what you mean by 'looked at.' I'm not going to a veterinarian if that's what you're suggesting. Birds molt."

Didn't they? I wasn't entirely sure. But also, I wasn't a bird. Mostly.

An odd stirring in the back of my mind reminded me of my raven's presence. She scoffed at the suggestion that I wasn't a bird, very much insistent that she wasn't going anywhere.

He chuckled and shook his head. "No, I meant we need to look at how to prevent this from happening. You need to learn how to shift."

"Do you think learning to shift is going to stop—" I looked at some of the feathers in the bed and pointed to them—"this?"

Tilting his head to the side, Dorian twisted his lips before answering. "Maybe. There's the possibility that this is just part of your shifter body now. You'll continue to molt at random, and it is what it is. The way you need to give blood as part of your vampire self. But there's also the consideration that your molting started, and continues, as a need to shift periodically until you understand that side of you. Much like your fainting spells before you give blood." He looked out of the window briefly, lost in thought, then returned his gaze to me. "You need to learn to shift, regardless. It's part of who you are now. Nothing bad will come of learning, but considering the way things have continued to go thus far, we can almost guarantee something will go terribly wrong if you don't."

That was an understatement. I had yet for anything to go right for me ever since I'd come back to Earth. I groaned in acceptance, throwing the sheets aside and pulling my legs over to the side of the bed. Reaching my arms up, I stretched, tightening my body and suddenly feeling every muscle that had clenched and unclenched over and over the night before.

"Fine. Let's get this over with."

"You really are charming in the morning, aren't you?"

I shrugged, getting up to walk to the bathroom. "I never claimed to be a morning person, but you're stuck with me now." I looked over my shoulder and winked at him as he blatantly stared at my naked body.

"Indeed," he said in a low rumble.

I laughed to myself as I shut the door and sat down on the toilet. I rested my elbows on my knees, letting the thoughts drift through my head.

How was I going to practice shifting? I didn't have the first clue where to start. It felt like it took forever when Rava had to help me learn to shift back. I wasn't sure I had the patience for it. If patience was considered a virtue, it definitely wasn't mine. I could feel my raven's irritability, but I didn't know what it meant. This was going to take some getting used to.

Was her emotion leaking into me?

No, I was never a morning person. Or an afternoon person. Mostly I wasn't a 'liked to be woken up' person. I didn't think she had anything to do with my mood at the moment.

I finished up and looked in the mirror, grabbing a brush from the drawer and combing my hair. It looked like it was on fire. Deep red, sticking out everywhere, and coated with sex sweat. I picked a small down feather off my shoulder, flicking it off my fingers as it got stuck. "Just-been-fucked hair and covered in feathers. Attractive," I said quietly to myself.

"You are," Dorian said from the other room.

Of course he could hear me. Supersonic bat hearing from the

shifter and the fae, and nosy mind-probing from the vampire. I had certainly found myself with an interesting group of mates.

When I came out, Dorian was again in his chair, but this time he wasn't reading. His heated gaze traveled the length of my body before he took a deep breath. Then I was clothed.

It took me by surprise, and I looked down to see what he'd chosen for me. Shapely black leggings, an incredibly comfortable green sweater, and low-heel leather boots that came just below my knees.

"Not going back to Houston?" I asked, knowing full well I would melt there if I were wearing anything short of a bikini.

He shook his head. "I spoke with Roman while you were sleeping."

"Well that was rude. What time is it there? Did you wake him up in the middle of the night?"

"He'll be fine," he said, waving it off. "Shifting needs to be a priority. You're much better at sifting now, and we know that'll improve as you continue to practice. Any other fae abilities you discover can be something we work on as well."

"What other powers could I have that would show up?"

"Elemental control. Persuasion. Glamour. Shielding. James is a hell of a baker," he said with a laugh. "I'm certain there's magic involved in his pumpkin streusel cake."

"Well, I am no baker. I don't even think magic could help me there." I thought through the others, thinking it would be cool if I had control of elements. With my luck I'd only be able to control something like fire. That'd be messy. I mentally shook my head, hoping that wasn't the case. Shielding, though . . . "Dorian? How do you shield someone?"

He raised a brow. "Do you think you have that?"

"I don't know. I knew about Lyra existing and somehow Ezra never saw that in my head. What do you think?"

He tilted his head, considering it. "It wouldn't surprise me if you could do it without knowing it. You're a natural, and sifting objects to yourself isn't an easy task. It's something we should explore." He tapped his head. "If you want to shield yourself, you're basically creating a mental barrier. Focus on it, building it around the thoughts you want to keep to yourself."

"Or in your case, around every thought," I pointed out.

"Yes. If that's what you want it to be." A small smile played on his lips. "In the meantime we have to get you started on shifting now that we know you're capable of it."

The memory of working through the frustration of sifting was burned into my mind. I thought of when he left me outside on the steps of the castle in Avalon, freezing my ass off. I wasn't keen on going through it again. If shifting was going to be anything close to that . . .

"Is it really necessary to work on that right now, like today?"

I felt my raven's anger as she crashed around.

Okay, okay. Message received.

Dorian looked at me in surprise, unaware of the exchange I'd had internally. "I thought you were a demon."

"I am," I said indignantly. "What's that supposed to mean?"

"I didn't expect you to be so averse to a challenge, much less whine about it." He smirked.

I narrowed my eyes at him. I knew what he was doing. And it was working.

"Touché, fairy." It was his turn to glare at me. "So when do we get this started? What's the plan here?"

He disappeared without answering, leaving me to stand alone in the middle of the room.

Well that was rude.

Fine. Leave me alone in the penthouse apartment. I was hungry anyway. I'd worked up quite the appetite.

I walked to the kitchen and opened a cabinet. A decanter of what I assumed to be fae wine was tucked next to other bottles of undefined substances. I grabbed it, taking a few swigs of the potent drink. I used the cuff of my sweater to wipe my lip marks off the crystal, wanting to avoid the shit I would no doubt get for not using a glass. Or just drinking in general. They'd laid into me for weeks now. It was getting old.

I turned to see a carafe of orange juice and a basket of bagels with some other assorted pastries I didn't recognize. Forgoing a glass once again, I sipped the juice and grimaced. Drinking that after fae wine was not a good combination. Grabbing the carafe, I picked up a bagel and stuck it in my mouth to hold, walking around the counter to sit somewhere comfortably and eat my breakfast.

As I entered the living room, Dorian and Roman popped in and I almost ran straight into them.

The juice sloshed, almost spilling, and the bagel fell right out of my mouth and landed on the floor with a thud.

"Really?" I asked them, annoyed with their choice of location.

"I didn't realize you would've left the bedroom. It's why I chose this room," Dorian said, looking at my discarded food on the rug with displeasure. "Also, I have plates, in case you were unable to locate them in the cabinet. The cabinets with clear glass doors."

Ignoring him, I turned to Roman. "Fancy meeting you here," I said, smiling obnoxiously and picking up my bagel.

Roman laughed, crossing his arms. "Nothing like orange juice and a lover's quarrel in the morning."

"He's got jokes," I muttered to no one as I sat on the couch and ate.

They took a seat across from me, uninvited I might add, and didn't even have the courtesy to wait for me to finish breakfast before they started talking.

"Dorian and I spoke this morning about your need to practice shifting," he said, leaning forward in the chair.

"I'm aware," I said around a mouthful. Swallowing a big chunk, I drank from the carafe. "I need to practice, yadda yadda yadda. I'm not disputing it. Let's go do the thing."

"We can't do it here," Roman said. "We'll need a safer location. It's going to be hard enough for you to learn this, but you need to be able to focus. When a shifter learns this part of their animal, it puts them in a vulnerable place. We can't do it at the compound, and this place is too —" Roman paused, looking for the right word—"unfamiliar. And clean."

I snorted. My mates most certainly lived two very different lives. I thought of Dorian's elegant castle. His estate in Houston and this penthouse. Clean lines, sterile, and organized. Then I thought of Roman's compound; earthy, rustic, and covered in dirt and nature.

I suppose I could see it. An animal learning to shift here wouldn't make much sense.

"Why not the compound?" I asked, wiping my hands on a napkin that Dorian had brought me.

"Lyra," he answered. "She knows about it and already came there once. Roman says you are vulnerable when you learn to shift. That's not a good position to put you in."

"We'll do it on Avalon," Roman finished.

I stopped fidgeting with the cloth and looked up. "Lyra is well aware of Avalon too. It's not only where she lived, but she kicked me off a cliff while we were there together. I fail to see how that's any safer." I looked at each of them. "Shouldn't we go somewhere else? Like the desert, or some remote island?" I liked the idea of an island, and I smiled to myself.

Dorian huffed a small laugh. He caught on to my train of thought about going to a beach. I hadn't done much resting in my Afterlife, and the beach wasn't a thing there. I wanted to go to one. A really pretty one that looked like it didn't belong on this earth, with shimmering black sand and sapphire blue water. I'd seen pictures. The contrast reminded me of, well—me.

"C'mon, Fury," Roman said. "We thought of that. We want you to be able to protect yourself further. We didn't plan on putting you in any danger while you practiced. Hades suggested—"

I snapped my head up. "Hades?" Shifting with him last time had been such a treat.

"You rang?" His familiar voice filled the room.

Where in this world or the next did he come from? How did he do that exactly? I wanted to ask. I wanted to know if I could do it too. It was a subject I would bring up once I mastered shifting.

Excitement rushed through me, but it wasn't my own. My raven heard the idea of mastering shifting, and she certainly seemed to like it.

"I guess I didn't expect to see you here," I said to him as he landed on the back of a couch.

He fluffed his feathers, reaching his foot up to scratch his neck. "Not sure why. I'm pretty crucial to the process, don't you think?"

I sighed. He was. Roman couldn't understand me in bird form. Neither could Ezra. If I needed help, I was screwed without him. Not that I would tell him that. Not in those words, anyway.

"I suppose you are," I conceded. Gesturing to my mate, I said, "Roman was saying you had made a suggestion?"

Roman held his hand out to the crow, letting him have the floor. So to speak.

"Mmm hmm. The cave," he said.

"The cave . . . the cave over the side of the cliff," I said flatly, trailing off.

"Yes, that cave. It's an excellent place for you to practice. Perfectly safe and away from humans." He watched me carefully, waiting for a response.

I hated that cave. And I hated how much he was right. No one knew that cave was there. It was pure dumb luck we'd found it to begin with, and it was only accessible depending on the tides and storm surges. I exhaled loudly. "Good idea, Hades. Point to you."

"I know it's a good idea," he said, his tone filled with snark. "That's why I said it."

"Well, aren't you pleasant this morning? Did you go play with a cat or something before coming here?" I asked, crossing my arms. Looked like we were having that kind of relationship today.

He fluffed himself up. "Considering you're also a bird—and not a very good one yet—I wouldn't joke about feline encounters."

I snorted. "I'm sensing there's a story there."

He glared at me in response but instead he chose to ignore me. Now I definitely wanted to know. Turning his head, he looked at Roman.

"Shall we?" he asked. "She's shifted once, but I have a feeling this isn't going to be like riding a bike."

CHAPTER 7
FURY

"I think we should toss her over the edge and see how that goes," Hades chimed in for the umpteenth time. I narrowed my eyes at the feather-brained asshole.

"You're here to be helpful, not"—I motioned to him—"*this*."

He snorted in a very un-birdlike manner. "I *am* being helpful," he insisted. "We've been waiting for over an hour for you to shift and I'm freezing my feathers off down here. If you can't shift on your own, what better way to kickstart it than tossing you over the ledge?" I crossed my arms over my chest as he continued. "Better yet, we could Sparta kick you off the cliff again? Now that would make this worthwhile."

"Sparta what?"

He cocked his head, his little dark crow eyes staring at me.

"Sparta kick. You know, from the movie *300*? Where Gerard Butler was all like, 'This is Sparta!' And kicked a messenger into a hole, like how Lyra booted you."

I stared at him blankly, not at all amused. "I don't know what you're talking about, so if you don't mind shutting your beak—"

"Oh come on! Really? You've seen every episode of *Grey's Anatomy* like fifty times, and you've never seen *300*? This is a travesty. Roman, we must fix this."

My mate scrubbed a hand down his face, amused and yet tired by the back-and-forth Hades and I had been volleying at each other since entering the cave.

"Not the time, Hades. As you pointed out, it's fucking cold down here and my balls are shriveled-up walnuts right now."

I choked on a laugh. My nipples were hard enough to cut glass and I wasn't even turned on. I understood the sentiment. None of us were crazy about the location.

"I'm sorry, shifting is just turning out to be as much of a pain in the ass as sifting was." And while Dorian's teaching method worked, something told me that wouldn't work here.

"Which is why wolf boy should toss you over the ledge and make you fall or fly—"

"Even if that would work—you still had to drag me to the edge of the cave last time. Forgive me for not being keen on the possibility of dying if you're not able to do it again, and instead I land on the rocks then drown in the damn ocean. I'm open to ideas that don't end in my death," I snapped at him, cocking an eyebrow.

Hades grumbled something about how I wouldn't drown if I flew—which I promptly ignored because it wasn't helpful.

Fucking bird. Why did he have to be the only one that could understand me in raven form? Ugh.

My inner raven also expressed annoyance over this. Not happy with him, and not happy with me. The best I could tell, she didn't like that it seemed as though he was better than me because he could shift. Like that was my fault. Somehow.

"Does your raven want to shift?" Roman asked me suddenly.

"Yes," I answered without having to think. "She's annoyed I can't."

"Hm," Roman hummed. "Have you tried letting her take over?"

I stared at him like he was speaking gibberish. "Take over?"

"When my wolf wants to shift, it's because he wants to be front and center—in control of us. It's a give and take with our animals. While we have to hold the ultimate upper hand, being too firm can lead to them lashing out. I'm concerned that's what the molting is—that she needs you to let go so she can take the reins."

My raven's immediate liking to this explanation answered the question.

"That's what she wants," I said. "But I don't know how to. Is this like a feeling? Is there an actual switch of who's in charge here?"

"Right now, you're the one calling the shots. Try closing your eyes and letting yourself step back for a moment. See what she does."

I pursed my lips. This sounded like a lot of mumbo jumbo, truth be told, but what better option did I have?

Closing my eyes, I let out a sigh and mentally envisioned my raven. I wasn't entirely sure what she looked like, but I knew she was there, flapping her wings impatiently. Her thoughts and emotions rushed forward, as if attempting to barrel me out of the way. I recoiled at first, wanting to snap back—but a firm hand caressed my back, reminding me of what I'm supposed to be doing.

"That's right, cherub. Let her out. She might be a bit aggressive at first because she's impatient to shift. We can work on that with her later." My raven disagreed with that idea. She thought 'working on that' was a hard pass. Bossy bitch, she was. "For now, just let her come forward. You'll be relinquishing control of your body, but don't fight it. It'll make shifting much easier if you give her the chance to guide you through this. You have to build trust."

As he spoke, a rippling across my back made me wince. My raven continued to wiggle her way forward, filling up every inch and crevice of who I was. Fire burned along my spine. I opened my mouth to cry out, but it didn't come. My raven had stepped into control and gritted our teeth against the pain. She pushed our body to accommodate her, and I knew the moment my wings popped free, and my bones cracked. Blackness closed in, but she kept pushing, unrelenting in this assault.

Unable to stop her even if I wanted, I got carried along for the ride.

And when the blackness faded and my eyes opened, the world looked quite different.

It was disorienting. Bright. A world of color opened up that I didn't know about before. Last time I shifted I was in shock. I didn't pay attention. This was different. It was startling and beautiful all at once, to realize how many other colors existed that I normally couldn't see. Ones that didn't have a name and were impossible to describe—even if I could talk.

"Well look at that. She grew her feathers, after all."

My raven turned her head and narrowed her eyes on Hades. She was not a fan of being insulted. Not when she knew what a majestic and rare creature she was.

I would have huffed a laugh if I could. *And Hades thought I was full of myself.*

He was in for a rude awakening when my raven charged at him.

Surprise flickered in his eyes before his wings snapped out and beat frantically, carrying him up.

"Not so bad now, are ya, you big heifer," Hades mocked.

My raven saw red, and her wings spread wide. In a mighty effort, half fueled by anger, the other half adrenaline, she took to the air after him.

"Oh shit," Hades squawked before ducking to evade us. Suddenly liking this dynamic a lot more, I egged my raven on, encouraging her to get him.

Roman doubled at the waist, letting out a booming laugh.

"You're going to regret talking shit now," he called out from the ground of the cave. Hades was more graceful, given he'd been at it longer—but my raven was a natural. She had this in the bag—and she preened under my praise.

Where he banked left, we followed, and when he skimmed the top of the cave, we closed in underneath him in an attempt to throw him off. When he did a wonky thing with his wings where he essentially rolled from the top of us to below us, my raven felt smug satisfaction.

All at once, she stopped flying and dropped onto him.

Hades let out a string of curses as we sank like a rock with us sitting on top of him, claws hooked into his sides. Hades went down, hitting the ground first, but my raven didn't let up. She continued to sit on him, lifting her head to gloat.

"Jesus Christ, you need to lay off the cheese fries—" he started.

She let out an indignant squawk at him and then shuffled forward. He tried to usurp us, but her larger size prevented him from making any real ground as she moved forward and then—

"YOU DID NOT JUST SHIT ON ME," Hades roared as she hopped

off and pretended to inspect her wings. Inside I was dying. Roaring with laughter.

"You're beneath me, peasant," my raven responded. Her voice sounded similar, but intrinsically different to my own. She was haughty and aloof in a way I wasn't. To Roman, it would have simply been a croak of some sort coming from deep in my throat. Given the way Hades was muttering to himself with dark fury, I figured he understood her perfectly well.

"I thought Fury was bad," he grumbled. "I think I prefer her lazy ass over—"

My raven cut him off with a beat of her wings as she threateningly towered over him—nearly twice his size.

"You don't get to talk bad about her," she growled at him. I found myself very pleased with her for that, mentally nodding along. "Only I can."

Okay, not where I expected that to go. I figured I could live with it if she was down to give Hades shit. Literally.

My raven liked this change in power dynamic. She liked it quite a lot. Enough so that I was beginning to think maybe she should have been a peacock or cat because she really was a bit full of herself. My raven turned a critical eye inward over that thought and I shrugged. We are who we are, and she was a high and mighty bitch boss. Could be a lot worse.

"Wolf boy, I think we should put her in a bird cage until she learns some manners," Hades chimed in, jumping back next to Roman when my Raven narrowed her eyes. "Maybe rig it up like a training collar and shock her every time she's bad."

Roman stroked his chin, a wicked smirk crossing his lips. "I'm not sure about the cage, but there are other possibilities in there." The rawness of his tone sent a shiver through me and my raven. I could honestly say I'd never considered that in my hundred and twenty-six years, but I was curious.

Hades flicked a glance between the two of us. "Oh—*oh*. You two are disgusting. Can't you at least save the freaky shit for Ezra's sex club?"

"Quiet, peasa—" My raven cut off in a croak.

Warmth ripped through me, burning like fire.

"I'm sorry, I couldn't hear that," Hades taunted in the background. "Cat got your tongue?"

We flipped sideways, curling inward as black edged into our vision. Without needing to be asked, she stepped back, letting me come forward in a panic.

The pain faded, but the blurred edges in my vision remained. I tried to lift my head but struggled to.

"Ezra," I rasped. "I need Ezra *now*."

CHAPTER 8
ROMAN

FEATHERS RIPPLED OVER HER HUMAN FORM, A WAVE THAT SPROUTED AND THEN receded as fast as it came. Beneath her bare skin that unearthly light of true power went off.

I ran to her, knees buckling at the sight. Cupping her face, I tilted it back to see her elongated fangs.

Fuck.

She needed to give blood again.

"Hades get to Dorian; tell him we need Ezra."

"On it," the crow said, all previous anger and bantering between them was gone in an instant. I heard the woosh of his wings as he took to the skies, but my eyes were all on Fury.

"Stay with me, cherub," I commanded, my wolf's power reverberating through me, making the ground quiver.

"Running out of . . . time," she said through a tight breath. "Need to bite."

My eyes flashed to the mouth of the cave where Hades had disappeared only moments prior. I wavered with indecision, knowing she wanted Ezra for this but that we might not have another option.

Dorian appeared, sifting in on a cold gust as if the frigid air itself had carried him here.

"I can't reach the vampire," he said. "He's not responding."

In my arms, Fury whimpered. Around us the cave started to shake, causing stalactites to fall from the roof and smash into the stone flooring. That wild light beneath Fury's skin started to glow. Something told me that it wasn't simply the blood trying to get out.

"I can do it."

Dorian narrowed his eyes. "Are you sure?"

"She needs to give blood and we can't keep waiting for that asshole," I muttered.

"We don't know if her bite could harm you," Dorian said. "She is part vampire."

"I'll live." I wasn't thrilled about the idea of being poisoned, but it was the only reasonable way to alleviate her pain. "She's also part wolf and she bit him."

Dorian tilted his head forward, conceding the point.

In my arms Fury began to tremble. Red colored her cheeks, and I knew we had seconds at most. Without hesitation or fear, I brought my wrist to her mouth.

"Bite," I commanded, pressing my flesh into her fangs.

Worry shone in her eyes, but the feverish need that was taking over won the fight the second I nicked myself—the very top of her fang pushing in. She latched on with incredible strength, a moan of relief escaping from her. I shifted us, pulling her back to my chest so I could wrap both arms roughly around her while not jostling my wrist. The bite itself stung a little, but not much. More than anything, it aroused my wolf, who quite liked the idea of its female biting him back. While this wasn't meant to be a claiming mark, he took it that way—practically purring inside me.

"That's right, cherub. Get it all out," I whispered into her hair. The soft words were meant to encourage, though my wolf's tenor refused to leave my voice.

The shaking in the cavern stopped. The rattling of the floors diminished. Everything around us went silent once more. Judging by Dorian's expression as he cast a look around the cave, I wasn't the only one who noticed the strange occurrence.

"Either her power is growing, or the vampire side of her is still settling. That was worse than previous events," he said quietly.

"Her raven only just shifted on its own. She's still learning how to use her fae magic. I'd say it's probably some of both."

"She managed to shift?" Dorian asked. "That was certainly faster than her sifting."

"I believe she and her raven came to an understanding of sorts."

Mouth still pressed to my flesh but fangs retreating, Fury snorted.

She lifted her face, fangs slipping free. My skin healed instantly, leaving only a smear of red blood as evidence it ever happened.

"You could say that," she grunted, stretching her mouth in odd directions as her fangs slipped back in—still longer than a human, but not ferally so. "We have a common interest at heart."

"Pissing off Hades?" I guessed.

"Precisely," she hummed, wiping her lips with the back of her hand and giving the blood a foul look, as if it were somehow at fault for this. "That and she's hilarious, and full of herself." She chuckled, clearly speaking to her raven when she added, "Oh hush, we both know you are."

"Glad to see you've figured that out," Dorian said. "Did you realize that you were starting to bring down the cave when you needed to give blood?"

Her face paled a shade, which said something—because my mate was already pasty white. "I was?" she asked. "I hadn't realized. I've had such a firm grip on that ability for decades. I didn't think it would be an issue again."

"Does it feel unstable?" he asked. "Out of control?"

"No." She shook her head. "I feel the same as always."

Dorian hummed in contemplation. "Perhaps it's a one-time thing, then. Or simply a development related to you needing to give blood."

"Must be," she said, leaning back into my shoulder. "Thank you, by the way. For letting me bite you." Her nose wrinkled on the word 'bite'.

I leaned forward, letting one hand skate over her collar bone and down her arm. "If it makes you feel better, my wolf quite enjoyed it."

She squinted at me like she found that hard to believe. "Neither me nor my raven are a fan of blood. Unless it's someone else bleeding. We're okay with that."

Dorian chuckled, and I lifted my eyebrows in amusement. "Torture. You're okay with torture, but biting is gross?"

"Yup," she agreed. "That about sums up our opinion."

"I shouldn't be surprised," I said.

"You really shouldn't." She pointed to herself. "Demon, after all."

I shook my head, hoping she never changed. The first thirty-three years of my life were a bleak place without her.

A flap of wings made us all look up. Fury stilled, going cold as stone for a moment, then she visibly relaxed when she saw it was Hades. It occurred to me that she'd momentarily feared it was Azrael. It killed me that that bastard could instill a fear response. It ran so deep I wasn't sure she recognized it.

"Found Ezra," Hades puffed, landing on a rock beside us. "He was busy dealing with clan business and didn't hear Fury."

"I checked his apartment and the club," Dorian said stiffly.

"He was in the dungeon, apparently. Kendrick helped me track him," Hades said.

"I guess it's a good thing we know he isn't needed now when *our mate* needs to give blood," he said, clearly not happy with the vampire. I wasn't either, but not quite as pissed as Dorian seemed.

"Um, you can relay that to him. I'm not getting involved with mate politics," Hades said, ruffling his feathers.

Fury snorted. "It's fine. I'm fine. Shouldn't need it again for a few days, right? Now, back to this shifting thing . . ."

For the first time in weeks, her eyes glowed with something close to happiness as she shifted back into her raven form and chased Hades around the cave. I wanted to capture the moment. Freeze it in place and hold it close. I hadn't done that enough in my past, and I didn't want to make that same mistake again.

CHAPTER 9
FURY

I TIGHTENED THE ROBE AROUND MY WAIST AND SAT ON THE EDGE OF THE BED, running a towel over my hair and squeezing out the excess water while I lost myself in thought.

Not bad for a day's work. I'd figured out how to shift, and I was pretty proud of myself for it. Wrapping my head around all the abilities was another story, but it would happen. In some ways it already had. I wasn't fighting it. It wasn't that I wasn't willing to accept it. It was still just a weird thing to understand when you really laid out all the details.

A lot had happened since I'd come to Earth , and I don't care who you were—supernatural, Bob-the-human, or a demon from the Afterlife—it was a lot to process.

Demon-vampire-raven-shifter-fae hybrid. And angel . Can't forget that.

In the Afterlife, I prided myself on being *The* Fury. I'd said I was one of a kind. I had no idea how true that would end up being.

Once we'd thought maybe Jules or someone else could find a multi-hybrid that existed. It didn't matter anymore. I knew deep down, even if we ever did find one, there wouldn't ever be one like me. I was okay with that.

I finally felt like I was in control of my body again, and after my human life, I despised not being in control. Yes, there were aspects to learning it all that were still fuzzy. I wasn't entirely sure of the pattern for the blood-giving. When that came on, it came on strong. But I was trying to analyze it and look for the telltale signs. I felt confident that I could figure it out and cut it off at the pass.

I could sift, and I didn't feel like throwing up when I did. Definitely a plus. I still had work to do and needed a lot of practice. My aim, so to speak, wasn't that great yet. I couldn't go far distances, but I could get myself from point A to point B in a nearby area, and that came in handy. Rava and Dorian said it would get better with practice. She assured me it had been the same learning curve for her.

Now I could shift with ease. Not only did I like mastering that, because let's face it, I hated failure, but it also put my raven at ease. I still felt her presence, but it wasn't as jarring. It didn't feel like a bird in a gilded cage, rattling her prison bars and desperate to get out. She felt at ease, comforted, and . . . rested. She lurked in the shadows of my mind. There was a trust there now, as weird as it felt. Handing over control was not my strong suit, but it felt different with her. She was me, and there was no way that Rava or anyone else could have explained that to me. It was something I truly needed to feel to appreciate it.

It helped me understand Roman a little more than I did before. If the way she fought inside me when I'd struggled to hand her the reins was even a tiny fraction of what Roman felt with his wolf . . . I shuddered at the thought. He and his wolf sounded like they had to work out some issues of their own.

Roxanne had said he killed relentlessly after he lost Maya. He let too much of his wolf take over. He became feral. Otherworldly. He'd said he was determined never to become that monster again.

My raven had her own personality. Her own thoughts, and in the same sense, her own emotions. That meant Roman's wolf did too. A part of me wanted to know his animal. A part of me didn't know that it would be possible. My girl had her own voice. What did his sound like? But how could a bird and a wolf communicate? We hadn't figured that part out yet. I couldn't rely on Hades every time I needed to shift.

At the mention of Hades' name, my raven stirred, huffing in annoyance. I chuckled to myself, reminding her that he had saved me right before I shifted the first time. He wasn't all that bad. I rather liked his company sometimes. The bantering was fun. She questioned my logic, but I reminded her that we didn't have to tell him. She could torture him all she wanted, but when it came down to it, we all had the same agenda.

I felt her acquiesce, reluctantly, I might add.

I stood up from the bed, walking to the vanity and sitting down to brush my wet hair.

"Whatcha doin'?" Jules said, appearing in the mirror three feet from my face.

I inhaled in shock, and spit smacked right into my windpipe, sending me into a coughing fit from semi-choking. The force of my surprise as I pushed away from Jules was too much. I tipped myself back, teetering on the bench as I hacked up a lung. My feet went up in the air while I windmilled my arms, hoping to stop the inevitable. It was useless. I landed on my back with a thud.

A cackling came from the mirror above me as I sucked in air while my confused body tried not to die. Death from spit. Add that to what would end up actually killing me. I just laid there on the floor, my arms sprawled out, waiting for it to end.

"It really never does get old," she said through fits of tears.

I gasped, clearing my throat. "You're a twat," I said, my voice hoarse.

She only laughed harder. "For a demon, you sure scare easily. I expected better."

Lifting my head off the ground, I glared at her. "Dude, the devil himself would jump out of his skin if you appeared right in front of his face and he wasn't expecting you." I let my head down, resting on the floor again.

I craned my neck when I heard a knock at the door. "Come in," I said, coughing again.

Roxanne peeked in, then opened it wide to enter. "Am I interrupting something?" she asked, raising an eyebrow when she saw Jules. "You did it again, didn't you?"

Jules grinned and Rox shook her head, coming to my side and extending her hand in a gesture to help me up. I shot Jules another dirty look, then threw my hand to catch hers. She helped pull me up and handed me a glass of water.

Taking it, I sipped it until my raw throat felt better.

"I heard you coughing," Rox said, answering the silent question.

"Thanks," I said, before turning to side-eye the poltergeist. "I choked on spit."

Roxanne tried to hold in her snort, but she only just managed. She quickly shook it off and mumbled, "Sorry."

"Laugh it up, you two. It's all fun and games until you piss off the demon."

"I'm trembling in my mirror realm," Jules teased, making the glass warble for effect.

I couldn't help but crack a smile. "Nice touch," I said as her mirror waved, then cleared my throat again. "I'd ask 'to what do I owe the pleasure,' but I feel like that would make me a liar. So instead, I'll ask, what do you want?"

She shrugged. "Nothing at the moment. Just saying hi. I've got eyes on Lyra, but nothing to note as of yet."

"What about Jo—" I stopped myself, knowing full well he never had been John. "Azrael. Where is he at?"

"Lying low. I haven't seen him." The disappointment in her tone was thick. "I'm sorry. I've been searching. But no news is good news, right?" Even she didn't sound convinced.

"Ha," I barked a laugh. "Not likely. He'll make himself known soon. He'll wait until we feel confident and comfortable. Then he'll show his face." It's what he did. I knew him. I wished so badly that I didn't.

A sense of grief washed over me quickly, and I pushed it aside, unwilling to let it grab ahold of me now.

"We'll be ready for him when he does," I finished. I pressed my lips together tightly.

I wanted nothing more in this afterlife than to make sure that bastard found a way to die. I didn't yet know how to actually kill the Archangel of Death, but it was now my mission to find out. Well, that and stopping the end of the world. Two missions.

Jules smiled big, showing her teeth. "You bet your ass we will."

Roxanne rubbed her hand over my back reassuringly and I looked at her with appreciation.

"You ready for tonight?" she asked me.

"Oooh, what's tonight?" Jules asked, her eyes brightening with excitement as she waited for an answer.

I turned to look at her. "It's a ritual with Roman and the pack. We're mates, so . . . we, um . . ." I tilted my head, turning to Roxanne in confusion. "What do we do here?"

"You're getting married, Fury," she answered, jutting her thumb over her shoulder and pointing to the door. "What did you think was going to happen? Rava is bringing your dress up any minute."

I felt the color drain from my face. "I . . . what?" I spluttered. My heartbeat raced and I could feel the pounding in my temples. *Married*?

Roxanne busted out laughing, doubling over, putting her hands on her knees. Jules snort-laughed, falling down in a hysterical fit and out of view in her mirror.

I glared at Roxanne, furrowing my brows. "You cackle like a swamp witch, you know that?" I got up while they had their fun, choosing to sit on the edge of the bed instead.

"You should've seen your face," she said, wiping the tears from her eyes.

"It wasn't that funny," I mumbled.

Jules reappeared, red-cheeked and catching her breath. "I assure you it was."

Rolling my eyes, I crossed my arms. "Care to tell me what really happens at this thing?" I huffed in annoyance. "For real this time."

Roxanne smiled, sitting on my vanity chair. "Oh, come on, Fury. It was funny and you know it. Don't tell me you wouldn't do something like that to me."

"She's more likely to strap you upside down on a St. Andrew's cross and leave you there," Jules said.

Roxanne nodded in agreement. "Probably. You should have seen it when she used a pool cue to deep-throat a douchebag shifter in my bar."

"What?" Jules exclaimed. "I miss all the fun."

I cracked a smile. "It was before I knew you."

"Will you promise to call me the next time it happens?" she asked, sounding hopeful.

I barked a laugh, thinking about how there would probably be a next time. "Why not."

Jules looked pleased as she smiled and watched Roxanne turn to the mirror, fluffing her gorgeous afro and playing with a curl.

"Rox?" I prompted. "The ritual."

"Right." She cleared her throat, turning back to face me. "It's the celebration of finding a mate. The whole pack is there, even the kids. It's really to honor the couple and to formally announce they're mated."

I nodded along as she spoke, not really picturing what it was. I only had one frame of reference, and that was the wake. "So . . . is there a bonfire and hot dogs again?"

Roxanne's smile was warm, and it reached her eyes. "I'm sure someone will start a bonfire somewhere, but it's more than that. To show the pack that Roman is worthy of you, he has to fight and prove himself."

"Fight? That seems pointless. It's Roman," I said. "He can't die. Why would anyone fight him?"

"That's the tradition."

"Okay, so who fights him, though?" I was trying to picture someone just raising their hand like an idiot and saying they'd fight Roman. The alpha. The immortal. No one would do that.

"For a hetero couple, the tradition is that someone from the female's family fights the male mate."

Not that any of it made much sense, but my heart sank. I didn't have family, and the evening was going to be really awkward in front of the whole pack when we all announced I didn't have someone.

"I don't have family," I said quietly. "So how do we . . . will the pack understand or make the exception?"

"I'm your family," Roxanne said. "I'm stepping in to fight for you."

What a weird turbulence of emotions. My heart swelled at the gesture and the notion that she considered me as her real family. The rush of worry swirled right through it, pushing it aside and taking hold. "You are going to fight your brother. You can't do that."

She threw her head back and laughed. "Oh yes I can. Just you wait."

She didn't seem worried in the slightest. She almost seemed amused by the idea of it, and that felt reassuring.

"How long do you fight for?" I asked.

"Well it used to be to the death," she said, using a hand to wave vaguely. "But that was a *very* long time ago when everyone was stupid. Now it's to first blood. Again, it's just following the traditions more than anything. It's more for show."

I sat there gaping for a moment, trying to process what she'd told me. It was Roman. This was his sister. Surely he'd pull his punches . . . right? He wouldn't draw blood on Roxanne. I scrubbed my hands down my face.

"You all need therapy," I said, exhaling loudly. "So you both fight. There's some blood. Then what?"

Roxanne pressed her lips together. "Then you fuck."

I stared silently, waiting for her to finish her sentence, but it seemed that was the end. "We fuck," I repeated.

She pressed her lips together in a smile, mumbling, "Mmm hmm."

"Are you going to elaborate?" I asked, holding my hands out in question.

"I don't think you need instructions," Jules piped up. "You're well-versed as it is."

I shot her a look that said, 'Shut up.'

"You're mates. So to prove to everyone that you have both been claimed, you do it in front of everyone," Rox said, watching me carefully. "I figured that wouldn't be a problem for you, all things considered."

A rush of heat coursed through my veins and shot straight to the place between my legs. Exhibitionism was certainly something I enjoyed. Damn, it was hot. In front of the entire pack . . . that would definitely be more eyes on me than ever before. The sex clubs in the Afterlife were a busy place, but you picked rooms. Areas. Not everyone was in one location. Even then, I'd stopped going long ago. Got weird when you saw someone that irritated you so much you wanted to drive a stake through their forehead for entertainment. Everything after that was smaller groups where someone lived.

Roman's entire pack was huge. I wasn't sure what to expect, but I had a feeling I would enjoy it.

I finally met Roxanne's curious stare, twisting my lips into a side smile, doing what I could to hide the excitement. "Yeah, no. I'm good."

"I know you are." She put her hands on her thighs, pushing herself up from the chair. "Finish getting ready. I'll come get you at sundown."

"You aren't staying?" I asked. It was unlike Roxanne to leave when it came down to me getting dressed or prepped for something. She enjoyed that sort of thing.

Walking toward the door, she stopped right before it and looked over her shoulder. A feral grin showed an elongated canine. A faint glow flashed in her eyes before she winked at me. "I have a fight to prepare for."

CHAPTER 10
FURY

Feet pounded the earth. A steady call. A battle drum.

The sound of over a hundred shifters, eagerly awaiting the upcoming ritual.

I heard them about a mile out. Their whoops and hollers in an otherwise quiet forest was akin to a bulldozer rolling through. Pebbles skittered across the ground the closer we got, jumping in rhythm with the deep boom of the earth as it shook beneath their feet.

It wasn't until we were right on top of them that I could really see it.

An arena for this ritual had literally been carved away into the land. Fifty yards in diameter, the massive circle plunged straight down, rows of makeshift seats acting as the stairs that led to the very bottom. Almost thirty feet below ground, where the dirt was thin and bedrock thick, was the center of where the fight would take place—followed by a truly indecent amount of sex that had my pulse hammering if Roxanne was to be believed.

I hoped she was.

"How long has this been here?" I asked as we approached the edge. It was mostly full, with a few scattered spots left open, apart from one section at the very bottom where I spotted a head of light purple hair. Rava.

"A hundred years or so," Rox said, waving at a few friendly faces that I was starting to recognize but still couldn't remember names. I smiled back in what I hoped looked like approachable politeness, but probably better resembled a grimace. "The mating ritual dates wayyyy back before Houston was picked as an official epicenter. Before shifters even came to America. Most of the larger packs have their own ieró zevgároma that's hidden by enchantments or what not. Kelly did ours, so unless you've been here, you'll never be able to find it."

"Clever," I murmured as we made our way around the side. "What was that word you called it again?"

"Ieró zevgároma," she repeated. "It means—"

"Sacred fucking? Coupling?" My eyebrows drew together.

Roxanne squinted at me. "You speak Greek?"

I tilted my head from side to side. "Somewhat. I'm rusty."

"Sacred mating," she said, correcting my translation. "You know, because shifters."

I snorted. "Why am I not surprised the ancient Greeks came up with this? Totally speaks to their quasi-orgy-fetish style."

She chuckled right as a kid around eight years old yelled, "AUNTIE ROXY," at the top of her lungs. I lifted both eyebrows.

"Um. Do you have another sibling I need to know about because Roman didn't mention he had any kids?" Not that it mattered if this was a child he'd had with another shifter, but this sure as shit wouldn't have been the time to tell me.

"No." She shook her head while smiling at the little girl. "She's Caitlin and Rava's daughter."

"Move, people!" the girl yelled. Some shifters scooted to the side to try to make space, but not everyone was listening . . . until wisps of hot pink magic shot from her fingers. It snaked straight up the seats to where we stood, shoving everyone to one side to clear a path for us.

My mouth dropped open.

"Pria!" Rava sighed, shaking her head. She shot a look of apology to the now bristling shifters, who immediately relaxed when they realized what had happened.

Beside me, Rox tried to hide her smirk behind a cough. "Pria is a hybrid. Like you and Rava. Half shifter, half witch."

"No shit," I said, watching as Rava scolded her daughter quietly. The girl didn't seem to be paying much attention as she watched Roxanne start down the seats toward her. Mirth shone in her dark brown eyes as she ignored Rava and bolted up the last few stairs to meet Roxanne. I followed down at a slower pace, nodding awkwardly to the shifters I made eye contact with on the way.

"I missed you sooooo much," the little girl said, throwing her arms tight around Rox's waist.

"I've missed you too, kiddo." She hugged her back just as tightly, putting her cheek to the top of Pria's poofy black curls. "How's school going? Magic lessons look like they're progressing."

Pria let her go to rock back and forth excitedly on the tips of her toes. "They're good. Ms. Jenn says I'm the best in the class. Which made Ashley maaaad. Her mom says I shouldn't be there because I'm not a full witch."

"Well, that's not nice," Rox said with a frown. "Did you tell Ms. Jenn this?"

Pria nodded. "She told me to be the bigger person and ignore it."

Roxanne hummed, sharing a look with Rava over the girl's head. Neither looked pleased with that answer.

"Pria, come down here so Roxanne and Fury can take a seat," Rava said now that the initial excitement passed.

A guilty smirk crossed the young girl's face before she turned on her heel and skipped down the seats till she reached the bottom. Rava crouched down in front of her, blocking her view as we followed behind. She spoke quietly; calm yet assertive as she scolded her daughter.

"We've talked about this, baby. You can't just use magic on people without their permission. You wouldn't like it if they used magic on you, would you?"

As I reached the bottom, I caught a flash of water welling in the little girl's eyes while she stared at her light-up sketchers. "No . . . but Mom , they weren't listening."

"First of all, you didn't give them a chance to. You yelled for them to move and then you made them. Second, not everyone is going to do what you want, when you want it. That doesn't give you permission to use magic on them."

Pria's bottom lip wobbled, but she sucked it in with her two front teeth, biting down to stop the tremble. Beside Rava, Caitlin sighed. "Leave it be for tonight. She's excited, and she misses the pack. We can cut her a little slack."

At her other mom's words, the girl perked up, all traces of guilt vanishing. Rava groaned. "Do you have to do that in front of her?"

"It's just for one night," Caitlin insisted, winking at Pria.

"It sets a bad precedent when she needs to learn about respecting boundaries," Rava replied, a little tersely. She let out a breath she must have been holding and slid back into the seat beside her mate. Pria sat next to her, followed by me and Roxanne. Below ground level, the thundering of shifter feet pounding the earth reverberated through my body, pulling me in. If not for the advanced fae-shifter-vamp-hybrid hearing, I wouldn't have been able to hear a damn thing.

"So Pria," I said quietly, trying to find a way to word my question. Rox must have sensed my confusion because she filled in the gaps.

"Was sent away after the first attacks on you, for fear the attacker might focus on people surrounding you—and their loved ones," she said without missing a beat. My lips parted.

"That was over a month ago."

"And Pria's been gone all that time. Caitlin and Rava enrolled her in a private school for witches so she could work on her magic." A trace of guilt flashed through me. I knew it wasn't my fault. Not truly. I didn't ask for my ex to be an archangel that was hellbent on killing me—again—because of my supposed angel blood I knew nothing about. I certainly didn't ask to put them or anyone else in danger, but still, being just a kid and taken away from everything you know, the guilt was there. "It was going to have to happen at some point," Rox added softly. "They'd just been putting it off despite Pria's growing magical outbursts. Don't beat yourself up too much. Sending her killed two birds with one stone."

I picked at a fraying edge of my jean shorts, ignoring the worming feeling beneath the surface. "This mating ritual must be a pretty big deal if they brought her back for it."

"You could say that." Roxanne nodded. "It's not every day the entire North American pack gets a second alpha."

My eyebrows rose as I stared at her dubiously. "They do know I'm not a wolf, right?"

Roxanne snorted. "Not all of them do, but it doesn't matter. You're Roman's mate and he's chosen to publicly stake that claim. Shifters respect that—if they know what's good for them."

It was my turn to snort at her. "Right. So Pria and the other kids are here to—"

"Watch the fight," the little girl chimed in. "Obviously."

I nodded once. Clearly, there was shit I needed to learn.

"I'll be taking Pria home after I beat Roman," Roxanne said under her breath. "Obviously," she added with a wink at Pria, who was swinging her legs while we waited for things to get underway. "I love you, but I have no desire to see what's going to happen after."

Given it was her brother and me, no other explanation was needed.

"You seem awfully confident about this," Caitlin said, speaking a little louder to be heard over the shifters around us.

Roxanne smirked. "Roman may be *the* alpha, but I taught him everything he knows."

All at once, the shifters quieted. Shouts turned to whispers as a hush fell over the crowd, and on the other side of the ieró zevgároma, Roman stood like a wolf god. His black locs were pulled back, showing the warpaint that dotted his cheekbones and outlined his jaw. Shirtless and glistening beneath the moonlight, the white paint travelled across his proud shoulders, down the hard edges of his chest, sweeping a story across every inch of his beautiful brown skin.

Suddenly I saw the appeal of this whole thing.

You know, apart from the very public and gratuitous sex that I was also totally down for.

"You can pick your jaw up off the floor whenever," Roxanne snickered.

I elbowed her in the side, which caused her to let out a demented cackle. "And to think, you told him 'hard pass' when he declared you his mate in my bar."

I did. Repeatedly.

If past Fury knew what present Fury did, she might not have run.

It had worked out so far, so I couldn't say I truly had any regrets about how things had run its course.

"You know what they say. Treat 'em mean, keep 'em keen."

From a distance, Roman heard what I'd said, and he lifted an eyebrow.

I had a feeling he was going to ask me about that later. Or better yet, take it out on me here. Tonight. My skin flushed at the prospect.

"Thanks for that. Getting him all worked up before his ass kicking," Roxanne whispered.

"That's a bad word," Pria said, semi-scolding Roxanne.

Caitlin snorted, which led to Rava throwing her another glare.

"She's an adult. She can say what she wants," Rava said under her breath. "Now quiet, unless you want Mama to take you back home and put you to bed."

Pria's mouth snapped shut with an audible clank of teeth that had even Rava grinning as Roman descended into the arena. Silence ensued for a suspended beat.

Then he spoke.

"My family, my pack, my people—" His voice carried loud and clear, yet low and intimate at the same time. "I stand before you to lay claim to my mate in the rite of ieró zevgároma."

With his final word, the pack let out a collective howl that not even the wind could compete with.

"Who here stands for Fury, to test my worth as a mate? Who here fights for her, to first blood?"

"I do."

Beside me, Roxanne stood, moonlight casting her face in partial shadows.

Across the space, Roman answered, "Very well. At first howl, we duel."

Roxanne stepped forward into the circle. She reached for the hem of her T-shirt , whipping it off to reveal a sleek black sports bra and spandex shorts underneath.

A certain swagger entered her step as she strode forward, stopping only feet from him. While he towered over her smaller form, the confidence she wielded was undeniable, and I was curious to see how this played out.

From the stands, a lone howl cried out, and others joined in.

Roxanne and Roman went from utterly still to a flurry of motion as he tried to grab her and she ducked, sending a knee to the kidney while she was at it.

Something brushed against my side. I glanced over at Pria who had scooted closer but was watching them with nothing short of awe.

"Who do you think is gonna win?" she asked me while Roxanne executed a perfect rolling maneuver to avoid his outstretched claws. She popped back up and turned to face him, but Roman had done some sort of movie-worthy flip over her head, landing behind her.

She must have sensed it, and swung a roundhouse kick in a full one hundred and eighty degrees.

"No idea," I said honestly as Roman caught her foot. He twisted it and she spun with the movement, landing on her back. Roman grinned down, thinking this was the end.

"I think Rox will," the little girl said, very assured. I didn't want to pull my eyes away, but the calm, collected way she said it made me want to read her expression.

"What makes you say that?"

Roman dived, going to strike against her forearm. I really thought it was over until Roxanne's legs shifted in a fraction of a second. They went from the human limbs of a woman to the ginormous, fur-covered legs of her wolf. The strangest and most extraordinary part was that they were the only thing that did. The rest of her remained in human form as she kicked him off with incredible strength.

Roman went flying straight up into the air.

In a flash, Roxanne shifted her legs back and rolled out of the way as he came falling back down. She was on her feet before he hit the ground.

Pria grinned smugly. "Because girls rule and boys drool."

I snorted. Her answer was so . . . eight. Roxanne was definitely gaining the upper hand, but it had nothing to do with gender and everything to do with her speed and strength.

Roman hit the bedrock hard and took a face full of dirt.

Rox flashed a victorious smile, sauntering forward to land first blood. Roman may have been down, but he wasn't out for the count.

He rotated his hips, kicking her legs out from under her, while getting his hands beneath his form and using his still moving leg to gain enough momentum to get his other leg up and under him to stand.

I half expected him to dive on her when she went down, but he seemed to have learned from the last time he tried and instead backed off, taking a breather to reconfigure his strategy.

Rox landed on her butt in a plume of dust but grinned up at him, clearly enjoying the duel despite the seriousness the ritual started with.

"You call this worthy?" she said, egging him on. His eyes flashed blue, his wolf surfacing at her insult.

"Watch it, sister," he said in a deep gravelly voice that I'd grown to associate as his more feral half.

"Watch yourself," she replied with a wink.

Roxanne charged him, shifting mid-stride without faltering for a second. Roman barely had time to follow her lead in their dance of claws and teeth. He shifted quickly, albeit not nearly as fast, in an attempt to stop her from plowing him over.

I wasn't sure how it would go when they met head on, but it seemed Roxanne had a plan. As she approached—he lunged for her, and she shifted back. She dropped into a slide that would have made any Major League Baseball team proud. She slipped straight between his legs, vanishing underneath him before he knew what was up. In the second that passed for him to realize, she popped back up behind him and leapt onto his giant furry back, gripping the scruff of his neck harshly.

Roman rolled, trying to unseat her, but Roxanne wasn't giving up so easily. She took the weight of his entire wolf form as her back hit the ground. Other than a wince, she didn't let it show that the action caused her any pain, instead persisting with the hold on him. Roman shifted to his human form, lifting up from the waist before slamming back down in an attempt to crush her—or at the very least, jostle his sister loose.

And to think I had assumed they would pull their punches.

Rox wrapped her arms around his neck in a headlock, then twisted her body, flipping them before he could do it. With his hands and knees flat on the ground, Roxanne sat on his back, choking the life out of him—so to speak.

I was just beginning to wonder how far they'd take the ritual when Roman lifted a hand from her arm and, in the moonlight, a dark red liquid smeared over his fingers.

"First blood," he coughed.

Roxanne released him instantly and took a step back.

"Is it?" She smirked, a red line running down her forearm but healing quickly.

Roman stood up and followed her line of sight to the matching red mark on his bicep that was healing and had left behind a swipe of blood where it had been.

Roman glowered, not pleased she may have kept going if she had been the first to draw blood. Roxanne smiled, shrugging a bit, and the crowd let out a laugh.

"We both drew blood, but who was first remains unknown. Roman, I declare you worthy of the sister to my soul. However, it is not my choice to make."

All eyes fell on me, and Pria elbowed me in the ribs, stage whispering, "It's your turn."

Caitlin and Rava chuckled at their daughter's antics, shaking their heads.

"Fury," Roxanne said, summoning me forward. "Beneath the night sky and before this pack, do you find him a worthy mate to bind yourself to, from now until the earth takes you both?"

My heart hammered, the silence around us screaming for me to answer.

"I do."

Roxanne smiled at me. "Then come forth and let the sacred mating begin."

CHAPTER 11
FURY

I APPROACHED ROMAN SLOWLY.

Roxanne patted my shoulder on the way back to grab Pria, who was excitedly chatting about their sleepover and how she was going to show off her rock collection and the stuffed animals she'd acquired. Other kids and their caretakers made their way up the seats. A few teenagers grumbled about how they wanted to stick around and were promptly told to come back when they were paying their own bills. I snorted, especially since I didn't currently pay my own. Then again, I didn't really live in any one place. I bounced between my mates and their homes.

Through it all, Roman and I stood toe to toe, staring at one another with something far deeper and more profound than lust. We shared each other's amusement in listening to the younger generations. We shared our impatience and delicious tension as we waited for what came next. We also shared a quiet sort of intimacy, just being near each other and not simply content—but happy.

I valued that more than I could ever find the words to say.

As the last of the kids left, Caitlin walked forward, carrying a clay pot with some sort of black substance. I cast a curious glance as Rava stepped up beside her.

"We will now paint you in the symbols of our pack to represent our acceptance," Caitlin said quietly. Around us, a subdued pulse of feet meeting earth began again, but unlike before, it didn't resemble a battle drum. Instead, an almost soothing sort of rhythm that seemed to aid the interpretation of them accepting me.

When I hadn't moved, Rava stepped in front of me and slowly reached for my shirt.

"May I?" she whispered. I wasn't sure if it was part of the ritual, but I appreciated it all the same.

I gave her a small nod and lifted my arms for her to begin undressing me.

With each piece of clothing that came off, my heart beat faster. A heat creeped over my skin.

There was a different sort of vulnerability in allowing them to undress me like this, for all to see. It wasn't driven by the same kind of heat that made me an exhibitionist, but instead was incredibly revealing.

Intimate.

Sacred.

When Rava pressed her fingertips to my cheek bones, I began to understand the ritual in a way I hadn't before. The paint was cool but not cold, and it thankfully dried quickly.

We stood in the center, not speaking as she painted my face and neck. Her fingers dipped in the bowl and then swiped across my shoulders in steady strokes. Down my arms and around the curve of my breasts.

Roman's eyes glowed an icy blue the entire way. His wolf was very much at the forefront and ready to claim its mate.

About halfway down my body, heat started to settle in under his watchful gaze. There was something erotic about being watched by him while Rava painted my naked form.

When she dropped to her knees to start on my thighs, her fingers brushed across a sensitive patch of flesh, and I shivered. A low rumble escaped his chest, the alpha starting to grow impatient.

My body flamed hotter. I was glad for the moonlight and shadows in concealing the flushed shade my skin was no doubt turning.

Rava's fingers moved quickly, painting the rest of my legs and feet. When she was done, she stepped back with Caitlin to observe me.

They both bowed their heads in respect, and the crowd behind them followed.

When I turned to Roman and saw that he was on his knees, doing the same, I wanted to combust. A cool wind whipped through the circle, lifting the sweaty strands of hair from the back of my neck.

No one told me what I was supposed to do now.

There were no instructions.

So I followed my heart.

Running my fingertips down the sides of Roman's face, I cupped his jaw and tilted it back. The eyes of his wolf met mine and the primal hunger I saw there—it shattered us both.

He stood up, pulling me into him, our lips meeting in a clash of teeth and tongues. I fisted his dreads, and a growl rippled through the clearing.

"Mine," Roman declared. His voice was mottled. Deeper. Rough.

He grabbed my ass with both hands and hoisted me up.

"My mate," he continued when he broke away to kiss down my neck. I tilted my head back, wrapping my legs around his waist.

"My equal," he purred, tilting my body in such a way his already hard cock touched my entrance. After minutes of standing in front of him, unable to touch, to tease, I was more than ready.

"My queen," he whispered reverently. Teeth pricked my skin on the opposite shoulder that he'd claimed before. I tipped my head to the moon, mouth falling open in pleasure as he bit me. A moan worked its way up my throat, turning to a gasp as he thrust into me.

My pussy spasmed, locking tight around his cock. Roman groaned into my shoulder, his fingers turning to claws that pricked my ass as he started working me over his length.

I dropped my hands from his hair to his shoulders, raking my own nails down his back. Roman released the flesh of my shoulder with a pop, throwing his head back to let out a howl. The wolves around us followed suit.

I opened my eyes to stare at them as they watched me, their eyes filled with lust. Several of them were touching themselves. Others undressing. Then there were the couples like Caitlin and Rava, who looked like they were most of the way to finishing the deal themselves.

Their ravenous stares urged me on, and I bucked against him. My hips bounced in rhythm against his, the smack of flesh meeting flesh and panting moans the only sounds now.

I couldn't remember a time in my life that I'd ever felt so alive.

I never wanted it to end.

That was the thought that filled me when my body tipped over the precipice. My cunt contracted. Blackness exploded behind my eyes as a visceral shudder ran through me.

Roman dropped to his knees, tipping me backwards. My head touched the ground, followed by my shoulders. He kept pumping into me, holding my ass and hips off the ground to guide them to his engorged cock as he fed it to me.

I gasped, looking down at where our bodies joined. The black paint on my body smearing and mixing with the white paint on his. It was the most erotic sight I'd ever seen. I loved it.

"So tight," he said through gritted teeth. "So perfect."

I was approaching another peak when he pulled out, then set me down. He maneuvered my legs around him, turning me over so that my face was pressed into the ground and my hips pulled up, ass in the air.

"I love this ass," he muttered, before biting it. My back arched and I let out a hiss as pleasure shot through me, putting me on the very edge.

"Need you," I groaned, rocking my hips back.

He released me from his bite and gripped me tight. I didn't even feel him at the entrance until he was shoving inside me, and I tightened around him.

My mouth fell open as I let out an anguished cry. My body wound up, then snapped. My legs turning to jelly. The second climax wasn't as strong, instead leaving me wanting more. Needing more to truly finish the job.

"Open your eyes, cherub," Roman commanded. "Look at them."

And look I did.

In the time between my first orgasm and my second, the seats around us had turned into an all-out orgy. Men and women fucked. Sometimes two men and a woman, one taking her from the front and the other behind. Then there were the groups where one man fucked another, and the one being fucked ate a woman out. No one was truly alone in the public act taking place, where we all embraced our desires together. I never felt more like I'd truly found my people.

"Roman," I breathed.

"What do you need?" he asked, his voice thick with restraint.

"You. Your cock." I groaned in frustration, reaching for that pinnacle again but failing to grab on. "I need to come."

Roman pulled out. I wanted to cry from the emptiness when my blood was pounding, yearning for a release only he could give me.

"What are you—" I started to protest, but my words were cut off when I felt him brush the inside of my thighs, his mouth covering me and latching onto my clit. He grabbed my hips, pulling me back so that I was sitting on him, spreading my pussy wide open for his taking.

I rocked into him, letting out another moan as his tongue swirled around my sensitive nub, then sucked.

"Yes," I breathed, finally gaining ground.

He blew on my clit, and I broke.

A mix between a guttural moan and scream escaped me. My body locked tight in the sweetest ecstasy. The best and worst sort of pleasure, where it felt so good it hurt.

My back arched so far back it threatened to snap as I clamped tight. He rubbed his tongue over me through the entire orgasm, drawing every last drop of pleasure from me until my body turned soft and pliable, too at ease to fight anymore.

With one last lick, Roman lifted my hips and pulled out from under me. I fell back, my butt hitting the heels of my feet when he let go. There I stayed, kneeling and half-dazed, when Roman stepped around in front of me. His cock was hard and heavy as it swung between his legs.

He gripped its base, lifting it to position the tip a few inches from my lips. I opened wide, taking his head. My tongue swirled around it, tasting my release and his precum.

"I'm close," Roman panted as he ran his fingers through my hair. I relaxed, taking him deeper. The rough pad of my tongue running along the underside of his length as I rocked into him and pulled back, going a little further each time.

My lips curled around my teeth to keep from hurting him. I pressed them tight to his skin, sucking hard. The way he twitched and pulsed told me how much he loved it.

"I want to show my pack who you belong to," he groaned. I hummed my approval around his member, bucking my head up and down.

Roman pushed in and out twice more before holding the sides of my head with both hands, twining his fingers through my hair, gripping tight. I parted my lips, widening my jaw so he could fuck my face.

I stilled while he thrusted in a fervent rhythm, his cock hitting the back of my throat repeatedly while I grasped his muscular thighs, keeping balance. A loud grunt sounded, then he shuddered as he erupted in my mouth. His salty release coated my tongue, mixing with saliva as it dripped down my chin, splashing against my chest, and running down the slope of my breasts.

Roman cupped my cheek, rubbing his juices into my skin, slightly possessive yet still sweet. "I love you," I said, the words slipping out of me.

Roman got on his knees with me and kissed me softly. "I'd destroy the world for you—and I don't even think I'd care anymore. That's how much I need you."

We kissed again, falling into the haze of lust and love that consumed the circle. But in the back of my mind, where I couldn't ignore it, I thought about what he'd said.

While I hoped it would never come to that, I believed him.

The part that scared me the most was that I was starting to believe that too.

I needed him. Them.

And I'd destroy anything that stood in the way. Even the Afterlife itself.

CHAPTER 12
FURY

JULES LEANED FORWARD ON HER ELBOWS, CRADLING HER FACE IN HER HAND while she watched me get dressed.

Kelly had put the final touches on my 'battle-ready' gala gown. We'd replaced the spaghetti straps with a thicker piece that clasped behind my neck. I twisted around, making sure it felt right and my boobs stayed in place. The black tulle of the skirt had been lessened as I requested, but it was still more than enough to cover my legs. Beneath it all, black leggings connected to my pale rose-colored halter , the rip-away function of the skirt cleverly hidden by a thick black ribbon tied around my waist.

The shade of pink was muted and not something I would have likely chosen, but Rox liked it and my hair more than made up for it. I put on my Doc Martens and double-knotted the laces for good measure. Standing in front of the full-length mirror, the boots were lost under the long skirt. Kelly had measured that tulle perfectly, and it touched the ground without dragging, but also without showing any part of my feet. I looked like I was floating.

"That's pretty," Jules said. "You look like a ballerina princess." Looking down at where she knew my boots were, she added, "Well, almost. Like a ballerina princess assassin."

I snorted. "I'd much prefer the latter. The whole pink tutu thing is not really my style," I said, trailing off. After a long pause, I added, "But it does serve a purpose. And it fits with the theme of that room. Gotta make it look real, after all."

"What's that mean?" Jules asked, pointing at my neck.

My fingers grazed over the intricate lines of the Celtic knot necklace. "It's, um, it's what Dorian gave me as his mate. It claims me as his and claims him as mine."

Jules waggled her eyebrows. "Fancy. So he gives you a necklace, Roman fucks you like a savage in front of everyone . . . what does Ezra do in this brother-husbands scenario?"

I busted out laughing. "Brother-husbands what?"

"You know that show, right? *Sister Wives*?"

"I've heard of it, but it's not really my kind of show. How have you seen it? Do you have TV in the mirror realm?" I asked, now genuinely curious as to what went down on her side of the world.

"I watch shows through mirrors in people's houses," she said and shrugged. "Anyway, it's like that for you, except the opposite. I don't know what that's called, or if it's even got a word for it. But you're the girl, and you've got three husbands."

"I do not have three husbands. I had one once, and that was enough," I said firmly. I wasn't so sure why the thought of calling them my husbands would cause such an adverse reaction. They weren't Azrael. They were my mates. I felt it. I knew it with every fiber of my being. This was real, and it was forever. Why it happened, I didn't know. I no longer cared about the why. It just . . . was. And I was happy for it.

Being called mate and allowing them to claim me while I claimed them didn't bother me. Why then did the word husband?

"Fine, *mates,* then. But it doesn't have the same ring to it," she said, frowning. "You still didn't answer the question, though. What does Ezra give you?"

"You know . . . I don't entirely know. Ezra is different. He's . . ." I paused, trying to find the right way to explain what I had with my vampire mate.

Ezra was the easiest in some ways. While his mind-probing was infuriating at times, he was also the one that could probably understand me more than anyone else. There was a comfort factor in that.

He'd been trying so hard not to invade my space, giving me peace of mind and not showing up or listening without permission. Or, as he said it, not reacting to it and allowing me to feel like my thoughts were private.

He was also more detached as a mate. I'd started to think on it as I accepted the mate bond with them all. Dorian and Roman were adamant about claiming. Dorian didn't like to share, but he acknowledged the bonds and wouldn't come between them. Roman wasn't that dissimilar, but I had a feeling he was maybe willing to share a little more than Dorian would. My cheeks warmed at the thought, reminding me of the ritual. Ezra was firm that he would never come between me and my other mates. He knew what pain it caused when you couldn't be with them. He certainly seemed like he would be fine sharing. He had no problem letting Kendrick watch us before. I assumed we'd easily take things further one day.

But the fact remained, he'd not only lost his mate, but he'd been burned so badly by her when she rejected him. It didn't make her loss any less, but I could see how it would be hard to fully open up to me. I figured he wore a mask when he was charming and flirtatious, in some ways getting close to me but still keeping me at arm's length. Before I had made my decision to stay, there was one thing I knew for certain. Of all three mates, he was the only one willing to accept me going back. Dorian refused to get close, and Roman would have followed me into the Afterlife if he had to.

I traced the outline of the scar on my shoulder where Roman bit me when he claimed me the night of the bonfire.

Who knew? Maybe I was wrong. Maybe I was overthinking things. I certainly had plenty of time in my afterlife to do just that. Now it would seem I continued to do it in my post-afterlife-life.

"Yo, Fury," Jules said, pulling me from my thoughts. I refocused my eyes, looking up from where I was staring off in the distance.

"Yeah. Sorry, I was just thinking," I mumbled.

"You sort of disappeared there. You were saying that Ezra is different?" she prompted.

"Mmm hmm," I answered, reorganizing my thoughts, and sitting on a cushioned stool. "He's just more laidback about the whole mate thing, I think. He believes in it without question, and he takes it seriously, but he was rejected once before. That probably takes a lot of time to get over."

She gestured toward me as she said, "Well, take a look in the mirror, no pun intended. It's been over a hundred years and you're still not over what your ex did to you."

I stared at her, wide-eyed. "Wow. Tactful."

She shrugged again. "Look, I don't people much anymore, okay? I call it how I see it."

Straightening my posture, I tossed my hair over my shoulder. "I don't think you can compare the two, but you're not wrong. There is, however, a massive difference between being rejected by a mate and being beaten repeatedly and then murdered."

"How do you know? You've never been rejected, and he's never been beaten and murdered."

I let out a frustrated sigh. "What is your point?"

"Not sure anymore. Maybe I don't have one. Who knows where thoughts come from?"

I groaned loudly, but before I could tell her off, she turned her head as though she were listening to something. Turning back to me, she said, "I'll be back. Lyra is on the move. I need to watch."

"Wait, how do you kn—" I stopped my sentence when she disappeared fully, knowing I wouldn't get my answer.

How did she know that, though? Was it possible she could be in multiple places at once? She had to have some system set up. I wondered if she would take me back in there when this was all done. I wanted to see more, and not when she was yanking me from the middle of Ezra's apartment and into her world, freaking everyone out.

I sat alone in my room at Dorian's Houston estate. Somewhere down the hall, Roxanne and each of my mates were getting ready.

I grabbed a lock of my hair, twirling it around my finger while I waited and mentally prepared myself for how the evening would go.

If Lyra was on the move, our plan had worked. She was coming to the gala. She'd been dormant for over a week, not causing trouble or showing up anywhere. Jules had seen Azrael with Lyra once, but nothing more. She couldn't hear them, but she'd said it looked like a quarrel. Azrael ended it the way he always did; striking her down, standing over her, and commanding her compliance.

Then he disappeared, leaving Lyra on the floor. Jules hadn't seen him since.

A knock on the door pulled me away, and I said, "Come in."

Ezra entered, his charming half-smile lighting up the room. His tuxedo jacket was on, but he'd opted out of a bowtie, instead allowing the inky black tendrils of his tattoos to peek out of the open collar.

"You look beautiful," he said, coming toward me and kissing me gently on the cheek. I held the side of his arm as he leaned in, lingering for a moment longer than I expected. "You smell delicious too."

"Thanks. Roxanne got me a perfume," I said by way of explanation. "I'm not entirely sure it was for tonight or for use in general. I'm guessing the latter because she said she could smell sex on me, and she thought it was gross."

The look on Ezra's face shifted briefly before he caught it and corrected it. If he didn't think I saw it, he was dead wrong. He reached into his jacket, pulling out a flask. After unscrewing the top, he took a swig, then another. He traced his fingers over his lips, wiping off the excess before extending it to me.

Thank the stars he was giving me a drink without being a prick about it. I took the offering, downing several gulps before returning it.

"I wanted to say thank you," I started, trying to steer us into a good conversation.

"For?" he asked, raising an eyebrow.

"Giving me space," I said, tapping my temple with one finger. "I know it's not easy to just stop listening and probing, but I know you're trying. Even if I know you're listening in, you've been quiet about it. I appreciate it."

"It's what you wanted." Reaching his hand out, he grazed his thumb and forefinger down my cheek, stopping on my chin and leaning in for a peck on the lips, leaving behind a tiny tingle. Pulling away and stepping back, he said, "I always want to give you what you want."

I smiled, looking him up and down in a suggestive way. I hadn't been able to spend much time with him, and I missed it. "I want to see more of you."

He looked at me in surprise, then turned to look at the door.

"What'd you have in mind?" he asked, giving me his full attention as he sauntered toward me like a predator tracking prey.

I walked backward, raising an eyebrow coyly. My back hit the wall, and Ezra ascended on me. Wrapping my arms around his neck and throwing one leg around him, I pulled him toward me in a deep kiss as I opened my mouth to him. Tracing my tongue over his, I inhaled deeply, drinking him in. His hands gripped my upper waist before he moved them up my body, pressing into me and following my curves. We released, and I gasped for air, feeling the familiar ache between my thighs when he moved his hips against mine, his hard length pushing against me.

"Hurry," I said in a husky tone, need taking over me. "I don't know what time we are leaving."

I reached between us, rubbing his cock with the flat of my palm, and started to unbuckle him. He let out a throaty growl, licking, kissing, and nipping down my neck, moving to my shoulder. As I turned my head to give him better access, I felt him freeze, and he inhaled sharply.

"What?" I said, my breathing somewhat heavy.

Ezra stared at the mark left by Roman.

"The shifter claimed you," he said quietly.

I looked at him in confusion. "Uh, yeah? I told you about this, and it's not like you can't see that shit in my head." I dropped my leg from his waist, taking my hands away from his trousers. Talk about a mood ruined.

"I didn't think I'd be able to see it. The bite should heal."

I looked at him incredulously. "I . . . the mating bite doesn't fade or heal. The mark stays there, even on me, apparently."

Ezra stepped back, eyeing between the necklace and the bite. He rubbed the bridge of his nose while the silence spanned between us.

I reached up, feeling the scar tissue under the pads of my fingers. Ezra's reaction felt awful. For a brief moment, I felt like I needed to cover my mark. Like I had done something wrong . . .

That moment quickly passed. Fuck that. We all knew what this was.

I took my hand off it, walking forward and pushing past him.

"Fury, wait," he begged, reaching out to grab my wrist. I yanked away.

"No, don't lay your bullshit on me, Ezra. It's not cool," I said, reeling on him. My hands were flapping wildly as I yelled, pointing at him and waving them about. "You can't make me feel bad for this. You were there when I said I would stay. I made a choice. My choice was my mates. All three of you. You said you would never come between us. They would never come between you and me. Honestly, I can't even process this right now. Out of the three, I expected jealousy least of all from you."

He held his hands up in surrender. "I know, I know." His entire demeanor had softened, and the appearance of jealousy melted away.

"What is this, Ezra? Tell me what's going on." I crossed my arms, jutting out my hip.

He put his hands back in his pocket and met my annoyed glare. "It's been a weird week, that's all."

I could feel the heat of my glower. It would melt an iceberg. "No. That's not enough."

He sighed. "I've spent the past week tracking Azrael, trying to keep you safe. Interrogating vampires across the southern borders. Roman has shifters out doing the same, but the only one I can rely on is Kendrick. Too many vampires were infiltrated last time. I just can't trust them."

I softened slightly. "What does that have to do with Roman claiming me?"

He frowned. "It's not jealousy. It's . . . longing for something I haven't had in a long time."

I held my hand out toward the wall where we had just been. "Um, you were about to have me over there, fangs. Not sure what you're longing for."

He huffed a laugh, looking at the floor. "Not exactly."

"Then what?" I asked, feeling the frustration starting to creep in again.

"I haven't claimed you, but they have," he answered.

Oh . . .

The tension and anger left me. "I . . . I'm not rejecting you, Ezra. We just haven't . . . you've not been around much. It just sort of happened with Dorian. The ritual with Roman was planned, but . . ." I trailed off, not knowing what else to say. I met his reluctant smile with one of my own. "What happens when vampires claim?"

"We tattoo each other," he said.

I raised my eyebrows in surprise. "Really? As in we are the ones that put the ink on each other?" I wondered what that would look like. That took artistry and skill.

Ezra opened his mouth to answer, then shut it quickly. He creased his eyebrows together in concentration and it looked like he was focusing on something behind me. Looking back at me, he rushed through his words quickly. "I have to go. Kendrick has something." He walked toward me, placing a hand behind my head, and kissed me on the forehead. "We'll talk more. I promise. I'll make this up to you," he said before going to the door.

I stood in the middle of the room confused as hell, wondering what had just happened. I'd managed to make Ezra feel rejected. I'd told him to give me space. To get out of my head. I couldn't feel bad for wanting privacy. I had a right to that. But still, that combined with the other two claiming me first probably felt like a giant slap to his ego.

I scrubbed my hands down my face and stormed over to the bed. I grabbed a pillow, took a deep breath, then screamed into it.

"Um . . . are you okay?" Jules asked tentatively.

I jerked my head up and saw her concerned look. "Yeah, I'm fine."

She deadpanned. "Did you really just say you are *fine*?"

I sighed. "Did you hear or see any of that with Ezra just now?"

She shook her head. "Afraid not. What'd I miss?"

"My first encounter with juggling the emotions and commitments to three brother-husbands, as you put it," I muttered, tossing the pillow back onto the bed.

"Oh, well, I don't actually know anything about marital bliss." She grinned awkwardly and looked away. "Anything you want to talk about?"

I laughed. I had made a friend with a girl in a mirror. She was significantly older than me, and younger all the same, but it didn't matter. Even if it made her uncomfortable, she was willing to listen to me vent if I needed to. Knowing that I had that with her felt good. At the moment, it was all I needed.

I waved my hand, dismissing the weirdness that had just taken place. "Nah, don't worry about it. I'll talk to him more later. I think I figured out what's wrong. Now we just have to make it better."

A subtle pop sounded in the room, and I turned to see Dorian as he walked toward me.

I smiled at him, feeling content that this encounter would at least not feel emotionally overwhelming. A warmness spread through my body, making me wonder if the temperature in the room had risen.

"You look stunning," he said, eyeing the necklace that he'd given me.

"Thanks," I started to say, but my tongue felt thick, and the word came out warbly.

Fuck. Not again.

I reached out, trying to grab something to hold me up as my vision began to swim, but I missed the edge of whatever furniture was next to me.

"Fury," Dorian shouted, catching me in an instant and bringing me gently to the floor.

So much for not being overwhelmed.

My fangs grew, pressing into my lips, and I groaned. The need to bite was increasing, and the buildup inside was creating a pressure in my head. "Need . . ." I slurred. It was all I could get out.

"Ezra just left," Jules said. I turned to see her mirror shaking just before she disappeared.

Dorian looked at the door, then back at me. He looked like he was vibrating. My vision distorted further, making it appear like the room was rattling.

I felt my consciousness fading as the room started to spin violently. I pawed at Dorian's arm, mumbling his name.

I had seconds to spare before blood would start pouring from my ears and eyes, and he knew it.

"Need . . . you," I managed.

Dorian looked up at the ceiling and around the room, muttering curses. He pulled his jacket off and readjusted our bodies, laying me between his legs, cradling my head and back with his right arm. With his mouth, he ripped the sleeve of his shirt, exposing the thick muscles of his left forearm. He pressed it against my mouth, my fangs piercing the skin as blood came rushing out.

Instant relief flooded my body as I poured into Dorian. He grunted through it, resting his head on top of mine as I reverse-fed. His fingers stroked my skin while whispering reassuring words I couldn't even make out.

When everything had been expelled, I let go, grimacing at the metallic taste leftover in my mouth. The puncture wounds started to close and heal.

"Sorry," I mumbled hoarsely. "I didn't—"

"There's nothing to be sorry for," he said, snapping his fingers to make a glass of water appear. I took it gratefully, gulping and swishing it in my mouth.

"Thank you for catching me and letting me . . . you know." What? Thank you for letting me bite you and inject you with an overflow of blood? Didn't feel right, so I left it at that. I looked at the tattered material on his arm and groaned. "You ruined your shirt. Did I ruin my dress?"

Dorian scrunched his eyebrows as he held me, staring at me with concern. "Did you just ask if you ruined your dress?"

"Oh, shut up." I smacked his arm, moving to sit myself up. "You know what I mean."

He chuckled. "I don't know. Seems like a situation where you'd be using a secret code to call for help, when you're worried about ruining your dress." He smiled at me while I rolled my eyes. "And you're welcome."

I squeezed my eyes shut, inhaling deeply. "That one came on fast. It felt faster than it did in the cave with Roman."

He pressed his lips together. "Mmm. You almost collapsed the cavern that day." He looked up, and I followed his gaze to see a crack in the ceiling. My mouth fell open. "Looks like that's part of the deal now."

I felt horrible. There were too many people in this house. Something could have gone terribly wrong. "I have to get this under control."

Dorian stroked my hair. "We're going about it all wrong. We need to tackle it from another direction."

I turned to look at him in question. "Meaning?"

"Maybe give blood before these symptoms come on. Perhaps it would lessen the severity of your reactions and cause less"—he gestured above us—"whatever that is."

I nodded along and sat up, my body starting to feel like my own again. "You may be onto something there."

I was willing to give anything a try. I was with my mates almost all the time, and I had given blood to each of them. They were fine. I was fine. We'd be able to figure it out.

I wanted to ask what could go wrong, but I honestly didn't want the universe to answer me anymore when I asked stupid questions.

CHAPTER 13
FURY

THE BALLET STUDIO TURNED BALLROOM WAS EVEN MORE BEAUTIFUL IN REAL life than it was in the pictures. The renovated building in the historical district was classic and restored on the outside. Inside, the wooden details in the columns, window trim, and archways showcased those characteristics missing in modern architecture.

The balance bars that lined the walls around the entire room were draped in sheer white and pink fabric. There were thirty large round tables covered in elegant black tablecloths, each one carefully moved away from the mirrored walls, leaving more than enough space for us to get Lyra near one when she showed up.

The centerpieces were grand vases filled with floral arrangements in different hues of pink and red. Sprigs of tiny white flowers filled the gaps between the roses and greenery. Each one sat on a mirrored plate, giving us one more opportunity to get her near Jules.

We weren't willing to unnecessarily risk anyone for this operation. Instead of hiring musicians, Roxanne opted for music playing softly through speakers. A bar had been set up at the end of the room, but I'd been informed it was all for show. No one was drinking on this particular evening. Each shifter, fae, and vampire invited tonight was here for battle. We even had a couple of witches on hand.

Roxanne had outdone herself. I had no idea how she was able to coordinate all of it, but she'd managed to make it stunning. I almost believed it was a real celebration to publicly acknowledge my acceptance of taking three mates. Almost.

Rox came to my side, handing me a red drink with a cherry. A 'drink.' I smiled and took a sip of the brightly colored liquid. I winced at the sweetness and coughed through the carbonation. "What is this?" I asked hoarsely.

"A Shirley Temple. It's a kids' drink. Grenadine and Sprite." She smiled brightly. "I thought you'd like to feel like you were having a drink at the party."

I frowned, setting it down on a table. "I appreciate the thought, but it's just a bit too sugary." And not enough alcohol-y.

She reached out, handing me another drink. A purplish red color filled the rock glass, a wedge of lime pushed into the rim. I grimaced, but she said, "Not sweet. It's cranberry and lime."

I took it tentatively, sipped it, and nodded. It wasn't bad. Whisky was better, but I would take it.

"It's your mocktail."

"My what?"

She pointed to the glass in my hand. "A mocktail. A mock cocktail. I serve them to pregnant customers, and some that just want to play pool or cards but don't like drinking."

"I'll keep that in mind." I pressed my lips together and held it up in a sign of 'cheers'. Mock cheers for the mocktail. I didn't plan on making this a habit. I liked drinking, and I sure as shit wasn't pregnant.

It was boring expecting someone to arrive when they didn't know they were even invited. I knew Lyra would show up, but the wait was mind-numbing. Everywhere I turned I saw mirrors. I knew Jules was watching, I just didn't know where she was. I patted my dress, feeling the orb in my hidden pocket. All around us, couples and groups were mingling. Holding mocktails in their hands while they had their fake conversations.

I saw Elena talking to Rya and Kendrick. Her high ponytail was traded out for intricate braids. She wore a rich black off-the-shoulder dress, but I knew full well she could sift into her armor at the drop of a hat. Kendrick and Rya appeared to pay attention, but I knew they were watching every move in their periphery.

I looked up to see Dorian on the balcony overhead, watching the entire room. His posture was relaxed but commanding. I knew he was tense, but somehow he didn't show it. I scanned to find Roman and Ezra as they spoke to each other quietly, strategically placed near the center of the room. I made eye contact with Ezra, and he smiled, winking at me. I hoped that was his way of telling me things were okay with us.

Caitlin and Rava were on opposite sides of the room, bringing Kelly around to chat with fae and vampires I didn't know. It was an odd thing. I was told the summit was the only time all three factions were on equal ground. The only time they conversed and socialized together. From what I was seeing, it looked natural. Like it could easily happen more often. The three groups were getting along fine. They all had a common purpose. I knew this was a façade, but they seemed at ease with each other. Their interactions didn't look forced or uncomfortable. It made me think it could happen more often if they didn't try to stay segregated. Nothing good had ever come from it. I wondered if I could talk to my mates about it. Would that be over-stepping boundaries? Getting involved in their duties as alphas?

Turning back to Roxanne, I asked, "Hey, do you think Roman would mind if I talked to him about the pack and working together with the vampires?"

She raised an eyebrow, giving me her attention. "Working how?"

I shrugged my shoulders. "It just looks like everyone here gets along better than I thought they would. Common goal and all. But maybe it's more than that. Maybe we can work together as factions and not need to have this need for a summit every decade."

Roxanne pursed her lips as she thought about it. "I imagine more would get done if everyone wasn't always in a pissing contest. Besides, we all hate the summit. Talk to Roman. He's a good listener. You're his mate. It's not out of line."

I nodded along. "I'm just thinking it would have been easier to spread out resources, especially now. Like with the southern borders. It just makes more sense to work together."

A crease developed between Roxanne's eyebrows, and she waited a moment before speaking. "The southern borders? What are you talking about?"

I stared blankly. "Ezra interrogating vampires at the southern borders? He said Roman had shifters out doing the same thing."

Roxanne gave a slight headshake. "We don't have any shifters at the southern borders. We aren't interrogating anyone, vampires or shifters."

I blinked several times, processing her words. "Maybe I misunderstood what Ezra had said. My bad." I bit my, lip feeling like I'd missed a part of our conversation earlier. "My point still stands about working together, though," I muttered. I excused myself suddenly, leaving Roxanne by the table with furrowed brows and twisted lips on her expression.

I walked toward Roman and Ezra, trying to give a small smile even though something ate at me inside. Why had he lied to me? I didn't miss part of that conversation. I wasn't crazy.

As I approached, Roman's attention went to Roxanne. I turned my head slightly, seeing in my periphery that she was waving him over. Her confused look was gone, now masked by a beautiful beaming smile, playing her part in the evening's charade.

Roman nodded, then bent down to kiss me before he left. I turned to Ezra, feigning happiness and pretended to start a general conversation like the rest of the supernaturals in the room.

"Hey angel," he said, giving me a half-smile .

I jutted my chin towards him in a casual gesture, acknowledging his greeting but hating that he'd called me that. "No kitten?" I asked, tilting my head to the side.

"Is this really the place for it?" he asked, looking around.

"I didn't know there was a place for it," I countered. "I just don't like being called 'angel'. Never have." I lifted my drink to my lips, sipping the cranberry juice. Ezra looked at it like I was drinking mud. "When you left earlier, I wasn't sure if we were okay. I know this isn't really the place to hash out the details, but we need to talk more, and I want you to know I want to talk about all of it. I never meant to make you feel that way, but I'm not sorry I asked for space."

Ezra looked at his shoes briefly, then nodded when he looked up. "We're good, I promise." He reached into his breast pocket, pulling out the flask from earlier. I glanced at Dorian on the balcony, and he rolled his eyes, shaking his head when he looked away. Ezra unscrewed the top, taking a swig and then offering it to me.

I cocked an eyebrow as I accepted it, tilting it back and taking a mouthful of real bourbon, no mock about it. I swallowed, letting out a heavy breath.

You're a fucking liar.

I waited.

Nothing.

Ezra waited patiently until I handed him back his flask and he tucked it away.

"Good. I'm glad we're okay," I lied in return, since that seemed to be what we were doing now. I reached down to smooth out the skirt on my dress for absolutely no reason. "I want to do that tattoo you were telling me about."

"Hmm?" Ezra mused. "When?"

"You tell me. Do vampires plan the claiming thing like the shifters do? Is it a public event, private? Does someone like Kendrick do the tattoo?"

Ezra and I scanned around the room, continuing to look for anything out of place. My eyes landed back on him, and I stared.

"We do it whenever we want, however we want," he answered, grazing his fingers down my arm from shoulder to elbow.

"I like the idea of that," I said quietly. "Will you show me what it looks like?"

"Of course. Anything for you," he said, taking my hand and leading me over to the fake-bar. I held my drink glass up to the bartender, asking for another as Ezra asked her for a pen.

She handed him one, and she handed me another drink. While he grabbed a cocktail napkin and started to draw, I waited, squeezing the lime into the cranberry juice and swirling it around with my finger.

I moved my eyes around the room, checking the location of my other two mates and their seconds. Everyone had shifted their places somewhat, finding a new person to talk to. Everyone looked casual and laid back. Everyone except Roxanne. Her gaze was pinned on me, watching my every move. Roman stood facing her, his back to me, but I saw him in the mirror. He watched me carefully.

"Here, kitten," Ezra said, sliding the napkin toward me. I took it from him, cocking my head to the side as I looked at the specifics of the tattoo. The symbol he'd drawn wasn't Chinese. They were runes connected to each other inside a circle. It was hard to tell where one began and one ended. "You look disappointed." There was a tone in his voice I hadn't heard before.

I shook my head. "I'm not," I said truthfully. "I thought it would be something in Chinese, to be honest. What does this mean? The only rune I can make out is 'eternity'."

He scooped his hand around my waist, pulling me closer to him. Setting the drink down on the bar, I slid into his embrace.

"It's a vampire thing, not a cultural thing," he said vaguely.

I moved the symbols through my mind, focusing on the curves and the details. It had to mean something. I felt like I'd seen it before. Runes were complicated. So many cultures had them. If there was a vampire language, I certainly wouldn't know about it.

I was willing to let it go, setting it aside in my mind. He was not okay yet, and he was pushing me away as a result. Fine. We'd deal with each other when Lyra was shoved into a mirror and I could think straight.

Ezra started to dance to the music, pressing me against him and taking me along for the movement. I tried to sway gracefully, keeping in time with him. My mind was tripped up, still trying to decode the symbols in my head, arguing with myself that I couldn't figure it out if they were in fact some sort of ancient vampire language. But I focused. They were attached to each other. Where did they break?

Ezra released me, turning me into a slow spin, holding my hand gently. I fixed my face into a demure smile as I separated from his body, falling back into a deep concentration when I came back to his chest, resting my hand on his shoulder. He hummed softly in my ear, sucked my earlobe, then whispered, "You'll be mine in life and death."

I stumbled over my feet in our dance. The runes. Where they broke apart . . . it meant life and death. I'd seen them before. I'd thought it was a hallucination back then. I'd been hit so many times, my vision was blurred. My eyes were swollen, nearly shut, filled with what felt like endless tears. I was balled up on the floor, covering my head with my arms as he'd yanked me up. I'd sworn I'd seen his hands glow with strange markings as he reached back to slap me again. It was when I knew my consciousness was waning. It was the only explanation at the time . . .

Bile rose in my throat, and I shoved it down, catching my breath. In an instant, I regained my steps. Then I put all my weight and strength into an uppercut into Ezra's jaw as I screamed bloody murder, shaking the room and cracking mirrors right down the middle.

My fist made contact with his face, shattering bone and sending him flying into the air. He crashed to the ground, breaking floorboards on his impact.

The room stilled, unsure of what to do. Dorian, Roman, and Roxanne were at my side in an instant, all three of them holding me back before I charged Ezra.

"What the hell are you doing?" Dorian said. I could feel an inkling of his persuasion crawling over my skin. He was trying. And failing.

My eyes flashed with anger and hatred as I looked at Ezra when he stood up, his jaw healing quickly. He rubbed it with his hands, opening and closing his mouth. "Where the fuck is Ezra, you piece of shit?"

"Fury?" Roxanne asked in panic. "What's going on?"

My chest was heaving as I tried to catch my breath, never taking my eyes off his body. "It's him," I choked out. "Azrael."

Azrael looked at me with Ezra's green eyes, but the fire and rage that filled them didn't belong to my mate. A feral grin widened on his face, and he started to clap slowly.

"Miss me, angel?"

CHAPTER 14
FURY

A CHILL OF DISGUST REVERBERATED THROUGH MY ENTIRE BODY, RATTLING MY bones, making my stomach roil. My shoulders shuddered, trying to shake it off. I wanted to get the slimy feeling away from my skin.

"Where is he?" I said through clenched teeth. He laughed at me in response. Roman threw his arm over my abdomen protectively, pulling me into him while a low growl sounded. Dorian's ire vibrated, moving the air around me.

Racing thoughts took over, clouding out reason. Ezra. My Ezra. I knew something was wrong. The distance. The silence in my head. He didn't look at me the same way. It was too much. He felt off. It was jealousy. It was Azrael's possession. It was never Ezra's. The sick feeling resurfaced, sending a flood of adrenaline and anger as it coursed through my veins.

I needed the ones I loved to get out. I didn't know how he trapped Ezra, but my mates were in danger of the same fate. If he could get one, he could get them all.

I didn't know if Ezra was safe. I wasn't even sure how long he'd been gone.

"Tell me where, or so help me—"

His laugh echoed in the room, cutting through the silence. No one moved. No one attacked. Dorian held his hand out to the fae, ordering them to stay still. Rya and Kelly stood with them, prepared to take direction from their friend. Roman's shifters remained alert, their hands fidgeting, their fingers twitching, aching to shift. The vampires froze in their confusion, looking to the other alphas for direction now that their own was absent.

"You'll what?" Azrael mocked. "Kill me? Go ahead. See what happens."

The torrent of emotions swirled inside me. Anger that he was standing in front of me. Frustration for what I was, why I existed, and why he even cared. Bitterness at the path my previous life had taken. A searing and intense rage that *he* existed at all—that he had been in my life just to torment and kill me. And an overwhelming fear that he had taken Ezra from me when I'd only just found him.

I hated him. I wanted him to die a thousand deaths, and I wanted to be the one to hand it to him. Could I? Surely my powers could end this motherfucker. Just blow him up. I couldn't have access to all this magic, just to have it end up being all for naught. What a sick joke that would be.

"What did you do with Ezra?"

He shook his head slightly, a crooked, vile smile on his face. "No, no, angel. You won't find him, and I have no intention of telling you where he is. What purpose would that serve?"

A tiny rush of hope surfaced. Present tense. He hadn't found a way to destroy Ezra. If someone could take my mates from this world, I didn't doubt it would be him that was capable.

I had been scanning the room all night, waiting for Lyra to show up. Hoping to see her crazy ass at any moment. Shove her in, then get us all out. Find a way to safety. I wasn't sure if safety existed or if it was just something we convinced ourselves we could find, but that was the only plan we'd had.

Yet here we were. Azrael wasn't supposed to be here. He wasn't supposed to be Ezra. My mate wasn't supposed to be gone. It was a show the entire time, and he'd been in on it. Everyone here was in danger. Every single fae, shifter, witch, and vampire in the room was in danger of becoming extinguished into nothingness. Lured here with bait. Bait I fed them. I wanted to choke.

"What, then? What do you want?" My words were strained. All

the powers I had within were dying to get out. Explode. Level this damned building if it would end him. Roxanne reached down, squeezing my hand. From the corner of my eye, I saw her. My friend. My sister. Giving me support . . . and the reminder to keep my cool.

"What I've always wanted." He reached into his pocket, taking out the flask. He looked down as he opened it, then brought his eyes up to meet mine. His tongue slid over the metal opening, licking slowly. The lewd gesture sent another wave of nausea through me. Then he hummed. "Tastes just like you."

"You're going to make me vomit."

His eyes narrowed briefly, a flash of his temper shining through. "Now, angel. That's no way to talk to your husband."

Dorian's and Roman's growl shook the walls. I was tempted to stop suppressing the need to throw up, just to make a point.

I turned my head slightly, never taking my eyes off the imposter in the room. "Get them out," I said quietly. "Now."

I could feel Roman's desire to protest as he tensed against me, but Dorian understood, though I felt his hesitance. For a moment he considered, then he met Elena's ice-cold glare, nodding his head once.

Fae had been strategically placed in the room. Always near vampires and shifters. Their safety net. Their escape route. We didn't want to lose lives. We just wanted to get Lyra into Jules' realm. Every fae was ready to sift the other supernaturals to a different location Out of this room. To a healer, if needed. Now? Now that plan was sift everyone out permanently. Don't return. Just go—anywhere but here. Take everyone with you, even the witches. There was no time for magic or spells.

In what felt like the blink of an eye, fae reached to the supernaturals nearest them, grabbing hold and disappearing from the room in droves.

Then it was just us.

A showdown with the Angel of Death.

"Why?" I shouted, feeling the hot sting of tears ready to come out. I pulled them back in, steeling my spine and swallowing the desire to cry. I would not give him anymore of my tears. Never again. "Why now? Why all this?" I shouted. "What is the fucking point? Why didn't you just kill me when you had the chance? You did it once. Why not just do it again and get it over with?"

He looked back at me, still wearing my mate's face. Still looking like Ezra, but the evil in his eyes and in his voice were one hundred percent Azrael.

"I could have, yes. I was going to. You shouldn't be here, angel. You shouldn't exist," he said, drinking from the flask and then tucking it away. He inspected his nails, drawing out the time between his answers. "But that first day you'd arrived back on Earth, I couldn't. You smelled too sweet. It would have been such a waste."

My jaw fell. He had been near me. He'd been following me for . . . how long? Was he there in the Afterlife, watching me and waiting? A fuzzy memory surfaced, reminding me of my initial arrival. "It was you. Outside the apartment . . . with the doors . . ."

He dipped his chin, the sneer on his face never dissipating.

"So, what? I smelled like a dessert, and you just changed your mind?"

"You were always my favorite, you know that? I wanted to watch you again. I loved the way you writhed and screamed."

"Kinda screwed that one up when you tried to have me killed by a shifter, huh?" I waved my hands around wildly, mocking his absolute failure in trying to torture and kill me all over again. "Azrael, the all-knowing. Didn't know that trick wouldn't work, did you?"

"It was certainly unexpected," he admitted. "That made it a whole new game. I like it. You're different now." He chuckled. "You think you're stronger, and you put up a hell of a fight, but you're still Sunny and I know how to break you."

My heartbeat pounded in my head when he said my dead name, but the only thing I did was roll my eyes. "Then why haven't you, hmm? Oh, maybe it's because you can't."

His expression darkened. "Give it time, angel. We've only just begun."

"There is no *we*," I scoffed. "There never was."

"You were mine once. You will be again." He closed his eyes, breathing in deeply. He opened them as he exhaled, pinning me with a glare. "I couldn't let these *animals* have you. No," he said, slowly shaking his head. "Nor could I have you fawning over them. *That* was unacceptable."

"They're my mates," I said through clenched teeth. "You can't have me."

He cocked his head, raising an eyebrow. "I almost did," he paused, looking at his watch, "about an hour ago, right?" My stomach sank as he winked at me.

"I'm going to kill him," Roman said, his voice low and rumbling. He moved forward, and I planted my feet, keeping his body behind me. Placing my hand over his arm that had been holding me protectively, I reminded him to stay back.

"I wanted Ezra," I snapped, looking him up and down in disgust. "Not whatever *you* are." The mere idea of it sent a shudder of revulsion through me. "But there you were, knowing you'd never be good enough, so you had to pretend to be a better man instead. You're so weak and cowardice that you couldn't show your own face. All it knows is rejection."

A rumble of thunder rent the air, a warning of an oncoming storm both inside and out. Had the weather been any different, I'd have assumed it was Azrael's wrath that sent the heavens into disarray. Maybe it was.

"Careful, angel," he warned, the furious tenor in his voice starting to shake. "This won't go the way you expect it to."

"Oh, go fuck yourself, John. Azrael. Not-Ezra. Whoever you are."

"I take it you don't care what happens to your dear vampire, do you?"

My insides twisted. He was lying. He had to by lying. I *needed* him to be lying.

Dorian put his hand on my shoulder, doing what he could to reassure me. He tapped my shoulder with his thumb, where Azrael couldn't see. Over my ex's shoulder was Jules, safe in her mirror realm, completely unable to help. She raised her hands and shrugged her shoulders, the panic and worry on her face unmasked. She disappeared just as quickly. A solid moment to let me know she was here. Moral support, but nothing more.

We didn't have Lyra. We couldn't beat Azrael. My mate was gone.

It was at that moment I realized what he was doing.

"You set me up," I said quietly. "How long? How long have you been Ezra?"

He smirked, but the darkness and anger that had been taking him over as I insulted him didn't dissipate. I hated seeing Ezra's beauty marred by the evil that encompassed Azrael. "I wonder if you already know the answer to that," he said, evading my question.

I shook my head, taking my hand off Roman's and beginning to move his arm. He held tight, refusing to let go. "You were going to keep me. That whole charade in my room tonight. The jealousy. Calling it 'longing'. Making me feel sorry for you. All the shitball qualities that have always been your piss-poor calling card. You were going to weasel your way into my life and pull me away from them because it amuses you to watch me suffer inside and out." I let out a humorless laugh. "You're nothing like Ezra. Never could be. He's my mate. You're just . . . death. To everything and everyone you touch."

A crease deepened between his brows, and this time, the rumbling came from him. I hated him. I didn't see Ezra anymore. Ezra would never look at me like that. He'd never enjoy my pain. He didn't look at me as though my existence was vile. The hate inside me was burning. I felt it crackling in my veins, begging for release.

"Oh, you're angry? You're gonna growl at me now? I'm not fucking scared of you. Sunny is dead. You killed her. Now it's me, baby," I shouted, throwing my arms out. "And you. can't. have. me. But I will end you, motherfucker."

"I told you, Sunny. You're mine, in life *and* in death." His arms shook as he held back, his temper rising, ready to strike me like he'd always done.

I met his glare with one of my own. "Then fucking kill me, asshole. Death is the only way you're getting me."

The words flew out of my mouth before I could think them through.

In that moment, two things happened, only one of which made complete sense.

Azrael retaliated, losing his hold as I openly defied his authority and challenged him. His palms glowed, his face straining with rage. He thrust his hand toward me while I stood with arrogance, not regretting the words I'd said.

Expected.

As I stared at his palm branded with the rune of death, I have to admit, I was taken by surprise.

His blast hit me in the chest, a crackling sound like lightning burning metal echoed in the room. My skin was searing, my veins burning, feeling like my blood was boiling. The air in my lungs expelled as I was knocked back by the force of his power . . .

And it fucking killed me.

Again.

Unexpected.

CHAPTER 15
FURY

I CRASH LANDED.

My head bounced forward then smacked into the hard ground, eliciting a crack. I groaned, rolling onto my side in the fetal position, waiting for the ringing to stop.

"What the hell are you doing here?" A familiar squawk broke through the static. I cracked one eye open, streams of light illuminating a flurry of dust particles around me. Through them, Hades sat on the edge of a familiar desk with papers strewn all over it.

"Hades?"

"Fury?" he quipped back, tilting his head.

I jumped up, turning in a full circle while patting myself down. It was my body. It was real. "Holy shit—motherfucker—we're in the Afterlife." That realization turned from excitement to dread as I repeated, "We're in the Afterlife. Fuck." I dropped my head in my hand, pinching the bridge of my nose.

"Yes. We've established that, but not the how—" Hades started, using a slow voice to speak to me like he would a small child.

"Because Lyra never showed up—" No, no, no. I stopped, feeling for the orb in my pocket. I came up empty. It was gone. I looked down at the ground, checking to see if it came falling out.

"And?" he prompted.

"And then my asshole ex, who has been posing as Ezra, killed me. Again."

I may have taunted him into doing it, but that was irrelevant.

"Ah shit," Hades groaned.

"Shit is right, because the other two now think I'm dead and—"

"That's not the actual problem," Hades interrupted. "Or at least not the immediate one."

"What are you talking about?" I demanded. "Of course it's the problem. Have you met my mates? Jesus Christ. They think I'm dead-dead." Even I thought I was dead-dead.

Instead of answering, Hades landed on my shoulder and said, "Stay quiet and don't move please."

My eyebrows drew together. This bird must be smoking crack to think I was just going to let this go. Before I could say anything, my body disappeared, along with Hades. We were still in the office. I still felt him there, nails digging into my skin through the straps of my dress.

No sooner did we disappear did Azrael storm into the office. I froze to my spot, fight or flight trying to kick in. He'd dropped the face of Ezra, instead taking the form of my ex-husband—albeit even colder and more beautiful than my true husband was. His high cheek bones were sharp enough to cut glass and his skin was so pale it looked like bone. He scanned the room, blue eyes cold and distant. I tensed when he looked straight at me . . . then kept searching.

He couldn't see me. Because of Hades.

Slowly he stopped, a cruel smile gracing his lips.

"You're mine now, angel. In life and death."

My heart froze, assuming we were visible again. But he disappeared in a blink, taking the chill his very presence exuded with him. I was slow to uncoil, not truly trusting that he was gone.

Another minute or so passed before Hades exhaled in a woosh. Our forms appeared again, and he sagged on my shoulder.

"What was that?" I asked, my voice quiet, deadly. It wasn't the outrageous cursing and yelling he was used to. No, this was a quieter kind of Fury. And far more dangerous. It was the Fury I'd become right after my death. The demon that underwent over a hundred years of anger management because the rage I'd held in was too much.

Hades must have sensed it because he didn't dance around the question.

"Jules isn't the only one with her own realm. A handful of beings from the Afterlife have the powers to unlock other pockets in reality. Azrael is one of them."

My lips pressed together. "I don't see how that has anything to do with what just happened, or how you knew he'd come for me."

"Azrael is the Angel of Death. The *literal* personification of death itself. When someone die-dies—like for good—they go to his realm."

My mouth popped open.

The air rushed from my lungs but wouldn't go back in.

I gasped, crushing my hands into fists to control the emotions rolling through me.

Because if he was death's true master . . .

"He looked for me here so he could finish the job," I said quietly.

Hades sighed. "But because he didn't find you, he's probably going to search his realm and see if you're already there. Judging by the creepy smile on his face, he thinks that's the case."

I turned toward the desk, putting my hands flat on the surface to lean forward.

"You've known that this entire time." The squeezing in my chest wouldn't let up. "As soon as we found out it was him, you knew he was trying to kill me—to trap me for *eternity*." My voice choked on the last word. I'd yet to truly understand time in that way, but I was beginning to. With it, all I wanted was to have that future with my mates.

I never knew the other outcome wasn't simply death, but a fate worse than that. While I was in a state of shock, a part of me said I shouldn't be surprised. Nothing about the Afterlife was what it seemed. But *this* . . . this was more than I could have ever imagined.

"Can you blame me, Fury?" he said, hopping off my shoulder to land on the desk. "I know what he did to you. I knew his end goal was to do it again—and that you'd truly rather die than face that. Except death wouldn't even give you peace. How could I tell you that if we lost this, if he got you, that's what you had waiting for you on the other side?"

"You should have told me," I snapped. "I had a right to know."

"Why?" he demanded. "So you'd be petrified with fear? So that you'd turn back into that shell of a girl you were when you came here? Why in the Afterlife should I have told you that if you lost, that your worst nightmare would come to pass?" I closed my eyes, looking away. "Telling you doesn't change it. All it does is let fear steal away the life you're currently getting to live with your mates, and if the only life you get is the here and now, I wasn't going to take that from you."

The tightness in my chest eased as I sucked in a breath and slowly released it. We'd shared some moments before. When the bantering was over and the emotions were real, he was something I'd never expected.

"Thank you," I said after a long moment. "For keeping him from finding me . . . and that."

"I do what I can," he said, dipping his beak down. "But you said he was posing as Ezra. Is he . . .?"

I shook my head. "He told me I wouldn't find him, but he didn't say he'd found a way to kill him, so there's that," I said quietly.

Hades exhaled. "Okay, first things first. We need to get you out of here."

I nodded, leaning back to stand. "Great plan, but I don't know how to use the portal, and Duke isn't here." I ran my hands through my hair. "I don't even know where to go. It's not like going back is safe. Nowhere is safe right—" I gasped, stopping mid-ramble. Something brushed my mind. A familiar presence I hadn't felt in days.

Water gathered in my eyes and my lips parted, making Hades cock his head as he looked at me in confusion.

"What is it?" he asked.

I couldn't speak, too overwhelmed for words, when a voice whispered through my head.

Fury?

CHAPTER 16
DORIAN

I WATCHED IN SLOW MOTION AS AZRAEL LIFTED HIS PALM IN RETALIATION, A glowing mark illuminating the magic that was ready to come forth as he rose to Fury's challenge.

I couldn't stop it.

It happened so fast I didn't even have time to sift.

It hit Fury squarely in the chest, its force sending her and Roman flying backwards. Roxanne and I had been standing next to them, all providing a level of protection. In the end, it meant nothing.

The force of the unexpected blast sent me flying to the side. The same for Roxanne as she landed with a thud on the ground, the floorboards rippling under our powerful frames.

For the first time in my very long life, I heard a ringing in my ears and the air felt heavy. It was a magic I had never come in contact with before.

A maniacal laughter echoed in the background, though it sounded further away than I knew it to be. The only words I could make out were, "You're mine now."

I heard Roxanne coughing, and I rolled over to the side, pushing myself up.

Across the room, Roman's arms were locked tightly around our mate where they landed, never having let go, keeping her protected as I knew he would. He groaned, but she didn't move or make a sound.

I looked for Azrael, but he was gone. For one foolish moment, just one, I felt relief. Clarity slammed into me, the voice in my head asking why he would leave. A part of me knew the answer.

Roxanne and I stumbled to them, regaining our composure as our bodies quickly healed from the injuries of being thrown.

As Roman turned to lay Fury on her side, the hoarse scream that came from him made my blood run cold and I stopped dead in my tracks. "Fury! No," he shouted, repeating her name over and over.

Roxanne rushed over, dropping to her knees beside her brother as Fury's body turned to ash, disintegrating before our eyes.

Roman grasped at what was left, as though he could hold on to her. But his hands came up empty, and he pounded into the ground, roaring, his body going into a shift as the electricity in the room sparked and flickered.

I stood there, looking at the empty space where my mate had been. My love. The one who had given me purpose again. She'd given me something I had lost so long ago. *Hope*. Hope for our future, and she'd further extended that prospect for my daughter's future. We were in it together. A family.

The loss was all-consuming. Grief tried to swallow me, reminding me I would never have another chance with either of them.

Everything I had ever loved had been ripped away from me. By the same. fucking. person. Hatred for that angel began to burn at the very core of who I was, devouring what little soul I had left.

The denial in me screamed for her to reappear. To come back to me. To us.

The air stayed silent.

A single tear streamed down my cheek while Roman howled, losing himself quickly.

She was dead. For real this time.

Azrael had killed her.

The anger inside me pulsed through my veins, but I was silent.

"No," a harsh whisper sounded in the room.

I snapped my head to the mirror, seeing Jules with her hands over her mouth, shaking her head softly.

A new flood of rage washed over me, and I stormed toward her.

"Where the fuck is he?" I hadn't even raised my voice and the entire building shook in my wake. In all my life, in all my loss, my power had remained under my control. Whatever restraint I had managed in my past was gone. The magic inside me swirled brighter, undulating as my emotions soared.

Her eyes widened, tears sitting on the brim. "I don't know. I can't see him. I don't know if he's even on Earth. I don't know what he did with Lyra, or where she is," she choked out. "They're just gone. I don't know."

"Then what do you know?" I shouted.

She threw her hands out, the glass between us warbling and moving like waves. "I don't know, okay! This wasn't the plan." She sniffed as she cried. "This wasn't supposed to happen."

"You were supposed to—"

"I was supposed to what, Dorian? Come out and fight the Angel of Death with you? I'm a poltergeist. I was supposed to grab Lyra and keep her safe with me here. I was doing that for Fury. My friend. I was doing that for you too. I was doing it so I could help save everyone, but you can't blame me for this!" The tenor of her voice started to make the mirrors shake.

I held my hands out in a gesture to show her I was giving in. "I'm sorry," I breathed. "It's not . . . it's not your fault . . ." I sighed and pressed my hand onto the mirror, giving what comfort I could to the dead girl on the other side. "It's not your fault," I said.

"She isn't dead," Roxanne whispered, but the sound of her voice carried all around the room. She was still kneeling beside Fury's ashes, holding a hand over them as though she wanted to touch them. "She's not dead."

Roman angrily pawed at the ground, communicating with her in a way neither Jules nor I could hear. She shook her head at him. "Turn back." He growled at her in response, baring his teeth, and she stared him down, repeating herself to him. "I just want to talk to my brother."

Roman took his time considering, and for all I knew, they shared more conversation. He shifted back, his chest heaving as tears marred his face. His icy blue eyes flashed as though streaks of lightning were hidden within them.

I walked toward them. "What do you mean?" I asked, coming to stand beside her.

She looked up at me, her silent tears dripping onto her chest. "She couldn't die before. She shouldn't be able to die now. It's Fury. I don't think the end of the world would have killed her." She let out a tiny huff. A humorless laugh.

"She's ash, Roxanne," I argued, pointing to the ground. "When she died before, *that* didn't happen."

She pressed her lips together firmly, humming her disagreement before speaking. "That was different. Before she had all this power. Think about it."

"Think about what, Roxanne? We turned her into a supernatural to save her life," I countered, shaking my head. "You heard what she said about death for our kind. They don't have anywhere to go. They just stop . . ." I couldn't finish it. I couldn't say it. Not out loud. Then it was real. I wasn't ready to speak those words. To admit what I knew to be true.

She shook her head vigorously, never taking her eyes off the place where Fury disappeared. "You're wrong. She was only part supernatural. Nothing about her was what we thought. When you all changed her, that should have been the end, but it saved her instead. Maybe he just killed the supernatural in her. Maybe her demon part is still there, and it's enough. She has angel in her too, and none of us knew that. She can't have survived this long to have those parts of her be worth nothing."

I didn't know who she was trying to convince.

"What are you saying?" Roman asked through clenched teeth. His nostrils flared as he exhaled forcefully between breaths.

Roxanne turned her head, facing her brother. "I'm saying give it time. Before either of you try to level the building." She looked up, and we followed her gaze. Cracks lined the walls, and a slow rumble in the room finally eased when she pointed it out. "And before you both try to destroy everyone and everything on this planet, give her time. Trust her. She'll come back to us."

Roman dropped to his knees next to his sister, defeated, staring at a pile of ash and waiting like an absolute fool.

I would do no such thing.

She was dead. Taken from me.

I didn't care what I had to do, or where I had to go. I was going to end Azrael myself.

He may have been the Angel of Death, but Duke had said angels could die. I was going to find out how and kill him.

I was immortal. He couldn't do shit to me. And if he could? What the fuck else did I have to lose?

I strode to the mirror and looked straight at Jules. Meeting her wide hazel eyes as she stared back at me in surprise, I took a risk, knowing it could lead to the end of all things, and I didn't even have it in me to care.

"I want you to take me to the Afterlife."

CHAPTER 17
FURY

"Ezra?" I whispered, scared to speak for fear that it was all in my head. That I'd cracked under the immense pressure that was weighing me down. The guilt that I'd failed my mate so horribly—

You haven't failed me, kitten.

Relief slammed into me, immediately followed by worry. While I was certain it was him, he didn't sound like himself. There was a heaviness in his mental voice. As if speaking to me was exhausting him.

"He's here," I breathed. "In the Afterlife."

Hades let out a low coo that I thought was his crow version of a whistle. "No wonder Azrael was confident you wouldn't find him."

"Ezra, I need you to tell me where you are. What you see."

White, he answered immediately. *White walls. White furniture. White everything. The minds around me are being tortured. I feel their pain, so I've pulled back. I can't . . . I can't hold on much longer.*

"He's in Hell," I whispered softly.

Azrael had placed him literally in the only real version of Hell that existed. The cookie-cutter houses on the bottom levels that housed billions of souls—each one living their punishment. It seemed he'd picked one that hadn't been assigned yet. The white on white on white was the Afterlife version of the base model. Before a soul was assigned to a demon and house, they simply existed as empty spaces waiting to be filled.

"The houses?" Hades clarified. I nodded.

"He put him in an empty one. Unassigned."

"Well, that's helpful," Hades said, shaking his head. "That only narrows it down to a few hundred million."

"I know," I sighed, rubbing the skin on my forehead as I tried to think. "We don't have time to search them all on foot."

"I sincerely doubt he officially logged it in the database," Hades said. "Even if we could break into the demon guild HQ without being noticed, the chance of us finding it before someone—namely Azrael himself—finds you, is slim to none."

I agreed, but that wasn't going to stop me. "I'm not leaving him here."

"I wasn't suggesting you do, but we need a plan and sticking around here isn't one."

Fair point. I inclined my head. "Got anything else in your bag of tricks, like you did back there?" I asked, somewhat hopeful.

Hades cocked his head at me. "I'm a crow. What the fuck do you think I can do?"

"Well, I don't know," I huffed. "You can pop up places and go between the realms, I'm guessing. You made me invisible. How am I supposed to know what you can or cannot do since you're apparently more than a messenger pigeon?"

Hades groaned. "I can cross dimensions. Veils. Slip between the realms. Like what poltergeists can do. It makes me good at watching and sending messages back and forth, but I'm not a homing device. I can't just find someone out of all the places that exist simply because I want to find them. If I could have, I would have found you instantly when you were stupid and got yourself captured by rogue supes."

I sighed, knowing he was right. Not about me being stupid, but the getting captured part.

"Fine, so you're basically useless here—"

"Hey," he squawked in protest. "Now hold up a minute there. Last I checked you're the one with all the badass powers."

"Because bleeding profusely then passing out is so helpful," I deadpanned, lifting an eyebrow. "Or maybe you mean my demon strength that is also useless here. As is blowing shit up. Or letting my raven take over. Or sift—"

Sifting.

That was it. My answer.

It seemed so obvious, were it not for my rudimentary skills.

"Sounds like we have a potential solution. Let's try it," Hades urged, jumping up and flapping his wings to push him high enough he could land on my shoulder.

"Wait," I hesitated. "I've never sifted very far. Let alone from Duke's office into one of the lower circles of the Afterlife. What if I don't make it?"

I wasn't sure what happened when someone failed to sift because of distance, but the idea of falling out of the sky or popping up in a random location didn't seem good.

"I don't think we have another option, unfortunately," Hades said. "Even if we could find a spare Apple Watch lying around, you still don't know where he's at. If you sift, you can focus on him to bring us to his location—or bring him to us."

I gnawed on my bottom lip, mulling over the options. "Ezra's in bad shape. If I fail to sift him to us, that's worse."

Hades dipped his head in acknowledgement. "As long as you don't land us in Upper Management, we *should* be okay." He tilted his head, thinking on it. "Probably."

So helpful, he was.

I closed my eyes and focused on my mate.

I'm coming for you, I thought, hoping he heard me despite the lack of response.

The ball of anxiety in my chest squeezed tight as all the scenarios of what could be happening to him right now ran through my head. Knowing what Azrael was capable of, it was all too easy to let the fear take over.

"Breathe, Fury," Hades said, pulling me back from the edge of a spiral I couldn't afford to go down.

I swallowed past the lump in my throat, nodding once. "What if Azrael's there? With him?"

"We hope you're not tapped out sifting and can grab him and go before the shithead tries to extinguish you."

Extinguish. Dead-dead. Or so I'd thought.

"If he succeeded . . ."

"Don't go there," Hades said quietly. "Cross that bridge when we come to it."

I took a deep breath and nodded. "All right, let's do this." Closing my eyes, I pictured Ezra. Focusing on the bond between us. I felt a tug, followed by the whoosh of my feet leaving the ground, but I didn't let myself get distracted in my destination for even a second.

Ezra. Ezra. Ezra.

His name became a chant, a calling as I pushed through the exertion that weighed me down, until I found him.

I could not fail. I refused. Success was the only option.

My feet slammed into the ground, sending me to my knees. I gasped, filling my lungs with air, and slowly releasing it. My fingers uncoiled, the dampness in my palms turned cool against the faint breeze.

I opened my eyes.

We'd landed on the porch of door number 19348.

I squinted, trying to recall why I recognized that number. It seemed familiar somehow . . .

"We're here," I said softly, slowly standing.

"You're sure?"

"Positive," I answered. "This was our house number when we were married."

Should have guessed that sick fuck would have found a way to make this even more unsettling.

Hades cursed as I reached for the doorknob—hoping, praying that Ezra would be alone.

The door turned easily. The wood panel swung without a single creak.

My breath left my chest as I laid eyes on my mate, but the relief didn't last for even a second.

Red.

It painted the walls.

Spilled across the carpet.

Stained the furniture.

And lying in the middle of it, on his back, breathing harshly—was Ezra.

"Jesus Christ," Hades uttered. I took a single step into the space. My heart shattered into a million pieces at the sheer carnage Azrael had committed. I'd tortured people in my time, but this . . . it was something else.

I ran to him, falling to my knees.

"Ezra," I whispered, brushing my hands over his face.

His eyelids fluttered.

Then he reached up, grabbing my hand. He squeezed it softly, as if in reassurance.

I knew you'd come.

I ran my hands over his face. His chest. I was looking for injuries initially. Until I noticed something that made my blood turn to ice.

His tattoos were gone.

Every single one of them.

I knew it was him with every fiber of my being. The voice in my head the only true way to tell. But if they were gone, that meant . . .

I slowly lifted my head, taking in the living room once more.

It wasn't simply blood that covered the walls. Beneath the smudged reddish-brown stains that were dry and peeling—was *skin*.

Ezra's skin. His tattoos mounted like trophies.

Bile rose in my throat, and I had to look away, swallowing it back down.

That son of a bitch.

"We need to go, Fury," Hades reminded me, staying on my shoulder as a mostly silent witness to what happened here, but he remained an unwavering voice of reason.

"I know," I said. "Can you take us through the birdie-back door or whatever veil it was you passed between earlier?" I asked.

"I'm afraid I can't. Hiding you was one thing. I can't take you and Ezra through veils to get to Earth. That's strictly a me-thing," he said. I could hear the apologetic tone in his voice.

I blew out a breath. Sifting it was, then. If I sifted us here, I could sift out.

Looking at Ezra once more, I mentally asked, *can you move?*

His answer was short and acted as a spear to penetrate the ice filling me.

Barely.

The part of me that was his mate shut down. I had to. The horrors I'd found here were too great to process. I just needed to function in this moment. So I rose, methodical and calculated.

I lifted my wrist to my face and bit down hard, grimacing at the pain. I snapped my neck to the side, tearing my fangs across my flesh to open the vein further.

Ezra's lips parted, scenting the blood.

You need your strength, he murmured.

"You need it more," I insisted, refusing to yield. Kneeling back down, I shoved my bloody wrist between his lips. At first Ezra did little more than lick at the wound. But slowly, some semblance of strength filled him. He reached up, grasping my wrist tenderly but still firm, as he sank his fangs in.

I watched as color filled his face. Still pale, but no longer deathly white.

A moment passed where he drank deeply before releasing my wrist and thrusting it away with great restraint. I tried to shove it back at him, but he refused, his lips clamping shut as he swallowed hard. A muscle in his cheek twitched, as if he were struggling to deny himself.

"No, no more," he rasped, voice hoarse.

"Yes, more," I argued. "You're not well—"

"And I won't be until we leave," he replied, then switched to mentally communicating. *It's going to take a lot of blood to deal with the extreme deficit I'm in. More than you can give right now. I can't sift. You're the one that needs to be strong for both of us right now.*

I pressed my lips together in a hard line, knowing he might be right but not liking it.

"Look at me," I insisted.

"Fury." The way he said my name was firm and harsh.

"You need to be strong enough to at least open your eyes. If I'm not strong enough to sift us out of here, it's going to hurt. A lot."

He sighed. *Don't ask this of me, kitten.*

"No," I said, voice flat. "I need to see—"

His eyelids lifted, and I stopped speaking.

Thinking.

Processing.

Where beautiful green eyes should have been . . .

There was nothing.

Pits of flesh. Hollow, empty holes.

I couldn't contain the bile this time. It rose, and I hardly moved fast enough, turning to the side as I vomited.

He'd been blinded.

It's not what you think, he said in my mind, sad and consoling.

"He took your eyes," I said once the saliva stopped dripping from my mouth. I wiped it off with my arm. "He fucking butchered you."

"He didn't take them," Ezra rasped. "I did."

Shock ran through me, followed by confusion. "Why would you do such a thing?"

"Azrael took your face when he . . ." Ezra let his voice drop off, not needing to explain further.

Azrael had taken my form to torture him, just as he'd taken Ezra's to fool me.

I couldn't bear to see that. I knew it wasn't you, but I wouldn't let him play with me like that. If he was going to take me apart piece by piece, he was going to do it without me looking at him wearing your face.

I shuddered. Just when I thought he couldn't get any worse—anymore fucked up—he'd found a way.

I reached down, placing his arm around my shoulder as I slid mine under his back. Then I twisted, putting my other arm under his knees. It was probably uncomfortable, and certainly looked awkward, but if he couldn't stand yet, I'd carry him.

I guess demon strength came in handy, after all.

I went from kneeling to standing, pulling him up with me.

Resolution settled in. The fight or flight I'd been struggling with fell away.

I was going to make that motherfucker pay.

Come hell, come death, I was going to end him.

But first, I was going to save my mate.

I walked out of the house of horrors and onto the porch. Lamplights filled the quiet street, warm and inviting. It was meant to be that way. You'd never know what happened here behind these doors. You'd never guess the pain inflicted on the inside.

It was exactly the same way on Earth.

I shook my head, ignoring the light, because the path I was taking led only to one place.

Darkness. Death. Destruction.

And for the first time, I would welcome it.

As I secured my grip on Ezra, preparing to attempt to sift out of the Afterlife and back to Earth—a force rocked the very foundation I stood.

I looked down, then up.

This explosion wasn't like something you would see on Earth. It wasn't like a building with a gas leak, and it wasn't as though dynamite went off. The night lit up in flashes like a bomb had been dropped, but that was clearly impossible. There was no impact prior. Buildings weren't on fire. It may have been Hell, essentially, but it looked nothing like the images of fire and brimstone.

Bolts of lightning shot out from another detonation, breaking apart and splintering across the sky. The entire display was the embodiment of rage.

I would know.

"What in the absolute . . .?" Hades said under his breath, flying up for a better view. "That looks just like your handiwork."

Not taking my eyes off the blasts, I asked a question even though I feared the answer. "Can Azrael . . .?"

"This isn't him. It can't be."

I breathed a sigh of relief. I was not ready to face that tool right now. Ezra was my main concern. I felt the heat of his body against mine as I held him, and it gave me a small measure of comfort.

"If you weren't standing with me, I'd think this was you," he murmured. "No one has this power, Fury. No one except . . . but he's—"

I snapped my attention back to him. "What?"

Hades looked at me gently, his bird eyes somehow softening. "No one except Michael. It's where your powers originated from. Make things go boom, yeah? That's not a demon thing. That was an angel thing. Specifically, Michael's."

“I’m descended from Michael?” I asked, breathing heavily. “Why didn’t you say something? How did you know?”

“I told you, I know a lot of things, and some things are better left unsaid.”

I looked back to the explosions. “Yeah? Then why say something now?”

“Because he’s dead, and we know this isn’t him. I don’t know what this is,” he said. “But I think that’s our cue to exit the Afterlife,” I said.

From above us, somewhere in the higher levels of the Afterlife—someone was using my power. And it sure as shit wasn’t me.

I briefly debated whether I should leave and let Upper Management deal with whatever was going on here.

That was until the wind carried a voice over the entirety of the realm.

A voice I’d know anywhere.

“Where is Azrael?” Dorian commanded. “Where is the angel who murdered my mate?”

CHAPTER 18
FURY

How did he even get here? I groaned internally and squinted my eyes, seeing the fires in the distance, trying to judge exactly where it was coming from. "That's headquarters, isn't it?"

"Ugh." Hades waited a moment before continuing, sounding exasperated. "You want to go get him?"

"Yup."

"Of course you do," he muttered. He swooped down to land on my shoulder.

"You're joking right now, right? Dorian is in the Afterlife and now shit is blowing up. It's like this realm is revolting."

"Probably because he shouldn't be here," he grumbled. "Supernatural and Afterlife magic don't mix well. Present company excluded, of course."

"All the more reason we need to get him out," I said slowly.

"I know, I know," he said with a sigh. "If it's not one mate falling apart, it's the other. Go on. Sift us there."

"You can't take us?"

He shook his head. "Like I said before, I can hide you, but I can't walk you through the veils. Not even here. You sifted us here. Just take us to HQ. No pressure. At least you aren't falling to your death though, right? That's an improvement."

"I would have just ended up here apparently," I said quietly, finding an inner focus so I could sift us there.

"Not necessarily. You may have only ended up here because of Azrael. Angel of Death and all that. There was no magic involved in those rocks and they could've just crushed you and you really would have been dead-dead," he said, tilting his head as he mused. "But dead-dead means—"

"Not the time, feathers," I said, and he snapped out of his contemplation. "I've got this. Even if you could take us, I can't rely on you or anyone else. I've got my own magic."

"Is this one of those 'put on your big girl panties' pep talks?" he asked.

"No." Maybe. "Let's go before Dorian fulfills the prophecy on his own." Which I really hoped wasn't possible.

He sighed through his beak, shaking his head. "Okay, I'm coming with you. You need all the practice you can get," he said, fluffing up his feathers like he was psyching himself up for the ride. "Onward, steed."

I side-eyed him, then turned my head and focused. Holding tight to Ezra, I imagined a hallway at headquarters. It had terrible geometric tile and reminded me of the carpet in *The Shining*. I turned my mind to it, pinpointing the details. The doors on either side. Their silver knobs. The obnoxious lighting. The color of the wood frames. (This place needed a makeover. We really did work in Hell, didn't we?)

SIFT, I told myself.

A sudden rush of wind brushed my skin while the ground I stood on felt as though it had been pulled out from under me.

Then I smacked my forehead straight into the doorframe, a loud resounding crack echoing the hallway. Hades had jumped off my shoulder in time, and my face politely blocked Ezra from hitting the wall.

I grunted at the impact, crossing my eyes at the sudden pain. It dissipated quickly, but the whispers of a headache were still there.

"Think about that wall a lot?" Hades asked.

"Clearly."

"Try thinking of the middle of the room next time," he offered, landing on me, shrugging a wing.

"Really? Right now?" I said, raising my voice.

"I'm being helpful," he said, flapping his wings to take flight.

"Be helpful and find where—" The entire building shook, cutting me off as I stumbled. I lost my footing, and my shoulder hit the wall while I held Ezra close to me. Hades fought the current in the air, trying to find space to fly.

Cracks appeared on the ceiling, traveling across like they were chasing some unknown creature. Thick pieces of what appeared to be concrete in nature crumbled, dropping chunks of it at random.

When I looked up, tiny pieces of lightning traveled the walls like electricity covering metal.

"Hades," I said, my voice trailing off. He landed back on my shoulder, and I turned to look at him. "You see that, right?"

He stared above us, and I followed his gaze, watching the crackles moving along the wall, rumbling as if they had a life of their own.

The room rumbled slowly, no lightning , just a deep resonance beneath the surface. Above us. In the walls. It was *everywhere*. We looked up again, watching the vibrations.

It was at that moment I felt a tingle across my skin. It sent a chill up my spine. I didn't know what it was either, but I sure as shit didn't want to stick around to find out.

I hoisted Ezra's sagging weight to give him more support, and he mumbled what I assumed was his thanks.

Shouts of frantic citizens of the Afterlife reached my ears as they ran away from the blasts. They were beyond confused. Nothing like this had ever happened. Our realm couldn't be attacked, and they knew this. Everyone knew it. On occasion, demons would lose their tempers, and yes, weird things happened. A building or two would get knocked over. Limbs were lost—and then they reappeared. Sometimes another demon was lit on fire. But it's not like any of them could die. It was the *Afterlife*.

I'd blown a few things up in my earlier years. I was *The* Fury. I'd made a name for myself.

I turned to my crow, pinning him with a stern look. The unnerved expression on his face was not at all comforting. Dorian's presence might have been driving this explosive bus, but I was worried that it would somehow attract Azrael's attention. Judging by the look on his face, I feared he shared the same concerns. “We need to find him,” I said. “Now.”

“Well, the screams are coming from that direction.” Hades took off down the hallway, flying quickly.

I needed a better way to carry Ezra if I planned on running. For someone that couldn’t die and was able to continuously heal, he was in a lot of pain. I mumbled my apology to him in advance, knowing what I was going to do wasn’t going to feel good. I set him down, but bent over, putting my shoulder into his belly, and lifted him over my back. Holding an arm and a leg, I got his weight situated on me and he moaned.

I took off after Hades, following him around corners and making turns I didn’t know were there. He’d said he couldn’t take me through his veil, but I no longer knew where we were, and it sure felt like he’d crossed some invisible lines at some point.

Another explosion.

More screams.

Another rumbling earthquake-like wave shook the floors and I almost toppled over. Holding my hand out to the wall, I felt the tremors rocking the ground beneath us as another surge of power pushed through. The energy it held throbbed against my fingertips, welcoming itself into my skin, edging around my very core, nestling itself like it was home. I gasped, pulling my hand back in shock. “Well that was weird,” I whispered, taking a step back.

Hades rounded in the air, coming back and hovering above me as he dodged bits and pieces of falling ceiling. “What are you doing?”

I looked at him, wide-eyed. “This is my power,” I whispered. “I’m doing this.”

“It’s not, you aren’t, stop talking, keep moving,” he said, speeding through his choice of words.

I snapped at him. “It is. I mean, I’m not blowing things up, but this is my magic. I can’t explain it. It’s like it’s reaching out to me. Calling me.”

“Well then tell it to lead you to Dorian,” he said. “Follow it.”

I stared at him in surprise. He was on to something. I put my hand back on the wall and my power spoke to me, the vibrations traveling through my limbs. I looked to a hallway on our left. “That way.”

He curved his body, rounding a corner when I felt a new burst of power—my power—readying itself like a current in the air.

Hades was in the path of the next shockwave.

Without giving it much thought, I dropped Ezra to the ground. The grunt as he landed made me grimace, but there was no time to dwell on it. I shouted for Hades to turn around as I rushed toward him, screaming for him to get out of the way. Like slow motion, I could see the streaks of lightning, the explosions ripping through space and time.

I ran towards it, letting it envelop me, pulling the magic back inside my body. Instead of reaching around my frame, it came straight to me as I blocked the damage from reaching Hades. My ears were ringing as I took the impact, my body absorbing the power it knew so well. Hades' claws sunk into my skin and dug into my back as he tried to pull me away with a strength I didn't know he had.

He cried out for my safety as I sank to the ground, shaking my head, trying to stop the tinnitus.

"What the hell were you thinking?" he shouted, landing on my lap.

"Saving your life," I said hoarsely. "You're welcome."

Before he could answer, Dorian's voice boomed in the corridors, the sound bouncing off the walls and carrying through. It was filled with anguish and a rage so deep it hurt my very soul, shattering the edges of my heart. Demanding to find out what happened. Demanding to know where I was.

I stumbled to a standing position when I heard him, my mind going into overdrive with the impossibilities that had become possible over the last few hours.

"Dorian!" I yelled.

My mate stormed around the corner, the room shaking as he did. When he saw me, he came to an abrupt stop. "Fury?" he asked, completely disbelieving.

His amber eyes were on fire. His tuxedo jacket was gone, his shirt ripped and shredded, hanging off his body in random tatters. Lightning crackled beneath his skin, traveling across his body like a stormy sky.

My mouth fell open.

I'd thought that somehow his presence in the Afterlife had shifted my magic. I was an abomination, and nothing about me made sense. My grief, Ezra's pain, Dorian's presence—I thought I'd inadvertently caused the explosions. It was my power. When I touched it, the source of it was enraged, but it still felt like home.

But none of this was my doing. It was Dorian's. My power had transferred to my mate.

I threw myself at him, wrapping my arms around his neck. He stood still for a moment before he returned the embrace, threatening to crush me. He buried his face in my hair, breathing me in, taking my scent to know it was truly me. If he questioned it and there really was an imposter-me running around, I don't think she'd be wearing a pink halter dress with a black tutu.

All the questions rushed out of me as I pushed him away, holding his arms. "How are you in the Afterlife? You can't . . . did you die? You can't die. You can't be here. How are you here? What are you doing here?"

"I . . . we thought you died. Azrael killed you. Your body turned to ash in the ballroom . . ." he said, struggling to get the words out. "I didn't know you'd be here. I thought it was real this time . . ."

If my body had turned to ash, I was pretty sure that orb went right with it.

"How the hell are you here?" Hades interjected, not at all caring for anyone's emotions at the moment.

Dorian snapped his head toward him, the room suddenly starting to shake again. "How about you tell me where the fuck you were when Azrael was killing her?"

I slammed my palm into my mate's chest, pulling on the power and telling him to calm down. "I'm not dead. Hades was here, working on his own part. Azrael wasn't supposed to be there."

My crow narrowed his eyes. "Unanswered question, fae. How did you get here?"

Ezra moaned from the ground, trying to push himself up and failing.

I cursed under my breath, rushing over to him. I stroked his hair, apologizing in a soothing voice. I glanced up and down his body. He wasn't healing. Worry shot through me.

Could he die?

Over the course of his life, attempts had been made on his life and none had succeeded. But had they tried this? Assassins on Earth went for the quick kill. That didn't work. In this case, the Angel of Death was no assassin. He was a sociopathic serial killer, and he enjoyed every minute of the pain and suffering he'd put Ezra through. I shuddered thinking about all the innocents he'd gone after in the past.

I turned to Dorian. "Azrael's had him here. He's been tortured, and he's seriously depleted in blood. I need to get him back." I started to lift him, getting him situated so we could sift when another familiar voice broke through the silence.

"I thought you got that temper of yours under control," Jake said. "But here you are, taking out the entirety of HQ."

Looking up, I saw him leaning against a wall, arms crossed, and his ankle crossed over his other. He looked like he did any other day. Khakis. Collared shirt. Bored expression, but just a twinkle of amusement in his eyes. Hades landed on his shoulder.

"I never thought I would say this," I said, sighing in relief, "but I am so happy to see you right now."

"I can't say the same. You're blowing up my building, Fury," he said, eyeing the cracks in the walls.

I shook my head. "It's not me, and I can explain, sort of. I only know the 'whats' and not the 'hows' at the moment."

Jake's gaze turned from me to Dorian, and his expression changed. His eyes narrowed in confusion, and he looked at Hades. "How did he get here?"

The crow shook his head. "He hasn't answered that yet."

Jake furrowed his brows, returning to my mate. He waved his hand in a circular motion. "Waiting for an answer. But add to it *what* you're doing here, if you don't mind."

The hallway began to vibrate in Dorian's anger.

I rolled my eyes. Now was not the time for a pissing contest. Dorian didn't know how to control these powers yet, and they were far more devastating than he understood. And what did Jake do? He *laughed*.

"I came here for some fucking answers," Dorian said. He balled his fists at his sides, but I wasn't sure if he was controlling the roiling anger or trying to contain it.

"Well. Ask your fucking questions," Jake retorted.

I smacked my palm to my forehead, scrubbing my hand down my face.

"Dorian, you can't burst into the Afterlife blowing shit up, acting like Karen the Horrible and demanding to see the manager of the Afterlife," I said, completely exasperated. Pointing to my co-worker, I added, "This is Jake. From AR. He's my case worker. Now isn't the time for this."

"Oh, I beg to differ. Now's as good a time as any," Jake said, uncrossing his arms and pushing himself off the wall. "Your mate here has figured out a way to get into the Afterlife—a feat that shouldn't be possible, might I add. He's come here to ask questions. To whom? Upper Management? Is that what you wanted, Dorian? You wanted to meet with them and find out what? Ask away."

From where I sat kneeled beside Ezra, I glanced at Dorian's arms, seeing lightning crackle across his skin.

"Dorian," I said quietly, slowly standing. "I need you to focus on me."

Without warning, Dorian sent out an explosion of power aimed directly at them.

My heart stopped.

The blast cut through Jake and Hades, shattering the nearby walls, sending their bodies into a million pieces of ash and flame.

It was my unique gift he was carrying, but he had no idea how to control it.

It was my unbelievable curse to bear, and he only saw it as a weapon.

I'd learned early how to wield the power. I had to. The destruction was immeasurable.

The quakes and the explosions? Those could be fixed. That was easy.

The core of my power? The boom? It could *extinguish*.

It had before.

Twice on accident, and once on purpose. All three were terrible mistakes in the end.

I screamed, unable to pull the power back before Dorian had done his damage. I watched as my power killed my friends. It felt as raw as though I'd done it myself. I reeled on him, hitting him in the chest with a force I didn't expect. He flew back, not prepared to take a hit from me.

"Why did you do that?" I cried.

Dorian shook his head. "I didn't know it would . . ."

Emotion clogged my throat, threatening to start pouring out of my eyes.

I was lost, in more ways than one. I had one mate that had just killed Jake and Hades. My other mate was in desperate need of blood and a healer. I was part angel. Azrael wanted to kill me and keep me as a bloody trophy. I was in the Afterlife, and all I wanted to do was go home. *Home*. That word repeated in my head, making the longing worse. At least the end of the world wasn't an issue when I had two of my mates with me in literal Hell. It was the only thing I had going for me. I wanted to scream. I ran my hands through my hair, trying to process what I could possibly do next.

"I really wish you hadn't done that," Jake said, breaking the silence.

I spun around in shock, finding Jake standing in the same place he'd been in, massaging the bridge of his nose. Hades' body shuddered, feathers flying about. "You're a dick, Dorian," he muttered, stretching a leg out and snapping his beak. "Ugh, I hate it when that happens."

I almost choked on tears, but confusion and curiosity overrode every other emotion I was feeling.

"Wait . . . how did you . . ." I was unable to find the words as I tried to piece it all together while I stared at Jake. He met my gaze, letting me trail off before he spoke.

"Your powers can do a great many things, but it would take more than that to kill the devil."

My mouth fell open once again.

"The *what*?" Dorian and I said in unison.

CHAPTER 19
FURY

I STARED AT JAKE DUMBFOUNDED. THERE WAS NO POSSIBLE WAY HE WAS anything more than another body behind a desk in Afterlife Resources. Not *Jake* . . . he was so . . . so . . . normal. I'd known him for over a hundred years. He was boring. And plain.

"Expecting someone else?" he asked, rubbing his temples as though a headache was coming on.

"I mean, technically, yeah." It was all I could manage. I looked at my feet, massaging my head in the same way. This didn't make any sense.

Dorian leaned into me as he whispered, "You said there were no such things as gods and devils."

I snapped my head up. "If you're Satan, is there a god too?"

He cringed. "Don't call me that." Turning to the side, he faced a door in the hallway that had not been there before. "Come into my office. I think we have a lot to talk about."

He twisted the knob, walking through with Hades perched on his shoulder, not saying another word. Dorian and I didn't move. I crouched down, feeling Ezra's skin. It was clammy and paler than it should have been. Dorian kneeled, scooping my other mate in his arms. "He'll be okay," he assured me. "I've got him."

In that moment, Dorian did more for me than he could have imagined. I was still angry at him for attempting to kill Hades and Jake. He had no idea what my powers could really do, and he made some terrible decisions in his anger. I would've expected Roman to lose his shit this way, but not him. When he picked up Ezra, the vampire he shared me with, it showed a strength and caring in him I didn't know was there. He didn't want to see me hurt, and that meant he didn't want to see my other mates hurt.

He'd said I was the only thing they had in common. It was true in a sense, but it was also more than that. A by-product of caring about me meant caring for each other too. We may never live together under one roof, but I had a feeling when all this was over, we'd still spend more time together than any of us realized. If the world didn't blow up, that is.

"Are you coming or not?" Hades called from the room they'd entered.

We followed them in, and the first thing I saw was Francine, Jake's secretary. I raised my eyebrows in surprise.

"Hi, Fury. He's already in there," she said, casually nodding to his office door without looking up from her crossword puzzle.

I narrowed my eyes. I knew it. Acting like she didn't know which Fury I was all these years just to agitate me. "Thanks, twat." I tossed the insult at her and stomped right into Jake's office.

It looked exactly the same as it always did.

"How can you tell me you're the freaking devil, then keep this shithole as your office?" I asked, crossing my arms and sitting down in a chair in front of him. Dorian held Ezra, standing up against the wall.

I'll get you home as soon as I can. I promise.

Ezra caressed my mind weakly. *I know.*

I shot Hades a look. "You've been keeping secrets."

"They aren't my secrets to tell, Fury. I know you understand that," he countered.

"What about you, then? What secrets are yours to tell? Are you someone special? Are you God? Are you really some hellhound dressed up in a feather costume?" A heat started to crawl up my chest, reaching my face and turning my cheeks red. My temper was on edge, and I didn't know what I was more angry about. There were too many things to choose from.

"There is no god," Jake cut in. "At least not the way you think."

"What is that supposed to mean?" I asked, throwing my arms out. "Everything I thought I knew has been a lie, so I don't know what to think right now. Up until five minutes ago, I didn't think there was a devil." My voice was rising, and the room began shaking.

I'd had these powers under control for years, but I was at my wit's end. There was entirely too much on the line right now, and I was done with the secrets.

"I think you and Hades have some explaining to do," Dorian said with authority. My fingers were pressing into the chair, and it started to splinter and crack under the weight of my hands. "Just tell her what she needs to know."

"This coming from you, who kept Lyra a secret, is that right?" Hades shot back, tilting his head. There was some obvious resentment that my mate had aimed a blast at him. I didn't blame him for it. I just couldn't find it in me to care.

"And look how that turned out," Dorian snapped in return. "I'll admit to my mistakes, crow. You should do the same."

I wasn't here for a standoff. "I don't care who admits to what mistakes. Just start talking. Here's what I know so far. I'm part angel. Azrael wants to own me in his hellhole pocket realm of madness. You're the devil. There is no god, at least not how I think. Tell me what that means. Let's start there."

Count to ten. No stabbing.

It didn't matter. What would I even stab?

Probably Francine.

Breathe and count to ten.

Jake cleared his throat before speaking. "The concept of a god and a devilish entity crosses over into multiple religions. Some have several on each side. The good and the bad, the dark and the light. It's all just made-up stories."

"I know this part. Where does that involve you?" I asked, impatience leaking into my voice.

He pointed his thumbs at himself. "I'm all of that."

I sat quietly, trying to process what he'd said. "You're all religions? Or you're all the entities?"

Jake shrugged his shoulders. “Tomayto, tomahto. It’s all the same. Yes to both.”

I inhaled, ready to respond, but the words failed me. I just blew out air, losing the ability to speak intelligently. After several suspended moments where they stared at me in the silence of the room, all I managed to say was, “But . . . you’re Satan. Lucifer. How can you be God ?”

“Because that’s how it is,” he answered simply. “I didn’t make the rules—well, that’s not true. I did make the rules. I didn’t make up all the stories that humans passed down.” He pointed to the table, wanting to emphasize his next statement. “I don’t go by all those other names, so don’t call me them.”

“He goes through phases. Changes his name over the years,” Hades supplied, rolling his eyes.

“If that’s the case, why did you call yourself the devil? You say there’s no god, but that there is. The story I knew was that Lucifer was an angel, and he pissed off God and fell from Heaven , but when I got here, I learned none of it is true.”

Hades snickered, then quickly apologized when Jake shot him a look. “That is indeed another made-up story. By someone who thought he was being funny.”

“I don’t follow,” I said, looking between them.

Hades avoided eye contact with Jake, who stared at him pointedly. He coughed quietly, then said, “Uh, that was me.” I waited for him to go further, and when he didn’t, I raised my eyebrows, motioning with my hands for him to get on with it. “I started that rumor. It was a joke. I didn’t think it was going to get passed along at the rate it did, but it got away from me. You know how things go. It’s a game of telephone, then it gets bigger and bigger and bigger until some guy writes a book and makes a religion out of it.”

“You . . . started a rumor . . . that included a god—and a heaven—and then said Jake rebelled and was cast out?” I asked incredulously, piecing it together in order. “Because you thought it was funny? And it started an entire religion?”

Hades nodded his little bird head. “Yep, that about sums it up.”

I blinked rapidly, not sure what to say, so I just looked at Jake and waited for him to speak.

"You asked why I called myself the devil. I said that because that's what makes sense to you. It's how you can comprehend who and what I am. How else would I explain it? This is part of why no one knows. It's a mind-numbingly frustrating conversation. In the end, I'm neither the dark nor the light, yet both at the same time. I'm everything. I just *am*."

"Well that clears that up," I said, not even trying to hide the sarcasm in my voice. I couldn't believe they kept this from everyone in the Afterlife. I couldn't even understand the point of it all.

Dorian cleared his throat, gaining the room's attention. "What about Upper Management?"

That was something I wanted to know as well, but Jake didn't immediately answer. Hades kept unusually quiet, which didn't exactly send warm fuzzy feelings through me.

"I'm what matters. It's like I said, I make the rules," he said, evading the question.

Every emotion came flooding through me as I listened to him. The circumstances of my life, and my death. Of how I came to be in general. What my mates had been put through. What my friends were beginning to suffer as a result of me being in their lives. The way Ezra looked when I found him sent another pang of anger through me. It was like the mercury rising on the thermometer, and it wasn't going to ever stop. It'd just burst through the top, shattering the glass.

"Well, you suck at it," I said, not considering any of my words before they came falling out. I was pissed. Jake looked surprised at my response, "If you're in charge, and you make the rules, then why was Azrael out there fucking humans, making babies? Why was Michael out there doing the same? How did Azrael start killing off other angels? That shouldn't even be possible. And more importantly, why didn't you stop it? You're all-knowing, right? You made the rules." My tone turned mocking while I waved my hands around erratically. "Azrael killed me in my real life, and you let him. Then he found his way back to me on Earth and is at it again, trying to end my afterlife and stick me in a place I didn't know existed but that I would apparently end up in for eternity. So if you are in charge, you are doing a piss-poor job at it, *Jake*."

He took my tongue-lashing, sitting silently as I let it all out. He pursed his lips and took a deep breath. "Are you finished unloading now?" I shrugged. "Right, well, I'll move on as though you are."

"Don't count on it," Hades muttered under his breath. I narrowed my eyes at him, giving him a dirty look.

"I needed a break. A vacation, if you will," Jake started.

"Wait," I said, interrupting even as he gave me an annoyed stare. "A vacation from . . . being Lucifer?"

He sighed deeply. "I. am. not . Lucifer. Stop calling me that. Satan, Lucifer, Beelzebub, Shaytan, Maara, Mephistopheles, Thanatos, Mors—these aren't my names. I'm vibing with Jake. You don't like your *other* name, right? So, I call you Fury, you call me—"

"Jake," I said through clenched teeth.

"Very good. And yes, a vacation from my role. I've been at it for a long time, you know. It's tiresome. It gets lonely. I'm as old as time. Look at your man here," he said, inclining his head toward Dorian. "He's been around fifteen hundred years, and time is crushing him slowly. That's a blip in my existence."

When I turned to see Dorian, his eyes were cold, but I knew he was trying to cover his pain. Jake was right. I knew he was.

Returning to him, I motioned for him to carry on. "Fine. You needed a break. So what?"

"I left Azrael in charge."

"You *what*?" Well, that fire and rage that had started to cool just crawled right back up my face. "Why would you do that? What's the matter with you?"

Jake held his hand out, palm facing toward me, then dropped fingers down until only his index finger was left. "Look, in my defense, he wasn't always like this."

"*In your defense*?" I repeated, my voice rising an octave. "You don't get to defend yourself for that. How long have you been on 'vacation'?"

"Eh, who's to say what time really is." If daggers could have come out of my eyes and stabbed him in the face, they would have. "I've been enjoying my work here in Afterlife Resources. It was a nice change of scenery. I jumped around, doing a little bit of work here, a little bit of work there. I found this role, and it's been surprisingly enjoyable."

An anger-filled sadness washed over me. Maybe all of this was fine. Maybe this was how he ran things, and this entire conversation was a total waste of time. "Do you care what's happening right now—what has been happening—or is this not something that matters to you?"

He softened for a moment, looking like the Jake I had known for a long time. The Jake that was my friend, who'd guided me through some rough patches in my afterlife. I really needed him to care. I wasn't sure I could take the heartbreak if he'd admitted that everything that had happened was of little concern to him.

"Very much," he answered. "That's why I've been doing what I can to help you through this."

While his answer was a relief and I released a breath I'd been holding while I waited, I couldn't help but scoff now. "You call this help?"

"Yes," he answered, clasping his hands together and setting them on the desk.

I ran my fingers through my hair, pulling on the strands. "Am I a pawn in some fucked-up game of Afterlife chess? Because that's what it feels like."

Hades flapped his wings in response. "Of course not. You were meant to stop the prophecy. Every bit of this is real." He hopped off his perch, waddling on the desk to come closer to me. "When I learned there was more to this than the basics of what your assignment had entailed, I came and told him everything. Your targets being your mates, Azrael waking Lyra, them coming for you. All of it."

"Did you know it was Azrael that sent that shifter to kill me?" I asked him point blank.

"Keeping that secret from you doesn't serve a purpose. I'll always tell you what you need to know," he answered. "That shifter knowing how to extinguish you was a tip-off that it was bigger than we realized, but no, I didn't expect him, and I didn't expect you to live through it, or their bites," he said, angling his head toward Dorian and Ezra. "There was a moment where I was certain we'd lost you."

I looked to Jake. "Why was that? How did I survive? Is that the angel in me?"

He shook his head. "It's because they're your true mates. Each one of them. It's happened a handful of times in history where someone from the Afterlife finds a mate on Earth, though three at once was a new development."

"Duke never found that in his research," I pointed out.

"Of course not. Why would he? I kept that out of the Divine Libraries for a reason. I don't need the dead taking assignments just to search the human population for a living mate. It could be catastrophic."

"The angels certainly did their share of damage without that knowledge written down," I tossed at him.

He cocked an eyebrow. "That they did."

I sighed, feeling some of my energy die out. "Why, Jake? Why were they allowed to do all this? Why didn't you stop him?"

"At first I didn't know what was happening. I was busy doing this," he said, gesturing to his office.

"Okay, but you know about it now. So? You say you're helping me, but why haven't you just made him stop? Ended him or extinguished him or *something*. Anything. You're . . . well, *you*."

He pressed his lips together, not disagreeing with me. "That's a complicated answer with a lot of layers to it. When I left Azrael to run things, I didn't look back. I'm not a micromanager. I trusted him. He wasn't what he is now. He was capable of running the show behind the curtain. Apparently he wasn't capable of handling what time does to us. I didn't know that Uriel was gone. Michael. None of them—"

Hades scoffed loudly, shifting his body, and fluffing his feathers up. I narrowed my eyes at him. "What was that for?"

He looked at Jake before answering. "I never liked Azrael."

"You didn't like him because you thought I favored him," Jake retorted, crossing his arms.

Hades bounced around to face him. "I don't care who you favored. I never liked him because he was a cunt, and I told you he was a bad choice. You just don't want to admit I was right." He squinted his little eyes at him, muttering, "Like I always am."

I was intrigued. Not that Hades thought he was right. He frequently was, and clearly he knew it because he never shut up about it. I didn't want to stroke his ego and tell him that even I agreed with him most of the time, but I hoped his emotions were running high and he'd tell me what I wanted to know.

"Why didn't you like him? Why was he a bad choice?"

"Because he *wanted* to be favored. He *wanted* to be in control of everything. Those that are good leaders don't want the power they are imbued with, like this asshole." He jerked his wing out in Jake's direction. "Despite some truly terrible decisions, he's good at his role. He doesn't relish in the control he has. Azrael is the Angel of Death, and he *loves* it. How anyone can be surprised that he went down a rabbit hole of fucking crazy is beyond me."

"You didn't want the job when I said I wanted a break," Jake said by way of explanation, but Hades just gave him a deadpanned look. It was quite the accomplishment for a crow.

"Of course I didn't."

"That's what a second is *for*."

"No it's not," Hades groaned. "By your side as a second, not in your place."

"Wait, what? You're a crow," I said, looking at him, then to Jake. "He's a crow." They both stared at me, as if they momentarily had forgotten that Dorian was here holding Ezra, and I was sitting in front of them. "What am I missing?"

"Nothing," they said in unison.

"Oh, that's believable," I said flatly.

"I don't care about who favors who, or why. What are you planning on doing about it?" Dorian asked, and the room rumbled with his frustration.

Jake tilted his head to the side, considering Dorian. "Fascinating."

I turned and exchanged a look with my mate. "What is?" I asked.

"He has your powers, but I'm not entirely sure how," he muttered. "You've done something to transfer it to him." He looked back to me in question.

I scrunched my eyebrows. "I don't know. I have aspects of their powers after they saved me. Maybe when they bit me—" I stopped, thinking about a newer development. I closed my eyes. "I bit them."

"You bit them?" he repeated.

"My vampire parts are sort of backwards. I don't need to take in blood, I have to give it. Ezra wasn't exactly available each time, so I've bitten all of them now. If I survived because they're my mates, I guess that works both ways." Which meant it wasn't just Dorian . . . fuck my afterlife.

He pursed his lips. "That would explain it." He looked Dorian up and down. "You need to work on your temper and managing those powers before you cause more damage than you're capable of cleaning up."

Dorian's mood darkened further. "Considering the cleanup you're involved in right now, I'm not sure you should be giving advice," he said coldly. "You left Azrael in charge, and he's wreaked havoc right under your nose for centuries. More. I don't know. Duke said he chased down every angel's descendants and was able to kill each one of them, including Fury, but she's evaded being extinguished. Now he's—"

I'd been pressing the palms of my hands into eyes as he was speaking, trying to massage the tension out from the overwhelming onslaught of discovery, but his last statement made me snap my head up, setting my train of thought aside. "You knew who I was."

The day I'd arrived came flooding back to me. I was a scared kid, just having found out I was dead. That I'd been murdered. Learning there was no god or religion as I had believed when I was brought up. Jake was there, gently leading me through it. Understanding. Soothing. He had a file about my life, and he knew everything in it.

"Of course I knew, but no one else would have. I was the only one who could know. Angels have a signature. I created them. I sensed it in you when you showed up in my office." Jake put his elbows on the desk, crossing his fingers and resting his chin on top.

My chest constricted, feeling the pain of that day all over again. I swallowed a lump in my throat. "Why? Azrael killed countless of Michael's offspring. Duke said I was an abomination. That's why I was being hunted by him. If you knew what I was, why did you let me in? Why didn't you extinguish me?"

He considered my questions, but the way he looked at me told me he already knew the answers. "Because I wanted to let you in. I liked you. I make the rules, remember? You interested me. I could see parts of Michael in you that I admired. His power flowed through your veins, but your heart was different."

"Ha," I laughed, but there was no humor in it. "By different, do you mean broken? Because that's what my life was. Broken. My parents despised my existence, my baby sister was taken from me, I married a guy I barely knew thinking I had a small chance at maybe being happy—or at least content—until Azrael wore his face and made sure the baby I carried never had a chance. Then he killed me, but not before he beat me senseless for years."

Hades looked away from me at that moment, and I could sense his discomfort. Jake dropped his hands, lowering his voice. "Your time on Earth was short-lived no matter what. You would have died in childbirth."

"I . . . what? How do you know?" The implications of what he said sent a spike of anxiety through me. Did he know the future? Was that written out? Was free will not a thing? Were we all about to die, anyway? That might have been easier to hear.

"Your mother, your real mother, died in childbirth. All women carrying an angel's descendent do. Humans aren't meant to contain that power. Men continue passing down the line, and females give birth to the offspring," he said. "They'd go on for years, trying to grow their line. It's why I forbid the coupling between the realms. It's suffering to humans, but it doesn't stop it from happening. Your suffering would have been greater. You are already part angel, and you were carrying an Archangel's child."

My jaw fell. My stomach roiled, threatening to let whatever I had left come out on the floor.

My eyes filled with tears. The loss and the grief I'd felt tore through me as fresh as the day it had happened. I'd held on to the memory of hope I'd had when I'd missed my first period. Then my second. When I realized I had a life inside me. To the dreams I'd had of being a mother. Of being with my child and loving it the way I loved my baby sister. Those memories were all made up, but they'd gotten me through so many days. Honoring my lost child and honoring the future we would have had together. My heart was ripped out now knowing it never would have come to pass. I would have died, and he would have killed my baby right afterwards. Learning it was kindness to have had a miscarriage instead of having a child shattered my heart beyond measure.

Ezra's breath stuttered as he felt my pain. It was too loud, and I knew I couldn't keep it from him.

I'm so sorry, my love.

Please don't listen to this . . . it's too much . . .

I'm not leaving you alone in this. I'm always here. He mentally caressed my face as though he were wiping a tear.

I knew the energy it took him to do that, and I could sense his exhaustion and pain as well. *I am going to fix you.*

I'm fine. Get the answers you need.

I turned back, directing my attention to Hades. "You knew," I said through my tears.

He shook his head. "I didn't. I pieced it together." He looked down at his feet. "Jake confirmed it."

I felt a small measure of comfort that Hades hadn't kept that from me. He had his reasoning for not telling me about Azrael's realm, and that I could accept. But this . . . Another thought crept into my mind.

"Azrael didn't stop me from having his baby. He stopped me from dying. To keep me longer. To just *keep me*. He killed me by accident." I met Jake's gaze, seeing the fire in his eyes. "He was going to hold on to me for as long as he could, torturing me until he extinguished me, then take me to . . ."

"Yes. But instead, you died and came to me. I don't think he expected me to allow you to stay. He'd lost you, and he wasn't getting you back. Until I sent you to Earth. Once he learned where you were, he had a chance again. And now we find ourselves here," he said, a dangerous undercurrent in his tone making its way to the surface.

An intercom buzzed and Francine's voice came through. "Boss? Risk Management is blowing up the phone, but I told them you weren't to be disturbed."

"Send them through."

Hades and I met each other's gaze, then I looked back to Dorian. We hadn't captured Lyra, but I had two of my mates with me. "We should be okay for now," I said. "If Dorian and Ezra are here with me, they can't cause the end of the world without Roman. We don't even know how they'd do it yet, but I figured it had something to do with . . . me . . ." I trailed off, feeling a tendril of something reaching out, begging to make the connection.

I rested my head in my hands as the call came in on speaker-phone. I looked up at Jake in question, but all he did was raise a single shoulder. "It's your assignment. You should hear what they have to say."

Static connected the line and a hollow voice greeted us.

"Speak," Jake commanded. That was it. No formalities, just authority.

"The prophecy has altered at an alarming rate," the voice said. "The supernatural trio are now joined by . . . others."

Jake leaned forward, toward the speaker. "What *others*?"

An uncomfortable silence spanned, freezing the moment in time. I could hear Hades' feathers ruffle. Ezra's shallow breathing. Dorian's quiet stewing.

Finally, the voice spoke again. "The Dukes are present."

Jake slowly closed his eyes, exhaling loudly through his nose. "What else has been seen?"

"It is the same ending, but the suffering and devastation leading up to it are significantly more," the voice answered.

"It would be with those twats in the picture," Hades said, gently banging his head into the desk on repeat.

Who? Ezra asked me.

I don't know, but it looks bad. His unease passed into me, furthering my own suppressed anxiety.

"Background?" Jake asked, running a hand through his hair.

"Night. The moon is a waning crescent. No location."

Jake hung up but didn't speak. Hades had the top of his head resting on the desk, as though he had stopped mid-banging.

"Who are the Dukes? What does that mean?"

"My asshole brothers," Hades muttered.

"My asshole children," Jake said, leaning back in his chair and rubbing his eyes.

"YOUR *WHAT*?" There was no holding back any longer. I was shouting at the 'boss' and I didn't care. I slammed my fist on the desk, sending a crack down the middle. "You both better explain this to me right now. RIGHT. NOW. What do you mean your brothers? What do you mean 'your children'—oh my god . . ." My eyes widened as I reached another conclusion. I did a double take between them, then I looked Hades up and down. "You're his son . . . you're a duke of hell . . ."

"I'm *The* Duke," he corrected, inclining his head as though he was bowing.

"But you're a crow." I had to sound stupid, stating the obvious. Who wouldn't be confused in this case?

"Yes, thank you for that astute observation." Hades flew over to a shelf, grabbing a book, and flying back to the desk where he dropped it. It landed with a thud, its dusty pages sending a plume of particles up in the air. "I wasn't always a crow. It's a form I take."

"Change back, then," I demanded while he flipped through pages.

"I can't. Punished. Bad choices and breaking rules and all that," he mumbled.

"Um, explain."

"We're off topic," he said, finding his page and turning the book to me and pointing his clawed foot at it. "Read."

I opened my mouth then shut it. We were so coming back around to this. He wasn't getting off that easy. Duke of the freaking Afterlife. Son of th—Jake. My head was going to explode from too much information.

I scanned the old text, trying to see what he wanted me to find that was so important. When I found it, I froze. I muttered to myself while reading, and then I heard Ezra's breathing change. Dorian felt the change, asking me what was wrong.

The bloodshed . . . the death and destruction they'd caused. It made Lyra look like the warm-up act. "The Dukes are . . . they're the Four Horsemen . . ."

Jake stifled a small laugh and shook his head. "They are definitely *not*."

Hades scoffed. "Oh, don't call them that. First of all, there's three of them—"

"Dude, you're their brother. Aren't you the fourth?"

"No." There was nothing more to it. Firm. Concise. To the point.

"He's technically the first," Jake supplied. At least now I knew where he was in the lineup. "And he never got on board with their little games."

Hades fluffed his feathers. "They are *not* the Four Horsemen. It's a stupid name they gave themselves like a shitty boyband and it stuck around with humans."

I snorted. "Well they can't be that smart. They can't even count." Something twinkled in Hades' eyes. Oh, we had so much to discuss now. "Are they like what humans think the Four—er, are they like what we think they are on Earth?"

Hades shrugged. "Depends on the lore you're reading."

That wasn't comforting. All the lore and legend was bad.

"Where are they?" Dorian asked, shifting his weight carefully while he held Ezra.

Jake placed his elbows on the table, rubbing the sides of his head with his eyes closed. "In Lethe. Azrael's realm."

"You extinguished them?" I asked in awe.

He opened his eyes, and I could see wisdom there I hadn't ever seen before. Old and ageless at the same time. The depths of knowledge, of happiness, and pain. It swirled in a black galaxy, flashing at me just once. If you could describe how time looks, that was Jake's eyes at that moment. Then it was gone. "They're imprisoned there. I had to," he said simply. His eyes traveled to the book in front of me. "You see what they were. The floods. The plagues. The decimation of entire civilizations. You see what they became. I can't allow that. I won't."

I nodded, not pushing the conversation. There was no reason to. He didn't need to explain it further. I completely understood.

A spark of hope made its way to the surface. "Wait, if they're in Lethe, they can't come out. Nothing comes back from that. The prophecy is wrong." When neither Jake nor Hades agreed and they sat there in silence, the ember faded. A pit grew in my stomach. "They can't come out, right?"

Hades closed his eyes, and Jake answered. "Azrael has the power."

"For the love of—*why* would you give him all this power? Why would you put these dangerous asshole kids of yours under his domain? That's a lot of freaking eggs in one basket, Jake."

"In my defense—"

"Enough with your defense! I don't want to hear about it. Azrael wasn't that bad, blah blah blah. Well he bloody is now!" I sucked in a breath, realizing I let all that out in one fell swoop. "Why would he let them out? Why can't these stupid risk witches even see Azrael doing this?" The answer slammed into me. All this time, they couldn't see me either. I jerked my head up, glaring at Jake. "They can't see angels, can they?"

He shook his head.

"Well that was a bit of an oversight, don't you think?"

"In hindsight, yes. You know what they say. Twenty-twenty."

"I can't believe you right now."

Fury . . .

Ezra's weak plea reached me, and I didn't need him to say more to know what was wrong. He was fading, and fast. What little I had given him had already pushed through his system, fueling what it could, but it was nowhere near enough.

"I'm going to go out on a limb here and guess you can't just stop your rogue boyband trio of death by snapping your fingers?" No answer. Great. "Are you planning on coming to Earth and stopping them?"

"I can't."

"What do you mean you can't?" I asked incredulously. "You made the rules. Don't you get to do what you want?"

"I mean I can't leave the Afterlife. Its very existence relies on my presence," he said, reaching into a drawer and pulling out a box and pushing it across the table. "But I can give you whatever you need to help you."

I blew out a breath. "These are the layers you were talking about, aren't they? This is why you haven't stopped Azrael. Lethe, the power he was given . . . and you're essentially imprisoned in your own realm." He inclined his head, confirming it all. This was so messed up. I threw my head back and groaned loudly. "How much time do we have until the waning crescent moon?" I asked.

Jake looked at his Apple Watch . "We have one day."

I grabbed the mystery box and stood up, walking to Dorian, then rested my hand on Ezra's cheek. "One day until Azrael unleashes your hellspawn on Earth and tries to take me back to his castle on nightmare island . . . no pressure."

"Tick tock," Hades and I said together quietly.

It'd be funny if it weren't true this time.

CHAPTER 20
FURY

We stepped out of Jake's and before the door could close, Hades swooped in from the back, landing on my shoulder once more.

"You should visit us more, Hades," Francine called out, giggling like a lovestruck fool.

"I'll see what I can do," Hades replied, with a little wink.

If not for the weight of everything I'd learned, I might have made a gagging noise at the flirting going on between them. As it was, exhaustion was hitting me hard, and it wasn't even the physical kind. It was mental, where my mind felt tired, my emotions felt raw and exposed.

I turned to Dorian. "I don't suppose you sifted here?"

"Uh, no. I had Jules give me a one-way ticket through the mirror realm."

"Unbelievable," Hades muttered.

I lifted an eyebrow at my mate. He and I were going to talk about all of this later. After Ezra was recovering and Roman knew I was safe.

"All right, in that case, let's hope my powers are strong enough to handle sifting us back." I wrapped my arms around his waist from behind, trusting he had a strong enough hold on Ezra. His muscles tensed under my touch.

"I'm not sure that's the best idea. You've never gone that far—"

I didn't let him finish.

For so long, I'd been *The* Fury, one of the biggest badasses in the Afterlife. Then I became their mate and took on new powers I struggled to control.

The truth of it was, I was just as strong as before. If not more. It was my own fear holding me back. Fear of the unknown. Fear of Azrael. Fear of getting close to them.

But after today, fear had no place in my life.

I couldn't overcome it when it was solely for my benefit. Not when it was just my life on the line. After seeing Ezra . . . I would overcome it for him.

And it started now.

If I could extinguish souls and blow up the Afterlife, I could sift us back to Earth.

I would.

Because success was my only option. I wouldn't accept failure. Not anymore.

Pressure crushed me as the sifting process began. It started in my head, then worked its way down, pushing me into Dorian so tight that if he weren't immortal, I'd worry there would be a Fury-shaped dent in his back forever.

My jaw compressed, teeth gritting in pain as the invisible weight that smothered me reached its peak.

I focused on Roman; on going to wherever my third mate was located. I knew without a doubt he needed to see me and know I was okay.

My feet slammed into the ground, pressure releasing at once. If not for Dorian's indomitable form holding me up, I would have collapsed to the ground in relief.

Hades croaked. "Remind me to never hitch a ride with you aga—" His statement was punctuated with gagging as he vomited onto the grass beside us. The longer trip must have hit him harder.

"Sifting can be a real bitch to get used to," I said, easing away from Dorian to look around.

"Your fae magic is stronger than I thought," Dorian said, casting me a wary look.

"What can I say? When the things holding you back are stripped away, we're capable of more than we think." I gave him a knowing look. We still needed to talk about teaching him how to control my power, but now wasn't the time.

"Fury?" Roxanne asked, disbelief in her voice. I turned to her and smiled almost sheepishly, if not for the sadness weighing me down.

"Hey, Rox."

"How—what happened—wait, is that Ezra?" Her questions spilled out one after another. In answer, I walked up to her and wrapped my arms tight around her shoulders.

"I can't answer everything right now, but yes. I died and showed up in the Afterlife. Turns out that still happens. Ezra was there, and we rescued him—"

"We?" she questioned, pulling back to look between Dorian and me.

"We meaning me and Hades in this case, but yes. Ezra's in bad shape and I need to take care of him. Dorian can fill you in, but first, I wanted to see Roman so he knows I'm not dead."

"About that," Roxanne sighed.

In the distant trees, an anguished howl warped the wind—followed by an explosion.

I turned to Dorian, sharing a look.

That explained why they were in the middle of nowhere. Roxanne took him to a secluded area to keep him from killing anyone accidentally.

"Rya and Kelly are out there doing damage control," she added. "He's destroying a lot right now. He's not quite . . . himself."

Yeah, about that, I thought.

"Can you help him without making things worse?" I asked Dorian.

He narrowed his eyes, seeming offended. I sighed and added, "It's not an insult. I'm being realistic. You don't have a handle on my power either. Do you think you can calm him down without accidentally using it? You two together could do a lot of damage."

Understanding flashed. He heard what I wasn't saying.

That the two of them may not end the world, but who was to say how much of it they could hurt with my power combined. As it was, Roman had to be trying to restrain it because this entire forest would be levelled if he wasn't.

Dorian nodded. "I can do this. Leave Hades here with me, though. In case he thinks I'm Azrael in disguise. He can't exactly impersonate a bird."

Hades puffed his chest in indignation. "I'm *far more* than a bird."

"We know," I said testily. "And we'll be talking about that when I can catch my breath for two fucking seconds."

He deflated, a guilty look crossing his beady eyes.

"I'm taking Ezra to your estate in Houston. Bring Roman and Roxanne there once he's not liable to blow it up—actually, take them to the compound and get Caitlin, Rava, and Pria. I want them kept close too. Azrael can impersonate anyone. We're safest in numbers right now."

I looked to Roxanne to make sure she understood the plan. Her chin dipped. "Thank you for thinking of them too."

One corner of my mouth dragged up. "Of course. We can't bring everyone, but I'll try to protect who I can."

She ran off, shifting into a wolf as she tore through the forest. I heard Roman's howling cut off . She'd shared with him that I was here, stopping him from causing more damage.

Dorian silently passed Ezra to me, then pressed his lips to my temple.

"Stay safe. Stay vigilant."

I lifted my chin. "I need you to do the same. Roman's in a vulnerable place right now. Don't let whatever he says get to you."

"For once, I understand completely where the wolf is. I was there myself. He'll be safe. I'll pull him out of it."

"Thank you."

I stepped back and focused on Dorian's mansion. Specifically, my room in it.

After crossing literal dimensions, this sift was nothing. The slight pressure didn't even register until after it was done. We landed in front of my bed, and I hitched at the waist to lay Ezra down.

"How are you hanging in there?" I asked quietly, retreating to the bathroom to grab several washcloths and running them under warm water.

I'll live, he answered, a hint of amusement in his mental voice despite his state.

"Is that meant to be a joke because you can't die?" I asked, unable to hide the follow-up thought, *that we know of. If anyone could have found a way, it would've been Azrael.*

Poor timing? Weariness leaked through his smartass comments despite the humor I knew he was trying to use to put me at ease.

"The worst."

I returned to his side and started to wash away the blood and grime that covered his skin. I had to bite the inside of my cheek, seeing his tattoos stripped away from him. Over a hundred and seventy years gone, just like that.

Tattoos can be reinked. He caressed my mind. *When all of this is over, I want to put mine on you.*

My hand froze where I'd been washing over his hips.

"That's real?" I asked, hesitant to show him what Azrael had done, but unable to stop it from playing through my mind. His jaw tensed.

It's real. We ink our mates ourselves with a design of our choosing. I've had mine picked out for you since that night in the pool.

The first night I gave into him. It seemed so long ago now.

"Will you show me?" I murmured, continuing to clean him.

When it's on you. Tradition is we don't show until after. You're trusting me to mark your body as I see fit because I'm your mate.

I pursed my lips in amusement, washing the rest of his waist before starting to peel his pants away. "That seems a little miso—"

The ring of dried blood around his cock made it hard for me to stay casual. I'd tortured enough people to know what that meant.

Ezra lifted his hand to mine and squeezed.

Don't blame yourself.

"I . . . I don't know how I can't. I feel like I should have known sooner."

There was no way for you to know. He's been doing this for thousands of years.

Perhaps. But Ezra was my mate. I should have realized . . . I certainly should've picked up on it before I nearly fucked him.

The thought stopped me cold. Self-loathing filled the space in my chest.

Kitten, we've been through a lot. We'll be through even more before this is over. I don't blame you for what happened. I'm not angry with you. If anything, I feel so incredibly lucky that you were able to find me. That destiny or fate or whatever it is that put us together gave me you. We're going to have to work through all of this later, but right now, more than anything, I just need you.

The raw need in his mental voice cooled the fire and put a cap on the self-loathing. I stuffed it away for another time and finished cleaning his body of the ordeal he'd been through. When a pile of dirty wash clothes sat next to the bed, I laid down next to him and pulled him toward me, placing his face at the crook in my neck.

"I'm here for you. Always."

Ezra groaned, his fangs testing the firmness of my skin. The bite was quick. The pain brief. While I wasn't into biting them, the heat that filled me as he took my blood had me squirming beneath him. I tried to keep still, knowing he was too weak for that.

So warm. He moaned, one hand curling around my waist and sliding up my ribs.

So sweet. He cupped my breast, rolling my nipple between his thumb and forefinger through the fabric of my dress.

My breathing grew shallow, and my chest heaved as desire coiled around me.

He drank deeper, pulling harder. His movements became stronger. Surer.

Ezra rolled onto his back, pulling me on top of him. My legs fell to either side of his hips, straddling his waist. He pulled back, releasing my neck with a pop. His hands drifted up, to the center of my neckline. He grabbed either side and pulled, ripping the fabric down the middle and baring me to him.

I gasped as he leaned up, wrapping his arms around my waist once more as he took my breast in his mouth. I groaned when he bit me again, feeling wetness between my legs as I shifted downward.

"You're not strong enough for this yet," I gasped, pushing through my own lust to be the partner he needed.

Ezra lowered his hands to my ass, grabbing a fistful of each cheek. His nails dug into my flesh as he pulled me down, running my center over his bare cock that was very much aroused at our friction.

"Do I feel strong enough to you?" he purred, pulling off my breast and licking the puncture holes until they shut. He lapped at my nipple, teasing it between his teeth.

"Hard enough?" he prompted, thrusting up against me. My lips parted in sweet agony.

"You haven't healed," I ground out, struggling to continue finding cohesive words to form an argument.

"Look at me," he commanded. I obeyed without question and found myself staring into his emerald green eyes .

I cupped his face between my hands.

Tears pooled as emotion overwhelmed me. My chest swelled with this feeling of completeness.

"I'm immortal, or as close to it as anyone can get. It's going to take a lot more to put me down."

I ran my thumbs over his cheek bones.

"You were in really bad shape."

"I was." He nodded. "But my mate's blood will heal me faster than anything else could." I didn't know that, but I was glad for it. "And thankfully, because she's exceptionally powerful, it worked quickly and I didn't have to drain her too much."

"I'd let you," I said, unable to stop myself. "It's not like it would kill me."

"I know." He pressed a soft kiss to my lips. "I'd rather avoid that if it's all the same to you."

The corners of my mouth drew upwards.

"Try not to get captured again and I won't need to," I said. He grinned up at me, that devilish gleam entering his eyes that told me he planned to fuck the sass out of me.

"Who's a mind reader now?" he asked, licking his lips. His fingers ripped into my underwear, completely shredding them.

He lined me up with the head of his cock, rocking my hips back and forth to smear my wetness over the tip. "Fucking tease," I groaned.

He dropped me on his length, filling me in one swift movement.

My head tipped back in ecstasy.

"What was that, kitten?" he growled, lifting me to bring me back down.

"Don't stop."

"As you wish." He thrust up into me over and over again, licking and sucking on my nipples while he did. My hands fisted his hair.

"Ah," I gasped when he hit a sweet spot. "Fuck, I love you."

Ezra turned, pinning me to the bed so he could fuck me harder. "My mate," he purred against my chest. "Such a romantic."

A chuckle escaped me before he took my mouth with his, devouring me whole. I moaned into him, and he worked me harder, taking my body with a fervor that one could only describe as need.

I pushed back against him, meeting his hips, thrust for thrust.

It wasn't enough. I needed more.

My hands curled into claws, raking up his back, but careful not to break skin. It was an effort to be so restrained and not cause him further pain.

Ezra broke away, giving me a hard glare.

"You're holding out on me."

I pressed my lips together. There was no point denying it.

He lunged forward, grabbing my bottom lip between his teeth, and biting down. Copper smeared my mouth as he sucked it clean. I groaned.

"If I have to make you come unhinged, I will," he growled.

His cock slammed into me hard enough the headboard hit the wall.

He reared back, pulling out except for the tip before entering me again. This time the drywall cracked.

My back arched, legs straining as I reached for my release. Ezra delivered on his threat, fucking me harder than anyone ever had. His hands grabbed mine, holding them above my head while he pounded into me, breaking the wall a little more with each thrust. I squeezed his hands back, giving him my mind, body, and soul.

His next movement made the bed rails snap.

We fell down, and the headboard tipped forward. He released my hand and caught it in one swift movement, not slowing for a second.

My pussy clenched, that peak steadily approaching. My lips parted as a groan left me. My legs went taut as every muscle in my body tightened.

"That's right, kitten. Milk my cock."

His dirty words made me see stars. I blacked out and came back to his cock twitching inside of me. His eyes were closed in something like rapture.

When the aftershocks faded and his shallow thrusts stopped, we both laid there. He tilted the headboard back, resting it against the wall so it wouldn't fall on us.

"For the record, I love you more than anything or anyone, but I'm romantic enough not to say it while fucking you."

I laughed as he pulled out. His come slipped down my thighs, but Ezra didn't seem to care as he pulled me into him, dragging one of my legs on top of his.

We stayed like that for a long time. Silent but content. Enjoying each other on a level more intimate than sex itself. Words didn't need to be said to convey everything between us. The love. The fear. The insecurities. The anxieties. The hope. But above all, the desire to protect each other from what was to come.

It was that thought that kept me from sleep, even after Ezra drifted off. His body relaxed as soft snores told me he was finally resting in the way he needed.

I slowly pulled away, careful not to jostle him. My feet were near silent as I padded into the bathroom and grabbed a robe, tying it around my waist.

As I exited the bedroom, I left the door cracked. The need to keep an eye on him after everything that had happened was all too real. The hallways were dark and the mansion was silent as I made my way into the kitchen and poured myself a glass of fae wine.

Then I took a seat and waited.

CHAPTER 21
FURY

SILENCE SCREAMED.

The ticking of the clock was like a hammer to my anxiety, chipping away at what little self-control I had.

With every passing second, the night turned darker. The living room grew colder. Emptier. I waited in the silence with my wine and drank to numb the feelings.

To numb the fear because it had no place here.

To numb the regret because I couldn't change it.

To numb the guilt because it wasn't going anywhere.

Not when I could see that house of horrors painted red every time my eyes closed. I could see the strips of skin decorating the walls. I could see his hollow eye sockets, all because he would have rather suffered losing his eyes than be mentally fucked over by Azrael wearing my face as he tortured him.

I could see it all, but I didn't want to, because all the feelings—the hollow ache in my chest that felt like a gaping black hole—they wouldn't go away.

So I drank.

And I drank.

And when the glass ran out, I turned to the bottle. Then another. Another.

I didn't know how much I drank. How fast. How much time had passed.

All I knew was the spinning in my head and the ticking of the clock that had turned into a mantra of sorts.

The end of the world was coming, and I had one fucking day to find a solution.

Azrael was an angel that couldn't die.

He controlled a realm where extinguished souls went—and apparently—the Dukes of Hell were trapped.

The Dukes that would end the world.

Subsequently sending us all to the Afterlife or Lethe.

All except my mates, right? Because unless Azrael knew of a way to kill them, they couldn't die.

But me? Something told me I could. That even if I couldn't die here, I could be extinguished and trapped in his realm forever.

Alone. Isolated. Tortured for eternity.

I shook my head, fighting the emotions trying to surge.

It wasn't enough. Me. My powers. Jake gave me this mission, and I wasn't enough.

The bottle of wine in my hand exploded. Glass cut my palm. Dark burgundy liquid mixed with blood, running down my forearm. I stared at it, unable to truly feel the pain I knew should be there.

A childlike giggle made me pause.

I tilted my chin, eyes narrowing in the direction it came from. The hallway shifted the harder I tried to concentrate.

I frowned, taking a step toward it. A strange light-headedness hit me. Or maybe it was heavy-headedness . All I knew was I felt weighed down, my feet dragging like lead bricks whenever I tried to lift them.

Somewhere beneath the haze that wrapped around me, I sensed my raven. Unlike me, she was very much not numb and fighting. For what? I didn't know, but I wasn't all that interested in finding out.

"Sunny," a lilting voice said, making me freeze. "Darling Sunny. Beautiful. Broken." I felt the air shift behind me before a soft fingertip was running over my shoulder.

"Blameless," Lyra breathed, the scent of lilac and pine filling my nostrils. I turned, or at least tried to. But my balance was off. All I succeeded in doing was stumbling into the counter.

"Azrael send you to fuck with me?" I groaned, liking the way the cool granite felt against my forehead. I lifted it, attempting to face the fae once more.

"Azrael," she repeated, his name sounding lovely and yet haunting in her voice. "The angel. My angel." I sensed it then. The burning fire in her eyes. The way she watched me with not just childlike cruelty, but something *personal.*

"Find Sunny. Play with Sunny. But don't kill. Never kill." Her lips pressed together, pursed tight in anger and hatred. "Sunny's too precious for Lyra to kill. She belongs to the angel. She's *divine.*"

I shook my head, wanting to deny it even though it didn't matter. Lyra wasn't listening to me. She came here with a purpose, and for once, I didn't think it was Azrael's.

"Did he send you?"

Lyra's eyes glowed brighter for a moment. "Yes."

Then she lunged. I barely had time to dodge, if you could even call it that. I fell to the side, landing on shards of glass. A low moan slipped between my lips as the world continued spinning.

"Lyra is worthless. Useless. A mistake." She spat the words with disgust. "The angel doesn't want Lyra anymore. Only Sunny. Always Sunny."

I squinted, seeing the amulet she'd previously worn was no longer hanging around her neck. I was starting to get a real clear picture of how we ended up here and it didn't look good. "He's using you, Lyra. He doesn't care about you, and he never did."

For a moment, her eyes turned sad. The rage dimming in the light of sanity.

"I know," she whispered. "But he's all I have."

Oh Lyra...

Some part of her knew and understood what this was. It was the same part that was buried deep beneath the trauma she'd endured. "That's why I can't take you to him. The angel wants Sunny for his queen. His prisoner." Her words broke through the numbness, filling me with dread. I twisted, trying to pull myself up and her foot came down on my back, pinning me to the ground. "Don't you see? I have to kill you to save us *both.*"

Well that was a charming notion. A part of me wondered if that tiny voice inside her was breaking through and influencing her. If she recognized the prison he'd put her in—that he would put me in—and she thought death was better. She couldn't die, after all, but as far as she knew, I could.

In her own fucked-up way, she might have been attempting to save me.

Or I was seeing something that wasn't there and she actually just wanted me out of the picture. Either way, it looked like Azrael learned I wasn't in the Afterlife or Lethe, and he wasn't pleased.

I just needed a mirror. I knew there was one in the room. It was framed in an ornate gold design, hanging on the wall. Where was it? I tried to picture it in my head. I had to get to it.

My body hurled through space before landing on something hard. A crack sounded before whatever it was collapsed downward. My body slid sideways, letting me get a quick look at the coffee table that had broken my fall. I rolled away and cursed, seeing I'd missed my location by more than half.

Not great. I just wanted to get to the other side of the obnoxiously large room. Why was the room so damn big? Stupid design.

I tried to haul myself up, as much as I was struggling to figure out which way that was.

A soft hand clamped around the back of my neck and Lyra hoisted me off the ground.

"Drop her," Dorian growled, appearing out of thin air. On one arm was Rox. On the other, Roman. Beside them, Rava sifted in holding Pria and Caitlin, with Hades on her shoulder.

Lyra bared her teeth at him in a snarl. "No."

"You can't kill me," I gasped. "I can't die."

"So sure of yourself," she said, lifting an object for me to see.

My heart spasmed in my chest. I stopped breathing.

She had a deathstick . I'm sure it had some official name, but I never knew it. I called it what it was.

The rod was made of stardust and the essence of death. It was said the archangels' combined power created them. The only tangible weapon that could extinguish a soul—that we knew of.

I had my doubts about their origin now and I knew that at least I had an ability that could do the same, but for Lyra to be wielding one . . .

She really could end me, sending me straight to Lethe.

No one came back from that. Unless you were Jake or Hades.

"I smell your fear. You understand," she said. I swallowed hard.

"How did you get that?" I whispered.

"I stole it from my master. He'll be angry, but with you gone, things will be better. They have to be." Her hand moved. The deadly end of the rod looming near me. It glowed with darkness, blacker than obsidian, emanating shadows.

"Goodbye, Sunny."

Her eerie words hit me in a way that little else could.

Then a wine bottle went flying. I saw it, almost as if time slowed down. The bottle appeared in my periphery, wielded by an unknown assailant. It slammed into the side of her head, cracking into a thousand tiny pieces upon impact. Her face caved, contorting in pain.

Lyra's grip on me slipped as she crumbled, releasing me as I dropped to the ground—right alongside the stick that lay on the floor.

Making a snap decision, I grabbed it just as someone grabbed me.

I twisted; weapon poised to end someone—before his mind brushed against mine.

Just me.

My body sagged.

Ezra grabbed me and backed up just as Dorian came forward.

"We don't want to hurt you, Lyra," he said, voice calm and controlled—even if his eyes were begging and pleading for her to understand. I knew it had to kill him to be doing this.

Lyra slowly lifted her head, sparkling glass shards embedded in her cheek, healing as the moments ticked by. The image made her into a strangely beautiful and terrifying piece of art.

"*You.*" Her tone was thick with disdain, haunted and plagued by centuries of hatred. "You're the reason he came to begin with. You're the reason Mathair is gone. Then you forced me to sleep . . ." Her eyes turned hazy, a faraway memory surfacing. "But there was no peace. Only nightmares."

The blue of her irises turned frigid.

Outside, the wind blew. Her skin began to glow a faint illumination akin to moonlight. The shards of glass stuck in her face created prisms that danced on the walls.

"You tortured me for a thousand years," she said, sounding strangely aware and not nearly as insane. "My angel may have broken me, but he also saved me."

Windows shattered.

Glass blew through like a hailstorm, wicked edges cutting anything in their path. They ripped through the drywall as if it were nothing. Pieces of fiberglass and insulation lifted in the air, creating a hazardous void that was going to consume everyone in this room.

My mates would have survived.

I probably would as well.

But Roxanne? Caitlin? Rava? Pria?

"I can't live this way," she said to me, completely at ease in the chaos she'd created. "He *wants* you, but I *need* him. Only one of us will survive tonight. Then he'll see."

I panicked, sifting to Lyra before she killed the ones I loved with the debris in the twisting tempest she'd created. Their bodies, supernatural or not, wouldn't provide protection from her destruction.

I forced power through me, slamming into her and sending her across the room. She smashed into that damned decorative mirror, her head leaving a star crack on its center before she landed on the floor. The glass shattered, raining fragments and slivers out of its gilded frame and onto the ground, the delayed sound ringing in my ears. But I'd overcompensated in my efforts, shooting that same blast outward and into everyone else.

Caitlin, Rava, and Roxanne went crashing into the hallway, rendering them unconscious. My mates went in different directions, breaking through walls. Even Dorian didn't see it coming.

Fuck.

I shook my head, trying to clear the fuzziness that was clouding my vision, squeezing my eyes shut so I could force away the haze, and focus.

When I opened them, Lyra was up, but her sights had shifted targets.

Hot pink magic hit her again, swirling around her body.

Across the room, Pria stood behind a piece of toppled furniture, laser-focused with a crease between her brows. Her powers wafted from her small fingers, sparking in bright bursts with her efforts. It shot out again, hitting Lyra in the chest. Its damage was minimal, but the follow-up Pria sent singed across Lyra's bloody cheek, leaving a singular line in its wake. Her face jerked in the opposite direction, and she turned back slowly.

"That was a mistake," she said, narrowing her eyes.

My stomach roiled, and a tight knot developed in my throat.

Lyra's eyes flashed, but Pria didn't move. I was going to be sick.

"Pria," I choked out, telling my body to sift to her. "Go," I shouted, hoping she would run away.

Concentrating hard, I sifted through space, and landed by a toppled bookshelf. I tumbled over it, slamming my shoulder into the splintered wood. I snapped my head up, trying to get my bearings.

Everything happened as though I was watching it from another dimension, peeking through a fuzzy veil. I had no control. My mind said to do something, but my body was frozen, impaired, and unable to follow any sort of proper direction.

Caitlin screamed, coming to and scrambling to crawl out of the mess and reach her daughter.

She wasn't going to make it.

My body flickered, trying to sift again, but nothing happened.

Lyra sifted, landing in front of Pria, claws extended and poised to swipe at her with a kill shot her tiny supernatural body couldn't survive.

I raged at myself to sift. I did, but not where I needed to be, landing on the other side of the room, opposite of where I had been. It changed my view of what was about to happen, and that was it. A scream built in my chest. Pria was about to die.

In a fraction of a second, a blur went by, and Pria was no longer in Lyra's path, her strike missing and going through thin air.

Ezra rolled out of the way, keeping the young girl tucked against his body. He came to a stop, and Lyra set her eyes on sifting to them.

"Dorian, catch," he shouted, then forcefully threw Pria away from him, knowing he was now the target. Pria shrieked, her body flying across the room, but Dorian sifted, grabbing her in mid-air, disappearing with her as quickly as he had appeared.

Lyra roared in anger, aiming for Ezra as she landed in front of him. He was crouched down, a hand behind his back, ready for her attack, but the look on his face wasn't grim. He smirked, a fang peeking through and touching his bottom lip.

I looked around the rubble, trying to find that stupid stick. I had nothing else to help me, so I ran. It was all I could do. My feet were as heavy as lead, and I had no speed. Just like Caitlin, I was never going to make it.

Ezra winked at Lyra, then pulled his arm from behind his back and thrusted the deathstick toward her chest.

My heart stopped. My emotions conflicted.

My mate would be safe. My mate's daughter wouldn't be.

Lyra gasped, stumbling back, clearly not expecting it.

Roman came from behind her, sliding a large shard of mirrored glass on the floor.

I watched as it swirled around, catching the light, twisting around in circles on its path, coming to a stop just behind Lyra as Jules' hand reached out, grabbing Lyra's ankle.

In a flash, she was gone.

With the exception of my heart pounding in my ears, silence filled the room. Roman was kneeling, resting on one knee with his forearm laid across it. He was staring at the spot where Lyra had just stood, unsure if it was over.

Ezra stood up, tossing the deathstick to the side and wiping his hands off.

Roxanne was pulling Rava out of a pile of debris, grasping her hands to help her.

Dorian was handing Pria over to her mothers.

Me?

I stood there. I did nothing. I said nothing. I helped with . . . nothing.

This was my plan, and I almost threw everything away.

I almost lost.

Pria almost died.

Lyra had said Azrael called her useless when he threw her away.

Not tonight. She'd been anything but.

I scanned the destruction of the room.

Caitlin and Rava held Pria's face, checking her body, crying and hugging her, then repeating it all over again.

Useless.

No, that title was reserved for me.

What had I done . . .

CHAPTER 22
DORIAN

I stepped into the mirror realm behind her. A perfect replica of my Houston mansion surrounded us, including the damage she'd done. In the center of the room stood my daughter.

Barefoot, dressed in one of the light, airy dresses she'd always preferred. Her white hair fell around her face in messy locks. Her blue eyes were vacant. Empty.

"I can't sift," she said. "I can't feel the wind. The cold." Her hands curled into fists. The action had previously filled me with dread. It meant she was planning something and preparing to strike. I'm not sure if she knew it. If the motions were intentional, or if I'd simply seen it too many times to know my daughter's tells.

"Your magic won't work here," I said quietly. "You won't be able to hurt anyone, and they won't be able to hurt you."

Her eyes lifted. Accusing. Damning.

I may have come off as a heartless bastard to most that knew me, but when it came to my daughter, I felt all too much. It suffocated me.

"You hurt me."

Her words did what they were intended, cutting worse than any blade.

I lowered my head and nodded. "I know," I answered gruffly. "I never meant to. I didn't know that nightmares plagued you the entire time you slept. I thought . . . it doesn't matter. I know I hurt you. I accept my fault in that choice. But I can't let you hurt anyone else either."

Lyra tilted her head, and I longed to know what was going through her mind. While her body gave away signs of emotion, her thoughts were a mystery to me. Just as they had been to Ezra.

For the first time, I wished the fae didn't have a predisposition to protect against mental attacks and psychic abilities. Lyra had never been taught. She was only a girl when her mother died and Azrael shattered her mind, but she was more powerful than any of us. Even me.

It didn't matter that she'd had no training. Her sheer strength allowed her to force her way into sifting, persuasion, and eventually —the wind itself. Elemental abilities were rare among the fae, even when I was born. It was a sign of truly remarkable power that came from our ancestors before us.

While I'd been able to manipulate the wind in limited ways with great practice, my daughter made what I could do seem like a parlor trick. Where the air might listen to me, it bowed to her.

I knew when she was born that she was gifted with my powers, and I suspected greater, but not even I knew how powerful she truly was. Since learning of the Afterlife and becoming privy to so many of its little secrets, I wondered if she were some sort of new god, brought into existence by supernatural magic but still beyond what this world understood. Maybe if we won this fight and Fury was able to help her, I'd find out.

"I won't go back to sleep," she said eventually, breaking the silence.

"I won't put you back to sleep." Stepping sideways, glass crunched under my feet. It littered every inch of the living room. "You can't use your abilities here, which means you're safe and so is everyone else."

She still hadn't moved, though I sensed her restlessness by the way her fingers twitched. "I'm a prisoner all the same. You won't lock me in my mind, but you'll make me powerless. Weak. A body in a cage—"

"No." I shook my head firmly. "You may see it that way, but I want to help you. Fix—"

"Me?" she said, her tone arrogant. Haughty. Above me. "What makes you think that you can fix me? That you can make the voices stop? Piece together my memories? Unravel the threads of the angel's influence?" She looked at me and waited.

"You're right," I admitted. It earned me a callous yet girlish laugh. "I can't, but that doesn't mean that it can't be done." Her jaw rotated as her teeth ground together. "Fury thinks she can help you."

"She and I are cut from the same cloth," Lyra said. "She is just as broken, even if her pieces broke differently."

I swallowed hard. She wasn't wrong. For someone with such a thin grasp on reality, she saw beyond the obvious, past the surface emotions, to the heart of people. She always had, ever since she was a little girl. It used to be unsettling, but also sweet. She wanted to help them. Fix them. That changed when Morvain died, and Azrael tortured her.

"She is," I said eventually. "Which means she knows better than anyone how to help you."

I stalled. Not sure what to say. This was my daughter. My one and only child. I loved her more than life itself, but in trying to help her I'd made things so much worse. No apology could fix that, and I wasn't sure if I'd even mean it. That was a harder truth. She was slaughtering people by the hundreds. The thousands. I couldn't let that continue. But if making her sleep had been a torture to itself, I'd have to live with that.

I didn't have a better way when I was forced to put her under. That doesn't mean there wasn't one, but I simply didn't know it. While maybe I could learn to live with that, she might not. The pain she'd endured could be too great for her to ever understand the choices I had to make.

But I'd live with that too.

Left without words to say, I turned to leave and go find Jules. She had to be somewhere around here, just far enough for privacy but still able to pop in when needed.

"I hope you're right."

She spoke softly. So quiet I might have mistaken it if not for the silence that weighed us down.

I pressed my lips together and took one last look at my daughter, knowing if we failed and Azrael could not be defeated it might be the last time. The only comfort I had, was that she was here, and he couldn't hurt her again.

"I do too."

CHAPTER 23
FURY

I SAT WITH MY ELBOWS ON MY KNEES, CRADLING MY HEAD IN MY HANDS.

I replayed that moment in my head, over and over and over.

Pria.

Lyra was moments away from killing her. Ending her existence.

I saw the fear in Pria's defiant eyes, but she stood her ground. There was so much fire and bravery in her little body. So much more confidence than any of us could have had at that age. She had so much potential. That was almost cut short, and no matter how hard I tried to picture it differently, I never made it there in time to save her. Each time it ended with her death. An outcome that was solely my fault.

This wasn't about guilt. This was about truth. I couldn't have prevented Lyra from showing up. That wasn't my fault. It was my fault that I wasn't in my right mind. It was my fault that I couldn't function. Had Ezra not been there, Rava and Caitlin wouldn't be tucking their daughter into bed right now.

A dull ache filled my head, throbbing in time with my heartbeat. My hybrid metabolism burned through the alcohol in my system, leaving only the echo of its presence. I could feel it leaving my veins as I began to sober up.

My eyes burned as they welled with tears. I couldn't believe that it almost happened.

"Fury." Roxanne's voice broke through my thoughts, causing me to snap my head up and look at her. My vision was clear. Nothing was rocking or fuzzy. I could hear every vibration in the room with clarity, including the sound of disappointment.

Maybe it wasn't theirs. Just my own.

I wouldn't blame them, though.

"Hmm?" I responded to her, watching as my mates all came to gather around me. We'd left the room of destruction when Dorian left, finding another place to sit and wait.

"He's back," she said gently. "And we all need to talk to you."

Understanding washed over me, and I cleared my throat before speaking. "Intervention?"

Ezra pressed his lips together, acknowledging my guess. Roman nodded his head slowly, and Dorian remained still. I knew he had so much on his mind, but I could see the answer in his eyes.

"Right. There's really no need—" I began.

"Fury, you have to listen to us first," Roman said, keeping his voice even. "Please. You owe us that."

Listen, kitten. I know what's in your mind, but they don't. Let them share their concerns before you tell them. Every single one of us has a right and a need to say these things out loud. Don't deny them that.

I inclined my head to him—to all of them, really. Mentally, I had that quiet support from Ezra, reminding me that everyone in the room was in it together. *Thank you,* I told him.

Hades flew to the couch where I sat, coming to sit beside me. At first, I wasn't sure if he was there to berate me or be a friend, but I was pretty sure I had an idea which one it was when he remained silent.

"I'm listening."

And I did.

I listened for an hour as Roman expressed concern for my long-term mental health. For how I would continue to make decisions that could affect the lives of others. I cringed as Roxanne said she'd carefully tiptoed around giving me drinks, trying not to feed the habit, but respecting me enough to give me control of my own life. That was no more. She wasn't going to look the other way when she knew I was sneaking bottles that I hid in drawers in my rooms. I listened as Dorian reminded me that he'd been there once, hundreds of years ago. It had changed nothing, and only made him feel worse. My past was my past. Liquor wouldn't change it. I felt another pang of disappointment as Ezra told me he didn't want to check every space we were in, emptying it of alcohol and treating me like I was going to raid the liquor cabinet.

Then I listened to how it affected them.

How they worried about what state I would be in from one minute to the next.

How they questioned if they could trust me around members of each faction, especially the younger ones.

How they hated watching me self-destruct.

When they'd finally said their pieces, I let it all sink in.

With the exception of Ezra, they were expecting pushback.

"So this is rock bottom?" I said, trying to break the ice. "I thought I'd been there before. Turns out I was wrong."

"You probably were there once. It just looked different," Hades said, dragging a claw on the sofa slowly. When he saw the questioning look on my face, he added, "It was rock bottom for where your life was at the time. Life, Afterlife, new life—whatever this is now, it's different. Your rock bottom has a different view. Your circumstances changed, but it's still the bottom. Still dark."

I nodded, whispering, "I suppose you're right."

Roman shuffled in his seat, shifting my attention to him as he spoke. "We've had our chance to say our piece. It's your turn."

I gave him a small smile. The concern in his voice ran deep. It was the alpha wanting to protect those he loved, wanting to fix whatever he could. He couldn't fix me, and he knew it.

"Okay," I said.

"What does that mean? 'Okay'?" Dorian asked, getting agreements from Roman and Roxanne.

Ezra smiled to himself, allowing me to speak on my own behalf. He gave a subtle wink, reassuring me as I continued.

"It means I'm done. You aren't going to hear any arguments from me. This was it tonight. My rock bottom. I blamed myself for what happened to Ezra and what he went through. None of you know the extent of it, but it doesn't matter if you did. I chose to try and numb it. The blame, the guilt, the self-loathing. When Pria . . ." I took a deep breath, shaking my head. "Her death would have been my fault, and not because I'm placing some bullshit blame on myself. My choices slowed me down."

"It's more than tonight, Fury," Roman said, leaning forward and clasping his hands together. "Your past . . . this is what you are doing to cope."

"Oh, I know." I ran my hands through my hair, keeping my fingers tangled in the strands at the base of my neck and I stilled. "Tonight was just the final straw. It was seeing her life in my hands, and seeing that I would have failed her, failed all of you, because I was plastered."

"You drink because of him," Dorian said, though he was careful as he spoke to me, worried I would react. "You always have, yes?"

I huffed a humorless laugh. "Pretty much." I let go of my hair, dropping my hands to my lap, and shrugged a shoulder. "It numbed the pain in my mortal life. I carried it into the Afterlife, though it didn't have the same effect there. Believe me, I tried."

Flashes of my past entered my mind. Strikes to my face. Kicks to my crumpled form. My body flying into furniture and door frames. Ezra winced, watching my memories as the uninvited thoughts played out in my head.

"It wasn't your fault," Ezra said. He tapped his head when my mates gave him a questioning look, sending his thoughts to Roman, with Dorian catching on.

"I know," I whispered. "I don't think I did know that for a long time, though. Maybe I wasn't willing to believe it." I straightened my shoulders, adjusting in my seat. "I know it now."

Roman and Dorian scrunched their eyebrows, hesitant that this was going their way. Which was to say, it was not as planned.

I frowned, mentally pushing to Ezra. *They don't believe me.*

Can you blame them?

I wanted to argue it, but I knew deep down he was right. I wasn't sure I would have believed me either if I were sitting in their seats. I sighed. *Not really,* I admitted. *I don't know what I can do here. They expected me to disagree and to pushback, but I'm not going to. Now that I haven't, they're unsure about what that means.*

It's not a level of distrust here. Don't take it that way. They desperately want this to be real for you. It's up to you to show them that. I can't.

I grunted under my breath, grabbing the attention of the room. It was real for me. As real as it could get. I refused to let Azrael scare me. I refused to allow his hold over me to carry on into my daily life. Into my psyche. Into my relationships. No more. It was done.

Rava walked into the room, rubbing her arms as though she had a chill. Her eyes were slightly red, but puffiness hadn't set in yet. "Pria's asleep. Caitlin fell asleep next to her."

I swallowed thickly. "Is she okay?"

She lifted a shoulder slightly. "As okay as she can be for now."

A thought came to me, and I knew I was risking something big if I attempted it and was turned down. But I had to try.

"Rava, can I ask you something?" I said, choosing my words carefully.

She raised her eyebrows in surprise, but she didn't have judgment on her face. She wasn't going to tell me to go back to Hell for what had happened. "Sure, I guess . . ."

I nodded, going with my gut. "I'm done with drinking. Like, done-done. I'd like to start—uh, well, I think I should start therapy of some sort," I said.

"And not like the 'therapy' you did with Vlad the Impaler," Hades interjected. When I shot him a look, he fluffed his feathers. "What? I'm being serious. Counting to ten before stabbing someone isn't an actual healthy coping technique. Rava will back me up. You know I'm right."

"That wasn't what I did. It was 'count to ten so I wouldn't stab'," I angry-whispered at him.

He gave me a deadpanned look. "And if you got to ten and you were still ragey?"

I glared at him. Through gritted teeth, I said, "Then I stabbed."

"I rest my case," Hades huffed. "Anger management, my ass. You always said you wanted to reform the guild, Fury. Start there."

I rolled my eyes, tempted to count to ten and stab him now that I knew he would just reappear. I shook it off, focusing on Rava and the hesitation she was exhibiting. Her mouth had fallen open slightly, taken aback. "Fury, I don't know . . ."

"Hear me out," I said, holding my hands up. I didn't want her making a decision without listening to me first. "This isn't about making amends for tonight. I know I screwed up. I can't change that. I don't want you to be my therapist so I can earn your forgiveness or anything like that. You're a hybrid, you're part of the pack I'm in, and I trust you. You're my family. I know you'll be real with me and hold me accountable. I need this. I need to work through my past, and I know it won't be easy. I know that. I need someone strong enough to walk me through it." Realizing I might have guilted her into it, I added, "If you say no, I respect that. I won't ask again. I'd only ask for you to make some referrals to someone. I can sift. They can be anywhere. The bird is an asshole, but he's . . . not wrong. I need it to be real this time."

Silence weighed heavily in the room. Dorian and Roman's expressions had changed from dubious to mildly shocked.

I met Ezra's gaze. *I didn't do it for them to believe me. I need this.*

I know. They know it too.

Even Dorian? I asked, wondering if he could read him now.

I can't read him, no. Just a hunch.

Rava closed her eyes, taking in a deep breath. "Our pack," she said.

"Huh?" I said, making the confused sound before thinking better of it.

"You said I'm part of the pack you're in. It's your pack. Our pack. You belong somewhere now, even if you never felt like you did before." She looked at Roman, dipping her head respectfully. "If this is what you want, I have provisions. We won't discuss what happened here tonight. I'm not the person for that, but we will hit hard on your past. You'll learn actual coping skills," she said, nodding in agreement with Hades, "but we can do it together."

I released a breath I'd been holding since she started to speak. "I've got to save the world first, but then we get started, okay?"

She barked a laugh, but there was still a seriousness to her expression. She met eyes with Roman, shifting to Dorian, and then Ezra.

"You're going to face Azrael again," Roman said, rubbing his hands together. "We all are. Are you ready for that?"

"I don't have a choice but to be ready. This is happening whether we like it or not. There's no time to dwell on it. I'm not letting him hurt the ones I love anymore. He's not in my head. I can deal with the past after I find a way to stop him," I said, steeling my posture. "And if destroying that motherfucker and extinguishing his soul brings me trouble up here"—I tapped my head—"then I'll deal with that in therapy too."

"There's the Fury I know," Hades murmured, tilting his head with a glint of fire in his eyes.

I looked around the room, seeing the expression on my mates' faces and they finally matched. Dorian and Roman could read and feel my sincerity. Ezra knew my heart, and there was no keeping the truth from him.

I stood up, walking to them as Roman wrapped his arms around me. Dorian stroked my hair softly, and Ezra placed his hand on the small of my back.

This was it. I was done. I'd lived a traumatic life and left this Earth when I died a tragic death. We'd escaped a potential tragedy tonight. It was a wake-up call, one that could have ended so differently. Azrael didn't own any part of me anymore. Not my heart, not my mind, not my body, and not my past.

That was all mine. It belonged to me. I owned it, I lived it, and I was over shoving it down and chasing it with a bottle.

It was the start of a new day. Or it would be, after I got some much-needed sleep.

Hades cleared his throat, sort of squawking as he did. "I hate to ruin this moment, but I wanted to get a word in here before we all started singing kumbaya."

"What now, feathers?" I asked, stifling a yawn.

"Nothing overly important. Just the small matter of the Dukes trying to rain fire on Earth here in a few hours."

Right. Just them.

I just wanted to stop the prophecy. Save the world, and everything in it. Prevent everything and everyone in existence from being wiped away. Was it too much to ask that the universe throw me a bone and help me out?

Apparently it was.

"I suppose we have to do this now, don't we?"

"Take a seat. Better to know the enemy now," Hades said as he nodded, seeing that each of my mates had agreed as well. I motioned for him to start. "Have you ever watched squirrels play in the road, dodging cars?"

I stared at him, gaping. This wasn't the best way to start, and I really hoped we weren't the squirrels in this scenario.

CHAPTER 24
EZRA

THE TALK HAD GONE BETTER THAN ANY OF US COULD HAVE EXPECTED. IT didn't take long for Fury to show me the sincerity in her choices. I saw the decision she had come to, and I could easily see why she did.

No one could read Dorian, but I listened to Roman's internal struggle. He had wanted to believe her, but when she's fought us on so many things before, it was hard to accept her being so agreeable. She was right when she knew he had the desire to fix her too. I'd seen enough people suffer from their own tragedies to know they could only fix themselves. She had our support, but she had to want that change.

I'd have to process with my own ordeal. I had no desire to, but moments of the torture and memories of the pain came in short bursts, flashing in my mind. That wasn't going to go away any time soon. I didn't want her to know how much it was simmering under the surface. It was new and raw, the same as my regenerating skin.

"Ezra?"

I heard my name, snapping my attention up to the room. I hummed in question before speaking. "Sorry. What was that?"

The crow fluffed up. "I'm sorry, was I boring you?"

"Yes, now that you mention it," I said, wiping my eyebrow and smoothing it out. "What were you saying?"

He glared at me in return.

"He was babbling on about analogies with squirrels that have no plans, taking risks that end up with them being flattened by a much more powerful machine," Fury answered, her tone dripping with annoyance. I reached out to her mentally, feeling her exhaustion.

"Well," Hades said, throwing out his wings. "Tell me I'm wrong."

Dorian sighed loudly before she got into a fight with him. "You're not wrong, but it's not helpful yet." He motioned for Hades to continue.

"Tell us what we need to know about the Dukes," I said. "All of us. Dorian and I know what we heard in Jake's office, but there's more to this. You said we need to know our enemy. They're your brothers. Start with that."

Roxanne looked confused. "Brothers?"

Fury snorted. "Wait for it."

"First off, there's three of them. They are not the Four Horsemen , no matter what they call themselves," he started. "Anubis, Typhon, and Orcus."

"Which one are you?" Fury asked. "What's your real name?"

He narrowed his eyes at her. "Hades."

I am going to find out who you really are, you bag of feathers. I have questions, dammit.

I chuckled under my breath when I heard her. She shot me a look, and I shook my head.

"Who I am is not important right now. They are," he said, trying to push the conversation forward.

"I thought—" Roxanne started, but Hades didn't give her the opportunity to finish.

"Look, everything you think you know, throw it out. Mythology, religion, history books, all of it. That's all manmade; nothing but stories passed down over generations. Not only was it lost in translation, but it was also embellished," he said.

"And in some cases, made up entirely as a rumor," Dorian added.

"In some cases," the crow mumbled. "Anyway, the point is, what I am telling you is real. Not what you think you know. Are we in agreement?"

The room nodded collectively, but Fury spoke instead. She had so many thoughts running through her mind, it was hard to hear them all. "I scanned through pages of a book that Jake had," she said, looking at Roman and Roxanne. "The destruction they caused was massive. Death everywhere. They enjoyed it. The events we know about in history are a warmup compared to the genocide they led."

"What happened?" Rox whispered. "I don't want gory details. Just —what happened to make them that way? Why did they do it?"

Hades shrugged. "Jake thinks they couldn't handle time and what it does to us. I think they were always a little unsure of their place. So close to control of everything, to leading the Afterlife, but it would never be in their grasp. Maybe time urged the crazy forward, and the combination is what caused them to explode. Who knows."

"And they did what exactly?" Roman asked.

"They almost wiped humanity from the face of the Earth," Fury answered quietly. I closed my eyes, seeing the pages in the book she'd flipped through when we were in Jake's office, looking at the details through her memory. The carnage. The lives lost. There wasn't a word bigger than genocide to give it the meaning it deserved. I didn't know how humankind had even survived it. So many parts of history were never written, and in this case, it was a good thing. "What man passed down as the story of the great flood? It was real, but it was them, and there was no arc to save anyone. Ancient plagues and wars that we know nothing about or that we only know as a myth—it happened. The Dukes came close to wiping out civilization. Then Jake imprisoned them in Lethe."

"Fantastic," Roxanne said sarcastically. "I'm going to take a wild guess here and assume that's Azrael's realm?"

"Bingo." Fury pursed her lips, pointing at Rox.

"And Azrael has the power to release them," I said. The silence in the room would have been deafening if I couldn't hear so much internal chatter.

"Which he plans on doing," Hades added.

"Tell me what their powers are," I said, running my hands through my hair, preparing myself for the worst of it. We needed to know what we were looking at. "And are their powers specific to them?"

"Of course they are. What kind of story would this be if they weren't?" Hades asked. He took a deep breath, no doubt troubled by what he was about to share. "Typhon has an elemental control that surpasses all, and he has no problem using them all at once. Anubis is much like a fae in his ability to control and persuade. He can turn throngs of people against each other on a whim, so keep him out of your head. Orcus is just a toxic octopus. He's going to wrap his poisonous smoke around you. Each of them is a master in their abilities, as you would expect."

"That's not great, but it's not too bad," Dorian said. "It sounds like they're supernaturals. You said they could end the world. What about them can—"

"It's the combination. That's what gives them the ultimate power," Hades said, knowing exactly where Dorian was going with his train of thought.

Like fucking He-Man, Fury thought.

I almost snorted. *Like what?*

She looked at me, somewhat surprised. *That cartoon? He was all like 'I have the power' because he was the master of the universe or something? That's what these dudes sound like. Totally full of themselves.*

I looked down at the floor to hide my smile while I shook my head.

I wonder if we can use that? she pondered, looking for my opinion.

I mentally shrugged. *Perhaps. You should ask.*

Fury relayed her thoughts to Hades, but he didn't seem on board.

"So, no hopes of convincing them to join our side?" Fury said playfully. "They sound like they want to be the winners, so . . ."

Hades huffed a laugh. "They are the winners, every time."

"Except when Jake extinguished them," I said.

"Yes, except then." Hades looked in my direction. "That is a luxury we don't have this time around. They know better than to go to the Afterlife, and Azrael has finally lost his last marble so he's just giving them a key to walk out the door."

"But they are vain," Fury said quietly, the wheels in her mind turning. "They know they're invincible."

"I'm not seeing how that helps us," Roxanne interjected. The sound of worry in her voice ran deep. "It sounds like this is a losing battle." I reached out, hearing her concern for the pack. The children in it. Stretching that fear out to every innocent life that would be lost.

Her empathy was overpowering, threatening to suffocate me. I pulled away quickly before it began to melt into me.

"It's not a losing battle," Fury murmured, as she tried to piece together a plan. "They want to end the world, and they don't see a way they could lose."

"Do you see a way we can win?" Roman asked.

She didn't answer, and neither did Hades.

He said their combined abilities was what gave them the unbridled power. I suppose the same could be said about you three, Fury said to me.

I shot her a look, wondering if that meant more than she intended.

What do you think that means? I asked.

She shook her head ever so slightly. *I don't know yet. I'm working on it.*

"We're not going to win without a plan," Dorian said, walking over to a window and looking out. "First light is in a few hours. Lyra is safe now. That plan worked. Now we have to come up with what to do for Azrael and the Dukes."

Roman blew out a long breath, and Roxanne leaned forward, placing her head in her hands.

Exhaustion was taking over everyone.

While it did, I listened to my mate.

She sat in the room silently, but her thoughts were racing. As I tried to see them all, hear everything she was saying in her mind, parts of it started shifting and becoming cloudy in my vision, like it was damaged and skipping.

A mild panic shot through me, feeling an odd disconnect between us.

What's happening? I asked her.

Do you remember when you were shocked that I'd kept Lyra's existence from you?

I mentally acknowledged my recollection. It hadn't made any sense.

Well, it wasn't intentional. But after it happened, I realized I had kept something a secret because it was important to someone else. I connected the dots and figured out it was part of my fae abilities. She met my gaze, her voice becoming gentler in her response. *I've been practicing how to shield my thoughts from you.* Before I could respond, she jumped to finish. *It's not because of privacy. I have all these powers. That has to mean something, so I'm trying to use it when needed. There are things I need to keep to myself, for your benefit and mine. I mean, how else am I going to buy you a birthday present if I can't keep secrets from you?* She smiled at me. *For this, I need to keep things close to the chest.*

I nodded, understanding and respecting her choice, even if I didn't want her keeping things from me.

I trust you, I said.

And I trust you.

She rubbed her hands on her thighs, leaving them to rest on her knees. "We're not going to do our best work when we're dragging. We need to think on it and get some sleep." When everyone nodded in agreement, she stood up, gesturing to Hades. "You," she said. "Come with me."

He tilted his head, but he went along with her request. He flew, landing on her shoulder. "I go where you go," he said.

"Wait—" Roman and Dorian said in unison.

"I'll be back in a little bit," she said, not bothering to explain herself.

Then she sifted from the room and disappeared.

They looked at me instantly, concerned and confused. "Where is she going?" Roman asked, frustration leaking in his voice.

"I don't know," I answered honestly. "But she's going to find a way to win this."

Dorian looked furious that she sifted and he didn't know where. Both he and Roman hated not having control of a situation. They hated feeling vulnerable, knowing that they couldn't follow her and protect her.

That made three of us, but I wasn't saying so.

CHAPTER 25
FURY

TICK.

Tock.

Tick.

Tock.

My fingernails drummed against the table, counting down the seconds till the end. Hades used to say the phrase goad me . Somehow, I'd adopted the saying as well, almost like a mantra of sorts. Now I sat, feet propped up on the chair across from me, staring into the early morning dawn through the wide dining room window.

Lyra and I had destroyed several rooms, including the main kitchen. But the formal dining room was on the other side of the mansion, accompanied by an industrial chef's kitchen. The smell of coffee drifted through the doorway, followed by the scent of cinnamon.

Ezra took a seat beside me, sans shirt, wearing only a pair of low-riding sweats that belonged to Dorian. "Eat," he said, pushing a plate and mug toward me.

My eyes flicked down, taking in the displayed cinnamon rolls.

I lifted an eyebrow. He shrugged. "Seems that Dorian's butler has quite the sweet tooth. It was this or candy."

I briefly thought about James, the fae assistant that had been by his side for over a century. I wondered where he was now. What he was doing. If he knew the end was upon us.

Ezra lifted a cinnamon roll to my lips and repeated in a harsher tone, "Eat."

I took a bite, then winced. Cinnamon dough covered in icing was a little sweet for my early morning tastes. I usually preferred a more bitter breakfast of gin and tonic.

But seeing as my drinking days were over, I chewed the sweet sticky bun and swallowed it down.

Ezra smiled faintly at me. "That so hard?"

"Yes," I responded stubbornly. Not that I meant it. I didn't give a damn what I ate for breakfast with everything else going on, but these little moments of happiness—bantering about something so inconsequential as a means to escape the crushing sensation in my chest—they meant everything to me.

Ezra leaned forward, his tongue flicking out to lick my top lip. "Mmm," he hummed, nipping softly at my bottom lip when they parted. "You know what else is har—"

"Now I know damn well you can hear our thoughts," Roxanne griped from the kitchen. "I feel like it's just a common courtesy to save that for when there's not an audience all of fifteen feet away."

My lips curled up at the devilish smirk in Ezra's eyes.

"If we're going to talk about my ability to listen in, Rox, then I feel obliged to say that you're quite the fan of watching—"

Another cup clapped down on the table on my other side. I glanced up at Roman, who was glaring at Ezra. "I don't want or need to know what my sister likes," he said, only just keeping the growl out of his tone.

Ezra dipped his head, acknowledging him. I lifted the mug to my lips, hiding my smile behind it as I took a tentative drink.

Probably not the best time to mention she'd totally be up for watching us in a group thing if not for this one over here, Ezra added mentally.

I choked, spluttering coffee from my nose.

"Ezra," I admonished. He ripped off a paper towel from the center of the table and passed it to me. I blotted at my face, semi embarrassed as Roxanne and Caitlin both took seats across from me.

"Yes, kitten?" he asked innocently, green eyes smoldering with heat and mirth in equal measure. I glared at him, pursing my lips.

"Don't 'kitten' me—"

The doorbell rang.

I paused, casting the rest of the table a wary glance. Next to me, Ezra stiffened.

Hades appeared out of thin air, landing on the table. At the same time, Dorian came striding into the room. If not for the briskness of his approach, I might not have stopped to take a second look. He wore jeans and a T-shirt of all things. His long hair was wild and unkempt. Golden eyes glowed with a ravenous sort of rage.

"We had a visitor," Hades said slowly, not taking his eyes off Dorian. "I think Fury should be the one to check it—"

Dorian was already moving. Despite the uncertainty of the moment, it struck me as off that something had worked him up. He never fell apart. Not in the same way I did. This was more than last night . . .

I sifted as I stood up, appearing on the front porch.

For a moment, time stood still.

I had to work to process what I was seeing.

A hand. A foot. An arm.

Pieces. A body that had been torn to pieces.

I tilted my head, trying to focus on the face. It was half hidden in the pile.

Biting my lip, I bent at the waist to grasp the hair—

Snarling rang through the air.

I didn't look up. I already knew it was Dorian behind me.

It took me a second to recognize the face. I'd seen many bloody crimes. Torture sessions that went beyond. Things that would turn most people's stomachs, but that's not what caused the delay. When someone died, their face took on an almost fake quality. Like plastic. There was a stiffness that wasn't there before. A blankness that occupied the shell where there was once a person.

Without his personality, it was hard to recognize, but when I did, I understood.

James.

It was James.

"Fury," Hades said, trying to get my attention. I glanced up to see light illuminating from beneath Dorian's skin.

It flashed like lightning, making his veins appear like dark streaks in contrast.

"Dorian," I said his name. Once. Twice. On the third attempt I grabbed his chin, forcing him to look at me. His golden gaze was nearly unhinged.

"Take a deep breath." When he didn't listen, I grabbed one of his hands and pressed it to my chest. "Do it with me."

In. Out. In. Out.

It took a few tries for him to finally listen and follow me. When I could tell I had at least part of his attention, I changed gears.

"What color is my hair?" I asked.

His eyebrows twitched. "Red."

"Like fire truck red?" I prompted. "Sunset red? Describe it."

He scowled. The flashes slowed. "It's dark, like liquid fire. At night it looks black until the moon catches it just right . . ."

Almost as if he realized what he was doing, he paused, looking from me to the pile at our feet.

"My eyes," I said, pushing forward. "Describe them."

It took him a second. Indecision warred in his features before he finally said, "They glow, similar to the wolf's, but it's not your raven. It's like the center of the flame. They're not gold like mine . . . they're light. Like the sun."

If not for the labored way he stopped and started, forcing himself to make words, it might have sounded flowery. As it was, I paid little attention to the compliments themselves and instead focused on the crackling beneath his skin and the way it receded to mere flickers.

"You'll need to learn to do that," I said. "When the power becomes too much and threatens to carry you away, focus on things you see. Describe them. Make the words. It will ground you long enough to take back control."

Dorian shifted, staring at the pile that was his butler, assistant, and closest thing to a friend.

"I'm sorry," I said quietly. We hadn't said who was at fault, but it's not like it was a question. This was Azrael's work through and through.

"He didn't deserve this," Dorian said after a moment.

"No," I agreed. "He didn't."

A gasp from behind Dorian drew our attention. At the door, Roman, Roxanne, Caitlin, and Ezra stood. My vampire was the fastest to react and grab Caitlin's hair when she bent at the waist and hurled.

"This is what I was talking about," Hades said, shaking his head.

"In what way?" I asked quietly. "I don't recall you mentioning *this* would happen."

"No, I mean Azrael being unhinged. After not finding you in the Afterlife or Lethe, he turned to tracking down anyone close to you, and he settled on someone close to your mate."

Whether Lyra was sent, or she'd gone rogue, she hadn't returned to him. I knew my ex, perhaps better than anyone. He'd lost his control over her, and this was the result.

It was that thought that made me take a closer look at the pile of limbs.

I squatted down, pushing my feelings aside. This wasn't James. It was a body. A shell. An empty vessel that was sent here for a reason.

So I looked for it.

My heart constricted when I found it. There, in one of the hands. A letter smudged in blood.

I reached for it without thought.

The parchment was rough against the pads of my fingers, and I pulled it from the severed body part.

Numbly, I opened it.

The first words drained me of whatever emotion I had left.

My Dearest Wife,

I miss you and the games we play. I long to taste your tears once more. Lyra's were never nearly as sweet.

I'll forgive your transgressions if you come home and submit to me. Refuse, and the Dukes will destroy everything you hold dear. If you bring one of those animals you've let touch you, I'll be sure to give them a warm welcome in Lethe.

I'll be waiting.

Yours,

Azrael

I don't know how many times I read it. Only that at some point, someone took the letter away. Arms wrapped around me, walking me back indoors. Sometime later, I put a name on the growing feeling inside me.

It was more than fear. More than dread. More than hate.

It was absolution.

Around us, words were flying. Everyone wanted to go after Azrael, and yet none of them could because the simple fact of the matter was he couldn't die.

He couldn't be extinguished.

Each one of us had tried to push away the tension. We had been taking time to appreciate the morning together. Be with each other. We knew what the night would bring. We knew Azrael was coming. We knew he was releasing the Dukes. Without saying so, we all wanted a moment to share where everything was normal.

That was long gone.

The few hours of peace we were trying to create were shattered.

War meant casualties. Always. And James' dismemberment was the startling reminder that more death was to come.

We all knew damn well I wasn't giving myself to Azrael.

The talking around me continued. The sounds of their voices were muffled, like they were speaking with their hands over their mouths, drowned out by my own thoughts.

I didn't say anything. I let them talk. Let them plot.

It would make them feel better and save me from having to tell them the truth.

That I would have to return to him alone to finish this—and neither life nor death would stop me from going through with it.

I scanned the room, focusing on each one of them.

Dorian, my refined brooding fae. In control, well-kempt, regal in so many ways. His heart hurt for his daughter, and his loyalty to the ones he loved was unending. He would do anything for me; remind me that I could have all that I had earned in right and name in my afterlife. Ensure that it was okay to want those things, and to enjoy them. That it was okay to be myself.

Roman, my nature-bound shifter. The protector. He was passionate in every way, and the love he had for his pack ran bone-deep. The responsibility he felt to every one of them was heavy, but he would always carry that burden—and he would never complain about it. He gave me a place to feel a connection. To be respected and seen as an equal. To let my raven be a part of something powerful and never-ending.

Ezra, my soulful vampire. My confidant in so many ways. My support. When it was hard to explain how I felt, hard to share what I was going through, he knew. It was effortless. There was so much he didn't take seriously, and he was just the balance I needed between the three of them. I could laugh with all of them, but he was different. He gave me a place to work and feel fulfilled. To continue the path I had set, so I wouldn't toss aside the purpose I had found. He gave me the gift of protecting my identity. More than anything, he always trusted me. I would need that now more than ever.

Roxanne, my first friend. My best friend. I loved her more than I could say. More than I realized I could love someone in a platonic way. I knew full well that friendships could come and go—I was a demon by trade, after all. I knew an awful lot of dead people, and I knew their stories. But I also knew there were times that people would meet someone, and it was kismet. That's what we were. Fights, disagreements, different viewpoints: none of that would separate us.

Rava, Caitlin, Pria . . . I could be an auntie too, just like Rox. I think I'd like it.

This was my family. It took death and an afterlife to find it.

I wasn't going to lose something so precious. Azrael would never take this away from me.

You aren't going to lose us, kitten. Ezra's gentle voice brushed my mind.

I smiled sadly. *Some hard decisions are going to be made today. I need you to be by my side. Trust me. I know what I'm doing.*

I'll always be by your side.

I lifted my chin, holding his gaze, shielding my thoughts once more.

I cleared my throat, rapping my fist on the table so they could hear me through the chatter. When the room silenced, and eyes looked my way, I spoke. "I want Roxanne, Caitlin, Rava, and Pria taken to an undisclosed location. I want them in hiding. This isn't their fight."

Dorian and Roman instantly agreed, taking no time to process it. They weren't willing to risk the lives of those mentioned. Roxanne opened her mouth to protest, but she snapped it shut, seeing the look in my eyes. I wasn't yielding. She appeared to reconsider her words when she took a couple of breaths but said nothing, and I gave her a moment to gather her response. "I agree that Caitlin, Rava, and Pria need to go, but this is my fight. This is my family."

I pressed my lips together and shook my head. "That's exactly why I want you in hiding too. You're my family. Azrael will come for all of you to hurt me in any way he can. I know you're powerful, and I won't dispute that for even a second. Your wolf is a force to be reckoned with, but you can still die. You all can. And if you're there, that is exactly what is going to happen. You can't beat them. All they need is that stupid deathstick and you're gone with a single touch."

Understanding reached her, and she sniffed, her eyes becoming glassy as they filled with tears. She nodded. "I know a place we can go. No one knows about it."

Roman's eyebrows raised in surprise, and she returned his gaze with a look of guilt. She'd kept something from him, but in this case, it turned out to be a good thing. She walked over to Roman and hugged him tight, whispering 'I love you' in his ear.

"Go. Take them now. There's no reason to wait," he said to her quietly.

"How will . . . how will I know?" she asked, unsure how to finish her sentence. Scared to say the words I knew she was thinking. How would she know if we survived? How would she know if we succeeded?

"You'll know because the world will continue spinning," I answered honestly. It was the cruel reality of what we were about to face. "Keep a mirror nearby."

She blew out an unsteady breath and whispered, "Okay." She approached me, wrapping me into her embrace, taking her time before letting me go. "I don't know what your plan is," she said in a shaky voice, "but I expect you to destroy them."

I huffed a small laugh. "I'll try not to fuck it up."

She released me, giving a nod to Dorian and Ezra as she wiped a small tear from under her right eye. "I'll go get them now."

"No goodbyes with them. Just have Rava sift you there. I don't want to put Pria through this. Tell them I love them too. Keep them safe."

She inclined her head in acceptance, then left the room to get our extended family and put them in hiding.

When the room was empty, I turned my attention to my mates. Hades was perched on the back of the chair, remaining quiet through the exchange. He waited patiently, knowing every bit that was coming.

"I'm sensing you already have a plan," Dorian said.

"I've been working on one, yes. But I can't share it in its entirety."

"Wait," Roman said, stepping forward. "Why not?"

Ezra urged me on silently, grazing a psychic hand over mine in reassurance.

"In case Azrael gets one of you," I said, not sugarcoating it. Glossing over the truth wasn't going to be helpful. We needed the facts, cut and dry, as harsh as they might have been. "I've figured out how to shield my thoughts from Ezra. Not fully blocked off like Dorian, but that part of fae that runs through my veins has given me access to it."

"Even I don't know all of what's going through her head. Parts of it are clouded, like there's a piece of opaque film over it," he admitted, confirming my ability.

Dorian crossed his arms. "He took Ezra with ease. He can take any one of us. I don't want to agree with you, but it's the smartest move."

Roman pulled out a hair tie, reaching back and securing his dreadlocks out of his face. "All of us except Jules and Hades."

"Exactly," I said, pointing to him. "They are the only ones that can't be compromised." I called out for Jules, and she appeared in a framed mirror above a credenza.

I had intended on greeting her but was taken aback for a moment. Her hands were on her hips, and she proudly wore a metal Vikingstyled helmet embellished with horns. "I . . . what is on your head?" I stuttered.

"A Veksø. I'm ready for battle," she answered like it was obvious.

Dorian's mouth popped open. "That's not a Veksø . . ."

She creased her brows. "It's close enough."

I pressed my lips together, trying not to laugh. "It suits you." She knew full well she couldn't physically help. If that's what motivated her for the small part she'd play, I was for it.

She dipped her chin in my direction with a smug look on her face.

I rubbed my hands over my thighs, feeling the friction of the material against my palms. It gave me something to focus on, readying myself to say the things I knew wouldn't go over well.

Say it, Ezra encouraged.

Dreading the pushback.

You might be surprised.

I sighed, taking in a deep breath through my nose, exhaling loudly through barely parted lips. "We aren't going to be together in this fight," I started, waiting for the immediate grumbled responses from the two mates who couldn't know what I was about to say. When none came, I sat in surprise for a moment, then continued. "Azrael wants me, and if he can find a way to go after you, it'll end up distracting all of us. You'll want to protect me; I'll want to protect you. We're going to lose quickly if our attention isn't where it needs to be."

Roman blew out a breath, and Dorian silently stewed. It was times like this I wished I could read them the way Ezra could read me.

"What do you suggest?" Roman asked after a suspended time.

"Azrael isn't the only one that needs to be dealt with. Even if we can take him out, there's still the Dukes. I need you three dealing with them so I can focus on Azrael ," I said.

"Wait, his brothers are in this?" Jules asked, raising her brows and looking at Hades.

I shot her a look, just as surprised. "You know about them?" Realization struck me. "Wait, you know Hades is a duke?"

She huffed in annoyance. "Oh trust me, I know. Imagine my surprise the first day you summoned me and standing beside you in crow form is the Great Duke of the Afterlife."

I gave Hades a curious look. "Yes. Imagine that."

He covered his face with his wing, no doubt wishing he could escape this. One day, bird. One day we would talk. My raven reminded me she'd shit on him if he didn't answer. I smiled at her internally, appreciating the support.

"The Dukes," Dorian said, bringing us back around. "So the three of us fight them. The question is how." I gestured to Hades, and he shuffled his body forward.

"They're more destructive than any group of supernaturals could ever be. Together, they're unstoppable," he said.

"Comforting," Roman said sarcastically. "So how do we stop the unstoppable?"

"Hades is going with you. He can slip between the veils and realms somehow. It's his power—"

Jules snorted, and Hades shot her a dirty look, narrowing his eyes.

"Apparently it's one of his powers," I amended. "We can't give these cards away too soon. Not yet. He's going to give each of you the piece you need when we know you are who you are."

Roman pursed his lips together, figuring it out. "And you'll know that because you'll be somewhere else with Azrael."

"I will," I said quietly. "And you have to let me. You can't protect me from him."

I waited for the arguing. I waited for the alphas to tell me how it would be, and that they wouldn't accept this plan. That they wouldn't leave my side. All of the things that would get us nowhere and would lead straight to death.

Instead, I was met with what could best be described as a reluctant accord as both Roman and Dorian paused before inclining their heads with a single nod.

I told you, Ezra said.

Did you already tell Roman? Did you tell him what I was going to say or tell him not to fight it?

I would never speak for you like that. Especially not in something as important as this.

A rush of warmth coursed through me. Appreciation and love for the mate who gave me exactly what I needed. For the mates that trusted me, just as I trusted them.

"What if you need us? He's death incarnate, is he not?" Dorian asked.

"I know where he wants me to be," I said. "I'll go to him, but not to surrender. I'm going to end him. I'm the only one that can."

Ezra smiled, but it didn't reach his eyes. "And you won't share the how."

I shook my head solemnly. The truth was, I wasn't entirely sure. I shielded all of that from him. I couldn't tell them I was flying by the seat of my pants. Hanging by a thread of hope that what I thought I could do would actually work. There was a tiny tendril of anxiety that whispered, 'this won't work'. And if it didn't, I would try again and again and again, exhausting every single idea I had considered.

I'd made a trip to the Afterlife post-intervention, spending the pre-breakfast morning hours having a conversation with Jake and Hades. I replayed it in my head. He'd answered my questions, helping me build the course of action I planned to take. He fueled the hope that I could finish this. Was it all a fool's hope? Maybe. I didn't care. It was all we had.

"Where does Jules fit in? The fight is here," Roman asked, he looked at her apologetically. "No offense."

"None taken," she said, shrugging a shoulder. "I know what I am."

"I'm going to fill her in on my plan, but she's the contingency in case"—I halted, hating the possibility of what I had to say. I sighed. "She's the messenger in case we don't fully succeed. She goes to Roxanne. She knows how to find her. If the Dukes are defeated, but in the end it still winds up being one crazy suicide mission, it's Azrael that's left. She'll keep them safe and protect them."

Understanding washed over their faces. Roman closed his eyes, struggling with that concept. I only knew a fraction of that pain. When he opened them, he looked to our favorite poltergeist, and simply said, "Thank you."

A small smile graced her lips. "I'll take care of them. It's all I can do."

The room went silent for a moment as everyone processed the information I'd given.

"Hey Jules," I said, "do you mind giving us a minute alone?"

She waved, the mirror warbling and going fuzzy as she disappeared. In a split second, it was back to a flattened glass, showing the reflection of the room.

I looked out the window, watching the sky change color, and I knew we didn't have much time before the waning crescent moon would be glowing high above us.

Before Azrael showed his angelically beautiful face. A face I hated with every fiber of my being. I wanted to feel better inside. I wanted to heal from the damage and from the trauma. I wanted to breathe freely for the first time.

I wanted to let go of the hate.

But if that hate would drive me, I was going to hold on tight and let it fuel every strategic move I had.

"A penny for your thoughts," Ezra said, choosing to share his comment with my other mates.

"Not sure there are enough pennies," I said, my voice flat.

"Try us," Dorian added.

I did have to force myself to smile as I looked at my three mates. They brought me genuine happiness. I didn't want to say goodbye. That felt too real. Goodbyes were permanent. They meant it was the end. This wouldn't be the end. We'd finish this, and it would be a new beginning.

"I love you," I said, settling on what I wanted to say. "I love all three of you, and I don't regret one second of our time together since I took that mission and ended up in this weirdness. I'd rather have it than anything else in the world."

I walked up to each of them, grabbing their face and pulling it to mine as I drank in their scent and lost myself in a kiss.

It wasn't goodbye. And I told them each that.

"I'd follow you to the ends of the earth," Roman whispered as he pressed his forehead to mine. "If you make me come to Lethe, I'm going to destroy it."

I chuckled, gently brushing his lips one last time.

I gazed at Hades. "Draw the Dukes out. Control this situation."

He flapped his wings, taking flight and hovering in place before landing on Dorian's shoulder. "I don't have anyone else I love-hate as much as you, so I'd appreciate it if you didn't die."

I snorted and my raven reluctantly hummed. "Wow. I'm touched."

I placed my hand over my heart. "I think you should put that on a greeting card. It would sell amazing."

"I'll cross-stitch it for you." He let out an obnoxious squawk, then he winked. He whispered into Dorian's ear, then turned to my mates as he said, "We're staying here."

"Where will you go?" Dorian asked.

"Where he asked me to meet him." I mouthed 'I love you' once more, then sifted out.

I appeared in Ezra's empty penthouse and walked to the bathroom in silence. I placed my hands on the counter, looking down at my feet.

I looked up, seeing my reflection. I stared at my eyes, seeing the glimmer of the girl I had once been. I saw the woman I had become. I saw love and rage, unwavering stubbornness, and perseverance. I grinned at myself devilishly. I knew who I was. Azrael didn't have a clue what I was capable of.

I wasn't afraid of him.

I just wanted—well, I wanted Death to die.

I straightened my posture, then whispered Jules' name. The glass waved, and she appeared, a questioning look on her face. "I need one last favor," I said.

She cocked her head, intrigued. "I'm listening."

I patted my pocket. "How do you feel about traveling?"

I wanted the impossible. I was going to make it happen.

Angel. Demon. Shifter. Fae. Vampire. Woman.

Fuck the Angel of Death.

I was as close to a god as one could get.

CHAPTER 26
EZRA

SHE'D SIFTED AWAY FROM US, REFUSING TO SHARE HER LOCATION. NONE OF US liked it. It went against every instinct we could have as a mate.

Honor. Worship. Guard. Protect.

There was one that was always left out. Trust. It was something that should have been there when you had a mate, or any type of relationship. For alphas, it was never at the forefront. It wasn't our nature. It wasn't a matter of loyalty or monogamy. The very nature of the mate bond was devotion, but if we broke things down, there wasn't the ability to trust they could do it without us.

Our first mates died. Trust wouldn't have prevented any of their deaths. That path, it would seem, was already set. With Fury, there was a great chance that not having trust in her would lead to everyone's demise. She wasn't cut from the same cloth. She was more than capable in so many aspects of her existence, yet she was vulnerable at times. She needed us, only in a different way.

Not to save her. Not to protect her.

To fight with her. To believe in her abilities.

She needed us to *see* her for who she really was, and not just see her as our mate.

We did. We listened, and we accepted . . . even if our baser instincts fought against it.

Although Dorian was shielded from me, I knew he understood. I could tell that he wasn't that different from the rest of us. He could wear the flat affect all he wanted, but I could see through it. Roman's voice was loud if I chose to listen, but he wasn't struggling to keep control. Something about Fury had changed him. Something had settled the fiery wolf within. He raged inside, just as I did, but she kept us grounded somehow.

It was trust.

The moments ticked on, and we sat in silence as the sun set further, the hazy disc slipping below the horizon.

The Houston pollution created a bright sunset, shooting streaks of color out in rays, illuminating the clouds in pinks and oranges.

It was our clock. The sand in the hourglass draining to the bottom. The moon was now visible, and it would soon be the only celestial orb in our sky.

Hades lifted a foot to scratch his neck, tilting his head to the side and closing his eyes as it clearly felt good.

"You'd think for as old as I am, waiting for this wouldn't feel like my soul was being sucked from my eyeballs," Dorian said, pressing his palms to his eyes and rubbing.

I snorted. "For as much as you stand by windows and stare out of them for what seems like hours on end, I find that surprising."

"Right?" Roman chuckled, leaning forward with his elbows on his knees. "In all seriousness, what do you think about when you do that?"

The fae smiled faintly and exhaled a light huff from his nostrils. "Everything. I'm a planner. In control of everything. Even with something that's out of my control, I'm making a plan for how to reverse that." The smile faded, and he looked down to the ground, almost as if speaking to his feet. "For a millennium I was searching for answers to fix my daughter. It was always at the forefront of my mind. Always pouring through the scrolls and ancient texts, then replaying it in my head. I was sure I'd overlooked something. I would try to consider what pieces of the puzzle I was missing." When he looked up, his eyes were slightly glazed over, but it faded quickly. "Now Lyra's safe."

I could see how that would take up a lot of mental energy. "So what makes waiting so hard right now?"

"I have no way to plan for the pure unknown," he said with a laugh. "I'm out of my element, and apparently that isn't something my mind is able to comprehend just yet."

I stood up, rubbing my hands on my jeans. "Well, I'm used to waiting, and this is still a nightmare."

Fury wasn't here, and I wouldn't pour a drink in front of her until she was ready. If that never happened, then so be it. I would respect that forever. Right now, it was me and her two other mates. Right now, we sat and waited for Jake's rogue offspring to make their world-ending appearance.

I walked to a bar cart, pulling the stopper out of a bottle of fae wine. I poured it into three small glasses and wrapped my hands around them to bring them to the coffee table. I set them down carefully, then handed one to Dorian and Roman. They accepted theirs, looking at each other cautiously.

I remained standing, raising my glass in each of their directions.

"A toast before we fight Hades' boyband of younger brothers." They each laughed, then stood up, and I continued. "There was a time when I didn't like either of you. We've done little to help one another, mostly tolerating each other over the years. Now we've passed toleration and we might possibly even *like* each other. The jury is still out on that one. What I do know for sure is that we share something else, aside from our mate. Respect for each other. Fury brought us together in ways we never saw coming. She brings out the best in us. Even you," I said to the crow and he snort-squawked. "With her, we look forward to the future, even if we see our futures differently. I never expected to have a mate again, much less have to share one. I never thought I'd be here, waiting to take on harbingers of death from the Afterlife. But here we are, and I'm honestly glad it's you two fuckers I'm standing with."

Dorian smiled, then dipped his head graciously before raising his glass. Roman laughed, pursing his lips, and nodding his head, then he shrugged. Glass poised in the air, we said 'cheers' and drank.

"Dear god, now you three are like a boyband," Hades said.

I barked a laugh, turning to his perch on the back of a chair, but I never got a response out.

A rumbling reverberated through the walls, shaking the floors, and making every item in the room rattle.

"Guess they're here," Hades said, sighing. He took a deep breath. "You should sift now. They're going to blow things up first." He shook his head, muttering, "So unoriginal."

"Then why aren't we outside?" I shouted. That damn bird . . .

He slipped into his realm, not answering.

Dorian grabbed us, sifting us away just as a blast forced its way through the outside wall.

A burst of hot wind blew over my skin just as the ground felt like it was pulled from beneath me, and then I landed hard, trying to secure my footing on impact.

Dorian grunted, letting us go. "Sorry about the rough ride."

We stood shoulder to shoulder, three immortal alphas, staring down the burning flames on the west wing of Dorian's estate. Smoke billowed from the fire, the debris of his destroyed home littering the ground.

Three beings emerged from the fumes, walking side by side, slowly approaching us. They each had shoulder-length black hair to match their black eyes, a stark contrast to the pallor of their skin. One had enormous wings, and if he didn't look like he was the walking dead, I'd almost describe his feathers as angelic. An unnatural wind blew around us, picking up the haze and swirling it around their bodies.

Hades appeared, landing on my shoulder. "Look at them walk like they're in a shampoo commercial," he huffed. "Tools."

I pressed my lips together in an attempt to hide my smile, focusing on the seriousness of what was about to happen. Hades didn't seem to have a worry. I had to believe he knew what to do.

Fury trusted him.

He trusted Fury.

Trust.

That's what would get us through this.

The winds grew, their speeds increasing, sending leaves fluttering across the ground as it quaked. Lightning split across the sky, sending a thunderous crack in its wake. *Typhon.*

A tendril of darkness appeared, snaking around a duke's arm, a pungent odor beginning to permeate the air. *Orcus.*

Psychic pressure made its presence known, pushing inward and demanding entry to my thoughts. *Anubis.*

"Hello, brother. It's been a long time," Typhon said. His voice had an eerie snake-like quality to it, dragging out the 's' in a hiss. "Yet, you come to us in your crow form. Father must have punished you as well, though not nearly to the same extent it would seem."

Hades sighed deeply. "Are we really doing this? You're gearing up to give your evil soliloquy before you attack? C'mon. You can't die," he said, holding his wing out in our direction. "They're immortal. It's pointless. You could just go back to Lethe and call it a day. Save me the trouble."

Orcus huffed a humorless laugh. "You should have joined us."

"Yes, clearly I missed out on the losing side," he retorted. "Have you changed your name to the Three Horsemen yet? It doesn't quite have the same ring to it."

Roman shook his head to the side, a loud sniffing sound coming from him as he did so.

Roman, are you still with us? I asked him, mentally reaching out while listening to the exchange between Hades and his brothers.

I am. The pressure from Anubis is getting stronger.

Fight it. We can't lose our control to him.

Anubis raised an eyebrow, holding his hands out and gesturing around us, extending his wings to show off. "*Losing*? We are here, are we not?"

Dorian chuckled, drawing their attention. Anubis' eyes widened as the fae mocked him, clapping slowly. "Your goal was to get *here*? In Houston?" he asked, looking amused at the mere thought. "Why? That's a hell of a long game if this was your intention. Poor planning. I'm guessing you're not the brains of the operation." He turned to Hades. "I really don't see the family resemblance."

Hades snorted. "In my father's defense, everyone makes mistakes."

I quietly laughed as his words rubbed them the wrong way. Fissures ripped through the ground, shooting columns of earth upward toward the sky. Pressure eased off my mind as Anubis' gaze was laser-focused on Dorian.

Flashes of unbridled anger reached me, and I realized Hades and Dorian had cleverly played to their emotions. As their rage increased, it became their focal point. Now they weren't even bothering to protect their minds. All their energy was moving toward fighting us, and Anubis had foolishly set his sights on the only supernatural present whose mental shield he couldn't break.

I mentally shouted to Hades and Roman, telling them I could read the dukes' minds. *It's jumbled, and disorganized, but it's there. Some of it's random. I can't see what their purpose is yet, but it's getting clearer.*

Purpose, Hades repeated in a jaded tone. *They have very little purpose, and they're sensitive as all get out. They react to any stimulus, good or bad. They're like walking testicles. That's what we're fighting.*

I nearly busted out laughing. *Well, I do like to fight dirty.*

Reading pieces of their disjointed thoughts, I saw it happening in their heads. Poorly planned, as Dorian said, but it was happening.

They had every belief they could kill us. They had some clever ideas. I'd died in many ways. Roman had been ripped apart as a young wolf. We always regenerated. The Dukes had every intention of incinerating us to ashes and taking us to the four corners of the world. So that was new. Even if we could regenerate from that, it wouldn't be fast, leaving more than enough time for them to wipe out every being on the planet. And they were angry enough to do it. They had stewed in that hatred for millennia. They wanted revenge.

I passed it on, letting them know what I could see in their thoughts. Roman nodded tersely in response. I wished I could tell Dorian, but he would catch on.

Hades' urgency reached me. *What we talked about, Ezra. Follow Dorian's lead. Make it happen. Without it, I can't do my part.*

The crow and I had shared pieces of the plan. Dorian had his portion, as did Roman. None of us knew it all. We couldn't. If Anubis was able to persuade and take control of us, if he could fully penetrate our minds, the entire thing could go to shit. The fae had the most solid barrier. Whatever was happening—whatever our plan was—would be safely hidden in there.

My job was to keep one of them busy. Distract. Make him aim for me. If the Backstreet Boys of the underworld focused their powers together, Dorian couldn't do his part.

I've got it, Hades. Go. Roman, Orcus seems like he's going for you. Typhon for me.

. . . *NOW.*

Hades let out a loud caw, flapping his wings and taking flight. He banked hard, gliding directly into his realm, disappearing before our eyes.

The Dukes' reactions were delayed, confused as to why their brother left the fight before it had even started. It gave us a brief upper hand.

In an instant, all hell broke loose. Roman exploded in a full shift, his wolf landing on all fours, cracking the ground beneath him with the impact of his weight. At full speed, his paws pounded against the earth in a steady beat. He aimed straight for Orcus, lunging, and flying into the air.

Tendrils of death and decay wrapped around Roman's body, slowly killing pieces of his flesh, but it hadn't slowed him down. In his wolf form, he was more powerful. He could regenerate faster. His paws landed on Orcus' chest, and he reached around with his gaping jaws, gripping hold of an arm right at the shoulder, ripping it right out of the socket. Tossing it to the side, Roman continued to nip at him as the poisonous rot attacked his body. Each of them would recover, but it would slow them down. Whatever his plan was, I had to trust he could handle it.

Dorian sifted, appearing across the massive lawn. Anubis' attention faltered for a brief moment. Lightning crackled beneath Dorian's skin, and the ground trembled beneath him. He was enticing him, and it worked. A harsh grin curled up Anubis' lips. He wanted more than anything to take control of the fae and use the powers he saw. He turned his full attention Dorian's way, walking toward him at a leisurely pace. He was too cocky. Maybe they both were. I had to fight my fight and watch Dorian simultaneously. *Follow Dorian's lead.* Those were my instructions.

Trust.

Typhon and I stared each other down. His hands rested at his sides, palms turned out while his fingers twitched. I was poised to run, using my speed to my advantage.

I reached out mentally, peeking into his thoughts. I saw his next moves. I smirked, then playfully winked.

He shot his hand up, throwing wind in an attempt to lift me from the ground so he could toss me into the fire. Hard pass. I'd had more than enough raw skin growing back in recent days. I just needed to keep him occupied. I wasn't going to let him mutilate me.

I dashed past him, his elemental grasp missing me entirely. He took chunks of broken earth, raising them high and using the air to catapult them toward me. I dodged them easily, watching his thoughts and predicting where each piece would land. He couldn't keep up as I darted away, never knowing where I was going.

He was infuriated with each miss, which was a delight for me, honestly. I laughed as his anger increased. His mind raged with thoughts of me on fire.

The problem was that level of wrath brought along an erratic desperation. He wasn't thinking anymore. He was just *doing*.

Shit.

A fire tornado burst to life, the gale force winds pulling the flames from Dorian's house, twirling them in a cyclone as it picked me up.

I spun within it, losing my sense of direction. My skin burned, melting away in patches, exposing muscle and nerves. Pain exploded through me, taunting parts of my psyche that had endured torture at the hands of Azrael. The fire and wind held me, sending me spiraling in its circle while smoke filled my lungs.

Burning flesh reached my nostrils and the olfactory memory pulled me into the house in the Afterlife. The moments before I took my eyes. Azrael wearing Fury's beautiful face, working to break me as he flayed my tattoos slowly. When the skin grew back, he did it again. My blood flowed freely, draining my power over and over and over as I tried to regenerate.

My mate flashed in my mind, and an anger grew within me. I knew what Azrael wanted to do to her. He'd told me repeatedly, and he relished in the idea he'd have her for an eternity. He knew how strong she was. He knew how long it would take her to break. He loved it. He wanted nothing more than to lick the tears from her face as he fractured her soul. His words echoed in my ears, replaying the sound of his voice while he stood over me, taunting me while every piece of me tried to grow back.

Michael hid her. He got to keep one of his line. I kept no one. *Destroying them was my punishment. Do you know what that's like, Ezra? Killing the very beings you created? It took a part of me that never returned. And it was all Michael's fault.*

He thought he could keep one. A final heir. Hiding the last descendent generation after generation after generation. But I found her, and she was just too perfect to destroy. Her pain was delicious. She was so much like Michael. I refuse to let her go.

The fire continued to lick at the regenerating skin, burning it off all over again in a sick loop. But ire coursed through my veins, and I felt a wave of light travel through my muscles, crackling over the pieces of skin that remained.

Fury's power . . .

I pushed it out with minimal force, not really knowing where I was anymore or how to control it. Just testing the water, so to speak. I may as well have set off a bomb. I was in the middle of it.

An explosion shot outward from my center, knocking Typhon down and blowing him back a hundred yards. The fire tornado dissipated, and I came crashing back down to the ground, landing on my back with a hard thud that almost knocked the air out of me. I turned my head to see I'd blown a hole in the side of Dorian's mansion. The entire side of the building was exposed, its walls crumbled all around it. A gaping hole showcased the damage, and I spotted the industrial kitchen fully demolished. A medium-sized metal object was on fire. It was the trash bin.

A literal dumpster fire.

Seemed fitting.

I groaned, sitting up and looking down at the skin that was regrowing at a record pace. Electricity ran over my body like I was a live wire. I surveyed the damage again, realizing I'd barely tried when I used that power. I just wanted the fire to stop.

That could be a problem.

I couldn't see Dorian. Off in the distance, Roman continued to shred at Orcus as his body took hit after hit of decay. It looked like acid wrapping itself around him, burning off fur and flesh, leaving a bubbling ooze before it went to find another piece of living skin to attack. I didn't know how much longer he could do that before he lost the ability to quickly recover.

He was apparently feeling that too.

Orcus reached a tendril out like a smoky black hand, closing its fingers around Roman's throat and I saw Roman's icy blue eyes flash yellow, the same shade as Fury's.

A sudden understanding hit me.

The prophecy had once said we three combined could end the world.

And here we were, carrying Fury's power.

If the Dukes didn't end the world . . . we would.

I reached out to Roman, panic filling my voice. *Don't use her power! You can't control it. We'll destroy everything before—*

I can control it. I've been in control of my own for longer than you know. A small smile crept up his wolfish jaw.

I didn't push back, but the uncertainty filled me quickly. I flicked my eyes between Typhon as he got up, and to Roman as fur melted off his body where Orcus held him.

Trust me, he said.

That damn word was going to be the end of us.

Then I watched as his wolf grew. Muscle regenerated and expanded, layering itself on top over and over. Bones popped as they enlarged to hold his everchanging frame. His fangs elongated, his jaw opening as drool dripped from his jowls.

Orcus lost his focus, removing his death smoke from gripping Roman's neck, but it wasn't simply the sight of Roman's monstrous wolf. When he growled, the very earth shattered beneath our feet. What looked like molten lava poured from his eyes.

What in the actual . . .

My mind went blank in pure shock. Motion in my periphery pulled my attention to the English-styled garden and hedge maze Dorian kept.

He and Anubis were fighting, disappearing, and reappearing in new places as they fought. They blinked in and out, sifting through Dorian's power and exchanging blows.

A small ripple appeared, just a tiny wave in the fabric of space.

Hades came flying through it, dropping an object into Dorian's outstretched hand, then vanishing through another split into his realm.

Anubis figured out what it was just as I did.

It was that deathstick Lyra had brought.

They couldn't be extinguished, but if that was part of the plan, he needed to use it.

Dorian sifted, but Anubis was prepared, moving himself quickly and planning his next move. I could see his thoughts. He'd taken note of Roman's hellwolf, and he had every intention of using that to his advantage.

He reached into Roman's unguarded mind, grabbing onto his psyche with determined persuasion, pulling him away from Orcus. He'd been stalking toward the Duke when he suddenly stopped and shook his head. Turning toward us, he ran in our direction. His paws shook the ground, breaking it apart like an earthquake chasing a fault line. He let out a roar as red magma poured onto the ground.

Fucking hell.

Typhon threw his arms deep into the dirt, pulling at it and creating an earthquake that sent splits shooting across the estate. Giant chasms appeared, creating a minefield to run through.

Dorian sifted, then disappeared, then sifted again, working to make his way to Anubis as he avoided him.

Mind reading and vampire speed. That's what I had to my advantage. I used it.

As I crossed the quaking terrain, I hopped over each crevice as it appeared, the separating increasing as Typhon shoved his elemental control into it.

I had no way to reach Dorian, but I saw my opening. Hoping he caught the reference, I shouted, "Dorian, catch!"

Fury's power crackled over my skin, building up. I only needed a little. Just a little.

As I came up on Anubis with lightning speed, I threw out what I hoped was just a small pulse of her power. The ground behind Anubis exploded, sending him flying forward . . . right to where Dorian sifted, landing in a crouch. He shoved the deathstick up and outward, his eyes filled with the same electric quality I had under my skin.

Anubis crashed into it, releasing his mental hold on Roman, who came to a sudden stop. The giant monster shook his head back and forth, regaining control of his mind and body.

Anubis fell to his knees. His form flickered in and out, as though it were trying to extinguish, but it couldn't. He coughed as he laughed, knowing his power would return momentarily.

"Your arrogance will be your end," Anubis said.

"Funny you should say that, brother." Hades' voice sounded as he stepped through his veil.

My jaw dropped when a man walked out. His jet-black hair was long on top, slicked back and away from his face. His dark olive-toned skin was covered in tattoos, hints of ink peeking out from his collar. The long sleeves of his crisp black shirt were rolled up, exposing extensive designs on his arms. I met his black eyes, but they carried a slight warmth I recognized.

Without a doubt, I was staring at Hades.

"Arrogance was always your downfall," he said, a cruel smile curved on his lips as he approached Anubis. His brother flickered quickly, trying to fully recover his power so they could be on equal footing, but Hades tsked, grabbing him and pulling him through the veil.

They vanished.

"Heads up," Dorian shouted, and it snapped me out of my trance. He tossed the deathstick at me, and I caught it. Following his gaze back to Roman, I saw he'd turned his hellwolf back around, aiming for Orcus.

I didn't have a clue where Hades had taken Anubis, but his brothers knew what was coming now.

"One down, two to go."

CHAPTER 27
HADES

I'd watched the fight unfold from the split between worlds. A place of veiled darkness, filled with silence that hummed in my ears. A place only I could go.

My realm.

It was uniquely mine, the way another realm had once been. I'd chosen to share that one. I gave it away to keep her safe.

I interfered.

I still didn't regret it.

Even if I lived the remainder of eternity in my crow form, she was safe.

She was worth it.

I closed my eyes, breathing in deeply as I readjusted to my human form. I felt my limbs, having long forgotten what it was like to use parts of my body. I extended my fingers, opening and closing them repeatedly, strengthening the joints and tendons. Tilting my head to the side, I cracked my neck, the popping sound and the relief filling my senses.

Exhaling, I readied myself to enter the battle once again. This time my brothers knew I was coming. The element of surprise was gone, but it needed to be this way.

Fury, Jake, and I knew what we needed to do. I carried more power than my idiot brothers. The 'Four' Horsemen , indeed. What a joke. But we couldn't cancel each other out. We were designed that way. Created from the same source, unable to destroy each other.

I didn't need to destroy them. I just needed them temporarily weak. I couldn't pull them through my realm at peak strength.

"One down, two to go."

My lips curled into a cruel smile.

Roman's hellwolf exploded in a run, aiming toward Orcus. I wouldn't lie. That was a bit of a surprise. We knew he was enormous in his power, but the tales of what he could become hadn't been shared. Perhaps his people were too scared. If you didn't speak of it, it wasn't real. The monster wouldn't return if you didn't give it a name.

Yet, he was real, and I watched him in awe. A true hellwolf, filled with so much anger and power it rippled across his body in waves. The icy blue eyes of his standard wolf were long gone, replaced by glowing yellow orbs dripping lava to the ground.

He pounded against the earth, my brother's poisonous tendrils of decay clashing with him in mid-air, throwing him to the side while his fur and flesh melted. Dorian sifted, trying to appear in front of Orcus, but he anticipated this, constantly changing his position. He threw out a black branch of smoke, wrapping it around the fae's arm, burning the skin off like acid. It shriveled, and Dorian's recoiled, catching the deathstick he'd been holding with his other hand before sifting out of the way.

Ezra was managing Typhon's erratic temper tantrum as best he could. God, what a twat. He always had been. He had the emotional range of a reptile.

I wanted to level the playing field.

And maybe have a little fun.

I shifted into my crow form, slipping through a rift high in the sky, flying fast and aiming toward Typhon.

My brother was shooting balls of fire, harnessing wind, and throwing chunks of whatever he could find. He never really was a man with a plan.

I twisted, curving in the air, keeping my body pressed together tightly as I dove down. My speed picked up, and I threw my wings out to break against the current, extending my feet out to grab. I cawed loudly, giving my position away on purpose. I wanted him to see me coming.

Typhon looked up just as I wanted him to. Legs fully outstretched, I hit my target, digging my claws into the squishy orb, curling my talons around the soft flesh, and ripping it out with a sickening, wet pop. I grinned internally as I flapped my wings hard, taking flight away from him, carrying my new prize with me.

He screamed in rage, glaring up at me with his one good eye. A deep pit in his face poured a black ichor from it.

I flew toward Roman, cawing again, tossing the eye out in the open like I was playing with a toy.

A feral grin curled up his wolf lips, and he jumped into the air, catching it in his mouth, chomping once for good measure, and then swallowing. He landed back on the ground, the impact shaking the ground and sending a plume of dust around him.

Did Roman just eat *your brother's eye?* Ezra yelled in my mind.

I laughed, mentally making sure he could hear my response. *He sure did. You know, I always liked that shifter.*

I'm not eating body parts for your approval. Making that clear right now.

I chuckled again, turning around in flight to return to the fight. *Awfully judgy for a bloodsucking vampire.*

Different and you know it, he said as he sped away from Typhon's fire.

Is it though? I hadn't pegged you for someone with a weak stomach, I taunted. I found a good current and hovered, taking in the carnage below me.

At least I didn't throw up when Fury sifted us, he retorted.

I shuddered. That was a rough ride, and I'd spent over four hundred years as a bird.

I floated, contemplating how to get Orcus out of the way. I just needed an opening. He was so good at keeping anyone away from him. Easy enough to do when you reeked of death.

I knew Fury would succeed on her part. She always would. She didn't know how to fail. That's why she was chosen. A piece of Michael was in her veins, yes, but that wasn't what made her unstoppable. It was her humanity. She was uniquely balanced in the gray area, accepting her faults and the darkness, always striving to increase the light. If we didn't complete our part, Azrael would win.

Equally as important, my asshole brothers would win.

I couldn't live with that.

I turned my attention to Roman, watching as he roared and prepared for his next move. He charged Orcus again, his great body protecting him from inflicting too much long-term damage from the tendrils of decay.

From my vantage point, I saw Dorian in the hedge maze, watching carefully as the shifter fought. Roman snapped at limbs, his razor-sharp teeth shredding at pieces of Orcus' body while my brother retaliated with poisonous fumes. Roman took a hit and rolled, getting back on all fours, and shaking his body.

Do me a quick favor and piss Typhon off, I said to Ezra.

He glanced up to where I was in the sky, half smirking, a fang peeking through and hanging over his lip.

Any requests? he asked.

Make me laugh while you do it. Yeah, we were fighting to save the world, but I was at least going to enjoy my brothers' misery. And yes, their misery made me laugh.

Ezra cackled, taking off at a breakneck speed. While Typhon was throwing all sorts of elements at the vampire, I needed one thing from him to pull off my next move. I was counting on his predictability.

In a sudden twist my brother didn't see coming, Ezra zoomed toward him, stopping for a fraction of a second, then poked him in his one good eye—speeding away before Typhon could retaliate.

He'd grabbed his face, screaming and cursing.

Immortal, supernatural, god-like creature, demon spawn: it didn't matter what you were. That hurt like a bitch.

I almost fell out of the sky as I squawked with unrestrained laughter. The sounds of my wheezing snorts caught my brother's attention.

I sent my thanks to Ezra, who gave me a salute and a wink.

Roman ate an eyeball, but you might be my new favorite, I told him.

Typhon's chest heaved up and down as clouds built above us, rolling like waves as they gathered and became larger. Lightning cracked and split across the night sky; thunder rumbled deeply, sending heavy vibrations to the ground below.

Perfect. Predictable. Just like the dumbass I always knew.

Tell Roman I need a decoy, I shouted to Ezra, knowing he would pass it on to the shifter. I had my own way of communicating with Dorian.

I cawed loudly in three short bursts, and the fae nodded, seizing the moment to sift in front of Orcus with the deathstick extending outward, aiming for his chest. He thrusted forward, but it fell short as Orcus pulled back, grabbing Dorian around the middle with his phantom smoky arms. He lost his grip on the weapon, and it bounced with a thud as it hit the ground. The decay burned around his waist, no doubt causing unbearable pain.

Fury's mates couldn't die, but I knew they could still feel everything.

Roman didn't hesitate and lunged haphazardly toward Orcus, right on cue.

Typhon threw one hand above him, pulling the elements from the sky, harnessing the lightning, gathering it like a ball of power in his hand.

Internally, I grinned.

I banked hard, flying into a rift, appearing in my realm.

I shook, feathers disappearing as I took my human form.

This is going to hurt, I said, preparing myself. Fucking my brother up was worth it.

I reached through the veil, my arm appearing right in front of Typhon as I snatched the orb of crackling electricity. It pulsed through my body, sending waves of burning pain in every direction. Shoving my hand through the fabric of space, a rift opened in front of Orcus, and I took another form. One that allowed me to pass directly through matter. I might have been a little out of practice, but it was like riding a bicycle.

I was the OG poltergeist, after all.

Orcus' mouth fell open in surprise when I shoved the ball of lightning into his chest. I yanked my hand back before the bolts shot from their confinement, splintering apart inside his sternum.

He looked down at his body, then gazed up at me in shock. I winked at him while I took my steps back.

He dropped his hold on Dorian and Roman, and they fell to the ground. Dorian rolled onto his back wheezing. "Fucking hell, you took long enough," he coughed as the skin on his abdomen bubbled and regenerated.

"Sorry about that. Great job, though. Give yourself a pat on the back," I said, reaching down to give him a hand.

He caught my extended offer, pulling himself up. "I don't want a pat on the back," he grumbled. "I want to not burn anymore."

Roman stood on all fours and vomited black poison on the grass. He shook like a dog, sending growing fur and pieces of rotting flesh flying off. I scrunched my nose and made a face.

"Well, that's new. I've never seen anyone ingest his power before."

Roman snapped his jaws once, then licked his lips, running his long tongue over his nose to the other side of his snout.

Dorian gave him a look of disgust while he rubbed his mid-section.

Crackles and pops sounded as my brother looked at his chest while he flickered in and out. His black toxic smoke wafted from his eyes, curling around his neck and his mouth.

I opened my mouth to speak, but snapped it shut when Typhon's scream of rage pierced the air.

Always interrupting. Nothing ever changed with them.

I turned around to see him throw his hands into the earth, reaching deep. Pebbles shook over the surface, and the earth quaked and began to get warmer. A stream of red and orange liquid rope came out of the ground, coiling like a snake under the control of its charmer.

I sighed.

Magma.

So predictable.

He stood up tall with his legs spread apart, manipulating his newest weapon.

"I'm coming for you," he called out to me.

I stared at him blankly. "Okay," I said mockingly. "To do what exactly? You can't kill me."

"I'm going to make you suffer." He narrowed his eyes on Dorian and Roman. "All of you."

For fuck's sake, his talking is enough to suffer through, Ezra said in my mind.

I shifted my gaze, realizing he wasn't in my sights.

Roman barked, grabbing my attention. A wind gusted past us, and I saw it then. Ezra. A blur in my vision, falling to the ground, sliding across the terrain like he was stealing home base. He dug his feet into the dirt, keeping them close together, sending up a cloud of dust as he came to a stop in front of Typhon, his legs sliding between my brother's.

Typhon looked down as Ezra smiled, thrusting the deathstick up into my brother's chest. His mouth formed an 'o' as his eyes rolled into the back of his head and he fell to his knees, convulsing. He flickered in and out, his indestructible soul trying to die. We had a few moments before they'd regain power. It was all I needed.

Ezra got up, swinging the deathstick at Typhon's head, landing it across his temple in a sickening smack. My brother tipped over to his side, pieces of electricity buzzing over his head. "You really are predictable."

He tossed it in the air, and I caught it. I extended my arm, shaking the vampire's hand. "Nice touch. Probably a bit overkill, but nice all the same."

He shrugged. "I haven't run like that in years. I'm pissed off."

I chuckled. He sounded so much like Fury, and he didn't even know it.

I held the deathstick up and looked at it. Lyra had no idea how helpful she'd be when she brought that. Make no mistake, she intended on using it. It just turned out to be useful for us. Azrael was a shitbag, and he never should've had something this powerful just lying around. It was going back to Jake's office to be hidden away safely. I tucked the weapon under my arm and reached for Typhon. I grabbed a handful of his hair and dragged him over to Orcus, dumping him unceremoniously.

"Well, this went better than I expected," I said to Fury's mates.

"Are we just going to skip over the fact that you're a person now?" Ezra said. "What the fuck is that about?"

"Of course I'm not just a crow. The three stooges here are my brothers and you don't see them covered in feathers. It's complicated." I shrugged. "I'm on a tight schedule. Only have a small window of time to get these assholes off this realm."

Dorian reached his hand out, patting me on the shoulder. "Where are you taking them, anyway?"

I placed a hand on Typhon and Orcus' shoulders. Their powers were still unsteady, but flashes and sparks were beginning to surface. Their strength was returning. It didn't matter. Where we were going, their power was useless.

"Back to our dad's place," I said, an evil smirk on my face.

I slipped into darkness, laughing while dragging my brothers back to Hell.

Contentment hummed through my veins. It was validating knowing my three siblings were about to get what was coming to them, but the real war wasn't over. The reality of that fact settled in my mind. Roman, Dorian, Ezra, and I succeeded, but winning here only got us to the halfway point.

Fury still had Azrael to contend with, and he was a much bigger problem.

CHAPTER 28
FURY

I SIFTED MID-STEP.

One moment I was walking out of Ezra's penthouse.

The next, I stood on the driveway of what was once my greatest nightmare.

Bright lights illuminated the dining room. The flowered wallpaper we had was long gone, replaced by a bright yellow paint. Inside two parents moved around a giggling baby with ginormous cheeks and a full head of dark hair. The kid flung food off its highchair toward the waiting Pitbull. The dog wagged its tail, happily chowing down whatever pureed mash it was given while the baby squealed in delight. They were definitely in cahoots. The mom shook her head in amusement while the dad scrambled to stop the baby from doing it again.

They seemed so happy. Picture perfect in the same house that haunted my dreams for decades. Sure, it looked different now. The exterior had been repaired over the years of natural wear and tear. It had a garage now. The ugly bushes that sat in front of the windows were long gone, replaced by a flower bed filled with color. The surface was new, but the bones of the place—the foundation it was built on—there was no changing that.

I walked around the front, toward the yard. A white picket fence surrounded it on three sides. I reached up, hooking my hand around the rough wood edge before jumping. My feet landed quietly on the other side. A soft breeze drifted up from the lake, lifting my hair, blowing strands over my shoulders. I started down the hill for the small dock at the edge.

A hundred years ago this lake was the place I went to when the walls closed in and the air felt stifling. John would come and go, but as a housewife, my duty was here.

Cooking. Cleaning. Dressing up like a living doll and going through the motions.

But when my makeup couldn't quite cover the bruises and the tears wouldn't stop coming, this was where I would retreat.

Azrael told me to come home.

I knew what he meant.

I half-expected him to have the house redone; reverted to the picture of our old life so that he could torture me just a little bit more with it. To make me play the doll—walking, talking, breathing in fear.

Perhaps he simply hadn't gotten to it yet. Maybe I was early. All I knew was that we had one last game to play, but this time the tables had turned.

He thought he held all the cards. That the rules were set and there was no escape.

He was mistaken.

"Sunny."

His voice was low and husky. Silky smooth. He always did know how to charm. After all, he was the greatest liar in history.

"Azrael," I answered, not nearly so pleasant. I glanced over my shoulder, taking in his pale blond hair, bone white skin, and icy blue eyes. He wore John's face. A tactic meant to throw me. Intimidate me.

But there was nothing intimidating about a coward who hid behind a mask.

"After all this time I would've expected you to show me your true face." Turning around, I looked at him. My reaction surprised him, and he tilted his head as he considered my words. "You're threatening to end the world just to have me. Seems a little strange you want me to spend the rest of eternity with you and I don't even know who my captor is."

His eyes narrowed on the word captor. To call it anything else would've been a kindness he didn't deserve. We both knew why I was here. He wanted to hurt me. Torture me.

This wasn't some long lost love.

It was obsession.

Madness.

"You have a very high opinion of yourself," he mused, stepping forward. Only four or so feet remained between. I brushed my damp hands against my jeans, then stuffed them in my jacket pockets. "It's not the most becoming quality in a lady, though I will enjoy slowly stripping it away."

I stayed silent, lifting an eyebrow.

"Because you followed my command and came alone, I will tell you a truth," he continued, taking another step. I might have broken past the fear, but I couldn't stop the way my heart rate picked up. Good. I needed him to believe he still had that effect on me. As if he heard it, Azrael smiled. It was lifeless and cruel. "They are all my faces. Whichever one I was made with, I forgot long ago."

I let out a soft exhale.

"I suppose it follows that you forgot who you were along with it. Was that before or after Michael saw to it that you slaughtered your children?"

He closed the distance between us, standing before me. His head ducked down, hovering only inches from mine.

In my first life, I'd sometimes thought I'd seen a glimpse of something in his gaze. Something inhuman. Something monstrous.

As I watched him, I saw it now in the way shadows drifted through the blue of his eyes, darkening it.

"You speak of things you know nothing about," he said, voice deadly.

"I know that's why you became obsessed with hunting angels' children," I replied. "And why you were after me." His hand came up as if to cup my jaw. Instead, it curled around my face, squeezing hard. I had to fight the sliver of panic that hit me, threatening to ruin everything.

"If you're looking for a reason why I am the way I am, you won't find one. If you're thinking there's something redeemable in my soul, that you can somehow coax it out—you won't. I've been the Angel of

Death a long time, Sunny, and I'm bored. The descendants of angels are no more. I ensured that when I beat the whelp out of you." His callous way of describing our child, *my child,* made me clench my hands. I was thankful they were in my jacket pockets, or he might have seen beyond the façade. He might have suspected that my heart wasn't beating simply because I had the desire to run, but instead, a desire to fight. To kill.

"I would have died anyway. You beating me just prolonged my torture."

"As I said, I'm bored. You were the first thing to interest me since I killed Michael. Needless to say, it's been a long time. Most of the angel hybrids were so far removed from the source. Their blood was diluted and they barely held any power, but you . . . you had his hair. I was struck by the unnatural shade of red that only he and his true offspring carried. Somehow your line wasn't weakened. I saw in you the same anger that filled him. This disgusting sense of what was just. You couldn't just lie down and take what life gave you, even when I used you. Broke you . . ." I flinched when his lips caressed mine, just the slightest of touches.

"Then I went too far. Hit too hard. I do regret that. Killing you so soon, especially when you weren't extinguished as you should have been. I was expecting you in Lethe, but you escaped me. I was saddened I didn't get to play with you. It was truly unexpected. I bided my time, watching you from afar. But there were times I missed you too much. I couldn't help myself. I took stranger's faces and met you at bars, sex clubs—enjoying my fill of you when you had no idea." My face drained of color. He smiled, pressing his body closer to mine, and I could feel his erection against me.

"You remember the night at Hail Mary's?"

I couldn't forget.

It was the night I'd hooked up with a demon I'd never seen before and went back to his place. We'd fucked like savages, but at some point, I'd passed out. Something that never happened. I awoke to my arms and legs bound while the same demon was using me . . .

I blew him up. It was one of two times I'd lost control of my power and extinguished someone.

That was the last time I'd fucked anyone outside of a group setting in the Afterlife.

"That was you," I said, fighting the acid crawling its way up my throat.

"I had to be more careful after that incident since my angel had finally grown into her powers. Still, you never knew. Not until I took the vampire's place."

"You're a sick fuck," I spat.

His grip on my jaw tightened, digging deep into the flesh, desperate to leave the bruises he'd so enjoyed. Making his mark.

"I've paid my dues. I ran this world and the Afterlife for thousands of years while Satan—I'm sorry, 'Jake'—fucked off. Forever is too long but I can't die, and I'm beyond caring about what is right or wrong or *just*. I want you, and I'm going to take you. You'll be my angel in a cage long after this world is gone. Existing for my enjoyment alone."

Hades said Azrael had lost his last marble. I didn't doubt it before. I wasn't searching for some hidden moral compass or compassion that would allow him to come back. It was just an incredible understatement.

I laughed once, cold as death himself.

Azrael tensed against me, not liking the sound.

I pulled my hand out of my pocket and flipped open the makeup compact.

A hand appeared, reaching through the glass. It fisted in his shirt, twisting the material.

Azrael saw it coming and he released my face, shoving me to the side without care. I twisted to avoid landing in the lake, and instead slammed my head into the side of the dock.

I blinked, clearing the stars in my vision. Azrael grabbed the wrist holding him. As the compact fell to the ground, more and more of Jules' body emerged. She couldn't escape.

Azrael looked down at me, ignoring the dangling poltergeist he held captive.

"This was your grand plan?" he asked me, incredulous. "I knew you wouldn't come easily. But really, this? You thought I'd fall for the same thing you did to Lyra?"

He laughed, then tossed Jules aside.

His foot came down on the compact, shattering it into tiny pieces that he kicked into the lake.

"I have to say, though, I do love that you give me excuses to punish you."

He knelt beside me, grabbed my ankle, then twisted—the entire time he watched my face, waiting for the reaction that would give him satisfaction.

Snap.

My lips fell open in a silent scream.

Oh that piece of shit was going to pay.

Gritting my teeth, I leaned up, using my elbows to brace me. Light danced on my hands and face. Any part of my body that had visible skin lit up like a star on the brink of going supernova.

Now he'd done it.

"Jesus Christ, you just love to hear yourself talk, don't you?"

Azrael narrowed his eyes. "And you just don't give up."

He reached higher, for my knee. I jerked forward, slamming my forehead into his.

He shot back, falling ass first on the dock.

"You're over here talking shit, saying you know me so well. If that were the case, you'd know I wasn't looking for anything redeemable in you. I know there isn't, and even if there was, who the fuck cares?" I rocked forward, sweeping my leg behind me so I could lean up on my knee. That ankle was broken; there were no doubts about it. It would heal, but I wasn't quite sure how long that would take. I was strong, but I didn't heal like Ezra who could regrow eyes in a flash.

I glanced up, taking in the crescent moon that was now high in the sky.

It reflected off the lake in front of us like an open portal into the universe.

"Maybe you weren't always a monster. I don't know. But you're a sadistic, evil shitbag now. If I'd been given your casefile, I'd tell them to extinguish you. But you can't die. That's the kicker, right?" He stared at me with unveiled hatred. I wondered if he saw his obsession and loathed himself for it. It controlled him. It drove him. He'd never be able to let it go. It owned him. Therefore *I* owned him. So no. He wouldn't blame himself for it. He'd save all that hate for me.

"You're going to regret that."

"No," I said firmly, fangs descending. "I don't think I am."

He launched across the deck at me.

I was ready for it.

I downright wanted it.

I'd positioned myself on the very edge of the dock. Coming at me from his angle, we'd topple clean over the side.

He expected me to block. To fight him.

He didn't expect my embrace. My arms closed around his shoulders, one going up to grab a fistful of his hair. Not to pull him away, but to bring him closer.

In the blink of an eye, between him slamming into me and us falling off the dock—I set my sights on the carotid artery in his neck.

Then I bit him.

Latching on, I pressed my fangs deep into his flesh, holding tight while I reverse fed.

It wasn't time yet. I didn't need to give blood, but I knew I could. Dorian was right when he said I needed to just get ahead of the urge.

The only urge I had now was to end Azrael. When he sent that shifter after me, I'd learned something of vital importance. The bite of a supernatural was lethal in Afterlife blood.

Unless you were mates.

Jake said mine saved me.

In return, I'd unknowingly claimed them.

But Azrael?

He was nothing to me.

My blood and power rushed into him as we went airborne. But where the water should have broken our fall, it didn't.

For one that had lived so long, he was horribly arrogant.

I'd banked on it.

The makeup compact was just plan A. One that both Jules and I knew would likely fail. It was too easy. He was too cunning. We'd hoped that it would work, but we knew better than to come without a backup plan. In demanding I come home, he'd positioned us next to a far larger mirror.

One he couldn't break.

One he'd never considered.

Lit by moonlight and reflecting our images on its calm and quiet surface, the lake provided just what we needed.

Jules was ready and waiting to open the door to her realm. When we should have hit water and sank into its depths, we crossed dimensions, falling through the entrance and landing on the other side.

Our bodies crashed into wooden planks, and the dock cracked under the weight of our combined ascent. Or descent, depending on how you wanted to look at it.

Fire licked along my back, or at least it felt like it as we skidded before sliding over the edge, landing in the shallows.

Azrael grasped either side of my head, wrenching me away from where I kept my teeth buried in his skin.

I took a chunk of his neck with me; blood dripped from my lips, down my chin. I spat his flesh out, baring my fangs. Water soaked my jeans, my shirt, my jacket. Every part of me was either dripping or submerged as a bitter cold settled over us.

I embraced it, maneuvering my stiff fingers to my jacket pocket. It was still there. It hadn't fallen out during the scuffle.

"There's no ending where you don't end up mine in Lethe. I should—" He paused, eyes narrowing as he cast a downward look at himself.

The light wasn't simply dancing beneath my skin.

It was under his.

Like a venomous bite, the mark on his neck turned black. It didn't heal as it should, instead gaping open and bleeding as his veins darkened—trying and failing to process my blood.

A harsh breath escaped his lips. His grip on me loosened. Chest panting hard as his heart began to slow.

"Clever," he spat. His blue eyes turned dark as obsidian.

"You don't know the half of it," I said. Using my free hand, I shoved him back. He tilted, giving me the space to crawl away, getting halfway up shore. I sagged against the grassy bank of the lake and looked up at the sky. "Over the next few minutes you'll lose the ability to move. Loss of speech comes next—although that seems to be setting in even faster than it did for me."

"This won't kill me," he said, straining to get the words out. He tried to turn and face me. To follow me. But he just ended up face-planting into the water.

"Jules," I said softly. I pointed to my unhealed broken ankle. "Help a friend out, will you?"

She appeared next to him and grabbed onto one black wing, using it to haul him up hill, toward me.

She managed to get the upper half of his body out of the water, taking more than a dozen feathers out while she was at it. Her face was set in a grim mask as she unceremoniously dropped him at my feet and then handed me a knife.

"This next step has to be yours." She gave me a knowing smile.

"Every bit of it." My hand closed over the blade's handle, and I nodded to her, giving her my thanks. "This part is my closure."

"Make him pay," she said before disappearing once more.

I maneuvered to the side, wincing as pain shot through my leg. I shuffled over , sitting just above his head so I could see every facet in his reaction. Every contortion of his face. Every flinch of his body as my power spread further in his veins. Deeper into his being. Embedding itself in him.

Part of me wanted to drag this out. Enjoy it. Make him feel the way so many others had when they suffered by his hand.

The rest of me was tired of it all.

I was ready for the games to end.

I was playing for keeps.

No more moves. No more strategy. Winner takes all.

"Still think you won't die?" I asked. His gaze flickered toward me. His eyes pitch-colored like pure evil. "I see the fight hasn't properly left you yet, even though you find yourself powerless—probably for the first time ever. In case you haven't put it together, I'm going to spell it out for you. You will die. Here and now. Killed by the supernatural powers I was imbued with when you tried to have that shifter extinguish me. My mates changed me in order to save me. Without that, I never would've evolved. I'd still just be an angel-demon hybrid, and nothing more. The part that I needed to defeat you? It was theirs, and neither of us knew it." My voice was cold and hard and unyielding. I didn't possess an ounce of power in this moment, but that didn't matter. Because neither did he.

"Supernatural magic doesn't mix with the Afterlife, Azrael. No exceptions. Except one. Me and the handful of others that found our mates. Our bodies accept that change. I'm not your mate, though. I'm not your wife. I'm nothing except your executioner. You will die from that bite, make no mistake." His arms began to shake. His hands curling to fists, but he couldn't lift them. He couldn't speak. He was well and truly immobile.

"But as you've continued to point out, you're the Angel of Death, so I've covered my bases."

I pulled the starlight orb out of my pocket.

"Without this, you'll die here in the mirror realm, but you'll still come back. You'd be trapped here forever, sure. And I could do that. Forever alone is a good punishment, but it's better than you deserve."

With my other hand I lifted the knife. It was a short blade. Sharp. Serrated. It would do the trick.

I tilted my head as I used it to cut his shirt away.

Beneath his skin the light was growing.

My time was almost up, but it would be enough. I'd carved up enough bodies in my time to know the fastest way to a man's heart. Between the fourth and fifth ribs, I stabbed at the flesh, hacking away at the organ desperately trying to beat in his chest. Blood coated my hands, making my grip slick, but I was determined.

Demon strength would have made it easier, but I'd create a five-inch pocket all the same. I set the knife down beside me and slipped my fingers into either side of the incision, then pulled.

His body jerked.

It was nearly time. I shoved the orb into the hole I'd created in his chest. Then used all my weight to burrow it as deep as I possibly could.

When I felt the surge of my power along his skin, I fell back, scrambling to get away. The broken ankle made it hard to move quickly, but Jules was right there. She grabbed my hand and blinked us away.

We sat on the mirror realm version of the Willis tower. Miles and miles away from the little Indiana town outside Chicago where my old life was. Where my ex lay on the shore of a lake.

Together in the darkness, we both waited and then watched as

Azrael self-destructed. Gold and orange and red wove together, exploding outward.

It was the best fireworks show I'd ever seen.

"You're sure he won't be able to use his powers anymore?" Jules asked.

"I'm sure."

The starlight orb was made of Afterlife magic, or maybe our magic was made from the orb. I didn't know. What I did know was that it could trap it. Hades said so. It's what prevented me from healing in Jules' realm. The orb didn't strip us of magic. Nothing could do that. But it could confine, and that's what I did with Azrael's powers.

I rendered him all but human.

"Take me home," I said as the light faded, and the darkness closed in once more.

"You don't want to get in one final hoorah?" she asked, legs dangling off the edge of the skyscraper. "I do love a good gloat."

I smiled. "Nah. His punishment begins now. He won't be seeing me ever again."

As she took me across the country, back to the mansion I hoped was still standing—I could have sworn I heard a cry of anguish on the wind. Almost like . . . death.

And I knew that Azrael—the Angel of Death, wearer of a thousand faces—was gone.

He may not have been able to die, but for the rest of eternity he'd wear the same face as John. He'd live his life as John might have.

Powerless.

There was no greater punishment for a twisted sadist like him.

And no greater peace for me.

CHAPTER 29
FURY

We stepped through a mirror in the hallway of Dorian's estate in Houston. Jules turned around, staring at it in silence for a moment. I wanted to give her time to say goodbye. She was technically leaving the only home she'd had for centuries. I could understand the longing she felt.

"Do you think you'll miss it?" I asked, knowing it was a type of grief she was likely going to experience.

She shrugged. "Maybe? Probably." She pulled her braid over one shoulder, picking at the ends of it absentmindedly. "Yeah, probably. But it'll be nice to socialize differently. See people again in a new way. Watch TV shows that I want to watch when I want to watch them. Even go to the beach," she said, smiling. "That'll be fun. Maybe we could go together."

I creased my brows, looking at her from the side. "The mirror realm has lakes but not beaches? You said it's an exact replica of this world."

"Oh, it is. But the beaches are empty. Lonely." She rubbed her arms as though she were cold. "I was safe, but that didn't mean I was comfortable. This'll be good. I'm excited to see what the future holds. You know, now that I have one."

I chuckled. "C'mon. I don't hear explosions and yelling, so that's a good sign." I turned, looking at the broken side of the house. Smoldering piles of rubble and ash littered the ground. I frowned. "Well, 'good' might be a bit of a stretch."

She followed me as I headed down to the library. I had no idea where the guys would be, so I walked the halls, calling out their names.

"Where are yo—"

Dorian sifted in front of me, and I walked headfirst into his massive chest, letting out a loud umph sound on impact. Before I could react, he wrapped his arms around me tightly, resting his cheek on my head.

Returning the embrace, I breathed in his scent as he no doubt breathed in mine.

A warmth bloomed in my chest, content and happy to have my mate with me.

Ezra's familiar voice filtered in my mind, stroking my jawline with his psychic touch. I felt the barest hint of a phantom kiss on my lips. *Welcome back.*

Hey, I said lamely. In all the years I had been rehabilitating troubled souls, no one ever treated me this way after a hard day at work. No, my job hadn't involved trapping the Angel of Death and preventing what boiled down to an apocalypse, but all the same. The greeting threw me off guard and I wasn't sure what to say. What I knew was I liked the contact with them. I liked seeing their faces and hearing their voices. *I see you blew the place up. Looks like Dorian is going to have to rebuild here.*

We'll help him.

I raised my brows in surprise. *Is that . . . comradery? If I didn't know for a fact it was you, I'd question whether or not you'd been kidnapped. What did I miss?*

He chuckled. *Let's just say we have a newfound respect for each other. There's trust there.*

I smiled against Dorian's chest. I never expected them to have a guy's night, but there was something nice about the possibility they might do more than tolerate each other for my benefit. They might actually get along.

I hoped they would. Eternity was a long time.

Roman's voice bellowed, echoing off the walls. "You plan on bringing her back here, or do I have to come to you?"

Dorian grumbled, then realized Jules was in the room with us. "I didn't expect to see you here," he said, dipping his head to her in a sign of appreciation. "We have a lot to discuss, it would seem." He held out a hand for her and she accepted, sifting us from the hallway to another room, one that hadn't been destroyed by fire or whatever bomb had gone off here.

He let me go, and Roman lifted me off the ground, pressing his lips to mine in a forceful kiss. He wrapped his fingers through my tangled hair, inhaled deeply, drinking me in. I hummed in response, kissing him in return.

Jules cleared her throat after an unknown amount of time. It didn't seem that long to me, but it was apparently enough for her.

Roman released me, looking at her and pointing in surprise. He gave me a questioning look about her presence while I wiped the edges of my mouth off, smirking and not at all ashamed.

I smoothed out the wrinkles on my shirt, moving my hair away from my face. Looking around, I said, "I see you tried to level the place."

Ezra walked over to me, giving me a soft peck on the lips. *I'll take more of that later. When no one can interrupt us.*

My cheeks heated and I pressed my knees together slightly. I had no arguments there. His greedy smile told me he already knew that.

"You and Hades set us up for success, really. We followed his lead, doing what you two planned, and we pulled it off," Ezra said, shrugging. He crossed his arms, tilting his head to the side in Roman's direction. "That one turns into a hellwolf too, so that didn't hurt."

I stared blankly for a moment, turning to my mate in question. "I'm sorry, what? A . . . hellwolf?"

"Oh yeah. Dripping lava and everything," Hades said. "You should've seen it."

I turned at the sound of his voice, finding myself looking for a crow, but staring instead at the tall, dangerously handsome son of Jake in human form.

"Hades," I said in greeting.

A smile curled up one side. "In the flesh."

"Have to admit, I was looking for feathers. I didn't realize you'd show up as a person."

"A person you and your raven can't easily shit on," he said with a grin.

"I'm not sure that's a challenge you should just throw out there. Never know what I'll do to prove a point." He twisted his lips and hummed in response. "You know, I think I liked you better as a crow," I said. My inner raven agreed. A smaller bird was something she could dominate. This new Hades was something else entirely. After being confined by mirror realm magic in my fight with Azrael, she was ready to pick a fight.

His hands were in his pockets while he leaned up against a doorframe. He lifted a shoulder in response. "I'm actually quite attached to both shapes. They serve their purposes." He turned his gaze to Jules who stood behind a chair, her posture rigid. He dipped his head to her. "Happy to see you're out of your realm safe."

A crease formed between my brows when I heard him change his tone while speaking to her. I looked back and forth, from Hades to Jules, then back again, piecing together something I hadn't caught before.

She knew him in *this* form.

His human form.

The way she looked at him spoke volumes.

My jaw fell.

"It's *you*," she whispered, her eyes traveling the length of his body. She looked surprised to see him, just not in the way I'd expected.

I held my hand up. "Wait just a damn minute," I started, walking toward them. "You know him when he's not a crow? Like, you *know* each other waaaay more than you let on. When did—"

"I'm sorry to interrupt you—" Hades said.

"No, you're not." I narrowed my eyes and pursed my lips.

"No, I'm not." He smiled at me. "That aside, it's time we head back. There's the final matter of my brothers' punishment that needs to be dealt with, amongst a few other things."

My mates shared a look of discomfort, and I had a feeling I knew what it might be.

"It's okay. Jake and I have an arrangement. I'm not staying in the

Afterlife." I could hear the collective relief they felt. "C'mon. We're all going for a visit. There's a lot to catch up on."

Hades held his arm out. "After you."

I walked over to Ezra and Roman, placing an arm on each of them. "Dorian, will you bring Jules?" He cocked his head in question.

"I can't—"

I pressed my lips together and smiled. "You can. Trust me. You have my powers, and I have yours. Jake and I figured this out. If I can sift there, you can too." He looked slightly unsure, but he agreed. I focused my energy on sifting us to the Afterlife.

We appeared in the waiting room, and Francine looked up. "Do you have an appointment?"

"I . . ." I sighed. "Not technically, no."

She picked up her phone, ready to dial Jake's intercom extension. "Name?"

I grit my teeth together. "Are you . . . are you fucking joking?"

She looked me dead in the eye with a flat expression, and not even the twitch of a smile. "I never joke."

I stormed forward, opening my mouth to give her a piece of my mind when the door flung open.

"Give it a rest, Francine," Jake said, gesturing for us to come inside. "You need to find someone new to pick on. Fury's off limits now."

I glared at her, motioning to my eyes and back to her. Twat. Then I led the way into his office, Jules and my mates following quietly behind me.

Hades was already in there waiting for us.

"Take a seat," Jake said, snapping his fingers. Four more chairs appeared, giving each of us a place to sit.

I plopped down in my familiar chair while everyone else sat. Dorian looked stoic, as usual, but he'd been in this room before. Ezra was taking it in, recognizing the scent of it, but considering he didn't have eyes the last time he was in the Afterlife, he was seeing it for the first time. Roman looked curious, but oddly comfortable. Jules looked downright concerned, assuming she was going to be extinguished or imprisoned at any moment.

I cleared my throat once everyone was settled. "So, where are they?"

Jake took a heavy ball out of his pocket, setting it on the desk. To the average person, it looked like a paperweight. A crystal ball, of sorts.

I pointed at it. "They're in there?"

"For now," he said. "It's a very, very temporary situation. This won't hold them, and it would be stupid of me to keep them confined where someone could let them out."

I cocked an eyebrow. "Yeah, in your defense, you wouldn't want to make that mistake again."

He narrowed his eyes playfully, letting me have my jabs.

Good. I'd earned them.

"I figured Jules would like to do the honor," he said, turning to the woman in question.

She looked at him with wide eyes. "Why? Hades knows how."

He shrugged. "You gave up your realm. You were an essential piece in stopping all this. If you want me to, I'll give it to Hades."

"Wait," Dorian said, shifting his body forward. "What do you mean? You're putting them in the mirror realm?" He turned to Jules. "You're not going back? What about Lyra?"

"Don't worry." Jules rested her hand on Dorian's arm, reassuring him. "We found another place for her. She's safe."

My mate's worried eyes met mine, and I gave him a small smile. "She's here, Dorian. It's okay." I nodded my head over to Jake. "We worked a few things out."

Jake locked his fingers together, resting them on his desk. "Fury drove some hard bargains—"

I scoffed. "No, I didn't."

"You did, actually. I don't give away favors."

"Whatever, Jake. I told you what I wanted to do to save the world. It was sort of a team effort here. I needed certain leniencies to get it done. It wasn't an ultimatum."

He considered me for a moment. "Weren't they? If I had said no to your demands, what would you have done?"

I sat for moment, letting the silence tick on. "I still would've saved the world, and I would have done what I wanted behind your back.

And if that didn't work, I'd have fought you until my dying breath, but the world wasn't going to end. That wasn't an option."

Jake smirked, nodding his head slowly. He turned to Hades. "This is why. I always saw this in her."

Hades tilted his head side to side. "She's all right. She grows on you. Like algae."

I scrunched my nose. "How is that a compliment?"

He shrugged. "It grows on sloths, and they're cute. It's not a bad thing."

I squinted at him. "You're the 'cute' sloth in this scenario. I'm a plant."

He grinned a Cheshire smile, saying nothing more.

Asshole.

My mates kept quiet, pressing their lips together as they looked down at the floor, but Ezra was laughing in my mind, getting a kick out of my bantering with Hades.

"At any rate," Jake said, starting up again, "I made some concessions. One of which was Lyra. We're going to keep her here in the Afterlife. She's not dead, nor will she be extinguished. Her case is specifically under Fury . . . and me."

I reached over, resting my hand on Dorian's knee. "I'm going to work here on special cases, mainly Lyra for now. I can sift into the Afterlife to work with her and sift back home for dinner. I can be the one to help rehabilitate her properly. She needs a level of compassion and empathy others don't have." I took a deep breath. "I dealt with Azrael's abuse. I know it, intimately. So does she. She needs me, and she'll be safe here."

Dorian placed his hand on mine, squeezing gently. He looked up to Jake, clearing a scratchy spot in his throat. "Thank you," he said softly.

Jake inclined his head. "Duke is back, and he's already set up a comfortable place for Lyra. She's getting settled in. You can see her when we're done here if you'd like." Dorian nodded once. "In the meantime, Jules gave up her realm entirely to imprison Azrael. Fury and I decided his fate."

"What about Lethe?" Roman asked, resting his palms on his

thighs. "What happens to it? That's where the extinguished souls go, right?"

Hades groaned. "I'm looking after it."

Jake turned to him with a sour expression. "Don't try so hard to hide your displeasure."

"Does that mean you're staying in Lethe like Azrael did?" Ezra asked. I tilted my head, listening closely to Ezra's thoughts. There was an admiration there. Whatever my mates and Hades had gone through fighting together, I think it bonded them in a way.

That and he found him far too entertaining.

"Hard pass." Hades shook his head. "I belong in the Afterlife, and on Earth." His gaze briefly flickered to another in the room, and I didn't miss it. "I'll manage it. The extinguished souls aren't all bad. As we've all learned over the courses of our lives, nothing is black and white."

Roman sat forward, his long dreads spilling over his thick shoulders. "What does sending the terrible triplets into the mirror realm accomplish?" Hades snorted at Roman's nickname for his rogue brothers.

"Well for one, they can't get out," I answered.

"And second," Hades said, "they'll be locked in there with Azrael, who is now powerless."

Dorian's eyes rose in surprise. "How so?"

I smirked, sharing a knowing look with Jake and Hades. "He'll live forever because *someone* here made him the Angel of Death—yeah yeah, I know, 'hindsight'," I said to Jake before he started to explain himself again. Turning back to Dorian, I added, "But he has no power anymore. The orb trapped it."

"She sliced him open and shoved it inside him," Ezra said, reading my thoughts.

I shot him a quick look. *I love you, but I still need you to at least pretend like you don't hear my thoughts. I don't want to shield you like Dorian does.*

Noted, he said to me, and the sincerity in his voice was strong.

My mates gave me an approving nod at Ezra's comment, and I couldn't help but preen under the quiet praise.

"Look, my brothers have no love for Azrael. He was their warden for a very long time." Hades crossed his arms, leaning against Jake's desk. "You saw them. They have temper tantrums and short fuses. Now they get to spend eternity in the mirror realm, tormenting Azrael."

Roman barked a laugh. I could tell that thought pleased him greatly. Dorian looked relieved. Not only was Lyra going to be taken care of, but her abuser was going to spend a literal eternity paying for his crimes. Ezra was just happy to be with me now that it was all over.

Jules sniffed quietly, picking at invisible lint on her jeans. "And *our* bargain, Jake?"

He swiveled in his chair. "I'm a man of my word."

She kept her head down, but lifted her eyes up, glaring at him. "You aren't a man."

"Fine. I never go back on my word," he amended. "Better?"

She pressed her lips together and gave him a single nod.

"Jules, you gave up your realm. What do you get out of it?" Dorian asked her, taking in the tension between them.

"Freedom," she whispered, a small smile playing on her lips. "No one is coming after me this time. I have no reason to hide."

Jake held out the crystal ball, waiting for her to accept it. "Toss them in, then come back."

She took it in her hand, then stood up from her chair. Hades moved out of the way, showing her a mirror that had been set on a bookshelf just for this occasion. Taking a deep breath, Jules pushed her arm through, quickly disappearing into the realm. Moments later, she pulled herself out, as though she'd just walked through a portal.

She wiped her hands off. "It's done."

Jake dipped his chin, then turned to my mates. "Dorian, I'll have Duke come take you to see Lyra. Roman, I imagine you'd like to see your sister and let her know everything is okay. Hades is going to take you and Ezra back to Earth while Fury and I settle a few other minor details."

"Jules?" Hades asked, offering his hand to her. "Are you coming?"

She looked to me in question. "You're family. You're coming home with us," I said, standing up to give her a hug. She squeezed me in return. "Roxanne will get you all set up. She lives for this kind of stuff."

"Think she'll make me a Bloody Mary?" she asked, a spark of hope in her eyes.

I chuckled. "She won't be making anything for me, but I bet she'll be happy to make a drink or two for you."

My mates stood up, walking over to me, grabbing the back of my elbow gently while they kissed my lips.

One by one, they left the room.

The extra chairs disappeared.

Now it was just me and Jake.

It felt like old times somehow, even though so much had changed.

I tucked one leg under the other, balling myself up in the chair, enjoying the silence.

Jake leaned back in his chair, putting his hands behind his head, interlocking his fingers. He exhaled loudly. "Man, tough day."

I snorted. "You barely did anything."

"I made decisions," he countered. "That's very, very hard work. I'm very busy and important."

I huffed a small laugh. It did feel like old times. Jake, my Afterlife Resources caseworker. He just happened to be running basically everything. Nothing serious. Death. The Afterlife. Existence.

I'd seen him countless times in my one hundred- and three-year stint, but none stuck out as much as the first day. The day he comforted me. The day he took a scared and broken girl and gave her another chance.

"The day you brought me in here to offer me the assignment, did you mean what you said?" I asked, picking at a nail. "You said if I succeeded, I earned my retirement."

He cocked an eyebrow. "Why does it matter? You succeeded and our agreement was you get to stay on Earth with your mates."

I gave him a doubtful look. "You didn't know I was going to have mates, much less three of them. By your own admission, it took everyone by surprise." He waited for me to finish, but he still didn't speak. Realization dawned on me. "You weren't going to let me retire, were you?"

A burst of anger shot through me.

"I don't know," he admitted. "I never go back on my word, and I did offer it to you. Retirement isn't what people think it is, and you weren't ready. I wanted to offer you something better."

I scoffed. "Like what? A seat next to you?"

He shrugged. "I'd considered it."

I paused, taking in his response. "I was just being an asshole."

"I know, but I wasn't."

"You really considered that? Why? What for?"

He gave me a disappointed look. "C'mon, Fury. You're Michael's descendant. I knew what you were the first day you landed in my office. You were something special. You still are. After you succeeded, and the alphas were reformed, I didn't want to see you quit. You have a lot to offer. There's a lot you can change." He leaned forward in his chair, placing his arms on the desk. "The trouble with the angels over the millennia was that they lost touch with humanity. You embody everything they'd lost. You hold on tight to it. It's what got you through every rough night you've had."

"I'm young, though, in comparison to them," I said, gesturing around me. "This place is *old*. Am I eventually going to be like the other angels? Descending into madness? I mean, if that's what runs in the family, I need to know now."

"Why?" he asked. "It's not like your mates can take you in the backyard like a rabid dog and end it like Old Yeller."

My mouth fell open. "No, but—"

"They never had what you had. You didn't live your first life as an angel. You were human. You have your own unique human spirit. Couple that with your angel heritage, and it made something special. I wasn't sure I wanted to let you give it up. Not when I knew you had potential."

I frowned. "That wasn't for you to decide."

"It's not," he agreed. "Which is why I said I don't know. I hadn't come to a decision, but I didn't like my options."

"I'm not sure you liked the options you had today either, but here we are."

"I made the trades I did because it was worth it. You weigh your choices the same as me. And look, we both got what we wanted. The alphas didn't end the world and Azrael and my other three sons are imprisoned, and Hades is going to manage Lethe. I can't complain about the outcome here."

Hades ruling Lethe seemed so strange to me. He clearly didn't want it. Though he'd mentioned that was exactly why Azrael had been a bad choice for all his roles. Maybe this would make him good at it.

Hades, crow and protector of extinguished souls. I needed to get him business cards made. Maybe that would be a good present.

A thought occurred to me, and I perked up. "Jake?" He hummed in question. "Do you think I can get one more favor?"

"You can ask," he said. That was fair.

"Now that Hades can control Lethe, is it possible that he can un-extinguish a soul?" I looked down at my feet, not wanting to meet his eyes. But he didn't speak. He waited for me to look up. When I finally did, his voice was calm. It was the same voice he used the day I first arrived in his office. That's when I knew the answer.

"I'm sorry, Fury. Truly. But no. Only Azrael carried that power." He met my gaze, holding it with gentle eyes. He knew what I wanted. The real John. It was my fault. My anger. And it was never him that'd hurt me. "We have to live with the choices we make, good or bad. You aren't in control of what happens to you. You're only in control of how you react. That's what life is. What you do with it is entirely up to you."

I pressed my lips together, taking a deep breath in. "It was worth a shot."

"I would give that to you if I could."

I saw the sincerity on his face. The one thing Jake wasn't was a liar. He may have kept his real identity hidden, but that was different. In all the years I had known him, he'd always been honest with me, even when I didn't want to hear it. "I appreciate that." I meant it.

I'd just have to add it to my list of things to work on in therapy.

"For what it's worth, that rule applies to everyone. Even me," he said.

I looked at him in question. "Which one?"

"We have to live with the choices we make," he repeated. "So do I. I don't get to turn back time and change it. Sometimes I wish I could."

"What would you change? One thing?" I asked him quickly,

hoping my fast speech would make him answer immediately and honestly.

"I'd bring back my daughter," he said.

"Shut the front door—what?" I was moments away from picking my jaw up from the floor.

He nodded slowly. "I told you, angels can't bear children." He looked at me, straight in the eye. "I was arrogant. I didn't protect her. I believed she was of my bloodline, and she would be indestructible, just as I was. All their mothers died. But my daughter would live. That's what I foolishly believed."

"But . . . you made them. Didn't you make all of this?" I asked in confusion.

He wobbled his hand from side to side. "It's more complicated than that. Everyone wants to point to some divine source, but they always overlook nature. Even me, it would seem."

"She died in childbirth too?"

He nodded. "It apparently doesn't matter what line you carry. A woman bearing a child of Afterlife magic can't survive it. The power is too great."

"I'm sorry," I said. It was lame. It felt so weak and insincere, but it really wasn't. I just didn't know the best way to respond. Then I realized, honesty was probably the best way to go. "I don't know what to say."

"Sometimes there's nothing you can say." He gave a half-smile. "She birthed a son, then she died."

"Did her son survive?"

He met my gaze. "He did. It was Michael."

My stomach tightened in a knot. "I . . . we . . . I'm from Michael, and he's from your daughter, and she's from *you,*" I stuttered, feeling like the wind was knocked out of me. "Why are you telling me this now?"

I'd come to terms with not having a child. I'd accepted it when I died and appeared in the Afterlife, but my newfound status as uber demon-angel-supernatural had given me the slightest inkling of hope. Just a little. When he told me in front of Dorian and Ezra what would have happened in my mortal life, I knew what that truly meant. This just solidified it. But more so, I was still technically dead.

The demon part of me was there. The living human girl that would age and grow was long gone. If I wanted children, I'd have them. They just wouldn't be from my body. I was okay with that.

But *this*.

"You deserve to know. This is your lineage. It wasn't some cruel joke that prevented you from bearing children. It was never intended to be a punishment. It just *is*. I didn't want to take that away from you or from anyone. I'm sorry for the way that turned out," he said.

"I . . . does this mean we have to invite you over for holidays?" I asked with a smirk, breaking the tension.

"Can't come," he said, snapping his fingers. "But I wouldn't say no to pie. I love pie. And cocoa bombs."

I blinked a few times. "You're the weirdest concept of a devil anyone could've ever imagined."

He shrugged. "You can guess how much I care what people think."

"Guess that runs in the family." I snickered, but saying those words made me think of something he'd mentioned. "When I was here the other day, you said you knew who I was the day I landed in your office. You let me live because I was Michael's descendent . . . but it's because I'm yours too."

"No," he said, a sad tone taking over his voice. "The angels did have to destroy their lines. When they arrived, they were extinguished. It was cruel and unusual punishment for humans to be damned the way they were, passing down a bloodline that was guaranteed to end every woman born. I lost my daughter. I wouldn't wish that on anyone. I wasn't going to allow it to continue for thousands and thousands of years. It's inflicting pain unnecessarily. I chose to keep you because I saw who you really were. You made the best parts of Michael thrive within. Not the other way around."

"It was cruel and unusual punishment to make them kill their line. What about those people? They were innocent too," I pointed out.

He sighed, but he didn't disagree with me. "You sound a lot like Hades."

"You just made me realize we're related. I don't know how I feel about that." I twisted my face, letting my head fall back with a groan. I was never going to hear the end of that. I snapped my head up.

"Wait. You gave Hades his body back so we could fight his brothers. Are you going to let him keep that form now that we're done, or is he still being punished?"

"He's back to his charming self. Saving the world gets him a pass." He tapped the desk a few times. "Besides, it's been long enough."

"What did he do?" I asked.

Jake shook his finger at me. "No, no. That's not my story to tell. You're welcome to ask him."

I pursed my lips, knowing he was entirely too secretive. He wasn't going to tell me shit. "Fine," I said. "I'll ask Jules."

I watched him carefully, but he said nothing. A spark twinkled in Jake's eyes, and he gave a half-smirk, and that was my answer.

I smiled, letting my legs drop to the floor.

"Get home, Fury," he said, moving to stand himself up. "You know where to find me if you need me."

I stood, reaching my arms above me to stretch. I was ready for a nap. I'd earned it. I could finally rest, not worried about impending doom or failing the entirety of the world.

I'd earned my retirement. It just looked a little different than what I'd imagined it would be. I was perfectly okay with that.

"I'll stop by tomorrow after I work with Lyra," I told him as I walked to the door. Turning over my shoulder, I added, "I'll bring pie." I saw him grin as the door closed behind me.

Francine sat behind her desk, smug as ever. "I like pie."

I glared at her. I'd read a book where a scorned woman baked shit into a chocolate pie. "I'm feeling generous. I'll bring you one too," I said, and she beamed in response.

I sifted out, laughing to myself. She was in for it.

I appeared in Roman's living room at the compound. It was just a guess, but it was the right one. Jules sat on a chair on the front porch watching the shifter cubs play while Pria used her pink swirling magic to chase them. I could hear Roxanne making sandwiches in the kitchen while talking with Rava and Caitlin.

Roman, Dorian, and Ezra were sitting on the deck, overlooking the lake. They weren't even talking, but they were together. Seeing their faces filled me with an overwhelming feeling of fulfillment. Something I had never really experienced before.

I had so much to tell them.

I supposed this is what people had meant when they talked about coming home to someone you wanted to share your day with.

I had that now . . . times three.

I had no complaints.

CHAPTER 30
FURY
THREE YEARS LATER . . .

"ALL RIGHT, EVERYONE. GATHER 'ROUND," I CALLED.

A dozen kids were on me in seconds as I placed a few discreet plastic bags on the table. A few other adults took notice, but for the most part no one seemed to be paying much attention. I glanced across the yard at my friends and family. Roman was grilling hotdogs, hamburgers, and brats on the grill, chatting with Caitlin and Rava. Dorian, Roxanne, and Ezra were deep in conversation about the enforcer program I'd created. It was a bit of a pet project of mine that I'd been playing around with for a while and finally launched about six months ago.

We'd come a long way since the end of the world. Physically and figuratively.

After our violent battle ended with the Dukes and Azrael, no one really wanted to stay in Houston. They'd only ever agreed on it as a central location for meeting. When they said they wanted to relocate, I certainly didn't complain.

Roman took his pack north to the Rocky Mountains and set up an amazing ranch there. Ranch was a bit of an understatement. It was closer to a town of all shifters, but there were the occasional fae and vampire that decided to join us. We welcomed it. Kelly said she couldn't let us have all the fun. She came along and worked with Rava to set up a school for hybrid kids like Pria.

I would soon be marking three years since I'd started therapy with Rava. It was hard in the beginning. After the initial drive to get sober had settled, I'd be lying if I said I didn't have weak moments. Days that I struggled to deny myself a drink. But I'd kept my promise and not picked up the bottle ever since that night. My life with them was too important to lose to alcohol.

Dorian restored Avalon to its former glory, pre-Lyra ransacking. It was still cold as ever, but the castle wasn't so frigid. Fae lived on the island again, working happily. He spent very little time there these days—preferring to visit me or play an active role in rebuilding communities his daughter had hurt deeply. Especially the shifters. It touched me that he took that responsibility so seriously. He wasn't simply funding the rebuilding, but also helping people relocate, finding homes for orphans, and keeping up with them to try to ease the tensions that a lot of the survivors had developed surrounding fae.

Ezra and I had a different journey to follow. Not in regard to our bond. We tattooed each other, just as he said we would. I loved every minute of it. But we were also connected in another way the others couldn't understand. Both of us had suffered horribly at the hands of Azrael, and that lasting damage wasn't going anywhere. Beyond therapy, I needed an outlet for myself. A purpose. For a while that meant becoming an enforcer for Ezra, but it didn't take long for me to see that changes needed to be made there—and in the Afterlife, for that matter. Too many people ended up in positions of power, lording it over others and too often it turned into abuse. Because of the trauma we'd been through, Ezra helped me come up with a plan to truly reform the way we handled punishments and infractions. I didn't just want to stop with the vampires, though. I wanted to make changes across the entire supernatural world.

But I'm just one person.

Badass mini-god though I may be.

So Roxanne stepped in and became my recruiter, of sorts. We went around the world finding supernaturals that were like us; those wanting to make a difference for the right reasons. Capable of reforming others without falling into their own darkness.

Don't get me wrong, there were still some broken kneecaps along the way. Reforming wasn't all sunshine and flowers, but there was a lot more to it than simply punishing.

That's how the Enforcer's Guild came about.

In the Afterlife, everyone belonged to one, but the supernatural world divided themselves by species. I wanted people from all walks of life to be a part of it, and while it was still new—I had this feeling that my work here was only just beginning.

My eyes dropped to Pria. Standing beside me with a toothy smile, she looked at me with admiration. She'd been saying for months that she wanted to be an enforcer when she grew up. Whether or not she would—only time would tell, but it didn't hurt the feeling inside that assured me I was *finally* where I was meant to be. Doing what I do best. Fixing people. Making a difference. Fury style.

"Now," I said, looking around the group of kids. "Everyone is going to take one." I opened the bag directly in front of me to reveal several colored glass bottles. I suppose I should have predicted the problems that would ensue when there were only so many pink and purple ones. "Color doesn't matter," I reminded them. "You're going to be blowing them up, anyway."

Rava's keen ears perked up, taking notice of my demonstration.

I pretended not to notice as she slowly turned her head, that inscrutable parent-eye falling on me. Pria giggled, completely aware of what was going on.

I pulled out two unmarked containers. They were filled with 100% alcohol.

Not the kind that would even come close to tempting me. Mix this stuff with acetone and you had nail polish remover.

"Set your bottles down so I can pour some of this in—*no*, you cannot drink it," I added, seeing the curious look on one twelve-year-old boy's face. I knew this one in particular because Pria had a crush on him. His name was Junior and apparently his wolf had 'the cutest little white paws'. I shook my head, a smile curling around my mouth as I filled the bottles—and then had to remind them a second time not to drink it.

One kid took a sniff and gagged, solidifying what I told them from the beginning.

"Fury . . ." Rava said, slowly trailing over.

Welp. They were going to find out soon enough.

I opened the last bag. It was full of rags in different colors. I picked up one of the spare bottles, and said, "You're going to stuff half of this in the bottle, but don't take it out or tip it over. Okay?" They nodded along, but I knew at least one of them wouldn't follow instructions. There was always *that one*. I stepped back, letting their little grabby hands go for the bag as Rava approached.

"What are you doing?" she asked, eyeing the table in question.

"Um, well," I started, shoving my hands in the back pockets of my pants. "In my defense, Pria asked for this—"

Out of nowhere, a deep, rumbling laugh drifted over the yard.

"Did you really just use that excuse?" Hades said, striding forward. "Because I remember your exact response when Jake tried to—"

I whacked him on the shoulder as he approached, pursing my lips. "This is completely different. I was put in charge of organizing a child's birthday party. Jake handed over the means to end the world to that shitbag—" I stopped; mouth snapping shut.

I was pretty sure 'shitbag' wasn't something I was allowed to say at an eleven-year-old's party. Even if said eleven-year-old was my niece.

Hades chuckled, throwing an arm around me. "It's good to see you too, Fury."

"We're ready!" Pria called, running up to me to present what she'd made. "Look Mama, it's a Molotov cocktail."

Rava gave me a not-amused look, though in a certain light her lip might have been curving up. At least I hoped so.

"I see that," Rava said, lifting her eyebrows as she looked between me and her child. Beside us, Hades started choking from laughing so hard. I elbowed him in the ribs, which didn't help. My raven asked to take control, wanting to tell him off, but I gently reminded her to wait until he was a crow. Then she could have a go at him. She bristled but was content to wait. Rava pinned me with her glare, adding, "I'm *so* curious on how Aunt Fury plans for you guys to set these off."

"We're throwing them into the mirror realm," Pria said happily.

On cue, Roman's garage door opened. Out stepped Jules wearing a light blue summer dress she'd picked up on our last trip to Hawaii. Her brown hair was bound in a long braid that went to her waist, decorated with flowers, courtesy of the birthday girl who'd asked for all this.

Beside me, Hades stopped laughing. His attention shifted, hyper-focusing on the poltergeist as she rolled out a large circular mirror on wheels. I glanced between them, noticing the change . Jules hadn't seen him yet, but Hades had definitely noticed her.

Rava's perceptive stare caught my eye, she was totally thinking what I was.

"All right, kiddos, line up in front of the mirror—" I didn't even have to finish the sentence before they took off like a herd of puppies that just heard a treat wrapper open. Pria dashed across the grass, her light-up sneakers blinking away as she approached the mirror first.

I gave Rava an apologetic smile and said, "It's better to ask for forgiveness than permission?"

To my relief, she snorted. "Under normal circumstances, I'd say you're a hundred and twenty-nine years old and you can do whatever you want. Next time, just a little heads up with what you're planning would be nice where it concerns my kid, though, okay?"

I nodded along, agreeing with her, while internally hoping Pria didn't ask for another unorthodox birthday activity. Last year was bad enough when I had to say no to base jumping off the Eiffel Tower without parachutes. 'Just sift us, Auntie Fury!' That girl. If Rava thought this was bad, she was in store for a hell of a time as her daughter got older. Pria was a total adrenaline junkie and Caitlin gave into it even more than I did.

As if she heard me thinking her name, Caitlin peeled away from Roman and pulled a lighter out of her back pocket. "Who's ready to make some bombs?"

Rava's mouth dropped open.

"Am I the *only* one that didn't know?"

"Yeah," Hades said.

"Kinda," I mumbled.

"Yep," my mates chimed in.

Rava lowered her head in her hand and sighed. "Apologies then, Fury. It seems my wife is the one I should be talking to."

As she spoke, Caitlin flicked the end of the lighter. The rag on Pria's bottle caught fire before she threw it as hard as she could at the mirror. Jules used her magic, and it went flying straight through. Pink glass exploded on the other side, causing an eruption of 'oooos' and 'ahhhhs' from the kids standing in line.

"If it makes you feel better, I still have to remind Ezra to put the toilet seat down," I said, resulting in Dorian and Roman laughing a little too hard. "Roman is a blanket hog and I wake up freezing. And Dorian has gotten my cat into the worst habit by bribing him to leave the bedroom with wet cat food. Now he stands outside the door screaming at me for food at six am." I grimaced at Dorian, who smirked and shrugged. Pretty sure he and the damn cat were in cahoots because that furball magically never did that when Dorian was over. The cat got his food, and Dorian still got to make me wake up early even if he wasn't there. It was a win-win for them.

"Rava brushes her teeth in the most obnoxious way, getting toothpaste all over the mirror," Caitlin said. "It drives me crazy."

"At least I clean the mirror," Rava huffed, blowing a strand of pale purple hair out of her face.

"You have it easy," Ezra chimed in. "Fury is incapable of picking up her clothes and shoes. Try waking up at five in the morning to take a piss and stabbing your foot on a belt buckle after you trip over a boot."

Roman and Dorian nodded in agreement. I pressed my lips together in an awkward smile. It's not like I could say much since I'd started the bantering session.

The truth was that I wouldn't change a single second of my life.

For over a hundred years I worked toward retirement, but I'd come to learn that the concept of retirement was highly overrated. I'd rather have our crazy family and friends—unconventional as it all was—over a life of complacency, just passing the time. The days didn't just pass by unappreciated. I treasured them. Birthday parties, lifted toilet seats, and all the in between.

EPILOGUE
DORIAN

I SIFTED ONTO HER FRONT STEP. THE HOUSE WAS SMALL, BUT ATTRACTIVE. She'd painted it yellow two decades ago when she decided to live on her own. There was a white picket fence out front and a little vegetable garden along the side. She enjoyed that, these days. She'd said that working in the dirt made her feel at peace in a way few things did.

I didn't care what she did to get to that point. I was just happy she was happy.

I lifted my hand to knock on the door, but the knob turned before I could, followed by the wooden panel swinging open.

Lyra smiled. It wasn't broken or chaotic as it had once been. It was soft. Sincere. There was a hint of an apology in it; the same apology I saw in her eyes. Fifty years had passed since she'd come to the Afterlife. It was here she was finally able to get the help she needed. Here that she found another family with Duke and his wife and girls. Here that Fury saw her multiple times a week to work with her—never missing a session and never giving up, even on the hardest of days.

I was almost sixteen hundred years old and I never for a second thought the day would come that I'd be having Sunday dinners with my daughter.

Because of my mate, I was able to.

I loved her for many reasons, but this—*this* went beyond my love for her. Fury gave me something irreplaceable when she committed to helping Lyra.

To say that my daughter was as good as new would be a disservice.

She'd been through immense trauma. The damage done to her psyche wasn't something she could simply heal from. She'd never be the same as before.

There was no going back.

No forgetting.

The only way she could go was forward, and with Fury and Duke's help, she did.

Years after years of therapy and working through her problems made it so that we could eventually connect again and build a new relationship.

One that involved us traveling back and forth between our worlds. While being mated to Fury and gaining her power somehow gave me access to sift into the Afterlife and use my magic here, Lyra could not. She was supernatural at her core—but she didn't care.

On Earth, she was essentially a god. Powerful in a way that only few of us were.

But here she had peace.

If you asked her, she'd tell you that was worth more than all the power in her veins.

Lyra opened the door wider and two excitable corgis rushed around her to greet me. She'd adopted them from the rainbow bridge. Strays that didn't have families waiting for them, much like Fury's cat that she'd taken from here back to Earth.

She and Lyra made weekly visits across the bridge, spending time loving on animals and getting something out of it themselves. After all the death and destruction, they both needed that extra support. Even beyond family, there was a certain kind of love that pets provided that helped heal beyond measure.

Fury found that in her cat, Mr. Waffles.

Lyra found that in her dogs, Sterling and Stitch.

While I wasn't one that ever needed the companionship of animals, I had to admit that watching them both with theirs softened me to the prospect of having one of my own. Fury often thought I'd benefit from the company of a dog but she didn't want to push the subject. I'd yet to tell her that I was getting an Old English Sheepdog I'd met on our recent day trip across the rainbow bridge. Something about the way he bounced up to me and looked at me with deep brown eyes that said 'you belong to me' had tugged a heartstring or two.

"I think they missed you," my daughter said, bending at the waist to pick up Sterling. He was a rotten dog, but perfect for her. The little monster made gremlin noises about being picked up that caused her to laugh.

I loved the sound.

Perhaps it wasn't as pure as when she was a young girl, but it was real. Genuine.

Which is why she could have all the dogs she wanted as far as I was concerned.

"I think they were hoping Fury was with me. She's the one that always brings them treats." It wasn't as if the Afterlife didn't have them, but she enjoyed the simplicity in going to the pet store. While we led interesting lives traversing the continents, her work with the Enforcer's Guild, and my own with rebuilding communities and improving fae relations around the world—it was the simple things she loved most.

Curling up with her cat on the lanai, overlooking the black sand beaches in Hawaii. Shopping for pet treats. Flying as a raven and teasing Hades to no end.

I shook my head, smiling to myself.

"There's probably some truth to that," Lyra said, chuckling as she closed the door behind me. She leaned over to let Sterling down and the corgi took off, doing laps around the kitchen table, Stitch following after him.

I looked at the pair of feet that I saw standing next to the pups.

We weren't alone.

"Jake," I said politely, but confusion edged my voice. While we still saw him from time to time, Fury more often than me—the last place I expected to see him was my daughter's house.

"Dorian." He inclined his chin in my direction while setting down a large dish on the small dining table. It smelled like Lyra's chicken tortilla casserole. Something she'd learned to make in her time here. Cooking was another hobby she picked up; one I certainly didn't mind benefiting from. My mate always appreciated any leftovers I brought home as well. She knew where her strength and weaknesses were. Fury may have been approaching two hundred now, but she still found a way to burn water.

"To what do I owe the pleasure?" I said, stepping toward the table. Lyra stalled between us, twisting her hands in her pleated skirt.

"Athair," she said, falling back to her Gaelic, something she did when she was trying to soften me up. I had an inkling of what it was this time, and I didn't like it. "Jake and I have been . . . seeing each other."

My mind blanked for a moment.

This was another first in my sixteen hundred years of existence.

"You're seeing one another?" I said slowly, resting my hands on the back of a chair. "As friends? Extended acquaintances?"

"I'm dating your daughter," Jake said bluntly. Lyra shot him a look of annoyance and the fucker just shrugged. "What? He knows damn well what seeing someone means."

"How long?" I asked, my hand slowly curling and uncurling around the wooden frame.

"Oh, just a little while—" Lyra started.

"Fifteen years," Jake said.

Fifteen years.

Fifteen. Fucking. Years.

Time wise, it was a blip. That was nothing to me. To Lyra. Especially to Jake.

But it was more than a little while. This wasn't some casual fling.

"Please tell me she knows who you really are," I said, torn between sitting in the chair and breaking it over his head. It wouldn't do anything, but it'd sure make me feel better.

Jake nodded. "She's aware."

I turned to her, forcing the aggression away. I had no problem beating the shit out of him, but I wouldn't come at her like that. "You know that he's essentially Satan, and yet you're still willing to pursue something?"

"Hold up now," Jake started. Lyra lifted her hand to call him off and he went quiet.

"One, that's rude. You know it's more complicated than that, and he doesn't go by that name," she said, sounding so much like Fury it made my heart ache. "Two, it doesn't matter who he is. He makes me happy. He supports my choices. He doesn't disrespect me or my boundaries. And he doesn't care what I've done." Her final admission made me flinch. It was a topic we rarely brought up. Fury had told me a long time ago to let Lyra choose when to talk about it and not a moment sooner. I'd always done just that. "Isn't that what you would want for me?"

Her pointed stare made me shift.

"I—yes," I sighed. "I am happy you have found someone that makes you happy. I just wish it hadn't been this fucker—"

"Athair," she chided.

"Really, Dorian?" Jake t'sked. "You don't have much room to talk. I know you and Fury fucked on my desk when I refused to build a statue in her honor—"

"So you date my daughter?" I snapped.

"Only because she hasn't agreed to the Aeternum ceremony."

That stopped me cold in my tracks.

"Aeternum?" I repeated, lowering my voice. I couldn't believe what I was hearing. "That ritual solidifies a union. Forever. It's the equivalent to a *mate* ceremony."

"I'm aware of that," he said coolly.

I didn't know what to say so I looked at Lyra instead.

"Jake, we talked about this . . ."

"I know we did," he said, walking up to me. "But he needs to know I'm serious and not fucking around with you. I can understand the concern, but I don't want the disrespect." She sighed. This conversation not new to her apparently. "Before you start blowing things up, this isn't me asking your permission. I've already asked her. Repeatedly. Lyra wants to take things slower, though. That included me meeting you as her partner and not just the deity you enjoy fucking with on occasion just because you can."

I sighed, rubbing my temples. "You're serious about him?"

Lyra nodded, pulling a seat out for her to sit. "I am."

I took a deep breath and sighed. Then slowly, I pulled the chair out and sat down at the table.

"You get her pregnant, I'll find a way to kill you."

Jake nodded once, understanding that I was being completely serious. One might find it funny, but I knew what happened to his son's mothers. Fury had a long talk with us about why she could never biologically have children, even if we wanted it someday.

"Oh that won't happen. We're safe. Fury helped me get a magical contraception from Kelly."

The fork I'd picked up bent in my hand.

"I don't think that helps, love," Jake commented.

"Lyra, sweetheart, I want you to be able to tell me anything—except that. Also, how long has Fury known about this?" I eyed them both.

Jake started scooping casserole while Lyra turned a bit red, staring at her cuticles.

"Fifteen years," she whispered, and my eyebrows shot up. "Fury was the one that convinced me we should tell you. I wasn't sure how you'd take it."

My mate had neglected to tell me something this big for fifteen years. I was going to have a long talk with her about what all she knew about Jake and Lyra's relationship. I could hear her now. 'It wasn't my secret to tell.' It'd be hard to argue with that, but I'd find a way.

"I am sorry if I've made you feel like you can't tell me things—"

"It doesn't help when you light up like a disco ball at the mention of it," Jake remarked. Lyra kicked him from under the table.

"It's not exactly that," she said. "I know that you worry about me, and I don't want you to. I know I've made a lot of mistakes, but this isn't one. I wanted to be sure before I told you *because* you mean so much to me—and also because I was a bit worried you might try to blow Jake up if you found out some other way."

She gave me a lopsided smile.

There was still an apology in it, one that didn't have its place there, but I smiled back.

He took her hand from across the table, squeezing her fingers lightly. Lyra visibly relaxed, her features smoothing as anxiety drained away.

It was then that I realized perhaps there was more to their relationship than I'd initially wanted to acknowledge or admit.

And that maybe, it was quite possible, that I was being overprotective.

Maybe.

She was my daughter, after all, and this was the devil. God. Jake. Whatever the fuck he wanted to be called.

The End.

Thank you for reading A DEMON'S GUIDE TO THE AFTERLIFE! We hope you are loved Fury and her men. If you'd like to read a super spicy scene with Fury and all her mates, CLICK HERE!

Join Kel and Aurelia's Newsletter at www.kelcarpenter.com

And I'm thrilled to offer a sneak peek of my bestselling why choose demon romance, Lucifer's Daughter. **Perfect for fans of Jaymin Eve, Tate James, and Ivy Asher.**

Sneak Peek of Lucifer's Daughter

Hell must have frozen over.

That's it. The only possible excuse for why Kendall Clackson, our resident Bible fanatic, was strutting through my favorite diner on a Saturday morning. She usually saved her shenanigans for earlier in the week, on days I didn't have off. Coincidence? Not likely.

I froze in my spot and considered bailing, but that thought only lasted about half a second before her smug face made me stomp across the diner and settle into my usual booth.

Fuck it. I've done the same thing every day for the last ten years. I'm not changing now.

Swinging my legs into the booth, I didn't even pick up the menu as Little Miss Georgia Peach approached me with all her southern charm.

"Ruby! What a pleasure seein' you here, hun."

I turned fractionally and nodded once, hoping she would get the hint. If there was anything that Kendall didn't understand, it was how insufferable I found her exaggerated southern accent to be. We lived in Portland for devil's sake.

"I hope you weren't comin' here lookin' for Josh. He's playin' golf with some of the other men in our church. Bless him. Found his way to the Lord through me."

I could barely contain rolling my eyes. *Oh, yes. I'm sure he did. Just as soon as you gave him what I wouldn't.* I snorted to myself, but didn't say anything. Kendall made it her job to remind me, and everyone else, that he had left me for her and God.

"What's so funny? You know, Ruby, you should find a church. It might help with your"— she dropped her voice low—"*issues.*" Several regulars threw us curious, and somewhat scathing glances. It was an unspoken rule with us Saturday folks that you kept to yourself and didn't start trouble. Like Kendall was currently doing.

"Issues?" I asked, pretending to be mildly surprised by her comment. I knew damn well what she meant. I had a bit of a temper, but in my defense, there's only so much you can do when you're half-demon.

I waved down Martha on the other side of the diner, and she took one look at Blondie before rolling her eyes. Yeah, this wasn't the first time this had happened, but clearly, *I'm* the one with issues.

"You know, your anger—"

"What can I get for you this morning, Ruby?" Martha asked, appearing beside Kendall and seeming not to notice her at all.

"Black coffee and four orders of bacon, please," I said, not bothering to look at the menu.

Martha chuckled under her breath. "I'm not even sure why I ask anymore," she muttered as she walked away.

Kendall resumed her preaching, knowing full well her advice was unwanted. "You know, Ruby, you really should lay off the fat if you ever want to find a nice Christian man."

Something like heat prickled inside me, but I clamped down on it hard. Kendall could pick at me all she wanted. I knew it wasn't actually me she was angry with. It was my cheating ex-boyfriend that wouldn't leave *me* alone, despite my repeated attempts to send him away. It wasn't unreasonable that she was pissed with him. It was unreasonable that she stalked *me* for it, and made *my* life hell. Particularly, when she was the one he had cheated on me with in the first place. Yet, somehow, she didn't see the irony in all of this.

"Hmmmm...let me think about that. Bacon or church? Bacon or church? Well, it's really a no brainer, Kendall. I'm atheist, so I think I better go with the bacon," I said, smirking at the way her mouth popped open. I did enjoy riling her up. What could I say? I have a penchant for trouble.

"Is that Satan talkin,' or just your jealousy, Ruby? You should've known that Josh would find his way to our Lord, with or without you."

This was too much. I couldn't hold back my laughter and I failed miserably when I tried to disguise it as a cough. "Kendall, I hate to be the bearer of bad news, but we split up because he fucked you in a broom closet, and unless 'God' is what you call your vagina nowadays, I think you're fooling yourself." I gave her my most mocking of smiles and made a shooing motion with my hand. Even beneath the orange of her spray tan, I could see her face reddening. She thought she could come here, in my sacred space, and offend me. Slander me and throw my break up out there for everyone to see. She thought it would embarrass me. What she failed to see was that I didn't care. Josh was someone to pass time with, and his dick got the better of him. As a half-succubus, it wasn't my nature to believe in love. Not when the "heart" could be swayed by a pretty face and a three minute fuck.

Kendall's anger seemed to intensify. She put on a saccharine smile as Martha came around the corner carrying my bacon and coffee, but I didn't miss the look in her eyes.

"Bless your heart," she sneered, turning on her heel. I breathed a sigh of relief, but it was a second too early. Her foot came out and caught Martha's black sneaker before I could say anything. Next thing I knew, heat flamed my chest as the coffee splashed across my maroon sweater. It wouldn't burn me, but she didn't know that.

Martha caught herself, but the damage was already done. My bacon lay on the table, soaking in a puddle of coffee that was dripping into my lap.

Her white apron and yellow shirt smeared with grease and coffee, Martha spluttered, "I'm so sorry about that, Ruby! Can I—"

"It's okay, Martha," I said, glaring at Kendall. The bitch had returned to her seat where three other Stepfords sat, each blonde and almost impossible to tell apart. They wore the same impossibly pleasant smiles with their impossibly perfect makeup. Kendall had strength in numbers and gave me a little wave for show as she took her seat.

I. Saw. Red.

Standing from my seat, I hastily helped Martha clean up the mess. She kept repeating to me: "She's not worth it, Ruby." Not that it mattered. Someone needed to teach Ms. Upstanding Citizen a lesson. This was the third time she'd tried to corner me this week, and while it was funny playing with her, what she just did was unacceptable. Not that I deserved any of this, but Martha certainly did not. She wasn't even involved. Kendall could fuck with me all she wanted, but dragging Martha into this and nearly hurting her crossed the line of bullshit I was willing to take. It was time for her to reap the consequences for being a shitty human being.

I placed a ten on the table and left the diner without another word. The door jingled as it swung shut behind me, and I turned my eyes on Kendall's baby blue Mustang.

A fit of glee came over me as my inner demon smiled. I went to my car and grabbed the baseball bat and a lighter I kept in the driver's side door.

Josh should have warned you what happens when you play with fire.

START LUCIFER'S DAUGHTER NOW

AUTHOR'S NOTE

While Fury is fictional, the abuse and trauma she experienced is a reality for countless people. She'll have an eternity to work on healing, but unfortunately, our time is finite. It's never too late to ask for help.

If you or someone you love needs help, please reach out to a friend, a family member, a counselor, or one of the resources below.

Alcoholics Anonymous
https://www.aa.org

The Substance Abuse and Mental Health Services Administration
https://www.samhsa.gov/find-help/atod

The National Domestic Violence Hotline
https://www.thehotline.org
800-799-SAFE (7233)

United Nations Domestic Abuse
https://www.un.org/en/coronavirus/what-is-domestic-abuse

www.ingramcontent.com/pod-product-compliance
Lightning Source LLC
Chambersburg PA
CBHW020720310726
48979CB00004B/996

* 9 7 8 1 9 5 7 9 5 3 3 9 7 *